'**Dennis Burton**' is the pseudonym for a professional novelist and biographer who was born and raised in Belfast but presently resides in West Cork. The two volumes of *Lagan River, Black Mountain* took him seven years to complete and were written between his 60th and 68th birthdays. He now considers himself to be in retirement.

Lagan River, Black Mountain

Volume 1

The Long Slide

Dennis Burton

Custom Books Publishing

This edition published in 2010 by Dennis Burton

ISBN: 1451539959

EAN-13: 9781451539950

The right of Dennis Burton to be identified as the author of this work has been asserted by him in accordance with the Copyright, Design and Patents Act 1988.

Designed on the Isle of Wight , Great Britain, by www.inkdigital.org

A Note to the Reader

There are some peculiarities to Belfast speech that could defeat even the most eagle-eyed, non-Irish reader. Here are some to be found in this novel...

'Donegal' and 'Donegall'. The latter spelling, when used in this novel, is correct. Most Belfast street names including 'Donegall' are named after Lord Donegall and should not be confused with such places as County Donegal.

'Mum' and 'Dad' are how Belfast Protestants generally addressed their parents. 'Ma' and 'Da' were the forms of address generally used by the Catholics living mere streets away from the Protestants. I have used them accordingly.

You will find the author alternating between 'Provos' and 'Provies' as used by various characters when referring to the Provisional IRA (PIRA). In Belfast, the word 'Provos' was generally used by those who did not approve of the Provisional IRA (mainly Protestants and the British media), whereas 'Provies' was the word generally used by those supporting them, mainly Catholics and other Republican sympathisers.

While most of the major events recounted in this novel are based on historical facts, they have in some instances been modified for the purposes of fiction. Fiction, after all, is not the pursuit of facts, but the pursuit of truth.

Dennis Burton
West Cork, 2010

The Long Slide

Prologue

The barrel of the pistol was aimed straight at him, the black pupil of an unblinking eye. As he lay there on his back, spreadeagled in the wreckage, he heard the gunfire and the bawling outside, smashing glass, sledgehammers unhinging locked doors, the repetitive explosions of petrol-bombs, women screaming hysterically. He could scarcely believe that this was happening, didn't want to believe it, but as he lay there, looking up at that unblinking black pupil, the steady barrel of that pistol, he was forced to accept that it was real and that his end might have come.

Lying there on the floor of the small, wrecked living room, waiting for the pistol to fire, for the bullet to pierce his heart, he saw the Pope and Virgin Mary, both gazing down upon him, framed and hung reverentially above the tiled fireplace, and wondered in a moment of hysterical clarity why the Prods who had wrecked this living room had left them untouched.

They must have not noticed them, he thought.

Then, returning his gaze to the man standing above him, aiming the pistol at him, trying to will himself to kill, the fear returned to squeeze the breath out of him.

He had only been on the floor for a couple of seconds, but already it seemed like an eternity.

What had happened to him? How had he ended up here? He was reminded by the clamour ongoing outside - the sharp crack of rifles and handguns, the savage roar of a distant machine-gun, the ear-splitting explosions of petrol-bombs, the bawling men and screaming women – of the breathless march from the Shankill, along that choked street to the Falls, the men armed with petrol-bombs and clubs, some with nails protruding from them, the women holding out aprons sagging with stones for throwing, the air dense with the smoke from burning houses, the flames snapping and hissing. They had advanced on the Fenians, wrecking their homes, settting them alight, forcing them to flee and then attacking them as they fled, using cudgels and stones, causing children to cry and mothers to weep as their men lay battered on the ground or offered futile resistance.

Shots were still being fired from illegal handguns. That single machine-gun was still roaring savagely. He recalled his exultation and fear, his perverse pride and shame, before being surrounded by three men who had attacked him with clubs. He had covered his head with his hands as the men set about him, but felt the sharp pain of the blows, the warm blood on his fingers, as they beat him down to the pavement and then kicked him and ran away.

What had led to that moment? What kind of ignorance lay behind it? Where was the beginning of the long road that had led to such madness? He had been there, surely, at the beginning of it all, somewhere in the distant past, in his childhood and youth, but he hadn't known what he was doing, what he was gradually slipping into, and had certainly not foreseen that eventually it would all come to this. Now, as he breathed deeply, prostrate on the floor, in the wrecked living room of a Catholic house, being threatened with death by a Fenian wielding a pistol, he could only wonder, in an instant of dazed comprehension, if what was about to happen to him would be justice well served.

Mere seconds had passed, but they were stretching out forever. The Fenian had just raised the pistol and was preparing to fire it, possibly working up the courage, and he, the Loyalist lying there on the floor, was numb with dread and disbelief. He had come in here of his own accord, on hands and knees like a hunted animal, hoping to hide from his assailants or any others who might attack him, desperate to escape from the general madness and gain a respite. But this Fenian had seen him and followed him in, planted his boot between his shoulders before he could rise, and sent him sprawling face-down on the floor of the small, wrecked living room. Still on the floor, scarcely aware of what he was doing, he had lain there for a moment, trying to get his breath back, listening to the rising crescendo of battle out on the street, of pain and humiliation both delivered and received, and then rolled over onto his back to look up into what he thought at first was a black, unblinking eye, but soon realised was the barrel of a pistol aiming down at him.

The face behind the pistol was that of a young man, handsome and pale, slightly ascetic, essentially decent, but contorted with an odd combination of rage and grief. He was staring down over the pistol held shakily in one hand, as if trying to will himself to shoot, but not yet able to do it.

There were tears in his eyes.

'You Protestant bastard,' he said, his voice hoarse, breathless, almost a whisper. 'You murdering Orange shite. You won't be killing any more Catholics. It all ends for you right now.'

As the Fenian aimed more carefully with the pistol, his hand visibly becoming steadier, sirens started wailing in the distance.

The Loyalist on the floor closed his eyes, waiting for the sound of the first shot, but hearing only the sirens...

Dennis Burton

Chapter One

1

The sirens wailed. It was not the sirens they were all dreading, but the ones they truly loved, calling an end to another long working day.

'Thank Christ,' a lot of them muttered, virtually speaking in chorus.

On the instant, over twenty thousand men – fitters, welders, joiners and electricians, lathe and crane operators, train drivers and truck drivers, labourers and apprentices - gratefully stopped what they were doing, wiped their oily hands, adjusted their ties, discarded their boiler suits and put on their coats or, in some cases, put their coats on over their boiler suits, exchanged their boots for shoes, though some preferred to stay in boots, placed their peaked caps or bowler hats on their heads, lit up cigarettes, traded weary witticisms or obscene remarks, and made their way out of the Harland & Wolff Shipyard, known to one and all as 'the Yard'.

They poured out of the Abercorn Wharf and other deep water docks, leaving deserted the steel-ribbed quays, floating platforms and slipways where recently completed ships were moored, immense but skeletal, waiting in the evening fog for final fitting, turned into ghost ships for another night. They poured out of the Gun Shop, the Brass Shop and the Pattern Shop; out of the huge Engine Works complex; out of the Musgrave Channel where the dry-docked, damaged ships, coated in rust, encrusted in seaweed, as forlorn as dying dinosaurs, were moored and repaired; out of the immense foundry, filled with molten metal and fire and smoke; out of the many other grim workshops, dwarfing those who worked there and certainly indifferent to them, where the gunmetal castings, metal pipes, valves, portholes, three-bladed propellers and galvanised fittings for the new ships were

13

made.

Pouring out in their thousands, in the dimming spring light, they hurried eagerly for freedom around the towering gantries and cranes, across the web of railway tracks used by the goods wagon trains, past the horse-drawn wagons piled high with piston rods and camshafts for gigantic diesel engines, the inhuman metallic squalor of the industrial world, to leave by the many exit gates. Once past the gatehouses and the heavy anti-aircraft Bofors-gun emplacements located near them, they went their separate ways, some heading for the nearest pubs, spirit-grocers, or chippies, some taking the electric trams that left from the harbour estate, others walking across the Queen's bridge, which would take them into West Belfast, or in the opposite direction to the equally grim suburbs of Ballymacarret, Strandtown, Bloomfield and points farther east.

Albert Hamilton was one of that twenty thousand.

Leaving the great shipyard by the Fraser Street exit, walking side by side with his red-haired friend, Roy Williams, both wearing thick jackets over their boiler suits, with peaked caps on their heads but no oil on their faces, joinery being a relatively clean profession, Albert glanced at the Bulkies standing by the gatehouse, arms folded, thick legs spread, eyes narrowed to slits as they suspiciously scanned all those who passed them in the evening's gathering gloom.

'Sure wouldn't you think,' Albert said, 'that those fat-bellied turkeys would have somethin' better to do than worry about us lads nicking a few wee bits and pieces for homers?'

The Bulkies were the vigilant Harbour Police who would stop and search any worker they suspected of trying to smuggle out spare parts, fittings, tools and scrap metal to use on outside jobs, known as 'homers'. This was done by a lot of the men on a regular basis, because without it they couldn't make ends meet. They didn't do it for greed.

'Somethin' better? Like what?' Roy replied, removing a Woodbine cigarette from its packet, flicking it into his mouth and lighting it expertly, cupping his hand around the match to protect it from the Belfast wind, which could be fierce even in the month of April.

'Like keepin' their eyes peeled for German bombers instead of decent, hard-workin' boyos, like you and me, pal.'

'Jerry's too busy bombin' England,' Roy said off the top of his head since, in truth, there wasn't too much under it as far as Albert or anyone else could see, 'to worry about us over here.'

'Don't bet on it,' Albert responded, dead keen, as always, for any kind of distracting conversation. 'Any day now - take my word for it - the sirens we *don't* want to hear will start wailin'. It's the shipyards those Nazi bastards are after - and it's those they'll go for.'

Roy sighed. 'Ackaye. I suppose you're right.'

'Take it as read, Roy.'

Walking along the Newtownards Road, past the still open grocery stores, shops, bookies and pubs, the pavements packed and vibrant with uninhibited conversation, they were indeed reminded that war was a possibility. Lampposts, telegraph poles and even the odd tree had been coated with bands of white paint in preparation for the blackout. Most of the transport vehicles had been coated in a dull blue and already were using dimmed headlights. Buses had been pulled out of service to be converted into mobile casualty posts and some cars had been turned into makeshift ambulances. A few concerned shopkeepers had already sandbagged their premises against blast damage. It wasn't a lot (and what there was had been done with reluctance) but it was a gesture, at least, towards the war between Britain and Germany. Few Belfast citizens believed that it would come here, but you just never knew.

Glancing about him, into cluttered shop windows, at women carrying their groceries, at the men sidling into pawnbrokers or stumbling from busy pubs, silhouetted in the pale light bleeding fitfully into the smog of this industrial city, this Victorian slum, Albert longed, as he did so often, to be somewhere else. Not because the city was rapidly changing, preparing for the war that few wanted and most believed would never come. No, he would have been happy to see the same thing in London, the Big Smoke, which is where he'd always wanted to go to. It was Belfast, in any way, shape or form, that he truly detested. Divided by the River Lagan and dominated by the Black Mountain, its soaring slopes of yellow gorse and brown bracken and wild green grass, the city was more scenic than was generally recognised, yet to Albert it held few attractions, being far too provincial. To Albert, who had dreams of greater things, Belfast was fart-boring.

Feeling a lot older than his twenty-two years, frustrated at being a shipyard joiner when he could have been so much more (a singer, an impersonator, a hoofer as good as Fred Astaire and sure as God he looked like him), he surrendered once more to the self-pity that always gripped him when he was walking in the evening's gathering gloom from the shipyard to his modest, unhappy home. He did, nevertheless, have the strut of a bantam-cock, arse out, chest forward, feet light on the pavement, nimble and quick, a natural dancer and dandy, with large rings on the fingers of both hands, demonstrating his yearning to be different, to be above his lowly station in life. Though short in stature, he walked tall.

'Do ya fancy a quick one?' he asked.

After glancing at the pub they were approaching, Roy furrowed his brow as if puzzled. 'What?' he said in his deceptively dim manner. 'You mean... *right now,* like?'

'Aye.'

'But it's not pay-day.' Slightly over six-foot tall and as thin as a rake, Roy had an odd, disorganised way of walking, as if he couldn't quite control his gangling limbs. His green gaze was perpetually distracted, always focused on the middle distance, possibly seeking out imagined horizons or, just as likely, more down-to-earth opportunities. 'Sure we normally only have a pint on pay-day.'

'You do, I don't. That mum of yours has you on a leash, but I'm as free as a bird.'

'Tell me another, Albert. Sure your Mary, she has a tongue like a razor blade and I've seen her draw blood with it.'

Not wishing to be reminded of his sharp-tongued wife, Albert stopped outside the pub, bathed in the churchly light of its stained-glass windows, and glanced at his wristwatch. 'We'll be in and out in twenty minutes, so what do you say?'

'Well...'

'Look at it this way,' Albert went on persuasively, needing a story to tell Mary, wanting someone to blame. 'We could be invaded by the Germans any day now, and if they come, there'll be no stout for anyone.' He gently, affectionately punched Roy's shoulder. 'Come on, pal, *live* a little! Just tell your mum you left the Yard a wee bit late. You were stopped by a Bulkie on the way out and searched at great length.'

Roy grinned admiringly. 'Good one, Albert. Sure you could always come up with a useful yarn. A born survivor, you are.' He pulled his pocket-watch out on its short chain, studied it, as if trying to work out the numbers, then put it back into his pocket and nodded affirmatively. 'Ack, why not? But only a quick one!'

'Aye, real quick,' Albert lied, already planning to have more than one, to stay away from home as long as possible. 'You can take that as gospel read and reverenced.'

Pushing open the twin doors of the pub, abruptly dazzled by bright light, they found it already packed with fellow workers, some from the Yard, others from the smaller factories scattered around the area. One of the older, traditional Loyalist pubs, it featured darkly varnished wood and brightly polished brass, with round tables and chairs in the centre of the main room, private booths with stained-glass windows along one wall. Being a Yard pub, located well away from the centre of the city, it was notably devoid of the British soldiers who had come to Belfast in their hundreds since the fall of Paris and the retreat from Dunkirk. Weaving between the tables, inhaling cigarette smoke, assailed by a riot of conversation, they made their way to the bar and found just enough space to rest their elbows.

'You standin'?' Roy asked, since he *had* been invited.

'Ackaye,' Albert said generously, always wanting to impress, raising his right hand, the index finger and forefinger extended, rings glittering on both, signalling to the immense, sweating barman. 'Two bottles by the neck, Danny.'

Blarney in Belfast took up a lot of time. Slightly over two hours later, after three more bottles of stout each, wreathed in cigarette smoke, as insubstantial as ghosts, Albert glimpsing his reflection in the mirror above the bar, slim, almost handsome, grinning, slightly shifty, they were engaged in a lively bit of crack with two of their fellow workers from the Abercorn Wharf.

'All this palaver about war,' Billy Gamble was saying, his slab of a face red with drink and slick with sweat, his pale-blue eyes bloodshot, 'and now them plain-clothed wardens are givin' out gas-masks. Have you had yours yet, boyos?'

'One for each of the family,' Albert said. 'They're strung from the back of the front door like Christmas decorations, though a fat lot of good they're gonna do if one of Jerry's bombs drops through the ceilin'. Take it as it comes, I say, and don't sweat till you have to.'

'There speaks a true hero,' Jim Hewitt said, rocking slightly, rhythmically, on the balls of his feet, as pale and gaunt as an undertaker, puffing on his pipe.

'Just being philosophical.'

'Sure you may not have to be,' Roy put in. 'I still say it might not come to that.'

'It'll come to that alright,' Gamble said, speaking, as he customarily did, with immense self-conviction. 'Sure ya can see it's gonna happen. Even those trenches in the parks, filled in after that so called crisis – '

'The Munich crisis,' Hewitt, with his intellectual pretensions, clarified sombrely.

'Exactly,' Gamble said. '1938.' He waved his index finger in the air, emphasising this important historical date. 'So though all those trenches were filled in, the crisis over, supposedly, they're now bein' dug out again.'

'Right,' Hewitt said. 'And accordin' to the radio, the government's drawin' up plans to evacuate all the school-kids in Belfast. Seventy-thousand in all.'

Roy gave a low whistle of appreciation. 'Sure that's a lot of school-kids to shift. Sounds like chaos to me.'

'Chaos is right,' Gamble said, 'though not because of the schoolkids. We're already practically at war with those Fenian bastards down south, so *they're* not likely to be any kind of help when it comes to war with those goose-steppin' German eejuts.'

'They'll stab us in the back.' Hewitt said. 'No question about it. If Jerry invades Northern Ireland, it'll only be because the South let him in through the back door, comin' in by the sea. We need the so-called neutrality of the South like a hole in the head. What do *you* say, Albert?'

'Sure I know nothin' about it,' Albert replied, lighting his first cigarette of the evening because, with the rationing and all, they were becoming as hard to find as food and drink. 'Politics isn't an interest, like.'

'He just wants to sing and dance,' Gamble said sarcastically, referring to Albert's part-time entertaining in the local music halls, 'while the Germans, at the invitation of De Valera, come rollin' in over us.'

'I don't think he'd do that,' Albert said, feeling uncomfortable as he always did with any kind of political or religious conversation. 'No, not even him.'

What Albert most hated about his hometown was all this damned talk about politics. Since partition in 1921 and the formation of Northern Ireland, people were talking about politics more than they'd done before – and none of it positive. Initial hopes for cross-border harmony had rapidly disappeared as the north became even more of a Protestant state, the Catholic minority became increasingly isolated, and north-south relations deteriorated to the degree where one side would barely speak to the other. Though Albert understood this much, at least, he didn't want to discuss it. He just wanted to sing and dance.

'He'd do it alright,' Gamble said, his face as flushed as a beetroot, his pale-blue eyes angry. 'Sure he'd do it because he hates the North so much, he'd rather see us taken over by the Germans than workin' with the Brits like we do. For Jasus sake, man, aren't those IRA bastards still bombin' and robbin' to their heart's content, takin' advantage of Britain's plight to put the boot in even more? For Christ's sakes, man, they virtually declared war on Great Britain in 1939 and they haven't stopped bombin' the mainland since.'

'Really?' Roy said, looking surprised.

Big Billy Gamble rolled his eyes in exasperation. 'Have ya lost yer marbles, or what? I mean, a year ago this month, even as the Germans were invadin' the Low Countries, the IRA bombed thirteen shops in Belfast, robbed banks and launched attacks on police barracks. Sure they were doin' the same damned thing when the Brits had their back to the sea at Dunkirk. No loyalty. None at all.'

'Right,' Hewitt said. 'Dead on. You're on the right track there, Billy-boy.'

'Sure I'm tellin' ya, lads, that traitor De Valera has reached an accommodation with Hitler, guaranteeing him neutrality on both sides of the border if he invades the mainland. Sure he *wants* to see the Germans in Whitehall and Buckingham Palace. It's in his own interests, ain't it? Hitler gets the United Kingdom while De Valera gets Ireland, north and south. That Fenian knows what he's doing.'

'It's a tragic truth,' Hewitt said, the drink making him even more portentous as he squinted through a purple haze of cigarette-and-pipe smoke, 'that Northern Ireland is the most politically divided place in the United Kingdom and that the Fenians are responsible for it. They just won't cooperate.'

'Right.' Gamble nodded affirmatively, then imbibed another mouthful of stout, his cheeks as pink as a pig's arse, wiping white foam from his mean lips with the back of his big hand. 'And until this war came along, bringing a lot of work to the Yard, we were also the worst off in the whole of the United Kingdom .'

'What's that mean?' Roy asked, seemingly as thick as two planks, though his distracted gaze shifted constantly, always looking for this or that.

'What it means,' Hewitt explained, 'is that up until a couple of years ago, when the war saved our bacon, we had approximately ninety thousand unemployed, the worst housing and education in Great Britain, and, of course, the highest death rate. If we can thank the Germans for nothing else, we can thank them for reversing that situation. Now the shipyards are booming.'

'Not much else, though,' Albert said without thinking, since he was actually more concerned with next Saturday evening, when he would be performing at a local music hall, singing, tap-dancing and doing impersonations of other, more famous, performers, his ears ringing with the applause of his fans, the eyes of women shining with admiration and the promise of a bit of the other after the show. Nothing else mattered to him. 'The shipyards have been given a lot of government contracts, but they're the only ones. Short and Harlands, for instance, and others like 'em, have been completely ignored. Our unemployment's still the highest in Great Britain.'

'But things are looking up,' Hewitt insisted, speaking with his pipe in his mouth, tapping down the tobacco prior to lighting it, impressing them all with his superior intelligence, boring them rigid.

'Not that you'd notice,' Albert said, returning the conversation to basics, 'with all this petrol-and-food rationing that's goin' on. I mean, first we can't get work, then, when we get it, they ration all of life's little luxuries. Know what I mean, like?'

'Ack, I do, right enough,' Gamble said, cooling down as he, too, returned to basics. 'Sure isn't my missus now servin' up pig's feet instead of real meat? It's enough to make a man throw up.'

'Ah,' Roy said, tapping the side of his nose with his index finger and widening his big, green, slightly crossed eyes to indicate that he had some secret knowledge. 'Sure ya still don't have to starve, boyos.

Where there's a will, there's a way, like.'

Gamble stared sceptically at him. 'And what would that be, Smarty-pants?'

'Eire,' Roy said, glancing furtively left and right, as if frightened of being spied upon. A lot of Belfast men did exactly the same in the course of a perfectly normal conversation. It was a local habit. 'Down south they've got everything we don't have. Butter, eggs, meat, cheese, bacon, jam, chocolates, and all the spirits and smokes you could want. Sure it's a regular wee paradise down there, compared to up here.'

'You traitorous shite,' Albert said without malice. 'So we have to take a train or bus across the border to pick up our wee luxuries. Sure it's not worth the effort.'

Roy picked something out of his nose with his little finger, studied it with furrowed brow, flicked it to the floor, then pursed his lips and shook his head from side to side, as if bewildered by his friend's pitiful ignorance. He then glanced furtively left and right again, this time lowering his voice when he spoke. 'This friend of a friend of mine...'

'Oh, yeah?' Albert interjected sceptically.

'Aye, right,' Roy insisted. 'This friend of a friend of mine, sure he makes this wee run to Carlingford Lough about once a month to meet some boyos who come in by night in an oil-powered motorboat, bringing everything a man could want - sugar, eggs, butter, clothing, you name it, fellas - in return for what *they* can't get down south: paraffin oil, rice, flour and tea. It's a good wee trade, like. So if any of you, bein' friends an' all, want anything, just let me know.'

'Sounds like a right load of blarney to me,' Hewitt said, setting fire to his pipe and exhaling a cloud of foul smoke.

'Now hold on there a minute,' Gamble said, interested at last. 'Roy might be telling the truth here – '

'For once,' Albert interjected sardonically, but then, thinking again, said, 'That whisky you've been getting for me, Roy... Was that...?'

'I mean, there's no question,' Gamble continued, ignoring Albert's question, 'that there's been a lot of smuggling going on since the start of the war, particularly along the Monaghan border and, of course, in Fermanah where, so I'm reliably informed, they have a train that's so full of smugglers, the locals call it the "sugar train".'

'I've heard of it,' Hewitt said. 'Women take the train in the morning, looking half starved, but come back in the evening looking pregnant.'

'*What?*' Roy was baffled again.

Gamble rolled his eyes while his friend, good old Hewitt, exhaling streams of smoke from his nostrils, patiently explained the situation. 'Because they stuff so many items into their blouses and up their dresses, they come back across the border lookin' pregnant.'

'Away with ya!'

'God's truth. An' they use their kids as well. I mean, the customs officers don't like to search kids, so the women use their wee'uns as carriers.'

'Aye, it's happenin' all over the place,' Gamble said, nodding affirmatively, 'so Roy's probably right for once.'

'Tellin' the truth for once,' Albert corrected him, though he resisted the temptation to mention the whisky that Roy had been selling him on the sly at a decent price.

'So can we give you our orders?' Gamble asked.

'Anything you want,' Roy replied. 'Nat'rally it'll cost ya a bit more than it costs me, but still cheaper than you'd pay if you bought it here - *if* you can buy it here at all. I think that's fair, right?'

'Right,' Albert said. 'Sure for someone who's as thick as two planks, you're a crafty bugger.'

'Ack, Jasus,' Roy said, staring wide-eyed at the stop-watch that he'd just pulled out of his inside coat pocket, extending the chain to its full length. 'It's after eight already, Albert. We've been here for hours. Sure I'll get killed by my mum when I get home. Let's finish our pints and get out of here.'

Watched by their grinning friends, who knew that Roy, still not married, was dominated by his fierce, widowed mother, Roy and Albert hastily finished their glasses of stout, poured from the bottle. When the glasses were empty, they wiped their lips with the back of their hands, picked their empty lunch cans off the counter and prepared to leave the packed, smoke-wreathed bar.

'Henpecked,' Gamble said.

'Under the thumb,' Hewitt agreed. 'Sure they'll both be wettin' their pants on the way home. They'll walk in with blue knees.'

'What?' Roy asked, bewildered.

'Yer knees'll be knockin' with nerves,' Gamble explained.

'They'll be blue from the knockin'.'

'Oh,' Roy said, his forehead wrinkled in concentration, though he still didn't get it.

'Just ignore this pair of eejuts,' Albert said, tugging Roy away from the bar, 'and let's make tracks. See youse tomorrow, lads.'

While Gamble and Hewitt grinned, waving airily with their free hands, Albert led Roy out of the pub, into the gathering night, the ever-present industrial smog, the threat of tuberculosis, then on along the Newtownards Road, passing through oblique ribbons of deepening shadow and clashing lights, jostled by others wearily homeward bound. Most of the shops were closed by now; only the chippies were open, the smell of fried fish and chips wafting out to the passers-by, though many had black-out curtains pulled across their plate-glass windows and some had sandbags piled around their doorways. Albert glanced about him, at the closed shops and shuttered pawnbrokers, the low clouds above, and yearned for the bright lights of London. He'd been planning to go there in 1939, to try and break into big-time show business (the smell of the greasepaint, the roar of the crowd) but with the coming of war, the air raids on the mainland, casual travel between the two countries had been banned and he'd been feeling frustrated ever since. Until this war ended - and it hadn't even begun in Ireland - he was doomed to his dreary life in the Yard.

'You ever feel like doing something else, Roy?' he asked, feeling the cold wind on his face, though it was April already, thus reminded that Belfast was a windy city and loathing it for that as well. It wasn't quite dark yet, but it would come soon enough and then the wind would be even colder. The Belfast wind could chip paint from a wall or strip skin from the face.

'Something else?' Roy enquired, not being too imaginative and so happy to accept what he had without thinking about it.

'Aye. Sure ya know what I mean. Doin' somethin' else or *goin'* someplace else. Like the Big Smoke: London. Somewhere like that. Where the real action is.'

'Never fancied England. A snobbish lot over there. And them Londoners are more stuck-up than most. Stick to your own kind, I say.'

'You like your life here?'

'Sure it's as good as life gets.'

'Fish and chips wrapped in newspaper, a couple of pints in the local, football matches, the odd game of billiards. That's enough to keep *you* happy, right?'

'I reckon,' Roy said.

Albert couldn't believe the sheer lack of imagination. Roy was a friend, but he lacked a little something up there: maybe because he was bullied by his mother and couldn't bring any women, or even his mates, home for a cup of tea or something stronger. Indeed, he appeared to live his life in a vacuum, as so many in this benighted city did. Glancing sideways, Albert saw his reflection in the glass of a shop window, a shadowy form, a ghostly apparition, there and gone in an instant, just like life if you didn't grab hold of it and shake something out of it. Albert wanted to do that: get out of the shipyard, into show business, something better than the pubs and music halls of this dismal, windblown town. Something grand and preferably in the Big Smoke, with its bright lights, restaurants, theatres and high-toned, reportedly loose, women. Of course, he couldn't do that now. The Germans were bombing London. On top of that, he had Mary to contend with - and she was more than a problem. Reaching the street where he lived, he sighed as if taking his last breath.

'Live on your knees or die on your feet. That's one hell of a choice, Roy. Okay, see you tomorrow.'

'Sure,' Roy said and continued along the road, clearly only concerned that he was late for his dinner and would get his head snapped off by his mum. Sighing again, Albert turned into his own street: terraced, two-up, two-down houses, no gardens, just a pavement along the front. He was reminded once more of the possibility of war when he saw the rectangular air raid shelters that had recently been raised along the centre of the road, built with red bricks, with flat, concrete roofs, eerily unreal in the smog. Not too many streets in Belfast had those. So far, they had only been placed in the most vulnerable part of the city - the harbour - and in areas that were near the danger zone, including the Newtownards Road and Mountpottinger.

We're real privileged, Albert thought.

Walking along the darkening street, shaking his head sadly as he passed the air raid shelters, he soon came to his own house, another dismal two-up, two-down, with a bricked-in yard out the back. After removing the door key from his pocket, he hesitated, not putting it in the lock. Instead, he stood there for a moment, just staring at the door, thinking of what was waiting for him inside, reluctant to enter.

'Jesus!' he muttered, again shaking his head, either in despair or simple denial, he wasn't sure which. Then he pushed the key into the lock, turned it, heard it click, released his breath and entered his humble home.

2

Albert's heart sank when he stepped into the small, cramped living room and saw that his mother and father had come for a visit. His mother, Doreen, was sitting on a wooden chair beside the pram, which had been positioned by the wall under the front window. She was looking down at the year-old baby, Marlene, with clear disapproval.

'This child's burping far too much,' she said abrasively, 'for someone her age. She must be gettin' the wrong kind of food. Or maybe not bein' fed regular.'

'She's getting the right kind of food,' Mary retorted, exhaling a stream of cigarette smoke, clearly trying to suppress her anger, 'and she's fed as regular as clockwork.' Looking up when Albert entered the room, she said, 'So where have you been, mister? You were supposed to be comin' straight home. Been in the pub, have you?'

'Just dropped in for a quick one,' Albert said defensively as he took his coat off and hung it on the hook fixed to the inside of the front door, beside the gas masks, only recently received, that also hung there like grim decorations. 'But big Billy Gamble and Jim Hewitt were at the bar and they insisted on buying a couple of rounds. You know what it's like.'

'Aye, I do, right enough. And I bet they had to force it down your gullet, with you complaining every second. Sure you're as full as the Lagan River, so you are.'

'Now, now,' Doreen Hamilton said, distracted from the baby by the need to defend her only son, whom she blindly worshipped. 'A working man, one who works as hard as Albert, has a right to a drop of stout now and then. Sure it builds up the energy.'

Albert's father, Brian, pink cheeked and grey-haired, his face reserved and kindly, raised his eyes at that comment, since he wasn't allowed to go near a pub without his wife's permission, which she gave but rarely and, indeed, usually only at Christmas time. Even then he was only given an hour. If he dared to stay longer than that there would be hell to pay.

'That's right,' Mary said, inhaling on her cigarette, but exhaling quickly enough to complete her statement. 'You defend him, why don't you, for staying out late and forgetting the very child that *I'm* being accused of ignoring. Thanks a lot. I'm in heaven.'

'Well, I never!' Doreen glanced dramatically at her husband and son in turn, her lips pursed as if about to spit, cheeks flushed, grey eyes bright with outrage. 'We come all this distance, walkin' every step of the way, just to see our grandchild and find out how the new one's comin' along - and *this* is all the thanks we get. May God strike you down dead!'

'Say that and it just might happen,' Albert said. 'So you'd better retract it.'

'Too late,' Mary said, exhaling another cloud of smoke, while automatically placing her free hand on her swollen belly, about to give birth to her second child, which Albert could not afford and didn't want. Also, he hated the sight of pregnant women, though he tried not to show it. 'If I keel over into that fire, we'll all know who's to blame.'

'Come, come,' Albert's father said mildly, shaking his head from side to side and offering a placating smile to the room in general. 'I don't think there's a need for…'

'And who asked *you* for your opinion?' Doreen said sharply, giving him a stern look. Her gaunt, prematurely lined face was framed by short auburn hair turning grey before its time. In fact, Doreen and her husband had both aged before their time. This was due, Albert believed, to his mother's puritanism and his father's relative lack of freedom. To the best of Albert's knowledge, the nearest his parents ever came to socialising was coming here to check up on the baby and, of course, on their only son and his wife. Otherwise, living in their own small house in a terraced street close to the Bog Meadows, they hardly ever went out and rarely spoke to their neighbours, most of whom had suffered at one time or another from Doreen's sharp tongue. Brian, a quiet, decent, determinedly optimistic man, endured this barren terrain stoically, though he had certainly been prematurely aged by it. Life had slipped away from him.

'Sorry, dear,' he said in response to Doreen's contemptuous question, 'I just thought I'd take the positive view by pointing out that…'

'And don't reach for them fags.' Doreen's gimlet eyes had seen the movement of his hand towards the pocket containing a packet of Gallagher's cigarettes. 'I won't have you blowin' that filthy smoke over the child,' she continued, blandly ignoring the fact that the child's mother, pregnant again, the shameless creature, was puffing away there by the black-leaded fireplace and the flames of its coal fire. 'God knows, life's dangerous enough for the young 'uns without them gettin' their lungs congested at an early age because of the likes of you.'

'Sorry,' Brian said, lowering his gaze as he withdrew his hand from his pocket, but managing to cast a quick glance at Albert, who grinned in return. An only child, Albert had been spoilt rotten by his mother even as his father was being oppressed. Now taking a chair beside Mary, he glanced at his mother, who was wearing an apron over her dress, with a shabby black overcoat covering both, and tried to imagine her in bed with his father, making love to conceive their only child. He tried and he failed. He could, on the other hand, easily imagine making love to Mary who, despite her pregnancy, was still attractive, her eyes as dark as her ink-black hair, the pupils more black than brown, but luminous with intelligence and aggression. Yes, he could certainly imagine making love to Mary, though he didn't actually want to and, in truth, had never wanted to. Just as he hadn't wanted the baby in that pram and didn't want the second child that was due. Unfortunately, Mary knew just how he felt and this knowledge, more than natural aggressiveness, explained her sharp tongue.

'Your dinner's in the oven,' she informed him, 'though it's probably cold by now. I gave up waiting after about an hour and turned the oven off. You can heat it up again if you like. It's only a fry-up.'

'Right,' Albert replied, wanting a cigarette but deciding not to light one while his mother was there. This despite the fact that Mary was puffing away like a train. 'I'll just warm my toes by the fire, then I'll go in there, treading on my warm toes, to heat up my cold dinner.'

'You do that, son,' his mother said, nodding affirmatively while casting accusing glances at Mary. 'Better to heat it up than starve, I say, though the food's always served fresh in *my* house.'

'Tripe and fried onions,' Mary reminded her. 'Easy to serve fresh.'

'Very smart, young lady, but that man of mine...' Doreen indicated Brian with histrionic affection. 'Sure he has the pan for breakfast seven days a week. Sausage, bacon, egg, tomatoes, potato bread, soda farls and buttered toast. If you find a man who ever ate better I'd like to shake his hand, like.'

'Your hand would break from all the shaking,' Mary said, 'with the queue of better-fed men stretching from here to Sandy Row.'

Doreen was about to make a retort when Marlene started crying. Instantly, she picked the baby up, flipped her over a shoulder and vigorously patted her on the back to bring up the wind caused, so she firmly believed, by Mary's indifference. Marlene obliged, burping healthily. When she had finished and seemed, from her silence, to be content again, Doreen let her rest face-up on her lap, stroked the fine hair of her precious head, smiled at her, then stared accusingly at Mary. The latter had just thrown the butt of her cigarette into the fire and was already, the common trollop, setting a match to another. She inhaled, exhaled, crossed her legs, which were shapely, and stared back steadily, in a challenging manner, at her hated mother-in-law.

'I still can't believe,' Doreen said, 'that any grandchild of mine would be called "Marlene". Sure what kind of name's *that* when you're writing home? Not an Ulster name, is it?'

'German,' Mary responded. 'Your beloved son, who's besotted with show business, insisted on naming his daughter after that mannish German singer, Marlene Dietrich. Naturally, I protested, but now we're stuck with it. So say your thanks to your revered offspring here.'

Mary had been born and raised in the upper Malone Road to middle-class parents and, though having married below her station (as she saw it), she still spoke 'proper English', particularly when she wanted to put someone down, as she was trying to do right now. Not that it worked with Doreen, who, after placing the baby back in its pram, removed her false teeth from her mouth, then proceeded to clean them, using a round tin of Gibb's pink, solidified toothpaste and a toothbrush, both of which she always brought with her when she came to this residence. She did, however, dip the toothbrush into a small dish of water that she had brought in from the kitchen when Mary wasn't looking. She enjoyed cleaning her dentures in front of Mary because she knew it annoyed her.

'S'cuse me,' she said, *sans* teeth and not sounding too coherent, gum flapping on gum to make revolting squelching sounds, 'but I've better things to do in life than argue with a twenty-one year old pregnant housewife about the merits of a foreign fillum star who can't even sing in proper English and flaunts herself half naked, like the brazen hussy she must be, on the cinema screens of decent, Christian countries.'

'No argument,' Mary said. 'But you just said you didn't like the name your son gave to our daughter.'

'I did *not* say that, Miss,' Doreen retorted. 'Don't put words in my mouth. I just said that the name wasn't Irish and wondered why you'd chosen it.'

'*I* didn't choose it. I repeat, your son did. And you've known why he chose it from day one. He's besotted with films, is why, fancying himself as a singer and dancer. He probably thinks *he'll* end up in films, duetting with his adored Marlene Dietrich - or maybe someone more *feminine*. Fat chance, I say.'

'Behind every successful man is a strong woman,' Doreen loftily informed her, 'but I can't say that this is the case here. Without encouragement from his wife, a man can't be expected to...'

'Alright, you two,' Albert interjected, grinning, 'don't get started. The war that's comin' with the Germans will be enough; we don't need another one in this house. Anyway, I'm goin' to heat up that dinner. Why not turn on the radio?'

'Good idea,' Mary said, preferring the slow death of the radio to an interminable conversation with her mother-in-law. 'I could do with some music.'

'Conversation's a dying art,' Doreen said, pointedly turning away from Mary and addressing her husband. 'Where would they be these days without the radio? Sittin' in mindless silence, is where, just scratchin' their backsides.'

Ignoring her, Mary turned on the radio as Albert gratefully took himself into the kitchen leading off the living room. It was a cramped, gloomy hole with cardboard covering a damp floor and more damp showing through the flowered wallpaper. The only hot water supply came from a gas geyser that ran into an earthenware jawbox, or sink. The gas cooker, though clean, had seen better days. The back door of the kitchen had two cracked windowpanes overlooking a small, grim back yard enclosed in brick walls. The yard contained an outdoor toilet, also built from bricks, with a sloping corrugated-iron roof. Clothes were hanging out to dry on strings tied to metal hooks fixed to the walls. Albert never looked out through those windows without feeling depressed.

Depressed again, he turned on the oven and listened to the radio in the living room while waiting for his meal to heat up. Bing Crosby crooned for a few minutes, then was followed by George Formby and Vera Lynn. Still waiting for his dinner, Albert glanced around the kitchen, which, despite its primitive condition, was immaculately clean, having been scrubbed down with bleach. Women around here took pride in their homes and Mary, despite her general lack of interest in domestic duties, was as determined as the others to keep up appearances. The back yard, he noted, had also been scrubbed down with bleach and, though remaining grim, was at least spotless. Sighing, thinking once more of the bright lights of London, temporarily out of reach, he turned off the oven, withdrew his dried-out, unappetising dinner, grabbed a knife and fork, and then went back to join the others in the living room. As he pulled up a chair between Mary and Doreen, the music on the radio was interrupted by the local news.

'Somethin' intelligent at last,' Doreen said, exhaling her breath and straightening her spine, as if about to give a sermon. 'I like a good bit of news.'

Albert listened to the radio while eating off the plate on his lap. Ever since the commencement of the war with Germany, the news had been rigidly censored and it was impossible, he knew, to separate the truth from propaganda. Nevertheless, as he ate his tasteless dinner, he learnt that the principle of treating the Ulster coastline as a protected area had led to the expulsion from Northern Ireland of more European refugees, including Czechs, Italians, Austrians and German Jews; that the belief in the Irish Republican Army as a potential fifth column had led to the internment of another sixty-four men suspected of being IRA members, some to be held on a prison ship anchored in Belfast Lough, others in the Crumlin Road jail; that the Local Defence Volunteers, now numbering over 40,000 men, was being criticised as a sectarian force because it had been formed mostly from members of the predominantly Protestant B-Specials and placed under the authority of the RUC Inspector-General, rather than under military command as it was in England; that the unionist government of John Andrews was widely viewed by its own backbenchers and junior ministers as ineffectual and heading for a downfall; that the aircraft, ship-building and munitions factories of Northern Ireland had the worst production record of any region in the United Kingdom; that Short & Harland had the worst strike record of all munitions producers; and, finally, that the absenteeism levels of Harland & Wolff were twice that of the worst British yards. When the news ended, Fred Astaire started singing, 'Cheek to Cheek', sounding as light as he was on his feet when seen on the silver screen.

'Did you hear that?' Albert asked of his father.

'You mean that bit about the Yard?' Brian replied.

Albert nodded.

'Sure it comes as a shock when you hear it, but I'm inclined to believe it. The men don't have the pride they once had. These days, they're only concerned with what they can get for themselves. They don't feel any urgency about the war because we haven't been bombed yet.'

'It's a lack of Christian values,' Doreen informed the room. 'You turn your back on the church and all your values come tumbling down like the walls of Jericho. That's what's happened in the Yard and elsewhere. The lack of Christian values corrupted them. They should all burn in hell.'

'Jesus Christ!' Mary muttered.

Doreen gave her a sharp glance, but said no more, letting Albert finish his dinner in peace... If peace you could call it. Not a peace that Albert recognised... Glancing into the open fire, he saw the yellow flames flickering over red-hot coals and felt that they were burning up his life. He was only twenty-two and already he felt that his light was dimming. There was Mary sitting opposite, undeniably attractive, and here he was practically breathing in her face, yet feeling washed up, oblivious to what would make her attractive to most other men. Both of them were imprisoned in this small, cramped house, with barely room to bend an elbow, just as the Protestants were in the Shankill area, the Catholics in the Falls, all equally deprived in their separate ghettoes, thus resenting each other. You could, of course, say the same about him and Mary, but certain words were best left unspoken. Albert thought it was pitiful.

Taking his plate into the kitchen, he placed it in the sink. Returning to the living room, desperately wanting a cigarette but reluctant to light up in front of his fierce mother, he sat in the chair again and said, speaking over Bing Crosby's dulcet crooning, 'You really think they had more pride in your day?'

'Ackaye,' Brian replied. He had worked as an electric welder in the Yard for most of his life, but had retired prematurely eighteen months ago when his eyesight, ruined by the welding, forced him to give it up. He had first gone into the Yard before the Great Depression of the 1920s crippled the industries upon which Belfast had been built, making life brutally hard for the workers; thus, when he recalled those distant days, he saw them through the golden glow of nostalgia, as if looking back on a totally different world

'Well,' he said, speaking softly, 'I suppose we had more reason to be proud then. There was a lot of work around and we were one of the most successful yards in the United Kingdom, building some great ships, including – '

'The *Titanic*,' Mary said with a melodramatic sigh, having heard this many times before.

'Aye,' Brian went on, unperturbed. 'We were proud of that one, I tell you, and maybe that's where our pride took its first fall. God, we really worked on that ship, for three years in all, giving it our very best, and when it was finished, when the gantries and wooden props were removed, letting it slide down into the water, when the tugboats towed it out of Queen's Island, you couldn't have seen a prouder bunch of men than we were at that moment. Sure we were laughin' and cheerin' and huggin' ourselves, because that ship was so brilliant.'

'And so *big*,' Mary whispered.

'God, yes, she was *big*! You can't imagine the size of her. So big that she had to be towed all the way down the Lough, past the thousands of spectators lining the shore, waving flags and handkerchiefs, all singing "Rule Britannia". Nearly nine hundred feet long, over ninety feet wide, weighing sixty-thousand tons: so big that her propellers couldn't be started until she was in really deep waters. It was only when she got near Bangor that the tug boats let her go, the boilers and propellers started up, and she was able to sail on to Southampton, to commence her maiden voyage.'

'Then she sank,' Mary said.

Doreen threw her a vicious glance and opened her mouth to say something. She closed her mouth again when Brian, oblivious to Mary's sarcasm, nodded in agreement and said sadly, 'Aye, she sank. We couldn't believe it when we heard the news a fortnight later. Some of us heard it on the radio, but others, like me, read about it in the *Belfast Telegraph's* one-page special. To this day I can't forget that single headline. "*Titanic* sunk!" Nothing else. Just that. "*Titanic* sunk!" Those words were burnt into my brain and made me choke up and... Well, I'm not ashamed to admit that – '

'You cried when you read those words,' Mary interjected flatly, wearily, exhaling a stream of smoke from yet another cigarette. 'You and a lot of your work-mates. You all cried when you learnt that your pride-and-joy had gone down on its first voyage. Not much pride *or* joy after that, right?'

Too sweet-natured to even notice her sarcasm, Brian nodded and said solemnly, 'Aye, right.' Doreen reddened up and gave Mary what she hoped was a withering glare. Mary smiled brightly, artificially, at her.

'So, yes,' Brian continued, not noticing the little exchange between his wife and his daughter-in-law, neither greatly loved by their men, 'I think that's when we lost our pride in our work. It never really came back.'

'It's nothing to do with that,' Albert said. 'Sure it's the management that's at fault. They don't give a damn about their workers and the workers know it, so they don't put themselves out too much. It's tit for tat, Dad.'

'Maybe so,' Brian said, this time with a sigh of sad and reluctant agreement. 'Ackaye, maybe so.'

'Dozers, all of 'em,' Doreen said. 'As lazy as sin. Cowardy custards as well. As mindless as bricks, not a decent spud amongst them, havin' no beliefs to sustain them, as devoid of Christian faith as a bird flyin' against the wind without a wing to stand on.'

'Birds don't stand on their wings,' Mary informed her. 'They might not have feet the same as you and me, but they can certainly stand on solid ground.'

Doreen shot her a withering look. 'Very smart, I'm sure. Too smart for me, naturally. *I'm* just a poor working-class woman, far removed from the Malone Road, not sophisticated like some, but at least I know that those who have childern born out of wedlock ...'

Albert straightened up in his chair as Mary's cheeks turned red. But before another word could be spoken sirens wailed in the distance.

These were not the sirens that Albert was pleased to hear at the end of his working day. They were the sirens that he had been dreading to hear and had hoped that he never would hear.

'Lord have mercy!' Doreen exclaimed.

3

'It's an air raid warning,' Albert said, pushing his chair back and rising to his feet as those eerie, discordant wailings were heard outside, coming from all directions.

'It's the Yard,' Mary said hopefully, though she bit her lower lip.

'No, it's not,' Brian said. 'The Yard's sirens don't sound like those. Albert's right. It must be an air raid.'

'Lord have mercy,' Doreen repeated. 'We're bein' attacked by the Germans.' She glanced in panic at the pram, as Mary, without thinking, spread the fingers of her right hand across her belly, feeling the baby kicking inside her. 'What'll we...?'

'We'd better get into that air raid shelter,' Albert said, hoping to sound more manly than he felt, heart pounding, throat dry. Already, as he had done so often in the past, he felt ashamed of his cowardice.

Galvanised into action by the continuing, spine-chilling wailing of the sirens, Mary rose to her feet and picked Marlene out of the pram. By now, her in-laws were also standing. Brian was staring at the nearest wall, as if trying to see through it, his eyes widening slightly, when they all heard, above the demented wailing of the sirens, a muffled bass rumbling.

'Those are aeroplanes,' Brian said.

'Let's get out,' Albert said, shocked when he heard his own voice sounding high-pitched and breathless. Who could tell what shame really felt like, except those who experienced it? And did anyone experience it like he did? Not likely, he reckoned.

'Do we need those gas masks?' Doreen asked.

'I don't know,' Albert said, licking his dry lips, blinking repeatedly, helplessly, seeing faceless forms in flickering light, not real human beings, 'but we'd better take them anyway.'

'And our coats and some blankets,' Doreen said, 'in case we're out there all night.'

'Not me,' Mary said. 'I won't be able to stand being cooped up in one of those things all night. I'm claustrophobic that way. I don't even like them in daylight. Those air raid shelters are *tombs*.'

'This house is likely to be your tomb,' Albert said as he made his way to the front door, vainly trying to suppress his rising tension, 'if you don't use that shelter. So come on, let's move it. I'll take the coats and these gas masks. Mum, you bring the blankets.'

'Aye, I will.' Doreen hurried up the stairs, disappearing into the darkness of the landing. Still holding Marlene, Mary glanced nervously at Albert. Realising that he was as frightened as his wife looked, if also inexplicably excited, Albert threw some coats over his left arm. Still holding the gas masks by their straps, he nodded at his father. 'My hands are full; you'll have to open the door for me.' When Brian did so, the wailing of the air raid sirens became dramatically louder.

'Jesus!' Albert exclaimed. 'It's really happening! That's the Germans out there!'

'Don't blaspheme,' Doreen said sharply, coming down the stairs with a pile of blankets slung over one arm, silhouetted in a pool of yellow light framed by wavering shadows,. 'And I'd recommend you take a couple of chairs. There's not much to sit on in those shelters.'

'Right.' Turning back into the living room, Brian picked up two chairs and glanced at Albert. 'After you, son.'

When Albert stepped into the dark street, he saw his neighbours doing the same, some with gas masks in their hands, others carrying blankets and chairs, most looking either frightened or disbelieving. Lights were still beaming out of many front windows, through open curtains, despite the blackout regulations, clearly illuminating those hurrying from their homes to the air raid shelters directly in front of them. They were not quiet about it. A few women were sobbing and being consoled by relatives. Their men were bawling at the children or shouting at each other, some pointing at the night sky, in the direction of the docks, from where that ominous rumbling was emanating. Searchlights swept the sky, criss-crossing each other to form an immense, shivering, phosphorescent web, a dazzling *son et lumière* spectacle, in which an armada of advancing aircraft, German bombers, could be clearly discerned.

'Good God!' Brian exclaimed like a child at a funfair, enjoying the spectacle, clearly feeling young all over again.

'They look like a flock of birds,' Albert said, touched by his father's rare display of unalloyed joy, though also tugged between his own fear and excitement, 'but that's not bird-shit they're dropping.'

'Albert!' Doreen snapped, scandalised by the obscenity. 'Mind your language in front of the childern!'

'Sorry, Mum, it just slipped out.'

Lowering his gaze, Albert waited until Mary had emerged from the house, holding the crying baby, before he locked the front door. 'Quick,' he said, pushing Mary towards the nearest air raid shelter.

Mary hesitated. 'I can't go in there. *I can't!*' But when Albert pushed her again, she reluctantly entered the shelter, followed instantly by Doreen and Brian.

Albert was just about to follow them when he heard a distant booming sound. Glancing in the direction of the docks, he saw a jagged, silvery-white, charcoal-edged light fanning across the night sky, instantly followed by another, then a third and a fourth, all accompanied by that distant booming sound, the noise of exploding bombs, and by billowing clouds of smoke that stained the sweeping beams of the searchlights, obliterating the stars. That sky, which Albert had rarely bothered to look at before, was suddenly alien, spectacular and terrifying. Heaven and hell were in that sky... and below it, people were dying.

'They're bombing the docks as they head in our direction,' the man beside him said. 'Best get inside, Albert.'

It was his neighbour, Patrick Lavery, a short, balding, good-natured Catholic in his early thirties. Even as he was speaking, his wife, Bernadette, tall and slim, was hurrying past him to enter the shelter with her sons, Teddy and Mark, ten and nine years old respectively. Both were grinning excitedly.

'Lord love us,' Bernadette said as she hurried past to enter the shelter, 'sure isn't this a desperate business?'

More bombs fell on the dock area, the explosions louder and brighter, tearing the dark sky with silvery flashes of light, filling the air with dense smoke that spread out and drifted toward the nearest houses. The German aircraft were black bugs under low clouds, outlined by pale moonlight.

Albert and Patrick stared silently at each other, then they entered the shelter.

It was already packed. Some of those inside, including Mary and Doreen, were sitting on chairs; others were resting on the old bus seats that had been placed on the floor by the Air Raid Wardens. The remainder were forced to stand, self-consciously rubbing shoulders. A couple of women had lit candles and the blue-tipped yellow flames moved back and forth though the darkness, illuminating frightened or excited eyes. Some men were silent; others chattered nervously. Babies cried and children sobbed, but most of the children, including Teddy and Mark, were clearly excited, accepting the sirens and the approaching explosions as an intriguing new experience.

Bernadette Lavery, always organised, had brought herself a wooden chair and when she sat in it, mere inches from Doreen, the latter visibly stiffened.

'Evening, Mrs. Hamilton,' Bernadette said, smiling brightly.

'Evening,' Doreen replied with glacial formality, then pointedly turned her head away to glance around the packed shelter, looking for signs of fear in her neighbours, most of whom she viewed as her inferiors, cowardy custards the lot of them.

The sirens had stopped wailing, but now the sound of the bombing was more distinct. The German planes were still concentrating on the docks, though some bombs were also falling nearby. When they exploded, the concrete floor of the shelter shook perceptibly, causing dust to drift down from the ceiling, through shadow and flickering light.

'We should've brought some bottles of stout,' Patrick Lavery joked nervously, 'and had ourselves a wee party.'

'Next time,' Albert said, taking courage from the sight of Lavery's nervousness, wanting to be the better man.

'Sure I never knew that was you, Albert, till you spoke,' Bernadette Lavery said, 'given the state this dreadful business has me in.'

'Oh, it's me alright.' Albert grinned at her. 'I'm pretty sure I'm still me.'

'Can't get rid of him,' Mary said.

Another bomb exploded with a nerve-shredding roar, showering the shelter with flying debris, making it shake dangerously, causing more dust to drift down from the roof. Some women screamed and their kids cried even louder, though the Lavery boys, both as bold as brass, only expressed their frustration.

'I wanna go back outside and see the explosions,' Teddy said.

'Me, too,' Mark added. 'I bet it's like a fireworks display.'

Both boys had flaming red hair and freckles. Bernadette's long hair was the same colour, though her pale skin had a flawless, alabaster perfection.

'You're not going anywhere,' Patrick told them, 'so just stay where we've put you.'

'Sure I don't want to be kickin' the bucket tonight,' Bernadette said, glancing upwards, her green eyes like saucers, 'with that roof fallin' in on me.'

'That roof's as solid as the Rock of Gibraltar,' Brian informed her, speaking calmly, reassuringly, though he didn't look as casual as he sounded 'It's thick concrete reinforced with steel rods. You're as safe as houses in here, love.'

'I'm not so sure of that.' Mary was still cradling Marlene in her arms, but the child had starting crying and the noise, adding to the general bedlam, grated on Albert's nerves. 'I don't like it in here,' Mary added, licking her dry lips, 'and I don't feel too good.'

When she glanced accusingly at Albert, he looked away, pretending he couldn't see.

'It's just the stress, pet,' Bernadette said, giving Mary's shoulder a reassuring squeeze 'I mean, having to take care of that wee baby, with another one due any minute, you're bound to feel a bit tense. Just take deep, even breaths.'

Glancing through a gloomy space between the people packed in front of him, Albert saw a rectangular hole about three feet wide, fitted with loose bricks encased in sand. One end of an iron lever, shaped like the figure 'S', had been embedded in the sand.

'What's that for?' he asked.

'It's a make-shift hand-lever,' Brian informed him. 'Pull that lever out and the bricks'll come tumbling down to form an escape hatch. It's an emergency exit. To be used if the rubble from a damaged building blocks the normal way out.'

'*What's* that?' Mary asked, sounding startled.

'Nothing,' Albert said.

'*What* was that you said about damaged buildings?'

'Nothing,' Albert repeated.

Luckily, Mary was distracted by the arrival of an Air Raid Warden, another neighbour, Barney Thompson, who appeared in the normal exit, proudly wearing his uniform, holding a couple of unlit oil lamps. Barney had weak hazel eyes, a greying walrus moustache, and an overhanging beer drinker's belly. He liked being in charge of things.

'Nothin' to worry about,' he said. 'Sure everything's in hand. Those German eejuts up there can't see a thing down here and they'll be gone before you can say "boo". Now I've got a couple of oil lamps here, to be hung from the roof of the shelter. Albert, me boyo, pass one of these wee items to the far end of the shelter, then fix this one to that hook in the roof and set a match to it. You'll all feel grand when it's lit.'

The second lamp was passed from hand to hand to the far end of the shelter and hung from the hook there while Albert did the same at his end. When both lamps had been lit, the shelter was filled with a pale, eerie light, which, if not particularly comforting, was at least more effective than the torch lights.

'Aye, that's grand,' Barney said. 'Sure it's almost as comfortable here as it is in your own homes. Now I have to attend to the other shelters. I'll see youse all later.'

'He's joking, isn't he?' Mary said when Barney had gone, trying to hide her growing fear behind mockery, but not quite succeeding. '*Almost as comfortable as it is in our own homes*? That man must be demented.'

Now that she could clearly hear the sounds of the air raid, she knew the bombs were falling not only on the dock area, but also over the whole of East Belfast. When the shelter shook, when dust drifted down from the low ceiling and spiralled up from the concrete floor, she was not the only one to twitch with nerves.

'God, I feel really awful,' she said, wiping sweat from her forehead.

'The Lord be praised, we'll survive,' Doreen declaimed, as if from a pulpit. 'Fear is all in the mind.'

'I still feel awful,' Mary insisted. 'It's the new baby... I'm convinced it's on the way... I can feel it coming, I'm certain.'

'How do you have babies?' Teddy Devlin asked.

'Shut yer gob,' his father said.

'It's all right, Mary,' Nelly Devlin, the local midwife, said. She was sitting on an old bus seat on the floor, beside her husband, Sammy. 'I'm pretty sure it's not on the way yet, but I'm here if you need me.'

'Thanks, Nelly,' Mary said.

'Babies come out of that hole in your belly,' young Mark Lavery helpfully informed his older brother.

'You shut your gob as well,' his father told him.

'God,' Mary said in frustration, 'I could do with a fag!'

'No smokin' allowed in here,' Doreen informed her with authoritarian pleasure. 'Because of the gas, like.'

'Gas?' Mary glanced left and right with bright, startled eyes. With her jet-black hair and marble-white skin, she looked, Albert thought with unexpected admiration, like a wild and beautiful gypsy. 'You mean from the explosions?'

'Stop worrying,' Albert said, having absolute faith in the benefits of white lies. 'They used gas in the First World War; they don't use it these days. And if we're allowed to use these oil lamps, we should be able to smoke.' He nodded at Mary. 'Go for it. It might settle your nerves.'

Indeed, some of the others in the shelter had already lit up and Mary, when she glanced about her and saw them, decided to do the same. 'Here,' she said, holding baby Marlene out to Albert. 'You take her while I have a quick drag.'

'I'll take her,' Doreen said, enthusiastically reaching out for the baby that she didn't believe Mary deserved. Mary gave the baby to her, but before she could light a cigarette, a couple of bombs exploded outside, nearby, creating a hellish bedlam, making the whole shelter shake dangerously.

A woman screamed. Another bomb exploded. The cataclysmic roaring was followed by the sound of breaking windows, collapsing walls, splintering beams and falling debris. The same woman screamed again. More kids burst into tears. Mary jumped to her feet, eyes bright with panic, hands exploring her belly and crotch.

'I'm wet!' she exclaimed. 'The waters have broken. The baby's on its way. I'm certain of it. I can feel it. Oh, Jesus! *I've got to get out of here!'*

'You're probably just imagining it,' Albert said, trying to sound calm, though secretly he felt a rush of panic. 'It's just being in here with the noise and all. Just relax and...'

But Mary had turned away from him and was staring wide-eyed at Nelly Devlin. 'Nelly! I think...' She lowered her gaze to her belly. Following Mary's gaze, seeing what she was seeing, Nelly jumped to her feet and pushed her way through those standing between them. Another bomb exploded, the noise shocking, reverberating, causing more dust to fall from the ceiling, swirling about them and choking them. Mary twitched and reached for Nelly's hand.

'Yes,' Nelly said, 'you're right. The baby's on its way.'

'We're gonna see it bein' born,' Teddy Lavery proudly informed his younger brother.

'Shut your gob,' his father said for the third time.

'We'd better get Mary back into the house,' Nelly said to Albert. 'And I mean *right now!'*

Another bomb exploded, this time dangerously close, causing the shelter to shake dramatically, filling the air with more spiralling dust.

'But the bombs...' Albert began, then dried up, lost for words, blinking repeatedly and feeling unreal.

'It's no safer in here than it is out there,' Nelly insisted, 'and Mary can't have the baby here. Come on, Albert, let's go! You, Sammy,' she added, turning to her husband as he was rising from the bus seat on the shuddering, dust-spitting concrete floor of the shelter, 'go back to our house and fetch my medical bag.'

'Right,' Sammy said, nodding.

'God Almighty.' Bernadette's eyes widened with concern as she stared at Nelly. 'Are you saying Mary's having her wee'un right this minute?'

'Not this minute, but soon.'

'Then we all have to help her,' Bernadette said, 'and to hell with these bombs. Can you..?'

'Yes,' Nelly said, anticipating the question. 'I can deliver anytime, anywhere, but I'd rather not do it here.'

'Sure that's sound,' Bernadette said.

'Christ, it's coming! It's coming!' Mary exclaimed between frantic puffs on her cigarette. 'Oh, Jesus, Nelly, *do* something!'

'*You* do something!' Nelly retorted. 'For a start, you can put that bloody fag out.'

'Absolutely,' Doreen said.

'All right, *all right!*' Mary wailed, dropping the cigarette and grinding it out under the heel of her flat shoe. 'Now, please God, get me out of here.'

'We will,' Nelly promised.

'I'm coming, too,' Bernadette said.

'And me,' Doreen added, still holding the crying Marlene, staring grimly at the attractive, though Catholic, Bernadette. 'It's *my* son's child, after all.'

'Don't we know it,' Mary said, regaining enough courage to be sarcastic.

'Let's go.' Doreen turned to Patrick Lavery. 'What about you and the kids?'

Patrick glanced at his wife, seeking her opinion, just as another bomb exploded outside, showering the shelter with debris that rattled, drummed and hissed, causing more women to scream, more children to weep. The shelter was now filled with swirling, obscuring dust. Those not choking and coughing were hastily putting on their gas masks.

'I'm not leaving my children in here,' Bernadette said, coughing into her clenched fist, 'so they're coming with us.'

'Right,' Albert said, 'let's go.'

They filed out of the dust-filled air-raid shelter, back into the hellish night.

4

Waves of heat and blinding light. The ground shaking underfoot. Aircraft were still growling overhead and more bombs were exploding, though thankfully a few streets farther on. The heat increased as the flaring light faded behind curtains of dust.

Running ahead of the others, withdrawing his door key from his pocket, Albert glanced to the side and saw that the waves of heat were emanating from a gas main that had burst and turned into a sheet of flame, ignited by the exploding bombs or red-hot debris. The pavement in front of the terrace farther along had been blown to pieces. The shell hole, charred black and wreathed in smoke, stretched out from the front of one of the houses to the air raid shelter in the middle of the road. The shelter was covered in debris - pulverised concrete, smouldering pieces of wood, twisted metal, glinting shards of broken glass - from other houses damaged by the blast. It was like a bad dream.

Albert's house was untouched. The Lavery house had escaped as well. But the house of Sammy and Nelly Devlin was a mess, its front windows blown out and the front wall badly cracked, with rubble strewn across the pavement, all the way to the road.

'Oh, Christ!' Sammy exclaimed. 'That's my place that's been bombed!'

'It hasn't been bombed,' Nelly said in her pragmatic, observant way, she being an Irish woman, with little patience for Irish men, mothers' boys, the whole damned lot of them, even including her own man, who, of course, she dearly loved and protected. 'It's only the windows that have been damaged from the blast of that bomb that fell in front of it. Now go and fetch my bag like I told you.'

'Well...' Sammy began doubtfully, obviously thinking of structural damage inside, perhaps imagining the roof caving in on him.

'*Go!*' Nelly snapped and Sammy, without another word, a loving husband, obedient, ran off along the moonlit, dust-obscured street.

'God, look at that, Mark!' Teddy Lavery said to his younger brother as they both stared, while on the move, at the ignited gas blazing farther along the street.

'It's like a bonfire on the Twelfth,' Mark said, 'but even better than that.'

'Get into that house, the pair of you,' Bernadette said, 'before I give you a hidin'.'

'We can't,' Teddy said. 'The front door's locked.'

'Don't give me your lip.'

Glancing skyward, Albert saw that the German bombers had indeed moved on and were now flying above West Belfast. Almost certainly they would be turning around to attack the docks once more, before heading back out to sea. Reaching the house, keeping his face turned away from the heat of the burning gas, an immense fan of incandescent yellow-white flame, he turned the key in the lock, pushed the door open, switched on the light, forgetting the blackout restrictions, then stood aside to let the others enter. He felt dazed and unreal.

Mary rushed in first, muttering, 'Jesus Christ, save us!' She was followed by Doreen, still carrying baby Marlene, then by Nelly and Bernadette. When Patrick Lavery and his two boys were also inside, Albert slammed the door shut. As he stepped into the living room, Mary was being ushered upstairs by Nelly. Meanwhile, Bernadette hurried into the narrow kitchen to start boiling water. Albert's father had tugged the closed curtains apart, a mere inch or so, to see what was happening outside. Patrick Lavery and his two boys were just standing there, looking bemused.

'Take a seat,' Albert said, still tugged uncomfortably between fear and excitement, yet noting, at the same time, that his racing heart had settled down, that his breathing was even.

As Patrick and his sons were cramming together on the sofa, facing the fireplace, Nelly came back down the stairs, saying, 'When that man of myine returns with my bag, send him straight upstairs. You, Albert, can help Bernadette bring up the water; the rest of you stay down here, keeping out of the way. I'd plug the ears of those two boys,' she added, 'to save them from hearing Mary's screams.'

'Let them learn at an early age,' Doreen said grimly, 'just how much a poor woman has to suffer for her man's sinful pleasures.'

'Your *son's* sinful pleasures,' Nelly reminded her with a wicked grin. Then, before Doreen could respond, she turned aside to bawl at the kitchen, 'How's that hot water coming, Bernadette?'

'It's on its way!'

'What's the water for?' young Teddy Lavery asked.

'None of your business, you nosey-parker,' his mother told him.

Nelly jabbed her thumb in the direction of the kitchen. 'In you go,' she said to Albert. 'You and Bernadette can form a chain gang; she fetches, you carry.'

'Right,' Albert said doubtfully, wondering how to avoid what was coming, keen to make his escape, preferring the bombs to the baby, the unreal to the real.

Someone hammered on the front door. 'That'll be Sammy with my bag,' Nelly said, emerging from the landing to open the door herself. Sammy stepped in with the bag. Upstairs, Mary screamed. Sammy winced and slammed the door behind him, shutting out flashing lights and explosions, then he passed the brown-leather bag to Nelly.

'How's the house?' Nelly asked him.

'Filled with glass. A few cracks runnin' down the front walls and dust all over the place. Truth to tell, it's a quare mess.'

'But fixable.'

'Ackaye.'

'That'll give you something to do when you're not in the pub with your drinking pals.'

Sammy grinned. 'Aye, I reckon.'

Mary screamed again.

'I'm coming! I'm coming!' Nelly shouted, hurrying back up the stairs, holding the leather bag in one hand.

Stepping into the living room, Sammy grinned and rolled his eyes. 'Fun and games for one and all,' he said.

'Not for that poor sufferin' woman upstairs,' Doreen retorted, defending Mary for once as she rocked Marlene into contented silence. 'Don't try talkin' to *her* about fun and games, given what she's about to go through. Sure isn't it always the women who suffer while you men have it easy?'

When Mary screamed a third time, Patrick's boys stared nervously at the ceiling, then at each other. Bernadette, emerging from the kitchen, carrying a basin of warm water, caught their reaction. They weren't too excited now.

'I think you should take those two home,' she said to Patrick. 'They won't like what's happening here. And let's pray that those planes don't drop any more bombs as you walk them back.'

Patrick opened his mouth to protest, but then, when Mary screamed again upstairs, he closed his mouth and nodded agreement. 'Right, boys, let's go.'

'Here,' Bernadette said to Albert, holding out the basin of hot water in which a clean white cloth was floating like a poached egg. 'Take this upstairs and come back down for another.'

Though feeling queasy at the thought of what he might see in the bedroom, well able to imagine what this water would be used for, Albert took the basin from Bernadette and started up the stairs. The front door opened and closed behind him as Patrick and his boys left the house. Brian was still at the front window, peering out, but as

Albert disappeared up the stairs, he turned back to the room.

'Can I help?'

'Yes,' Bernadette said, emerging from the kitchen with another basin of warm water. 'You can take this one up.'

'Right.'

'What about me?' Sammy asked.

'Plant your backside on a chair and don't do anything that Nelly might disapprove of.'

'Wouldn't dream of it, love.'

Brian carried the basin of water upstairs as Albert was coming down, pale from what he had seen in the bedroom.

'Tell you what,' he said to his father, as if trying to be helpful. 'You stay at the top of the stairs and I'll pass the next basin up to you. We'll be quicker that way.'

Mary screamed in the bedroom. 'Ah, Jesus, oh mercy, sure I'm bein' torn apart!'

'Just take a deep breath and push,' Nelly responded, 'and none of your nonsense.'

'Is it coming? Is it happening?'

'Yes, it is. It's the shock of that air raid.'

'Ah, Jesus! Oh, no!'

When Albert winced, Brian grinned and nodded, saying, 'Ackaye, that's the way to do it, son. I'll take this one up and wait for you to bring up the others.'

As his father went up, Albert went down to find his mother still sitting by the fireplace, holding baby Marlene in her arms and staring grimly at Sammy Devlin, who had, the Fenian upstart, taken a chair without being invited.

'Christ, I'm parched,' Sammy said.

'Is it comin?' Doreen asked, ignoring Sammy, looking at Albert.

'I think so,' Albert replied, avoiding her gaze as he hurried past her to the kitchen.

'It's all that smokin' has done her nerves in,' Doreen said, 'and loosened up her insides. If anything happens to that new-born child, she'll have only herself to blame.'

Bernadette, in the kitchen, rolled her eyes as Albert walked in. 'Here,' she said, handing him another basin of warm water. 'That's the last one for you to take up. You look so ill, I wouldn't have the heart to ask you to do it again. I'll take the last one up myself and stay there to help Nelly until it's done. You can stay down here with your dad. Have a drink and smoke to settle your nerves. *If* your hand isn't shakin' so much you can't light your fag.'

'Just let go of the basin,' Albert said, though he managed a weak grin, 'and give me none of your lip.'

Bernadette smiled, releasing her grip on the basin, turning away to fill up the last one. Leaving the kitchen, Albert saw his mother placing Marlene back in her pram. Ignoring that sight, he nodded at the beaming Sammy who indicated, by jabbing his index finger at his mouth, that he wouldn't say 'No' to a drink. Albert nodded in return, agreeing with the sentiment, then carried the basin up the stairs. Brian was waiting on the landing to take the basin from him.

'You can come down when you've taken that in,' Albert said. 'Bernadette's bringing up the last one and then she'll stay in there until it's over.'

'Good,' Brian said, turning away to take the basin into the room.

When Mary screamed again, Albert winced and hurried back down the stairs.

Having pulled a ball of wool and needles out of her handbag, Doreen was knitting with fierce concentration. Since she wasn't looking at him, Sammy pointed again to his own throat, indicating that he was desperate for a drink. Before Albert could even nod, indicating that he, too, had a thirst, Bernadette emerged from the kitchen with the final basin of warm water. After waiting until Brian had come down the stairs, she hurried back up into the bedroom.

This time, when Mary screamed, Albert hurried into the kitchen, emerging with a bottle of Bushmills whisky and three tumblers. He waved the tumblers at his father and Sammy. Both men nodded gratefully.

'And who said you could drink?' This was Doreen to her husband.

'Special occasion,' Albert said before his dad could reply, determined to let him have one this time, while having one himself. 'A wee drink and a smoke,' he added, 'as recommended by Bernadette. Good for the nerves, she said.'

'Humph,' his mother responded, putting her nose up in the air, though continuing with her knitting, the needles moving rapidly up and down, clicking like chopsticks. 'Any excuse, I suppose. Next thing you'll be pretending it's Christmas, but don't mind *me*. Just pretend I'm not here, like.'

'You want one as well?' Albert asked.

'Well, I wouldn't normally. As you know, I can't drink much. But if you two are going to have one, I don't see why *I* can't.'

'Sure, why not, indeed?' Brian took the three tumblers from Albert, handed one to Sammy, then held up the other two. When Albert had filled those and was turning to Sammy, Brian passed one of the tumblers to his wife. Still holding the bottle, Albert hurried back into the kitchen and returned with a fourth glass.

Upstairs, Mary screamed yet again, then cried out, 'Oh, God!'

Albert, with heart pounding again, poured himself a stiff drink and had a good swallow.

'Sounds like she's doing well,' his father said, as if discussing the weather. 'Bearing down strong, I'd say.'

Sammy sipped and gasped ostentatiously. 'Sure that's a good wee drop. It should soothe the pain of waiting for Mary's delivery. Here's to you all.'

He raised his glass.

'To your health,' Brian said.

'To *Mary's* health,' Doreen retorted with emphasis, 'and to the health of that poor wee unborn child.'

'Right enough,' Sammy said, having beaten everyone to the first drop and already needing another. 'God, that's good!' he exclaimed after his second sip, licking his lips.

Albert lit a cigarette, feeling rotten, despite the whisky, not wanting another baby in the house to clutter up his life. In truth, he couldn't *afford* another baby, but he had only himself to blame. A man did these things when he was out of his head with lust, then spent the rest of his life paying for them. This second child was his penance.

'And during our first air raid!' he said. 'I can't believe this is happening.'

'It's the air raid brought it on that wee bit prematurely,' Doreen informed him in a confidential manner. 'The shock loosened up her insides, like I said; now the child's being pushed out before its time. Not that the constant smoking of your wife has helped matters, but it's too late to discuss that now, isn't it?' She drank most of the whiskey in one gulp, then held her tumbler up to the light, thoughtfully scrutinising it. 'A fine medicine,' she said, 'if you drink it in moderation, though that glass was more moderate than most, if the truth be known.'

Albert inhaled on his cigarette, exhaled a cloud of smoke, dutifully filled up his mother's glass and then turned to his father. 'Do you think the bombers will return?'

'They're on their way, son. Sure I can hear them in the distance. They're circling around over the Black Mountain, to come back to the docks. They'll bomb the docks one last time, then escape out to sea.'

'Which means they'll bomb *us* again,' Sammy said. 'They're almost certain to do that.'

Cocking his ear for that ominous, distant sound, Alberrt heard it soon enough: an armada of bombers flying back towards East Belfast. They would aim to hit the docks, which included this area. Sure you couldn't tell the difference from up there; it was all hit and miss, like.

Mary screamed again upstairs. The scream faded away into a pitiful moaning that made Albert shudder and close his eyes. He wanted to be in a music hall, somewhere else, *anywhere*, tap-dancing and singing (*the roar of the greasepaint, the smell of the crowd*) women staring up at him, wide-eyed with admiration, all willing to give him anything he wanted. Which, God help him (he thought with self-pity), he had rarely received in real life.

He'd always loved his part-time work in the music halls; to him, it was more real than reality, more true than the lies or ingenious self-deceptions of his childhood. The music halls of Belfast, between the Lagan River and Black Mountain, his suffocating boundaries and unbreakable perimeters, were where he felt that he truly belonged. Not here in this cramped two-up, two-down house with a screaming wife about to have a second child. Domestic life was his prison.

'I thought whisky was hard to get these days,' Brian said, looking appreciatively at his glass and hoping to engage in normal conversation, to distract himself from what might be coming any minute now... a German bomb through the ceiling. 'Everything bein' rationed and all.'

'It *is* difficult to get,' Albert replied. 'Like cigarettes and matches and God knows what else, but in this case I have a friend with connections, though he works in the Yard.'

'Roy,' his father guessed correctly.

'No names and no pack drill,' Albert retorted. 'Ask no questions and I'll tell you no lies.'

'No questions asked,' Brian said, raising his gaze when Mary screamed again. The bass rumbling of the German bombers grew louder, now approaching East Belfast.

'Here they come,' Sammy said.

'Oh, God, it's coming!' Mary wailed.

'The good Lord will protect us,' Doreen informed Albert, 'because the shameless screaming of that wife of yours will surely shake the very portals of Heaven.'

'She's bearing down really hard now,' Brian said. 'I take the screaming as a positive sign. That wee child's on its way.'

'You think they know what they're doing up there?' Doreen asked the room in general. 'Maybe I should help them. The old-fashioned ways are always the best, and those two up there, both Catholics - no offence meant, Mister Devlin - almost certainly have their new-fangled ways.'

'Nelly uses the old-fashioned ways,' Sammy said, seeming not to take offence, though God knows what he was actually thinking, this being sectarian Belfast with its multitude of subterranean hypocrisies. 'Sure you've no cause for fear there.'

'Leave them be, love,' Brian added, pouring oil on troubled waters. 'I'm sure they know what they're doing. Nelly Devlin has never lost a child. I take that as a positive sign.'

A bomb exploded directly behind the house, its roar reverberating, shaking the very foundations, as Mary released her most piercing scream so far.

'I don't know what's shakin' the house most,' Doreen said. 'The bombs or your Mary. Now a little bit of screamin' sometimes helps the child come out, but it has to be said that in *my* day – '

She didn't complete the sentence. Albert saw his mother vanishing in an onrush of flaring light that filled the whole room, washing out the normal light, shocking, unfamiliar, too vivid to be real, and only then did he hear the noise, terrifying, cataclysmic, a demoniac roaring and whistling, followed abruptly by silence and the feeling that his eardrums were bursting. *Oh, Jesus Christ, I'm deaf!* The moment stretched out forever, only humanised by fear, as he was bathed in an alien heat that sucked the air from his lungs, scorched his chest, made

50

him retch, the walls and floor shaking around him, the window-panes blown to pieces. Luckily, the flying shards of broken glass were blocked by the closed curtains and showered onto the floor under the window frame, instead of into the room, though they still added their own musical tinkling to the greater, all-encompassing bedlam.

Upstairs, Mary screamed like a stuck pig.

Nelly, responding, bawled words that were lost in the continuing reverberations of the blast.

Blinking, shaking his head to clear it, Albert realised that he had automatically thrown himself to the floor and that his father had done exactly the same. Pieces of broken glass were glinting on his father's back, but his face was pressed to the floor and there were no visible bloodstains on his clothing. To prove that he was still alive, he pushed himself upright, even as Albert, dazed and temporarily mindless, stared dizzily at him.

'Jesus,' Sammy said from where he was seated on the couch behind Albert, 'I thought the whole house had gone. Thank God for that whisky.'

Glancing back over his shoulder, Albert saw that Sammy, also, was unharmed. 'I spilt all my drink,' Albert said. 'I didn't realise what was...'

Hearing Mary screaming again, he rubbed his stinging eyes and saw his mother still seated in her chair, covered in dust like a ghost but seemingly unharmed. Baby Marlene was crying, shredding his nerves again, but while he was still on his knees, willing himself to stand upright, his mother rushed to the pram that was, like her, covered in the dust raining down from the ceiling and spiralling out of the cracked walls. Reaching the pram, she picked Marlene up, turned her this way and that, checking that she was unhurt, then said, 'Thank the Lord, this wee creature's all right. Not a scratch on her. So what's happening upstairs?'

Finally forcing himself to his feet, Albert glanced left and right, up and down, at floor and ceiling; and saw fresh cracks with dust spewing out of them. Eventually, seeing dust boiling down the stairwell, through that pool of yellow light framed by shadow, when Mary's final scream turned into moaning, he rushed up the stairs.

Ascending, he noticed that the walls and ceilings of the landing were cracked as badly as those downstairs, that the air was filled with the spiralling dust of broken mortar, and that pieces of plaster and brick were scattered underfoot. Though frightened by the thought of what he might find in the bedroom, he pushed the door open.

An exhausted Mary, stark naked, sweat-slicked, was stretched out on bloody sheets.

Albert heard the stabbing cry of a newborn baby.

He started to enter the bedroom, but then stopped himself, still frightened of the unknown, and was grateful when Nelly Devlin stepped in front of him, blocking his way.

'They're both fine,' Nelly said with a smile. 'You've lost half of the upstairs of your house – that last bomb did its worst - but Mary and your son are right as rain.'

'Now go and find out what's happened to *my* family,' Bernadette said, from where she stood behind Nelly, wiping her hands with a bloody cloth, 'while we clean up this mess.'

But Albert didn't have to do anything. Even as he was turning away, he glanced down the stairwell to see Brian opening the front door. Patrick and his two sons were outside, framed in a vertical rectangle of darkness, fitfully illuminated with flashes of light from the bombing and burning. The boys were wide-eyed with shock.

'Our house has been destroyed,' Patrick said, almost weeping, 'but me and the wee'uns are okay. What about youse in here?'

'We're all safe and sound,' Brian said, 'though I think we might have lost our house as well. Jesus, Patrick, come in.'

When Patrick and the boys entered, Brian glanced outside, into that darkness still fitfully illuminated by flashes of light. 'At least the bombers are leaving.' He closed the front door and turned back into the room as Albert came down the stairs. 'The explosions are moving away from us,' Brian continued, 'crossing the docks as the planes fly out to sea.' Sirens wailed all over the city. 'The air raid's over,' he said.

Albert sighed. 'Sure they're all okay upstairs and I have a new son. Sit down, Patrick. Hey, kids,' he said to the wide-eyed boys, 'take a seat on the sofa. Your mum'll be down in a minute. Now who's for a drink?'

'I think congratulations are in order,' Patrick said.

'What for?'

When Albert heard his new son crying upstairs, he knew exactly what he meant by his thoughtless statement: his repudiation of the need for congratulations. Because he didn't believe, at bottom, that they were in order. He hadn't wanted, and did not want, this child.

'Jesus Christ,' he added forlornly, shaking his head from side to side, wearily denying the truth of his own words.

'You can't call him *that*,' Sammy said mischievously, 'despite the fact that you sing and dance like an angel. So what *will* you call him?'

'John,' Doreen said without hesitation, picking up her empty glass and holding it out to be refilled with whisky. 'Let's all drink to John Hamilton.'

And so they all drank to John.

Born in violence.

Born *for* it.

Chapter Two

1

The air raid was being discussed on the radio as Barry Coogan washed himself from the waist up over the sink in the primitive kitchen of his parents' house in the Pound Loney of the Falls Road area. Barry had watched the air raid the previous evening from his upstairs bedroom window and taken a grim satisfaction from it. It had been a spectacular sight, with bombs exploding all over the harbour as well as the nearby Newtownards Road and Mountpottinger areas. Buildings had blazed and collapsed, fountains of crimson sparks had illuminated the night sky like a fireworks display, then black smoke had boiled up, as if emerging from Hell's fires, to obscure all that had gone before it, including the few stars previously visible *and* the German bombers. Now, the following afternoon, as he dried his face, neck and shoulders with a towel, Barry heard the BBC radio commentator describe the 'bravery' and 'fortitude' shown by the Belfast people during what had been an 'inhumane' attack on the city. Shaking his head in disbelief, grinning at his youthful reflection, distorted by the crack in the mirror above the sink, he put on his shirt and tie, slid his braces back over his shoulders, then went into the living room for his coat.

His father and mother were sitting in old, elbow-smoothed armchairs by the prepared fire in the open grate under the mantelpiece. The fire wasn't lit because this was an unusually warm day. It was a small, cramped living room, immaculately clean, with a framed Virgin Mary on one wall and a framed Pope on the other, both surrounded by family photos and reproductions of Irish landscapes and biblical scenes, purchased cheaply either along the Falls or in Smithfield Market. Eddie worked for a local haulier, delivering coal for him. It wasn't a great job and he worked for slave wages, but it was better than being unemployed like most of his friends. Most of the decent jobs in Belfast went to the Protestants.

Just turned forty, Eddie Coogan was still a handsome man with a healthy head of slightly greying auburn hair. He was wearing his dark-blue overalls and had his horse-and-cart parked outside, the animal tethered to the nearest lamppost. Eddie only delivered around the Falls and could come home for lunch, so right now he was having a thick salad sandwich, washed down with a cup of tea, while cocking one ear to the radio. As the news was just ending, he switched the radio off and had another bite of his sandwich.

Barry's mother, Lizzie, a heavily built woman who had aged before her time, was wearing a flowered apron over her dress and cardigan - the standard wear for married women in the Falls. Normally she worked long hours as a weaver in a Falls Road textile mill, but she had been laid off a week ago and was presently looking for a new position. Given the increase in work caused by the war and the urgent need for uniforms and other military clothing, she would probably be working again quite soon. Right now, she was knitting herself another cardigan.

Barry, the youngest of what had once been five children, three boys and two girls, was nineteen years old, highly intelligent and unemployed. There wasn't much work for men his age around the Falls and when he tried to get work elsewhere, such as the Harland & Wolff shipyard or the Short & Harland aircraft factory, invariably he was asked what his religion was. The answer to that question, at least outside the Falls Road area, invariably led to prompt rejection.

'Did I hear right?' Barry said, lighting a cigarette to relax before he went out. 'That bit of news about the bravery and fortitude shown by one-and-all during the air-raid.'

His father chuckled. 'Ackaye,' he said. 'The usual propaganda. What I heard from some pals is that frightened people, mostly Prods, fled from their homes during the raid and headed wide-eyed for the open countryside. Even now, with the raid well over, a lot of those in East Belfast are leaving with their belongings stacked up in carts and prams. They're convinced there's going to be another air raid soon, so they're heading for the open country, hoping to find safer accommodation. You wouldn't credit it, would you?'

'I would,' Barry said, inhaling gratefully and then exhaling again, pursing his lips to blow a couple of smoke rings. 'They didn't prepare for war at all, they refused to accept that it was coming, and now that it's here they're scared out of their wits. The only thing the Orangemen are good for is marching to Lambeg drums.'

'Lots of damage, though.'

'I missed that bit,' Barry said. 'What *was* the damage?'

'A lot killed, even more badly wounded. Hundreds of minor casualties due to blast, shock and, as you'd imagine, flying glass and stones, smashed beams, pieces of piping, and so on. Also, lots trapped in the rubble, some dead, but others, the poor souls, still alive and suffering.'

'Let's hope they were mostly Prods,' Barry said.

'They'll still be suffering something terrible,' his father said, 'if they're alive but trapped in the rubble. What a nightmare that must be.'

'Aye, I suppose so. Is it really bad over there?'

'The radio's playin' down the damage, but from what I heard, when I was doin' my rounds this morning, it was pretty bad.'

'How bad?'

'Scores of homes wrecked. Hundreds more so badly damaged that even Africa's starvin' couldn't live in 'em. A lot are still burning right now. You can see the smoke over the Albertbridge and Mountpottinger junction, where a lot of bombs fell, and over Castlereagh Street and most of the streets off Templemore Avenue. Gas mains were fractured and ignited and are still burning. More smoke's coming from smouldering wooden beams - all that's left of the houses. Tramlines were mangled and at least one tram took a direct hit. Most of the people from the ruined houses are being relocated to the Shankill and Sandy Row. It's a pretty big exodus.'

'Rather them than us,' Barry said.

'It might be us the next time.'

Barry was always surprised by how little malice his father felt for the Prods, despite what they had put him through in his lifetime. Eddie had still been a boy, twelve years old, when the Ulster Volunteer Force was instituted and Sir Edward Carson, the southern Unionist, led Ulster's bloody resistance to Home Rule. He had only been fifteen when the Easter Rising of 1916 and its horrendous aftermath, the execution of all of the rebel leaders by firing squad, turned many young Catholic men, formerly uncommitted, into fervent nationalists. Eddie had been one of those young men. In 1920, when he was nineteen years old, civil war broke out in Ireland. The following month, Belfast exploded, with hundreds of Protestant apprentices marching into the Harland & Wolff shipyard to assault Catholic workers. Some were kicked and pummelled with fists, others were badly injured when steel rivets were thrown at them, yet others were forced to dive into the harbour and swim for their lives. One of the latter was Eddie. When he reached the shore and made his way home, soaked, frozen and badly bruised from the beating he had taken from a Protestant gang, he learnt that fierce fighting between Catholics and Protestants had taken place all over Belfast. Enraged by what was happening, he'd gone back into the streets to join the fight against the rampaging Prods. He fought with other Catholics for three days and nights, using anything he could get his hands on, including stones and petrol bombs, until British troops fired on both sides and order was restored. A month later, however, Protestants went on the rampage again, attacking Catholic areas, burning pubs and business premises, eventually driving almost all of the Catholic residents out of Belfast. Shortly after that bloodbath, Eddie, deeply embittered, formally joined his local battalion of the IRA. After training, he took part in raids against army barracks and police stations. Though successful for a couple of months, he was eventually picked up in a wide swoop on suspected nationalist sympathisers and incarcerated for three months in the Crumlin Road jail.

Now, gazing down at his mild, kindly-faced father, Barry could scarcely imagine him engaged in fire fights, blowing up buildings, or serving time in prison - not even as a 19-year old, which he had been at the time.

'You really don't hate the Prods, do you?' Barry said, exhaling a stream of cigarette smoke. 'Not even after all you've been through. Sure I find that amazing.'

'Why hate 'em? They're Irish, just like you an' me. True, some of them are wicked, but so are some of our Catholics, and a lot of them, also just like us, believe in what they're fighting for.'

'They're fighting for British rule,' Barry said, still trying to find the bottom line of his father's decency.

'Thousands of 'em died valiantly at the Somme for the Brits,' Eddie responded, 'and that, right or wrong, gives them a heavy emotional investment in that country. Prods like that - those whose sons died at the Somme - feel more British than Irish. Sure I think that's an awful sad thing, but I *do* understand it.'

'You think we'd do that?'

'Ackaye. We couldn't really avoid it. It's something that would just gradually happen. Life's not fair to anyone.'

Barry didn't share his father's equanimity about the Prods and was still too young to grasp how he could have retained it, given his personal, painful history. He did, however, understand why his father had gone back to the fight after being released from his first time in prison. Set free shortly after the signing of the Anglo-Irish Treaty, he'd gone straight back to the IRA to take part in its bid to destabilise Northern Ireland. The campaign was launched in January 1922 when eleven IRA men from Country Monaghan were arrested; by March it had exploded in Belfast where both sides engaged in brutal assassinations, intimidation, house-burning and rioting. In April, the Royal Ulster Constabulary was formed, thus turning Northern Ireland into what was virtually a Protestant-controlled police state. In the same month, the Civil Authorities (Special Powers) Bill became law, enabling special courts to hold suspects without trial for unspecified periods and impose sentences of penal servitude or death. Despite this, the killing in Belfast increased, which led in turn to the imposition of internment. All two hundred men arrested in the first sweep were Catholics - and Eddie was one of them. Incarcerated in the Crumlin Road jail for the second time, he was severely and repeatedly beaten.

'Well, I have to say, Da, that given what I've been reading upstairs, I can't find it in me to be as understanding as you are. When we wrest Ireland back from the Brits, making it an Ireland for the Irish, I won't lose a minute's sleep over the thought of a bunch of fat-bellied Orangemen pining for their lost Loyalist heritage. They used that heritage to keep us firmly in our place and we both know where that place is - right here, at the bottom of the heap. As Catholics, we're second-class citizens with precious few rights.'

Eddie chuckled, shaking his head in bemusement, gazing out the front window, seeing only a row of small terraced houses at the other side of the road. The sun was shining for once. 'All that reading you've done has filled you with convictions,' he said, 'but you're young, so that's as it should be and I'm not saying it's wrong. I'm simply saying that at my age, a man tends to take a more objective view and be less judgmental.'

'So why did you go back to the fight after you'd been released from prison for the second time?'

'You know why,' Eddie said.

'Yes, Da, I know why. Because by the time you got out of prison, over five hundred people had been killed in Northern Ireland, most of them Catholics, thousands of Catholics had been driven out of their jobs, thousands more had been forced out of their homes and businesses. That's why you went back.'

'Aye, that's true enough.'

'And you weren't too thrilled when James Craig abolished proportional representation, were you?'

'No, son, I wasn't.'

'And you were even less pleased when the Northern Ireland parliament's permanent home became Stormont?'

'That didn't please me either, I'll confess.'

'But then, by the time you went back to your battalion, most IRA activity in the six counties had ground to a standstill.'

'Aye, that's right.'

'Which is when you got out.'

'That's right as well, son. So, what's your point?'

'The point, Da, is that although you got out, you didn't stop being active - and you paid the price for it.'

'You take your chances and pay your dues.'

'Yeah,' Barry said sardonically. 'With a third term in prison.'

He knew what he was talking about because his Da had told him all about it. Given the collapse of all IRA activity, Eddie had gone to work in the Hughes Dickson flour mill, an immense, grim edifice that loomed over the Falls and the Divis Street Methodist Church located adjacent to it. Though working conditions there were appalling, the air dense with choking flour-dust, Eddie had managed to hang on for a couple of years, making just enough money to marry Lizzie and father the first two of their five children. However, just when he needed money the most, when a third child was due, the Great Depression of the early 1930s caused thousands to lose their jobs. Eddie was one of those unfortunates. Soon he found himself deeply in debt, threatened with the prospect of losing his home and entering the poor house. Outraged again, he joined the

Unemployed Workers' Committee and helped organise a series of public marches and demonstrations. When the outdoor relief workers began a strike to force their demand for an increase in assistance, 60,000 other workers from all over Belfast, Catholics and Protestants alike, marched from the Frederick Street Labour Exchange to a torch-lit rally at the Custom House. Violent demonstrations erupted in the days following, leading to clashes between the police and the workers. Caught throwing cobblestones at attacking police, Eddie was badly beaten up. With a split head and one broken leg, he was thrown into a 'cage' and driven away to be treated. A few weeks later, still in crutches, he was taken to court and sentenced to eighteen months in the Crumlin Road jail. That was his third prison stretch.

'Does it still bother you to recall what they did to you in prison?' Barry asked.

'Never mind what happened in prison,' Lizzie said sternly, interrupting for the first time. That's all in the past now. We've no shame about your Da's spells in prison, but that doesn't mean we want to remember them. Some things in life are best forgotten and that jail is one of them.'

Eddie grinned. 'No,' he said, 'it doesn't hurt to think about it. But I've told you all about this before, so there's no need to repeat it.'

'You don't have to repeat it,' Barry said, ''cause I've been thinking about it.'

'You think too much,' his father said. 'I don't want you to get involved like I did. No good will come out of it.'

'I'm not involved,' Barry lied. 'I just like to know these things. It's like my personal history.'

'It is that, right enough, son.'

'You kept going back to the fray, though didn't you, until that last time? You just couldn't stay away.'

'No, I couldn't stay away until the last time. But that last time was too much for me. I gave up after that, though I don't want to talk about it now. Not now and not ever.'

Barry thought he understood why his father couldn't talk about that particular period. While serving his third term in jail, he was beaten repeatedly by the wardens, thrown repeatedly into solitary confinement and, worst of all, informed that two of his three children had died from the tuberculosis that was decimating those living in the cramped, damp houses of the Catholic ghettoes. That news devastated him; more so when he was refused permission to attend their funerals. When eventually he emerged from jail, he was a greatly changed man. Knowing that if he was arrested for the fourth time, he would receive the harshest sentence possible under the law, he determined to be more careful. Initially, after taking on a modestly paid job, driving a horse and cart for a local haulier, he stayed well away from politics, including the neutered IRA. Nevertheless, he continued to be outraged by the inflammatory outpourings of Unionist politicians and to agitate for social and political reforms. Thus, when in 1935 violent demonstrations erupted again, he couldn't resist the call to arms. After more days of violent rioting, in which he took part, he found himself lying on a bed in a Catholic 'safe' house, being treated for gunshot wounds to his left shoulder. Kept in the safe house until his wounds healed, he was then transferred, under cover of darkness, to his own home in the Pound Loney. When eventually he was able to leave his house, when the wounds were completely healed and the bandages were removed, he was left with a shoulder that would never be as mobile as it had been. Luckily, the haulier he worked for was a nationalist sympathiser and he not only let him return to his old job, but ensured that he was only given the kind of light deliveries that he could manage with his disabled shoulder. According to what he had confessed to Barry, Eddie, morally and physically exhausted, had then become a much changed, more passive man who kept well away from politics, including the IRA. He was, however, still a socialist at heart and in principle still supported the IRA. He just couldn't cut it anymore and Barry understood why.

'So what are you up to today?' his father asked him, clearly wanting to change the subject.

Barry shrugged. 'Ack, the usual,' he lied again. 'Got a couple of jobs to apply for, then see a few pals and maybe cadge a pint of stout off one of them.'

'You still seeing that nice wee girl, Eleanor?'

Barry nodded. 'Yep.'

'Is it serious?' his mother asked him.

'Maybe. It's early days yet. Don't worry, Ma. Sure when it gets really serious, I'll let you know.'

His mother smiled. 'You do that, son. It's time you settled down.'

'I can't *afford* to settle down,' Barry said, 'until I get another job.'

'If you're serious about her, you'll take that chance.'

'I don't take chances.' Barry threw his cigarette butt into the open grate and then turned to Eddie. 'So what are *you* plannin' for this evening? Got anything lined up?'

'Just goin' for a game of darts in Walsh's pub, up in the Clonard.'

'And a couple of pints, of course,' Lizzie said.

'Those, too,' Eddie admitted.

'Well, I'd better be makin' tracks,' Barry said. 'I'll see youse both later.'

'Enjoy yourself, son.'

'And take care of yourself,' Lizzie added.

'I will,' Barry promised.

2

Barry and his parents shared a dilapidated two-bedroom house in a terraced street in the heart of the Pound Loney, within sight of the twin spires of St. Peter's pro-cathedral. The Pound Loney, best known and most loved district in the Falls, was the maze of streets that lay between Albert Street and Pound Street. Its inhabitants, of which there were an unusually large number for such a small area (hardly more than half a mile square) were known as 'Loney hoppers'. While the origin of the name was in dispute, the most widely held view was that the area had once been the location of an animal pound reached by way of a 'loanin', or lane, named Pound Loanin, or Pound Lane, and that this gradually became translated as 'Pound Loney'. The terraced streets of the area had been built by Belfast industrialists to house the growing numbers of lowly paid workers required for their huge mills and factories. Nevertheless, while the 'Loney hoppers', living in tiny houses in narrow, packed streets, suffered from a lack of space and privacy, they had developed an uncommon sense of community and interdependency. Certainly, it was a tight, caring community and Barry was proud to be part of it.

After stepping outside, he walked along the street and saw three girls swinging around a lamppost, using ropes tied to the high metal upright, other girls playing hopscotch on the paving stones, yet others skipping with ropes. Ignoring the girls, whom they traditionally disdained at that age, the boys, all wearing short pants, pullovers, open-necked shirts and shoes or boots with knee-high socks, were playing football and marbles at an 'opening' farther along, where the street intersected with another. Women in dresses and flowered aprons were sitting on chairs outside their front doors, some with babies in their laps, others surrounded by children or grandparents, all taking in the unusual warmth of this mid-afternoon. On good days like this, some left their prams by the front door while they continued with their housework inside, confident that the baby in the pram could benefit from some sunshine without being harmed by passers-by. Older women were sharpening the blades of their kitchen knives by rubbing them vigorously against the stone windowsills of their houses. All in all, it was a pleasant scene, indicating community harmony, but when Barry then saw another local, the robust and good-natured Jimmy Ryan, serving a queue of women with water from his wheeled water-carrier, pouring it from a container into the buckets they held out to him, he was bitterly reminded that certain basic amenities of life, such as proper plumbing, were missing from many of the Falls Road homes. The Catholics lacked a lot that the Prods took for granted.

'How are you, Jimmy?' Barry said as he passed, tipping his peaked cap to the water-carrier.

'Ack, sure I'm grand,' Jimmy replied, flashing his big grin as he poured water into the bucket held by old Mrs Dogherty, who was wearing an ankle-length black dress, with a black shawl wrapped around her shoulders. 'If this weather keeps up, I'll do a quare bit of business, like, so I'm not complainin'.'

'That's the ticket,' Barry said.

At the end of the street, he turned into the Falls Road, heading uphill. Known affectionately as 'the Falls', this was the heart and soul of West Belfast, running all the way from Divis Street, just above Castle Street and the centre of town, up past the revered Milltown Cemetery, and then on to Andersonstown Park, which marked the city boundary. Almost exclusively Catholic, the road was lined with grim Victorian mills - textile, rope and flour mills – and with churches, cinemas, and dance halls. There were also pubs, social clubs, grocery stores, butchers, cobblers, electrical repair shops, and second-hand furniture shops which, in good weather, such as today, displayed their wares out on the pavements. Last but not least were the pawnbrokers without whom many of the locals could not have survived. Indeed, the abysmal wages of the Catholic workers ran out quickly, paid on a Friday, spent by midweek, with the rest of the days generally lived off 'tick', or credit. Thus the pawnbrokers were, for many, a vital, albeit sometimes shameful, source of secondary income.

As Barry walked up the Falls, nodding at the groups of men (the unemployed in shabby suits, the employed in overalls) gathered on street corners or outside pubs and newsagents, hearing the noisy clanging of the electric trams to his left, he saw the two mountains, the Black and the Divis, soaring high above him, covered in bracken and heather, with Cave Hill, Napoleon's Nose and the Hatchet Field (so called because it was actually two adjoining cultivated fields which, together, formed the shape of a hatchet) clearly visible and, to his eyes, serenely beautiful in the afternoon sunlight.

Indeed, despite its proliferation of grim industrial buildings - the great textile mills; the spinning, weaving, rope and flour factories - Barry thought that Belfast was more beautiful than most gave it credit for. Raised on the banks of a river, called in Irish the Béal Feirste, meaning 'the mouth of the sandy ford', the city was set superbly on the shores of Belfast Lough, with the mountains of Antrim soaring up on one side, the green hills of County Down rolling away on the other, and the Lagan River meandering through the pastoral, wooded fields that lay in abundance in every direction. So, despite the fact that the city itself was rendered acutely ugly by its many industrial buildings and warehouses, despite the fact that the atmosphere was choked with smoke, Barry loved it and could not imagine living elsewhere.

After walking about five minutes, he passed another group of mostly unemployed men who were hanging around outside a corner pub, smoking and having a talk, maybe hoping that some employed friend would turn up and invite them in for a drink. Nodding at those he knew by sight, though he knew none of them personally, Barry skipped around them to enter the pub. Even at this time in the afternoon, the pub was doing good business, with most of the tables taken, but it was still a grim barn of a place, with a long, darkly varnished counter, tables and chairs to match, the walls covered with photos of local sporting heroes, including the popular Shelbourne junior soccer team, which had recently won another cup, the Belfast Celtic team, which had more prizes than any other and was widely revered, the Brookvale and the St. Gall's football teams, the Dwyer's hurling team, and the Hib's dart team. There were also photos of Eamon de Valera, Michael Collins and other nationalist heroes.

Seated around a table at the very back of the large room, well away from the other customers, were Frank Kavanah, Seamus Magee and Kevin McClusky, three IRA men respected by Barry. All had pints of Guinness in front of them. Barry ordered himself a pint at the bar, waited patiently for it to be poured, then went to join the others. Taking the chair directly facing Frank Kavanah, he raised his glass and said, 'Cheers.'

'Cheers,' they replied in chorus, raising their glasses to him. Barry took a deep draught of his drink, then placed the glass back on the table and lit up a cigarette.

'So what's cookin'?' he asked.

'You know what,' Frank Kavanah said. 'The fuckin' Germans have bombed us at last and they're gonna come back again. As this could work out to our advantage, we have to exploit it.'

'Do we have enough men left to do that?' McClusky asked him.

'Just about,' Kavanah said.

Barry knew what he meant. In May, 1938, the government, concerned with what had been described as 'the potential fifth column of the Irish Republican Army', had rounded up all the principal officers of the Belfast Battalion and interned them in a camp at Ballykinlar. In May 1940 a further 700-odd suspects were rounded up and interned, some in the Crumlin Road jail, the remainder on a prison ship anchored in Belfast Lough. Now, though the total IRA strength, including the south, had been estimated at 2000, the number remaining in the north was unusually low. It was, however, more than they had left down south, where the military sweeps had been even worse.

'Just enough *is* enough,' Barry said. 'We can do an awful lot with a little, so let's do as you say and exploit this war.'

'What I'm worried about,' Kavanah, their leader, said, 'is that yesterday's bombing, with more air raids expected, is gonna make the government feel even more insecure and maybe encourage them to round up more of us.'

'I don't think they'll do that,' Barry said. 'They don't have an excuse.'

'They don't need much of a fuckin' excuse these days,' Seamus Magee said, looking angry, which he always did, even when he was happy. It was his red hair and freckles that did it. Either those or his naturally flushed cheeks and high-pitched, abrasive, young man's voice. 'They didn't need much of an excuse when they declared the Ulster coastline a protected area and forced the refugees there to leave at a few day's fuckin' notice. Those poor bastards ended up in a concentration camp at Huyton on the Isle of Man. Most of 'em were accused of being Nazi spies, though some had come here only after *fleeing* from the fuckin' Nazis. So if the government can do that, they can surely dream up an excuse, particularly with this war begun, to round up the few of us left.'

'Right,' said McClusky, lean and mean, his youthful gaze intense. 'They'll raise the spectre of an IRA fifth column again and we'll end up, with our pals, in the Crumlin Road jail or that prison ship in Belfast Lough.'

'Bastards!' Magee exclaimed automatically.

Kavanah, his green eyes as hard as jade, his barrel chest heaving, lit a cigarette, exhaled a stream of smoke, then pursed his lips thoughtfully and said, 'They might, they might not. No use waiting around to find out. Let's do as much damage as we can *before* they move against us. Let's wring this rag dry.'

'How?' McClusky asked.

'We could plant a few bombs in the docks,' Magee proposed, not being too bright, 'and blow some of those fuckin' Prods to Kingdom Come. A lot of Catholics have had a bad time in there - *when* they could get work there at all - so this'd be the time to pay 'em back.'

'Not possible,' Barry said. 'Since the beginning of the war in England special constabulary patrols have been steadily increased; now the docks are being guarded by armed police. Here and in Derry, docked ships are inspected on a regular basis and the RUC's patrolling the port areas, some in plain clothes. Besides, what's the point in bombing the docks when the Germans are already doing that for us? No, I'd leave the docks out of it.'

'We have that problem everywhere,' Magee said impatiently. 'Right now, the British army's all over the place, with units of the 53rd Welsh Division deployed at Derry, Ballymena, Lisburn and, nat'rally, right here in Belfast. You can't step into the streets anymore without seeing those fuckers.'

'Not to mention the Look, Duck and Vanish Brigade,' McClusky said sardonically.

The Local Defence Volunteers was the organisation they all feared and loathed the most. Formed in May 1940, ostensibly as an anti-invasion militia, the Northern Irish LDV was composed mostly of the hated B-Specials. Now effectively a branch of the constabulary, almost totally Protestant, it was widely viewed as a sectarian body whose aim was to keep the Catholics suppressed. In 1941 it had been renamed the Ulster Home Guard, but most people still thought of it as the LDV and derided it as the 'Look, Duck and Vanish Brigade'

'Far be it that I should sound like a fuckin' traitor,' Kavanagh said, 'but in my opinion, none of this would have come about - the British army in Belfast, the formation of the LDV, the rounding up of our men - if those dumb bastards down south hadn't virtually declared war on England, then followed up that declaration by bombing the shite out of a lot of English cities, even as England was up against the Germans. That's what started all this.'

'And are those dumb bastards down south,' Barry asked, 'still having their talks with the Nazis?'

'Aye,' Kavanah said, 'but they don't seem to be getting very far. According to my sources, the Nazis have virtually given up on 'em. In fact, they may have murdered Sean Russell during his submarine voyage back to Ireland, after his so-called *secret* visit to Germany. Died of stomach ulcers and buried at sea, they said. More likely, if you ask me, he was poisoned to prevent him from compromising de Valera and Irish neutrality with another bombing campaign on the mainland. I mean, de Valera made it clear that the activities of the IRA down south were jeopardising Ireland's neutrality. So if he thought that, why wouldn't the Germans?'

'The IRA's been talking to the fuckin' Nazis?' Magee asked, clearly amazed and outraged.

'Right,' Barry said. 'They've been conducting negotiations with the German intelligence network, the *Abwehr*, since 1936, when Sean MacBride was Chief of Staff.'

'Are you kidding me?'

'No. According to information received by Irish military intelligence, the Nazis were hoping, with the help of Irish Republican collaborators, to prepare the ground for a peaceable invasion of the island.'

'Jesus, man,' McClusky said, clearly just as surprised and outraged as Magee. 'That could have turned Ireland into a Gaelic Vichy!'

'Aye, right. But that's what those boyos down south were discussing, either with Nazis who arrived in Ireland by submarine, in de Valera's so-called neutral waters, or during visits that IRA men made secretly to Nazi Germany.'

'I don't believe it!' McClusky exclaimed, disgusted.

'*De Valera* believed it,' Barry said, grinning. 'That suspicious bastard was convinced that any German invasion would go hand-in-hand with a Republican uprising. The Brits believed that as well.'

'Jesus Christ!' Magee exclaimed, his face flushed and sweaty.

'Meanwhile,' Barry continued, grinning, amused by the disbelief showing in the faces of Magee and McClusky, 'our own lot here in the north, out there at Stormont, were watching the Anglo-Irish trade talks with shite in their pants, frightened that de Valera would abandon Irish neutrality, letting the Brits use the south's airfields and ports in exchange for the ending of partition.'

'Which de Valera, in the end, didn't do,' Kavanah said.

'No,' Barry agreed. 'Instead, he rounded up hundreds of IRA men and threw them into the concentration camp of the Curragh military base.'

'From what I've heard of that place,' McClusky said, 'it's even worse than the prisons up here.'

'Aye, it is. IRA prisoners in the Curragh are repeatedly made to run a gauntlet of soldiers armed with batons and guns. Some spent as long as three months or more in solitary confinement. And in at least one instance, prisoners were lined up outside their huts and then fired at indiscriminately by Irish soldiers. Five were shot; one in the back.'

'Bastards!' Magee exploded again.

A lingering silence, born of disbelief and rage, was broken only when Kavanah said, with a weary sigh, 'Still, while de Valera's breakin' the spine of the IRA down south, it's more important than ever that we stick to our separate command and deal with the north in our own way. I mean, for fuck's sake, those boyos down south are out of touch with the situation up here, so we'd be better dealing with it ourselves.'

'Aye, right,' Barry said. 'The Irish government's moves against the southern IRA have fucked it so much, we're now better off here in the north.'

'What does that mean?' McClusky asked.

'What it means is that despite our own problems, we now have more men than our friends down south have. We're also better equipped. In other words, we're better off than we think.'

Kavanah nodded approvingly. 'The proof's in the puddin'. According to my reckonin', durin' April and May of last year alone, we managed to bomb thirteen shops in Belfast and country towns, not forgettin' the occasional raid on banks, police barracks and milit'ry camps. So we did okay, lads.'

'And can continue to do it,' Barry said.

'So what *do* we do?' Magee asked, always slow on the uptake.

'Kill more fuckin' Protestants,' Kavanah said. 'Are you in or out, boyos?'

'I'm in,' Barry said.

3

Informed of what he had to do and where he had to do it, Barry took his leave of the pub in the late afternoon and walked all the way to Eleanor's rented house in Stranmillis Gardens. Barry liked to walk. He loved this city so much, he liked to see it at his leisure; also, walking gave him time to think. Besides, as what he was about to do would be done under cover of darkness, he had plenty of time to spare but didn't want to spend too much of it with Eleanor.

As he made his way back down the Falls, the sun, sinking slowly over the mountains, was behind him and the city was spread out before him, with even its imposing industrial buildings not hiding the high gantries of the shipyards, the glorious sweep of Belfast Lough and the Holywood Hills. While still a good distance from Divis Street, passing the immense mills and factories, all belching smoke, their stone walls dark with soot, he could see the gantries and cranes of the various docks that lined both sides of the Victoria and Musgrave channels, now covered in a different kind of smoke - the smoke from the buildings still burning after the previous evening's air raid. However, once he had turned into Grosvenor Road, passing the sprawling Victorian edifice of the Royal Victoria Hospital, known locally as 'the Royal', which doubtless was busy today, his view was cut off by the high buildings in the centre of town, mostly retail stores such as Woolworth's and Robinson & Cleaver's and, north of them, the gigantic mills and factories that were spread out in a pall of choking industrial smoke around the grim vicinity of York Road.

Wanting to avoid Sandy Row, a fervently Protestant enclave, he walked on until he reached the beginning of Howard Street, leading to Donegall Square, containing the City Hall and, more important to him, the Linenhall Library, where he had spent many an hour reading books about Ireland's bloody past. Instead of going to the library, which he would have done normally, he turned into Great Victoria Street, filled with horses and carts, automobiles and open-topped electric trams, and walked along to the Crown Liquor Saloon, located directly opposite the Great Northern Railway Terminus. Pulling out his stopwatch, he checked the time and saw that he had plenty of it, so he put the watch back into his pocket and entered the pub.

The Crown Liquor Saloon was a glorious establishment and one of the many in Belfast that Barry was willing to fight for and, if necessary, die for. Not that it was in any way threatened by the Protestants, who used it even more than the Catholics, given its close proximity to Sandy Row, but certainly it represented the kind of heritage that Barry wished to preserve. Ironically, though the pub dated back to 1826, the decor for which it was famed had been created by Italian craftsmen who came to Belfast years later to work on the great liners being built at the Harland & Wolff shipyard. It was, at heart, a baroque Victorian gin palace with lots of stained glass, mosaic tiling, intricate wood carvings and gas lighting. The bar, which contained no tables or chairs, ran along the left-hand side of the main room and was, even as Barry entered, packed with dedicated drinkers. Along the right-hand side were ten 'snugs': small rooms with tables and bench-styled seating, enhanced with intricately carved wooden doors and stained-glass windows that protected the privacy of those inside. The snugs had bells that could be rung when food or drink was required. All in all, the pub was a haven for those who drank like fish, smoked like trains and enjoyed a good bit of *craic*.

Going straight to the bar, Barry squeezed in beside his friend, Brendan Coghill, forty years old, good-humoured and artfully dishevelled. Brendan came here as regular as clockwork every evening at five, drank four or five bottles of stout, then took himself back to his home in the Pound Loney where, in the company of his ageing mother, he would write the poetry for which he was famed locally and also do the homework required for the Falls Road primary school where he was a popular, engagingly eccentric, teacher. Now, when Brendan saw Barry, he simply grinned and raised his index finger to silently indicate that the barman should set up another pint of stout.

'*Remember now thy Creator in the days of thy youth,*' Brendan intoned, '*while the evil days come not, nor the years draw nigh.*' He grinned, showing bad teeth, and wiped his moist lips with the sleeve of his ancient tweed coat. 'The evil days are, however, upon us right now, so even *Ecclesiastes* is redundant.'

'So says the jaded, mature man to unblemished youth.'

Brendan nodded and grinned even more broadly. 'Yes, indeed. So how are you, Sunny-Jim?'

'Sure I'm doing okay,' Barry said, lighting a cigarette and exhaling a stream of smoke to the already smoky atmosphere. 'So what are these evil days you're talkin' about?'

'The days that are coming, Sunny-Jim. That air raid last night was only the first of many - a trial run, I'm sure - but the ones that are coming will be worse. We're going to have a Blitz as bad as the one on London. The Germans are going to bomb us until the whole city is flattened, not only the shipyards, so the Falls won't be let off the next time. Evil days, indeed, boyo.'

'Every evil has its good side, Brendan, as you surely must know.'

'What good side can a Blitz have, I wonder?'

'It could keep the enemy, the Brits, otherwise engaged while we get on with our business.'

'The enemy? Our business? You speak in riddles, my young friend, and I think I know why. Don't tell me you're still involved with that bunch of assassins whom you only *imagine* are your friends.'

Barry nodded. 'Aye, I am. And they *are* my friends. You should join us and play your part in making history. This country needs men like you.'

'I don't need friends like *your* friends,' Brendan said, 'and I think I'd rather let the country sink than keep it afloat your particular way. I disapprove and you know it, you wee eejut.' He glanced left and right to note, with relief, that the people next to him had finished their drinks and departed, leaving a safe space between him and those farther along the bar. A man had to be careful about what he said in this bar or any other in Belfast. Which explained why Barry was speaking, if not exactly in riddles, at least without specifically mentioning the name of 'the enemy' (the IRA) or 'our business' (sabotage and assassination). Barry was being bold and certainly mischievous, but he wasn't being dumb. 'You're not *actively* engaged, are you?' Brendan asked.

'Aye, I am,' Barry said.

'Jesus!' Brendan exclaimed, shocked. 'I don't believe it. Does your Da know?' He and Barry's father were approximately the same age and the best of friends, though Brendan, while sharing some of Eddie's nationalist leanings, had consistently refused to join the IRA.

Barry shook his head from side to side, indicating, 'No.'

'And do you think he'd be pleased if he found out?'

'We both know he wouldn't, though I've never understood why. I mean, when *he* was my age, he was doing exactly what I'm doing now, so I can't understand why he keeps telling *me* to stay out of it. The only thing that stopped *him* in the end was that bad shoulder of his - that and the knowledge that if he was sentenced one more time, he might have to spend the rest of his life inside. I mean, he didn't stop because he *disapproved*, but only because it wasn't practical to go on.'

'Those were certainly good reasons,' Brendan said, 'but there may have been others.'

'Such as?'

'From various things he's said to me over the years, I believe he simply became sickened by the violence and decided there had to be another way. I think he saw one too many weeping women or children and decided, like my beloved Dostoevsky, that the single tear of a single child in all the world was too high a price to pay.'

'Maybe.' When the barman brought Barry's pint of Guinness, he picked the glass up and had a taste of it. It went down a treat. Wiping his wet lips with the back of his hand, he said, 'So what about you? Do you still believe that the problems of this country can be solved by peaceful means?'

'*Accursed be he that first inventeth war...* Ackay, my young, foolish friend, I still believe, at least, that every peaceful means possible should be explored before a single shot is fired.'

'Sure that sounds real romantic,' Barry said, 'even if it's impractical.'

'How do you know it's impractical if you haven't actually tried it?'

'Because history has shown that the only way anyone's ever got rid of the Brits is by taking up arms against them. Sure there isn't one instance, in the whole history of British imperialism, of that country packing up and leaving without a fight. So no way are they going to get out of Ireland if we don't push them out. You could help us do that.'

'Even if I agreed with you, which certainly I do not, I can't imagine becoming active at my ripe old age. So how could I help you?'

'You're only forty, Brendan. Hardly a ripe old age. And you're a schoolteacher, aren't you? You could do a lot in your classroom. Emphasise Ireland's long struggle against the Brits and...' Barry glanced left and right to ensure that he couldn't be overheard... 'And the Orange State.'

'Sure my poetry's well known for its nationalist leanings. Like you *and* your Da, I want a united Ireland and I make that perfectly clear in what I write.'

'I know you do. But I also know, being one of your readers, that your poetry takes the pacifist line. You could do more to emphasise the iniquities of the Brits, the inequalities of the Orange State, and to impress upon the young that a country has to fight to defend itself. So what about it, Brendan?'

'Now would that be poetry or propaganda? Teaching or brainwashing? I don't write propaganda - I write poetry - and that's what I intend to continue writing until I kick the proverbial bucket and win my eternal rest. As for teaching, I'll continue to encourage my innocent wee'uns to think for themselves; I won't attempt to brainwash them into a blind acceptance of anyone's party line. Propaganda, no less! What's come over you, Sunny-Jim? Where are you getting all these bin-lid ideas from? That fascist mongrel, Frank Kavanah?'

'Aye, amongst others,' Barry said. 'But Frank isn't a fascist.'

'Oh, no?'

'No. He's simply following in an honourable tradition - and that's exactly what I'm doing as well. Sure I'm following in m'Da's footsteps, aren't I? What's wrong with that?'

'Your Da erased his own footsteps a quare while ago to make sure that you *didn't* follow in them. If you think that what you're doing is so honourable, why haven't you told him?'

'Because it would worry him. It would certainly worry m'Ma. She doesn't even like to talk about what Da did a few years back; she wants it all dead and buried, like.'

'Understandably,' Brendan said.

'So that's why I don't tell him. It's not because I don't believe in what I'm doing, or because he'd disapprove, but because he'd worry about me ending up in prison like he did or, even worse, ending up prematurely in a pine box. That's the only reason I don't tell m'Da - and I think it's a good one.'

'The good son,' Brendan said.

'That's sarcasm. Sticks and stones.'

'I'm not trying to break your bones. I *do* think you're a good son. I just happen to think that what you're doing is wrong and that you *could* end up in that proverbial pine box if you stick with those so-called friends of yours.'

'You won't tell my Da, will you?'

'No, I won't. It's not my place to do so. I just happen to think that you're still too young to understand what – '

'Don't even say it, Brendan. I'm not too young for anything. Sure m'Da was my age when he was doing what I'm now doing and I tell you, I really admired him for it. When I was growing up, each time he was thrown in jail I was *proud* to know he was willing to endure that for what he believed in. And what do *I* believe in? What *he* believed in! So as far as I'm concerned, I'm just carrying on the family tradition and have no cause for guilt.'

Agitated, he stubbed out his cigarette and then caught Brendan's quick, sideways smile.

'Ack,' Brendan said, 'who knows what's right and wrong these days? Sure these are truly the days of the plague. Maybe we should all get out of this vile, accursed city, which will surely go up in smoke and flames, sooner or later. Maybe we should all go and live in the

75

countryside, breathe the fresh air, contemplate nature and live the simple life. Sure a man could do worse.'

Turning away from the bar, he raised his hands in the air, then boomed melodramatically, as if speaking to the gallery:

'I will arise and go now, and go to Inasfree,
'And a small cabin build there, of clay and wattles made:
'Nine bean-rows will I have there, a hive for the honey-bee,
'And live alone in the bee-loud glade.'

'Sure you'd die of fucking boredom,' Barry said as some of the other customers applauded and Brendan histrionically took a bow, 'and don't kid yourself otherwise. Yeats can write that, but it doesn't mean he could have actually lived it. And believe me, *you* certainly couldn't. You're a city-man and bar-crawler.'

'A true poet, in other words.'

Barry chuckled. 'Aye, that's right.' He finished off his stout, placed his glass on the counter and wiped the foam from his lips with his fingers. Then he nodded at the empty pint glass. 'Are you standin'?'

'Another one?'

'No, that one. I have to be makin' tracks.'

'It's already on my tab,' Brendan said. 'I'm a local celebrity, as you rightly pointed out, and in this bar I'm treated as such. Would you have me give up my local fame for a fugitive life?'

'I guess not,' Barry said. 'Thanks, Brendan. I'll see you around.'

'Fare thee well, for I must leave thee. Do not let this parting grieve thee. And remember that the best of friends must part.'

'Jesus!' Barry exclaimed, shaking his head from side to side and grinning as he left the pub. Brendan, despite his lack of commitment, always made him feel good.

The sun was well down, sinking behind the Black Mountain, as he continued on along Great Victoria Street to Shaftesbury Square, where people were jumping on and off electric trams at the end of their working day. This was a predominantly Protestant area, but Barry felt at ease in it, as indeed he did in most of Belfast, because sectarian harassment only extended to stopping people in the street during times of riot and other forms of open conflict. Right now, the main concern of most people in this city, both Catholic and Protestant, was the previous evening's air raid and the air raids that were bound to follow. So Barry had little fear of being stopped by some Protestant hoodlums out for blood. He had the Germans to thank for this.

After crossing Shaftesbury Square, he headed up University Road, mercifully devoid of the mills and factories that defaced most other areas of the city. This was a pleasant, tree-lined area, packed with shops and cafes where Protestants and Catholics mixed, united by the common need for higher education. Less than ten minutes later, after passing Queen's University and the Botanic Gardens, he came to Eleanor McFarlane's street.

Walking to Eleanor's house, he noted that the sun had nearly set, though sunlight still streaked the road, turning it into a moody mosaic of bright patches and shadow. Few of the residents were outside their houses, as invariably they were in the Falls and other working-class areas. This was a middle-class area where the population was predominantly young and transient - students attending the university - so the sense of community that Barry was used to was sadly absent. For this very reason, however, it was a good area for Eleanor, offering relative anonymity and rarely drawing the attention of the police. Few would think it odd that Eleanor, a twenty-three-year-old, unmarried Catholic, originally from Dublin, lived here alone. There were plenty of unmarried women of Eleanor's age living alone in this area, attending the university as mature students, working as teachers, administrators, cooks and cleaners, toiling locally at other jobs, or, if they were employed farther afield, living here simply because it was a safe and pleasant area.

It was, in other words, an excellent base of operations for a secret member of Cummann na mBann... the female wing of the IRA.

4

Stopping at Eleanor's red-brick terraced house, which she rented, Barry hesitated before using the brass knocker, again feeling the fine edge of tension that always came just before he actually saw her. Realising, with a shock, that his heart had started racing, he took a deep breath, composed his features, then knocked on the door. Eleanor came to the door promptly, obviously expecting him. Seeing him, she smiled and stepped aside to let him enter. Brushing past her, he caught a whiff of scent, the seductive smell of newly washed hair, and felt a sudden, familiar rush of tingling awareness: a heightened reality. Upon entering the living room, he turned back in her direction and found her leaning against the closed door, staring steadily at him. He took a step forward, wanting to hold her, but she raised her right hand.

'Not yet,' she said. 'Business first. Take a seat on the sofa.'

Though only a few years older than Barry, she made him feel like a child and, just like a child, he did what he was told while glancing about him. The living room lacked space and was functionally furnished, with two soft chairs facing the sofa placed to one side of the fireplace, a dining table under the window overlooking the street, and a glass-fronted, varnished oak sideboard filled with dishes and bric-a-brac. The wallpaper was hideous, painted flowers on a light blue background, not enhanced with the cheap reproductions of rural scenes that were hanging here and there on the walls. It was a rented house and all this had come with it, so Eleanor could hardly be blamed for it. She lived where the work took her and she took what they gave her, which included, at least for a month or so, this small, dismal dwelling.

'So you've come,' she said, using that oddity of Belfast speech as a greeting.

'Aye, I've come.'

'They told you what you're to do?'

'Sure. Why else would I be here?'

Eleanor smiled. 'Oh, I thought you might be here for another reason.'

'Ackaye, that as well.'

Eleanor nodded, still smiling, standing in front of him to look down upon him. Medium-height, healthily plump, with a moon-shaped face, full lips, chocolate-brown eyes and short-cropped black hair, she would never have stood out in a crowd, though she was quietly attractive. Barry thought her more than that. He was intoxicated with her. His relationship with her was supposed to be impersonal, strictly professional, but they had made the mistake of going to bed together shortly after his first job. Now they were in love. At least Barry was in love. He wasn't too sure about Eleanor, who seemed more mature than he was, more sexually experienced, and who had mood swings that he couldn't get to grips with, first close, then distant, blowing from hot to cold in seconds.

Maybe all women were like that. He wasn't experienced enough to know. He only knew that what he and Eleanor did in bed together always made him feel like a grown-up man. Now Eleanor, though smiling warmly, was being strictly professional by insisting that he keep his hands off her until after the job. She was right, as usual. It was always best to keep your head clear until the job had been done.

'Do you have what I need?' Barry asked.

She couldn't resist the obvious. 'Are we talking about the job or something else?' she asked with a wicked smile.

'The job,' Barry said.

'Yes, I have what you need.'

Eleanor did a lot of things, but essentially she was a courier whose task was to transport, deliver and hide weapons, both in Ireland and on the mainland, for the IRA. Dedicated and experienced, she had been responsible for delivering the explosives that had led to many of the outrages that had taken place in England over the past few years. However, as the war with Germany had seriously restricted travel between Ireland and the mainland, she was presently operating only in the former, though covering both sides of the border, depending upon where her services were required.

'It's a foot job,' she said. 'You have to walk there and back. There'll be no one in a car to pick you up after it's done, because you're going to be too far inside their turf. Do you understand that?'

'Ack, Eleanor, for Jesus sake, you know I do!'

'Which means that once you've done the job, you're on your own and can't be helped if you get into trouble.'

'Yeah, yeah,' Barry said impatiently, 'sure I know that as well.'

'Well, all right, then.'

'It's grand, love. Don't worry.'

Eleanor sighed, as if doubtful. He was touched by her concern. 'You're still a bit early,' she said, checking her wristwatch. 'We don't want you to go out until it's dark. Would you like a drink?'

'Aye. What have you?'

'You can't have any alcohol,' she told him. 'What I meant was a cuppa tea.'

Barry shrugged, disappointed. 'Okay.'

'Good. It's already brewing in the kitchen. I'll be back in a minute.' Disappearing into the kitchen, she returned shortly after with two cups of tea and a plate of biscuits on a tin tray. Decorated with paintings of snow-covered Christmas trees, the tray was a true antique. After placing tit on a low table in front of the sofa, she sat beside him, her thigh pressed against his. He was instantly aroused by her body's heat. 'Help yourself to the sugar.'

'Right,' Barry said.

After stirring sugar into one of the cups, he drank some of the hot tea. Eleanor was sipping as well, staring at him over the top of her cup with those big brown eyes. He felt uncomfortably that she was still sizing him up, but he might have been imagining this because he was still slightly insecure with her. He often wondered how many men she had been with, but he didn't dare ask.

'Why are you operating for us,' he asked instead, after having had another sip of his tea and a couple of biscuits, 'instead of working for the IRA down south?'

'Because most of our men down there were rounded up in the sweeps conducted over the past months by the Garda, under instructions from that traitor, de Valera. Now most of those men are rotting in prison and we've precious few left on the ground. Certainly not enough to do anything worthwhile, so those left are just lying low. You're in a stronger position up here, so I decided, since I'd nothing to do down there, to come up here and lend a hand.'

'That shows a lot of dedication,' Barry said, 'particularly since we're not too keen on you lot down there. And vice versa, I take it.'

Eleanor chuckled, shaking her head in mock weariness. 'Sure that's true enough, Barry, but it's not enough to stop me doing my duty. My aim is to help bring down the Orange State and get the Brits out; so if helping your lot helps to do that, then I'm all for helping them.'

'Like I said, it shows a lot of dedication.'

'Aye, I'm dedicated alright.'

'Is it because of your Da?'

She nodded. 'Right. Him and my whole family, but mostly him, because he's suffered a lot for what he believes in. We're a really tight, committed Republican family and we always have been.'

'Did they catch your Da in one of the recent round-ups?'

'Aye, they did. Now he's back in the Curragh, where they had him last year, and they'll probably give him a worse going over than they did before.'

'What did they do to him?'

'What they did to all the others and none of it nice. I'm tellin' you, Barry, the Irish are worse to their IRA prisoners than they are to the Brits. They're bastards. They really are. The Curragh is a concentration camp, no more and no less. It's just Nissen huts ringed with barbed wire. No heating. No washing facilities. And what they did there, to my Da and to others, simply doesn't bear thinkin' about.'

'I've heard a bit about it,' Barry said. 'Months of solitary confinement, running gauntlets of soldiers swinging batons, even being shot at random by the guards. Did that kind of shite really happen?'

'Yes,' Eleanor said. 'That's what it's like being a prisoner in the hands of our own Irish soldiers - worse than it would be with the Brits, except, maybe, the Black and Tans.'

'That may be so, but the Irish wouldn't behave that way towards their own if it weren't for the Brits. It's the Brits who've turned the Irish against each other and they'll keep doing it as long as they stay here. The Brits are masters of divide-and-rule, so every time one Irishman kills another, it's the Brits who're responsible.'

'Will they be responsible for this evening?' Eleanor asked.

'Yes,' Barry replied without hesitation. 'I'll feel no guilt at all.'

'Good.' Smiling enigmatically, Eleanor put her empty cup back on the low table, then swung her legs, which were heavy, away from him, to stand up and move to the stairs. 'I keep everything upstairs,' she said, 'in the second bedroom. I'll be down in a minute.'

Barry wanted to go up those stairs, to follow her into the main bedroom where he had been before - the one not used as a storeroom for illegal weapons - and there, in that narrow bed, on that hard mattress, make love to her as he had done so often in the past couple of months. He visualised her soft breasts, her hard nipples, the smooth belly, slipping into a timeless, erotic trance until she came back down the stairs. When she entered the room, he had to cross his legs to hide what was happening down there, blinking repeatedly, wrenching himself back to reality, to focus upon her, the *real* Eleanor, once more. She was now standing in front of him, looking down at him, a leather-holstered German pistol in her right hand, some shells in the other. She held both out to him.

'Can you use this?' she asked, nodding to indicate the pistol.

Barry nodded. 'Aye.'

'Have you been trained *specifically* with this weapon?'

'Yes,' Barry said. 'That and a lot of others.'

'Good.'

'I know that these weapons come courtesy of our German allies, but how the hell do you get them into the country?'

'They come in the same way that German agents come in for negotiations with our GHQ staff: by submarine. The same way that men like Sean Russell went to Germany for talks with Ribbentrop and Canaris.'

'I have a friend who believes that Russell's unexpected death at sea, during his last voyage back from Germany, was engineered by the Nazis because they didn't want him to compromise de Valera's neutrality by starting up another bombing campaign. Do you agree with that?'

Eleanor shrugged. 'Who knows? If you deal with the Nazis, you have to be prepared for anything. Maybe Russell *did* die from ulcers and was buried at sea. On the other hand, maybe he was poisoned aboard the submarine. Then, again, maybe they surfaced and put a bullet through his head and then threw him overboard without ceremony. What does it matter? You deal with the devil you know or you don't deal at all. And if the Nazis can help us bring down the Brits, then let's deal with the swine. Here,' she said, handing him the holstered pistol and a fistful of bullets, 'take them.'

Barry positioned the holstered pistol on his left hip, almost behind his back, which would hide it from view under his jacket and also enable him to make a rapid cross-draw with his right hand. When he had buckled the belt, he removed the pistol from its holster, took the bullets from Eleanor, slipped them into the chambers, leaving one chamber empty, then applied the safety catch and placed the pistol back in its holster.

'Fine and dandy,' he said.

Eleanor checked her wristwatch, then nodded as if speaking to herself and looked up again.

'Right,' she said. 'He should be home by now. You'd better start making tracks. Good luck. See you later.'

She hesitated, then stood on tip-toe to kiss him full on the lips, but when he tried to slide his hands around her waist she pulled back again, smiling and gently waving her index finger from side to side, indicating, 'No.'

'Later,' she said.

Barry nodded. 'Sure. I'll see you later, right enough. Keep the kettle on the boil.'

He left the house, stepping into the evening's lamplit darkness, and made his way back to University Road. Once there, he walked down to Shaftesbury Square, which was packed with evening revellers, the pubs doing great business despite the previous evening's air raid, trams clanging to and fro in the flickering yellow light of the gas lamps. Turning into the Donegall Road, he passed Sandy Row, which ran up from the Royal Bar directly across the road on his right, and also passed the Victorian Orange Hall, dominating the short street to his left. Though reminded that this was a Loyalist stronghold where the locals would be as anti-Catholic as those Prods up in the Shankill, he didn't feel threatened in any dramatic, immediate way. Nevertheless, he instinctively tensed up and became more alert when he passed men loitering on street corners, which they traditionally did, blowing smoke from their nostrils, having a good bit of *craic*, or conversation, out of sight and earshot of their wives. Barry empathised with their boredom, their lack of work or a hopeful future, but when it came to politics and religion, the Catholic-Protestant divide, United Ireland or Orange State, they disappeared in his mind as human beings, becoming merely symbols, enabling him to undertake this task with a clear conscience.

It would not be long now.

He had just passed the tram yard, the library and a lot of dead-end streets that looked as grim as the ones up in the Falls. Most of the shops had closed by now, though the pubs along the road were open, their lights beaming out into the night to merge with the flickering yellow glowing of the gas lamps along the pavement, illuminating the men entering and leaving, turning them into silhouettes. Though not particularly nervous, Barry certainly breathed easier when he had crossed the railway tracks and turned down Donegall Avenue, heading for that small network of streets located near the Windsor Park football grounds. That was where a lot of hardline Prods lived, so it mattered symbolically.

Donegall Avenue ran a good distance (terraced houses along its whole length with not a tree in sight, the rows only broken up by side streets of more uniform terraced houses) before terminating at Windsor

Park. The gable ends of the houses, Barry noted, were all covered with huge paintings, most of them badly done, showing the same kind of tripe that the Prods had on their Orange Lodge banners: King William crossing the Boyne River, the Battle of the Diamond, the Siege of Derry (which the Prods called 'Londonderry') and so on. It was enough to make a civilised man puke, though Barry simply grinned, amused at the stupidity of it, oblivious to the fact that the gable ends of the Falls were covered in equally bad paintings, though the subject matter was Catholic instead of Protestant.

'Fucking barbarians,' he muttered as he turned into Broadway, not impressed with what he was seeing. The area was, in reality, no more than a square-mile or so of criss-crossing streets composed of small, two-bedroom, terraced houses, with no gardens out front and only brick-walled yards and entries out back - a Protestant version of the Pound Loney. Broadway itself, along which Barry was now walking, led past a short block of shops, including a fish-and-chips shop, or chippy, to the marshy steppes of the bog meadows, through which the Blackstaff River wound, filled with rubbish, and upon which the tinkers always camped with their horse-drawn caravans. Beyond the river was the Black Mountain or, as the Prods called it, the Mickey Mountain (the Catholics' Mountain), now visible as an irregular dark mass outlined against a cloud-streaked, starry sky.

Down here, on the ground, life was less picturesque, with the streets of terraced houses running off to both sides and the unswept roads illuminated in the pale, flickering light of the gas lamps. As usual, groups of men were loitering on street corners, even at this late hour, while children were still playing football at the 'openings' or having games of marbles on the pavements.

Ignoring them, Barry stopped beneath a gas lamp to check the address that had been written by Eleanor on a small piece of paper. Memorising the address, he refolded the paper, tucked it back into his coat pocket, then turned into the next street and walked along until he found the number he wanted.

This was the home of Robert Moore, a sergeant with the Royal Ulster Constabulary. Moore had done nothing to deserve what was coming to him. He had been selected only because it was felt by Frank Kavanah that an attack right here, where the Prods felt safe, would have a devastating effect upon them and, just as importantly, cause bad feelings between them and the Catholics who had lived in the same area, in relative peace, for years. It was Kavanah's belief that the segregation of Catholics and Protestants was vital to the ongoing struggle; that Catholics ghettoised in their own areas would be easier to manipulate into becoming more supportive of the IRA. The important thing, according to Kavanah, was to select someone who lived in the very heart of this largely Protestant area; the second most important thing was that the one selected be well known to the locals. Sergeant Moore, a popular RUC sergeant, fit the bill nicely.

Conveniently, Moore's house was located near the end of the street. Though darkness had fallen, three boys, all about ten years old, were playing marbles on the pavement at the opening, but luckily there were no men loitering about there.

Satisfied, Barry glanced left and right, saw that no one was coming, and withdrew the pistol from its holster. He took a deep breath, let it out evenly, then hammered the brass knocker on the door. The instant he heard footsteps inside, approaching the door, he raised his weapon into the two-handed firing position, intending to charge into the house if anyone other than Moore materialised.

Luckily, the door was opened by Moore, a big man with fair hair and a good-humoured face, wearing an open-necked shirt with V-necked pullover. He stared directly at Barry, his eyes widening in disbelief as his gaze dropped lower to take in the weapon aimed at his chest.

Squeezing the trigger, Barry felt the pistol jolting and heard the harsh crack of the shot. Moore jerked convulsively, arms flying out to his sides, knees bending as the impact of the bullet sent him staggering backwards into the hallway. He struck the frame of the stairwell, practically bounced off it, arms flapping, legs like rubber, then spun to the side and fell into the living room.

His wife and two kids were seated around the fireplace, the former listening to the radio, the latter reading comics.

Mrs. Moore screamed. It was a dreadful, demented screaming. The two kids, a boy and girl, about seven and eight respectively, looked up bug-eyed as Barry stepped boldly into the living room to give his victim the coup de grâce.

Moore had fallen face down on the linoleum-covered floor and was now rolling onto his back, breathing harshly and groaning as blood splashed out of his torn, smashed chest and soaked the floor around him.

Mrs. Moore kept screaming. The kids were open-mouthed and still bug-eyed. Barry knelt over Moore, who was staring up at him, eyes dazed, their light fading, then he grabbed Moore by the hair, jerked his head up off the floor, placed the barrel of the pistol to his temple and squeezed the trigger again.

The pistol roared. Moore's head exploded. Pieces of bone and dollops of brain matter spewed out to splash over the kids, who instantly added their terrified crying to the relentless, hysterical screaming of their mother.

Barry released Moore's hair, letting his bloody head, the white bone exposed, fall back to the floor, then he straightened up, turned away and left the house, slamming the front door behind him to cut off the noise from inside.

Glancing across the road, he saw pale faces peering tentatively out from behind opening front doors or shifting curtains, but no one so far had been foolish enough to venture into the street. Holstering his pistol while on the move, he walked quickly, deliberately not running, to the corner of the street where the boys with the marbles, all still on hands and knees, had stopped playing to look up at him with frightened eyes, indicating that they had heard the gunshots. Ignoring them, he turned the corner and kept walking, not increasing his pace, then he took the next street and went along it, past rows of terraced houses, heading for the Tates Avenue Bridge. Though there were groups of men loitering at various openings, they merely cast curious glances in his direction, strangers being a rarity here, then went back to their smoking and talking.

Barry kept walking, not increasing his pace. He knew that news of the assassination would have swept that street by now, but experience had taught him that no one would follow him for fear that they might be shot themselves. Also, people in this area didn't have telephones and it would be some time before the police were notified. By the time the police turned up to investigate, he would be well away from the area - just another face in the evening crowds.

Still, as he walked towards the Lisburn Road, hearing the clanging of the trams and the honking of horns, seeing the drivers of cars trying to pull out around horse-drawn carts and cyclists, their lights merging to form silvery webs in the darkness between the weaker glowing of the overhead gas lamps, his heart was racing from an unruly combination of excitement, relief and exhilaration. The latter finally took him over, making his skin burn, illuminating his mind, making him feel electrically alive and vibrantly sensual; and as he crossed the Lisburn Road to enter Eglantine Avenue, tree-lined and quiet, he couldn't wait to get back to Eleanor's place and lay his trembling hands upon her.

He was there soon enough and found Eleanor waiting for him, stepping back into the living room as he entered and closed the front door behind him.

'How did it go?' she asked.

'It was grand. No problem at all. The copper's dead as a doornail.'

'Good,' Eleanor said.

Barry took his jacket off, draping it over the nearest chair, then unbuckled the strap of the holster and handed the holstered weapon to her.

'There's some bullets left in it,' he said. 'I only had to use two.'

'You're breathing heavily,' Eleanor noted.

'You know why,' he replied.

Eleanor smiled. 'Let me get rid of this upstairs,' she said, indicating the weapon in her hand. 'And you might as well come up as well.'

'Damned right, I will,' Barry said.

He followed her up the stairs. While she went into the small bedroom to hide the weapon with the others kept there, he entered the main bedroom, kicked off his shoes, then threw himself down on the bed. Lying there face up, hands clasped behind his head, he heard the metallic snap of the pistol's chamber being opened and knew that Eleanor was removing the remaining bullets before hiding the weapon. He admired her expertise, her professionalism and dedication; indeed, he loved her all the more because he felt that he and she had so much in common.

We're made for each other, he thought. This was all meant to be.

He felt spiritual, religious, removed from himself, even as she was leaning across him, making the mattress sink and sigh like a living thing. Opening his eyes, he saw her gazing down at him, propped up on her hands and knees above him, blouse unbuttoned to show the heaving of her breasts, her lips curved in a slight smile. She lowered herself slowly, tormentingly, upon him, melting over his burning loins, making him drain down to his centre, until he was conscious only of her soft skin and lambent warmth. They fell into each other, into chasms of pure feeling, thinking wild, disordered thoughts, losing themselves in pure sensation, and somehow managed, at length, to undress each other and be joined at the hip. They moved together in silence or, at least, without speaking, communicating with sighs, groans and gasps, reduced to the basics, two animals in heat, consuming each other in order to feel as free as any human can. This bed was a place for life. Death did not have dominion here. Joined together in what they both believed to be a fight for freedom, they briefly found the only true freedom, creating life in that instant.

Barry poured himself into her, transferring his essence to her, knowing even as he spasmed and lost all control that his seed had found that place where new life would be germinated and his future, or at least his continuance, was at last guaranteed.

His childhood had ended.

Chapter Three

1

Johnny came out of sleep through a vale of wondrous dreams to find the world still in darkness. Beside him, in the cramped, single bed, his younger brother, Billy, was asleep, softly snoring, his moon-shaped face already scarred on cheeks and chin from his many fights and other misadventures. Billy was only eleven, but he was always in trouble whereas Johnny, a year older, was rarely in trouble. Marlene, now thirteen, was sleeping at the other side of the small room, in a narrow bed made by their dad; her face was hidden in the tangle of her hair, itself hidden by darkness. Johnny had awakened early because he was excited. Today the Avenue was going to celebrate the Coronation of Queen Elizabeth with a party beginning at noon. The party would take place outdoors, in the road and up the side streets, with free food and drink and games to play. Johnny was really keen for it to commence, but noon seemed an eternity away.

Sighing, he closed his eyes again and tried to recall his dreams. He'd had lots of different dreams, but recalled them only vaguely; the only one he remembered with any great degree of clarity was the one about an immense balloon that had picked him up and carried him high above the earth to where he could see its curved surface. Indeed, two years ago, when Johnny was only nine, he had gone with Billy, without his parents' permission, all the way to the King's Hall, Balmoral, to see a real gas-filled balloon that was going to ascend and carry its passengers, a man and a woman, across the Irish Sea to Scotland. Johnny and Billy had tried to get there early, but they didn't get there early enough because when they arrived, the grounds outside the King's Hall were already packed with spectators and the huge balloon was about half a mile away, still tethered to its restraining poles and only partially visible above that sea of bobbing heads. They did, however, see it fully when it began its ascent, rising slowly, silently, with a square wicker basket dangling beneath it, the man and woman clearly visible in the basket, silhouetted against the greyish sky. It drifted off in a northerly direction and eventually disappeared over Cave Hill, heading for Larne. Johnny was entranced with that sight, an ethereal vision, and even hours later, when he and Billy were back home, even after their mother had clipped their ears for having gone all that way on their own and, worse, without permission (naturally blaming wee Billy for it), he kept imagining himself in the basket of the balloon as it drifted across the sea, through candy-floss clouds, carried up by gas but borne on the wind, and eventually landed in the wilds of Scotland, that far-off, foreign land that he only knew about from books. He was therefore disappointed when he learnt from a neighbour, Teddy Lavery, that the balloonists had decided against flying all the way to Scotland, that they had thought it too risky, and that they had, instead, vented the gas and descended in Larne, still right here in Ulster.

It seemed to Johnny that he was always being built up only to be let down again. Nothing was ever what it appeared to be.

'Hey, Billy,' he whispered, nudging his younger brother with his elbow, 'waken up. It's Coronation Day.'

Billy groaned in response.

Lying there, the blankets up to his chin, warm enough to still be feeling sleepy, Johnny glanced at the window and saw that daylight was coming. Closing his eyes again, he cast his thoughts back as far as they would go, to the absolute beginning that always somehow eluded him, and was defeated yet again, only managing to recall fragments that always contained his Mum and Dad, surrounded by the walls of this very house. It seemed to him that his Mum and Dad had always been here, right from the beginning that he could never remember, and though he thought the same of the house, these familiar walls that seemingly had always been here just like his parents, he knew that this wasn't quite true.

His Mum had told him many times that he had not been born in this house, but in another house near the Newtownards Road, and that the house had been half demolished by a German bomb the night he was born.

'I thought we were all going to die,' she told him, 'but instead you were born. A few hours before the house was being destroyed. Sure I thought it was magical.'

To Johnny, his own birth seemed magical as well, though when he asked his Mum exactly how he had been born, how children in general were born, she always answered by looking away from him, her cheeks flushed, and talking about something else. Nevertheless, though Johnny didn't know exactly *how* he had been born, he knew that it had happened (whatever *it* was) just before a German bomb exploded, the whole house shook violently, the walls cracked and plaster rained down from the ceiling to fill the air was a choking dust. He knew this because his Mum and Dad had both said it was so. And this was why they were now living in this long avenue, instead of the Newtownards Road, which was in another part of the city, far away where Johnny had never been. Some day he would go there and find out exactly how he had been born and, maybe, where he had come from, in order to end up, a living being, in a house that no longer existed, having been blown to pieces.

He nudged Billy again. 'Come on, Billy! Sure it's Coronation Day! Let's get up and get out, like.'

But Billy just groaned again. Unlike Johnny, once he clambered into bed, he slept like a bird. It was because he was always getting up to mischief and burning up all his excess energy. At least, that's what their Mum said.

'Come, on Billy! Waken up! Sure it's time to get out and see what's happening.'

'Give over,' Marlene said from the other bed. 'Sure you're gonna waken up the whole street. There's nothin' happenin' outside yet and I'm tryin' to get some sleep here. So just shut yer gob.'

'Sorry,' Johnny said.

Marlene was one year older than Johnny and that made her almost grown up. Johnny was in awe of Marlene because of her age, though he sometimes thought it strange that she cried an awful lot and had terrible tantrums when she threw things and threatened to kill herself, which was more the kind of things that children his age did, not someone a whole year older than him. To Johnny, a single year seemed like a million, so the year between him and Marlene might as well have been an eternity.

On the other hand, he didn't feel all that much older than Billy, which is probably why they played together a lot. Though Billy was smaller than Johnny and younger than him by a year, he protected Johnny by fighting his fights for him and generally acting as the leader of their gang. He did this because Johnny was frightened of being hurt and also scared of getting into trouble. Billy was always getting into trouble and he seemed to enjoy it.

'Hey, Billy!' Johnny tried again, though this time in a whisper that he hoped Marlene wouldn't hear. 'Waken up, Billy!'

Billy groaned and opened one eye, which seemed to roll unnaturally in its socket as he sleepily surveyed the room.

'Wha...?'

'Coronation Day!' Johnny whispered in his ear. 'It's time to get up! Look! The sun's almost shining.'

In fact, it wasn't as early as Johnny had imagined because he could hear his Mum leaving the bedroom, muttering complaints, to pad downstairs in her slippers, light the coal fire, have the first of many cigarettes and then prepare breakfast. Normally, she would then have gone to work in the stitching works of the Albion factory, but everyone, including her and his dad, who worked in the Harland & Wolff shipyard, where Johnny hoped to work some day, had been given the day off in order to celebrate the Coronation. With luck, this meant that she would treat today like a Sunday and give them all the pan for breakfast: a good fry-up with bacon, egg, fried tomatoes, soda farls and potato bread. Johnny prayed this was so.

'Ack, it's still dark outside,' wee Billy said. 'Whose leg are ya pullin'?'

'We've gotta get up early,' Johnny whispered. 'Mum said so. She said we have to have breakfast early 'cause she has to do a lot for the celebrations - lay the tables an' all that. If we don't get up when she calls us, she said, she'll give us a clip on the ear.'

Their mother often gave them clips on the ear, for this crime or that, though it was more like a brush with a feather duster. It was her voice, when she shouted in anger, that did more than the clipping. Her voice could move mountains.

'Sure that's just a lot of blarney,' Billy said.

'CHILDREN!' their mother bawled from downstairs. 'Marlene! Johnny! Billy! Get your backsides out of your beds and come down here and wash! You, too, Albert Hamilton!'

'Light the lamp!' Billy said, abruptly galvanised into action and sitting upright, wiping the sleep from his eyes. 'Hey, Marlene,' he added, glancing across the cramped room to where his older sister was sleeping. 'Mum's callin' us down. Sure ya better get yourself out of there.'

Marlene groaned in response. 'I'm sick, so I'm stayin' in bed. Sure I've got a bad stummich. When ya get down there, tell 'er I'm in agony. Say I'm white as a sheet, like.'

'She won't believe that,' Johnny said as he pulled the chain to operate the valve that turned on the bedroom's only gas lamp. When the gas was ignited, the room filled up with a flickering pale-yellow light. 'And besides,' he added hopefully as he swivelled the metal sleeve covering an aperture that could be reduced or enlarged to control the brilliance of light emanating from the glassed-in mantle of the lamp, 'she might treat today like a Sunday and give us the pan for breakfast.'

'My stummich couldn't hold a fry-up,' Marlene replied, trying to sound like she was at death's door. 'I'm at death's door, I tell ya. So tell her – '

'That's Dad getting' up,' Billy said as Johnny finished adjusting the gas lamp and the room filled with a brighter, more cheerful light. 'Sure ya might get away with that with Mum, but ya won't with our Dad. Better get out of bed, Marlene.'

'Ah, God!' Marlene groaned, but she rolled over and then, with a mournful sigh, pushed herself upright. 'You think we'll really get a fry-up?' she asked.

'It's a holiday,' Johnny said, feeling confident.

As he stripped off his striped pyjamas, he glanced through the window and saw that some of the houses opposite were lit up inside with the steadier light of electricity. He wondered why those houses had electricity when this house didn't. He'd ask his dad about it, if he seemed in good mood, when they were all downstairs having their breakfast.

The door to the other bedroom squeaked open and then slammed shut, then footsteps advanced to, and stopped outside, the door of this bedroom. Their dad hammered his knuckles on the door.

'Downstairs!' he called out.

93

'Comin'!' they called back in ragged chorus as they wriggled out of their pyjamas and put on their clothes. Once dressed, they left the room and went downstairs to join the queue for the sink, which was in the tiny kitchen located between the living room and the bleak, bricked-in back yard. Their mother was, indeed, doing a fry-up in the pan on the gas burners right beside the sink. The smell was mouthwatering. Their father, Albert, stripped to the waist, had just finished washing (face, neck, chest and armpits) in the sink and was drying himself with a towel as he left the kitchen, brushing past Mary. He stopped when he saw Mary about to pick up another couple of eggs.

'What are those for?' he asked.

'The kids,' Mary replied. She was wearing a flowered apron over her dress and frying with a cigarette in her mouth. Johnny thought she was beautiful with her marble-white skin, ink-black hair and big, glistening dark eyes.

'This isn't Sunday,' Albert reminded her.

'It's a holiday,' she replied. 'Coronation day, no less. So I thought we'd treat it just like a Sunday and give them the pan. Here,' she added hopefully, scooping the fry-up into Albert's plate and handing it to him. 'Here's yours.'

Lining up in order of age, which placed Marlene to the front (also 'because she's a girl' as their mother had once explained) Johnny and Billy waited just outside the kitchen, each with his own towel in his hand, as Marlene went in to the sink and their father took the delicious smelling fry-up from his wife. He glanced down at his plate, nodded with satisfaction, then looked up again.

'Have you lost your marbles?' he said. 'Sure this isn't a Sunday. It isn't even a weekend. We have a fry-up once a week, every Sunday, and that's all there is to it. If we give 'em fry-ups every time we have a holiday, we'll end up in the poor house.'

'*You're* having a fry-up,' Mary retorted. 'You *insisted* on having a fry-up.'

'I'm a working man and I have to keep up my strength, but this lot are a bunch of strapping youngsters. They can wait until Sunday for their fry-up. Today it's porridge as usual.'

'I just thought – ' Mary began as Johnny's heart sank and he exchanged glances with Billy, both built up only to be let down, this being the way of the wicked world.

94

'I *know* what you think, Mary. You think we're made of money, but we're not, so give these kids porridge. Besides, they're gonna get their guts filled with free cakes and sweets when they go to the Coronation Party. I say "free" but we had to contribute, so view that as their Sunday treat.'

'Aye, right,' Mary said.

'I'm finished,' Marlene said, emerging from the kitchen, shivering from having to wash her face in cold water. 'Are we havin' a fry-up?'

'No,' her Dad said, then he took a seat at the living room table and placed his plate emphatically upon it. 'You're having porridge as usual.'

'Oh,' Marlene said, disappointed.

'Put your backside on that chair,' Albert said.

Marlene sat at her usual place and looked on forlornly as Albert attacked his mouth-watering fry-up with his knife and fork. When Johnny and Billy had also washed, taking it in turn, they, too, sat at the table. Johnny smiled at his grumpy sister. Marlene had a pretty face, moon-shaped like Billy's, but with lovely hazel eyes and full lips. She was, however, when not being hysterical, withdrawn, even secretive, and Johnny rarely knew what to say to her.

Mary served them their porridge.

'Dad?' Johnny said as his mother, having completed her duties, sat down at the table with her customary cup of tea and cigarette.

'What?'

'Why do some houses in the street have electricity while others don't?'

'Always one with the questions,' Albert replied. 'A real smartie-pants, aren't you?'

Johnny blushed. 'I just...'

'We don't have electricity,' Albert informed him, 'because it's just been introduced to the main roads and certain side streets, but the corporation, in their capitalist wisdom, only took responsibility for the laying of the wires to the front doors of the houses. If you want, you can have it extended into your house, but you have to get it done privately, at your own expense, and I can't afford that right now. Any more questions, smartie-pants?'

Johnny shook his head. 'No.' He was eyeing his dad's fry-up.

There was bacon, eggs, fried tomato, soda farls and potato bread - and it all smelt delicious. Johnny wanted to die.

'What are you lookin' at?'

'Nothin', Dad.'

'Yes, you are. Sure you're lookin' at my fry-up and resentin' me because you're not havin' the same. Well, just remember this, smartie-pants. I'm the head of this household and I work my guts out, so I need all the energy I can get. You can have a fry-up every day of your life once you're making your own money and can afford it. Until then, as long as it's *my* money we're depending on, you'll have your fry-up once a week, while I have one every day. Now finish your porridge and be grateful. There are children starving in Africa and don't you forget it.'

Johnny wanted to kill his Dad, but at the same time he loved him. His Dad, after all, was one of the two pillars of his life (the other one being his Mum) and had done an awful lot for him. For one thing, his Dad rarely beat him like most of his friends' Dads did; for another, he did a lot of things that his friends' Dads never did: cycled him around the town in a special two-wheeled metal carriage that he'd had a friend weld together secretly in the Yard; made him a magic theatre out of cardboard and wood, complete with stage, curtains and trap doors; taught him how to draw and paint; dressed up and performed for him and the other kids at Halloween and Christmas; took him to the Custom House steps to hear the preachers and politicians and other crazy people ('Sure they're all a bunch of lunatics,' his Dad had often told him); and, even better, got him into the music halls where he could see the whole variety show, including his Dad's performance, free of charge. Though he made his living by working as a joiner in the Yard, Johnny's Dad was a part-time hoofer and all-round performer who, apart from tap-dancing like Fred Astaire, sang, performed magic tricks, acted the clown with a funny hat, false teeth and rubbery legs, and also did impersonations of other, more famous stars, particularly Paul Robeson, Bing Crosby, Frankie Laine, Dean Martin and Jerry Lewis, Frank Sinatra (whisky glass in his hand, singing 'One More For the Road'), George Formby, all of the Goons, Tony Hancock, and even females such as Vera Lynn, Rosemary Clooney and Marilyn Monroe. When he did the latter, he always rolled his trousers up to show the audience his white, hairy legs and striped socks with gaiters. Johnny thought he was brilliant.

On the other hand, despite how brilliant he thought his Dad was in certain ways, Johnny was often hurt by him, convinced that his Dad didn't really care for him - nor, indeed, for Billy or Marlene. He felt this because his Dad, though never physically mistreating them, rarely touched them, didn't like to be touched by them, and never showed the slightest interest in them. Marlene, in particular, was desperate about this, always trying to please him, always wanting to do things for him, but he never gave her any encouragement, always pushing her away when she reached out to hug him. This often either reduced her to tears or caused her to have a destructive tantrum, screaming and throwing things about the house, smashing anything she could get her hands on. She wouldn't stop until their Mum shook her rigid and then sent her up to bed.

Mum never had cause to shake Johnny because he never had tantrums.

Billy, of course, angered both his Mum and his Dad. He was always in trouble. He played truant repeatedly, insulted his teachers, stole sweets and fruit from shops, smashed neighbours' windows by throwing stones through them, beat up other kids, particularly Catholics, and tormented Marlene until she was in hysterics. When he did that, Marlene seemed more like a child than Billy, the youngest in the family, was. In truth, most grown-ups thought Billy was a right wee terror who would end up serving time in a Borstal, or boy's home. They thought Billy was bad news.

Now, with everyone's belly stuffed with hot porridge, Billy said, 'Can we all go out now, Mum?'

'Aye, you can,' their Mum replied. 'I've got to help with laying out the tables and chairs for the celebrations, so I don't want you under my feet. But make sure you're back by twelve noon or, believe me, you'll all get a good hiding.'

'Ackaye, Mum,' Billy said, unconcerned. 'Come on, Johnny, let's go.'

He didn't invite Marlene because she was a girl and real boys didn't play in the streets with girls. Boys who did that were sissies.

Relieved that the request had been made by Billy, Johnny gratefully followed his younger brother out of the house.

2

They lived in what was known as the 'short end' of the avenue, between the football grounds and a series of arches over which a road ran all the way down to the Bog Meadows. The houses were terraced with small gardens out front, fenced in and with wooden gates, and back yards that led into the entries. The back yards, bricked in, contained only a coal shed. Johnny's house was near the end of a terrace adjoining a factory that produced metal containers and looked like a prison behind its tall, black-painted fences. The football ground was located at the southern end of the avenue and a lot of big matches took place there. Each time a game was played, hundreds, maybe thousands, of men would pour along the street, right past the front gate of the house, on their way to the grounds, which were only a couple of minutes walk away. When the match was over, the same men would flood back down the street, though now visibly more excited and in many cases drunk, some cheering or booing, waving their team scarves or flags, others bawling abuse and even having fist fights, and an awful lot of them, filled with booze, urinating under one of the three arches, which is why the arches stank night and day. One of the arches spanned the avenue, from one pavement to the other, while the other two filled the space between one side of the avenue and the wall of the Great Northern Railway, which ran along the back of the terrace facing the house in which Johnny lived. Supported on iron pillars and red-brick walls about thirty feet high, the arches had winding steel stairs connecting the avenue to the road that ran above it, forming a bridge that the local children often played on.

'Let's slide down a pillar,' Billy said, the minute they stepped out of the house and saw none of their friends in the sunless street.

Traditionally, a boy wanting to join a local gang had to go to the top of the arches, about thirty feet above the avenue, clamber over the railing, place his feet on the inch-wide metal collar that ran around the top of all the pillars, lower himself to just under the rim of a chosen pillar by holding on to the railing with one hand while gripping the rim with the other, then slide down the pillar with his legs and arms wrapped around it. The first dangerous part of the exercise was when the boy had to remove one hand from the railing and grope blindly under him to find the rim. The second, even more dangerous, part was when the boy, holding the rim with one hand and gently lowering himself to a position under it, with his legs curled around the pillar, had to release the railing entirely and balance there for the few seconds that it took to grab the rim with that free hand. Over the years more than one boy had slipped and fallen thirty feet to the ground, breaking bones or cracking his skull, but though most parents forbade their children to slide down the pillars, they could rarely stop them from doing so.

Billy had slid down a pole even before Johnny had done so, but Johnny had finally done it last year and now, like Billy and the other boys, he often did it just to give himself a thrill.

'Naw,' he said, not being in the mood for it today, 'let's go to the bogs.'

'Okay,' Billy said, always game for anything.

Together they walked along the street, towards the arches, but just before they reached the end of the terrace a friend, Dan Johnstone, came out of his house. Though Dan was the same age as Billy and in his class at school, he was big for his years, had the muscles of a wrestler, and was constantly dirty and dishevelled, which made him look oddly threatening, like some of the tinkers who lived on the Bog Meadow. Dan took after his dad, Barney Johnstone, who was the size of an elephant and aggressive with it, constantly picking fights with other men in the Yard, where he worked, and also known to beat up his three sons (Dan being the youngest) and, just as frequently, his wife. Edna Johnstone was a washed-out woman who rarely left the house, only going out for the groceries, and she spoke to no one when she ventured forth. Dan's two brothers, Ian and Bobbie, eleven and twelve respectively, were as wild as Dan and, like him, were quick to bully anyone they sensed was scared of them. Most of the neighbours gave the Johnstone family a wide berth, but Billy and Dan were close and, together, were trouble.

'How are ya, Dan?' Billy said, staring up at his big friend.

'Not bad, Billy. Just got a clip on the ear from that oul bastard in there, so I ran out before he could hit me properly. Where are you two goin' then?'

'We're just off to the bogs, like.'

'What for?' Dan said, falling in beside them as they turned the corner and went along the street that ran below the bridge formed by the arches. There was a painting of King William of Orange on the wall of the bridge. He was sitting astride a white horse and pointing with his sword, clearly urging the men behind him to attack the vile Fenian hordes.

'Dunno,' Billy said. 'Just thought we'd go for a run around, like. Maybe try to catch some tadpoles. Maybe throw stones at the fuckin' tinkers. Maybe beat up a Catholic.'

'You shouldn't beat up Catholics,' Johnny said. 'Mum says they're just like you and me.'

'Are ya joking me?' Billy responded. 'Are you sayin' we're the same as fuckin' Fenians? You tell *me* I'm like a fuckin' Fenian, Johnny, and I'll knock your teeth out.'

Dan and wee Billy always swore like troopers when they got together. Johnny didn't swear at all because he knew it was a sin and that his mother, if she found out, would be mortified.

'I just meant…' he began to protest.

'Them Fenians are filthy,' said Dan, who hadn't had a bath in a month. 'They keep their coal in their bath tubs an' they use their outdoor toilets for storin' things, so they have to piss and shit in the back yard. That's why they're all filthy.'

'Who told you that?' Johnny asked.

'My Dad told me that. He hates the fuckin' Fenians. He said that Fenian snipers used to shoot at the trams that were takin' him and his mates to the Yard. He said some of his friends were killed in the trams and them snipers, them Fenian murderers, did it.'

'What I asked…' Johnny began, but was instantly silenced when Billy pointed excitedly to where Frank Wilson's motor van was parked by the side of the road a few yards ahead, near where the bridge levelled out to become the road that ran down to the Bog Meadows.

'Hey, there's Frank's van!' Billy said. 'Let's wait till he starts up again and then – '

'We shouldn't really do that,' Johnny interjected nervously, knowing what they were planning. 'Sure Frank's a quare good man who's never done us any harm. So I don't think we should – '

'Ack, for fuck's sake,' Billy interjected, 'it's only a wee bit of fun we're after, Johnny. Let's hang about here.'

Frank delivered milk to the locals from a large drum that had a brass tap fixed to it and was located at the open back door of his van. As the boys looked on, women wearing aprons and shawls were lining up to have their containers filled with milk from the tap or obtain buttermilk from a second drum. Frank normally had a helper to keep an eye open for young mischief-makers like Billy and Dan, but he had no helper today, almost certainly because he had given him the day off in order to let him celebrate the Coronation.

'Great,' Dan said. 'This is gonna be dead easy.'

'I still don't think we should do this,' Johnny said.

'Shut yer gob,' Dan said belligerently. 'Jesus, Billy, your big brother's such a softie.'

'No, he's not,' Billy said.

'There he goes!' Dan exclaimed.

The last of the customers in the street had just left and Frank was clambering back into his van to drive off again.

'I'll take the milk,' Dan said to Billy, 'and you take the buttermilk.'

'Aye, that's grand,' Billy said.

'I'm goin' on to the bogs,' Johnny said and immediately started walking, preparing to run if necessary.

'Go!' Dan bawled, the instant Frank's van moved off, going slowly in order to turn into the next side-street. Giggling like lunatics, Billy and Dan raced after the van and caught up with it as it was turning the corner. Still running behind the van, each boy grabbed one of the brass taps and opened it, running slightly to the side of it, to let the milk and buttermilk shoot out all over the road. Frank must have seen this happening in his rear-view mirror - or maybe someone else had seen it and bawled a warning to him - because he braked to a sudden halt and started clambering out of the van just as the boys, now giggling uncontrollably, turned away and raced off in the direction of the Bog Meadows.

'You wee eejuts!' Frank bawled at them, waving his right fist but unable to pursue them for fear of losing more milk and buttermilk. He was frantically closing the taps, standing in a rapidly expanding pool of milk, when Billy and Dan, both flushed with excitement, still giggling, caught up with Johnny.

'Run!' Billy shouted.

With his heart suddenly hammering, imagining that Frank was pursuing them, Johnny ran after his young brother and wild Dan. They ran all the way down the road, past the chippie and other shops, until they reached the broad, green expanse of the Bog Meadows. It was a serious bog with piles of rubbish everywhere and the tinkers' camps scattered untidily along the meandering banks of the Blackstaff River. The tinkers lived in battered caravans or tents of rags, had their horses tethered nearby, cooked their meals on open fires. They often turned up in the avenue, either to beg for money and unwanted household items or to sell some of the rubbish they had collected or, perhaps, stolen. Johnny and his friends often came here to explore the narrow, winding river, which was filled with its own kind of rubbish, and to collect tadpoles in jam jars. They usually did this around the short bridge that spanned the narrow river and was a good distance away from the tinkers' encampments. The bogs at the other side of the bridge led to the cemetery and, more importantly, the Whiterock Road. This led in turn to the Sheep's Path that wound steeply up the Black Mountain to the white farmhouses, the spring, and the Hatchet Field. Unfortunately, while being the only route to the mountains, the Whiterock Road ran between the City Cemetery and Ballymurphy, in what was a predominantly Catholic area.

'Feel like goin' up the mountain?' Dan asked, as they stood on one side of the bridge, regaining their breath. They viewed everything on the other side of the bridge as belonging to 'the Mickeys'. Cross the bridge and you were in enemy territory.

'Naw,' Billy said.

'What's the matter? You scared of the Mickeys?'

'Ack, away with ya,' Billy said. 'Sure you know we've both been up there lots of times. It's just that it'd take us too long to get there and back in time for the Coronation celebrations. Let's just hang about here.'

'Alright,' Dan said, casting his intense, slightly deranged glance towards the sprawling cemetery that ran up the western side of the Whiterock Road. 'I bet *they're* not celebratin' the Coronation,' he said. 'Them fuckin' Mickeys have no loyalty to the Queen. My Dad told me that.'

'Your Dad tells you a lot,' Johnny said.

'Only when he's goin' on about the Fenians. Apart from that, he

102

only grunts and shouts and gives the lot of us hidings. Sure I'm black and blue night and day.'

'You should run away from home,' Billy said, having done that a lot himself, though he always returned in time for tea.

'If I tried that an' he caught me he'd kill me,' Dan said, 'but when I'm bigger I'll knock the shite out of him.'

'Ackaye,' Billy said, sounding impressively grown up. 'Sure that's the way to do it, Dan. So what'll we play?'

'Cowboys and Indians,' Johnny suggested.

'That's for sissies,' Dan scoffed. 'Let's see what we can find in the river. There could be treasure down there.'

'Good idea,' Billy said.

They pottered about in the river on both sides of the bridge for an hour or so, dragging their fingers through the muddy, rubbish-and-glass strewn bed to see if they could come up with buried treasure and, when they failed to do so, blaming the tinkers for having already done so. They blamed the tinkers for a lot. The tinkers were scavengers, thieves and general layabouts only one step removed from the Fenians. (Of the three of them, Johnny was the only one who refused to accept this view of the Catholics; not only because he had Catholic neighbours, including the Lavery family, but also because his Mum had told him otherwise and he believed her in all things.) Though none of them would admit it, they were all deadly scared of the tinkers, particularly the older ones, who could cast the evil eye upon you and do you serious damage. In fact, it was precisely *because* they feared the tinkers that they tormented them in various ways - they had to prove to themselves and to each other that they were *not* frightened of them. So, as they wandered up and down the banks of the river, getting covered in mud and finding nothing worth having, they talked each other into doing some damage to the tinkers before going back to the avenue for the celebrations.

'Sure those gypsies,' Dan said, using another word to describe the tinkers, 'would eat the fuckin' grass if you let 'em. They've been up and down this river, I can tell you, fishin' for everything they could find. Now all that's left here are the tadpoles and they'll probably pinch them as well. They think they own the whole bog, like.'

'Ackaye,' Billy said, looking up with big eyes, his scarred baby-face covered in wet mud. 'Sure you're right as rain, Dan. Let's give them somethin' to think about before we turn back.'

'I don't think…' Johnny began, but was cut short again when Dan looked up, raised his eyebrows and said, 'Sure who are those two comin' along here? Who the fuck do they think they are? Obviously comin' to cross the bridge, like, so they must be two Mickeys, headin' back to their pigsty houses in Ballymurphy or Turf Lodge. Let's give them a bollickin'.'

'They might be Protestants,' Johnny protested, 'just goin' for a walk up to the mountains.'

'So what?' Dan responded, clearly bored out of his mind and wanting *any* kind of action. 'Let's have some fun with 'em. We'll ask them if they're Protestant or Fenian - and whatever they say, we'll say we're the opposite and then make 'em turn out their pockets. Here the wee shites come.'

The two boys were no more than eight or nine and both of them were carrying empty jam jars, which indicated, to Johnny, that they were planning to catch tadpoles in the river and go no farther than that. This meant that they were Protestants from his own area, but it was going to cut no ice with Dan when he stepped out in front of them and, being big for his age, could look down upon them.

'So where do you think *you're* goin'?' he asked them.

Both boys stared up at him with widening, frightened eyes. One was blond and the other had red hair, though both of them had pimples.

'Just goin' to catch some tadpoles,' the blond-haired boy said.

'On the way up the Whiterock, are ya?' Dan asked, while Billy, standing beside him, a lot smaller than he was, grinned and clenched his fists.

'We was just comin' here,' the red-haired boy said, his voice already shaky, 'to catch some tadpoles. That's why we brought these jam jars.'

'Are you Fenian or Protestant?' Billy asked, flexing his fingers before clenching his fists again.

'Protestant!' both boys declared in unison, recognising fellow Prods when they saw them. 'Sure we've just come up from Ebor Parade.'

'Well, we're *Fenians*,' Dan lied, 'and we don't like you Prods comin' over to our side of the river.'

'We weren't goin' to cross the river!' the blond boy insisted.

'Look!' he added by way of proof. 'We've both got jam jars. Sure we were only going to catch some tadpoles and take them back to Ebor Parade.'

'Sure you're a right pair of lyin' wee shites,' Dan said, towering over both of them and looking as threatening as he sounded because he hadn't had a wash in a month and his hair was dishevelled. 'You were goin' to use those jam jars to pay for your tickets into the Broadway. That's *our* picture house.'

'No, we weren't!' the blond boy protested, clearly trying to look calm but not quite succeeding. 'We weren't plannin' to go to the fillums. We just wanted some tadpoles.'

'You're a lyin' Prod shite,' Dan said, sounding more ferocious with every word. 'Now put them two jam jars on the ground and empty your pockets.'

'I've no money,' the blond boy said.

'And no sweets,' the red-haired boy added.

'Just empty your fuckin' pockets,' Dan said, 'before the three of us beat you up.'

Both boys emptied their pockets, producing marbles, a few pieces of chewing gum, a couple of torn cigarette cards and, in the hands of the blond boy, a couple of two-penny pieces. While Dan looked on, his fists clenched, Billy grabbed everything. Johnny burned up with shame.

'Ya wee liars,' Dan snarled. 'Typical fuckin' Prods. Ya tell us ya don't have any money and now look what I find. A good hidin's what you both deserve.'

'Swear to God,' the blond boy said, 'I didn't know I had that money. It musta gone right out of my head, like. Musta been there for days.'

'Alright,' Dan said, 'take your Protestant arses back to where you came from and don't come here again.'

'Okay!' the blond boy said.

'Sure!' the red-haired boy added.

They both bent down to pick up their empty jam jars, but jerked upright again when Dan snarled at them, 'Let them fuckin' jam jars alone and go back where you came from.'

'Aye, okay!' both boys said in chorus, then they turned and hurried back the way they had come. When both of them were well out of earshot, Dan and Billy broke up. They both laughed until tears rolled down their cheeks, though Johnny wasn't amused.

'If Mum found out what you'd done,' he said to Billy, 'she'd give you more than a hidin'.'

'Ack,' Billy replied, 'sure they were only a couple of wee eejuts from Ebor Parade. What's the harm in it, like?'

'I think it's time we went back,' Johnny said, feeling flushed, his heart racing, visualising his Mum's accusing face and trying to turn away from it. 'The celebrations'll be startin' pretty soon.'

'Here,' Billy said, displaying the booty in the upturned palms of his grubby hands. 'Have some marbles and chewing gum.'

'I don't want anything,' Johnny retorted primly. 'I just want to go back now.'

'I want those green-and-blue marbles,' Dan said, reaching down to grab them, 'and some of this chewing gum and one of them two-penny pieces. A fuckin' good mornin', wasn't it?'

'Aye, it was grand,' Billy agreed.

Johnny had already turned away and was about to commence the walk home when Dan, the lunatic, said, 'Hey! Look at those fuckin' tinkers over there. Aren't they the ones that dredged the whole river and left us nothin' to find?'

'Ackaye, they are,' Billy said.

'So why don't we...?'

'Aye,' Billy said, always keen on some mischief. 'Let's go and do it.'

'I'm goin' home,' Johnny said, though he didn't actually move, not knowing what Billy and Dan were planning.

'Just come with us,' Billy said, 'and then run with us when we tell you to.'

Johnny didn't like it, but he had to go with them. He kept imagining his Mum staring at him with her big, dark, accusing eyes. He kept thinking of himself taking the punishment for his younger brother's vile crimes. His younger brother, less troubled and in the company of mad Dan, led him by a roundabout route, all three crouched low like soldiers, across the Bog Meadows, truly a swamp of mud and rubbish, to where the tinkers' horses, five in all, were tethered by ropes tied to steel rods hammered into the marshy ground. Once there, practically down on their hands and knees, while Johnny simply knelt on one knee, frozen by fear (or, perhaps more accurately, self-consciousness), Billy and Dan surveyed the tinker encampment, ascertained that their approach to the horses had not been witnessed and then, satisfied that it had not been, urgently untied the restraining ropes, jumped back to their feet and started screaming like Tarzan while slapping the horses on the flank. Finally, as the five horses broke apart and started galloping off in different directions, Billy bawled, 'Run!'

Johnny ran. One of the horses ran after him. The horse was in a panic, as Johnny certainly was, and as fast as Johnny ran, the horse came after him and started catching up with him. Johnny glanced back over his shoulder. He saw the horse looming large. There was steam coming out of its nostrils and its white flanks were rippling. Johnny thought he was going to die. The horse would trample him to death. It would run over him and leave him face down in the mud, before innocently galloping on to freedom. Johnny sobbed and kept running. He was stripped clean by fear. He heard the horse close behind him, imagined its flaring nostrils, heard its hoof beats unnaturally amplified and wanted to die. Death seemed preferable to life in that moment of fearful transcendence. Johnny wanted to die because life terrified him and he didn't want to go through this again.

Then he stumbled and fell.

Face down in the mud.

Glancing up, he saw his younger brother Billy running across the field towards him, still screaming like Tarzan - that jungle-call they all knew so well from their Saturday morning matinées in the Broadway cinema -and waving frantically to make the horse turn away.

Which it did.

Abruptly veering to the right, making a sharp turn, its hoofs kicking mud all over Johnny where he lay belly-down on the ground, it galloped off in the opposite direction, leaving him safe and sound. He raised himself to his hands and knees. From there, he climbed back to his feet. Wee Billy walked up to him. With mad Dan coming up behind him, he gave Johnny a cocky grin.

'That was fuckin' great, wasn't it?' Billy said. 'Sure those tinkers are all steamin' from the ears and dancin' like Apaches. What's the matter? You alright?'

'I'm fine,' Johnny said, burning hot and cold, dizzy, but

controlling himself, trying to look unconcerned. 'But I think it's time we all went back home. The celebrations should be starting any minute now.'

'Dead on,' Billy said.

'Aye, dead on,' Dan added.

3

Grandma Doreen sat at a table in the middle of the avenue, mere yards from the decorated main arch, twelve years older than she had been when the bombs were falling on the Newtownards Road and her grandson, Johnny, was born. Now Doreen was fifty-two years old and not wasting one second wondering how the ground had slipped from under her feet. The ground *hadn't* slipped from under her feet, because the Lord was her shepherd. Which was more than you could say for those she was looking at right now, including some Catholics who should have been elsewhere.

'The Lord works in mysterious ways,' she said. 'Ours not to reason why.'

'*What's* that, Mum?' Albert asked.

'Nothing,' Grandma said, casting a baleful look, first at her husband, Brian, seated beside her, then at Patrick and Bernadette Lavery, both on chairs beside Albert and Mary, now in their early thirties. Nelly and Sammy Devlin were also present, both now nearing forty, which still made them a few years younger than the Laverys. All of them were seated around a table covered in plates of sandwiches, cakes and sweets, as well as bottles of stout, whisky, orange-juice and lemonade. All were wearing paper hats. The arch that spanned the road had been decorated with dreadful murals of King William of Orange, the new Queen, Elizabeth, other members of the Royal Family, diamond-studded crowns, the banners of various Orange Lodge districts and, of course, Union Jacks. The whole street was filled with tables and chairs, most taken, and kids were running wild all over the place. Some of the neighbours, those with electricity already installed in their homes, had put extension cables on their radios and placed the radios on the pavements to enable them to listen to reports of the

Coronation as it was taking place. When the Coronation was not being reported, music was played.

'Sounds like a real swell do over there,' Albert said, referring to the ceremony taking place in Westminster Abbey.

'As befits the Royal Family,' Doreen responded loyally, tucking strands of loose grey hair back into place. 'Sure they deserve nothing less.'

'If you ask me,' Mary said, exhaling smoke through her nostrils, her dark eyes flashing brightly, casting a quick, sympathetic glance in the direction of her Catholic friends, 'I think it's a shocking waste of money that could be better spent. You could feed half the unemployed of Belfast on what that marriage is costing.'

'Sure I don't believe I'm hearin' right!' Doreen said, almost apoplectic. 'That's a disgraceful thing to say! You've always had a careless tongue, missus, but that remark takes the cake. This is the Coronation of *our Queen* we're talking about, and all *you* can think about is...'

'The money,' Mary retorted boldly, always keen to needle her hated mother-in-law. 'All that pomp and circumstance. I bet it costs the earth and moon - and *we'll* be made to pay for it in the end, you mark my words.'

'Money!' Doreen exclaimed, practically breathing fire from her nostrils. 'Who are *you* to talk about *the money* when it comes to something like this? You that smokes like a runaway train with no thought of the cost. Why you...'

'No doubt it costs a lot,' Patrick Lavery began tentatively, 'but – '

'And I suppose you agree with her,' Doreen interjected, turning her outraged gaze on the unfortunate Laverys. 'Since of course you're not as loyal to the Crown as some of us are.'

'Now, *hold on* there, Doreen,' Bernadette Lavery said. 'Just because we're Catholics doesn't mean we're not loyal to the Crown. I mean, Pat and me, we – '

'I'm sure if de Valera's government spent exactly the same money, you'd – '

'Now, now, Mum,' Albert said, throwing Mary an angry glance, knowing that she'd started this deliberately just to aggravate his mother, 'Pat and Bernadette said nothing about the money being spent. It was *Mary* who said that, and – '

'That's it,' Mary said, puffing another cloud of smoke. 'Blame me for everything. Sure that's all I'm here for, it seems. I'm just sitting here quietly, minding my own business, and the next thing – '

'I was just about to say,' Patrick continued, 'that though it costs a lot of money, I'm sure it's worth it in the end, because the people need this kind of thing every so often. I mean, it's a special, an *historical*, occasion. And all that pomp and circumstance, though maybe expensive, makes it a day to remember. That's why the money's well spent.'

'Truer words were never spoken,' Doreen said, 'and it took a Catholic to speak them. Trust your own kind to stab you in the back when you're least expecting it.'

Mary ignored Doreen's baleful stare and instead glanced about her, at her celebrating neighbours, before saying to Albert, 'Where are those two wee tykes of ours? They should've been here by now.'

'In my day we looked after them,' Doreen said. 'We didn't let them run wild.'

'They're in the house getting washed,' Albert informed them as he poured stout from a bottle into his glass. 'They came back from the Bog Meadows all covered in mud, absolutely bloody filthy, so I sent them inside and told them not to come out till they were clean.'

'They were probably playin' in the river,' Marlene said, leaning out of her chair with her shoulders slumped, clearly desperate for someone to play with. 'That's why they were covered in mud. It was the mud from the Blackstaff.'

'If I've told them once, I've told them a million times,' Mary said, 'that the water in that river is filthy and they're not to play there. It was probably wee Billy leading Johnny. I should take the strap to him.'

'You're always talkin' about the strap,' Nelly Devlin said, 'but you've never strapped one of them. You're a real softie that way.'

'Here, Marlene,' Mary said, holding out a plate of sandwiches to her rag-and-bone daughter, 'have one of these.'

Marlene shook her head from side to side. 'I don't want one,' she said. 'I'm not hungry. My stummich's upset.'

'Then have a cake or something.'

Marlene shook her head again.

'There's children starvin' in Africa,' Doreen informed Marlene, 'while you sit there turnin' down food. Spoilt rotten, I say. So what do you think *you're* doing?' she asked of her husband when she saw him opening another bottle of stout. 'Isn't one enough for you?'

'There's plenty more where that came from,' Albert said, jumping to Brian's defence, indicating the many other unopened bottles on the table with a backwards jab of his thumb.

'That doesn't mean he has to drink them all himself,' Doreen retorted while glaring at her husband.

'We'll be here the whole afternoon,' Brian said in his mild-mannered, quietly determined way, 'and I'll be drinking them slowly.'

'Just make sure you do,' Doreen said.

'There's Donna!' Marlene jumped out of her chair and looked across the road at a girl with blonde hair and a skipping rope. About the same age as Marlene, she was dressed in a lime-green dress and flat shoes. 'I'm goin' over to see her.'

'Aye, you do that.' Albert was always relieved to get rid of his kids, finding it easier to talk to adults. 'Go and have a good time there.'

Marlene ran off, weaving between the people crowding the road, the tables and chairs. The sound of a brass band wafted through the air, but was cut off abruptly as a voice solemnly described what was happening that very moment in Westminster Abbey. Princess Elizabeth was being crowned Queen Elizabeth, but that, in Albert's view, wouldn't change a damned thing for the common folk. Certainly not here in Belfast.

'I was in the centre of town yesterday,' Nelly Devlin said, 'and saw them pulling up some of the tram lines.'

'Aye,' Brian said. 'And that's only the start of it. Sure they say that by next year the trams'll all be gone, replaced by the new trolley buses. They don't need tram lines. They run on pneumatic tyres and get their power from overhead cables. First the horse-drawn carts go, now the trams. Soon you won't be able to recognise this town, it's all changin' so fast.'

'Not for the better,' Doreen said. 'These newfangled things are so quick, sure they're a menace to everyone. There'll be dead bodies strewn all over the streets when them... whatyoumaycallems...'

'Trolley buses,' Brian offered helpfully.

'Aye, when them trolley buses start runnin'. Sure you'll be scraping us off the roads like jam when those things run amok. I don't like them at all.'

'So what have we here?' Bernadette Lavery said with a smile when Johnny and Billy, both with clean faces and hands, walked up to join them. 'Sure butter wouldn't melt in their mouths, they look so immaculate.'

'We just washed,' Johnny explained.

'Aye, we're clean,' Billy added.

'What are those dark marks on your pullovers?' Mary asked. 'Streaks of mud, aren't they? Mud from the river, isn't it?'

'Well...' Johnny stuttered and blushed.

'It was you, wasn't it?' Mary said accusingly to wee Billy. 'I bet it was you who suggested that both of you go to the Bog Meadows.'

'So what?' Billy said, not bothering to deny it, though in fact it wasn't true. 'We just went there for a wee walk, wanting to pass the time, like, and some of those tinkers threw handfuls of mud at us. That's why we were filthy.'

'And a filthy wee liar to boot,' Doreen said. 'Sure that's as tall a story as ever I've heard. Have you no shame, you sinful child?'

'I'm starvin',' Billy said, ignoring his granny and reaching out to grab a sandwich. 'Sure I could eat a whole horse, I could.'

But Mary leaned forward and slapped the back of his wrist. 'Keep your paws off that table until you've asked politely,' she said. 'I've a good mind to starve you, like them poor children in Africa, as a punishment for going to the river when I told you not to. What about you, Johnny?' she continued, turning to her favourite child with a loving smile. 'Would you like something to eat, son? A sandwich? Some cake?'

'I'll have a sandwich,' Johnny said.

'Help yourself, son.'

'Can I take one for Billy as well?'

'Of course you can, son.' Mary turned her big dark-eyed gaze on wee Billy, whose battered baby face remained pugnacious. 'See how your brother looks after you?' she said. 'Asks politely instead of pawing the table like some scavenging animal. Aren't you lucky to have him?'

'Yes, Mum,' Billy said, then turned to Johnny. 'I'll take that big fat one right there. The one with eggs and tomato. And gimme one of them glasses of lemonade.'

'Aye, right,' Johnny said.

He passed Billy a sandwich and drink, had the same himself, and then the two of them stood there, side by side, munching happily and drinking while listening to the conversation of the grown-ups. Johnny liked to hear adult conversation because it seemed so intelligent.

'Ack, sure isn't this a grand day?' Sammy Devlin said. 'Just sittin' outdoors, havin' a bite and a drink, listenin' to the Coronation on the radio. A pleasant afternoon, to be sure.'

'I bet the Queen looks really lovely,' Bernadette said. 'A real little princess, straight out of a fairy tale.'

'She *was* a princess,' Sammy corrected her. 'Though now she's the Queen, right enough.'

'You know what I mean, Sammy.'

'She's a quare wee beauty alright,' Doreen said. 'We should all be proud of her.'

'She looks prettier than de Valera, that's for sure,' Sammy said with a broad grin. 'Even a good Catholic like me can't be denyin' that.'

'There's nothin' wrong with you, Sammy,' Albert said generously. 'Sure a man couldn't wish for better neighbours, Catholic or not. You and Nelly are as good as they come, and there isn't a Protestant in this street who wouldn't agree with that.'

Doreen's lips moved in agitation, but she kept her mouth shut. Mary nodded and said, smiling, 'Ackaye, that's right enough. Sure we spend more time in your place...' - nodding to Patrick and Bernadette... 'than we do anywhere else. Except for you two, of course,' she added hastily, addressing Nelly and Sammy. 'Sure we're all friends together in this street and that's all that matters.'

'Hear, hear,' Patrick said.

'All the rest is just politics,' Albert continued, sounding unusually emotional. 'It's just dirty tricks dreamed up by the politicians and a lot of them that professes to be religious, no names, no pack drill.'

'Where would we be without the church?' Doreen asked sternly, determined not to have her religion denigrated, not even by her beloved son. 'Without the church, all order would collapse and Belfast would be Babylon.'

'We should be so lucky,' Brian muttered.

'What's that, mister?'

'Nothing,' Brian said, putting his second bottle of stout to his lips in the hope of hiding his blushes.

'Sure there's good and bad in everyone,' Sammy said as he removed the metal cap from another bottle, 'and that includes the priests and politicians. It's just a matter of who has the scissors when it comes to cutting the cloth to fit.'

'Personally, I take the positive point of view,' Brian said. 'Given the right attitude, things will work themselves out in the end. And I think it's true to say that everyone here has that attitude. That's what makes good neighbours.'

'Hear, hear,' Patrick repeated.

'If I may say so,' Doreen said, proceeding to say her piece without fear of contradiction, 'there's two sides to every fence, and if only people remembered what side they were on - and *stuck* to that side – life would be a lot easier.'

'What you mean,' Mary said, moving in for the kill again, 'is that Catholics and Protestants - say, the Laverys and the Hamiltons - should remember exactly who they are, *what* they are, and stick to their own side of the fence.'

'Don't tell me what I mean, missus.'

'What you mean is – '

'So what's this about you going to work across the water?' Nelly Devlin asked of Albert, diplomatically changing the subject.

'Aye, it's true,' Albert said. 'I think it's about time. Sure there's no future in this country at all, so I thought I'd give it a go over there.'

Johnny and Billy looked up in surprise.

'Liverpool?'

'Birkenhead. Doing joinery work for a company that builds and maintains the ferries. You get a long weekend home every six weeks and the wages are better. Of course, you have to pay for your own accommodation, which takes a bit out of it, but all in all you still come out a good bit better.'

'About two shillings a week better,' Mary said bitterly, pouring herself another bottle of stout, the smoke from her latest cigarette coiling about her white face and black hair. 'Sure he's only going to get away from home and have himself a good time.'

'Ack, now, Mary, that's not true.' Albert tried a weak grin. 'I'm goin' because there's more opportunities over there and because I want to chance my arm at real showbusiness. I'm fed up with all the music hall rubbish that we have over here. They're all amateurs here.'

'*You're* an amateur,' Mary said.

'Oh, he's a lot more than that, Mary,' Bernadette insisted. 'Sure he's as good as any *I've* seen on the stage, I can tell you that much.'

'He's brilliant!' Doreen declared emphatically, defending her only son.

'A real trooper,' Patrick said.

'Ack, sure I know I'm not that good,' Albert said modestly. 'But I think I'm good enough to chance my arm across the water, first in Birkenhead, then, if I make it there, maybe in the Big Smoke.'

'Where's that?' wee Billy asked.

'London,' his Dad explained, before addressing the grown-ups again. 'I mean, I'll stick with my job, I'll work at my joinery, but on the weekends I can try some things over there that you can't do on this side of the water. Sure it's just a dead-end street over here when it comes to showbiz.'

'Jesus!' Mary whispered.

'Don't blaspheme,' Doreen said. 'That's it, son, you do what you think is right. It's bound to be the right thing.'

'And if it doesn't work out,' Albert said, though he didn't sound too convincing, 'sure I can always pack it in and come back here. Meanwhile, I'll be back every six weeks for a long weekend. I mean, it sounds grand to me.'

It didn't sound grand to Johnny. It didn't sound grand at all. At his age, six weeks seemed as long as six years and he couldn't even imagine his Dad being away that long, let alone repeatedly. Johnny sometimes hated his Dad, though he loved him as well, and no way could he imagine life without him. His Dad belonged in their house. He was part of the furniture. If he went away for six weeks at a time the whole world would be changed. Johnny trembled to think of it.

'So when are you going?' he asked.

'In two weeks time,' his Dad said.

'Right,' Johnny said flatly, blinking repeatedly and finding it hard to think straight. 'Can me and Billy go off and play now?'

'Aye,' his mother said with a sigh. 'You go off and enjoy yourselves.'

Johnny nodded at Billy and then led him away from the table, weaving his way through the noisy crowd, passing people singing, others dancing, until he had reached the front gate of their house. The front door was unlocked.

'Wait here,' Johnny said to Billy. 'Don't come in. I'll come back out in a minute or two, so just wait for me right here.'

'Okay,' Billy said.

Johnny went into the house. He sat down on the small sofa. He glanced about him, wondering what he could smash, then he started to cry. The tears fell long and hard, shaking him leaf and bough. He cried until there were no tears left and he felt a bit better. Then he went into the kitchen, splashed cold water on his face, dried his face on a towel and walked back out of the house. Wee Billy was waiting loyally for him down by the garden gate.

'So what are we gonna do?' Billy asked him.

'I dunno,' Johnny said.

<h2 style="text-align:center">4</h2>

Walking back along the pavement, avoiding their parents' table in the centre of the road, they immediately ran into Dan Johnstone, who was standing at his garden gate at the end of the terrace with his enormous father and two brothers, Ian and Bobby. Johnny was frightened of Dan's father. In fact, he was frightened of all the Johnstones, including Dan. He was even frightened of Dan's mother, Edna, because although she had never said an unkind word to him, she had never said a word of *any* kind, and her silent stare, grey eyes dulled by daily fear and despair, no doubt caused by all the beatings she received from her monstrous husband, was even more frightening to Johnny than the possibility of physical violence.

Right now, with Edna doubtless cowering inside the house, Dan's father, Barney, about as big as an elephant, wearing an open-necked shirt and threadbare pants held up by braces, was removing a bottle of stout from his lips and glaring contemptuously at those enjoying themselves in the middle of the road. By now the Coronation was over and the radios were blaring, so people were dancing between the tables and singing to the music. Some of the men had put on their Orange Lodge sashes and black bowler hats. Children were running to and fro, screaming and giggling.

'Jasus,' Barney said. 'All of this for the fuckin' Queen of England. When will these eejuts ever learn?'

'I thought we supported the Queen,' Bobby, twelve years old, said nervously. Bobby and Ian were always nervous when they spoke to their father. Only Dan seemed fearless.

'We don't support the Queen or any other English bitch. We support the Orange State to keep the Fenians in their place and we need the English to help us do that. That doesn't mean we have to behave like this just because young Tin Lizzie's been crowned. I could puke just to look at that. And you,' he continued, looking down at Johnny, 'I suppose your dad's out there, toasting the Queen and generally acting like an eejut.'

'Aye, he's out there,' Johnny said, outraged by the insult but not willing to defend it because right now he had good reason to hate his father. He was being deserted.

'Aye, I can see him,' Barney said, squinting as he gazed across the crowded road. 'Sittin' there shamelessly with them Fenians, the Laverys, the same neighbours they had in Newtownards before they were bombed out. Trust the Fenians to get themselves a good house in a Loyalist area when Protestants bombed out of their homes were shoved into prefabs. Between breedin' like lice and infiltratin' Protestant districts, the Fenians will soon be runnin' Belfast. Sure it's a damned disgrace!'

'Comin' to play, Dan?' Billy asked.

Dan stared up at his father. 'Aye,' Barney said, 'you run off and get into more mischief. Maybe pull the chairs out from under the Laverys while they're sittin' there pretendin' to be Prods on Coronation Day. Do some good for a change.'

Grinning, Dan joined Billy and Johnny. Together they made their way back into the road, weaving between the dancing people, grabbing sweets off the tables as they passed. When they reached the far side of the road, they found Marlene skipping with a rope while Donna King stood by, waiting her turn. Blonde and pale-skinned, Donna was wearing a lime-green dress that matched her eyes. Donna had cats' eyes, beautiful, enigmatic, always steady, and after flickering automatically over Dan and Billy, they came to rest gravely, steadily, upon Johnny. He felt himself blushing.

'Hi,' Johnny,' Donna said.

'Howya doin'?'

'Alright, like.'

Marlene stopped skipping. Donna kept staring at Johnny with her steady green gaze and he felt the blood rushing to his head, though he didn't know why. When Donna smiled, as if knowing something that Johnny didn't know, the blood rushed even quicker to his head and made him feel all confused.

'Here, gimme that skippin' rope,' Dan said, stepping forward to grab the rope from Marlene.

'No,' Marlene said, putting her hand behind her back, keeping the skipping rope out of Dan's reach. 'What for?'

'No friggin' business of yours, what for. Just give me that rope.'

Dan made a grab for the skipping rope, but Marlene shrieked and jumped out of his way. 'Get away from me, you binlid,' she said. 'Go and play someplace else.'

'Who do you think you're talkin' to?' Dan said. 'Sure you're just a friggin' girl. Gimme that rope or I'll take it off ya and strangle ya with it.'

Dan made another grab for the rope, but as Marlene shrieked again, jumping backwards, wee Billy darted between the two of them and, always prepared to defend his family, raised his balled fists.

'Are you threatenin' my sister?' he asked, staring up at Dan.

'For fuck's sake, Billy, I just want the skippin' rope and...' Big Dan glanced down at Billy's clenched fists, then stared into his fearless eyes. 'You threatenin' to hit me, you wee shite?'

'Aye, if you lay one fuckin' hand on my sister.'

A hand came out of nowhere and slapped Billy across the left ear, making him yelp and raise his balled hands in protection. 'Watch that language!' Albert said, having turned away from Bernadette, his temporary dancing partner, to administer his vigorous slap to the head. Mary had been dancing with Patrick Lavery just behind them and she, too, now glared at Billy.

'Where did you learn language like that?' she said. 'Certainly not at home, you didn't.' Her fire-and-brimstone gaze moved inevitably to Dan Johnstone. 'Learnt it from you, did he? Sure I wouldn't be surprised. You're likely to end up in Borstal, you are, taking my Billy with you. Get out of here before I clip your ear and send you home howlin'.'

Dan ran off, grinning, and Billy, giggling, ignoring a warning shout from his mother, ran after him, leaving Johnny standing there on his own, burning up because he was being stared at by Donna King, whose steady green gaze was unnerving.

'Hey, Johnny, love,' his mother said with a big smile, while still holding Patrick Lavery's right hand in her left hand, her own right hand being pressed to his back, both preparing to start dancing again, 'why don't you take Donna, standing there all forlorn, for a wee spin around the road? If you can't dance, I'm sure she can teach you. Don't you think, Pat, they'd make a lovely couple?'

'Ackaye,' Pat said, then he and Mary burst out laughing simultaneously and went spinning away into the other dancers, followed by Johnny's dad and Bernadette.

Johnny felt so hot he thought he was going to burst into flames. Donna was still staring at him. Still smiling. Still breathing.

'Hey, what are you starin' at?' Marlene asked him.

'What?'

'Sure your eyes are like two great big spoons when you turn them on Donna.' Marlene turned to Donna. 'He's only eleven, but he's gone all soft on you. That's why he standin' there as speechless as a deaf-and-dumb eejut. Just pat him on the head and watch him pant like a wee puppy dog with a fresh bone.'

Johnny spun away from them and made his way, running, through the grown-ups dancing in the pearly-grey afternoon light to the music blaring out of various radios. Reaching the far side of the road, two doors up from his own house, he found wee Billy and big Dan playing marbles on the pavement. Both looked up when he approached, both giving him wide grins.

'Hey, Johnny,' Billy said, holding up one of his marbles, 'these are the marbles we got off those two wee Fenian eejuts in the bogs.'

'They weren't Fenians,' Johnny reminded him. 'They were Prods from Ebor Parade.'

His correction was ignored. 'You wanna play marbles?' Dan asked him. 'We could play for the money we took off them. I mean, gamble just like the grown-ups do.'

'No, thanks,' Johnny said. 'Teddy didn't come to the party, so I wanna go and see if he's home.'

'He is,' Billy said. They were on the pavement just outside the garden gate of the Lavery house. 'Sure we saw him at the window while we were playing. He was wearin' his Navy uniform an' all.'

'Then I'll go in and see him,' Johnny said.

'Okay, see ya later.'

Johnny walked up the short garden path to the Laverys' front door. As the door was open, he stepped into the small, square-shaped hallway and knocked on the frosted-glass window pane of the living-room door.

'Yes?' Teddy Lavery called out.

'It's me. Johnny.'

'Johnny! Come in!'

Opening the door, entering, Johnny found the Lavery brothers slumped side by side on the sofa, drinking stout straight from the bottle while listening to the radio, now broadcasting Mantovani's string orchestra. Teddy was twenty-two, red-haired like his brother, and too plump in his Royal Navy uniform, having already developed a beer-belly. He was, however, healthily flushed from the hot sun of the exotic, foreign countries that Johnny wanted to visit. You could practically see the palm trees in his eyes. Golden beaches, too.

'You're back,' Johnny said.

'Aye, I'm back,' Teddy replied. 'But just for a coupla days, then I'm off to Gibraltar and points farther east.' He put his bottle of stout on the low table in front of him, then jumped to his feet and grabbed Johnny by the ears to tug them lightly, affectionately. 'So how're ya doin', kid? Sure it's good to see you again!'

Johnny revered Teddy because he was in the Royal Navy, had seen a lot of the world, and had a terrific sense of humour. Teddy had been able to join the Royal Navy because, although Irish by birth, he was also a British citizen, which was something that Johnny had never understood, though he knew that he was the same. He wasn't too pleased with this because the British-Irish, according to his parents, were not all that popular with the British. This confused him even more because people in Ulster, his Ireland, were more patriotic about England than were the English who, according to what Teddy had told him, tried to rush out of cinemas even as the National Anthem was playing. If you tried, during the National Anthem, to rush out of a cinema in Belfast, someone would stick his foot out to trip you up and others, once they saw you falling, would be likely to give you a good kicking for insulting the King - now the Queen, of course.

'Ack, I'm doin' fine,' Johnny said, grinning and shaking his head free of Teddy's grip. 'Good to see you, too, Teddy. So why aren't you two out there at the party? I was expectin' to see you there.'

Teddy grinned and rolled his eyes, then slumped back down on the sofa beside his brother. Though a year younger than Teddy, Mark looked older than him, not being healthily flushed from the sun of foreign climes and, more crucial, not wearing a handsome Royal Navy uniform. In his open-necked shirt, V-necked pullover and corduroy trousers, Mark looked ordinary.

'Ack, tell him, Mark,' Teddy said, having another swig from his bottle of stout. 'Tell my wee friend Johnny here why we're not outside celebratin' the Coronation.'

'Celebrate the Coronation?' Mark asked rhetorically, sounding disgusted. 'Are ya fuckin' kiddin' me, or what? The fuckin' Orangemen can go out and celebrate their new Queen, but don't fuckin' ask me to do it 'cause I'm no fuckin' mug. I'm a fuckin' Catholic in a fuckin' Protestant state - a fuckin' *British* state - so I'm not about to join a fuckin' party that's celebratin' the fuckin' Coronation of a fuckin' British Queen.'

Mark never swore when his parents were present.

'And I'm tryin' to tell him,' Teddy said, talking to Johnny, as he'd always done, as if Johnny was a grown-up, for which Johnny also revered him, 'is that we live in a Protestant street with good Protestant friends and so joining them in *their* celebration is simply bein' polite, like.'

'*Polite!*' Mark almost screamed. 'Are ya fuckin' kiddin' me, or what? Would you sell your soul to the fuckin' devil just to be...' He was practically gibbering now. '*Polite*?' He almost jumped off the sofa. 'Well, fuck *that* for a joke!'

'So I can't join the party,' Teddy calmly explained to Johnny, 'because my wee brother wouldn't approve and I don't want to hurt his tender feelings.'

'Oh, very fuckin' funny,' Mark said. 'My fuckin' sides are splittin' to hear *that* fuckin' remark from an Irishman who thinks he's fuckin' English - my own brother, for fuck's sake! You've already joined the British Navy to defend the fuckin' British Empire, so why don't you join the fuckin' Orange Lodge and get it over an' done with? I'm sure they're desp'rate for some fuckin' Catholic members to make 'em fuckin' respectable.'

Teddy was about to retort when the living room door opened and his father walked in. Patrick, being forty-four years old, was flushed from his drinking. He was also breathless from dancing.

With my Mum, Johnny thought, though he liked Patrick almost as much as he liked Teddy and didn't mind the dancing at all. Grown-ups liked to dance, like.

'God,' Patrick said, gasping. 'Sure that's a grand wee time we had out there, but I thought it was finally time to quit. Not as young as I used to be, though Bernadette's still out there having a quare good time. Ack, you've come,' he said to Johnny, stepping forward to ruffle his hair with rough, friendly fingers. 'Sure isn't your Mum one hell of a wee hoofer? Sure she coulda been on the stage like your dad. She swirled me around there, I tell ya. Fred Astaire and Ginger Rogers we were. So,' he went on, turning to his sons, 'what have you two misery-guts been up to? Missing the party an' all.'

'Just havin' a drink and listenin' to the radio,' Teddy said, winking at Johnny. 'Enjoyin' the Coronation from afar with a bottle of stout.'

'And him, too?' Patrick asked, nodding to indicate Mark, whose pale cheeks, untouched by foreign sunshine, disguised his simmering outrage. 'Has he been enjoying the Coronation more inside than he would have done outside?'

'Lay off it, Dad,' Mark said.

'No sweat, son. Just joking. But there's a lot of nice neighbours out there and it's a pity you missed them.'

'No sweat here either, Dad. I just didn't feel like partying. Sure we've had enough parties in this house with the Hamiltons to last the average vampire a lifetime. I just wanted to have a quiet time alone with my elder brother - and that, I hope, is what we've been having.'

'Dead on,' Teddy said.

'Well, you obviously had a good time, da,' Mark said, not offering a single swear word.

'Aye, it was grand,' Patrick said. 'Sure didn't wee Mary, like I said, sweep me off m'feet and have me swirlin' about there like a regular hoofer?' He turned to grin at Johnny. 'Between your Dad and your Mum, it's real showbiz out there. It must run in the veins.'

'Not in mine,' Johnny said.

'Give it time,' Patrick told him.

'Here,' Teddy said, suddenly standing up and going to his Navy overcoat, hanging behind the living room door. He pulled a package out of the coat's big inside pocket and gave it to Johnny. 'A wee present for you, Johnny. Sure I saw it in the bum-boat of an Arab in Aden and thought of you the minute I laid eyes on it.'

He handed the package to Johnny. Though it was wrapped in plain brown paper, Johnny's fingers were tingling. It had come from far-off shores and Teddy, his friend, had brought it all that way just for him. Johnny trembled with gratitude.

'Well, open it, why don't ya?' Teddy said.

Johnny sank into the chair beside the sofa, placed the package in his lap and then carefully opened it, trying not to tear the paper. Inside was what looked like a big wallet, pale-pink in colour, about ten inches high and eight inches wide, with sailboats and Arab hieroglyphics carved into the leather. When Johnny opened it, he found pens, pencils and crayons on one side, sheets of heavy white paper on the other.

'It's a drawing kit,' Teddy explained. 'Sure I've seen all them drawings you did and I knew that you had a lot of talent and thought you might like this.'

'I do,' Johnny said.

'What I mean,' Teddy said, 'is that you'd like this more than something you'd find in the Smithfield Market, because this one was made by the Arabs. I mean, look at it! It's hand-tooled out of pure leather. They probably made it in one of them Bedouin tents - out there, in the middle of the desert, where white men don't go - so I knew you'd like it for that alone.'

'I do,' Johnny said, all choked up.

Teddy ruffled his hair. 'Sure you're a grand wee kid,' he said. 'We've always been mates, right? I bet when you grow up, you're gonna join the Navy just like me and travel the world.'

'I will!' Johnny said fervently.

'Don't,' Teddy said. 'Sure it's not as grand as it's cracked up to be. I only did it 'cause I didn't want to go into the Yard, which is all you get here - assumin' they'd even have a Catholic like me. But you, Johnny, you're not like me. I mean, you've got a lot of talent. Some day you're gonna be a great artist and that's why I bought this. Take it home, kid. Use it.'

'I will,' Johnny said. He didn't want to cry with gratitude in front of Teddy, a real man, a *worldly* man, so, instead, he looked at Teddy's dad, Patrick, and said, 'What are my Mum and Dad up to out there?'

'When last seen...' Patrick began, but then losing his train of thought, he turned to his younger son, Mark. 'I'll have one of them bottles if you're still pouring.'

'Ackaye,' Mark said, still not uttering a single swear word. 'Sure we're still pourin', Dad.'

'Then pour me a bottle,' Patrick said and then turned back to Johnny. 'When last seen,' he repeated, 'your dad was givin' one of his showbiz performances - much appreciated, I might add - and your Mum was pouring herself another stout and smokin' a fag. I think the dancin' exhausted her.'

'Thanks for the present, Teddy,' Johnny said.

'Draw me a masterpiece,' Teddy replied.

When Johnny went outside again, the sun was going down and a pot-bellied amateur photographer, Barney Thompson - who had been an Air Raid Warden in Newtownwards during the war and was in no way related to the monstrous Barney Johnstone - was trying to persuade his neighbours that the photos he was taking in the dim light would still come out and could be purchased at a real bargain price. Unfortunately for Johnny, when he went back to the table occupied by his family and their friends, his dad had finished performing and was talking to *his* dad about their experiences during the war, having been reminded of it, Johnny assumed, by the presence of Barney Thompson.

'So you know what I mean,' Albert was saying as Johnny knelt on the ground beside his mother, wildly, darkly beautiful, exhaling cigarette smoke from her nostrils. 'It wasn't easy back then.'

'God, yes, sure they were desperate days, indeed,' Johnny's grandfather Brian responded, looking unnaturally flushed and bright-eyed while clutching a bottle of stout in his right fist. 'I mean, that first air raid wasn't so bad; it was restricted to the dock area – '

'Including where we lived then,' Mary grimly reminded him.

'Ackaye, but it was only *our* area. The raids that came later... God, they were terrible! Sure Belfast was almost flattened. Over a thousand dead. Nearly sixty thousand houses damaged. More than a hundred thousand left homeless. Sure wasn't it so bad that the mortuary services were overwhelmed and the public baths on Falls Road and Peter's hill had to be used to house all the corpses?'

'*And* St. George's market,' Sammy Devlin said. 'That old fruit market, remember? Instead of fruit, it was filled with coffins. Row upon row of the awful things, with a stench to knock you down comin' off them.'

'Aye,' Nelly Devlin said. 'Sure I remember it well. There I was, on the one hand delivering babies; on the other...' She shrugged her broad shoulders. 'Well, what can I say? When I wasn't being a midwife, I was checking out the dead to see if the husbands of those poor women had died, even as the women were givin' birth. And because of that, I ended up in St. George's market and...'

'Don't even say it, love,' Sammy interjected, always willing to speak up for her. 'Sure the dead, in their hundreds, were only half covered with oul rags or blankets, all still wearin' their original clothes, no time to clean them up or treat them with dignity, all just lyin' there, unattended, and every one of them rotten with maggots. Dear God, it was terrible.'

'They didn't have it that bad in Britain,' Brian said, running his fingers through his grey hair and blinking, as if trying to focus his gaze. 'Sure the Brits never appreciated just how badly we suffered over here from those German bombings. Our Blitz was even worse than theirs.'

'Amen,' Doreen murmured.

At that point wee Billy ran up to Johnny and, always trying to impress him, showed him a clenched fist with torn skin and bloody knuckles.

'Look at that,' he said proudly. 'Sure I got that from beatin' up a Fenian who was bigger than me. He ran away with a bloody nose and wet eyes. He probably came from the Falls.'

'We were lucky, though,' Albert said, not even hearing wee Billy's boast. 'Most of those bombed out of their homes during the Blitz were moved into those awful prefabs, but being among the first to lose our houses, we were moved into proper homes. So here we are, fine and dandy in this avenue, still in one piece and celebratin' the Coronation of our beloved new Queen. Sure life's filled with surprises.'

'What's the difference if he was a Catholic or not?' Johnny said to wee Billy. 'Sure Teddy and Mark, though Catholic, are our friends. Look,' he added, holding out his leather wallet, 'Teddy brought me this from somewhere in Arabia.'

Billy examined the artist's wallet, turning it this way and that for a closer inspection. 'Gee, that's brilliant, Johnny.'

'Yeah,' Johnny said with pride.

'I bet he didn't bring *me* anything,' Billy said, looking disappointed as he handed the wallet back. 'He only brings *you* things. No one ever brings me anything from anywhere - not even dad. That's why you like Teddy, though he's Fenian. He's always givin' you presents.'

'Take the wallet,' Johnny said, meaning it, holding it out to his younger brother.

'Aw, fuck off,' wee Billy said, embarrassed, pushing the wallet away from him. 'Aw, Jesus, here's Mum and Dad comin' and they've got Marlene with her. That means we have to go home.'

'Yeah, I reckon,' Johnny said.

'I'm more tired than your beloved new Queen is,' Mary was saying to Albert, 'because she's only had a crown placed on her head. But I had to sit there all afternoon, watching you make a fool of yourself with your singing and dancing. So don't complain because I'm calling it a day.'

Johnny's Granny and Granddad were there, also, the former looking as stern as always, the latter flushed with drink.

'Charming!' Doreen exclaimed. 'A man entertains his neighbours and has them applauding - and that's the only thanks he gets from his wife. Well, God forgive me for offering criticism, but a mother's heart *can* be broken.'

'Jesus!' Mary exclaimed in disgust, exhaling another cloud of smoke. 'I'll never utter another word.'

'I'm tired,' Marlene said, 'and I've got a bad stummach. I've had a bad stummach all day but no one believes it. Sure I feel so bad, I could kill myself.'

'Just take the bread knife from the kitchen,' wee Billy said pragmatically, 'and stick it into your bad stummach and twist it, like they do in the fillums. You'll die before you feel any pain and we'll all laugh ourselves sick.'

'Mum, don't let him say that!' Marlene exclaimed. 'He's just tryin' to ...'

But Mary had already clipped Billy on the ear and was practically throwing him into the house. 'Get in there, you wee larrakin, and go straight up to bed and shut your ugly gob. One more word and I'll brain you stone dead.'

Billy went up the stairs like a rat up a drainpipe as his Mum and Dad said goodbye to *their* parents. Doreen and Brian only lived a few streets away, so they didn't have far to go.

'See you when we see you,' Mary said.

'God willing,' Doreen said.

She and Brian turned away and walked off as Johnny entered the house and followed Billy up the stairs to the bedroom. Marlene took more time to get there because her mother, fed up with her complaining about her stomach, made her take a good dose of Cod Liver Oil.

Cod Liver Oil was magic. Once you had it, you never wanted it again and so your stomach was cured. Marlene came up to the bedroom, looking sick, though in fact she was cured. Refusing to talk to either of the boys, she soon fell asleep. Billy, never troubled by his conscience, also fell asleep quickly.

Alone in all the world, raised on high by his gift from Teddy, Johnny went to the window and looked down upon the avenue. Though darkness was falling, there were still lots of people down there, many clearly drunk. The lamplighter, wearing his Belfast Corporation uniform with peaked cap, was coming along the pavement, carrying his lightweight ladder and tubular rod, which had a hook at one end. As the lamplighter approached the lamp at the far side of the street, almost directly opposite, two girls, one named Donna King, she of the lime-green dress and matching eyes, were swinging around the lamps, having tied one end of their skipping rope to the crossbar that supported the lamplighter's ladder. When the lamplighter, Ernie Kerr, chased them away, Johnny, an innocent voyeur, in love though not knowing it, swallowed deeply as he watched them depart, gradually vaporising in the lamplit darkness.

That lime-green dress fluttered like a distant banner before disappearing.

As Johnny looked on, Ernie reached up to the lamp-housing with his long rod, opened one of the hinged sides, then hooked the valve of the gas lamp and turned on the gas. Ignited from the tiny pilot light that burned continuously, the burning gas blossomed like a phosphorescent flower to cast its pale-yellow, flickering illumination on the pavement below.

There were eight lamps in all, four on each side of the road, and now they all shed their benevolent light on the dwindling crowd of revellers. The avenue was littered with discarded paper bags and flags, all of which would, tomorrow morning, be conscientiously picked up by the neighbours and put in with the other rubbish to be taken away. People in the avenue were inordinately proud of their reputation for cleanliness.

Only two of the streetlights did not need attention by the lamplighter on a nightly basis, because they were turned on and off by a clockwork mechanism inside the glass interior of the lamp. Those two lamps would stay alight until dawn, when they would be extinguished automatically. The lamplighter would come around each night after midnight to manually extinguish the other six lamps in the street. It was only at weekends that he would have to attend to the automatic lamps, to rewind the clockwork mechanism.

One of those two gas lamps shone outside Johnny's bedroom, barely more than three feet away. And so, this night, as he did most nights, he lay in his bed and watched the large grey moths flying around it, attracted to its fluctuating, seductive light. He could even hear the lamp's clockwork timer which, beating as steady as a metronome, had a soothing, even mesmeric effect that helped him forget the lime-green dress and matching gaze of an alien creature.

A mere girl. A sissy.

Johnny lay there, a mere child, holding his gift to his chest, filled with love for his friend, Teddy, even as he was swept away on a tidal wave of confusion caused by green eyes, a lime-green dress and awkward, feminine limbs, unaware of his dark and bloody destiny, misinformed by God.

Johnny lay there in innocence.

Chapter Four

1

Barry felt his age. He didn't know where the years had gone. Though only thirty-two, he felt middle-aged because he had done so much in such a short time and that had made the time stretch. Even now, sitting in the living room of his small house in the Pound Loney, just around the corner from his parents' home, having a bottle of stout and a cigarette, fully aware that he was drinking too much but unable to stop himself, he looked back on his life as he imagined an old man would: not fully trusting his memory, feeling that his own history was a dream, far removed from reality. Too much killing, too much death, too much fear. And what had it all been for? What had been gained by it? The answers to those questions were written on the wind and the wind, in its blowing, was unpredictable. Barry shivered to think of it.

He could hear the Lambeg drums of the Prods pounding away in the distance.

Did he want to go on? Yes, of course he did. Naturally. Because despite the disappointments of his life, the cause still had meaning. The cause, right now, was in a precarious state, with not much happening anywhere, but that would change, for good or for ill, after tomorrow night. Either the cause would be put back on its feet or it would die a death. Tomorrow night meant a great deal.

'No!'

'Yes!'

'No!'

'*Yes*!'

Hearing Sean and Theresa arguing in their bedroom upstairs, he raised his eyes to the ceiling and bawled, 'Quieten down, you two!' The argument ceased, there was silence for a moment, but then he heard muffled, hysterical giggling from both of them. Grinning, feeling better, being fond of his kids, Barry inhaled on his cigarette, exhaled a stream of smoke, then had another sip of his stout and glanced distractedly around the small living room, made reasonably cosy with dove-tail cabinets engraved with inlaid wood and filled with china dogs and other bric-a-brac. The hysterical giggling continued upstairs and Barry smiled again.

He only had two kids. Most of his neighbours had more. The Prods thought that the high birth rate amongst Catholics was a deliberate plot designed to make the Catholic minority in the six counties the majority, but it was only because the Catholics, by Papal decree, were forbidden to use contraception. Barry and Eleanor, both still dedicated to the fight for Catholic rights in the north and Ireland's freedom in general, had solved the problem by employing *coitus interruptus* during sex. While this had solved the problem of having too many kids, which they certainly could not afford, it had spoilt the sex for both of them, causing a great deal of mutual frustration. The itch was still there and it had to be scratched, but Barry often found himself thinking that he would rather do without sex entirely than have to withdraw at the crucial moment. Of course, it took more than that to dim the lustre of a marriage, and his own, though certainly solid on the surface, was no longer exciting. Familiarity had gradually worn the romance away and left only that itch to be scratched. The excitement was gone.

He was thinking about this because Eleanor was due back any moment from work and, indeed, when a key turned in the lock of the front door, he knew that it was her. Presently unemployed, as he had been so often throughout most of his adult life, he always felt a fleeting shame when Eleanor came back home after another twelve-hour day as a stitcher in the Crumlin Road Linen Mills and Weaving Factory. She had been there for the past three years and that was a dangerously long time as the working conditions were atrocious, with over five-hundred women slaving at sewing-machines in the same vast, long chamber, in dreadful, relentless noise and draining heat, in an atmosphere dangerously thickened with the flax dust that drifted in from the spinning and weaving areas. Barry felt guilty because he was unemployed more often than he was employed and Eleanor was working a twelve-hour day in that awful place to make up for his lack.

The worst thing about being unemployed, apart from the boredom, was the guilt a man felt. That cut deepest of all.

Eleanor closed the front door behind her, stopped in the hallway to cough a couple of times, and then entered the living room. She was a vastly different woman from the attractively plump, sexually provocative girl that he had first made love to in 1941, twelve years ago. Now, apart from being constantly dark-eyed from exhaustion, she had put on a lot of weight and was far too heavy for her short stature. This, Barry knew, was due to a mixture of stress and the wrong kind of food: too many sandwiches, chips and fry-ups. She was, however, rendered even less attractive by the brown shawl wrapped over her head like a hood, her thick, heavy overcoat, and the broad, heavy boots that she had to wear at the mill. She had also lost her sense of humour, the wickedness that had enlivened her otherwise average features and lent them the teasing sensuality that had so strongly aroused him when they first met. The constant struggle (the IRA struggle combined with her daily battle to survive economically, which the IRA could not help her with) had taken its toll. She was therefore also embittered and it showed in her face, the soft features of which had hardened to make her seem older than she was. Now she removed the shawl from her head, revealing short-cut black hair turning grey. Taking off her overcoat, she hung it and the shawl on the hook behind the front door, then sank into the armchair facing Barry, to gratefully light up a cigarette.

'If the flax dust in the mills doesn't do in your lungs,' Barry said, 'those cigarettes will.'

Eleanor raised her eyebrows, stared steadily at him, then inhaled on her cigarette and exhaled a thin stream of smoke.

'How can you be saying that to me when you're sitting there smoking yourself?'

'Aye, I smoke alright,' Barry confessed, 'but not nearly as much as you. You smoke like a train these days.'

'It's for my nerves,' Eleanor said.

'I used to think you didn't have any nerves; I used to admire you for that. Way back then, when you were a courier up from Dublin. You didn't seem to have a nerve in your body and that really excited me.'

'I was younger then, Barry. I believed in what I was doing. I thought I was respected for what I was doing; I didn't imagine that eventually I'd be pushed out for not still being young enough, or attractive enough, to act as a courier.'

'I doubt that they dropped you for that,' Barry said, referring to her work as an IRA courier during World War II and for quite a few years after it, up until about five years ago when they gradually stopped asking her to help them. 'It was just one of those things. Like when the people who were using you were replaced and the new men had their own people. Sure it happens all the time, everywhere.'

'Not to the men, it doesn't,' Eleanor responded. 'They look after their own kind. But the women...' She shrugged. 'Sure they use them when they need them, then discard them... Just like in most marriages, I suppose. It's always been that way, hasn't it?'

'Don't judge me by them,' Barry said.

'Why not?' Eleanor responded brutally, as disillusioned with the marriage as he was. 'Aren't you one of them? Don't you toe the party line?'

'Not to that degree,' Barry said. 'And I'm only a member of the organisation - which is why we met, remember? I don't run it and I don't make the rules.'

'No, I suppose not.'

What she was saying was true: the organisation in those days *had* favoured younger women as couriers because, it was believed, they could charm their way out of awkward situations or seduce men who could be useful to them and might not otherwise be sympathetic. In truth, Eleanor had aged more than her years and was no longer of use to them, but Barry could hardly tell her that. She knew the truth, however - *she knew* - and the truth had embittered her.

'How are things at the mill?' he asked her, still hearing the Lambeg drums pounding in the distance, reminding him of the conflict, and deciding that it would be wise to change the subject.

'Not good. That bloody Korean War again. Ever since that war ended the prices here have been collapsing and now they're saying that the Irish linen trade's in terminal decline. That's why some factories have already closed down and more are going to close in the near future. There's even talk that the linen trade in this country's eventually going to disappear altogether. That'll mean an awful lot of people out of work and I'll probably be one of them. One and one makes two, Barry.'

'What's that mean?'

'If I lose this job, we'll both be out of work.'

'I'll find something,' Barry said, though he didn't hold out much hope. 'Don't worry. It's just a matter of time.'

He tried to sound more confident than he actually was. In truth, he had been unemployed so often, it had come to seem like a natural condition. His problems stemmed largely from the fact that he, like his father, Eddie, was widely known as a Republican activist who had served time in the Crumlin Road jail for his IRA activities. While Eddie had done the same, he was now fifty-two years old and no longer active, so he wasn't viewed with the suspicion accorded to Barry. Also, Eddie had remained with the same haulier company, a local Catholic company, for years, though now, with his damaged shoulder often seizing up, he was working in the stores rather than making deliveries. This was his reward from a boss who was an IRA sympathiser and viewed his venerable employee as a war hero. Barry, on the other hand, was only thirty-two, and that relatively young age, combined with his so-called 'criminal' record as a convicted IRA member, had made him suspect in the eyes of even Catholic employers, who didn't wish to hire anyone with a police record, particularly if related to the IRA. So even when Barry *was* offered a job, invariably it was something menial, dreamed up as a favour by a friend or forced upon him by the Labour Exchange, and usually not lasting long. He knew that he was paying for his life-long dedication to the cause, for his sins, but when he saw Eleanor's black-ringed eyes, sallow skin and heavy body, that knowledge didn't make him feel less guilty.

'Aye,' Eleanor replied. 'You'll find something in Australia or America, maybe, but you won't find much here. If you want work, you're going have to emigrate like half of the Irish nation has done since time immemorial. The Irish don't emigrate because they want to; it's because they have to. And you might have to do the same if things don't pick up here.'

Barry knew his Irish history. It was a history of relentless, enforced migration that had begun as far back as the reign of Henry II when Anglo-Norman nobles first came to Ireland to take over the estates of the country, sometimes with intermarriage, but just as often at the point of a sword. Either way, families that had owned their land for centuries had been expelled, reduced to poverty, becoming the chattels of their new masters. Greedy and merciless, those early colonists had deprived Irish priests of the right to enter their own churches and monasteries, forbade marriages between Irish and English (just as, centuries later, they would forbid marriage between Catholic and Protestant), denied Irish people the benefits of English law while forbidding them to use their own centuries-old laws, and, most crucially, used their tenants as cheap labour, paying them only enough money for basic subsistence and dispossessing them for the slightest infraction, sometimes simply because they wished to expand their personal property, or merely on a thoughtless, cruel whim. Later, in the reign of Henry VIII, the confiscation of Church property, which had been used nobly by Irish priests for the benefit of the poor and homeless, only made matters worse by casting thousands more families upon the mercy of the new landowners whose will was the only recognised law. Subsequently, poverty and homelessness had increased and countless thousands of Irish had been forced to emigrate in order to survive. That same iniquitous system continued throughout the Plantation of Ulster, commencing in 1608, when more estates were confiscated and new colonists, English and Scots Protestants, cleared the estates completely of native Irish inhabitants and planted on every thousand acres twenty-four Protestant British, thus turning Catholic Ulster into a Protestant state. Thousands of those ejected from their own property, or forced to pay rent that they could not afford for what had formerly been their own homes, again took the only possible route to survival: emigration, invariably to America. From those grim days to the present, emigration, no matter how painful, had often been the only recourse left to Irish people deprived of their property, their livelihood and their basic rights, though, in truth, it was more like a Diaspora that left generations of dispossessed Irish people living overseas and pining for their homeland. Now, in 1954, the Catholic Irish, young and old, were still emigrating, mostly to America or Australia, where they would not be under the rule of the British or, even worse, under the yoke of the Orangemen. Barry wasn't quite ready to join that exodus, but his day might yet come.

'Have you been thinking of that?' he asked of Eleanor as she inhaled and exhaled cigarette smoke, then coughed and inhaled again. 'I mean, emigrating to somewhere like Australia, the whole bloody kit and caboodle of us.'

Eleanor smiled wearily. 'Yes, I've thought about it,' she said. 'I mean, they're begging people right now to go to Australia. Sure you can get there for ten quid.'

'What's the catch?' Barry asked.

'You just surrender your passport for two years. If you want to leave before then, you have to pay the Aussie government back the cost of the fare; if you stay for two years, your passport is returned automatically and you can then leave or stay, as you wish. Pretty tempting, isn't it?'

'I don't think you could live in Australia, any more than I could. What about your Ma and Da? The cause? Everything we've fought for? You'd give all that up, would you?'

Eleanor's Ma and Da, both fervent Republicans, from whom she had picked up her own fierce beliefs, were still living in Dublin. Eleanor did, however, see them at least three or four times a year, which she would not be able to do if she went to Australia. As for the cause, though she was feeling bitter towards her old IRA comrades for the way that they had, in her view, neglected her, she was still totally committed to the overthrowing of the Orange State and, eventually, the formation of a united Ireland. She would not give that up easily. She had paid too much for it.

'No,' she confessed, 'I suppose not.' She inhaled on her cigarette, exhaled while coughing raggedly, and eventually regained normal breathing. Barry had started to worry about that cough because tuberculosis was rife in the community, due to the appalling working conditions in the factories and, also, to the primitive living conditions in the Falls. This house, for instance, though prettified by Eleanor, was still damp and cold, with running water but no hot water, no bath, and only an outside toilet. It was certainly not a healthy way to live, and Eleanor, her lungs already congested with flax dust, wasn't helping herself by smoking so much. 'Maybe I just want to get out of this damned house, this damned area, into somewhere better.'

'You want a new house?' Barry said. 'You'll be lucky! There isn't a single Catholic on the local council - all those bastards are Unionist - and most of the council housing, the decent housing, is allocated to the Prods.'

'And we can't do a thing about it. Is that what you're trying to tell me?'

'No more than we can do anything to stop those bloody Lambeg drums and all the rest of that Loyalist nonsense.' Barry was angry now, only too aware of what was going on and feeling helpless because of it. 'You know damned well that ever since the abolition of proportional representation, Protestant gerrymandering's ensured that we Catholics get nothing. You won't be getting a new house - at least not for a long time - so don't bother me with your wishful thinking. Jesus, to think of what we both sacrificed when we were young, only to come down to this. I could kill – '

'You *have* killed.'

'And could again, just thinking about it. God, I feel so... *frustrated*!'

'Don't blow a gasket there, Barry.'

When she smiled, he relaxed, though he *was* surprised. It was so rare to see her smile these days. Studying her weary face, as he had not done in a long time, he suddenly found himself travelling back along that thirteen years to when they had first met, introduced by a mutual IRA friend in a pub near Queens University. They had both been so young then, less then twenty. Now Barry remembered vividly just how Eleanor had looked at that time: not yet fat, though healthily, sensually plump, full lips in a moon-shaped face, brown eyes, short-cropped black hair, with a slightly mocking, mischievous, alluring smile that made her seem worldly-wise and, to him, seductive. They had been excited with each other, drawn together by the cause, glued together by sex, in love with the romance of being in love and fighting for their country at the same time, both risking their freedom at best and their lives at worst. Eleanor had delivered weapons and organised 'safe' houses; Barry had used the weapons that she gave him to create bloody mayhem and spread fear in the Protestant community. Both of them had thrived on the excitement, the risk, exalted by the thought that they were not merely existing, drifting from dawn to darkness in a dream without substance, but helping to regain their country's freedom and perhaps change the course of Irish history. Possibly naïve, they had certainly been idealistic and wilfully ignorant when they needed to be (the maimed and the dead, those who paid the price, stricken from the record), and their romance, at once personal and political, had certainly made life seem more glamorous than that lived by the common herd. Then he and Eleanor married and the real world rushed in: two children to look after, careful sex instead of great sex, material concerns intruding upon Republican convictions, the IRA itself rendered increasingly irrelevant and then virtually digging its own grave with a series of failed campaigns and divisions within its own ranks. Deeply disillusioned, more so because she was no longer being used as a courier, Eleanor had eventually turned her back on the conflict to become a working housewife. But she never really forgot it.

Barry had kept going, of course, still believing in the cause, but also needing the organisation to help him fill up his unemployed days and give him a sense of purpose when Eleanor, nearly always the breadwinner, went out to work and, in so doing, helped the family survive, even as she was, unintentionally, making him feel less than a whole man. His IRA work helped him to keep his equilibrium, letting him cling to his self-esteem with a shooting here, a bombing there, but as the organisation was gradually whittled away, both in the north and in the south, even the few jobs that he was getting were beginning to seem like a waste of time, a mere treading of water. The south was now formally the Republic of Ireland and here, in the north, the Unionists were more firmly in control than ever. In order to survive, the northern IRA needed a propaganda victory - so tomorrow night's operation, in which Barry was taking part, would either give them that or put an end to their activities for a long time, maybe even for good. It was a job so important that Barry, even thinking about it, felt his throat going dry. For the first time in all his years at this game, he was truly frightened.

'You know I'm going out tomorrow night?' he said.

'Yes,' Eleanor replied, 'I know. Let's not talk about it. Just do it and get it over with. Have the kids had their tea yet?'

'No,' Barry said, 'but it's ready.'

'What is it?'

'Fish pie.'

'This being a Friday.'

'Aye, that's right.'

Eleanor smiled again. 'A decent enough Catholic meal,' she said, 'to be done by someone who can't really cook.'

Barry smiled in return. 'It's my wee speciality,' he told her, 'and the kids always like it.'

'Then call them down while I lay the table.'

'Right,' Barry said. He went into the small hallway and called up the stairs as Eleanor went into the kitchen. 'Hey, you two! Stop all that gigglin' and come down for your tea!'

The giggling stopped temporarily.

'Right, Da!' Sean shouted.

'Coming!' Theresa trilled after him.

The two children, twelve and eleven years old respectively, came rushing out of their bedroom, collided on the landing, giggling again, disentangled themselves, then came down the stairs one after the other, Sean first, Theresa second. Breathless, they rushed into the living room.

'Jesus, I'm starving!' Sean said.

2

'Don't blaspheme,' Eleanor said automatically, without anger, as she carried four plates and eating utensils into the living room and started laying the table placed against the wall, under the front window, letting them watch the activities in the street while they ate and drank. 'Sit down, you two.'

Barry sat at the table with the children, glanced out at the street where darkness had fallen, and saw the rain-dampened pavements glistening in the light of the gas lamps. In the new Protestant estates, electric lights had been installed, but so far that hadn't been done here. The Falls was always low on the list of priorities with the Unionist councillors.

'So,' Barry said, turning back to face his children while Mary returned to the kitchen to fetch the fish pie, 'what have you two been up to?'

'Doin' our homework,' Theresa said, staring boldly at him out of eyes the same brown as her mother's. The skin of her face was as smooth and white as marble; her features, though delicate, were shaped by a decided pugnacity. She was one tough wee girl.

'Aye, that's right,' Sean added. 'We were doin' our homework.'

'I bet,' Barry said. 'So what was all that giggling I heard? Your homework was filled with jokes, was it?'

'Sure we were just havin' a wee bit of fun,' Theresa said, 'because we'd both finished. What's wrong with that, then?'

Though pretty and well looked after, Theresa had the look of a street urchin, aggressive and wily. She was a bit of a tomboy, really, and hard to control. Sean, on the other hand, while generally good humoured, was essentially serious, curious and keen to learn. Some of this was, undoubtedly, due to Barry's personal tuition, his insistence that both his children should learn the history of Ireland, which wasn't taught in the state schools and which Barry had, therefore, taken it upon himself to teach them, but most of it came from Sean himself, since he was naturally studious. Dark-haired and brown-eyed like all the family, already handsome for his age, of medium height and build, he looked after his sister when she got out of control and charmed most of the adults with whom he came into contact, including his schoolteachers, one of whom was the local poet, Brendan Coghill. According to Brendan, Sean was one of his best pupils and destined to go far. Right now, however, he was rubbing his nose with the palm of his hand, saying, 'M'nose is itchy. That means I'll get money.'

'From where?' Theresa asked.

Sean shrugged. 'I don't know. But an itchy nose means money. Maybe I'm gonna find it in the street.'

'No such luck,' Theresa said.

'So *did* you finish your homework?' Barry asked.

'Yes!' they both affirmed in chorus.

'Then you've earned your supper,' Eleanor said, coming in from the kitchen, holding the dish containing the fish pie in one hand, a serving spoon in the other. Both kids picked up their forks even before she started serving and tucked into the food without ceremony when it was served. Eleanor took the empty dish back to the kitchen, and then returned to join them at the table. She had only served herself a small portion, but even that she merely picked at while the others hungrily gobbled theirs.

'You still keeping up with your reading?' Barry asked of Sean, since he didn't push Theresa to do much at all, her destiny being to get married and have kids while Sean's destiny, Barry hoped, was to attend university.

'Aye, Da, but it's been hard to concentrate 'cause those Prods have been practisin' all week with their Lambeg drums.'

'Deafenin', they are,' Theresa said. 'Sure you can hear them from miles away.'

'Aye, that's true, right enough,' Barry said. 'They want us all to know that the Twelfth of July celebrations are next week. They want to rub our Fenian noses in it.'

'I'm gonna rub my nose in money,' Sean said. 'That's why it's itchy.'

'They're practising in the Shankill,' Eleanor said, 'and also in Sandy Row. The noise of the drummin' in both those places carries all the way up to here.'

'They're practising all over the city,' Barry corrected her. 'There's hardly a street you can walk down without seein' them there, paradin' with their bloody orange sashes and King William of Orange banners, rehearsin' for their grand parade on the Twelfth. Sure you'd think they own the whole damned city. It's a quare disgrace, if you ask me.'

'They *do* own the city,' Eleanor said bitterly. 'Sure they've put up their decorated arches and hung Union Jacks from their windows and they're already startin' to build their bonfires. I feel like a foreigner in my own town, having to be doubly careful where I walk. You two remember that,' she added, sternly addressing both children. 'At this time of the year you've got to be doubly careful where you walk. Don't go near any Protestant areas. They're all excited at this time of the year and on the lookout for Fenians to interfere with, so keep well away from them.'

'Sure we never go near Prod areas,' Theresa said. 'We're too scared to do that.'

'I'm not,' Sean said.

'Yes, you are,' Theresa insisted. 'You're a real wee yella guts when it comes to the Prods. You and all of yer cowardy-custard pals.'

'No, we're not!' Sean responded, turning red in the face. 'Sure last year me and Tommy Molloy actually saw the Twelfth of July parade. We watched all them Orangemen gathering at Carlisle Circus and then marching off. We watched them until they'd all gone and no Prod laid a hand on us.'

'You watched them?' Eleanor asked, shocked.

'*Last year?*' Barry asked, also shocked.

Realising that it was too late to deny it, though he hadn't meant to tell them in the first place, Sean blushed an even deeper red while nodding affirmatively.

'You went all the way to the centre of town,' Eleanor said, 'to Carlisle Circus, when you were only... *eleven*?'

Sean nodded again, then glanced at Theresa with anger for what she had made him say.

'With that wicked wee dozer, Tommy Molloy?'

'Aye, Ma'

'And you watched the gathering of the Orangemen?' his father said. 'You stayed there till they left?'

'Aye, Da, of course. I mean, that's what we went there to see.'

'Without ever telling us?' Eleanor said. Then she glared at Barry. 'I can't believe my own ears! Sure they could have got themselves a damned good hidin' from some Protestant hooligans. They could have been killed!'

'There were lots of Protestant kids there,' Sean said, 'but they didn't even look at us. They were too busy watchin' the Orangemen and the bands to think about us. There were flute bands and pipe bands. It was really brilliant to see. We're always bein' told that the Prods can recognise a Catholic by his eyes, just by looking at him, but none of them Prod kids, if they *did* look at us, recognised us as Catholics. Sure we had a grand day there.'

Recovering from his shock, Barry couldn't help grinning. 'I never knew he had it in him,' he said to Eleanor. 'This lad sure has some guts.'

Eleanor's eyes grew wide in outrage. 'Guts?' she said. 'Am I hearin' right? Are you actually tryin' to *encourage* him?' Turning back to Sean, who had seen his da's grin and was now grinning himself, she wiggled her index finger and said, 'Don't you ever do such a thing again without asking me first. As for that binlid, Tommy Molloy, who's more trouble than he's worth, you tell him that the next time he comes to this door I'm going to...'

But she trailed off and looked towards the front door when she heard the bell ringing.

'Who's that?' she asked.

'It must be Grandda and Grandma,' Theresa said as Barry stood up to answer the door. 'They always come here for a cuppa on Friday evening.'

'Oh,' Eleanor said, relaxing, recalling that this was indeed Friday, the evening when Eddie and Lizzie generally dropped in to see them. They still lived in their old house around the corner, but were clever enough not to overdo the visits. Perhaps for that very reason, Eleanor and they had always had a good relationship. As in-laws, they weren't the interfering kind and Eleanor liked them for that. She also liked them because they stood in for her own parents, who still lived in Dublin. 'If it's that wee troublemaker, Tommy Molloy,' she called out to Barry as he opened the front door, 'give him a good boxing on the ears for me.'

'It's m'Ma and Da,' Barry said, stepping aside to let Eddie and Lizzie enter. Now in their early fifties, they were both grey-haired, though Eddie looked a lot younger than Lizzie, who had spent most of her life working twelve hours a day in the hellish conditions of the textile mills. Though only fifty-two, Lizzie looked about ten years older, with dark-ringed eyes and badly wrinkled, greyish skin. Eddie, on the other hand, having had an easier life, despite the prison terms of his early years, was flushed with good health and energy. His only problem was the stiffness of the shoulder that had been wounded long ago, though that was only noticeable when he tried raising the arm above his head. Apart from that, he seemed as fit as a fiddle.

Lizzie never looked healthy. She was, however, always in good humour when she came to see her grandchildren, both of whom adored her. Leaning over them where they still sat at the table, she kissed them on the top of the head and then gave them each a quarter of Liquorice Allsorts, wrapped in newspaper cones.

'This is for after your dinner,' she told them. 'From me and Grandda.'

'Gee, thanks!' Sean exclaimed, taking his paper cone from Grandma.

'Hey, that's great,' Theresa said, being less polite, as she snatched her cone and placed it on the table beside her plate of unfinished fish pie.

'But you have to eat your dinner up before you eat those,' Eddie informed them, grinning broadly as he sank into one of the wooden-

142

framed chairs beside the fireplace where no fire was burning, this being July. 'If one scrap is left on your plate, you can't have the sweets.'

'I'm practically finished,' Sean said.

'Me, too,' Theresa said, rapidly scooping up some pieces of fish and shoving them into her mouth in a race to beat her brother.

'Hey, miss,' Eleanor said. 'Sure you're going to burst those bulging cheeks of yours if you try to shove any more food between them. You eat your food a lot slower and *digest* it or I'll take those sweets off you.'

'Look who's talkin',' Theresa retorted when she had hastily gulped another mouthful, thus reducing the size of her bulging cheeks. 'You finished hours ago, ma.'

'Minutes ago,' Sean corrected her.

'That's because I had less to eat than you,' Eleanor said, lighting up a cigarette. 'It's not because I *ate* quicker.'

Theresa defiantly shoved the last of the fish into her mouth, swallowed it without chewing, then put her fork back on the table and said to Sean, 'Beat you to it!' Then she opened her newspaper cone.

'You wait until your brother's finished,' Lizzie said, pulling a chair up to sit near the table. 'That's simple good manners.'

'Aw, Granny!' Theresa exclaimed, then glared at Sean and added, 'Shut your gob and just swallow it, you eejit, or I'll be waitin' all day for these Allsorts.'

After dutifully swallowing the last of his fish, Sean opened his bag of sweets, though not before Theresa had started chewing at least one of her own.

'Sure wouldn't you think they'd never had anything in their lives,' Eleanor said, 'the way they're goin' at those sweeties like wolves? Have you heard, by the way,' she continued, turning her chair around in order to blow her cigarette smoke into the room while facing her in-laws, 'what our innocent wee Sean has been up to? And, even worse, last year... *when he was only eleven*!'

'Sure what's that if you're writin' home?' Lizzie asked.

'Last Twelfth of July, without saying a word to us, the wee tyke, with that troublemaker Tommy Molloy, he went all the way to Carlisle Circus to watch the Orange parades.'

'He did not!' Lizzie exclaimed, casting a shocked glance at Sean.

'Ack, Ma,' Sean said, 'don't start all that up again.'

'He did,' Theresa confirmed, though her cheeks were bulging from half-chewed Liquorice Allsorts.

'Well, I never!' Lizzie exclaimed. 'Have you no sense, Sean? Sure you could've gotten yourselves a damned good hidin' from some Protestant hooligans. You could've been kilt!'

'Now who'd bother a couple of wee boys on the Twelfth of July?' Eddie asked more sensibly. 'All them Prods, they'd've been too busy enjoying themselves to take notice of a couple of childern that age. Sure they'd think they were just another couple of Prod kids, out for the day. So *did* you have a good day, Sean?'

'Aye, Grandda, it was brilliant. Me and Tommy had a grand time.'

'That's the ticket,' Eddie said. 'Well, you can certainly go back there next week, 'cause it's all gonna happen again.'

'Have you no sense of responsibility, Eddie Coogan, tellin' *that* to the child?' Lizzie was appalled. 'Sure the Protestants are out all over the place, dead set on more mischief.'

'Aye, they are that, right enough,' Eddie said. 'Doin' up all their streets as usual.'

'All them decorated Orange arches straddlin' the roads,' Lizzie reminded him. 'And Union Jacks flapping in our faces. Sure isn't it awful?'

'Lots of arches, right enough,' Eddie said. 'Sandy Row alone has six of them, going the whole length of it, and the kerbs are painted red, white and blue. King bloody William murals painted on the gable ends and, as Lizzie said, Union Jacks flying from every upstairs window. If they could fit Buckingham Palace into the middle of the road, I've no doubt they'd do it.'

'That's why those filthy B-Specials are out there in the streets again,' Eleanor said. 'Not prowling around their own areas where all the trouble-makers are, but here in the Falls where we're minding our own business and not flaunting *our* history in the faces of the Prods.'

'They're out there now?' Barry asked.

'Aye,' Eddie replied before Lizzie could say more. 'At least they were when we came here - and we only live around the corner, after all. Up to their usual shite - excuse me, children. They know damned well who I am, they know me by sight, yet they stopped me and demanded my name and address and identification. It was just the usual

144

harassment, the Protestant bastards, but it's always worse in the run-up to the Twelfth.'

'That's right,' Eleanor said, coughing out a few puffs of smoke. 'Not only do we have to let the Orangemen parade anywhere they like, even right past our doorsteps, but we also have to take twice the harassment from their wonderful police force, especially those pig-ignorant B-Special bastards.'

'Mind your language in front of the childern,' Lizzie said, addressing the three adults and staring sternly at each of them in turn. 'Sure we don't want to corrupt them with that kind of talk.'

Theresa giggled and Sean grinned at her.

'Did Grandma say something funny?' Eleanor demanded, staring grimly at both children.

'No, Ma,' Sean said, but Theresa just turned her head away to giggle again.

'If that gigglin' means you use that kind of language behind our backs...' Eleanor began, but was distracted when the doorbell rang again. 'So who might that be?' she asked.

Barry opened the door to find Brendan Coghill standing there, his silvery-grey hair thick and dishevelled, his cheeks flushed with drink, a bright smile on his fulsome, wet lips, his dentures, which had recently replaced his bad teeth, gleaming white and proud. With the door open, the beating of the Lambeg drums in the Shankill was much louder. Brendan, now fifty-two, was Eddie's friend, Barry's friend and, this year, Sean's schoolteacher. All in all, an old family friend, always warmly welcomed.

'My boy, how are you?' he said. 'So good to see you again. I was in the next street, intending to call in on your father, and found the front door closed and locked. So can I take it he's here?'

'Yes, he's here with m'Ma,' Barry said, stepping aside to let him in. 'We were just going to have a cuppa tea, so if you want...'

'Come, come,' Brendan interjected, withdrawing a bottle of Bushmills whisky from under his coat and waving it in front of Barry's nose as he passed him to get into the living room. 'If the Prods are already beating their drums in the Shankill, then surely we can have our own party, which requires more than tea. Eddie! Lizzie!' he bellowed by way of greeting as Barry closed the door behind him. 'How are you both doing? My best wishes to you - and to *you*, Eleanor, as beautiful as always,' he lied blatantly, bowing slightly to her, 'and, of course, to my best pupil, young Sean there, and, last but by no means least, his exquisite young sister, Theresa, who steals my heart, as always, with her lovely smile.'

Theresa stuck her tongue out at him, then shoved her finger down her throat and pretended to vomit.

'Charming!' Brendan exclaimed histrionically, unperturbed, then returned his beaming smile to Eddie, while holding the bottle of whisky on high. 'Far be it that I should deprive you of a cup of tea,' he said, 'but I assumed that with all that Prod drumming going on, you wouldn't mind a little anaesthetic.'

'No, I wouldn't,' Eddie said.

Closing the front door, which muffled the sound of the distant drums, Barry stepped back into the living room and pushed a wooden-framed chair up behind Brendan. 'Rest your backside on that,' he said, 'while I get us some glasses.' He glanced at the others. 'Anyone else for a whisky?'

'You really shouldn't have,' Eleanor protested to Brendan.

'I was desperate for a couple of swigs myself,' Brendan said, acting the role of drunken poet, 'so bringing a bottle was my way of being excused. Naturally, if all join me for a sip, I can drink without guilt.'

Brendan was being disingenuous. He knew that they weren't well off and could afford to drink but rarely, so this was his way of giving them a treat without embarrassing them, Barry in particular. Barry was touched by the gesture - more so because this wasn't the first time that Brendan had done this. 'So,' he said. 'Anyone else for a whisky?'

'Yeah, I'll have one,' Theresa said. 'In a big glass.'

'Shut your cheeky gob,' Eleanor retorted, then she turned to Brendan. 'Ack, why not, indeed? Sure those drums are driving me mad. A drink might calm me down.'

'I don't need an excuse,' Lizzie said. 'If Eddie can have a whisky, so can I. You can fetch me a glass, son.'

'Excellent!' Brendan said. He proceeded to screw the top off the bottle as Barry went into the kitchen and returned with five glasses, three in one hand, two in the other. He distributed the glasses. Brendan poured and then sat back in his chair and raised his glass in the air. 'To the Twelfth!' he said mischievously.

'To hell with that!' Eddie retorted, raising his own glass. 'I hope the rain pisses down on their parade and puts out their bonfires. I say to... the Pope!'

'To the Pope!' the others cried out in chorus, then touched glasses and drank.

Wanting to join the adults, Sean and Theresa slipped off their chairs and sat on the floor, the former between Brendan and his father, the latter between her Granny and Grandda. They were both systematically removing Liquorice Allsorts from their newspaper cones and shoving them into their mouths.

Having had a good slug of his whisky, Brendan put his head back, closed his eyes, and smacked his lips. 'Ah!' he said, almost sighing with pleasure. 'Wonderful!' He opened his eyes again and smiled at them, clearly pleased with his new dentures. '*Let schoolmasters puzzle their brain,/With grammar, and nonsense, and learning,/Good liquor, I stoutly maintain,/Gives genius a better discerning.*'

'You think you're a genius, do you?' Theresa asked him, as slyly mocking as any adult.

Brendan smiled fondly at her. 'Be careful, young lady. Next year you'll be in my class, as your brother is now. Next year you will be at my mercy.'

'Sure Sean isn't doin' badly at all,' Barry said. 'If you can do the same with Theresa, me and Eleanor will be more than content. You're a good teacher, Brendan.'

'Teachers shouldn't drink in front of their pupils,' Theresa said, sounding like she was forty-five years old. 'It sets the childern a bad example, like.'

'*Man, being reasonable, must get drunk/The best of life is but intoxication...* Lord Byron, my dear.'

Theresa stuck her tongue out again, but Brendan ignored her. 'So how are my *grown-up* friends?' he asked, looking at each of the adults in turn. 'All well, I trust?'

'Ackaye,' Eddie said. 'As right as rain, Brendan. Certainly no dramatic changes since we saw you last week.'

'A week's a long time at our age,' Brendan said. 'You go to bed at night and waken up the next morning to find that yet another friend has gone.'

'Gone where?' Theresa asked.

Brendan ignored her. 'So a week, at our age, can be a long time, though I'm glad to note that in this particular instance, this particular week, all my friends are still doing well.' He turned to Eleanor. 'And you, dear? How are things at the factory?'

'Grim,' Eleanor said. 'They've laid off a lot of workers and there's talk of them laying off a lot more. The whole industry's dying.'

'Cheap labour overseas,' Lizzie explained. 'In Korea and such like. There's no call for our linen anymore, so the trade's bein' kilt.'

'That's what I've heard,' Brendan said. 'And, of course, seen with my own eyes. Mills and factories of all kinds are being closed down - the spinning mills, the flour mills, the tobacco factories. Half the buildings in the city are standing empty and might soon be knocked down. Belfast's changing alright.'

'Not that anyone would miss those Victorian monstrosities,' Eleanor said. 'Sure they're as ugly as sin and an awful lot of decent souls went too early to their Maker because of them. They covered this city in a pall of smoke and dust that made life unbearable. Good riddance to bad rubbish, I say. Except that we need the work and God knows where it's going to come from if all those industries disappear.'

'Which they will, eventually,' Eddie said. 'Sure even ship and aircraft construction is dropping off and isn't likely to come back to previous levels. We're headin' for another Depression, I think, but down there...' He nodded at the fireplace, indicating the general direction of the Shankill and Sandy Row, from where the muffled sound of pounding Lambeg drums could still be distantly heard... 'Down there, they're celebratin' our defeat at the hands of King William of Orange - and also celebratin' the rise of the Orange State that keeps us impoverished. Sure it's a quare queer world when you think of it, but life is as life is, like, isn't it?'

Brendan smiled at Eddie's unconsciously adroit use of language. 'Eddie,' he said, 'sure you're more of a poet than I am. Your use of alliteration and repetition is truly, grandly original. Poetry is as poetry is, like - and you certainly know it's quare queer.'

'What?' Eddie asked, puzzled.

'Never mind, Grandda,' Sean said, holding the last of his Liquorice Allsorts up in front of his nose and clearly reluctant to part with it by swallowing it. 'He's just playin' word games with you. Sure he does that to us every day at school. It's just 'cause he's a poet.'

'Thank you for that recognition, my child,' Brendan said. 'It comes so rarely from adults that to hear it come from the lips of one so innocent does this old heart a power of good.'

'How old *are* you?' Theresa asked.

'That's not your business, young missy,' Lizzie said, trying not to smile. 'Just shut your cheeky wee gob and try to learn some manners.'

'I only asked,' Theresa said.

'So you asked, now shut up. Sure I was hopin' that those Liquorice Allsorts would glue your chattering teeth together and keep you quiet for a change. What a waste of my money!'

Theresa smiled. 'Sure that's not why you bought them, Granny.'

'Never mind why she bought them,' Eleanor said. 'Just say your thanks that she did and then take yourself up to your bed and read one of your books. You, too, Sean.'

'Aw, Ma, that's not fair! I'm a year older than her, so I should go to bed later.'

'No, you shouldn't,' Theresa said. 'It's 'cause you're older than me that you have to come up with me and look after me. I'm just a poor wee girl, after all.'

'A *clever* wee girl,' Brendan said. 'A wee girl who has a way with words that should take her far. I can't wait to get you into my class. My cane is twitching already.'

'He never canes anyone,' Sean informed Theresa. 'He's just trying to scare you. Come on, let's go upstairs.'

Theresa stuck her tongue out at Brendan, but then reluctantly followed Sean up the stairs.

'That boy is so diplomatic,' Brendan said, shaking his head from side to side as if bemused. 'So quietly intelligent. I think we should consider the Civil Service - or perhaps Sinn Féin. They could do with a good diplomat right now and that boy has everything they need - except age, of course. But give him time and he could do great things. He has the gift of innate maturity.'

'It's Theresa who has maturity,' Barry said. 'She talks just like a grown-up. Just wait till you get her in your class, Brendan. She'll drive you right up the wall.'

Brendan smiled and again shook his head from side to side. 'No. She's not mature. What that girl is... is *wilful*. She has a mind of her own, that's for sure, but it doesn't necessarily mean that she's mature. I suspect she's a girl who'll be true to herself, but who knows where that's going to lead her? She's the great unpredictable.'

'A chip off the old block,' Eleanor said sardonically while staring at Barry. 'Another great unpredictable.'

Barry ignored her. 'So what about you?' he said to Brendan. 'If Sinn Féin's in need of a good diplomat, why not help them out? You're one of our better known poets, a respected schoolteacher, and you've given lots of interviews and radio talks. Sure you're a natural when it comes to talking - particularly on radio and to journalists - so you could do Sinn Féin a power of good as their public voice. Why not help them out, Brendan?'

'I *am* helping them out,' Brendan replied. He had another sip of whisky and then lowered the glass to his lap. 'Sure aren't I writing their propaganda leaflets and the speeches for the ones presently doing all the squawking? I'm their voice behind the scenes, as it were, and my voice carries far.'

This was true enough. Brendan had repeatedly refused to become involved with the IRA in any way, shape or form, but over the years, when he saw no change in the system, no sign from the British that the Catholic lot would be improved, the old injustices rectified, he had changed his way of thinking and eventually let himself be persuaded to help Sinn Féin by drafting their propaganda leaflets and speeches. Though now totally dedicated to overthrowing the Orange State, he still preferred to do it behind the scenes and refused any more overt kind of involvement. This was a pity, Barry felt, because Brendan had a large personality and could charm the birds out of the trees. With a man like him as spokesman, a respectable and much loved figurehead, Sinn Féin could gain a lot more than they were gaining at present. As things stood, the organisation had little support in the local community, let alone in the wider sphere of politics. The IRA could continue the armed conflict, but it needed a more respected Sinn Féin to win the support of the community and carry on the long-term political battle. It needed men like Brendan.

'Sure your voice carries far,' Barry agreed. 'The problem is that no one knows it's *your* voice. The propaganda leaflets and the political speeches are a help, but they'd be a hell of a lot more effective if people knew who was writing them. And if you delivered those speeches yourself, Brendan, standing up to be counted, sure you'd gain us a lot more attention than we're getting right now.'

'I can't stand up to be counted,' Brendan said. 'I'm risking enough as it is. I'm a local schoolteacher, teaching in a state school, and that precludes me from taking an overtly active role. If it was known that I was involved with Sinn Féin, I'd be out of a job, and then I'd be of no use to anyone. I'm doing all I can, handsome.'

Barry sighed. 'Maybe.'

'But you, Barry, once my wee Sunny-Jim, sure you're never content. No matter what I do, it isn't enough for you. You've been at me since you were nineteen years of age. You were a regular wee enthusiast then and you haven't changed since.' He turned with a big grin to Barry's father. 'How did you raise such a mad dog, Eddie? Once he bites, he never lets go. I have his teeth marks all over me.'

Eddie chuckled. 'I'm not sure he's a mad dog, but he certainly has more passion for the cause than I ever had. I had it once, but it faded away, though now it lives on in him. It must be in the blood, like.'

'He's only still involved because he can't get regular work,' Eleanor said with finely suppressed contempt. 'It's a vicious circle, isn't it? He can't get a decent job because of his IRA involvement, his couple of prison sentences, and now he has to stick with the IRA because he can't get a decent job. Give him steady work and regular money and he might not be so keen.'

'That's not true,' Barry said. 'I'm proud of my involvement and I'm willing to pay the price for it. Steady work and regular money have nothing to do with it. You're insulting me, Eleanor.'

'Now, now, you two,' Lizzie said quickly, gazing down at her unfinished whisky to hide her embarrassment. 'We're just here to have a brief, pleasant evening, so let's not get into any political arguments. They always lead to trouble.'

Though a Republican, Lizzie had always disapproved of her husband's involvement with the IRA, insisting that the problem could eventually be solved by peaceful means. She and Eddie had fought a lot over that throughout their long marriage. The marriage had held together, though. She and Eddie were still a close couple.

'Ah, yes,' Brendan said, unperturbed. '*Politics* is trouble in general and always best avoided. Alas, it can't *always* be avoided, as all of us know.' Smiling, he finished off his drink, then stood up to place his empty glass on the mantelpiece over the Devon grate. 'Anyway,' he added, 'I have to be off now. I'd love to help you finish the bottle, but I have to meet a friend and I note, from your clock, that I'm already late, so I'd best be making tracks.'

'Take the bottle with you,' Barry said. 'Sure it's still over half full.'

But Brendan shook his head again. 'I'm meeting my editor for a few drinks in the bar of the Grand Central Hotel in Royal Avenue. We're going to discuss my next book over a meal in their excellent restaurant - on him, of course. Now I can't be seen entering that high-toned establishment with a bottle of Bushmills sticking out of my coat pocket. It's just not done, my dear friends, in the august circles to which I am accustomed as poet and scholar. So just finish it, enjoy it, sleep well on it, and I shall see you anon. Good night and God bless.'

When Brendan opened the door to leave, the sound of the distant Lambeg drums rushed in again. When he left, closing the door behind him, the sound of the drums was still there, but mercifully muffled.

'Well,' Barry said, holding up the bottle of whisky, 'let's not disappoint Brendan. Who's for another one?'

Everyone wanted another drink, so Barry filled their glasses, then sank back into his chair to drink with them. They drank in thoughtful silence for a moment, then Lizzie offered a sigh that was as loud as a sigh could be, while nodding, as if conversing with herself.

'Poor Brendan,' she said. 'Sure he's as decent a man as you're ever likely to find, but he hides it all behind drink and careless talk, pretending that nothing really matters. I just wish he'd found himself a decent woman instead of the bottle.'

'Why did he never marry? Do you know?' Eleanor asked.

'What does that mean?' Eddie said. 'Sure lots of men don't get married.'

'*Most* men get married,' Eleanor corrected him. 'And as for Brendan... Well...' Her shrug was a question mark. 'He's a man who's got everything going for him, at least as far as the women are concerned. Good looks, charm, financial security and - irresistible to women - a quare bit of fame. So what went wrong with him?'

'Does something have to be wrong with him,' Eddie asked, sounding affronted, 'just because he never tied the knot?'

'Well, no, but...'

'Sure he was lookin' after his ill mother,' Eddie said, 'and had to do it for years. By the time she died, which was only last year, he was fifty-two years old. I think that explains everything.'

'Well...' Eleanor looked at Eddie and then shrugged, as if not convinced. 'Maybe...'

'You don't think he's...?' Lizzy began, but couldn't even speak the words.

'What?' Eddie said, sounding harsh.

'Well, one of... *them*... And him being a schoolteacher an' all. I mean, it...'

But she lost the power of speech again and was only rescued when Barry said, 'Sure he's just an oul bachelor, for Christ's sake. That's all there is to it. He's one of them natural-born bachelors who likes to live alone because he needs privacy to write his poetry. He's a poet and he likes his wee drop as a lot of poets do. Apart from that, he's as good a man as you're likely to find, so I think we should all drink to him with the drink he gave us.'

'Right,' Eddie said. 'To hell with those Prods who're keepin' us awake as they rehearse for their bloody Twelfth. Let's all drink to Brendan.'

Agreeing, they raised their glasses and drank to Brendan in his absence. As he drank, becoming drunk, Barry contemplated tomorrow evening, which could mean a lot to so many, and wondered fearfully - more fearfully than was usual - how it would turn out. He drank to forget it.

3

'I wanna go with ya,' Theresa said, the minute they were out in the street, having finished their breakfast. 'Sure I've nothin' else to do.'

'Go and play with your girlfriends,' Sean replied. 'Me and Tommy don't want no wee girl to look after when we're tryin' to have a bit of fun. Go and knock on Martha Donovan's door and invite her outside. Tell her to bring her skippin' rope, or play hopscotch or somethin'. Just don't bother me.'

Some girls were already playing hopscotch on the pavement, leaping from one marked paving stone to the other in the early morning's grey light, but they were all too young for Theresa to play with.

'I don't wanna play with Martha. Sure she bores the knickers off me. I wanna go up the mountain with you and have some real fun.'

'Climbin' mountains is for boys.'

'I can do anything you can do. I'm as strong as you are.'

'No, you're not.'

'Yes, I am.'

After rolling his eyes, Sean started off along the street, past terraced houses that had no gardens, looking up to check if the sun was going to emerge from behind the clouds. Theresa followed him. Right now the sky was dark and low, but streaks of light could be seen here and there to fill Sean with hope. Lambeg drummers were already beating their instruments in the Shankill, wakening up the late sleepers. Sean stopped, with Theresa bunching up behind him, when he came to Tommy Molloy's house. Before knocking on the door, he turned back to face Theresa.

'I told ya,' he said, staring down at her pretty, pugnacious face and badly combed dark hair, 'you can't come. Go and play with the other girls.'

'I wanna go up the mountain with you.'

'We don't want girls along, so go away before I give you a good hidin'.'

'I'm not goin' away and you're not givin' me a hidin'. If you don't let me come with you I'll tell ma and da you're playin' with Tommy Molloy again. You're the one that'll get the good hidin' if I tell them that.'

'Tell them that and I'll kill ya,' Sean said.

'Sure they'll put you in a home if you kill me, so you're not gonna do that.'

Sean grinned. 'No, I suppose not. But you're a terrible wee blackmailer, Theresa, and I should at least box your rabbit-ears.'

'Take me with you or I'll tell ma and da.'

Sean sighed. 'Well, alright, then.' He turned away from her and banged the brass knocker on Tommy's front door. Tommy had three brothers and two sisters, but he was expecting Sean's call, so he was the one to answer the door. Like Sean, he was dressed in a white open-necked shirt, a grey V-necked pullover, short pants, socks and the white canvas shoes known as 'gutties'. Though twelve years old, he was even smaller than Theresa and had a face that would have been cherubic had it not been for the scar over his left eyebrow, a lower lip slightly twisted from having been split and badly stitched, and a nose that had been broken in a fight and improperly reset. His eyes, which were bright blue and perceptive, turned to take in Theresa. He stepped out of the house, closed the door behind him and said, 'What's *she* doin' here?'

'She's comin' with us,' Sean explained.

'No, she's not,' Tommy said contemptuously. 'She's a *girl*!'

'So what's that to you?' Theresa asked him.

'Fuck off,' Tommy said. 'You're not comin'. Sure Gerry Donovan's comin' as well and he can't *stand* girls.'

'He can't stand his sister, Martha,' Theresa said, 'but he doesn't mind me.'

Tommy turned to Sean. 'Tell her to take a powder,' he said, 'before I do somethin' drastic.'

'I can't,' Sean said. 'If I don't let her come she's gonna tell my Ma and Da that I went with you.'

'So what's the matter with *me*?'

'Our Ma and Da can't stand you,' Theresa explained, 'because they think you're trouble.'

'Well, fuck them,' Tommy said.

'If we don't take her,' Sean said, ignoring the insult to his parents, 'she'll tell on us and then we won't be able to play together again, so let's take her, Tommy.'

'As long as you look after her.'

'I will.'

'Alright, let's get goin'.'

'Where's Gerry?'

'He said he'd wait for us at the bottom of the street 'cause he didn't want his Ma or Da to see him with me.'

'Why not?'

'Because they think you're trouble,' Theresa said. 'I heard them sayin' so the last time I was in their house, playin' with Martha.'

'Well, fuck them,' Tommy repeated.

Turning away from the end of the street that gave a view of the twin spires of St. Peter's pro-cathedral, they walked in the opposite direction until they reached the Falls Road, where they found Gerry waiting for them at the corner. The same age as Sean and Tommy, he was in their class at school, but was bigger than both of them. Unlike Tommy, he had a soft spot for Theresa.

'So you've come,' he said.

'Aye,' Tommy said.

'You comin' with us?' Gerry asked of Theresa.

'Aye,' Theresa said.

Gerry didn't seem surprised. He just gave her a friendly grin, then frowned and turned his head, looking north, cocking an ear to the sound of the Lambeg drums being played in the Shankill, not much more than half a mile from here. 'Holy Jesus,' he said, having a fondness for blasphemy, 'but can you hear them Prod eejuts with their drums? Sure some of them started up even before I had m'breakfast. They'll still be playin' at midnight, I bet, just to keep us awake. Sure I'll be glad when the bloody Twelfth is over.'

'Maybe we should go over there,' Tommy said, 'and see what's goin' on. I bet they're all out in the streets already, makin' eejuts of themselves by rehearsin' what they're gonna do next week. As if they didn't do it every year and now know it by heart.'

'You wanna take a look?' Gerry said.

'No,' Sean responded. 'Theresa told my Ma and Da that we went to town last year to watch the Orange parades and both of them got really annoyed.'

'More annoyed,' Theresa added, 'when they heard that he went with Tommy here.'

'Oh, why?' Gerry asked.

'Because they think Tommy's trouble.'

'Well fuck them,' Tommy said. 'So are we goin' up to the mountain or not?'

'Ackaye, let's go,' Gerry said.

Being the biggest of all of them, also a natural leader, he marched off first and let them catch up with him. Though it was still pretty early the Falls Road was busy, this being a Saturday, with lots of housewives already doing their weekend shopping while the men entered and emerged from the bookies or stood on street corners, smoking and having a bit of *craic*, just passing the time until the pubs opened. The new trolley buses went up and down the road, making less noise than the old trams, but the road was still a riot of honking car horns, bicycle bells, the trundling wheels of horse-drawn carts, stubbornly clinging to the past, the music blaring out of the open doors of various shops, the shouting of grown-ups, the shrieking and giggling of children at play. Gerry led them southwest, past butchers, bakers, cobblers, bookies, closed pubs, pawnbrokers, and grocery and fish shops. Often they had to make their way around or between the sofas, chairs and beds put out on the pavement in front of the second-hand furniture shops. Eventually, however, they had passed the more commercial part of the Falls and found themselves crossing the Clowney Bridge, which led to the Donegall Road and, only two streets beyond it, the Whiterock Road. The former was a Protestant enclave; the latter was Catholic. As they passed the former, the pounding of Lambeg drums was almost deafening. When they glanced along the road, they saw a lot of Prods out in the street, looking on as a couple of men, dressed in normal clothes, fiercely hammered their huge, gaudily decorated Lambeg drums with sticks, making a dreadful, insistent, warlike din.

'Jesus, look at them go!' Gerry exclaimed. 'There's just a blur where their hands should be.'

'Keep walkin',' Theresa said. 'Those Donegall Road Prods are all Fenian-haters, so God knows what they'll do if they see us and recognise us as Catholics.'

'How the fuck could they do that?' Tommy asked. 'Sure we look just like them.'

'They'll just see that we're strangers,' Sean said, 'and that'd be enough for them to come up here and question us. So let's keep walking, like Theresa says.'

They continued on until they reached the Whiterock Road, turning into it with a feeling of relief that none could admit to. They felt safer here. To their right was Ballymurphy, a Catholic estate; to their left, beyond the rows of headstones in the Belfast Cemetery, was Turf Lodge, another Catholic estate. Nevertheless, as they started up the Whiterock Road, they could still hear the relentless rhythm of the Lambeg drums.

'Them and their fuckin' parades,' Tommy said. 'Sure those Prods are paradin' all the time, like they've nothing better to do. They must all be eejuts.'

'We have our own parades,' Gerry reminded him. 'Marian parades. Corpus Christi processions. The Men of Clonard Confraternity who wear their own sashes and march through the Falls with banners and flags.'

'That's only for men,' Tommy said, staring pointedly at Theresa. 'No wimmen allowed, like.'

'So what about the Children of Mary procession,' Theresa said promptly. 'That's for wimmen only an' they have their own banners. No men allowed, like.'

'Though they often get men to carry their banners for them,' Sean pointed out. 'And of course they always have priests along, so that's at least a *couple* of men.'

'Aye,' Theresa conceded, 'but men aren't allowed to join the Children of Mary. Sure they'd just spoil it, wouldn't they?'

'Only a sissy would want to join it,' Tommy said, determined to have the last word, 'so that leaves me out.'

'But we still have our parades,' Gerry insisted, 'just like the Prods. We have our sashes and banners, too, so I don't see the difference. The Prod parades are just bigger, that's all, and they take a lot longer to pass. That's the only difference I can see. We're just like them, really.'

'If your Da heard you saying that,' Theresa said, 'you'd get a quare hidin'. He's real fierce against the Prods, is your Da. I've heard him with my own ears.'

'I *like* parades,' Tommy said, changing the subject just a little. 'I want to play drums for the Saint Malachy's Scout Pipe Band, but you have to be in the Catholic Boy Scouts of Ireland to get into the band.'

'So why don't you join?' Theresa asked him.

'I did, but they threw me out right quick. They said I was trouble.'

'You're jokin'!' Theresa exclaimed with raised eyebrows.

'You should join the Saint Peter's Girl Guides,' Tommy told her, offering his pearls of wisdom to a lesser mortal. 'Sure you get to go on field manoeuvres in Colin Glen. I mean, you get an awful lot of trips like that. I wouldn't mind that m'self.'

Straight ahead, soaring high above them at the end of the Whiterock Road, was the bracken-and-heather covered Black Mountain, with the small white house in the Hatchet Field barely visible. That was the house of the madman they all feared, though none could admit it. To the right, on the lower slopes of the mountain, were other white-painted farmhouses.

'Holy Jesus, it's hot!' Gerry exclaimed, wiping sweat from his brow. They were now nearing the end of the Whiterock Road, approaching the path that wound steeply up the face of the mountain to the spring located near the farmhouses. They could have a drink of cold water up there and they were, in the rising heat of noon, looking forward to it.

'Hey, look how far up we are already!' Tommy shouted, glancing back over his shoulder.

Looking down, Sean saw the whole of Belfast spread out in bright sunlight, row upon row of tiled rooftops, redbrick houses, with cranes towering over them where new homes were being built. Soaring above the houses were the high chimneys of the many factories, smoke belching out of them to darken the sunny sky. Beyond the houses, the factory chimneys and the high stores in the town centre, the three channels of the docks, lined with ships and the cranes used to load them, merged into one and flowed into the sea, which swept out as a rippling, silvery sheet to the heat-hazed horizon. The whole of Sean's world was down there and he was, as always, overwhelmed by it, scarcely able to comprehend that he was part of it, a mere ant in an anthill.

Turning away, he followed Gerry and the others up the torturously steep, winding path, past grassy glades, beechwood trees and shrubberies covered with juicy blackberries. There they stopped for a while, to pick and eat handfuls of the berries, their lips and faces covered in blood-red juice; then they clambered higher still, until they reached the gushing spring and could lie belly-down on the ground beneath it to drink the ice-cold water as it rushed out in a delicious, gurgling, swooping stream.

Thirst quenched, they moved even higher up the face of the mountain, passing the white farmhouses until they reached the open stretches of heather and bracken and, beyond them, the Devil's Punchbowl, a great amphitheatre of soaring black cliffs. There were caves in the cliffs, two joined by a subterranean passage that they always had to goad each other to enter. But enter it they did, instantly finding themselves in a damp, chilling darkness illuminated only fractionally by the light that could be discerned at either end.

Going through that passageway, more like a tunnel really, claustrophobic and scary, Sean, who was well read because of his father's urging, thought of the primitive human beings who had lived here thousands of years ago, between 7000 and 6500 BC. It struck him as incredible that those primitive men had almost certainly come from the Isle of Man, walking from there to Ireland when land bridges connected them, settling on a high bluff overlooking the lower Bann, just south of Coleraine, and gradually spreading out until some of them found their way to these caves and made their home here. As he continued on through the subterranean passageway, hearing the steady, metronomic dripping of water, the crunching of gravel underfoot, and, more nerve-wracking, soft rushing sounds in the darkness beneath the walls of rock, almost certainly rats or some other form of wildlife, he felt his heart starting to race and wished he hadn't come in here. Even worse: Gerry and Tommy were well ahead of him, obviously hurrying to get out again, their courage already failing them. Theresa, right beside him, wasn't saying a word, though her heavy breathing told him all there was to know about the fear she was feeling.

'Here,' he whispered, reaching out to her. 'Give me your hand and stick close to me until we're out of here.'

Theresa didn't say a word, but he felt her fingers slipping between his fingers and squeezing gently, gratefully. This tactile contact was as much a comfort to him as it was to her.

Looking straight ahead, Sean saw a jagged circle of bright sky and, silhouetted in the middle of it, Gerry and Tommy. They both whooped like red Indians, the way the Indians did in films , then raised their hands to the sky and started jumping up and down, as if doing a war dance. Sean knew what they were doing. They were exorcising their fear. They were also pretending that they hadn't been frightened, though he knew that they had been.

When he reached the mouth of the tunnel, where he released Theresa's hand, he burst gratefully into the light and did exactly the same thing. He and the other two boys jumped about and hollered while Theresa just sat on a rock and stared silently at them. Eventually, when they had all settled down, Tommy, flushed with excitement, turned to the silent Theresa and said, 'Sure you look as white as a sheet, Theresa. Saw a ghost in there, did you?'

'No,' Theresa said. 'And I'm no whiter than I normally am, so don't tell me different.'

Tommy leaned forward, resting his hands on his knees, practically shoving his face into Theresa's, to say mockingly, 'Go on, admit it! You were pissin' your knickers in there. That's why we didn't want to bring a girl like you. Sure we knew you'd be scared, like.'

'You were scared as well,' Theresa said, looking pugnacious again. 'That's why you got out of there so quick. You practically ran the whole way.'

Tommy straightened up again. 'Ack, don't give me yer shite,' he said. 'Sure there's nothing up here that scares me, I can tell you that straight.'

'Yes, there is,' Theresa said.

'Oh, yeah? What's that?'

'The madman who lives in the Hatchet Field,' Theresa said. 'I bet you wouldn't have the nerve to go all the way up to his house and knock on his door. I'll go if you go.'

Tommy's eyes widened, then he glanced at Sean and Gerry. The latter two glanced at each other, then stared down at their own feet. A light breeze ruffled their tawny hair.

'You're fucking kidding me, aren't you?' Tommy said at last, when it was clear that he was getting no support. 'Sure that old madman's known to kill children and then chop them up into pieces and have them as food. That old bastard's a cannibal!'

This was something they all believed through having talked themselves into it. Some solitary person certainly lived in the dilapidated farmhouse at the far corner of the Hatchet Field (where the handle meets the blade, as it were) and most of the children who climbed the mountain had convinced themselves that it was a crazy old man who abducted children and chopped them up and then ate them. Neither Sean nor anyone else of his acquaintance had ever actually *seen* the tenant of the farmhouse, but because it was in such a dilapidated condition, they were convinced that whoever lived there was mad. Perhaps some of their friends had, indeed, been chased off the Hatchet Field (which was, in reality, two adjoining fields) by the owner of the farmhouse and from that, given imagination and gross exaggeration, the legend of a crazed old man who abducted and ate children had sprung into being. Certainly, Sean and most of his friends, though often trying to pretend otherwise, were frightened of approaching the farmhouse. Now Theresa, stung by Tommy's mockery, was cleverly challenging *his* courage. If she, a mere girl, was willing to go with him, he could hardly refuse to go.

'You mean you're frightened of him,' she said, 'because he's crazy and eats the childern he catches?'

'Well, no...' Tommy was almost stuttering. 'I just mean...'

'I'll go if you will,' Theresa repeated. 'Just to prove I'm not frightened, like.'

'Well...' Clearly Tommy wanted to refuse, but he had no way out. Now as white as he'd accused Theresa of being, he shrugged forlornly and said, 'Fuck it. Okay. I mean, it's nothin' to me, like.' Then he turned to Sean and Gerry. 'What about you two?'

'What?' Gerry responded, looking more than a little nervous. 'Sure you're not serious, are ya?'

'Aye, I'm fucking serious,' Tommy said. 'You think I'm frightened of some crazy oul bastard? Well, I'm not. And I bet if I go all the way up to his house, Theresa won't go that far with me.'

'Yes, I will,' Theresa insisted.

'Holy Jesus,' Gerry whispered.

'I'll go,' Sean said. He truly believed that the crazy old man lived in that house and, though terrified at the very thought of approaching it, he wasn't going to let Theresa go without him. 'I mean, he doesn't scare *me*.'

'See?' Tommy said to Theresa. 'We don't give a shit, like.' Then he turned to Gerry, who was distractedly kicking up the soil with the toe of his mud-covered white gutty. 'What about you, Gerry?'

Gerry didn't raise his head. He was studying his mud-covered gutties with deep concentration. 'Aye, okay,' he said after an eternity.

'That's it then,' Tommy said triumphantly to Theresa. 'Let's go. Follow me.'

The others followed Tommy as he led them towards the Hatchet Field, compensating for his lack of size by moving skilfully across the breast of the mountain, from patches of bracken to heather, passing limestone quarries, pursing his lips to look fearless, ignoring the broad swathe of Belfast, spread out far below them, hazy in summer sunlight, until he reached the edge of the field and could see the farmhouse. Once there, he dropped onto his belly and they all followed suit.

Looking across the emerald-green, carefully cultivated field, they saw the farmhouse with frightening clarity. Though painted white, it seemed more dilapidated than ever, with piles of wood and various pieces of machinery scattered haphazardly around it. Sean, whose heart was racing, didn't know if he was actually seeing that farmhouse or simply imagining it.

'Sure that oul house looks haunted,' Gerry whispered, wiping sweat from his forehead.

'It's not haunted,' Theresa said, sounding as calm as could be, 'but I bet there's bodies buried all around it, just waitin' to be dug up and eaten by that oul mental case.'

'So why are we gonna knock on his door?' big Gerry asked, looking forlornly, perhaps yearningly, at Theresa, who had, up until this bitter moment, always been treated lovingly by him. 'I mean, he's bound to grab one of us.'

'Well...' Tommy began, still as white as a sheet, but pursing his lips to demonstrate that he was fearless. 'Maybe we should just...'

'We're gonna knock on his door,' Theresa said, sounding adamant, giving no one a get-out, 'and stand there until the oul bastard opens it. Then, before he can grab anyone, I'll shout, "Fuck the Orangemen!" and we'll all run away.'

'What?' Gerry said, sounding strangled.

'Listen, Theresa...' Sean began.

'Anyone who doesn't do it,' Theresa interjected, still sounding incredibly calm, 'is a cowardy custard who'll be branded a yella-belly for the rest of his life. Now I'm goin', so who's comin' with me?'

Raising herself onto her right hip, she stared steadily, boldly, at each of them in turn. Gradually, one by one, they all rose to their feet. When all of them were standing upright, Theresa did the same. When, after a long time, nobody had moved, Theresa turned away from them and started briskly across the Hatchet Field, towards the farmhouse.

'Okay, I'm comin',' Tommy said, hurrying to catch up with her, with Sean and Gerry falling in behind. 'I was goin' to go first, but you took me by surprise, like. Just stay a wee bit behind me and you should be okay. If that oul bastard makes any kind of move, I'll punch his teeth out.'

'Right,' Theresa said.

Now committed, or out-manoeuvred by Theresa, Tommy forged on ahead, racing across the field, crouched low and zigzagging like a soldier, with the others coming up behind him and doing the same. Sean felt sweaty and unreal. He could feel his heart racing. He didn't want to go near the farmhouse, but he was worried about Theresa, knowing how bold she could be and imagining her standing her ground when that mad old bastard opened his front door. If he managed to grab anyone, it was bound to be Theresa and she'd then disappear for all time. The very thought of that terrified Sean and made him stick close to her.

They were about halfway across the Hatchet Field when the front door of the farmhouse opened and someone, a shadowy, faceless figure, stepped outside and bawled something at them.

'Oh, shit!' Tommy wailed.

Sean remembered little else. It all dissolved in a blur of panic. He remembered running down the Hatchet Field, towards the city spread out below, hazed in summer sunlight, obscured in clouds of industrial smoke, his heart racing as if it was going to burst while his breath scorched his lungs. He forgot all about Theresa. He even forgot his own name. He turned into a football composed of raw nerve ends, rolling on forever down the slopes, stripping him bare. He ran down the whole mountainside. He fell and scrambled about gasping, stung by nettles, cut by bracken. He glanced back and saw Theresa behind him, her lips curved in a sneaky smile. He hated her at that moment. He also loved her for her courage. He kept running, scrambling, rolling down the mountainside, and eventually came to a rest, huddled up with his two friends, the three of them sprawled around the gurgling spring.

Tommy and Gerry were laughing, though the laughter wasn't natural. The laughter was hysterical, contagious, a disease, and it caught Sean and made him laugh as well, though his stomach was churning.

Theresa came down the slope. Sean caught her sneaky smile. He kept laughing, pretending to have a great time, but then he walked away from the gurgling spring until he came to a quiet glade. He threw up in violent spasms, getting rid of his secret shame, then returned to his friends and his sister as if nothing had happened.

'Jesus, look down there,' he said, pointing to Belfast. 'Sure you can see the Protestant arches and the banners and even hear those drums. Wouldn't you think the Twelfth of July was today with all that's going on down there?'

'Aye, you're right,' Tommy said. 'Fuckin' amazin'. Sure we should go down there and check it out.'

Relieved to be distracted from their cowardice, they made their way back down to Belfast, their familiar home, for good and ill.

'Sure we should never have brought a girl,' Tommy said. 'I mean, they're always bad news.'

'Aw, fuck off,' Theresa said.

4

Sitting in the back of the windowless van as it rattled and banged its way out of Belfast, heading for Antrim, Barry felt an unaccustomed dryness in his throat and wondered why, after so much experience of this kind, he was suddenly suffering from a case of bad nerves. In fact, ever since turning thirty, two years ago, he had felt a subtle change within him, something not quite comprehensible but certainly there, a kind of overnight ageing that had opened the door to self-doubt and guilt. When he raised his eyes to glance at Frank Kavanagh, seated directly opposite, and saw those ageing but still hard green eyes, seemingly harder with each passing year, he found himself wondering if his secret life as a guerrilla fighter would make him go the same way. The possibility was infinitely disturbing and did not help his dry throat.

'That dozer drivin' needs more lessons,' Kavanagh said. 'I've had more comfortable rides in a dodgem car than I'm havin' right now. Where the fuck do they find these boys?'

'It's just the van and the roads,' Barry said. 'The van's obviously seen better days and this particular road isn't a good one. The kid driving is okay.'

'Good old Barry,' Kavanagh said sarcastically. 'Always stickin' up for the underdog. Sure you're a man in a million.'

Grinning crookedly, with little real humour, he flipped a cigarette out of its packet and into his mouth, then lit it with a match and exhaled a stream of smoke. Looking at him, Barry wondered how they had managed to remain friends for years and could only assume that the IRA was the one thing they had in common. Certainly, while he had once admired Kavanagh, a long time ago, when he had been young and naïve, he had come to like him less over the years, seeing him more clearly with maturity. Either Kavanagh had changed, becoming hardened by his vocation, the repetitive violence, or he had always been hard and Barry had only gradually come to see him for what he really was. One thing was certain: Kavanagh *enjoyed* the violence, was addicted to it, and would be at a loss for something to do if it ever ended. Barry, on the other hand, though he had previously killed without conscience, or, more likely, when his conscience was overwhelmed by the idealism of youth, was increasingly having doubts about what the violence was doing to him and that, in turn, was making him nervous when jobs like this came up. In this instance, however, he was also nervous because the job was so important. If it failed, it would set the whole of the northern IRA back for a long time to come.

As the van continued to make its shaky, noisy way across the hills and glens of Antrim, which Barry could not see because the vehicle had no windows, he lowered his gaze, avoiding Kavanagh's steely gaze, and looked down distractedly at his own booted feet, lost in the semi-darkness of the oily, cluttered, vibrating floor. Increasingly, in the past few months, he had found himself reliving his younger days, the days of World War II, when he was eighteen or nineteen years old and an enthusiastic novice in the IRA, passionately committed to Republicanism, all too willing to fight and die for it. Now, thinking back on the first time that he had ever killed a man, in a doorstop assassination, it amazed him that he could not recall feeling any fear, but only a heart-racing excitement and, when the job was done, triumphal exultation and pride. He had not been able to understand, at that time, why his father, who had gone before him, doing exactly the same things, had eventually given it up because, at least as Brendan Coghill had interpreted it, he had lost his taste for violence. Now Barry was glimpsing what his father might have experienced: an immobilising guilt and self-doubt that all the idealism in the world could not extinguish. Barry, who still had faith in the cause, was losing faith in himself.

'I'm gonna enjoy this one,' Kavanagh said abruptly, exhaling smoke and nodding his head. 'I'm so fuckin' sick of listening to the Prods rehearsing for the Twelfth - those Lambeg drums night and day, not to mention the pipe bands - that I'm gonna feel really good pullin' this caper while they're all still rehearsin'. This should put a real pissin' dampener on their fuckin' parades.'

'If it's successful,' Barry said without thinking.

'And why shouldn't it be successful?'

'Well, they haven't always been in the past and this one could be tough.'

'What past are you talkin' about? Sure we've hardly done a thing these past few years. We've been lyin' low, like, lettin' those boyos down south get all the glory. Now those same fuckin' boyos are tryin' to tell us we're not to take action in the north because they're frightened that a Loyalist reaction couldn't be contained. Well, fuck 'em, we don't have to toe *their* line. We'll pull off this job - and if there's a Loyalist backlash, we'll use that as an excuse to go back to war. Fuck the south. De Valera betrayed us on partition, so we don't owe them anything. We're better off on our own.'

'Maybe so,' Barry said.

'Damned right, we are, pal.'

There was a certain amount of truth in what Kavanagh was saying. Many Catholics, north and south, had become disillusioned with De Valera's failure to end partition. That sin had been compounded when the Cold War began and De Valera rejected an invitation to be part of NATO and abandon the principle of neutrality, insisting that as long as partition was in place, Eire could not join the Allies. That blunt refusal had only reinforced the British belief that Northern Ireland was strategically important to Britain and Europe - and that, in turn, had increased the Republic's isolation internationally. As a result, in July, 1949, only a month after Eire had formally become the Republic of Ireland, the British Parliament passed the Ireland Act, confirming that Northern Ireland was constitutionally part of the United Kingdom and that it would not cease to be part of the United Kingdom without the consensus of the Stormont Parliament. In other words, the British government had handed the Unionists the power of veto over the decisions of any future Catholic majority. The IRA had no choice but to strike back.

Yet as Barry recalled, the violence had never entirely gone away. Even before the passing of the notorious Ireland Act, there had been violent conflicts in the north. In February of that year, when a Northern Ireland election was called, Orangemen had marched through Catholic areas, announcing their triumphalist right to parade anywhere in the country and, even worse, inciting the Catholics with confrontational banners that stated, 'No surrender!', 'No Pope Here!', 'Dublin rule is Rome rule', and 'A Protestant Ulster for a Protestant People.' As usual, fire bombs were thrown, people on both sides were beaten up by angry mobs, and a certain number were injured or killed. Barry had not taken part in those particular riots because he couldn't risk being caught by the police when he was still engaged in covert operations for the northern IRA. Nevertheless, having witnessed them, he had been confirmed in his belief that there would be no peace in the province until the Orange State was demolished. Even now, despite his nervousness and doubt, he believed this to be true.

'We'll soon be there,' Kavanagh said, checking his wristwatch, then looking up again, squinting through drifting skeins of cigarette smoke. 'I can't wait to get started.'

'I just want it over with,' Barry said.

'What the hell's the matter with you, Barry? Getting' soft in yer old age. Well, I'm twice the age you are, boyo, but I'm still rarin' to go. I want those Orangemen to quake and I want those IRA bastards down south to know just what we can do. I mean, fuck it, they get it easy. We have to do it the hard way.'

'What does that mean?' Barry asked, not really caring, but preferring even Kavanagh's conversation to a silence only broken by the rattling and banging of this old, beat-up transit van.

'Think about it,' Kavanagh said. 'Those boyos down south are always boastin' about how they boldly cross the border into the north, do their business, then flee back to the south. *Boldly*? I ask you! Sure wouldn't we be doin' the same - pulling jobs off down south - if we had the same protection as those dozers have?'

'What does that mean?' Barry repeated, lighting a cigarette to calm himself, breathing in, breathing out.

'What does it mean? Sure didn't the IRA down south formally declare, way back in '49, that they'd never again undertake operations against the security forces in the new Republic?'

'Yeah,' Barry said, 'I remember that. So what?'

'So fuckin' *what*? I'll *tell* you what! Why do you think those bastards did that?'

'I don't know.'

'Because they were fuckin' clever, is why. Because they needed bases in the Republic for any future campaigns in the United Kingdom and, because of that, they didn't want to antagonise the Irish authorities. They did it because they knew that a deliberate policy of non-aggression in one part of the island would encourage the authorities to turn a blind eye to the southern IRA when they used Irish territory for the launching of attacks in the north. So while tellin' us not to mount any attacks here, for fear of arousing the wrath of the Loyalists, those boyos crossed the border, made their own attacks, then crossed back over the border in the confidence that they wouldn't have any aggravation from the fuckin' Gardai. Clever bastards, alright! So now they get all the glory while we're told to put a cork in our arses and make no noise of any kind. Well, we're gonna make a bit of noise tonight and they're gonna hear it even down there in the south. About time an' all!'

Barry hoped that Kavanagh was right, that the mission would be a success, but he wasn't too sure that it would be. There had, of course, been similar operations in the past, between the ending of World War II and the present, but not all had been as successful as they might have been. In 1951 the Derry unit had raided the British naval base at Ebrington, using inside information gained from Catholics who worked there. The raid, which was successful, had resulted in the seizure of a large number of .303 rifles, submachine guns, machine-guns and ammunition; but it also gave the Unionists a good excuse to re-equip the RUC and reintroduce repressive measures against suspected IRA members, resulting in many more arrests. Approximately two years later, another IRA raid on a British Army officer training barracks at Felsted, Sussex, resulted in the capture of scores of rifles, machine-guns and ammunition, but the weapons obtained were so heavy that they prevented the escape van from moving more than a few yards and most of the weapons had to be dumped. The van was then spotted by a police patrol car in Bishop's Stortford, Hertfordshire. The three IRA men arrested were sentenced to eight years in prison. That farcical raid had made a laughing stock of the IRA. On the other hand, only last month, an IRA raid on Gough Barracks in Armagh, the largest army barracks in Northern Ireland, had resulted in the capture of eighteen Royal Irish Fusiliers and the seizure of over 300 weapons, including Bren guns and submachine guns. The success of that raid had put the southern IRA back in business and now the northern IRA, under the command of Kavanagh, were hoping to do the same tonight with a raid against an RUC barracks located in a village near Antrim city and known to have a large arsenal of weapons. If they succeeded, they would be resurrected like the southern IRA; if they failed, they would be humiliated and have to lie low for the foreseeable future. It was therefore a high-risk operation with a lot at stake.

No wonder I'm nervous, Barry thought.

'Sounds like we've arrived,' Kavanagh said as the van ground to a groaning halt, shuddered violently, then rapidly coughed itself into silence.

Instantly, Barry threw the remainder of his cigarette to the floor of the van and ground it out under his boot. He then moved up behind Kavanagh, who had already opened the rear doors of the vehicle and was lowering himself to the ground. Barry followed him out. It was close to midnight, but the summer sky was resplendent with moonlight and stars, forming a vast, glistening umbrella over the silhouetted hills of Antrim. Apart from knowing that he was in Antrim, Barry didn't know much else - he hadn't been here before and didn't know what area he was in - but he saw that the driver had parked in a siding behind a dark-blue Ford saloon car. The siding was bordered by high hedgerows, behind which were beech trees, offering a good deal of protection from passing motorists. Seamus Magee and Kevin McClusky, both wearing dark-blue overalls, were standing by the Ford saloon, both smoking. They threw their cigarettes away and walked up to Kavanagh and Barry, both also wearing dark-blue overalls, as soon as they emerged from the van. Though Magee was Barry's age, he still looked surprisingly youthful because of his red hair and acne. McClusky, who looked every minute of his thirty-five years, was still lean and mean.

'So you've come,' he said to Kavanagh, giving Barry a curt nod.

'Aye,' Kavanagh replied. 'No problem. We didn't even see a police car, let alone get stopped by one, so the weapons are safe and sound in the back. How far's that police station from here?'

'Approximately five miles,' Magee said.

'Right, boys, let's get started.'

At a nod from Kavanagh, Barry clambered back into the van, raised the false bottom, located between the opposing bench seats, and reached down to start passing the weapons up to Kavanagh, who had come in behind him. Magee and McClusky were each given M1 Thompson submachine guns, more widely known as 'tommy guns', along with spare ammunition and half-a-dozen pineapple-shaped '36' hand grenades, widely used by British troopers during World War II. Barry and Kavanagh armed themselves with stolen British Army 9mm Sten submachine guns and four extra box magazines. When everyone had their weapons, Barry pulled two home-made bombs out of the false bottom. Relatively primitive and easy to make, they consisted of a Thermos flask packed with low explosive gunpowder and detonated by means of a firing cap and a simple timing device based on the principles of the stopwatch. Barry gave one bomb to Kavanagh, the other to McClusky, then he replaced the lid of the false bottom and covered it up with a rubber mat. The four of them then left the van.

Kavanagh told the driver to wait here until they returned, then he and the other men transferred to the Ford saloon, which had been stolen earlier that night and hot-wired. In the Ford, Magee took the driver's seat and drove at no more than forty miles an hour along an empty, moonlit road that led them, less than ten minutes later, into the main street of the village they were seeking. It was basically a one-street village, about half a mile long, with a couple of rows of terraced houses, a scattering of detached houses in their own grounds, a few shops, a petrol station with the pumps at the edge of the road and, a few yards from the latter, the RUC station that they were planning to raid. This being close to midnight, the village was sleeping, with not a single person in sight.

'Stop here,' Kavanagh said. He was sitting up front beside Magee. Barry and McClusky were in the rear.

Magee slowed the car, then braked to a halt at the kerb, on the same side of the road as the RUC station, but about fifty feet away from it. It was a single-storey, red-brick building, raised about six feet above the road, with steps leading up to it. The front door was closed, but a gas lamp was burning above it, casting a flickering pale-yellow light over the pavement. There were iron bars across the front windows.

'The building's bigger than it looks,' Kavanagh said. 'Though it's narrow at the front and has only one floor, it runs back a good distance. Our informant used to work here as a maintenance man and he did me a drawing of the place. It's a real simple structure. One long corridor runs straight along the side of the building, from the front door to the back. Leading off that corridor, on the right as you go in the front, are the administrative office, a rest room, two toilets, a couple of holding cells and, at the very back, a kitchen. There's a trap door in the floor of that kitchen, leading down to a basement that's as big as the floor area. Their arsenal is kept down in that basement.'

'So how do we go in?' Magee asked.

'Front and rear,' Kavanagh said. 'Though the station is closed, there are two men on duty every night, both awake and armed. They could be anywhere in the building - maybe one in the administrative office or rest room, another in the kitchen at the back. So we go in front and rear, blowing the doors off, despatching both the guards, then taking as much of their weapons and ammo as we can get in the car before the other cops, who live right here in the village, can get out of their spermy beds and get to us.'

'It'll take a lot of runs to get the weapons out of that cop shop and into this car,' Barry said.

'We don't have to do that,' Kavanagh replied. 'There's a car park at the rear of the station, right there where the back door is. Seamus will stay here, in the car, until we blow out both doors simultaneously. The instant those bombs explode, Seamus will drive the car round to the rear of the station, reversing it up to what's left of the back door. By that time, we'll have at least started to clear the building and Kevin should already be down in the basement, ready to hand the weapons up to us. Seamus will help to transfer the stolen weapons and ammo from the building to the car. You'll keep the front of the building covered while all that's going on, ensuring that no one either comes in the front or gets around to the back. When we've got as much as we can carry, we'll call you to come and join us, then Seamus will drive us out of here.'

'Why aren't we using the van instead of this car?' Barry asked. 'The van would hold a hell of a lot more weapons.'

'Aye, but it'd also be too slow when we're making our getaway. Forty miles an hour, for fuck's sake. Swings and roundabouts, like.' Kavanagh swept the lamplit street with his gelid gaze; seeing that it was still empty, he said, 'Okay? Are we set?'

'Let's do it,' Barry said.

'You sound like you have a dry throat,' Kavanagh said. 'Can I take it you're nervous?'

'Yes,' Barry confessed.

'Sure that's always been a good sign,' Kavanagh said. 'The only ones who aren't nervous are eejuts. Okay, let's go.'

Leaving Magee behind the steering wheel, the other three men clambered out of the car and immediately made their way to the police station, not bothering to hide their weapons or Semtex bombs, because the street was deserted. Kavanagh and McClusky had their submachine guns slung over their shoulders and were carrying the bombs in their hands. Barry had already cocked his Sterling submachine gun and was holding it across his chest, preparing to give covering fire if necessary. They were all wearing rubber-soled, lace-up military boots and approached the station without making any noise. Once at the steps of the station, they stopped to let Kavanagh and McClusky check the luminous dials of their synchronised wristwatches. It was now five minutes after midnight.

'Set your bomb to explode at precisely ten past,' Kavanagh whispered, getting enjoyment out of playing the general. 'I'll set mine for exactly the same time. The minute the doors are blown away, you go in shooting. Okay?'

'Aye,' McClusky said, nodding.

'Right. Off you go.'

As McClusky made his way along the narrow alleyway formed by the gable ends of the police station and adjoining petrol station, carrying his home-made bomb, Kavanagh went up the steps to the front door. There he was clearly illuminated in the flickering light from the overhead lamp. Instantly, Barry held his submachine gun at the ready and kept his gaze on the barred windows of the building. The lights inside were still on and Barry could see rows of thick black files on shelves running along the far wall of what had to be the administration area. There was no sign of movement. While Kavanagh knelt on the top step to place his bomb against the door and then set its timer, working as quietly as possible, Barry alternately scanned the street and those barred windows, preparing to fire the instant he saw human movement and praying, as his heart started racing and sweat formed on his brow, that no civilian materialised in the street.

Luckily, no one appeared.

In less than a minute, Kavanagh had positioned the bomb, set the timer and was coming back down the steps, unslinging his Sten gun from his shoulder while on the move. Together, he and Barry slipped into the narrow alleyway formed by the gable ends of the two buildings. They pressed their backs to the wall while Kavanagh checked his wristwatch.

'One minute to go,' he whispered, keeping his arm raised, watching the hand on his wristwatch count off the seconds. That sixty seconds seemed to take an eternity, but then the two bombs exploded, one out front, one at the back, splitting the midnight silence with their shocking, head-tightening clamour.

Instantly, Barry and Kavanagh raced around to the front of the building to see the scorched front door lying on the pavement under a cloud of swirling smoke and choking dust. Barry heard the roar of McClusky's tommy gun at the back of the building, indicating that he was already inside. Slightly deafened by the explosions, feeling remote from himself, though his heart was still racing, Barry rushed up the steps ahead of Kavanagh, crouching low as he went in through the smoke-filled doorway. He pressed the trigger of his submachine gun as he went in, not waiting until he saw someone, simply moving the barrel left and right, keeping his finger on the trigger to cover as wide an area as possible.

Someone screamed inside.

A shadowy form, hands raised in the smoky gloom, staggered backward and then disappeared as he fell to the floor.

Barry unclipped a hand grenade and flung it into the smoke-filled room, the administrative area, and hurried past the doorway even as the grenade exploded, making another calamitous din. A submachine gun roared behind him. That would be Kavanagh. Barry advanced in a dream along the corridor until he came to the rest room, the door of which was open, revealing that it was empty. But he flung another grenade in, just to be sure, and raced past as it exploded with another deafening roar, producing more smoke and the acrid stench of cordite. Then he reached the toilets.

He didn't open the toilet doors. He simply peppered them with bullets, shooting both locks all to hell. When the locks had flown away in a shower of wood splinters, he kicked the first door open, saw that the room was empty, then kicked the second door open and found exactly the same.

McClusky's submachine gun roared again from the rear of the building. Kavanagh's weapon roared from the administration area. Men screamed (or so it seemed, though this may have been imagined) as Barry advanced along the corridor and came to the two holding cells. He looked in. Both were empty. The stench of cordite pinched his nostrils. He moved on until he came to the kitchen doorway, where he stopped, his finger on the trigger, and gingerly looked in.

A man in an RUC uniform was stretched out on the floor in a spreading pool of blood, his pistol lying a few inches from his outstretched right hand. Beyond his head was an open trapdoor.

After checking again that no one else was in the kitchen, Barry stepped over the back door, which was lying splintered and still smouldering on the floor, and looked out through the smoke-filled doorway. The Ford saloon was reversed up to the back of the building and Magee was hurrying away from it, holding his tommy gun in both hands. Barry waved to him, then stuck his finger up in the air, indicating that the building had been cleared. Magee nodded in acknowledgement, then hurried up the concrete steps to the doorway. Kavanagh came up behind Barry at the same time.

'We're in,' Kavanagh said. 'You get back out front and keep us covered while we fill the car up with whatever we find down in that basement. If you see anyone - I mean anyone at all - put their fuckin' lights out.'

Barry nodded. 'Right.' He hurried back along the corridor, through the swirling, choking smoke, until he reached the front of the building. Passing the administrative area, he glanced in and saw two men in RUC uniforms sprawled out on the floor, both shredded by bullets and the shrapnel from the hand grenade, bloody and frozen in a welter of debris: wood splinters, broken glass and scorched, scattered papers. Trying to control the churning of his stomach, he went to the front of the building and looked out on the lamplit street.

'Oh, Jesus!' he whispered.

The explosions and the gunfire had awakened the whole village. Now lights were blinking on along the whole length of the road and people were stepping out of their houses. Some of those people were off-duty police officers, two of whom were running towards the police station, one still jerking the braces of his pants up over his shoulders, the other with his handgun at the ready.

Barry let them come. He tried to buy as much time as possible. He waited until the first man was about fifty feet away, in the middle of the road, then he fired a short burst from his submachine gun, stitching the ground directly in front of the man, hoping to make him turn back. The man did not turn back. He *jumped* back, spinning sideways, then cut directly across the road and ran towards the police station, hugging the front wall of the petrol station. When he was between the petrol pumps and the office of the petrol station, he fired his first shot. It was a wild, blind shot, clearly fired on impulse, and the bullet struck the wall high above Barry's head to shatter the bricks and shower him in debris. Barry fired back instinctively, holding his finger on the trigger, a sustained burst, and the policeman went into convulsions before practically somersaulting backward and falling against a petrol pump.

Barry stopped firing. He was frightened of hitting the petrol pump. He turned back to the front and saw the second policeman, also wearing civilian clothing, letting one side of his braces snap down on his shoulder in order to wrench his handgun from its holster. He looked comical out there. He looked terribly human. Barry closed his eyes, shutting out what he was doing, but opened them when he heard his weapon firing and felt it jolting his arms. He saw the man staggering backwards, an epileptic, limbs flailing, as other bullets made a quilt work of the road around his feet, spitting powder that formed smoky arabesques when he fell onto his back.

The other people, who had opened their front doors, irresistibly curious, now fearfully stepped back into their houses and slammed the doors shut.

All but one.

Another man, obviously a third policeman, came out of a nearby house, wearing an open-necked shirt and pants held up with braces, holding a pistol in one hand and lowering it to fire at Barry even as he was crossing the road. At precisely that moment, the Ford saloon came roaring out of the alleyway to Barry's right, between the police station and the petrol station, to make a sharp right turn and screech to a halt. Ignoring the policeman racing towards him, Barry went down the steps, taking two or three at a time, hardly aware that he was doing so, and fired his submachine gun on the run, covering a broad arc that took in the advancing policeman. The policeman's kneecaps exploded. His anguished screaming cut like a knife. His legs bent outwards at unnatural angles and then gave way beneath him. He fell face-down on the road and rolled over, then went into spasms caused by pain as he screamed at the moon.

The rear door of the Ford was flung open and Barry dived in.

'Go, for fuck's sake!' Kavanagh bawled.

Barry closed the door behind him. The Ford roared and raced away. Barry huddled up in the back seat, beside McClusky, and burst into tears.

'We fuckin' did it,' Kavanagh said, sounding brutally excited, sitting up there in front beside Seamus Magee, who was driving hell for leather out of the village. 'We got most of what was down there. A really great haul of weapons and ammunition and...' Hearing Barry's distraught sobbing, he glanced back over his shoulder. 'What the hell's the matter with you? We pulled it off, boyo. *We did it!*'

But Barry kept sobbing. He couldn't stop the tears from flowing. He was seeing the three policemen, all just out of their beds, all in pants and braces, all comically, pathetically, human as they went to their deaths. He was seeing the pieces of bone that had exploded from the kneecaps butchered by his wide arc of gunfire. He was seeing, perhaps for the first and final time, the harsh reality of what he had been doing. He was seeing his destiny.

'You're fuckin' out of it,' Kavanagh said, sounding disgusted, 'for the foreseeable future. We pulled it off, we've resurrected the whole movement, and this is how you respond. You've just blown it, you eejit.'

Barry sobbed like a child.

Chapter Five

1

'I don't want to go and see Granny,' Johnny said as Albert put on his coat and wee Billy, who was keen to go for his own reasons, stood patiently waiting.

'You're goin',' Albert said, 'and that's all there is to it. She'll be expectin' to see you and her feelings will be hurt if you don't turn up. More so because of her tragedy. She needs the company, like.'

He was referring to the loss of his father, Brian, who had passed away a couple of months back. Brian had died suddenly in the middle of a flu epidemic, catching a fatal dose of it and dying as so many others, though mostly children, had been doing at that particular time. Johnny, Billy and Marlene were surprised by this because they all thought that only children could die of the flu and so far neither one of them had, though other children they knew had. Granddad had died of it, however, and their dad had come back from England to help his mother sort out the funeral and bury Granddad up in the Belfast Cemetery.

It had all happened quickly, with no warning, and was over soon enough to hardly affect the children, none of whom had really fully comprehended it. Their Dad had only cried once, the evening after the funeral, and their Mum hadn't shed a single tear, though she had smoked an awful lot of cigarettes, so it didn't seem too bad. Only Doreen, their Granny, had been affected by it, but she didn't live with them, so they only saw the change in her when they went to visit her.

Johnny was slightly frightened of Doreen these days because she had changed since the funeral and now seemed to be slightly mad. That's why he didn't want to go and see her. The thought of mad people frightened him.

'I still don't want to go,' Johnny insisted.

'I do,' Marlene said. 'Dad says Granny's got a dog now, and I want to see it.'

'And besides,' wee Billy said, 'we might get some money. She normally gives us money to spend on the Twelfth.'

'That's right,' Marlene said. She was now fourteen and had developing breasts that she always tried to hide by slumping her shoulders. She was already at the door, wearing a loose skirt and overcoat, ready to leave, and her shoulders were distinctly slumped. 'She'll probably give us some money to spend at the field tomorrow, so come on, Johnny, let's go.'

'I don't – '

'Shut your gob,' his mother interjected, 'and put your coat on and get out of my sight. I'm exhausted looking after the lot of you, so I could do with a wee break - have a smoke, play some music. So out you all go.'

'Well, alright, then,' Johnny said reluctantly and walked across the small room to take his coat off one of the hooks behind the door. 'I just don't want to, that's all.'

'Move it, kiddo,' his Dad said, affecting the kind of American vernacular that he was fond of, particularly since going to work in England where, presumably, they spoke it in the showbusiness circles that he claimed to move in during his spare time, when not working as a joiner in a factory in Birkenhead.

'So where are you goin' after you've seen your Mum?' Mary asked of her husband.

Albert shrugged. 'Haven't thought about it,' he said. 'After sayin' hello to Granny, Marlene's comin' back to play with Donna King, so I'll take the other two for a wee wander around town - maybe Smithfield market and down to the Yard to see the boats. Don't worry about us. We'll be back by tea-time.'

Johnny wished that *he* was going to play with Donna King, even though her steady green gaze still unnerved him. Johnny thought of Donna King a lot. That was his secret sin, though everyone seemed to know about it. At least, they were always pulling his leg about it, particularly Marlene, Donna's dearest friend.

'Just you keep away from the pubs,' Mary said as she sank into a chair in front of the fireplace and lit up a cigarette. 'I don't want them children hanging around a pub while you're inside havin' a good time.'

'Look who's talking,' Albert said.

'What does that mean?'

'Nothin',' Albert said.

He had been working in Birkenhead, England, for just over a year now, normally coming home for a long weekend every six weeks, but was now home for the two weeks of his summer holidays. Normally, when he was away for his six-week stint, working as a joiner during the day and performing in various variety halls in Birkenhead and Liverpool in the evenings, Mary would occasionally, say four or five times a week, go off to the pub, taking Johnny with her when he asked, which he often did, being the only one who was home at lot in the evenings, not running wild in the streets, like Billy, or practically living in Donna King's house, like Marlene. As women weren't allowed to go into the pubs alone, Mary would wait outside, smoking fag after fag, hoping to see a male friend who might take her in with him and, in the meantime, asking any single man who was entering to do just that. Invariably, if some man agreed to do so, she would send out a fizzy drink to Johnny and, indeed, would emerge every thirty minutes or so to check if he was all right, ask him if he didn't want to go back home on his own, and, when he insisted that he didn't, which he always did, offer him another drink to keep him going. It wasn't that Johnny didn't want to go home alone, but, rather, that he was fascinated by the kind of people who would go into pubs on a regular basis, which his Mum did, even though a lot of the neighbours disapproved. So Johnny spent a lot of nights standing outside pubs, feeling lonesome on the one hand but somehow adult on the other. Either way, he thought it was a perfectly normal situation and he really enjoyed getting those fizzy drinks.

'Nothing?' Mary said to Albert. 'What are you getting at?'

'Nothin',' Albert repeated. 'Come on, Johnny, get that coat on properly, for God's sake, and let's get out of here.'

'Just make sure you keep my kid's away from them pubs.'

'I will,' Albert said.

As Johnny was putting on his coat, with a great show of reluctance, he failed to understand why his Mum was so worried about his Dad leaving him and Billy standing outside a pub when she did the very same thing in his absence. Sometimes, when his Mum left the pub at the end of the evening, she left alone; at other times, though, she left with the man who had escorted her in and often brought him back to the house for what she daintily described as 'a wee nightcap'. At such times, Johnny, Billy and Marlene were sent up to their beds.

Mum was really popular. She had lots of men friends. Invariably, when Johnny, Billy and Marlene were out on a whole day's jaunt, which she often encouraged them to do, making them sandwiches and giving them hot or cold drinks in a Thermos flask, they would return in the late afternoon to find the front door locked. In such cases, they would, as instructed, go round the back of the house by way of the entry, stinking of urine and littered with those rubber things used only by grown-ups, to enter the back yard and find the window of the kitchen slightly open, enabling them to climb through and enter the house that way. When they did so, they often found their Mum stretched out on the sofa with a man friend, obviously having shared some drinks and cigarettes with him. Invariably she told them that she and her friend had been listening to the radio or playing records on the phonograph: Hank Williams, Tennessee Ernie Ford, or Frankie Laine.

Johnny, Billy and Marlene never talked about this, though Marlene often fell into her sullen silences while the men were there. Johnny sometimes thought about it, but found himself trying not to and instead concentrated on the fact that even while his dad was away, which he was most of the time these days, Mum always looked after them really well, ensuring that there was food on the table and that their clothes were washed and pressed for school. She asked for nothing in return, except that they not talk about her men friends to their dad - and so far none of them had, because they liked their Mum so much.

'Bye, Mum,' Johnny said when he had finally put his coat on properly.

'See ya later,' Billy said.

Marlene said nothing.

'Youse all have a good day now,' Mary said, 'while I have a well earned break.'

'Sure they will,' Albert said, opening the front door and clearly keen to be away. 'I'll make sure of it. Okay, kids, let's make tracks.'

Mary was already puffing away when they left the house, stepping into the late morning's pearly-grey light and instantly assailed by the pounding of Bert Wilson's Lambeg drum. Preparing to lead his own Lodge on the following day's march to Finaghy Field, wearing an open-necked striped shirt, trousers held up with braces, and his bedroom slippers, Bert was standing out in the middle of the road, under a recently constructed ceremonial arch, beating away at his huge, vividly decorated drum for all he was worth, making a blood-stirring racket. A lot of the neighbours were out on their doorsteps or at their garden gates, watching him with amused or admiring grins while conversing with each other or doing up the front of their houses: washing the front-door steps or the outside of the windows, putting up even more red-white-and-blue streamers. A lot of the windowsills were worn away where the housewives sharpened their knives on them, year in and year out.

'He's up early,' Albert said, gazing at Bert Wilson with no great deal of admiration. 'They should place that oul goat and his Lambeg drum on the stage of a proper music hall and watch the audience flood towards the exit. Come on, kids, let's go.'

They walked along a road that could have been in another world. A mass of brightly-coloured bunting criss-crossed the street, from window to window. Union Jacks were flying from all the houses except those of the Catholics, including the Laverys, who, with the other few Fenians in the avenue, were keeping a low profile this week and would continue to do so until after the Twelfth. Even though the brick arches still existed, the annual triumphal arch of wood and cardboard, spanning the whole width of the street, had been built between two houses on opposite sides of the road. Painted a vivid orange, it had been further enhanced with garish paintings of members of the Royal Family, King William crossing the Boyne on his white charger to defeat the Catholic Stuarts, various royal crowns, Jacob's ladder, open Bibles, the insignia of various Orange Lodges, and an enormous rainbow that swept from one side of the arch to the other. The real arches, the ones of brick, had been similarly decorated and the whole street was a riot of red-white-and blue paper, and linen rosettes.

What the Laverys thought of all this was anybody's business, though Johnny certainly felt a little embarrassed for them and was pleased that Teddy, at least, was back at sea at this particular time.

At the opening on the near side of the arches, a big bonfire, about fifteen feet high, had been raised with tree trunks and branches, broken-up furniture, sticks, cardboard boxes and lots of other burnable material. It was surmounted with a six-foot high cardboard effigy of the Pope, who would be burned to a cinder once the bonfire was lit that evening. When Albert led his children under the real arches, they saw crude paintings and effigies of the Pope and other Catholic heroes propped up at street corners. They had been there for days, ironically collecting pennies for Protestant charities. Later that evening, when the bonfire was lit, they would, like the painting of the Pope, now resting on top of the pyramidal bonfire, be ritualistically consigned to the flames - burnt to death, as it were, for their sins.

Albert led his three children farther along the avenue, heading for the heavily Loyalist street, located just off the Broadway, where his mother Doreen still lived, though with a dog instead of her husband these days.

'What did you say Granny's new dog is called, Dad?' Marlene asked.

'You,' Albert said.

'What?'

'She calls it "you",' Albert explained. 'That's all she calls it. She says "you" this and "you" that, and if you ask her about it, she'll say it's just a mindless dog and if you say "you do this" or "you do that" to it, it's going to do it. So she just calls it "you".'

Marlene glanced at Johnny and Billy. Both were rolling their eyes.

'So when are you gonna bring us all over to England, Dad?' Johnny asked. 'I mean, it must be real great over there. Real exotic, like.'

'What's that mean?' Billy asked.

'Colourful and foreign,' Johnny explained. 'So is it exotic, Dad?'

'It's a piss-hole just like here,' Albert said, 'but it has its good sides. I mean, there's more opportunities over there if you're willin' to go for them.'

'So when are you gonna take us over there?' Marlene asked, still desperate for any kind of sign that he cared for her and missed her when he was away. The first time he had come back for a long weekend, after an absence of six weeks, Marlene had rushed at him and threw her arms around him. In response, he had stiffened, then gently

184

but persistently took hold of her wrists, tugged her arms apart, then pushed her away from him. Marlene had run up the stairs to cry for hours in her bedroom. She had not tried to embrace him since that day and he had not embraced her.

'Ack, I don't know,' he said. 'I mean, the place might not suit youse. Sure you'd probably prefer it here, with your friends and the like, than you would over there with them English. I don't know that yer Mum would like it either, but who knows? It might come to that.'

'I wanna go on the boat,' Billy said. 'Even if it's just for a wee holiday.'

'Sure I'll fetch youse all over for a few days,' Albert promised as they turned into the street where Granny lived.

'When?' Johnny asked.

Albert raised his hands in the air, palms turned upward, while shrugging his shoulders. 'Who knows?' he said.

'Is it a nice wee dog?' Marlene asked.

'Ackaye,' her dad said.

He hammered the brass knocker against the door. Instantly, a savage, shockingly loud barking and snarling emanated from inside and something heavy thudded repeatedly against the other side of the door, making it shake. Marlene and Johnny both took a step backward, terrified by the noise, watching the door shake, realising that the thudding was the sound of large paws coming down repeatedly on the wood-panelling.

'Sounds like King Kong,' wee Billy said, though he didn't look as fearless as he sounded.

The barking, snarling and thudding continued unabated, becoming, if anything, even more ferocious.

'She uses it as a watchdog,' Albert explained. 'It's a big bastard, right enough. Hey, Mum!' he bawled through the shaking door, trying to make himself heard over the barking, snarling and thudding. 'It's me! Albert! Quieten that animal down, for God's sake, and open the door!'

'YOU!' Granny snapped, her voice cracking like a whip from inside the small living room. 'Shut yer yappin' and get back in this room or sure as chickens make eggs you'll get a good tannin' with my belt. YOU! You hear me? I said YOU!'

The barking, snarling and dreadful thudding continued, with the front door still visibly shaking each time the monster's paws hammered against it. Then Granny spoke again, this time sounding louder, having advanced to the hallway, saying, 'YOU! Get away from there, you brute! Sure I warned you! *Take that*!' Crack, crack, went the strap, followed by a piteous howling far removed from what had preceded it, then the thudding on the door abruptly ceased. 'You hear me? I'll teach you to be disobedient! Take that, you dumb brute!' Crack, crack, went the strap again, followed by more piteous wailing, this time fainter because it was in the living room. Then merciful silence.

When the front door started opening, Johnny and Marlene took another step backward. Granny appeared in the doorway, looking the same as always - as hard as nails. She stared from Albert to each of the children in turn, not offering a smile.

'Ack, you've come,' she said to Albert.

'Aye, Mum.'

'Sure that's grand. Come in.'

Albert started into the house, following his mother, but none of the children behind him moved.

'I'm not going in there,' Marlene said.

'Me neither,' Johnny said.

'Sure it's only an ould dog,' wee Billy said, taking a resolute step forward.

The sudden barking of the dog reverberated throughout the whole house, making wee Billy step back again.

'Sure didn't I tell you to shut yer gob!' Granny snapped in the living room. Crack, crack, went the strap and the barking again collapsed into piteous whining.

'All right, kids,' Albert said, stepping back out to grab wee Billy and Johnny, dragging them both inside before they could protest. 'It's quietened down now. No sweat. You, too, Marlene. Close the front door behind you when you come in.'

They all entered Doreen's house.

2

In the dark, damp and dusty living room, they found a huge brute of an Alsatian dog resting on its belly in a narrow space formed by the end of a threadbare sofa and the wall. Granny was standing over it, holding a leather strap in her right hand, glaring down at it. The dog, which was breathing heavily and dribbling slightly from its mouth, was looking up at her with big, brown, terrified eyes, clearly begging forgiveness for its sins. When Albert and the children entered the living room, a low growl emerged from the beast's throat, but when Granny raised her right hand the growl turned into another piteous whimper. Granny nodded, as if satisfied with what she was seeing, then lowered the strap to her side and went back to her chair at one end of the table positioned beneath the front window. Normally she sat there all day long, looking out on the street and its daily flood of sinful riffraff. Now she indicated the torn, threadbare sofa with an airy wave of her right hand.

'You childern can sit there,' she said. 'Sure that wee dog won't bother you at all.' Turning to Albert, she indicated the chair facing her own across the table. 'Put yer backside down there, son.'

Albert sat down while the kids stared at the dog which, though now whimpering, was huge in that small corner and still had what looked like flecks of foam around its impressive jaws.

'Sit down, for Jasus' sake,' Albert said as he flipped a cigarette into his mouth. 'Sure it's not gonna bite you.'

'I'll sit here,' Marlene said, practically diving at the far side of the sofa, well away from the dog.

'I'm the smallest,' wee Billy said, 'so I'll sit in the middle.' And he sat there before Johnny could respond, thus forcing him to take the only remaining space, at the near end of the sofa, right beside the huge Alsatian, which had stopped whimpering, but was now panting noisily.

'Can I get you all a wee cuppa tea?' Granny asked, smiling for the first time.

'No!' the three kids cried out simultaneously, being frightened of what the dog might do if Granny left the room.

'Ack, away with ya!' Granny retorted, climbing to her feet and heading for the kitchen. 'Sure I knew you were comin' and the kettle's already on the boil.'

'I still don't want any tea,' Johnny said. 'I just had a cuppa back in the house, Granny.'

'Me, too,' wee Billy said.

'Me, too,' Marlene added.

'I'll have one,' Albert said, thus destroying any hope that Granny might remain in the living room with her savage beast. 'Sure I could do with a cuppa.'

'Right, son,' Granny said, pleased. 'I'll be back in a minute.'

While Doreen was in the kitchen, Albert enjoyed his cigarette, distracting himself by blowing smoke rings and watching them dissolving above his head. None of the kids said a word. They kept glancing sideways at the huge, panting Alsatian, but obviously, frightened of Granny's belt, it had given up trying to protect the house. Like most of the houses around the Broadway, it was a cramped two-up, two down, similar to their own, but with no front garden. It had once been a well kept house, but now it was gathering dust and the flowered wallpaper, badly faded, looked mouldy in places. This being a Protestant household, there were no religious icons on the walls or cupboards, though a framed Coronation photo of Queen Elizabeth had pride of place over the Devon grate and was surrounded by framed hymns and Psalms. There were also fading photos of Doreen and Brian when they were younger – to the kids, unimaginably so - plus a couple of photos of Albert, who had clearly once been a handsome man. Significantly, there was no photo of Mary, either with or without Albert.

Doreen soon returned with a pot of tea, two cups and two plates, one containing biscuits, the other pastries that looked like currant squares. She poured the tea for herself and Albert, gave the latter a cup, then passed around the plate of currant-filled pastries.

'Here, have a fly's graveyard,' she said. 'Take one or two each.'

When each of the kids had grabbed a currant pastry, Granny offered the plate to her beloved son. Albert took one to be polite, gobbled it down while holding his second cigarette in his left hand, then immediately proceeded to smoke again while sipping at his hot tea. Granny returned to her chair at the other side of the table, stared grimly out on the street, her personal Sodom and Gomorrah, then glared at the panting Alsatian dog. Its sad brown eyes turned towards her, but then, having caught her fierce glance, it whimpered and lowered its gaze to the floor.

'So when did you get the dog, Granny?' Johnny asked, feeling the desperate urge to make conversation.

'Couple of weeks back,' Doreen replied.

'Where did ya get it?' wee Billy asked, managing to speak even as his cheeks were bulging with a piece of undigested fly's graveyard.

'In the pound,' Doreen said. 'They told me it'd been handed in because it was too vicious an' I wanted an animal with a bit of spirit, like. Sure a poor windowed woman needs protection.'

'Protection from what?' Marlene asked.

'Filth and vermin,' Doreen said grimly, then nodded to indicate the street at the other side of the window. 'All them an' their kind.' She nodded again to indicate the kitchen and the entry beyond the back yard. 'Not forgettin' those who get up to their obscene animal antics out there in the night. Sure it's clear they've no shame - and those without shame are unprincipled and open to anything. My husband used to protect me - he was a decent, Christian man - but now the Lord in His wisdom had taken him away and left me here, all alone. That dog's my protection.'

'Sounds to me,' Albert said with a wicked grin, 'that the folks you're talkin' about - the ones out back at night - would be too busy to attempt breaking in here.'

Doreen didn't see the joke. 'The sinner's never too busy to dream up some more ways of sinnin'. Once they know that a poor widow's unprotected, who knows what they might do?'

'Just be sure that dog doesn't eat *you* alive,' Albert said, still grinning, 'before he gobbles up a potential burglar.'

'He's only vicious with strangers,' Doreen said. 'Sure I've beat the rest out of him. That's a dog that knows his place and will know what to do when it's necess'ry.' She turned to the children. 'Lookin' forward to tonight and tomorrow, are ya?'

'Aye, Granny,' wee Billy said promptly, giving her his big smile in the hope that she might open her purse. Billy wasn't frightened of Granny. Johnny hadn't yet told him that he thought Granny wasn't right in the head.

'What about you, Johnny?'

'Aye, I am.'

'Me, too,' Marlene said.

Granny took no notice of Marlene because she reminded her too much of Mary.

'Aye, sure it's a grand time of the year alright,' she said, nodding vigorously. 'A time to remind ourselves that this is a Protestant country and intends to remain that way.'

'Sure we'll see you tonight, won't we, Granny?' Billy asked because she still hadn't reached for her purse.

But Doreen shook her head gravely from side to side. 'No, not tonight. I'm not up to it this year. It's still too close to the passing away of your granddad, God bless him, and I simply wouldn't have the strength for it. Sure a tragedy like that weighs upon a woman and leaves her drained of all life.'

It seemed to Johnny that the last year had been filled with deaths. First Granddad, struck down by the same flu epidemic that had killed a lot of children and adults in Belfast. The epidemic had hardly passed when a local boy, Bobby Dixon, who had been in Johnny's class at school, was killed when he went to some woods beside the Lagan River to chop off the thicker branches of trees for a Halloween bonfire. One of his friends had swung his axe at a branch while Bobby was kneeling down, sorting out the branches already chopped off, and Bobby had stood up just as the axe was swinging, thus having his head practically chopped off and, of course, dying instantly. Another friend, Jimmy Pearson, had died by simply jumping off a trolley bus when it was still moving, falling onto the road, and then getting run over by a passing car. Other people, adults and children alike, had died, as they did every year, from TB. It had therefore become almost commonplace for Johnny to see black-cloth bows tied to door knockers, wreathes of wax-paper flowers being delivered to the houses of the bereaved, blinds drawn for three days and, finally, the long black hearses pulling up in front of local houses to take the dead away in their coffins. The hearses used to be pulled by big horses; now the hearses were long, black limousines.

Worst of all, however, was when Granny, who loved visiting the dead while they lay at rest in their parlours at home, would insist on taking Johnny to view the corpse and then, most nightmarish of all, pull back the black veil over the coffin and make him give the corpse a 'final kiss' on its wax-like forehead. Johnny often had nightmares about kissing the dead and he blamed Granny for them.

'You children have a good time without me, though,' Granny was now saying, sounding funereal. 'Don't let my personal suffering effect you. I'll be as right as rain sittin' here at home, listenin' to the radio and watchin' all them out there getting' up to their filthy, unChristian antics. Sure that street's a disgrace.'

'Aye, that and the entry behind you,' Albert said, having his sly little dig.

'That as well,' Granny said, missing the humour entirely. 'So where are you all off to this afternoon?'

'Just a walk around town,' Albert said. 'Keep the kids out of mischief until tonight and give Mary a wee break from us all.'

'Oh, it's a wee break she needs, is it? Her that's rarely at home. In my day, a woman did her duty, no matter what, and that duty included lookin' after the childern and keeping a clean house, all spit and polish, like.'

Johnny glanced around Granny's house to take note of the mouldy paper and dust. Their own house was a lot cleaner than this, despite the fact that his Mum insisted on doing her housework only in the evenings, between when she stopped working at the weaving mill and when she went out for an evening's fun. Johnny looked back at Granny, trying to stare into her eyes, but he either saw, or imagined seeing, the mad gleam in their glassy greyness, so he lowered his gaze on the instant, feeling slightly fearful.

'Mary doesn't do so badly,' Albert said, always quick to state the opposite to what he truly believed if it helped to avoid any kind of friction. 'The kids are clean and well fed, which is more than can be said for some of their friends. Are you sure you don't want to come along to the house tonight? To join in the celebrations, like?'

'What? And me still in mourning? Sure I'd end up bein' the talk of the street. Get away with ya, son!'

Albert sighed, put his empty cup back on the table, then stubbed his cigarette out in the ashtray. 'Okay, then. I just thought I'd ask. Now we'd best be makin' tracks. I promised the kids I'd take them to a fillum this afternoon, the matinée show, so we'll have to hoof it if we want to get there on time. Right, on your feet, kids.'

Glancing wide-eyed at each other, having been promised no such thing, but hoping it might be true, Johnny and Marlene jumped to their feet and started for the door. Wee Billy, however, sat on. He gave Doreen a big smile and said, 'A real pity you can't see the parade tomorrow, Granny, 'cause I'm holdin' the string of a banner for my Lodge.'

'Sure you're not! Away with ya!'

Billy nodded vigorously. 'Aye, Granny, I am.'

'Did you join the Orange Lodge then?'

'Aye, Granny, I did. I mean, I thought it was the thing to do, like. I mean, at my age an' all.'

Johnny, who had not joined the junior Orange Lodge, either last year, when he was Billy's age, or this year, felt like killing his younger brother for that remark. Granny, on the other hand, was visibly excited by this wonderful news and immediately climbed to her feet to reach out for the purse on the mantelpiece.

'Sure that's a grand thing to do,' she said, picking the purse up and opening it. 'Pity some others didn't think of doing the same thing at your age,' she added, glancing accusingly at Johnny, 'but then we can't expect everything.' She beamed down at wee Billy, who had formerly been, in her eyes, a real trouble-maker, bound for Borstal, but had seemingly changed overnight to become a real, or at least an Orange, saint. 'I'm so proud of you, Billy. Here! I nearly forgot. Take this shillin' and buy yourself somethin' with it when you get to the field. We can't let a boy holding the string of a banner go unrewarded.'

'He gets paid for doing it,' Johnny reminded her.

'Never mind that,' Granny said. 'Sure that's the Lodge's business. But here,' she added, handing Johnny and Marlene each a sixpence, which was half a shilling. 'You get yourselves something as well, when you go to the field to congratulate your brother.'

'Thanks, Granny,' Johnny said.

'Yeah, thanks,' Marlene said. 'Can we go now, Dad?'

'Aye, we'd better get out of here quick if we want to catch that fillum. See you, Mum.'

He turned his cheek to Doreen, to receive a sodden kiss, before hurrying out of the house.

'Oh, my wee Billy, I'm so proud of you,' Doreen repeated, then she kissed each of the children on the cheek, receiving a smile only from Billy.

'Sure I'll do ya proud, Granny,' Billy said.

'I'm sure you will, son.'

Johnny and Marlene were already outside when Billy finally left the small, gloomy house, closing the door behind him.

'Sure I thought that dog was goin' to eat us alive,' he said.

'It should have eaten *you*,' Johnny retorted.

'Let's hoof it,' Albert said, heading off along the street at a cracking pace, as if he really *did* want to catch that film.

The kids rushed to catch up with him.

3

'Can I go now, Dad?' Marlene said, clearly relieved to have done her duty by her hated granny and now keen to go back to the avenue to join Donna.

'Aye, you go off now,' Albert said, 'and leave us men to do the things men do.'

'What's that?' Billy asked.

'Never mind,' Albert said. 'Away you go, Marlene, but don't you spend all of that sixpence. Leave some for tomorrow.'

'Aye, Dad. Sure I'll see youse all later.'

As Marlene hurried back to the avenue, Albert led the boys in the opposite direction.

'Are we really going to see a fillum, Dad?' Johnny asked hopefully when they reached the Donegall Road, just across from the Windsor Picture House.

'Are ya kiddin' me or what?' Albert responded, affronted, leading them away from the picture house, obviously heading for Sandy Row. Cars and trolley buses passed by in both directions, creating a lot of noise and exhaust fumes. 'Do you think I'm made of money? I mean, it's bonfire night tonight and the Twelfth tomorrow - all fun and games, like - and you want to go to the pictures as well? Are you out of yer mind or what?'

'But you said…'

'Never mind what I said. Sure you know what Granny's like. Give her the slightest excuse and she'll keep you there yarnin' all day. Now is that what you wanted?'

'Well, no, but you said...'

'So I got you out, didn't I? Stop complainin' about the pictures and instead say yer thanks that you're not still sittin' there, smellin' that mouldy oul dog and listenin' to yer Granny talkin' nine to the dozen about nothin' that makes any sense. I mean, show me some gratitude!'

Johnny was crushed with disappointment, but there was nothing to say. He was, at least, sixpence richer than he had been, though that made him a lot less rich than wee Billy, whom he still felt like strangling.

'So where are we goin', Dad?' Billy asked. 'Are we goin' to Smithfield Market, like you said?'

All the kids loved Smithfield Market, which they thought was a kind of Treasure Island, filled with fabulous things. Even Johnny was keen to go there.

'Aye,' Albert replied. 'Don't worry about it. I just thought we'd take in the Row first, to see what's happening there.'

Johnny's heart sank as they continued along the Donegall Road, passing the public park, side streets of terraced houses, all with their individual arches and the traditional paper streamers and Union Jacks; then the public library, which was also displaying a Union Jack, a real big one, and gradually approaching Sandy Row which, as he knew, contained an awful lot of pubs. His dad liked to drink in those pubs and had often performed in them, singing, dancing and doing impersonations, so he was unlikely to be able to walk the length of the Row without meeting at least a few of his old cronies and fans, some of whom would invite him in for a drink. As Johnny knew, his dad rarely refused a drink and was unlikely to do so today. In fact, it was the drink that almost certainly was making him cut through the Row to get to Smithfield Market. Fat chance that he would make it that far.

'Why don't we go down Great Victoria Street instead,' Johnny said, still hoping. 'We can have a look at the railway station, like.'

'Sure you've seen that railway station a million times,' Albert responded, 'and can see it any day of the year.'

'Or we could check on what's showing at the Royal Hippodrome,' Johnny said desperately.

'Jasus, lad, this is the eleventh! Tomorrow's the Twelfth! I mean, you've got to see the Row at this time of the year 'cause it's done up real grand. It's the best done-up street in town. I mean, it's something you really shouldn't miss. So we'll cut through that way, have a gander at the Row, then, dependin' on what's happenin' there, we'll decide what to do next.'

Johnny and Billy glanced at each other with raised eyebrows, though neither said a word. Their eyebrows were raised even higher when they turned into Sandy Row.

The long main street was done up like their own street, but even more so, with no less than three arches straddling the road, all covered in garish Loyalist murals. There were so many streamers criss-crossing the street, from one side to the other, it looked like a sky made up of fluttering papers of many colours, instead of clouds. Every single upstairs window had a Union Jack fluttering from it and there were huge painted letters on the gable ends, stating:

NO POPE HERE!
GOD SAVE THE QUEEN
REMEMBER 1689
NO SURRENDER!

'No surrender!' was the cry that had first been made by the beleaguered Protestants of Derry during the siege of 1689. Going to national schools, Johnny and his friends had been taught practically nothing about Irish history and only a little about English history, though they were certainly stuffed with tales about the Protestant faith and the horrors of Rome. They had also been taught about the attack on Derry by Catholic Redshanks and Jacobites led by King James II and of how, refusing to surrender during a siege that lasted for 105 days, enduring a daily rain of shells, bombs and cannon balls, then further decimated by fever and starvation, the Protestant defenders of the city had been reduced to the eating of horses, rats, mice and dogs fattened on the meat of slain Irish. Nevertheless, even after 15,000 of them had died, including most of the children, they had refused to surrender, and eventually the enemy had retreated. According to what Johnny had learnt at school, that epic defence, in the short term, had given King William of Orange the breathing space he needed in his war with Louis XIV, enabling him to have the base that he required in Ireland in order to drive out the forces of King James. The Battle of the Boyne, the following year, won by William of Orange, secured parliamentary rule over Ulster and ensured the survival of the Protestant plantation. In the long term, however, the same epic defence, combined with the Battle of the Boyne, had given inspiration to Ulster Protestants for more than three centuries - an inspiration that survived to the present day.

Right now, Sandy Row, a fervently Loyalist enclave, was in a state of high excitement, with a lot of people out in the streets and a couple of Lambeg drummers making a ferocious din. Sandy Row had always been a lively place packed with shops named Sarah Jane's, Wee Mack's, Ginny Dickson's, Mary Best's, Tommy Thompson's, the Guttery Gap and, incongruously, Le Taste, selling vegetables, fish, meat, bread (including potato bread and soda farls), cakes, newspapers and cigarettes and sweets, clothes (McCance's for shirts and socks, McCurry's for shoes) school uniforms, furniture, wallpaper and paint. It also had a wide variety of pubs (the Big Boyne, the Wee Boyne, the Aghalee, the Albion, the Mayola, the Klondyke and the Clock), billiard halls, bookies, chippies and, of course, pawnbrokers. As many of the local housewives were preparing for the festivities of this evening and tomorrow, while their men worked themselves into the festive mood in the pubs, most of these establishments were doing great business. Being off school and waiting impatiently for Bonfire Night to begin, a lot of kids were out in the street, playing Pirrie 'n Whip, Swinging Around the Lamps, Marbles, Churchie-one-over, Hopscotch, Rolling Hoops, and, of course, though only at the 'openings' in the side streets, football.

'Sure isn't this a great sight to see?' Albert said, as he flipped another cigarette into his mouth and led them along the colourful, frantically busy, noisy thoroughfare. 'Would you wanna miss this for the pictures?'

Johnny would have happily missed almost anything for a chance to see a film, but now aware that it wasn't going to happen, he tried to compensate by letting himself be swept up in the excitement of the street.

'Aye,' he said, 'this is really great.'

'Aye, it's grand,' Billy said. 'But it's gonna be better tonight when they light those bonfires.'

A lot of bonfires had been raised in this area, at least two in the Row itself and others, smaller ones, in its web of terraced side streets. By midnight, when all the bonfires were burning, it would seem as if the whole city was ablaze.

'Hi, Joe! How are you?' Albert said, giving a nod to a big brute of a man who was leaning against the wall of a corner pub, smoking a cigarette while watching the world go by.

'Not bad at all, Albert. How's yourself?'

'Sure I'm doin' grand, Joe. See you later.'

'Aye, you will, right enough.'

Walking on with his two boys in tow, Albert offered a nod here, a wave there. He was well known along the Row as a local entertainer, doing all the pubs and, occasionally, something really posh like the Grand Opera House (though well down on the billing list) or the Ulster Hall, the city's main concert venue, where he was a barely listed, though always a well received, minor turn. So, he was a well-known personality, much beloved by all, and could certainly not walk the length of the Row without being greeted by fans and old friends. Unfortunately, at least for Johnny and Billy, most of the latter were seasoned boozers who enjoyed Albert's showbusiness blarney over a pint or two.

'Sure it's grand to see you back, Albert,' one of those friends, Victor Fletcher, now said, having just crossed the beribboned road from the side street in which he lived, emerging from a cloud of his own cigarette smoke to shake Albert's hand. A dishevelled, undernourished creature in a badly stained, frayed grey suit, he had a nose as angular and red as a parrot's wing, a prominent Adam's apple, and pale, watery blue eyes tinged with the crimson light of a tropical sunset. Another boozer, as Johnny instantly ascertained. 'We've really missed ya since you've bin workin' over there in the Big Smoke.'

'Not London,' Albert instantly corrected him. 'Birkenhead.'

'Ackaye, sure that's right. So let's have a wee get-together jar, Albert, and you can tell us all about it.'

'Well...' Albert hesitated.

'Smithfield Market,' Johnny reminded him.

'Aye,' wee Billy said. 'Either that or the pictures and we're too late for them, so let's go, Dad.'

'For Jasus sake,' Fletcher, said, 'we haven't seen you for months and today's the fuckin' eleventh, for fuck's sake, tomorrow bein' the Twelfth, like, an' some of the lads will be already in there...' He nodded, indicating the door of the pub they were standing outside... 'so they'll be quare disappointed if I tell 'em you were here and didn't want to come in. Sure it's just a few wee jars, Albert.'

'Aye, right,' Albert said.

He pondered for a few seconds, his conscience flickering on and off before blinking out entirely, then he dipped into his trouser pocket and withdrew a couple of coins, transferred one to his free hand, then clenched both fists and held them out to the kids. 'I'm just goin' in for a quick one with Dan,' he said, looking utterly sincere, 'so why don't you two – '

'Smithfield Market,' Johnny interjected.

' - take yourselves down to Smythe's, buy yourselves somethin', have a wander up and down, then come back here in an hour or so.'

'Smithfield Market,' Johnny stubbornly repeated.

'Aye, right,' Albert responded without a pause. 'Buy yourselves somethin' at Smythe's and then wander along to the market and, you know, maybe pick up a comic or book at Harry Hall's with what's left of the money. See you back here at, let's say...' He checked his recently purchased wristwatch. 'Five o'clock.'

'That's four hours away,' Johnny said.

'Great,' wee Billy said, snatching the coin from his dad's left hand. 'We can do everything we want in that time and still be home in time for the bonfire.'

'Right,' Albert said, flushed with gratitude, as Johnny took the coin from his other hand. 'My thought exactly. I can have a few wee pints with the lads here, while you two have a boy's day out without your Mum, or even Marlene, complainin'. Everyone's happy, like. Okay?'

'Okay,' Johnny said.

'Good boys,' Albert said, patting each of them on the head, then giving both of them a gentle push to encourage them on their way. Without looking back to see their dad enter the pub, they walked straight to the end of the Row, turned into Hope Street, and stopped in front of the plate-glass window of Smythe's shop, which was dominated by enormous, mouth-watering slabs of home-made honeycomb, yellowman, and rhubarb rock, surrounded by jars filled with all kinds of sweets, including teeth-cracking brandy balls. They both stood there, staring at the window, in an ecstasy of anguished indecision.

'What are you havin'?' wee Billy asked.

'I dunno,' Johnny said. 'Maybe the yellowman. I love yellowman.'

'I love honeycomb.'

'So do I,' Billy said.

'Why not get a quarter of each?' Billy suggested astutely.

'Aye, I think I'll do that.'

'I love that rhubarb rock as well.'

'And the brandy balls are great.'

'We could have half a quarter of honeycomb and yellowman and just a wee bit of rhubarb rock and some brandy balls.'

'Aye, we could,' Johnny agreed. 'But the honeycomb doesn't last. I mean, it melts really quickly in your mouth and is gone before you can blink. The yellowman and rhubarb rock last longer, so I might get a half of honeycomb and a bit less of the yellowman and the others.'

'Aye, that might be worth thinking about,' Billy said.

Thus they negotiated with each other for five minutes or so, making various calculations, positively writhing with ecstatic frustration. Having made their independent decisions, they entered the shop, started ordering, kept changing their minds, but somehow or other managed eventually to walk out, each carrying a paper cone filled with mixed sweets. As they walked towards Smithfield Market, their jaws crunching and chewing pieces of honeycomb, yellowman, rhubarb rock and brandy balls, they were assailed on all sides by immense gable-end paintings of King William of Orange and other Protestant heroes, as well as with painted slogans. One of these stated:

KICK THE POPE!

'All the popes should be kilt and buried,' Billy managed to say while still chewing a melting lump of yellowman.

'Dead popes aren't buried,' Johnny informed him. 'They're all embalmed like that oul Egyptian Mummy in the museum.'

Both of them inwardly shivered at the very thought of the Mummy, Takabuti, the sight of which gave them the shivers, which is exactly why they went regularly to the museum to see her: they liked to shiver with fear.

'Some day I'm going to Egypt,' Johnny said. 'They have Arabs and camels there. Pyramids as well. Teddy says he saw Arabs and camels along the banks of the Suez Canal, though he didn't see any pyramids. So when I'm old enough, I'm gonna do what Teddy did and join the Navy.'

'Aye,' Billy said. 'That'd be more fun than school. I'd do anything to get away from school. I'd rather clean a public toilet than go to school. That's how much I hate school, like.'

They both hated school. All of their friends hated school. At school they had to sit for hours on plain seats that had no backs, writing with pen and ink taken from the inkwells on their wooden desks, using blotters to dry the ink, or with pencils and rubbers that could be used to rub out misspelled or wrongly used words. At school they had to study English, Maths (generally called 'sums'), Geography and History, using phenomenally boring books known as School Readers. At school they had lots of Bible Studies, including interminable lectures by visiting clergy from Anglican, Presbyterian and Methodist churches, and were presented with certificates proving that they had gained Proficiency in Scripture Knowledge. At school, while learning very little about the history of their own country, Ulster, they were taught a lot of the stories in the New Testament. At school they were caned brutally, on the hands and on the backside, for the slightest infraction - say, giving the wrong answer to a question or sneezing while the teacher was talking - and the pain was something that didn't bear thinking about. At school, if a teacher decided that caning wasn't a brutal enough punishment, he or she would repeatedly strike the back of a pupil's knuckles with the sharp end of a wooden ruler or sometimes even slam the lid of the desk on the pupil's fingers. At school, in the bleak, bricked-in yard that stood in for a playground, they played marbles, swapped cigarette cards, kicked a football, beat one-another up, and tugged the hair or pinched the bottoms of the girls. At school they did a lot of crying, a lot of begging for mercy (both from the teachers and from other pupils), though mostly they suffered a hell of boredom and endless, enervating days. At school they all felt slightly crazy and couldn't wait to get out.

'Oh, great,' Billy said, his cheeks bulging from being stuffed with too much at once, 'there's the market.'

'Great,' Johnny echoed him.

Formerly a square-shaped area used as a cattle market opened in 1780, Smithfield Market was now an immense, glass-roofed building containing a virtual warren of mostly second-hand shops that had their goods spilling out into the criss-crossing, cobblestone passages: mountains of books, seas of magazines and old sheet music, pools of keys and locks, boxes piled high with tools, drawers filled with nuts and bolts, trays heaped with mysterious mechanical parts. Elsewhere there were cameras, bicycles, paintings, records, fire irons, coal buckets, curtains, carpets, clothes hanging from the rafters or from hangars on steel or wooden frames, rows of shoes on the feet of invisible people, antiques and bric-a-brac of all kinds, including exotic items from foreign lands. Strung across the cobblestone central walkway, about fifteen feet above the ground, were signs advertising the bigger, well known shops. The first sign Johnny and Billy saw when they walked in was:

HARRY HALL
BOOKSELLER

Harry's was to their immediate right, a heavenly emporium of plywood walls and wooden uprights, its shelves packed with row upon row of books, magazines and comics of all kinds, both new and second-hand. You could spend hours in there, boldly reading anything you fancied, or just browsing endlessly, because Harry, a good-natured legend in his own time, wouldn't say a word. Directly facing Harry's was a second-hand shop selling everything from pianos to gramophones, radios, sideboards, tables, chairs, pots and pans, cups and saucers and plates, and buckets piled high with old cutlery. Along the whole length of the market on both sides of the central walkway, now webbed in striations of sunlight beaming through the glassed-in roof, were shops selling a wide variety of goods, with another big bookshop, Hugh Greer's, at the far end. Running off the main walkway, in both directions, was a web of narrower, darker passages, all packed with stalls, compartments and alcoves run by shawled women and grimy men selling every imaginable kind of used goods.

Leaving the best to the last, Johnny and Billy plunged into the web of cluttered passages on both sides of the main walkway and made their way up and down, left and right, imagining that they were in another world, an Arab bazaar complete with crowded *souks*, exploring every shop that took their interest, sometimes dropping onto their knees to do so, picking their way with increasingly dirty fingers through piles of junk that included old turbine engines, tyres and tubes, compasses, broken rifles and pistols, Zulu shields and spears, Moroccan knives, Indian saris and silks, cigarette packets from many different countries, Salvation Army tambourines, other musical instruments of all kinds, and cracked, dusty mirrors in which they could make funny faces. Generally they were ignored by the withered old men and women who presided over their grimy warren holes, drinking, eating, smoking or reading while waiting for an offer; though some of them, it is true, would shout out to passers-by while demonstrating their wares, trying to suck in the suckers, and it was these ones who would shake their fists at Johnny and Billy, telling them to clear off 'or else', in which case Johnny and Billy would run away, giggling and breathing hard with excitement.

Eventually, when after a couple of hours of exotic, dusty exploration they had exhausted all possibilities, buying not a single item, they retired to Harry Hall's Bookshop where, greeted warmly and then kindly ignored by Harry, they roamed from shelf to shelf, drawer to drawer, scanning books, magazines and comics. Neither bought anything (Why waste money when Harry let you read for free?), but when they judged that about four hours had passed since leaving their Dad (not having wristwatches, they had learnt to judge time accurately), they left the shop and made their way back to the pub in Sandy Row. The clock on the wall above the door of the pub informed them that the time was 5.15pm. Their Dad wasn't outside waiting for them, but they hadn't really expected him to be.

'He must still be inside,' Johnny said.

'Or in some other pub,' Billy retorted.

'If he's in another pub, we'll never find him. There's too many of them.'

'You'd better go in and see if he's there.'

'No,' Johnny said, embarrassed at the very thought of entering a pub on his own. 'Dad would only be upset if I did that. Let's just wait here and see if he comes out.'

'Wait for how long?' Billy asked.

Johnny shrugged. 'Half an hour,' he said. 'If he doesn't come out by then, we'll start home and maybe, when we pass the other pubs, we'll find him waiting for us outside one of them. If we don't, we'll just go on home. We'll still get there before they light the bonfire.'

'Half an hour's a long time to be standin' here like eejuts doin' nothing.'

'Well, we'll just have to do it.'

'Maybe one of Dad's pals will come along and go in for a drink. If that happens we can ask him to see if Dad's in there or if he's gone somewhere else. We'll tell him to tell Dad, if he's in there, that we're waitin' out here.'

'Aye, okay,' Billy said. 'It's just that I'm gettin' hungry, you know? And it's nearly tea-time.'

'We'll get home for tea-time.'

They stood there for another fifteen minutes, almost deafened by the continuing, relentless pounding of the Lambeg drums, but distracting themselves by watching the drummers and the many other activities taking place in the street between and under the high, vividly decorated arches. Men were pouring in and out of the bookies and pubs, women were packing the shops and stores, and children were running under the arches or playing a variety of games on the crowded pavements. The pungent, vinegary smell of fish and chips, as well as meat pies, being taken home wrapped in paper for tea-time, wafted through the cooling air to torment their nostrils.

'Jesus,' wee Billy exclaimed, 'I'd kill for some fish and chips!'

'We'll probably get some when we get home,' Johnny said hopefully.

'But when's that gonna be?'

At that moment, the door of the pub opened and their Dad peered around its vertical edge. His face was flushed with drink. When he saw them he raised his eyebrows, as if really surprised.

'You're back already!' he exclaimed histrionically.

'It's half past five, Dad,' Johnny said. 'Near to tea-time.'

Albert's eyebrows went up even higher, then he glanced disbelievingly at his wristwatch. 'Well, God Almighty, you're right! Who'd have believed it? Sure time flies like one of them jet planes when you're having a wee jar. Okay, kids, just hang on there for another minute. I'll pop back in an' say goodbye to the boyos and then I'll come out again. Just give me a minute, like.'

They were beginning to think he had forgotten them again when, about fifteen minutes later, he emerged looking even more flushed and happy.

'Right,' he said, 'let's get back to the house before your Mum kills us all.'

He led them back to the avenue, walking straight and steady, not bothering to ask them how they had spent their afternoon, content to know that they were both still alive. The light was starting to dim by the time they reached home, but darkness was still a few hours away and the bonfires would not be lit until dusk. Nevertheless, a lot of neighbours had already gathered at the unlit bonfire or beneath the decorated arch to drink and talk, with children playing and shrieking noisily on all sides. Clearly, then, the fun and games would soon be starting.

'What are we having to eat?' Billy asked, the instant they stepped into the house to find their mother sitting in front of the grate, having a sherry, smoking a fag, and reading a copy of *People's Friend*.

'Fish and chips,' Mary said.

4

Thrilled though they were to be having fish and chips, Johnny and Billy were disgruntled when informed that they had to go straight out again and walk to the chippie to buy the food. Each of them insisted that only one of them was required for this task and that the other should be the one to go, but Mary insisted that they both do it. When the boys then suggested that their Dad could do it, Albert retorted, 'Ack, you're bloody jokin', aren't you? Sure I've been on my feet all day, runnin' you two all over the town, so the least you can do is let me have a rest before the evenin' starts.'

'What do you mean, you ran us..?' Johnny began, but was promptly cut off by his Dad, who, not wanting the truth revealed, quickly said, 'Either you go to that chippie or you starve. Me, I'm not fussed one way or the other. I'll just have a couple of fags and they'll set me to rights.'

Johnny glanced at wee Billy, who shrugged his shoulders in defeat. 'Alright,' Johnny said, 'we'll go. What'll we get?'

'I'll have cod and chips,' Albert said, 'with a helping of mashed peas.'

'I thought you were going to smoke a couple of fags instead,' Johnny said.

'Not if you're going to the chippie,' Albert retorted without a pause, taking a chair and tugging off his shoes to wiggle his toes and fill the air with the aroma of his sweaty socks. 'So cod and chips with mashed peas, thanks.'

'I'll have the same,' Mary said. 'You two can have what you want.'

'What about Marlene?' Johnny asked.

'Don't worry about her. She's still across the street with Donna and she'll probably eat there. Here...' Mary reached into the pocket in the apron she was wearing over her dress and pulled out some coins. She passed these to Johnny. 'That should do it,' she said. 'And don't dilly-dally on the way. We've people coming here for a wee party, which is why I'm not making the supper. You come straight back here, right?'

'Right,' Johnny said.

Reluctantly, he and Billy left the house, walked along the street, past the decorated arch where the crowd had clearly grown rapidly and was becoming a lot rowdier, then turned left at the arches and made their way to the fish-and-chip shop, located near the beginning of the Bog Meadows. The mountains loomed beyond the bogs, the sky darkening as the sun sank behind them. The streets here were virtually seas of fluttering Union Jacks and the fish-and-chip shop, known as 'the chippie', had a really big Union Jack fluttering proudly above its front door. The chippie was packed, the customers were excited, preparing for Bonfire Night, and the people serving were pouring sweat as they raked in the money.

While waiting in the queue, Johnny and Billy heatedly debated what they should have from the extensive menu - fish and chips, fish patties and chips, meat pie and chips, sausage and chips - but eventually, becoming confused, even a little panic stricken, they decided to make life easy by simply asking for four helpings of cod and chips with mashed peas, all drenched in vinegar and salt. When served, they divided the order between them, each meal wrapped in newspaper, and hurried home as quickly as they could without actually running, wanting the food to be still hot when they ate it. Nevertheless, the newspaper-wrapped parcels soon became greasy and warm, giving off a mouth-watering smell that made both of them ravenous.

Back in the house, Johnny gave one of the parcels to his Mum, Billy gave one to his Dad, then the four of them, seated around the fireplace, in which no fire was burning, unwrapped the newspaper and ate off their laps, using their fingers. They were still eating when the front-door knocker banged three or four times.

'It isn't locked!' Mary called out. 'Come on in!'

The door opened to reveal Mary's sister, Barbara. Looking like a taller, slightly heavier version of Mary, with the same ink-black hair, marble-white skin and luminous brown-eyed gaze, she was wearing a fashionable light-grey overcoat over a high-collared sky-blue dress and had a patterned scarf tied loosely around her throat. The clothes looked like money and so did the silver brooch pinned to the lapel of her coat.

'Aunt Babs!' Johnny called out with a big smile.

'Hi, Aunt Babs!' wee Billy added, grinning delightedly.

Auntie Barbara, known as 'Babs', was beloved by all three of her sister's children.

'Did I come in the middle of tea?' she asked, talking the way Mary talked when she wanted to impress people, with the accent they had gained from having been born and raised in the Upper Malone Road. 'Well, given what I see you all eating, I'd say I made the right move.'

'Hi, Babs,' Albert said, taking her in with a swift, devouring glance, then lowering his gaze to guiltily stuff more chips into his mouth.

Babs closed the door behind her, stepped into the living room, placed a shopping bag on the table beneath the front window, then took her overcoat off and hung it up behind the door. Removing a packet of

Gallagher's and a lighter from a pocket of the coat, she lit up a cigarette, inhaled luxuriously, then exhaled with what sounded like a sensual sigh.

'Ah, Jesus, that's good!' she said.

'Still disapproves of you smoking, does he?'

'Nothing's changed, Mary.'

Babs was married to Malcolm Craig, a well paid civil servant who worked as a senior administrator out in Stormont and was widely viewed as a pillar of Protestant rectitude: tight, teetotal, non-smoking, and invincibly boring. Ironically, Babs, who was one year older than Mary and had three children of her own, was revered by Mary's children because, when not with her husband, she was a real live wire, smoking, drinking, always generous and wickedly good humoured. She also had a thrillingly husky voice that made her seem, certainly to Johnny, more glamorous than other women her age.

'So how are my favourite boyfriends?' she asked, ruffling the hair of Johnny and Billy in turn, while blowing a stream of smoke over them. 'Getting up to mischief as usual?'

'Sure we've done nothing worth talkin' about,' Johnny said.

'We're as clean as whistles,' Billy added.

'Yes, I'm sure,' Babs said, smiling and taking the chair beside Albert, then crossing her long, curvaceous legs, showing off expensive stockings, and blowing another thin stream of smoke. 'A pair of wee angels, as usual. I believe you where thousands wouldn't. So how are you, Albert?'

'Ack, I'm grand,' Albert said, glancing at Babs' crossed legs, then just as quickly looking away. 'No complaints, like.'

'You like it across the water, do you?'

'Well, you know...'

'Go on, admit it.'

Albert grinned and nodded. 'Aye, you're right,' he said. 'What's the point in denyin' it? Sure it's a damned sight better than here. More opportunities, like.'

'Not that the benefits are noticed much over here,' Mary said, holding a couple of chips between her fingers and waving them to and fro. 'No champagne or caviar or steak; just the usual fish and chips.'

'You wouldn't recognise caviar,' Babs retorted, 'if it was shoved down your gullet with a spade, so you haven't lost too much.'

Albert grinned. 'Aye, right.'

Not amused, Mary suddenly wrapped up what was left of her fish and chips, which was most of it, and tossed the package into the open grate, presumably to be burned at a later date. 'So that makes it alright, does it?' she asked rhetorically, taking a cigarette from the pocket of her apron and proceeding to set a match to it. 'The fact' (puff, puff) 'that I've never had caviar or champagne' (puff, puff) 'means that I'm not allowed to complain about the lack of money coming from Birkenhead. Well, excuse me' (puff, puff) 'but I was under the impression that he' (puff, puff) 'was going over there to make his fortune as a joiner and also become a showbiz star in his spare time. So excuse me' (puff, puff) 'for expressing mild disappointment.'

Babs merely grinned at that, then turned to Albert. 'So how's the showbusiness coming along in England?'

'Not bad at all,' Albert said, glancing nervously at his wife. 'Not brilliant, but pretty good. I mean, I've done a fair bit of work in pubs and workin' men's clubs and now this new-fangled thing, television, is bound to offer a lot of opportunities. I mean, there isn't much television over here yet, but there's a lot across the water and it's growin' all the time. So, you know, if I just keep at it and bide my time, I think I've got a good chance of getting' in there. Television's the coming thing, like, so that's what I'm now aimin' for.'

'Jesus!' Mary exclaimed softly, exhaling a cloud of smoke. 'If dreams only came true...'

'You do that,' Babs said encouragingly to Albert, ignoring her sister's sarcasm. 'Sure what have you got to lose? Nothing but a little bit of pride and I'm sure you can spare that.' She raised her eyebrows and glanced about the room, looking for the booze and sandwiches. 'So when's the party beginning? When's the first drink being poured?'

'Right now,' Albert said, crumpling up his piece of greasy newspaper, having finished everything, and throwing it onto the other rubbish in the grate as he stood up. 'What'll you have, Babs?'

'A whisky will do for starters,' Babs said, squinting at him through a veil of cigarette smoke.

'Right,' Albert said. 'What about you, Mary?'

'I'll have the same,' Mary said. 'It's not really a party,' she explained to Babs as Albert disappeared into the kitchen. 'We just told some of the neighbours to drop in any time after six for a bit of a drink and a sandwich. Then we'll all go out for the bonfire. What's up with Malcolm? Is he comin' or not?'

'Yes,' Babs said, not bothering to hide her lack of enthusiasm, 'he's coming straight from the office. He should be here any minute now.'

'Better smoke yourself to death before he gets here.'

'Oh, he never tries to stop me smoking when I'm with company - in someone else's house. Only in our own place. That's why I go out visiting a lot. I'm looking for a life.'

'Sure don't they all give us grief?' Mary said. 'We'd be better off without them.'

'I'm not so certain...' Babs began.

'Now, now,' Albert interjected, coming back into the living room with a tray containing a bottle of whisky and enough glasses to get the party going, 'we don't need your cynicism, Mary. Where would you women be without us? Sure you'd be at a loss.'

'You reckon, do you?' Mary said.

'There's good and bad on both sides,' Babs said, smiling warmly at Albert, who could not quite meet her gaze, though his frequent sideways glances took her in. 'Live and let live, I say.'

'Let the whisky make equals of us all,' Albert said as he started pouring and distributing the drinks.

'So are you two going to watch the parade tomorrow?' Babs asked of Johnny and Billy.

'I'm carrying a string on the banner of the Sandy Row Lodge,' wee Billy announced proudly.

'You're not!'

'Aye, I am. I joined the Lodge a couple of weeks ago and then got picked to help with the banner.'

Shocked, Babs looked wide-eyed at her sister. 'Sure I can't believe my ears. I thought you were dead-set against the Orangemen, Mary. Always saying they caused more trouble than they were worth. Now I'm told that wee Billy here has joined the most fanatical Lodge of them all.'

'Not with my permission,' Mary said, glancing sternly at Billy. 'The wee eejut joined without my permission. He joined secretly, without tellin' us. Now I can barely look the Laverys in the eye.'

'And what do I say to Teddy,' Johnny asked, 'when he comes back from sea?'

Johnny still worshipped Teddy because he was travelling the world with the Royal Navy. Indeed, he came over all emotional when he recalled the artist's wallet that Teddy had given him last year. Everyone, including Johnny, had been given a Coronation Book as part of the celebrations, but Johnny was the only one with that exotic, hand-tooled leather wallet, bought from an Arab in his bum boat in the port of Aden. Johnny's Coronation Book was gathering dust under his bed, but he often used the pencils and carbon sticks in the wallet to improve his drawing because he wanted Teddy to know just how much he appreciated the gift. Now wee Billy had gone and joined the Orange Lodge, which was known to be dead-set against the Catholics. Johnny was really embarrassed.

Aunt Babs wasn't embarrassed. Though pretending to be shocked, she was clearly amused. 'So what on earth made you join?' she asked of Billy.

'Sure I only joined 'cause I wanted to march in the parade on the Twelfth,' Billy replied. 'I wanted to carry the string of a banner. I get sixpence for doin' it.'

'That's a secret organisation,' Johnny said disapprovingly.

'Naw, it's not all that secret,' Billy said. 'It was all just a bit of a geg really.'

'So what happens when you join?' Johnny asked, intrigued despite himself.

'Just a wee enrolment ceremony,' Billy said. 'I went down to the Sandy Row Lodge hall and was made to wait outside the locked doors of a room called the Inner Chamber. They call the doors of the Inner Chamber the *Sacred* Doors.' Billy grinned at that. 'When the sacred doors were opened, the Orangemen sponsoring me, one standin' on each side of me, led me into the Inner Chamber. It was full of other Orangemen - Blacks and Purples, as well as Orange – standin' there in a couple of lines. One of my sponsors told me they were called the Loyal Sons. I was marched between the two lines of Loyal Sons, stood in front of a long table with Blacks and Purples sittin' behind it, all really stern, like, and told by one of the Blacks about the Lodge I was goin' to join.'

'Told what?' Johnny asked.

'That the Sandy Row district is the Number Five district of the County Grand Lodge of Belfast, that it has seven Lodges, that its headquarters is the Orange Hall, and that it was first opened in 1868.'

'That boy has a good memory,' Babs said approvingly, despite her disapproval of the Orange Lodge.

'So what happened next?' Johnny asked.

'I was made to take the secret oath.'

'What's that?'

'I can't tell you 'cause it's secret.' Billy's expression was conspiratorial. 'Then, when I'd taken the secret oath, I was given the Lodge password and had to swear not to tell it to anyone outside the Lodge. An' that was it, really.'

'So why did they chose you,' Babs asked, 'as one of the four boys holding the string of their banner during the march to Finaghy Field?'

'Pure luck, Aunt Babs. I went to a couple of meetin's and then, last week, when it came time to pick some junior members to hold the strings - which nat'rally we all desperately wanted to do - a senior Lodge member wrote our names down on pieces of paper, put the pieces into an upturned bowler hat, shook them about, then put his hand in and pulled out four names. I was one of the names pulled out.'

'Amazing!' Babs exclaimed. 'And you only in the Lodge a couple of weeks! Some of the other boys must have been really jealous!'

Billy grinned. 'Aye, they were. Sure one of 'em made a smart remark to me as we were leavin' the Lodge, but I gave him a punch in the gob. That soon shut 'im up.'

'If you tell the Lodge about that,' Babs said, 'they might throw you out.'

'I don't care,' Billy said. 'Sure I only joined for the chance to march in the parade and get sixpence for holding the string of the banner. I won't be goin' back after the Twelfth. I can't be bothered with anything regular, like.'

'They won't like you for that,' Babs warned him.

Billy merely shrugged and grinned. Then the front door opened and Marlene came in, wearing a loose dress with a flowered pattern and buckled brown-leather shoes, her auburn hair untidy. Seeing Aunt Babs, she shrieked with pleasure and threw herself into her auntie's arms, nearly burning her hair on the latter's cigarette. Laughing, Babs patted her on the back and then released her, but held her by the shoulders as she studied her.

'So how are you, gorgeous?' she asked.

'I'm great, Aunt Babs. I was just over playing with Donna, but now they're havin' their tea.'

'They didn't feed you?' Mary asked crossly.

'Aye, Mum, they fed me, but now Donna's gettin' washed before going out to watch the bonfire.' Marlene turned her smile back on Aunt Babs, who gave her the affection that she rarely received at home but so desperately needed. 'Are you stayin' all evenin', Aunt Babs?'

Babs stroked Marlene's hair and smiled at her. 'Aye, love, I am.'

'That's great!' Marlene said, beaming.

Someone knocked on the front door.

'It's not locked!' Mary called out. 'Come on in!'

The door opened and Babs' husband, Malcolm Craig, entered. A big man, well built, with a handsome, humourless face and brown hair turning prematurely grey, he was wearing a pinstripe suit with shirt and tie. When he saw Babs smoking and drinking he shook his head from side to side, expressing disapproval, though he didn't say anything. Not one of the children smiled when he entered the room; because he felt himself a cut above the Hamiltons. His own smile was slight and forced.

'Evening all,' he muttered.

'Hey, you!' Mary snapped to wee Billy. 'I can see that you've finished your fish and chips, so get your backside off that chair and let your Uncle Malcolm have it.'

'Then where will I sit?'

'You can sit with Johnny on the stairs or take yourselves out into the street to watch them light up the bonfire. We'll all be out later.'

'I'm goin' out now,' Billy said, rising from the chair and then pushing it reluctantly towards his uncle, who sat on it without offering a word of thanks.

'Me, too,' Johnny said, getting off his chair and then following Billy out of the house.

'And what about you, Missie?' Mary said.

'I'm staying here,' Marlene replied, possessively looping her right arm around Babs' shoulder.

'Then you can help me lay the table,' Mary said, flicking her dead butt into the grate. 'You can bring out the sandwiches.'

'Alright.' Marlene gave Babs another warm smile as she followed her mother into the kitchen.

Albert and Malcolm glanced at each other, wondering what they might say to one another. Malcolm always carried a heavy atmosphere with him and now it was dampening Albert's spirits. He longed for the first neighbours to arrive and help him carry this dead weight.

'Would you like a drink, Malcolm?' he asked.

'No, I'm fine,' Malcolm replied, obviously longing to be somewhere else.

'So how did your day go?' Babs asked of her husband, trying to rescue Albert.

Malcolm shrugged. 'Just the same as always,' he said mournfully. 'Nothing unusual.'

Defeated, unable to think of anything else to say, Babs glanced at Albert with what seemed like desperation.

'Still payin' you a small fortune,' Albert said to Malcolm, 'for all yer important work out at Stormont?'

'What does that mean?' Malcolm asked. 'Are you being sarcastic?'

'Well, no, what I meant was...'

'What's so wrong with being a civil servant?' Malcolm asked. 'Just because I don't work in the Yard or James Mackie's doesn't mean that I – '

'Sorry, Malcolm, sorry. I wasn't tryin' to imply anything. Just askin' if things were goin' okay with you. Nothin' else intended, like.'

'Things are fine,' Malcolm said, turning his head away from Albert in order to stare steadily, without warmth, at Babs. She deliberately exhaled a cloud of smoke that obscured her reaction.

'What exactly do you *do* out there?' Albert asked.

'I can't say,' Malcolm replied. 'It's confidential. Government business, naturally.'

'Oh,' Albert said.

'So,' Babs said ambiguously.

'Right,' Albert said, sounding strained. He was groping for something more to say when, mercifully, Marlene emerged from the kitchen, carrying a plate of sandwiches in each hand, followed by

Mary, who was holding a tray containing a bottle of sherry, another bottle of whisky, and a lot of glass tumblers. They placed these on the dining table under the front window of the living room, then returned to the kitchen for more. As they had to make three trips to and from the kitchen, they helpfully filled the silence that lay like lead between Albert, Babs and Malcolm. Luckily, before the final run was made by Mary and Marlene, the front door opened and Patrick Lavery's flushed, smiling face appeared.

'Okay to come in?' he asked.

'Aye, come on in,' Albert said, relieved to see his Catholic friends from a few doors up.

Patrick and Bernadette entered, the former holding another bottle of Bushmills whisky, the latter carrying a couple of plates of home-made cakes, which she placed beside the sandwiches on the table. They both greeted Babs with a big smile, Malcolm with mere nods of the head. When Bernadette took the last vacant chair, Patrick stood beside her. Asked by Albert what they would like to drink, they both settled for whisky.

'Give us a fag, Pat,' Bernadette said to her husband. Patrick passed her a cigarette, then lit one for himself. Exhaling a cloud of smoke, Bernadette said, 'You're looking good, Babs. You never seem to age, like.'

'Thanks,' Babs replied. 'But it was only a year ago today when we last saw each other, so you can't expect much change in that time - not for either of us. You're looking great yourself, Bernadette.'

'That's a wee white lie, Babs, but I appreciate the kindness. I turned forty-three last April and I feel every bloody second of it. The years are dragging me down, like. So how are *you*, Malcolm?'

'I'm doin' alright,' Malcolm said, then fell silent again as Mary and Marlene came back into the living room to place the last of the sandwiches on the table.

'Well, for Jesus sake!' Mary exclaimed melodramatically when she saw the whisky and cakes that had been brought by the Laverys. 'Will you look at that! I told you two not to bring anything, since this is our day, not yours. Sure it's decent enough of you to come, you bein' Catholic an' all. I mean, they'll soon be burnin' the Pope on that bonfire, despite what you believe in, so I don't see why you should contribute to *this* particular Protestant celebration.'

'Sure it's just a neighbourly gesture,' Patrick said, taking a whisky from Albert and giving him the wink, which was returned.

'Aye, that's right,' Bernadette said, also taking a whisky from Albert while blowing a cloud of smoke in his face. 'I mean, we might draw the line if they burnt the real Pope out there, but since it's only that awful painting we've been lookin' at for days, I think it'll be an act of mercy to us all when it goes up in flames.' She raised her glass of whisky in the air. 'Cheers!'

'Cheers!' everyone else, except Malcolm, said more or less in unison as they held up their glasses. Then they had the first formal drink of the evening.

'Ah, Jesus, sure that's grand!' Patrick said after his first sip, wiping his lips with the back of his free hand.

The front door opened again and Nelly Devlin, the local midwife, also Catholic, stuck her head around it, smiling.

'Are you all still sober?' she asked. 'Is it safe to come in?'

Marlene ran up to the door and said, 'Ackaye, come on in, Nelly!'

Nelly entered the living room, holding a plate of cakes in each hand. She was followed by her husband, Sammy, who was carrying a cardboard carton filled with bottles of stout.

'Would you look at that now!' Mary exclaimed as if surprised, though the bringing of such items was traditional. 'Sure wouldn't you think we couldn't afford to do our own entertaining on Bonfire Night?'

'Ack, it's just a wee gesture,' Nelly said, placing her plates on the table and then turning back to face the room. 'So how are you all?'

The words 'grand' and 'great' were offered from various sources, then someone banged the knocker on the door and Marlene, who was enjoying playing hostess, went again to answer the call. 'Ack, come on in, Roy,' she said.

Albert's old Yard mate, Roy Williams, entered the room. Still tall, thin, loose-limbed and deceptively simple-minded, he grinned like an idiot, offered his greetings to all, then placed a couple of paper bags on the table.

'My wee contribution,' he said.

'So what's this, then?' Albert asked, dipping into the two bags in turn, withdrawing a couple of bottles of Jameson whisky, a couple of bottles of Sandyman Port, and two cartons of cigarettes.

'Jasus!' Albert exclaimed. 'Where did this lot come from?'

Roy grinned and tapped the side of his nose with his index finger. 'Ask no questions an' I'll tell you no lies,' he said.

'Down south,' Albert ventured.

'No comment,' Roy retorted.

'I think I'll go outside for a wander,' Malcolm said. Being a respected civil servant who worked for the Stormont government, he preferred not to even *see* smuggled goods. 'If you'll all excuse me...'

'Aye, right,' Albert and a few others, including Babs, said simultaneously, clearly glad to be rid of him. 'See you outside later.'

'Right,' Malcolm said, stepping out into the street as Marlene, who loathed him, enthusiastically held the door open for him. She shut the door behind him with a loud bang.

'Here, let me top your glasses up,' Albert said, doing the rounds with the bottle of whisky and receiving approval from all concerned.

'What about me?' Marlene asked, now leaning against her beloved Babs again. 'Don't I get a drink?'

'Not of whisky, you don't,' Babs said. 'Not even from me!'

'What do you want, love?' Albert said, hoping to impress Babs with his concern for his normally neglected daughter.

'A lemonade,' Marlene said, knowing what her father was trying to do and taking full advantage of the situation.

'Right, love,' Albert said, speaking to Marlene but smiling brightly at Babs, while avoiding actual eye contact. 'I'll be back in a minute.'

Albert disappeared into the kitchen as Mary, having laid the table with Marlene's help, lit a cigarette, blew the smoke all over the food, and said, 'All right, everybody, food's up. Just help yourselves.'

Big Roy Williams, already standing by the table, promptly grabbed a sandwich and the others, leaving their chairs, followed suit. Albert returned to give Marlene a bottle of Grattan's lemonade and she, too, grabbed a sandwich, even though she'd just had a supper of fish and chips over at Donna King's place. At that moment, the front door burst open and wee Billy rushed in, all excited.

'Hey, they're startin' to light the bonfire!' he shouted, then he saw the sandwiches and cakes on the table. 'Oh, great!' he exclaimed, hurrying across the room to grab a sandwich. 'God, I'm starving, I am!'

His mother slapped his wrist, making him jerk his hand away, then squinted down at him through the smoke spiralling up from the cigarette between her lips.

'Get your hands off them sandwiches,' she said, 'you greedy wee bugger. Sure haven't you just had your fish and chips?'

'But I'm starvin' again,' wee Billy insisted.

'Ack, let him have one, Mary,' Babs said. 'He's ravenous because he's excited and this is Bonfire Night.'

'Well, alright,' Mary said, coughing up more smoke and wagging her finger at wee Billy. 'But mind your manners and don't take more than one until you've finished the first one.'

'Aye,' Billy said, grabbing a sandwich, 'but I need another one for Johnny. He's starvin' as well.'

'Then take it,' Mary said, 'but if I find out that you took it for yourself, sure you'll get a good hidin'.'

'Okay, Mum,' Billy said.

Grabbing a second sandwich, he rushed out of the house.

'They must have lit the bonfire early,' Roy Williams said, his brow furrowed, trying to work this one out.

'Aye,' Albert said. 'Sure isn't that a brilliant deduction?' He glanced at Babs and just as quickly looked away. 'Well, I think we should eat and drink first, then go out there when the bonfire's ablaze.'

'I'll second that,' Babs said.

'She's your sister-in-law,' Mary said to Albert, 'so I suppose she can give you her support.'

'What?' Albert responded, looking baffled.

'Never mind,' Mary said.

Two hours later, when they were all filled with grub and drink, therefore drunk, at least all except Marlene, they tumbled out into the street to find the bonfire roaring and snapping, sending fingers of flame and smoke to the night sky. Malcolm was there, arms folded across his chest, out of place in his pinstripe suit amongst the plebeian hordes, his solemn face erratically illuminated by the flames of the enormous bonfire, which turned his features into a jigsaw of shadow and light. Being drunk, glancing at him, Albert just couldn't imagine it - Malcolm and Babs in bed together, making children together - and his heart, which he had always denied, almost skipped a beat. Looking away, he saw Mary and Babs, two sisters together, both smoking, both with drinks in their hands, and they glanced at him to send him different signals, neither of which he could read. He felt the heat of the great fire. He saw the Pope burning up there. The Laverys and Devlins had gone back to their own homes, because even with their rare kind of tolerance, the consignment of Catholic effigies to the flames would have been too much for them. Albert watched the Pope burning. It meant not a damned thing to him. He looked across the road and saw his eldest son, Johnny, standing beside Marlene and Donna King, all shading their eyes with their hands as they looked up at the fiercely burning bonfire, a fountain of sparks rising from it, to pattern the darkness with crimson dreams.

Donna King turned to Johnny. She gazed steadily at him. Johnny tried to hold her gaze, but he was still too young to do that, so he turned away instead, pretending to look elsewhere, and then took a step sideways and dissolved into the darkness just beyond the reach of the light thrown on the street by the flames.

The bonfire continued burning for most of the night and when it died down the painted Pope had gone. Most of the spectators had gone as well, but silence did not prevail. All over the city other fires were still burning and the Lambeg drums continued pounding. Those drums were still pounding, resurrecting old passions, when dawn broke on the Twelfth of July.

Wee Billy was the first to waken up.

He had to march with the banner.

5

The ashes of the bonfires were still smouldering when Billy dressed himself, had a hurried breakfast, then ran off to join his Orange Lodge in Sandy Row. Letting Billy leave first, since this was his big day, the rest of the family had a more leisurely breakfast and left the house later in the morning. The instant they stepped outside, they heard the noise of Lambeg drums and pipe bands coming from every direction, as various Lodges geared up for the march to Finaghy Field. Marlene did not go with them, since she was going, instead, with Donna King and her parents.

'See youse all at Finaghy Field,' she shouted, running off like the wind, leaving Johnny with only his Mum and Dad for company. This did not greatly thrill him.

'Ack, stop worryin' about it,' his Dad said. 'Sure you're bound to meet some friends up on the Lisburn Road and then you can go off on your own, like, and we'll all meet up later at Finaghy Field.'

'I could go with Dan Johnstone,' Johnny suggested hopefully.

'Are ya jokin' or what?' his Mum said, outraged. 'Sure Dan'll be goin' with his parents, and his Dad has promised to give your Dad a hiding if he gets within arms reach.'

This was the secret shame of the family. A couple of years back, Albert had made the mistake of giving Dan Johnstone a clip on the ear for involving Johnny in a highly dangerous prank. Dan had told his dad about it and big Barney had gone mad, saying that no one except him could strike his children (which he did a lot) and that he would give Albert a good hiding the next time he passed Barney's house on his way to the Yard. As big Barney was built like King Kong and certainly renowned for his violent nature, Albert had taken the coward's way out (the 'sensible way', as he had put it unconvincingly to Mary) by changing his daily route to the Yard. When leaving each morning, instead of turning left to go along the avenue, which would have taken him past big Barney's house, he had gone in the opposite direction: turning right at the garden gate, then right again , then another right into the first of the streets that ran parallel to the avenue, only returning to the avenue via the Broadway. That brought him out a safe distance beyond Barney's place.

Johnny and Billy might have believed their Dad's contention that this was a sensible move had it not been for the fact that their Mum constantly mocked him for it, saying that he was a cowardy-custard and yella-belly who was scared of Barney.

'What a humiliation!' Mary had said more than once. 'My own husband taking the long way round, just to avoid a big, dumb brute like Barney Johnstone. Sure it shames me to think of it.'

Nevertheless, despite Mary's mockery, Albert had never again walked past Barney's house and, indeed, must have been greatly relieved when he 'crossed the water' to work and didn't have to worry about it any more. Which didn't mean that he was about to walk past the house even now, let alone let Johnny join up with Barney's sons this particular day, when socialising with the neighbours was next to unavoidable.

'No way are you goin' down to knock on Dan Johnstone's door,' Albert said to Johnny, 'and remind his Dad that I'm back in town. You're comin' with us.'

'Dan's my friend,' Johnny ruthlessly reminded him.

'He may be *your* friend,' Albert said, 'but his Dad's no friend of mine, so no way are we goin' to join them on the Lisburn Road or anywhere else.'

'You're just scared of his Dad,' Johnny said contemptuously.

'Who isn't?' Albert retorted without shame. 'If that man was remotely normal he wouldn't scare me a bit, but as we all know, he's as mad as a hatter and has fists like sledgehammers. Scared? I'm just sensible, kiddo. So keep your gob shut and do what you're told. You're comin' with us and we're goin' by way of the Stoney Bridge - not past where that mad bastard's house is.'

'That means I'll be with you and Mum all day.'

'No, you don't have to be. If you happen to see Dan Johnstone up on the Lisburn Road, you can run off with him and do your worst, but not if his mad Dad is with him. I'm only here for a fortnight and I don't want any trouble while I'm here, so don't give me anxieties.'

'You don't want a punch in the gob,' Mary retorted. 'Let's be straight about that much.'

'Grand, Mary. I hear you. Sure it's David and Goliath for you, but I won't be your David. Isn't it typical of a woman to despise a man who simply doesn't want to lose his perfect teeth to the knuckles of a lunatic? You want Errol Flynn? Go to the fillums. As for me, I'm goin' up to the Lisburn Road without aggravation. Now are you comin' or not?'

'Aye, I'm comin',' Johnny said, glancing across the road to see Marlene rush up to Donna King, who was standing at her garden gate, wearing another lime-green dress (her favourite colour, matching her eyes) that was flattened against her developing curves by a restless breeze. Brushing the blonde hair from her eyes, Donna glanced across the road at Johnny, but he was still too young to hold her gaze. Embarrassed, he turned away. 'Well, let's go,' he said.

With his parents, he walked along the avenue to the waste ground in front of the football grounds, then crossed the bridge and walked up to the Lisburn Road, where hundreds of people were already lined along the pavements to watch the procession. Lambeg drums pounded dementedly; pipe-and-brass bands wailed. Having left Carlisle Place about forty minutes ago, the first of the Orangemen had already passed this spot and the rest of the procession, which would take nearly three hours to pass by, was on the march from the centre of town. A lot of the spectators lining the road were waving small Union Jacks; others were cheering or singing the lyrics to the songs being played by the various pipe bands, including those that had come over from Scotland.

Sure I'm an Ulster Orangeman,
from Erin's Isle I came
To see my Glasgow brethren
all of honour and of fame
And to tell them of my forefathers
who fought in days of yore
All on the twelfth day of July
in the sash my father wore.

The Orangemen passed by, one Lodge after the other, behind the big, flapping banners illustrated with garish paintings of the Battle of the Boyne, King William of Orange, other heroes or heroic events of Ulster history, members of the Royal Family; and, of course, the identifying insignia of the individual Lodges. The men marched in strict order. Passing first were the Orangemen wearing black sashes trimmed with a heavy gold fringe - the black denoting that they were those of highest rank within the hierarchy of the Order. Next came the men with purple sashes, also fringed with heavy gold, these being one rank below the Blacks. Coming up last were the ordinary Orangemen with plain orange sashes. Most of them, despite their rank, wore grey or black suits, with shirt and tie and bowler hats. Orange was, however, the predominant colour, flaming in the summer sun from the hundreds of sashes and banners, but also in the orange-lily worn by a lot of the spectators or twined in bunches with sweet-williams on top of the standards. Sweet-williams was as sacred to the Protestants as the shamrock was to the Fenians.

As the bands played the ancient, beloved tunes, the crowds watching them continued singing the lyrics that had been passed down from Protestant generation to generation.

It's ould, but it's beautiful,
and its colours they are fine,
It was worn at Derry, Aughrim,
Enniskillen and the Boyne;
My father wore it in his youth
in the bygone days of yore,
And on the Twelfth I love to wear
the sash my father wore.

A Lambeg drummer preceded each Lodge, face flushed, sweat on his brow, flaying the taut hides with his sticks, his hands a blur of incredibly rapid movement, his body twisting and turning like a whirling-dervish as he played, spinning like a top, leaping like an athlete, sometimes bending so far backwards that his huge drum, about six foot in diameter and strapped to his shoulders, seemed to be welded to his upturned chest. Like the wind-whipped banners, which seemed, to Johnny, to be the size of cinema screens, the Lambeg drums were garishly decorated with crests, royal coats-of-arms, famous Protestant heroes, and extraordinary colourful but indecipherable patterns. The noise they made was so loud that it seemed to be announcing the Millennium and would certainly have been capable of sending men rushing off to war. Also positioned between the various Lodges were brass and pipe bands, flutists, ordinary drummers and men clashing cymbals, which flashed blindingly in the summer sun.

Eventually, wee Billy's Lodge came into view. It was preceded by a Scottish bagpipe band, the players wearing their kilts, the leader throwing his baton high in the air and spinning around dramatically to catch it, sometimes when his hands were behind his back - a trick that always drove the crowds wild. The Scotsmen were the descendants of the original Ulster plantationers, more Loyalist than the Loyalists, more patriotic than the English, passionately in love with Northern Ireland and living for this one day of the year when they could prove what they were worth. As they played the melody of 'The Sash My Father Wore' on their bagpipes, the crowd lent their support by singing the words that had long united the Scottish Protestants to the Irish:

> *So here I am in Glasgow town*
> *youse boys and girls to see,*
> *And I hope that in good Orange style*
> *you will welcome me,*
> *A true blue blade that's just arrived*
> *from that dear Ulster shore,*
> *All on the Twelfth day of July*
> *in the sash my father wore.*

The bands played as if they were in fierce competition with each other - as noisily and as tirelessly as could be humanly managed - and their clamour, combined with the relentless pounding of the Lambeg drums, filled many a heart with dangerous excitement.

'There's wee Billy!' Donna King cried out.

Donna and Marlene had come out of the crowds lining the road and were now standing right beside Johnny. Donna was wearing her lime-green dress, and her blonde hair, which fell only to her neck, was being tossed by the wind. Either deliberately or unconsciously, she placed her hand on Johnny's right shoulder. The very touch of her fingertips electrified him and made his cheeks burn.

'Aye,' he said, bereft of words, falling to pieces, though determined not to let Donna know it, 'there's our wee Billy. As proud as punch, isn't he? Sure who'd have believed it?'

Billy was obviously in his element, holding the string and making sure it was always taut, not letting the banner waver, while the pipe band out in front of the marching Lodge members gave the onlookers what they wanted to hear. As the Scottish pipers wailed out the melody, with Billy practically dancing on the end of his string, more excited than he would ever admit later, the onlookers continued singing the lyrics that had stirred more than one formerly gentle heart to violence:

> *And when I'm going to leave yeeze all*
> *'Good Luck!' to youse I'll say,*
> *And as I cross the raging sea*

my Orange flute I'll play;
Returning to my native town,
to ould Belfast once more,
To be welcomed back by Orangemen
in the sash my father wore.

The crowd roared at the closing of the song, while wee Billy, holding the string of the banner in one hand, threw his other hand above his head, grinned like a loon, and did the kind of jig that he had certainly not learned at home, though it made the crowd break into applause.

'Hey, Billy!' Johnny cried out.

Billy grinned and waved at him, then at all the other familiar faces, including his parents, Uncle Malcolm and Aunt Babs, Marlene and Donna, and even Roy Williams, who had appeared, seemingly out of nowhere, to join the excited group.

'You look great!' Johnny called out.

'It feels great!' Billy shouted back.

'Brilliant!' Marlene added.

'See you on the field!' Albert shouted, recognising another performer when he saw one.

'Me too!' Mary called out, temporarily forgetting that she hated the Orange Order, only aware of the fact that her wee boy was there, holding the string of a banner, being viewed by the thousands lining the roads. 'Sure you look lovely, son!'

Billy grinned and waved at her.

'A proud day,' Roy Williams said.

'What?' Albert responded.

'To have a son holding the string. That's surely worth the remembering.'

'Aye,' Albert said. 'Right.'

'So how are you, Johnny?' Donna asked, as wee Billy gave them all a last wave and marched on with the others, heading for Finaghy Field.

'What?' Johnny responded, feeling hot and confused, as he always did when with Donna.

'How are you?' Donna repeated.

'Oh, fine. Doin' great, like.'

'You must be proud of wee Billy.'

'What?'

'Holdin' the string an' all.'

Johnny shrugged. 'I dunno.' His heart was racing, but he tried not to show it, tried not to blush. 'Proud? Why should I be? Sure Billy's doin' it for sixpence and a bit of excitement, so I don't know why I should feel proud. Billy's Billy, if you know what I mean, and that's all there is to it. He's carryin' the banner for a bit of a lark and to earn himself sixpence. Pride doesn't even come into it.'

'Would you like to hold the string?'

'No,' Johnny said, straight out. 'I think all of it's - excuse me - a lot of shite, and I can do without it.'

'That's because you like that Fenian, Teddy Lavery.'

'And his family,' Johnny clarified.

'Come on, Donna,' Marlene said, tugging at her best friend's arm, trying to pull her away from Johnny. 'Let's follow Billy's Lodge all the way to the Field. Sure we can have a good time there. If we don't go there, we'll just stand here for hours, waitin' for the whole procession to come back the other way, while this eejut brother of mine looks at you with calf's eyes and I go...' She poked her index finger into her throat and then pantomimed vomiting.

'Ack, shut up!' Johnny said, embarrassed and blushing.

'Go with them,' Mary said, blowing a cloud of cigarette over him as she spoke. 'No point staying here with us. We're going to the Field as well - a whole crowd of us; all grown-ups - and we don't want you kids around our feet until we get there. So you go off with Marlene and Donna. Though try to stop your knees from turning blue from all that knocking they do when you're with Donna.'

This comment, from Mary, made her and Albert burst out in laughter.

'Aye, dead on,' Albert said.

'Sure, look at him,' Roy Williams added. 'Isn't the poor wee lad as red as a beetroot? He must fancy her, right enough.'

'Just shut up, the whole lot of you,' Johnny said, as Marlene and Donna, both giggling, ran away, determined to follow wee Billy's Lodge all the way to Finaghy Field. 'You hear me? *Shut up!*'

Leaving his parents stunned, since they had never heard such rage from him before, he ran after Marlene and Donna, not wanting to join them, but determined to do what they were doing, which was to follow wee Billy's Lodge all the way to Finaghy Field, running alongside the marching Orangemen, in front of the crowds lining this side of the road, waving their small Union Jacks and singing the other traditional songs being played by the Scottish and Irish bands. He stuck with Billy's Sandy Row Lodge, keeping within sight of Marlene and Donna, but deliberately not trying to catch up with them, content to watch his younger brother strut proudly with the string of the banner in his clenched fists, following the wailing pipe band, its leader pirouetting as he repeatedly threw his baton high in the air and caught it again, behind a whirling-dervish Lambeg drummer. The crowds lining the Lisburn Road, all the way to Finaghy Field, waved Union Jacks, clapped and cheered, and sang along with the bands.

It was so exciting you didn't care what it was about; you were just consumed by it. At least Johnny was.

At Finaghy Field, which seemed to stretch out for miles in all directions, thousands of Orangemen and spectators mingled together on the grass and in the large white tents where food and drink were being served. Lemonade, stout and a wide variety of cakes, buns and sandwiches were liberally dispensed and just as eagerly received, while voices amplified by loudspeakers announced various events or, just as often, asked mothers to come and collect their lost children. Speeches were made. 'Kick the Pope!' was shouted a lot. Johnny ran into Dan Johnstone who said, 'Jesus, Johnny, I was wondering where you were. I thought you might call in and collect me. I was praying you would, 'cause my dad was beating up on my Mum, giving her a right bloody tannin' for somethin' or other, an' I thought he was goin' to turn on me, so I just bolted, like. I mean, you wouldn't miss this for the world, would ya? Fuckin' great, isn't it? Hey, look! There's Marlene and Donna King. Christ, that Donna's a real looker, isn't she? I mean, she's got tits already. Can you imagine unbuttoning that dress and...'

'Hey, did youse all see me?' wee Billy said, rushing out of the crowd and beaming, his face flushed with excitement. 'Did youse all see me with the banner? Bloody great, wasn't I?'

'Aye, you were,' Johnny said.

'I saw everyone we know and they all waved and cheered me on. Jesus, it was great! And I've got to march all the way back this evenin', so they're all gonna see me again. Sure it's grand bein' cheered, like. Where's Mum and Dad?'

'Dunno,' Johnny said.

'Let's go and find them. I want to know if they saw me.'

'Okay,' Johnny said.

They were about to move off when Marlene and Donna King came running up, both flushed with excitement. Marlene threw her arms around Billy and gave him a hug.

'Did you see me?' Billy asked.

'Aye,' Marlene said. 'Sure didn't you see us waving at you?'

'Aye, I did, come to think of it.'

'He's a celebrity,' Donna said to Johnny, mesmerising him with her steady, green gaze. 'Sure your wee brother's famous.'

'Famous for a fuckin' day,' Dan said, annoyed that Billy was receiving so much attention, particularly from the girls.

'That's one day more than you'll ever get,' Donna replied sarcastically. Then she turned to deliberately smile at Johnny.

'Fuck you,' Dan said.

Johnny threw a punch at him, impulsively, without thinking, consumed with a fierce, blinding rage that blew up out of nowhere. The blow glanced off Dan's cheek, making his head jerk to the side, then Johnny hit him again, first on the left cheek, then the right, a fourth time on the nose, before Dan even knew what was happening. He staggered backwards, reeling from the blows, shaking his head from side to side, blinking and weeping, wiping blood from his nose, then, when he saw the blood on his hand, he let out a kind of animal growl and hurled himself forward.

They fell as one to the field, each punching wildly at the other, as Marlene shrieked, Donna gasped, and the adults on all sides looked on, either amused or outraged. Johnny and Dan fought like hell, wrestling each other, throwing punches, until the former managed to roll on top of the latter, when he grabbed him by the throat and start throttling him, banging his head repeatedly, brutally, against the grassy ground. He had no thought of stopping. Impelled by a fury unknown to him before but now blotting out all else, he was determined to kill his former friend. Indeed, he might have done so had not Billy grabbed him by the shoulders and tried to drag him off his wildly kicking, wriggling victim.

Johnny didn't come off Dan. Instead, he turned instinctively, blind with fury, to throw a punch at his brother. Billy ducked and the blow missed him. He was just about to grab at Johnny again when Albert came running out of the crowd, pushed Billy aside, and roughly hauled Johnny, still swinging wild, blind punches, off his battered, bloody friend.

'What the hell's goin' on here?' Albert said, having dragged Johnny away and now hauling him up onto his knees. 'This is the Twelfth of July celebrations, not a bloody war. Now calm down, you two.'

Both boys clambered back to their feet, wiping blood from their noses, embarrassed because everyone standing around them was staring at them.

'What started this?' Albert asked of wee Billy.

Billy shrugged. 'I don't know.'

Mary also came out of the crowd, followed by Aunt Babs, Uncle Malcolm and Roy Williams.

'You!' Mary snapped, pointing her index finger at Dan. 'Get away from here. *Now!*'

'It wasn't my fault!' Dan protested.

'Yes, it was,' Marlene said. 'He swore at Donna here. That's what started it. He told her to...'

'You foul-mouthed wee bugger,' Mary said to Dan before Marlene could utter the swear word. 'Disappear. Take a powder.'

'Aw, fuck you all!' Dan exclaimed, wiping blood from his nose, but then, when Mary took a swipe at him, he turned away and rushed off.

'Just as well you missed him,' Albert said. 'Otherwise we'd have trouble with big Barney again.'

'To hell with big Barney,' Mary said. 'As for you,' she continued, looking at Johnny in disbelief, not believing that he, her favourite son, the *good* son, could have fought with anyone, let alone Dan Johnstone, since it was wee Billy who had the reputation for fighting. 'As for you,' she repeated, having temporarily lost her train of thought, 'sure I can't believe that you'd do such a thing, particularly on a day like this, with all these Orangemen standin' around gawping and having a giggle. And just because that eejut Dan Johnstone swore at Donna here.'

'It must be true love,' Auntie Babs said.

Marlene giggled. Donna simply smiled. Johnny burned up with embarrassment as he wiped the blood from his face. His heart was racing and he was secretly shocked by what he had done, not believing himself to be capable of it. Though that didn't help him with his embarrassment when Donna stared at him.

'Well, he gave that Dan Johnstone a quare hidin',' wee Billy said proudly.

Mary gave him a good clip on the ear for that remark. 'Just you shut your gob,' she said, 'and don't encourage him to be like you are. One's enough in this family. Are you alright, Johnny, love?'

'Aye, I'm fine,' Johnny said, though he was trembling, heart racing, cheeks burning, only capable of looking down at his own feet, avoiding their stares, wanting the ground to open up and swallow him.

'Okay,' Albert said. 'Let's forget it and go back to our table before some Orangeman pinches our food and drink.'

'Aye, let's do that,' Mary said. 'And you,' she said, turning to Johnny. 'You keep well away from that Dan Johnstone. You hear what I'm saying?'

'Yes,' Johnny said.

'Disgraceful,' Uncle Malcolm said as the adults started back to their table, just beyond the nearest catering tent, where the Orangemen and their wives and children were already eating and drinking. 'And right here on the Field on this day. Sure it beggars belief.'

'True love,' Babs repeated.

Wee Billy waited until the adults were out of earshot, then he took hold of Johnny's arm and shook it affectionately. 'Sure that was one hell of a fight,' he said. 'You're a real champion, Johnny. Now let's go and get something to eat and drink in one of them big tents. We'll spend the rest of the money that Dad gave us earlier on.'

'Aye, let's do that,' Johnny said.

He wanted to get away from Donna. Her steady gaze was disconcerting. He saw Marlene smiling at him, as if reading his mind, amused by his confusion, and that made him even more confused.

'Let's go,' Billy said, starting off.

Johnny was just about to follow Billy when Donna stepped in front of him, stopping him, deliberately standing close to him, her breasts grazing his chest. Gazing deeply into his eyes, smiling enigmatically, like a beautiful cat, she whispered, 'Who loves me?'

This was the Twelfth of July, 1954 and Johnny would never forget it.

Chapter Six

1

Eleanor was dying and Barry didn't know what to do about it. He had just been to see her in the Forster Green Hospital and been so shocked by her wasted appearance that he had wept outside in the corridor. Her lungs had gone. She had been coughing for years, of course, getting worse every year, and finally the flax dust from the mills, combined with her heavy smoking, had done her lungs in. She was dying of pulmonary tuberculosis, the common disease of the disadvantaged, politely referred to by the locals as 'decline', and she would not last much longer. It was only a matter of days now, maybe hours, and Barry could hardly bear to think about it.

Leaving the hospital, he gratefully took in lungfuls of fresh air. The hospital was located in one of Belfast's greener areas, between the Cregagh Hills and Belvoir Park with its lakes, woods and golf club, all of which, on this fine summer's day, looked pastoral and welcoming under an azure sky, far removed from the stench of death that Barry, rightly or wrongly, was convinced he had smelt in Eleanor's ward. There were others dying in that ward, all women, all young once, not imagining that they would ever age, let alone find themselves at death's door with no chance of reprieve. Nearly all of them, like Eleanor, were dying prematurely because of the atrocious working conditions in the factories owned and run by Protestants. When Barry thought of this, he wanted more than ever to bring down the Orange state.

Turning into the Saintfield Road, where the middle-classes resided, where Catholic and Protestants mixed, united by money, not in conflict because of the injustices that were inflicted upon the disadvantaged of the Falls and the Shankill, he glanced at the nearby houses, spacious, detached, with expansive gardens front and rear, hidden behind trees and high hedgerows. How ironic, he thought, that Eleanor should be dying of TB, the disease of the poor, in this pretty, well tended, bourgeois area. The employers partially responsible for Eleanor's fatal illness lived in areas just like this: certainly, if not right here, then in the upper Malone Road at the other side of the river. They were enjoying the good health of the privileged, even as she was dying well before her time.

Though Eleanor was four years older than Barry, she was still only thirty-nine and would not live to see her fortieth birthday.

Barry stopped walking, closed his eyes and choked up, then he wiped a few tears away and started walking again. He was hoping to find Kavanagh and his gang in Sean McGeown's bar, the Dacent Man, in the Pound Loney at 1.00 pm, which gave him an hour to spare, so he decided to fill the time by walking at least as far as the centre of town. Once out of the Saintfield Road, he took the Annadale Embankment, snaking around the River Lagan, offering another soothing vista of pastoral greenery. The playing fields of Wellington cottage were spread out on his right; tennis courts and the rowing club could be seen at the far side of the river, also nestling on smooth, hilly lawns and shielded by more woods. The air above the river was clear and did not contain flax dust. Death did not have dominion here.

Death did, however, seem to have dominion elsewhere and was making Barry feel twice his age. His mother, Lizzie, who had also slaved most of her life in mills owned by Protestants, had died the previous year from the same disease that was wasting Eleanor, though she had, at least, live to a decent age. Eleanor's illness, coming so soon after Lizzie's death, had plunged Barry into a nightmare from which he thought he might never escape. He felt trapped in it right now.

'I don't want to die,' Eleanor had said to him that very morning, desperately holding his hand, as if his energy might revitalise her. 'I'm scared, Barry. Oh, Jesus, I'm scared and that makes me ashamed.'

'You've no need to be,' Barry had replied, squeezing her hand, trying not to cry in front of her. 'Jesus, Eleanor, I...'

'I don't want to see myself. I'm frightened to look in a mirror. When I think of the children seeing me like this, then I *want* to die and get it over and done with it. I want to die, but I'm frightened.'

She was indeed gaunt and pale, a mere shadow of her former self, her breathing harsh and anguished, her brown eyes unnaturally large and luminous, staring at him and through him, at that great wall of darkness that only she could see right now, coming towards her to carry her away. She trembled and moaned in the face of it.

Barry hadn't recognised her. She had aged beyond her years. The woman lying on that bed, bathed in sweat, fighting for breath, was not the woman he had loved and married and shared his life with. She was another creature, desperate and alone, beyond all hope of rescue. She was going to that place he could not imagine and she filled him with fear.

Barry had squeezed her hand and promised to return in the afternoon, then he had rushed gratefully from the room. He had cried his eyes out in the hallway of the hospital, oblivious to passers-by, thinking only of that implacable wall of darkness that was coming towards her. He felt a different kind of darkness growing within himself, but it was not yet definable. He merely sensed its imminent arrival.

Yet the sun was still shining, contradicting his inner darkness, as he turned off the Embankment, crossed the King's Bridge to the Lyric Theatre, then headed down the Stranmillis Road, eventually passing the Ulster Museum and the Botanic Gardens: more sun-splashed green lawns, more hedgerows, more shivering trees; more people, young and old, out enjoying themselves as if they had all the time in the world.

We're all fools, Barry thought. Betrayed by God and cheated by Nature. There is no sense to anything.

When he reached the beginning of University Road, he glanced to his right, at the rambling buildings of Queen's University, and thought hopefully of the day when Sean would be the first of the Coogans to enter those august halls of learning. Sean was presently attending St. Mary's Grammar School, where he was proving to be an exceptional pupil, winning high marks in all subjects and, encouraged and helped by Barry, showing a natural bent for Irish history. Since his own belief in the value of armed conflict had faded, it was Barry's dream that Sean would carry on the family tradition of active Republicanism, though not with a gun. Instead, Barry wanted his only son to go to university and then perhaps become a lawyer specialising in civil rights, working on behalf of the Catholic community. If that happened, something at least would make sense to Barry, compensating him for Eleanor's premature, meaningless death.

Neither Sean nor Theresa had been told the truth about their mother's condition, but Eleanor had been in hospital for over three weeks, growing worse daily, and they must surely suspect something by now. They would learn the truth soon enough, certainly when Eleanor died, and Barry was praying that Sean, in particular, would not be thrown too far off the rails by his brutal, untimely loss.

He was not so worried about Theresa because she had little interest in school, was rebellious by nature, and would probably find her destiny in an early marriage. This was, in Barry's chauvinistic view, the way of the world. Right now, Theresa was obsessed with rock & roll music, which, spearheaded by Elvis Presley, had recently swept the teenage world; she spent most of her spare time in her room, playing records of her favorite singers, mostly American, and mooning over magazines containing pictures of them. For Barry, who was essentially conservative, musically and otherwise, that just about said it all.

By now he had left Shaftesbury Square well behind and was reaching the centre of the city, packed with people and clamorous with traffic, despite the relative quietness of the trolley-buses. Belfast had often been described as a dour city, but Barry had never seen it that way. As he made his way around the immense City Hall with its high dome and colonnades, its statue of Queen Victoria, an ostentatious monument to British Imperialism, he saw the red-and-yellow flowerbeds, dazzling in the sunlight, and the many people relaxing on the well-mowed, green lawns, some eating packed lunches. Likewise, the pavements of Donegall Place were packed with men enjoying their lunch break, many entering and leaving pubs, flushed with drink and grinning or laughing. Farther on, Corn Market and Castle Lane were packed with attractive girls dressed in figure-revealing summer clothing and bubbling with pent-up high spirits. All in all, then, this legendary 'dour' city was lively and colourful, offering Barry some distraction from his troubled thoughts. He loved this city and always would.

But the city, he saw, was changing. Though the shipyards and aircraft factories were still going, and while the rope works remained the biggest in the world, though British Oxygen and the Hughes Tool

Company remained, many of the old linen mills had shut their doors and were being knocked down, gradually opening the city to the sky and reducing the former density of its smoke and flax dust. Despite that, this was still a Protestant city, a city of churches, tabernacles and mission halls: Methodist, Presbyterian, Unitarian, Pentecostal, Anabaptist and good old fashioned gospel. Catholic churches remained in the minority, as were the Catholics generally.

Suddenly tiring, thinking again of Eleanor in the hospital and drained by the very thought of going back there, Barry decided to take a bus for the remaining short distance to the Falls. Boarding a Belfast Corporation Transport double-decker at Castle Junction, he took a seat up front in the Upper Saloon where he could gaze down into the stream of cars, motor bikes, bicycles, milk floats, various delivery vans and the odd, though gradually disappearing, horse and cart. The times were certainly moving on.

Getting off at a stop by one of the streets of the Pound Loney, Barry skirted around a parked Inglis' bread-van and made his way along to the Dacent Man pub. Entering that cozy, smoky gloom, busy as always at this lunch hour, packed with men wearing peaked hats and speaking with cigarettes virtually glued to their wet lips, their hands being used to hold a glass of stout or dramatically demonstrate a point, he saw Frank Kavanah, Seamus Magee and Kevin McClusky seated around a table near the counter, all drinking and clearly deep in conversation.

Nodding silently at them, Barry went to the counter and ordered a pint of stout. Close to his elbow, at the centre of the counter, was a high pillar of coins that were destined, when eventually broken apart, for the Nazareth Lodge Orphanage. Though the glittering pillar looked precarious, as if the slightest movement would bring it tumbling down, it was actually cemented together by the wet stout each coin had been dipped into before being added to the ever growing pillar by generous boozers; when the stout dried, it made a sticky paste that glued one coin to the other. Receiving his pint, Barry dipped a sixpenny piece into his glass of stout, glued it to the top of the pillar of coins, grinned automatically, then went to join Kavanagh and the others at the table. Despite the fact that Eleanor was dying of a pulmonary tuberculosis partially brought on by her heavy smoking (the other part being the deadly flax dust in the mills), Barry instantly lit up a cigarette and inhaled with relief.

'How's Eleanor?' Kavanagh asked in his blunt manner. Now in his early sixties and, though still as broad as a barn and clearly fit for his age, he looked every minute of his age, though his features had not been softened by time. He was still a hard man.

'As bad as can be expected,' Barry said. 'It won't be long now. I'll be goin' back there this afternoon. I just came here for a break.'

'You want something to eat?' Kavanagh asked. He and the others had already eaten and three used plates, smeared with gravy and littered with uneaten vegetables, were piled up in the centre of the table, waiting to be collected. 'It might do you some good.'

'No, I'm fine,' Barry said. 'I couldn't stomach anything right now. The stout and fag will do fine, thanks.'

'Sure it's a right shitty business,' Seamus Magee said.

'Aye, it is,' Kevin McClusky agreed.

'How are the kids takin' it?' Magee asked.

'They're a bit confused, I think. I haven't told them anything too specific, but I reckon they sense what's happening, like. I just can't bear to tell them outright.'

'Sure it's always hard to know what to do,' Magee said, 'when it comes to the kids. I had the same problem when my missus passed away. That was TB as well.'

Magee was now thirty-five and his wife had been the same age as him. She had, however, worked in the mills since leaving school at ten (child labour was commonplace in those days) and the flax dust, combined with her heavy smoking, had done her in a year ago. Those who worked in the mills all their lives rarely lived long. Now, thank God, the mills themselves were dying out, though clearly too late to help Eleanor.

'Those fuckin' mills have killed hundreds,' Kavanagh said, as if reading Barry's mind. 'Their disappearance might give us a few problems in the short term - I mean the growin' unemployment - but they're not likely to be missed in the long run. Sure didn't they kill as many poor souls as they fed?'

'No question about it,' McClusky said. Now two years short of forty, he was still lean and mean, still dark-eyed and dangerous. A man with few friends.

'So what are you boyos up to?' Barry asked, wanting to change the subject.

'Not much,' Kavanagh said. 'Not much we *can* get up to, having been ordered by those down south not to take any action in Belfast while the border campaign is still goin' on. It's bloody frustratin', I can tell you, an' I'm not sure they're right. I mean, what could be wrong with *us* causin' a little aggravation while they're doin' the same with their cross-border raids?'

'Damned right,' McClusky said. 'We haven't done a thing worth the mentioning since that raid in '54. A few things here and there, true enough, but nothin' special, like.'

'And since the beginning of the southern IRA's border campaign last year,' Magee added, 'we haven't been *allowed* to do a damned thing. I don't think that's right, sure I don't.'

Barry had not taken part in *any* overt action since that raid against a police station outside Antrim town three years ago when he had, to his horror, broken down in tears. He knew what had caused the tears. It was the sight of that RUC policeman with his kneecaps and, possibly, his shinbones, shattered by bullets, his legs bending in unnatural directions as he screamed in dreadful pain and collapsed. That sight, more than anything else, had given Barry an inkling as to why his father, Eddie, while remaining loyal to the cause, had finally turned his back on violence. Barry had wept, he now believed, because he had realised at that moment, when he heard the policeman screaming and saw his shattered legs, that he, too, could no longer deal with the violence and that there had to be some other way. He now saw that other way in his son, Sean, and, hopefully, others of his generation, who would carry the fight into the political arena instead of the war. Barry, who had bombed and shot more than he could stand, now believed in a non-violent solution. Unfortunately, few of his friends agreed with him.

Naturally, whatever his reasons, his tearful breakdown had been enough to get him dropped from all further IRA covert actions, though he had remained with his own unit, Kavanagh's unit, as a general driver and courier. He wasn't remotely ashamed to be so reduced; in fact, he had welcomed it.

'What I can't get over,' Magee said, 'is how, despite the success of that last big raid, which netted us a lot of arms and gained the northern command a propaganda victory, it eventually backfired on us.'

'It backfired,' Barry said, 'because the very success of the raid gave the Unionist government an excuse to warn people that the IRA was still a real threat to the six counties. It also enabled them to announce further spending on the security apparatus, including an increase in weapons for the B-Specials and even more repressive legislation against the Catholic minority.'

'Right,' Kavanagh said. 'In particular, it gave those Unionist bastards an excuse to introduce their notorious Flags and Emblems Act.'

'What's that?' Magee asked, ruffling his red hair with restless fingers, looking a lot younger than his years, though clearly not matured in intelligence.

'Someone tell the dumb bastard,' Kavanagh said, rolling his hard green eyes in exasperation.

'The Flags and Emblems Act,' Barry explained, 'permitted the RUC to remove any flag or emblem displayed on public *or* private property, if its display, in their view, could lead to a breach of the peace.'

'So?'

'What it meant, in effect, was that the displaying of the Irish tricolour was banned and only the flying of the Union Jack was permitted.'

'Well, fly me to the moon!' Magee exclaimed, seeing the light at last. 'Sure them Prods can never sink low enough. There's no bottom to 'em.'

'They always do that,' Kavanagh said, nodding his head as if talking to himself. 'Every time we get the better of them, they use it as an excuse to put us down even more. Remember the Westminster elections a couple of years back?'

'Aye,' McClusky said. 'The Republicans secured the biggest anti-partition vote since 1921.'

'Right. And the government's response was to declare that Orangemen could march wherever they choose, with no holds barred. Brian Faulkner then proved it by marching at the head of 15,000 Orangemen, protected by loads of B-Specials, through Longstone Hill in Mourne, despite the protests of the Catholic majority of that village.'

'A deliberate provocation,' McClusky said. 'A calculated display of arrogant, fuck-you power, designed to hammer home the fact that this was a Protestant country for a Protestant people. And those fucking bigots won the day again!'

'Maybe,' Barry said, glad to discuss anything other than Eleanor. 'On the other hand, it was that particular march that encouraged the IRA to launch Operation Harvest - still going strong after two years.'

'Goin' strong?' Kavanagh said contemptuously. 'Are you pulling our legs, like? That campaign was supposed to take Northern Ireland out of the United Kingdom once and for all; yet here we sit, still part of the fuckin' UK, still ruled by the Orangemen.'

This was true enough. Operation Harvest had been planned as a series of daring cross-border raids by the southern IRA, using the help of the Northern Units, but not letting them take an overt part for fear of a Loyalist reaction that could not be contained. The opening of the campaign, however, had been a botch, with little being achieved, while producing, in the case of a planned raid on a police station in Brookeborough, an absolute disaster in which six of the raiders were wounded and two killed. From that day on, while the IRA attempted to make propaganda out of the deaths of its two men, claiming that they had been 'executed' by the RUC, it was secretly forced to accept that it did not have the capability to defeat the Northern Ireland security forces. The weakened position of the organisation then worsened when De Valera was returned to power and, more crucially, when, a mere month ago, the Irish Special Branch arrested scores of IRA activists and reintroduced internment. Right now, there were over a hundred internees in the south and more than two hundred in the north. Since then, the IRA had been lying low on both sides of the border and Barry, at least for now, was no longer the only IRA man with time on his hands.

'Look on the bright side,' Barry said. 'That Suez disaster of last year left the Brits with egg on their faces, so right now they might be willing to compromise.'

'The Brits never compromise,' Kavanagh said. 'They don't have to; they divide and rule instead. They did it in India, they did it in Africa, and they've been doin' it here for three hundred years. As long as they keep supporting the Unionists they won't have to give an inch.'

'I think we can win this war by peaceful means,' Barry said. 'I think that after Suez, which really humiliated them, they'll be more open to political remedies than they've been in the past.'

'Ackaye, you'd say that, wouldn't you,' Kavanagh responded brutally, 'after havin' your wee breakdown during the last raid you were on? You couldn't stand the screamin' of the man you shot to hell and since then you've tried to justify your weakness. Well, don't try it on me, boyo. I haven't turned that soft yet. We've still got internment, a lot of friends are rotting in the Curragh prison, the border roads have been spiked, and between the Brits and the Unionists, both helped by that traitorous bastard, de Valera, we're virtually livin' like prisoners in our own country. So until we're set free, until we *set ourselves* free, we have to keep usin' the guns and the bombs to get what we want.'

'But we aren't doing that,' Magee said. 'Our friends down south won't let us. While they keep making insignificant raids across the border, into the six counties, we're not allowed to do a damned thing on our own. It's a fuckin' joke, if you ask me.'

'It's not a joke,' Barry said. 'The authorities have already rounded up too many of our men and a Protestant backlash would see the rest of us inside with our friends, which could mean the end of the organisation altogether. That's why we've been forbidden to take covert actions while those down south are making their cross-border raids. They need our support and they don't want to give the government an excuse to round up the rest of us. It's as simple as that.'

'Nothing's that simple,' Kavanagh said, always reluctant to give credit to anyone, 'but what you say is the truth of it.' He glanced at his wristwatch. 'Jasus, man, look at the fuckin' time! I have to be down at the dole office ten minutes from now. I'd better start makin' tracks.'

'Me, too,' Barry said, also glancing at his wristwatch. 'I want to go back and check up on the kids, then get straight back to the hospital.'

'The sooner it's over the better,' Kavanagh said with his customary pragmatism as he pushed his chair back and stood upright. 'It's always worse when it drags on. Well, the best of luck, boyo.'

'Thanks,' Barry said.

He finished his pint while Kavanagh was leaving the pub, then he, too, pushed his chair back and walked out, leaving Magee and McClusky still sitting over their pints, both looking bored.

The sun was shining over the Pound Loney as Barry made his way back home. The narrow streets of terraced houses were as busy as always, with housewives sunning themselves outside their doorsteps as their children played in the roads and on the pavements. Barry knew most of the adults and either nodded a silent greeting or said hello, receiving sympathetic smiles and encouraging comments in return, since they all knew about Eleanor's condition and sympathised. When he entered his own small, terraced house, he found that it was empty, the kids obviously out somewhere, so he made himself a cheese sandwich, opened a bottle of stout and sat down to wait for them to return.

It was time to tell them the truth and it wouldn't be easy.

2

The whole history of Ireland could be imagined by the banks of the Lagan Canal and the river that sometimes verged with it. Flowing all the way from Lough Neagh in Antrim, the canal snaked for twenty-seven miles down through Aghagallon, Soldiers Town, Trumery and the Lagan Valley to Lisburn, on from there to Lambeg and Belfast, then finally into the Victoria Channel and out into the Irish Sea. Along the stretch normally explored by Sean and his friends, from Shaw's Bridge to the Belvoir Park area, the river curved for about two-and-a-half miles between rich woods, meadows, playing fields, marshes and private grounds surrounding grand houses. Cattle stood in the long, lush grass of the upland fields. Other fields were golden with ripening corn and bright yellow daffodils. The light also lay golden on the river, which reflected the drooping willows along the towpath. There were eerie green-hued shadows under the tall hedges, breeze-blown and rustling, that stood on banks thick with weeds and tall, swaying bulrushes.

Sean knew from his voluminous reading that it hadn't always been like this. He knew, for instance, that the boulder-clay scattered about the area had been produced when the reddish material of the marls and sandstones had been ground up and scattered eons ago. Now, as he made his way along the towpath with Theresa, Tommy

Molloy and Gerry Donovan, he tried imagining what it must have been like, a wondrous spectacle in slow-motion, taking thousands of years, when the ice of the Ice Age withdrew, letting the Lagan valley emerge as dry land, though the adjoining Lough and the sea outside it were still vast tracts of water. The ice had formed a great wall, a veritable dam, and behind it, around the site of Belfast, a great lake had been produced as the withdrawing ice melted. Numerous streams from the highlands had carried into that lake the sediment which settled as red sand or as the fine red clay presently used for the bricks out of which most of Belfast's buildings had been constructed. It was hard to imagine.

'This river,' Sean said, pointing to the Lagan where it flowed glittering beyond the dense weeds and bulrushes growing out of the water running alongside the towpath, 'used to be a great lake, a sea, really, that covered where all of Belfast stands now.'

'Ack, away with ya!' Tommy Molloy exclaimed in disbelief as he let fire with a catapult, sending a stone flying towards a bird resting on the branch of a crab-apple tree in the field sloping away to their left. The stone missed and the bird flew off, unharmed. 'Aw, fuck!' Tommy exclaimed, disappointed again.

'You're a vicious wee shite,' Theresa admonished him, 'trying to kill an innocent wee bird like that. Sure you should be in a home with the other delinquents.'

'Fuck off,' Tommy said.

'No, it's true,' Sean went on, ignoring their bantering, glancing about him in wonder, trying to imagine what those green and golden fields, now speckled with white-washed houses, had looked like in ancient times, before the grass and corn had been cultivated.

'When Neolithic men lived in this country, the land around Belfast stood lower than it is now and the tide from the sea flowed a lot farther into this valley. In the post-Glacial age those fields we're seeing were a lot higher than they are now and filled with creatures that don't exist anymore.'

'You mean dinosaurs?' Tommy asked. Although he was now sixteen, like Sean and Gerry, he seemed younger because he was, so small and still as wild as a kid. He was still trouble, too.

'No,' Sean said. 'Not dinosaurs. Red deer, wild boar and loads of insects that don't exist anymore. Sure there were all kinds of creatures.'

'The thought of them gives me the shivers,' Theresa said, shivering melodramatically. 'Sure I hate creepy-crawlies.'

'Ack, they don't bother me at all,' Tommy boasted.

'They bother *me*,' big Gerry said, glancing down at Theresa (who, though growing, was still small, slightly under five-feet tall) and giving her his oddly bashful smile. Because he liked Theresa more than he could say, he was often tongue-tied in her presence.

'Then, you know what?' Sean asked, trying to stir their flagging interest.

'Okay, tell us,' Tommy responded. 'Bore the pants off us.'

'The land - that land out there; all those fields and hills - began to sink until it was buried about fifty or sixty feet under water. That sea covered what's now the whole of Belfast and it reached as far as Balmoral.'

'You're kiddin' me!' Tommy said, impressed despite his former lack of interest.

'No, I'm not,' Sean said. 'Sure the sea once covered the whole of Belfast. But then the land rose again, pushing up above the sea, and Belfast was built on what had previously been the sea-bottom, though the Lough and the sea around it remained. So that land out there - and even this towpath we're walkin' on - was once sixty feet under the water. That's a scary thought, isn't it?'

'I can't imagine it,' Tommy said.

But Sean *could* imagine it. He had a vivid imagination. Encouraged by his Da, he had read a lot of history books, some of which were illustrated, and based on what he had read and what the illustrations had shown him, he had often tried to visualise what had occurred as if it was happening all over again. He wanted to do that now, desperately needing some form of distraction. His Ma was ill and he sensed that it was worse than his Da had said, so he wanted to put it out of his mind by going back to the past. It was there in his head. If he closed his eyes he could see it. He saw the first Stone Age settlements around Mount Sandel, a Gaelic fort overlooking the lower Bann River, just south of Coleraine, where human beings had lived between 7000 and 6500 BC. The chronological history of Ulster, let alone the world at large, seemed to Sean, who had only been on Earth for fifteen short years, absolutely incredible. For twenty-five million years Arctic conditions had made Ireland inhospitable to humans, but then temperatures started to rise. Fifteen thousand years ago, when Ulster still lay under ice about one hundred feet thick, the real thaw began. The last great ice sheet, advancing south, tore and crushed rock from the mountains, then dumped it as it retreated, leaving it as huge heaps of boulder-clay that stretched in an irregular arc from Donegal Bay to Strangford Lock. Known as drumlins, those low rounded hills, about thirty miles long, would shape the whole future of Ulster.

As he walked with the others along the sunlit towpath, Sean saw, in his mind's eye, how the ancient drumlins, blocking the normal flow of water, became surrounded by loughs and dangerously dense fens which, overgrown with thickets and separated by more water, eventually divided the northern province from the rest of Ireland. Though not completely impenetrable, access to the north from the south was possible only through a few areas, including the fords of Erne in the West and the Moyry Pass in the east. By 11,000 BC, when all the ice had disappeared, as plants and animals returned to Ireland, bands of early humans migrated north from the Mediterranean region. Then, between 10,000 BC and 9000 BC, another 1,000-year cold spell wiped out everything except the hardiest plants. When the climate warmed again and melted the ice, land bridges were formed between Ireland and Britain.

Sean could scarcely imagine it: a tract of dry land that stretched most of the way from Ireland to the English mainland. But it had once existed, enabling primitive peoples to travel by dry land from as far as Cumbria and the Isle of Man before having to take to water - and those people, mysterious and, to Sean, magical, became the first inhabitants of Mount Sandel. From there, they had made their way to the caves in the Black Mountain and, possibly, to this very towpath.

Glancing left and right from the towpath, now resplendent in summer sun, the river flowing on one side of it, trees and sloping fields on the other side, Sean imagined his early ancestors, Mesolithic man, traversing it as he was doing right now. The very thought of it made his flesh tingle.

'God, I'm hot!' Theresa exclaimed, wiping sweat from her forehead with a hand muddied from being trailed through the reeds and bulrushes by the riverbank near Shaw's Bridge.

'Me, too,' Gerry said. 'Sure we've been out a long time.'

'I'm fine,' Tommy Molloy said, firing another stone from his catapult and grimacing with disappointment when it made the leaves of a tree explode wildly while missing the bird it had been aimed at. 'I'm not bothered by heat or cold, like. I'm not bothered by anything.'

'He thinks he's Superman,' Theresa said.

'I could've lived in a cave,' Tommy responded, boasting, 'and it wouldn't have bothered me at all. Sure you could put me in one of them caves up the Cave Hill and I'd be happy as Larry, like.'

'There used to be people living in those caves,' Sean informed him. 'Primitive people. Hunters. Fishermen. Later, they moved into huts and started farming. Some would have lived in those fields over there and maybe even fished here in the Lagan. That was thousands of years ago.'

Now, in his mind's eye, he saw the first Mesolithic camps in Ulster, the dome-shaped huts of spaling covered with bark or deer hide, each hut sheltering up to perhaps a dozen people who fished for salmon, flounder, sea bass and crab, using sharp-edged flints fixed to sticks that turned them into harpoons. They also hunted wild pigs with flint-tipped spears and arrows, for birds and wild fowl, for eagle, goshawk, red-throated diver, widgeon, teal and song birds, all of which were supplemented with hazelnuts, crab apples, goose-grass and seeds of water lilies. They ate better than Sean and his family had ever done in this state ruled by Protestants.

'My Da,' Gerry said, 'insists that people who believe we're descended from the apes are unChristian heathens.'

'Then *I'm* an unChristian heathen,' Sean said, 'because *I* believe we descended from the apes.'

'My Da calls me a right wee monkey,' Tommy said, 'and I used to think he was jokin' me. Now you tell me he's right.'

'I know *you're* descended from the apes,' Theresa informed him, 'because you still act like one.'

'Sticks and stones,' Tommy said, then glanced across the sloping field beyond the trees lining one side of the towpath. 'So some of those early men lived in huts in those fields over there?' he asked.

'Yes,' Sean said. 'They crossed the North Channel to Ulster with their cattle, sheep and pigs in the first half of the fourth millennium BC. At first they stayed near the shores of Strangford Lough, farming the land, but then, when the clearings became barren, they moved on, settled down in a new location, then moved on again when they had to. They kept doin' that until they reached Ballynagilly, County Tyrone, where they build the first known Neolithic houses.'

'What's "Neolithic" mean?' Tommy asked, growing interested despite his normal aversion to learning.

'The last period of the Stone Age.'

Tommy gave a low whistle of appreciation. 'Jesus, that's a long time ago!'

'Ackaye,' Gerry agreed, nodding and smiling at his beloved Theresa, 'it is, sure enough.'

Sean briefly closed his eyes, letting the sun warm his face while he visualised those same Neolithic settlers constructing protective stockades, growing corn, making pottery, working the land, breeding livestock, and building court cairns, the earliest megalithic monuments, almost certainly as temples, as well as portal tombs, or dolmens, using the enormous, bizarrely shaped stones that could still be seen all over the six counties. By 2100 BC the people of Ulster, the Ulaidh, were making a wide variety of objects from metal. By 2000 BC they were making weapons and domestic items from mixtures of copper, tin and lead, using gold in their ornaments and ceremonial artifacts, constructing immense stone circles and monuments as ceremonial sites or as pointers to the rising and setting of the sun, the moon and the stars. They were also building great forts and were constantly at war with each other, one tribe against the other, year in, year out, until united against a common foe: the Celts.

Sean was fascinated by the Celts. According to the books that he had read, the Celts had emerged into recorded history in the second millennium BC, spreading out from Bohemia and the east bank of the Rhine. By 500 BC they were the dominant force in Europe, setting out from their hill forts in chariots or on horseback to conquer all in their path. In 278 BC they sacked Rome, looted the temple of the oracle at Delphi and then crossed the Hellspont to settle in Anatolia. Though they did not actually invade Ireland, they infiltrated gradually over the centuries, beginning in 1000 BC and arriving in increasing numbers, advancing on horseback, with iron weapons, around 500 BC, to subjugate the people and, over time, to produce the Gaelic civilisation of early Christian times.

To Sean, who was obsessed with his own history, his country's history, it seemed that from the arrival of the first Celts to the present day, the history of Ulster was a stream of constant conflict, one war after another, each following the other so rapidly that they all seemed to merge seamlessly together. In those wars, or in that single, epic battle which was, in a sense, still being fought today, a spectacular epic of blood and death, there had been horrors aplenty, certainly enough to give Sean nightmares and make him shudder in dawn's eerie light.

In 59 BC Julius Caesar began his conquest of Gaul and the Celts collapsed before the might of Rome. Caesar invaded Britain in 55 BC, but his legions never advanced as far as Ireland, then known as Hibernia. In that relatively small, isolated island, Ulster was an area protected by defensive walls such as the Dane's Cast and the Dorsey: massive linear earthworks that extended for miles and were intended to defend the inland routes between the bogs, loughs and drumlins of what are now known as counties Down, Armagh, Cavan, Fermanagh and Donegal. The people of Ulster, the Ulaidh, also built huge, circular hill forts such as the Grianan of Aileach of the Uí Néill dynasty on the Inishowen peninsula in County Donegal. Those fortresses still stood all over Ulster and Sean had seen most of them. Each time he had gazed upon them, he had felt a ghostly shiver slithering down his spine.

However, those massive defensive walls and forts were not enough to protect Ireland from Viking invasion or Norman and Tudor conquest, nor from bloody intercine warfare. Sean was both enthralled and horrified by what he had read about these wars: the Vikings arriving in their long ships to plunder Bangor, destroy the coastal monasteries and slaughter all those in them, including the bishops and clergy; then moving inland up the rivers, carrying their long ships overland past rapids and falls, to plunder Armagh, destroy its churches and, again, ruthlessly slaughter all those found in them. When the Vikings were finally defeated in Ulster (though establishing themselves in the south), it was the turn of the Normans, who, after capturing the Viking cities of Waterford and Dublin, as well as the kingdoms of Leinster and Meath, conquered much of Antrim and Down, built the mighty Carrickfergus and Dundrum castles, and renamed the territory

'Ulster', from the Viking Uladztír, an adaptation of the Irish *tír* (land) and *Ulaidh*.

After the Normans came the Scots, led by Robert Bruce, who 'spared not saint or shrine, however sacred, nor churchmen or laymen or sanctuary, but went wasting and ravaging across Ireland from the Shannon in the south to Coleraine and Inishowen in the north'. However, the Scots, having wasted and ravaged, sparing nothing, eventually settled in Ulster, mainly in the Antrim Glens.

Following the Scots, came the English. Fearful of Ulster's position as an independent Gaelic province that could threaten the security of the realm, Elizabeth 1 determined to drive the Scots from the Antrim Glens and settle Englishmen in their place. This task was given to Walter Devereux, the Earl of Essex, who, in the autumn of 1573, arrived at Carrickfergus with a thousand soldiers and proceeded, for the next three years, to wreak havoc with massacres, hangings, the burning of crops, the slaughter of farm animals and even more inventive acts of politicised barbarity. Following Essex's downfall, other English expeditions were sent repeatedly into Ulster only to be repeatedly defeated by the 6000-strong conscript army of Hugh O'Neill, Earl of Tyrone, until, in 1602, after nine years of relentless war, a force of 4000 foot soldiers and 200 cavalry, led by Lord Mountjoy, disembarked at Culmore, on the south-western shore of Lough Foyle, marched from there to Derry, and gradually, over the winter, wore down the forces of O'Neill and his ally, Red Hugh O'Donnell. Aiding Mountjoy, Sir Arthur Chichester, governor of Carrickfergus, crossed Lough Neagh to create dreadful havoc on its western shores, killing, burning and spoiling, and, in his own words, sparing 'none of what quality or sex soever'. Finally, despite an attempt at rescue by the Spaniards, the forces of O'Neill and O'Donnell were defeated in the battle of Kinsale and the subjugation of the whole of Ireland was guaranteed. Mountjoy then went on to lay waste to the countryside, seizing cattle and destroying corn, creating a dreadful famine as a consequence. O'Donnell died in Spain, where he had gone in vain to seek help. O'Neill and the cream of Ulster's aristocracy also fled to Spain. With O'Neill, O'Donnell and most of the Irish aristocracy gone, the thousand-year history of Gaelic Ulster was swept away, leaving the country under the control of the English.

England's plantation of Scots and English Protestants then began, giving birth to the Orange State.

The horrors of those wars lingered in Sean's mind and sometimes resurfaced, as they were doing right now, to haunt and disturb him...

The captured wife and infant son of William de Braose, Lord of Limerick, being deliberately starved to death in prison.

The defenders of the garrison of Carrickfergus first reduced to eating hides, then killing and eating their Scots prisoners.

The Scots, in their turn, forced by hunger into Ulster after sweeping as far south as Limerick, reduced to eating the bodies of the dead disinterred from the cemeteries while their women devoured their own children.

Sir Brian MacPhelim O'Neill, Lord of Lower Clandeboye, plus his brother and his wife, put to the sword and then cut up in quarters.

The bloody slaughtering of every man, woman and child, over four hundred in all, in the honourably surrendered castle of the Gaelic lord, Sorley Boy.

And finally, worst of all, starving children, during the famine caused by Lord Mountjoy's pitiless scorching of the land, eating the entrails of their own mothers after feeding for twenty days on their corpses, roasting them continually on a slow fire and devouring them piece by piece, from the feet up to the shoulders and head, until only the entrails remained. Once they had eaten the entrails, those children, too, were doomed to starve.

This was the history of Ulster.

This was Sean's history.

'Hey, Sean,' Gerry said, oblivious to Sean's history. 'Do you remember how they once pulled the barges along here with horses that used the towpath?'

'Ackaye,' Sean said, glad to be returned to the present, being all too easily haunted by the past. 'Sure I do.'

Up until three years ago, horse-drawn barges known as black lighters (so-called because they were made of pitch pine and retained the blackish appearance of the original wood) were either motor-driven or pulled along the canal by heavy horses led by their haulers. Sean could clearly recall seeing them only a few years ago. The barges had moved from lock to lock, bridge to bridge, weir to aqueduct to quay, mainly to discharge coal for the mills, though boats returning from

Lough Neagh also carried flour, turf, tiles, sand, canned goods and farm produce. A few of the mills along the river remained, set back in the fields, but most were now boarded up and derelict. There used to be sweet shops along the towpath, usually located at one or other of the locks, but they, too, were starting to disappear.

This is history, Sean thought. The present is flowing back into the past even as we speak. This river is already ancient history, just like the great Megalithic sites scattered all over Ulster. Soon this river that we remember will be no more, existing *only* in memory.

That thought made him feel funny. What if his ma, so ill in hospital, also became only a memory?

No, he couldn't even consider it.

'There's one of the old locks,' Gerry said, placing his left hand on Theresa's shoulder to stop her from walking on and pointing with the index finger of his free hand to an overgrown, disused lock and the derelict house on the stretch of towpath that passed it. 'That's where the Lock-keeper used to live, but he's moved on as well.'

Originally there had been a total of twenty-seven locks along the Canal, with eighteen lock-keepers to look after them, most living in boatman's sandstone cottages surrounded by wild roses and creeping honeysuckle, in the shadow of sally trees. A few of the cottages were still in use, since river traffic still moved in both directions between Belfast docks and Lisburn, but most were now derelict and overgrown just like the old mills. Now, though the upper reaches of the Canal had been closed to traffic, coal delivered by boat to Belfast Docks was taken upriver by barges towed by tugboats, linked in groups of four, two up front, two behind, to the Belfast Gasworks located at the bottom of the Ormeau Road. Each tugboat had a hinged funnel that could be lowered flat to enable the vessel to go under the many low bridges. The barges going upriver to Lisburn were heavily laden, usually with coal, while those heading downstream, back to the Belfast Docks, were empty.

Sean and the others enjoyed watching the barges entering the locks and then slowly rising as the water on the high side of the river was poured in until the boat was on the same level as the water in the river at the upstream side of the huge, dark, moss-covered, somehow frightening sluice gates. Then the lock-keeper, using a long crank lever, would open the sluice gates to let the boats through and close them again once the boats had left the lock.

'I'm gonna be a lock-keeper when I grow up,' Tommy said. 'Sure that's a grand job. Bein' on your own, like, either spendin' all day in that wee shed, readin' comics an' the like, or bicyclin' up and down the river, from one lock to the next, takin' orders from no one. The life of Reilly, that is.'

'My Grandda told me,' Sean said, desperately trying to put inchoate, disturbing thoughts of his sick mother out of his mind, 'that he could remember when the canal burst its banks near the Molloy Ward lock. Millions of gallons of water poured into the fields on that side, leaving barges in this part of the river stranded on the dry bottom. And because that part of the towpath was missing, no one could use the canal for months. Loads of boats were stranded on the Sand Quay.'

'Oh, yeah? So how did they fix the burst bank then?' Tommy asked skeptically. 'I mean, how did they replace that missing section of towpath?'

'Dead clever,' Sean said, already looking forward to university and keen on lecturing. 'They took an empty steel barge and towed it up to where the burst bank was. They towed it using horses and draggin' it along the dried riverbed. Then they maneuvered the steel barge until it was blocking the big hole formed by the burst bank. When it was in position, they filled the barge with stones until it sank deep down into the hole, filling it completely. Finally, they poured cement over the barge and let it harden to form a solid bottom. Then they opened the lock further downstream - in the direction of the docks - and let the water back in. Now, when you walk along this towpath, you're actually walking over that sunken barge.'

'Jesus!' Tommy exclaimed, raising his eyebrows. 'You mean it's under our feet right now?'

'Aye,' Sean said.

A hundred yards from the Sand Quay was the Boat Club, located by Stranmillis and used for various recreational purposes, including dancing. At the Boat Club, a rowing boat was permanently attached by a looped rope to each side of the canal. This meant that people could get in the boat and pull themselves across the canal from either side without having to use oars. Sean and the rest of the gang had walked a good distance before returning to this point. They had walked a mile or so beyond Shaw's Bridge before turning back. During their walk they had collected apples from the crab-apple trees, some to eat and some to be used for the making of apple jelly. They had also collected chestnuts, which could be eaten when roasted. However, when a hole was bored in a chestnut and a length of knotted string wormed through the hole, the chestnut became a 'conker' that could be used in a competitive game in which two opponents took turns at swinging their individual chestnut, or 'conker', on the end of a string in an attempt to smash the conker of the opponent. If the attacker failed, his opponent then attempted to do the same in reverse. The loser was the one whose conker broke first.

Though all the boys felt that they were now too old for conkers (Theresa, being a girl, didn't play the manly game) they still occasionally played it just for fun, invariably cracking their knuckles instead of the conkers and either yelping with pain or bursting into fits of hysterical giggling.

During their long walk, they had also stopped at just about every stone bridge they came to, to fool about in the shallows at the side of the river, trying to net tadpoles in old socks, to simply have a rest, or, as at Shaw's bridge, to eat their packed sandwiches and drink from a bottle of fizzy orange juice or lemonade.

Sean's favourite spot was Shaw's Bridge, named after the English captain who built an oak bridge there in 1655 to transport the guns of Cromwell's army across the river. Rebuilt in 1709 from the stones of the demolished Castle Cairn, the bridge had five arches and was surrounded by grazing fields, gently rolling hills and woods. Unusually, at Shaw's Bridge, the towpath passed under the arches, but also changed to the opposite side of the river, so you had to cross the bridge in order to continue your journey along the river. Despite his love for the pastoral beauty of the bridges, Sean could not help recalling that in former times men had been hanged from them for stealing sheep and that other unfortunates had been murdered near them, then either dumped into the river or left to rot under the arches until found by someone using the towpath. The bridges were beautiful during the day; at night they gave you the shivers.

'Jesus!' Theresa exclaimed when they had all reached the Boat Club and flopped on the grassy verge of the towpath to cool down in the shade of some yew trees which were reflected, distorted and wavering in the flowing waters of the broad river. 'I'm all hot and sweaty and we've still got to go all the way through town to get back to the Falls. Who's goin' to carry me?'

'I will,' Gerry said.

Theresa smiled at him and patted the back of his hand. 'Aye,' she said, 'I bet you would.'

Theresa was as tough and as wild as most boys; only Gerry, so big and awkward, could bring out her gentler side.

Sean wondered what she was thinking. Theresa rarely expressed her emotions, other than through aggressiveness, and neither of them had mentioned their mother's illness, as if by not talking about it, it might go away. Sean was worried. Their Da had been pretty vague about their Ma's illness, but Sean sensed that he was a lot more worried than he let on. Ma had been in the hospital for over three weeks now and there had been no mention of when she might be coming out. Also, it seemed to Sean that his Da had been visiting Ma with increasing frequency, his original one visit per day recently increasing to two or even three times a day. When Sean started wondering why, his thoughts shifted and slid, moved on elsewhere; though now, gazing down at the river, thinking of how the river he had known throughout his childhood was already disappearing, real only in recollection, he thought of his mother as being like the river, her life flowing back into the past that they had all shared a long time ago. He saw his mother gradually disappearing as the present moved inexorably into the future. He thought of her disappearing entirely... and then...

Shivering, suddenly shaken leaf and bough, he scrambled hastily to his feet and said in a strangled voice, 'Come on, let's get goin'. We've still got a long walk ahead of us and our Da's expectin' me an' Theresa back no later than three.'

'What time's it now then?' Theresa asked as she clambered to her feet and brushed loose soil off her flower-patterned dress.

'Ten past two,' Sean said.

'Jesus!' Tommy exclaimed, also jumping to his feet with big Gerry rising beside him. 'I was supposed to be back for lunch. Sure I'm gonna get kilt.'

'Let's go,' Sean said.

Growing more fearful with every step he took, he led them towards the centre of town, heading for the Falls. The walk, which took about forty minutes, seemed to take forever. Once back in the Pound Loney, Sean and Theresa bid their friends goodbye, then entered their house. Their Da was in the small, gloomy living room, slumped in an armchair by the fireplace, smoking and drinking. He looked extremely uncomfortable.

'Sit down,' he said gruffly to both of them. 'I've something to tell you.'

3

Walking back to the hospital, fearful of what he might find there and putting the moment off, Barry felt the world closing in upon him and starting to choke him. He felt that he was suffocating, the blood pounding in his head, and when he glanced about him, he hardly saw a thing, being locked up in the cell of his nightmare, succumbing to interior darkness and thoughts best avoided.

It had been a hellish experience trying to explain to the children, or, at least, trying to decide *how much* to tell them. He had intended telling them the truth, that their mother was dying, that her time was coming soon, but try as he might, he just couldn't do it, could not get his lips to form the words, 'Your mother is dying'. Instead, though fully intending to say just that, he had sat them down on the sofa in that cramped, gloomy living room and found himself saying, his voice hoarse, almost mumbling, 'Listen carefully to me, kids. I've got something to tell you. As both of you know, your Ma's been in hospital a long time, nearly a month now, so I suppose you've guessed she's not well at all.'

'Ackaye,' Sean said, trying to sound calm and mature, though his jaw muscles were working as he ground his teeth together. 'Sure I guessed that alright.'

'Me, too,' Theresa said, her expression revealing only confusion and, perhaps, instinctive fear. She glanced at him and then lowered her gaze to study the floor at her feet. Barry's heart went out to her.

'Well, it's bad, kids. No use pretending otherwise. I have to tell you that... I mean, I don't know how long... Well, damn it, I have to tell you to be prepared for the worst and to look after each other until I get home again.'

'You're goin' out again?' Theresa asked, not sounding her customary saucy self.

'Aye,' Barry said. 'I'm going back to the hospital right now, to keep your Ma company, and this time I might be there a long while. I mean, I may not be back before the morning, so you'll have to look after yourselves. I've asked Grandda to call in this evening, just to check if you need anything, and I've already prepared a salad for you.' He sighed, rubbing his hands on his outspread knees, trying not to scream and kick the walls. 'So do you think you'll be alright?'

Sean's jaw muscles were still working and his eyes were glistening wetly, but he managed to keep his gaze steady. 'Why can't we come with you? We haven't seen Ma for three days. Every time we want to go and see her, you say it's not the right time. When will that be?'

Barry glanced at Theresa. She looked like an urchin from a Charles Dickens novel. Though pretty, she was a tom-boy who ran wild in the streets, more so than her brother, and was always disheveled and streaked with dirt, as she certainly was right now, doubtless having been fooling about where the waters of the Lagan River were shallow, around one of the bridges. Unlike Sean, she was uncertain about what was happening, exactly what she was hearing, her gaze still showing her confusion and inchoate dread. Barry, not wishing to witness that, turned his gaze back on Sean.

'Your Ma's feeling weak at the moment,' he said, 'and hasn't the energy to talk too much. The fewer visitors she has, the better. Best to let her just rest, like.'

Sean's gaze remained steady, unblinking, but his voice was a strangled sound. 'You said we should prepare for the worst. What does that mean, Da?'

Barry sighed again, too loudly, as he pushed his chair back and stood upright. 'Sure I don't know,' he said. 'I don't know. Ack, Jesus, don't ask. *I don't know!*'

Suddenly trembing, trying to choke back his tears, he leaned down to grab each of the two children by the shoulder. He squeezed them, shook them affectionately, forlornly, then before they could see the state he was in, he expelled his breath in another lingering sigh and rushed from the house.

'Christ!' he now exclaimed softly, speaking only to himself as he walked along the Saintfield Road, blind to the green fields and shivering trees, oblivious to the first drops of a rainfall. 'Jesus, never again!'

As if to reflect his thoughts, the sky had turned dark, with clouds drifting across the mountains and a chill wind rising to slap the rain gently against his face. He scarcely noticed. Turning into the grounds of the hospital, he nearly stopped walking, as if physically repelled by the very sight of it. In truth, he did not want to go in there. Instead, he wanted to avoid this particular grim reality, wanted to disappear from the face of the Earth rather than see Eleanor pass on, leaving him and the children behind. Yet he kept walking despite himself, drawn to the hospital like a lemming to the sea, impelled by pure instinct, while the faces of Sean and Theresa materialised spectrally in front of him, disembodied in thin air, wholly imagined, vividly real, their eyes seeming to shine unnaturally with bewilderment and fear, with the inexorable rise of uncontainable grief.

He had hurried out of the house in order to avoid those eyes, unable to deal with them, despising himself for his helplessness in the face of the pain they were soon to suffer, hating God for inflicting it. Nevertheless, because he didn't have a choice, he entered the hospital.

Inside, it was cool and orderly, clean and tidy, almost welcoming, with people coming and going in a constant stream: doctors, nurses and relatives. The nurses smiled a lot, offering comfort to one and all, not falsely but automatically, living every day with suffering and death, dealing with it as best they could. They smiled at Barry when he entered. They smiled at him in the corridors. The nurse just coming out of Eleanor's ward smiled at him as well.

'How is she?' Barry asked.

The nurse stopped smiling. 'Not too good, I'm afraid.' She shook her head from side to side, while offering a sigh of defeat. 'Not too good at all.' Then she smiled again, trying to offer him encouragement. 'But you go on in, Mr Coogan. Sure she'll be real pleased to see you. Father Connolly's with her.'

'That's grand,' Barry said.

Entering the ward, he went along the central aisle, between the opposing rows of beds with their white-faced, wasted, constantly gasping, tubercular patients, the visitors either seated or standing around them, all speaking in hushed, reverential voices, as if already in church for the funeral service. The whole ward was a riot of flowers, all brought by visitors.

Eleanor was in a bed near the far end of the ward, not propped up by the pillows as high as she had been before - an ominous sign. She was holding her rosary beads in her trembling hands as she painfully gasped out her Confession to Father Paul Connolly, the local priest and a family friend.

Barry froze, not wanting to hear the Confession, preferring not to know his wife's sins. He turned away to walk back to the corridor just outside the ward. Once there, he went to the window to gaze out at the pouring rain and windblown trees, the pastoral, wild, dark beauty of the Cregagh Hills. He let five minutes pass, an eternity, never ending, then turned back into the ward and walked reluctantly, numbly, to Eleanor's bed.

Father Connolly was holding Eleanor's right hand while staring courageously at her wasted face and large, unnaturally bright eyes. Barry knew what that luminosity signified. It was the glazed light of dread. He had seen that same light in the eyes of some of the men he had killed. He had seen it just before he had killed them, when their eyes had focused, with disbelief and growing fear, on the weapon aimed at them. Their eyes had always turned luminous at that moment - the moment of death. This was Eleanor's moment.

'Bless you for coming, Father,' Barry said, stepping up behind the priest as Eleanor's gaze turned towards him, looking at him and through him, searching instinctively, perhaps hopefully, for the Great Unknown, beyond the reach of the mortal world. 'Oh, Eleanor... My...'

But Eleanor choked and coughed, groaned and moaned, gasped and sighed, as Father Connolly stood up, took hold of Barry's wrist, pushed him down onto the chair, then pressed his hand around Eleanor's hand as if to make them as one. That hand was as cold as ice. It was the hand of the living dead. Barry shuddered to feel that hand when it suddenly grasped his, as if clinging on for dear life. Gazing into Eleanor's glazed, fearful eyes, he saw eternity's doorway.

'Ack, Jesus!' he exclaimed in a whisper, not knowing what he was saying.

Father Connolly squeezed his shoulder and whispered, 'Don't blaspheme, my son. Sure she's received the ministrations of Holy Religion, made her Confession, repeated the act of contrition, received Extreme Unction and Last Blessing and Holy Viaticum. She's been comforted, my son, and is now prepared and in a state of acceptance. Listen to her. Talk to her.'

'The children!' Eleanor croaked, then choked and gasped, fighting for her last breaths, shivering, the sweat glistening on her browning, wrinkled skin, formed by premature ageing, ice and fire at war in the living flesh, given life by her dying. 'The children!' she managed to croak again as her eyes rolled back in her head to take in a dissolving world.

'Yes, love,' Barry whispered.

'Sean!'

'Yes, love.'

'Theresa!'

'Yes, love!'

'Ma! Da! Barry! *Yes, Sean!* No, Theresa, you silly wee thing... *Yes, Theresa!* Bless me, Father, for I have sinned... Where am I? What...?'

As far as Barry could see, she was not prepared for anything, was hardly aware of anything, except the pain of her final, dreadful suffering. Her body rose and fell, twisting this way and that, trying to break free from its bondage, incarcerated in light and shadow, imprisoned in space and time, but then she opened her eyes to look directly at him, deep into his soul, drawing him to her for the last time, leaving him mortified.

'Barry!' she cried out, her grip tightening around his hand, the ice of her fingers numbing his very bones. 'Barry! The children! Sean and Theresa! God, *where are my children?*'

'They're here,' Barry lied desperately, since it now made little difference. 'They're here, love,' he added, squeezing her frozen, sweat-slicked hand. 'They're right here beside you. Me and the kids. We're all here with you, darlin'.'

But she no longer heard him, was beyond him, in her own world, her mind reeling back through its own history, before the absolute darkness claimed her.

'Ma! Da! Barry! Yes, Sean! No, Theresa! Yes, Theresa! Yes, Ma! Bless me, Father, for I have sinned. Where am I? What?' Gasp, gasp. 'Why?' Gasp, gasp. 'Who?' Gasp, gasp. 'Sean! Theresa!' Gasp, gasp. 'Oh, God, please forgive me for I have sinned.' Gasp, gasp. '*I can't breathe!* I can't...' Choking again and coughing, gasping painfully for breath, her skin stretched so tightly on the cheekbones that it looked transparent, exposing the skull beneath. 'God! Oh, my God! Why did I? Why did *you*?' Gasp, gasp. 'Sean! Theresa! Oh, my Barry! Dear God, help me...' Gasp, gasp. 'What is it? That light! Ah, God help me, what's happening? Where am I? What's...? Where...? When...?' Gasp, gasp. Then, in a rushing tide of expiring air, her final word: '*Jesus!*'

She died gasping and choking as Barry held her hand, as Father Connolly squeezed his shoulder, as the world spun and turned and the sky fell about him, the cosmos imploding, as her icy grip on his hand tightened for one last, desperate moment, in pitiful, forlorn hope, before finally letting go, his tears falling on the back of her wasted, shrunken wrist to stain the white sheets, flooding and obliterating the whole world for all time, to eternity.

Barry wept as she died, wondering what he had lost. He wept because he had never really known her and she had never known him. He stared down at her dying face (not dead, though death had come), not recognising her at all, repulsed by what he saw, not even remembering her as she had been when they were both stirred by passion.

Passion? Oh, yes. Passionate politics, passionate sex. Romantic love born out of a love for their country, a shared commitment to the cause (a cause greater than the self?) until the cause betrayed her, or, at least, discarded her, leaving her with nothing but bitterness and the pain in her choked lungs. She was dying, her fingers gradually relaxing around his hand, in a disillusionment that had possibly destroyed her long before her lungs failed her. She was dying deprived.

Barry choked back his tears.

Father Connolly compassionately squeezed his shoulder once more. 'The Lord be praised, it's over,' he whispered, 'but life will continue. Have faith, my son. Pray for her. Now please let me...'

But Barry had no faith. Though a Catholic, he was faithless. His only son, Sean, appeared to have that faith, but Barry, though he would not discourage Sean, preferred to live without faith.

Where was God when Eleanor needed Him? Not here. Not out there. He was neither in the wind nor in the rain, and His silence was absolute. God did not have dominion here. Only death had that. Eleanor lay here, a corpse, unrecognisable, beyond rescue, while Father Connolly, a good man and family friend, prayed for her supposedly immortal soul and took his faith from that prayer.

Barry wanted to believe. He cried out to believe. He wanted to pray with Father Connolly, to confess all his sins, but his sins, which included murder, the execution of the innocent, the creation of the luminosity that he had seen in Eleanor's eyes, were too great to be absolved with mere Confession. In Eleanor's final, anguished gasp, in the dreadful, unnatural luminosity of her dying, he was convinced that she was saying what he had often imagined his own victims to be silently, desperately saying just before he blew them to Kingdom Come: 'Please don't do this to me. I, too, despite my weaknesses and vices, am one of God's children. Please have mercy upon me.' Where was God when they needed Him? Had He been there for Eleanor when her time came? Barry couldn't believe it.

He broke down and wept more bitterly, with no shame, with real pain, while Father Connolly, a man who truly believed in God, wrapped his arms about him and rocked him like a child in its cradle.

'Oh, Christ!' Barry sobbed. 'Jesus!'

There was no reprimand from Father Connolly, who, in his innocence and faith, translated the blasphemous words as Barry's prayer of acceptance.

4

Shortly after Eleanor was buried in the Belfast Cemetery, friends and relatives poured into the house to pay their respects. The men arrived with bottles of stout and whisky, the women brought cakes and sandwiches, and all of them tried to bring good cheer. Knowing how small the house was, they did not all come at once, some heading off to the nearest pub for an hour or so, others attending to personal business first, but the house filled up anyway, with people packed tightly together in the small living room and kitchen, as well as the bricked-in back yard upon which the sun was mercifully shining.

'Sure isn't it grand to see how popular Eleanor was?' Brendan Coghill said, glancing about the packed living room while sipping from his glass of Bushmills whiskey. 'This is a really swell turn-out.'

'Aye, it is that, right enough,' Barry's father Eddie said, while also holding a glass of Bushmills, sipping it more slowly than Brendan. 'Eleanor would've been pleased.'

Sean wasn't pleased. Still in a state of shock, he was sitting beside Theresa at the top of the stairs, looking down on the adults at the bottom and frequently glancing through the banisters at the people packed together in the living room, most drinking, all wreathed in cigarette smoke and making a lot of noise. Apart from his Da, his Grandda and Brendan Coghill, both in their late fifties but still with heads of thick grey hair, he saw Father Connolly, Gerry Donovan's parents, Tommy Molloy's parents, and his Da's three boozing companions, Frank Kavanagh, Seamus Magee and Kevin McClusky. He hadn't seen any of them in a long time, as they rarely came to the house, and he was shocked by how old Frank Kavanagh, in particular, now looked. Kavanagh was in his sixties, but he looked even older than that and was clearly still as mean as he had always been. Sean had never liked him and often wondered why his father bothered with him. Probably because they were both in the IRA, as were Magee and McClusky. The latter also seemed mean to Sean; while the former was simple-minded and hot-tempered. Sean loathed most of his father's friends, the one exception being Brendan Coghill, whom he deeply respected.

'Sure somethin' good always comes out of a death,' Magee was saying between sips from a bottle of stout. 'Old friends and relatives gettin' together, for instance, after not seein' each other for years. It's compensation, like.'

'Aye, maybe,' McClusky replied, his voice sounding abrasive, 'though personally I could do without my relatives, most of 'em more trouble than they're worth. Nice to have a drink, though.'

'That's true, right enough.'

'Real sorry about your troubles,' Mr. Molloy, Tommy's father, was saying to Barry, while resting a hand consolingly on his shoulder. 'Just try to bear up, lad.'

'I will,' Barry replied.

'Sure that woman of yours was a grand wee girl,' Mrs. Molloy said, sniffing back her tears and dabbing at her eyes with a handkerchief. 'It breaks m'heart to think of her goin', but sure God has his reasons.'

'Aye, right,' Barry said.

'She's in a better place now,' Mrs. Donovan, Gerry's mother, said, nodding affirmatively. 'No longer sufferin' in this earthly vale of sorrow and tears. She's up there with the angels now.'

'I hope so,' Barry said.

'Let's have a good time while we recall her,' Mr. Donovan said, 'and put the misery of the funeral behind us. I know Eleanor would have wanted us to do that.'

'She would indeed,' his wife said. 'Sure that woman had a heart of pure gold, as I always told everyone. A real saint, she was.'

'Absolutely,' her husband said.

Looking down from upstairs, Sean failed to understand how all those people could be in such good mood. Of course, some of the men looked uncomfortable and some of the women occasionally cried, recalling some virtue of the dearly departed, but for the most part they seemed, to Sean, to be using the death as an excuse to have a good time. Sean resented this, particularly when he saw his Da drinking and smiling at his friends, even though, no doubt about it, the smile was pained and possibly even forced. That, however, wasn't good enough for Sean. He wanted his Da to burst into tears, to openly show his grief, but all he was doing was getting drunk with his drunken friends. This deeply offended Sean.

Beside him on the top stair, Theresa was alternating between whispered swear words and tears. 'Fuck, fuck, fuck,' she would whisper and then grit her teeth, her lips forming a grim, defiant line, before the tears came again. Sean squeezed her hand reassuringly, as he had been doing a lot today, first in the church, then in the cemetery, and finally right here in the house.

'It's alright,' he said repeatedly, ineffectually, not even knowing what he meant. 'It's alright, Theresa.'

Because it *wasn't* alright. Nor was it *all right*. In truth, the past few days had been a nightmare and he could still hardly credit what had happened. Most of it had taken place in an unreal blur, a kind of waking dream, and now, when he looked back on it, his recollections were both hazy and fragmented.

His Da had returned from the hospital, obviously distraught, hugging them both and saying, 'I'm sorry, kids, but your Ma's passed on. She won't be comin' home, now or ever. You understand? She's passed on. She's up in heaven now. Oh, God, kids, I'm sorry...'

Sean had known instantly what his Da was talking about: his Ma had *died*, she was *dead*, but Da couldn't bring himself to utter those words, so Sean's Ma had 'passed on'. But his Ma had *died*, she was *dead*, she was gone *forever*. When this sank in - and it didn't take long - Sean felt his whole world collapsing.

Theresa had turned away and ran up the stairs to lock herself in the bedroom. She had cried for hours and refused to come out until the next morning. Sean, who still shared the bedroom with her, was forced to sleep on the sofa.

He vividly recalled that night, only a couple of nights ago, though it seemed like a million years away. He had spent most of it sleepless, alternately sobbing and having bad dreams, to awaken the next day feeling shattered. Later, when his mother's body was moved to the funeral parlour, where people could go to pay their last respects, their Da had insisted upon taking Sean and Theresa to see her. Neither had wanted to go, but their Da had made them do so, saying that they'd regret it if they didn't see her for the last time. So both of them had gone in fear and trembling. Now, when Sean recalled that visit, it seemed like another bad dream, not remotely real: Theresa and him taking turns to look into the coffin at the alabaster-white face of their mother, skin stretched tight on the bone, eyes closed, lips tight, all expression drained away, both by death and by ghoulish make-up, everything that had made her familiar erased for all time. Yet much worse was when, at the urging of their Da, they had each leaned over the coffin to kiss their dead mother's forehead. Sean now shivered to recall the coldness of her skin, the absence of tactile sensation, the revulsion and terror that had swept through him at that moment, only to be followed by a scourging shame aroused by the knowledge that it was his formerly beloved mother who had caused the revulsion.

He was ashamed of himself even now, as he sat on the landing at the top of the stairs, beside his equally stricken sister, scalded by hot waves of guilt, to think of how he had reacted to the sight of his Ma in her coffin, to the coldness of her dead skin against his lips. He was convinced that he had betrayed her at that moment and deserved to be punished.

'How are you two?' Father Connolly asked, emerging from the packed people below, framed by two banisters, to look up at them, smiling in his kindly, understanding way. Father Connolly, in his black suit and clerical collar, looked younger than his forty-five years because his face was so pleasant, good-humored and decent, though his reddish hair was thinning at the top. He was a popular priest with the locals and Sean, too, was fond of him.

'I'm fine,' Sean replied.

'I feel sick,' Theresa said. 'I don't feel fine at all. I wish all of them people would clear out and leave us alone.'

'They're just paying their respects,' Father Connolly said. 'When you're older you'll understand how important that is at a time like this. Just be patient, Theresa.'

'All that smoke,' Theresa said, meaning the cigarette smoke. 'Sure it's stinkin' out the house. No wonder I'm feelin' sick right now. All that smoke's gettin' to me.'

Barry, who had been standing in the centre of the living room, talking to Tommy Molloy's parents, turned around and stepped forward until he was beside Father Connolly.

'If you're bothered by the smoke,' he said, 'go outside and find a friend to play with. The sun's blazin' out there and it's really hot. You can breathe some fresh air – and playin' with friends will give you a wee bit of distraction. You'll feel better doin' that.'

'Aye, I might,' Theresa said. 'Sure I'd be better off out there. My Ma died from the smokin', yet you're all smokin' like trains and not carin' about the damage you're doin' to us. You should be hung from a gallows.'

'Now, now, Theresa...' Father Connolly began. But before he could say more, Theresa burst into tears again and rushed down the stairs, rudely pushing aside those sitting further down and then bolting out through the front door.

'Theresa!' Barry called out , clearly about to follow her.

'It's all right, Da,' Sean said, getting to his feet and starting down the stairs, 'I'll go out and stay with her. You stay here and look after the guests.'

'Aye, right,' Barry said. 'Thanks, son, you do that. Don't let her do herself a mischief.'

'I won't,' Barry promised.

Making his way down the stairs, stepping around the others sitting there with drinks in their fists, smoking like trains, he went out into the street to find his sister. The sun was indeed blazing out of a cloudless azure sky and the neighbours not already in Sean's place were taking advantage of the good weather, sitting outside their terraced houses, enjoying a good bit of *craic*, watching their children playing on the pavements. Sean saw Theresa across the road, disappearing through the doorway of Gerry Donovan's house, obviously seeking the company of Gerry and his sister Martha while their parents were having drinks in her own house. The door closed behind her as Sean started across the road, aware that some of the adults sitting out on the pavement were giving him looks of commiseration. Ignoring them, he went up to Gerry's front door and knocked on it with his bare knuckles. Gerry opened the door and nodded, not smiling, faintly embarrassed because he didn't know how to respond to the death of Sean's Ma.

'Aye, she's in here,' he said, stepping aside to let Sean enter. Theresa was sitting on the sofa beside the fireplace, sharing a cigarette with Martha. Sean knew that she smoked the odd cigarette, as a lot of kids her age did, though it surprised him that she was doing it right now, just after her outburst of a few minutes ago. When he stepped into the living room, stopping in front of his sister, Gerry closed the front door behind him and then entered the living room to join him.

'Are you alright?' Sean asked of Theresa.

'Aye,' she said. 'I'm fine. I just had to get out of that place, away from all them hypocrites. Pretending to be payin' their respects, while they stuff their bellies and knock back the drinks. My Ma's dead and buried and I don't want to know anything more about it. I don't want to sit there all afternoon, bein' reminded it of it by their presence. I don't want to hear them sayin' how wonderful she was when they barely spoke to her when she was alive. And there's some that Ma despised and refused to speak to, yet there they are, singing her praises like they'd loved her with all their might. So I didn't want to see or hear anymore. I'll go back when they're gone.'

'Give us a drag of that fag,' Martha said. 'Sure I'm sittin' here gaspin'.'

Martha, like her brother, was big for her age, already running to fat, with a face totally lacking in good looks or humour. Her short brown hair was dowdy, a double chin was already threatening, and her constant sobriety made her look a lot older than her twelve years. Theresa tolerated her, rather than being best friends with her; she only came here a lot to see Gerry, who, though big as well, was not running to fat and, though sometimes shy in her presence, had a quiet sense of humour. Also, Gerry adored her. And Theresa, though she behaved like a tomboy, could not resist being wanted.

She had another quick drag on the cigarette, then passed it to Martha.

'Hey, Gerry,' she said.

'What?'

'Go upstairs and bring down your record-player and let's have some music.'

'All right,' Gerry said. Always keen to keep Theresa happy, he turned away and bounded up the stairs.

Sean followed Gerry up into the bedroom that he still shared with his sister. The room was a mess, with photos of movie stars and popular singers, cut out of magazines, stuck up on the walls and lots of 78 rpm records scattered carelessly over Martha's bed. Though Gerry liked rock & roll as well, it was Martha who bought most of the records.

'You take the record-player down,' Sean said, 'and I'll bring the records.'

'Okay,' Gerry said.

A couple of minutes later they were downstairs again, the record player was spinning, and Elvis Presley was singing 'All Shook Up'. Theresa and Martha were tapping their feet to the music while sharing another cigarette.

'Where'd you get the fags?' Sean asked.

'Nicked them from a packet m'Ma left in the kitchen,' Martha said. 'She smokes so much, she'll never notice they're missing. There's lots more where these came from. You want a drag?'

Sean shook his head from side to side. 'No.'

'He's so pure,' Theresa said.

Elvis was followed by Paul Anka, Gene Vincent, the Coasters, the Everly Brothers, Fats Domino and Jerry Lee Lewis, by which time Sean had had enough and decided to go outside again and take in some sunshine.

'You wanna go out for a walk?' he asked Gerry.

But Gerry, who loved his records almost as much as he loved Theresa, didn't want to leave either. 'Naw,' he said. 'I'd rather stay here and dig the music.'

'Okay,' Sean said, slightly annoyed at Gerry's use of that American word 'dig' and certainly not in the mood for loud, uplifting music. 'I'll see youse all later.'

'Right,' Theresa said. 'See ya.'

Leaving them to their music and cigarettes, Sean left the house and headed for the Falls Road. Seeing the twin spires of St. Peter's pro-cathedral soaring arrogantly above the rooftops of the terraced houses of the poor, he recalled the funeral service that had been held that morning for his mother and was deeply disturbed by the recollection. Still in a state of shock over his mother's passing, he had been almost traumatised by the service and found himself wondering about his own faith, which was, for him, inextricably tied to the Irish history that so enthralled and horrified him. He was not attending a British-controlled state school, where the curriculums carefully avoided Irish history, including the history of Ulster. Instead, he was attending a Falls Road school, run by the Christian Brothers, who were strict disciplinarians, but taught Irish history, including the politics of

Republicanism, using the same books that were used south of the border, as well as Irish-language books. Even the sports were orientated to Ireland, with hurling, football and handball. Yet even though the Christian Brothers gave him the kind of Irish learning that he would not have received at a state school (where history was English history, geography was concerned solely with the countries of the Commonwealth, and literature was Kipling and British Imperialism), including the literature of Yeats, O'Casey and Synge, he had noticed that the Irish history he was learning was all about Dublin and the southern counties, not about Belfast and the north. It was as if his own city, based squarely in the six counties, did not exist. Nevertheless, Ireland, his country, had at least been placed on the map for him, alongside the Catholic religion. Thus, he had been increasingly drawn to religion and had even considered entering the Church.

Now, as he walked towards the cathedral, hardly knowing that he was doing so, he recalled taking his first Holy Communion. In the company of hundreds of other seven-year-olds drawn from all over the Falls, all nervous and self-conscious, he had paraded through the narrow streets of the Pound Loney in his short-trousered suit, white shirt and breast ribbon with a picture of Our Lady on it, while the locals, including his parents and relatives, lined the pavements to watch him and the rest of the procession pass by. Shortly after, in the cathedral, kneeling in front of the altar, listening to the epistle being read in Latin as, for the first time, he drank the blood of Christ and swallowed the host, he had found himself trembling with awe and a queasy sensation borne of the thought that the host might now be within him as a spectral presence. He wondered if the citadel of his body might henceforth be haunted. He had, however, soon been distracted from that thought when, after the ceremony, he received his personal prayer book, had the page in front signed and dated by his parents, then went on to collect a small fortune in two-shilling pieces and half-crowns from just about every relative and family friend known to him. His parents then made him put the money into a post office account and holding his first savings book in his hand had made him feel really grown up.

Religious studies made him feel the same way and thereafter he had rarely neglected them. Once a week, from that time on, he had attended religious instruction at confraternity in Clonard Monastery and always found himself oddly moved by the sight of the altar boys in their white gowns and long, red soutanes, magically illuminated in sunlight that slanted down from the stained-glass windows as the priest's incense drifted across them like ectoplasm. Sean enjoyed listening to the sermons and singing hymns with the congregation; it gave him a feeling of solidarity with family and friends and, indeed, with the whole of the Pound Loney community. He even took Confession seriously, which most of his friends did not, though he didn't necessarily confess his worst sins because the priest was Father Connolly, a personal friend to his father and mother, though only the latter truly had the faith. Nevertheless, sitting on a bench beside the Confession box, waiting his turn to go in, he had always felt deeply spiritual.

Entering to kneel beneath the opening shutter, he would hear his own whispered words resounding eerily in that gloomy, confined space. 'Bless me, Father, for I have sinned. It is one week since my last Confession and these are my sins...' Then enumerating his sins, none too great, and receiving Father Connolly's absolution: '*Ego te absolvo...*' plus the penance of some 'Our Fathers' and 'Hail Marys' to send him on his way, he kissed the cross at the side of the shutter as he left the Confession box, released from his guilt.

At least that was the way it was then...

Now, nearing the cathedral, he saw Father Connolly hurrying between the big wooden doors, under the Gothic arch, having left the gathering in Sean's home and now on his way to take the early-evening Confessions. Still not knowing precisely what he planned to do, aware only of his churning emotions, the mixed pain and guilt and, yes, even outrage, caused by his mother's death, Sean did not increase his pace as he approached the cathedral doors, though he experienced a rising urgency and resolve that made him feel stronger.

Entering the cathedral, advancing into striations of rainbow-coloured light that fell obliquely through the stained-glass windows, he felt its eerie silence as a palpable presence, sensed the ghosts of its long history, and was almost drawn back to what he had been just a few days ago.

But that was all over now. The rock of his faith had crumbled. As he crossed the vestibule, feeling the cold stone under his feet, approaching the few men and women sitting on the benches that hugged the walls beside the Confession boxes, he knew at last what it was that he had come here to do.

He had come to purge himself of his former beliefs.

Sean sat on the bench beside an old lady who was wearing a black shawl over her head and shoulders. She held rosary beads in her hands and kept twisting them this way and that, frequently kissing them, as she muttered her prayers. Sean waited patiently, having nowhere else to go, determined to do this thing and put it behind him. Other penitents came and went. Most were older than Sean. He sat there, isolated by his young age, though he felt like an old man.

Striations of sunlight fell across him, forming a pool of light on the floor. He saw motes of dust at play, beheld a microscopic universe where God had no presence, felt as small and as insignificant as those drifting motes of dust, yet remained determined to do what he had to do. Breathing deeply and evenly, trying to still his racing heart, he watched the old lady entering the Confession box beside them, waited patiently for her to leave, took another deep breath, released it in a sigh, then slipped into the cramped gloom where he knelt just below the opening shutter.

'Good afternoon, my son,' Father Connolly said, his voice eerily disembodied, but still sounding kind when it emerged from the open shutter above Sean's head.

Sean took another deep breath and only slowly released it, still trying in vain to slow his racing heart.

'Bless me, Father, for this is my final Confession and I won't be coming back here again.'

There was a lingering silence, but eventually Father Connolly said, as if he couldn't quite believe his own ears, '*What's* that, my son?'

'Bless me, Father,' Sean repeated, 'for this is my final Confession and I won't be coming back here again.'

There was another lingering silence, perhaps expressing shocked disbelief, then Father Connolly said, 'My son, I – '

'My sin is this, Father. I no longer have faith. I don't believe that a just God would have taken my Ma from me, would have caused her such pain, would have caused such pain to me and my sister and my Da, and I can't see what purpose that kind of suffering can possibly serve. My sin is also this, Father. I don't believe in a caring God. I don't believe that a caring God would let the devil have his way, yet everywhere I turn I see what can only be the devil's work.'

'Please, my son, consider what you're saying. Try to think it through. Please don't make quick – '

'My mother suffered like the damned. We've all been made to suffer, too. There are children dyin' of starvation in Africa and other places, and grownups being tortured and killed, and what's it all mean? What's the purpose in a famine or a flood or a tornado? What's God's purpose when he causes pain and fear and nightmares and hunger? A caring God wouldn't do that. Not if He cares for us. And so I don't believe in God - at least, not in a caring God - and without Him, there's nothing to believe in, except what's here and now.'

'*Please*, my Son, let me – '

'I've lost my faith, Father. I won't ever get it back. Now I only believe in what's here and now, the good and the bad. I believe in the real world.'

'And what do you think that is, my son?'

'My family. My home. My city. My country. Everything I can see and smell and touch.'

'That isn't enough, my son.'

'It is for me, Father.'

'No, my son, you are wrong.'

'Bless me, Father, before I leave here. Bless me for the last time.'

'No, my son, I can't do that.'

'Sure I knew you couldn't,' Sean said bitterly. 'I just wanted to check, like. Thank you, Father. Good day to you.'

He left the Confession box, not kissing the cross at the side of the shutter, then rushed out of the cathedral's gloom, into dazzling sunlight, choked up and with tears in his eyes, no longer a child.

Chapter Seven

1

Working in the James Mackie & Sons foundry, wearing a set of overalls just like the other workers, Johnny felt like a grown man at last. Though he had passed the Qualifying Examination and could have gone on to grammar school, he had chosen, despite the protestations of his mother, to leave school and go into the great foundry that dominated the Shankill Road area and soaked up so many of the school-leavers in the Protestant community. Mary had been deeply disappointed with his decision; more so because Marlene had failed the Qualifying Examination and Mary believed that the failure had shamed the whole family, this being a typical case of working-class snobbery. Having left school, Marlene was serving in a shoe shop in Great Victoria Street with no great prospects for the future, except perhaps marriage. Mary wanted more than that for her favourite son. Luckily, wee Billy had also passed the Qualifying Examination, had attended grammar school, and, surprisingly, considering his childhood penchant for trouble, seemed content to be working as an electrical apprentice..

Johnny had surprised everyone, including Marlene and Billy, because they had assumed that he would be the one to go on to grammar school and, later, university. No one had remotely considered that he, the reserved, studious one, would turn his back on grammar school and opt to go into the foundry at fourteen. But just as he had surprised them by exploding into violence on that Twelfth of July four years ago (that kind of behaviour was expected from wee Billy, not from Johnny), he had surprised them again by insisting on leaving school the instant he could do so. Now, a man at seventeen, he was working in the foundry, earning his weekly wage and paying his mother for his keep, which is why he now felt like a grown-up.

Though he wasn't particularly thrilled to be working in Mackie's, he preferred it to school and felt that he had gained some freedom at last. Every morning, five days a week, when he rolled out of bed in the darkness, put on his overalls, went downstairs for a quick breakfast of hot porridge and tea, then left, still in darkness, for the thirty-minute walk to the foundry, he was pleased that despite the drawbacks he had finally gained the kind of freedom that he hadn't even been able to imagine when at school. In truth, he had hated school. It had made him feel like a victim, at the mercy of his teachers as well as some of the other pupils, and he had spent most of his time, when not concentrating on schoolwork, gazing out the window and dreaming of the world beyond the grim, red-brick walls of the playground. Johnny had wanted then, and still wanted, to get out of Ireland.

He had come to hate Ireland - or, at least, Belfast. He loathed the provincialism of it, the narrow-minded bigotry, the ever-simmering hatreds between the Protestants and the Catholics, the constant domination of the Church on both sides of the divide. In all of his life to date he had witnessed no overt act of antagonism between Protestants and Catholics and, indeed, he still was deeply fond of the Lavery family, especially Teddy, and his mother's friends, the Devlins, all Catholics; but he was constantly aware of the buried resentment between the two sides and knew that a border war, with IRA men from the south crossing into the north to launch armed attacks against police stations and army bases, had been continuing quietly for years. He also knew that few Catholics had been able to get a job in Mackie's and that when the odd one *did* get in for some obscure reason, invariably he would be treated so badly by his Protestant co-workers that he would soon leave of his own accord. Again, Johnny had never witnessed this himself, though he had picked up stories from co-workers in the foundry. It was the same situation, as his father had informed him, in the Harland & Wolff shipyard and the Short & Harland aircraft factory. Belfast was a Protestant city and it fully intended remaining that way.

James Mackie & Sons was a Protestant foundry with a Protestant labour force numbering in their thousands, a vast complex of machine shops, tool shops, drilling shops, smelting foundries, supply stores, loading bays and, separated from the rest, across the road from the foundry entrance, a building housing the draughtsmen, accountants, administrators and other white-collar workers. During World War II, the foundry had manufactured munitions and aircraft components; now it was manufacturing the components for the machinery of a dying textile industry. Johnny had been taken on as a potential apprentice textile machinist, a job he would commence at sixteen; for the first two years, however, he was to prove his worth as a message boy for the Jig & Tool Shop, either running errands for the machine operators who worked there or carrying official messages, spare parts and tools from there to the many other workshops and offices, including those of the draughtsmen. Like most of the boys his own age, his ultimate aim was to serve his apprenticeship as a machinist, then graduate to being a draughtsman, when he could wear a suit with shirt and tie, sit at a drawing board all day, designing machine parts, and mingle with the attractive young female secretaries, instead of the oil-smeared, rough-tongued women who worked in other areas of the foundry.

Still sexually inexperienced and desperately shy, Johnny often had to screw up his courage to enter a particular workshop, where all the machinists were women. Knowing that he blushed easily, those women would mercilessly make fun of him, shouting bawdy remarks or mocking requests for a date, or making even more lurid demands, then laughing raucously when, as anticipated, he blushed furiously. In fact, Johnny blushed a lot in the factory because even the men, bored with the repetitive nature of their work, would often distract themselves by making fun of the message boys and then watching them squirm with embarrassment. Johnny would also blush a lot when they told sexual jokes, talked crudely about sexual matters in general, or told extravagant tales of their often invented sexual encounters. Making the message boys blush was a daily sport.

On the other hand, Johnny had a great deal of freedom in the foundry, running all over the place, from the Jig & Tool shop to other workshops and departments, meeting a wide variety of the workers, blue-collar and white-collar, and gradually making a lot of friends amongst the older men, the other message boys, and the apprentices.

Though still only a message boy, he was determined to get ahead with all possible speed and so had taken it upon himself to attend evening classes for mechanical drawing and maths at the Belfast Technical College, known as the 'Tech'. He attended the college three evenings a week, straight after leaving the foundry, and often went on from there to a nearby cinema, to see the final performance of a movie, alone more often than not, except for when he met Donna King. He knew all of the cinemas: the Alhambra in North Street, the Royal in Arthur Street, the Picturedrome in Mountpottinger Road, the Stadium in the Shankill, the Broadway in the Falls, the Windsor in Donegall Road, the Coliseum in the lower Grosvenor Road, the Royal Hippodrome in Great Victoria Street, and, biggest of all, the Ritz in Fisherwick Place. He was awed by the Broadway, which had uniformed attendants at each side of the entrance, intimidated by the Ritz, simply because it was so big and posh, and slightly shocked by the Alhambra where adults could watch the film while having a drink in the bar. He also knew his theatres, some of which doubled as cinemas, including the Grand Opera House, with its golden elephants and fancy boxes, and the Empire in Victoria Square, which was the first to show 'flicks' in Belfast, in 1896, and the first to broadcast the first live theatre, in 1937. In truth, he was fanatical about the flicks, perhaps because he was sexually aroused by them, often watching them in a trance of erotic distraction with an erection that could scarcely be contained and, indeed, sometimes wasn't. He often left a cinema in a state of acute embarrassment, trying to conceal the evidence of his helpless outpourings. Yet despite the shame engendered by this, he always went back for more.

A romantic by nature, wanting to live somewhere less bigoted and more exciting, to travel the world as Teddy Lavery had done while in the Royal Navy (though Teddy had recently completed his term in the Navy and was now working as a labourer for a Catholic builder in the Falls), Johnny distracted himself from his secret longings, including acute sexual frustration, by taking long trips outside the city on his Raleigh bicycle, sometimes as far as Portrush or Bangor; by going to the cinema three or fours evenings a week, straight after his two-hour sessions at the Tech, seeing practically every new movie; by saturating himself in the rock & roll played every evening on Radio Luxemburg and on the 45rpm records that he was constantly buying out of his wages; and by playing in a skiffle group consisting of himself, Dan Johnstone and another two friends, Ronnie Campbell and Rob McKenzie.

Dan, who could play three or four notes on the guitar, was the lead guitarist and singer, modeled ineptly on a mixture of Lonnie Donegan and Gene Vincent. Ronnie played a crude upright bass made from a wooden packing crate that had a broom handle shoved through a hole drilled in the top of it. A piece of normal cord was nailed to the bottom of the soap box, ran up through the same hole and was tied taut to the top of the broom handle. When plucked, the cord, its noise amplified by the hollow packing crate, gave off an unmelodic but insistent bass throbbing. Rob McKenzie hammered out a relentless rhythm on his second-hand drum kit; as, invariably, this was the only instrument that could be heard properly by the audience, it galvanised the dancers and also helpfully drowned out the musical imperfections of the rest of the group. And Johnny, though he didn't know a lick of music, tunelessly strummed an acoustic guitar while shaking his legs like Elvis Presley. This caused the girls in the audience to scream hysterically, as if they were seeing the real thing.

Mostly they played in local church halls, though occasionally, when the management was desperate, they managed to get the odd date as a last-minute supporting act for the lead band in one of the many local dance halls, including the Tivoli in Christian Place, the Floral Hall out in Hazelwood, and even, despite the fact that they were Protestants, in the notorious Jig, in Coates Street in the Falls. The latter was a dance hall owned by Catholics and renowned for the number of brawls that erupted either inside or outside on the pavement. Indeed, so frequent were such brawls that Johnny and his group were under strict orders to keep playing, no matter what was happening on the dance floor. They certainly witnessed a great number of fights there, but were never personally involved and had no trouble with the Catholic audience, despite the fact that they were known as a Protestant group.

Girls in the dance halls would often swoon over the members of the group, as if the players were real stars, and practically throw themselves at them after the show, when the boys were cooling down with fizzy drinks at the bar or hanging hopefully around the dance floor. Invariably, trying to screw up the courage to dance with a girl was agonising. The girls usually stood in groups on one side of the floor, eyeing the boys and giggling, the boys at the other side, always tried to act 'cool' to cover their nerves before, egged on by his mates, one of them would venture forth to brave the girl of his choice, not knowing if he would be victorious or be publicly humiliated when, in front of the other girls and his own friends, she said, 'Ack, away with ya! No, thanks!' Being a member of the skiffle group, however, was a considerable help, because the girls often transferred their passion for real rock & roll stars to this bunch of amateurish impersonators; they were therefore more likely to say, 'Okay,' or 'Why not?' Thus, being a member of a skiffle group, good or bad, had distinct advantages.

Despite this fact, Johnny rarely asked a girl for a dance and was usually glad to get out of the dance hall and return to the avenue where, with a bit of luck, he could drop in on Donna.

Johnny was in love with Donna, but she remained a mystery to him. His so-called 'bass player', Ronnie Campbell, was in love with Marlene, but she resolutely ignored him. As they lived only a few streets away from each other, and as Dan Johnstone and Rob McKenzie, both bold and girl crazy, always hung around the dance hall to pick up 'birds' after the performance, they often walked home from the dance halls together. This meant that Johnny, who had his guitar slung over his shoulder, could help Ronnie carry the dismantled 'bass' - the broom and the cord and the packing crate with the hole in it - and they could both discuss their separate romantic problems out of earshot of their more down-to-earth friends.

This is what they were doing this particular snow-bound winter's evening, making their way home after another evening at the Jig, up in the Falls. They were hawking the packing crate between them, holding it by handles that Ronnie had fashioned out of coiled masking tape. The top of the crate was covered in snow and their hands were numb with cold. The snow was still falling.

'How can I get Marlene to talk to me?' Ronnie asked forlornly. 'Every time I speak to her, she just turns her nose up at me and then flounces away. Sure she makes me feel really daft, but I can't let her go. I mean, I fancy her too much.'

Though Johnny certainly fancied Donna and had done so for years, he couldn't imagine how anyone could possibly fancy Marlene. She was attractive, all right - pretty face, good breasts, long legs - but she was his sister and that made her asexual to him. When he had to listen to Ronnie talking about Marlene, he moved from amusement to embarrassment and then sheer disbelief. Ronnie couldn't possibly feel for Marlene what he, Johnny, felt for Donna. It wasn't in the cards.

'Ack, just keep after her,' he said. 'Every time she turns away, jump in front of her and make a joke out of it. Exhaust her. Wear down her resistance until she hasn't the energy to say "No". I mean, she probably just acts that way because she's embarrassed to have you – or anyone else – chasin' after her. Either that or start pretendin' you don't give a damn anymore. That might turn her around, like.'

'You think so?'

'Aye.'

They were now struggling along the avenue, nearing the arches, and the snow was falling thicker than ever, making even the terraced houses look picturesque in the light of the street-lamps. The snow on the road was crisscrossed with footprints, though few people were out and about at this late hour. Christmas was only two weeks away.

'What about you and Donna?'

'What about us?'

'You've fancied her for years,' Ronnie said. 'Sure we all know that. So how did you get finally together with her? Did you just ask her out?'

'I invited her to the flicks,' Johnny said. 'That's all I did. We went to the Windsor, saw the fillum, then walked home and parted outside her door. Before we parted, I asked her if she'd like to go again and she said, "Why not?" So we went again a week or so later. After that it became a regular thing and seemed perfectly normal. Dead easy, it was.'

He was being disingenuous, if not actually lying. In fact, it had taken him months of anguish before he could find the courage to ask Donna out to the movies. He'd almost fainted with relief when she said, 'Why not?'

Girls never seemed to say 'Yes' to anything. It was always 'Why not?' Or 'I suppose so.' Or 'I don't know. I'll have to think about it.' Or 'Away with ya! Do ya think I'm soft in the head?' They never said 'Yes' straight out, although, as Johnny had slowly come to learn, a 'Why not?' was often as good as a 'Yes'.

Not that his anguish had ended with Donna's consent. Indeed, once it was known that he was taking her to the movies at the end of the week (she told Marlene within the hour and Marlene told everyone else), he was compelled to endure four days and evenings of relentless bantering from his mother, Marlene and wee Billy, as well as from his mother's friends and any relative who happened to drop into the house to be informed of the great event. By the time Friday evening came around, he was so traumatised by self-consciousness that he could scarcely force himself out of the house to cross the road to Donna's place. Even worse, when she invited him into her house, to wait for her while she put on her coat, her mother and father were grinning so much, so clearly amused at seeing him there, that his agony of self-consciousness was doubled, rendering him virtually speechless by the time he left the house with her.

The rest of the evening was a disaster because he simply couldn't speak, refused to meet her gaze, and sat stiffly beside her in the back row of the Windsor cinema, practically jumping out of his skin if she made the slightest move. His discomfort was made all the more acute because the back rows of the cinema were filled with couples, many of whom were passionately necking, this being the only place that most of them could be alone together, since few of the local families possessed a car.

Emerging from the cinema a couple of hours later, Donna broke the torturous silence with, 'Did you like it?' and he replied, 'Ackaye, it wasn't bad.' He didn't say another word until they were back on her doorstep, when he muttered, 'What about next week?'

'Why not?' she replied.

He practically ran away from her.

Naturally, when he entered his own house, the whole family, except his father (still working in England) was waiting up for him, dying to know how the 'date' had gone. They didn't actually ask him any questions - they simply *stared* at him - until, attempting to break the lingering silence, wee Billy said, 'So what was the fillum like?'

'Sure it was great,' Johnny said, then, with an ostentatious yawn and a stretch, trying to avoid Marlene's grin in particular, he added, 'God, I feel really tired. I'm goin' straight up to bed.'

Thus ended his first evening out with Donna, though other evenings followed, each following the same pattern, with him inviting her to the cinema and her saying, 'Why not?' until gradually, after they had been four or five times, he relaxed to the point where he at least *talked* to her, before, during and after the film. Nevertheless, he still hadn't held her hand, let alone kissed her. He only did that when dreaming.

'So do you think,' Ronnie asked, sounding pitiful, almost deranged, 'that if I ask Marlene out to the flicks, she'll at least say "Yes" to that?'

'Maybe,' Johnny said.

'So what do we talk about,' Ronnie asked, sounding ever more desperate as he wiped falling snow from his eyes and nose, exhaling steam from between frozen lips, 'as we walk to the Windsor? I mean, what did you talk about with Donna?'

'I can't remember,' Johnny lied, having been struck dumb that evening. 'I mean, we just talked, you know? About the movie we were gonna see, other movies, rock an' roll, and so on. Nothin' special. Just normal crack. Then, when we came out of the picture house, we talked about the movie we'd just seen. It was all really natural, like, so don't worry about it.'

Ronnie let his breath out in a sigh, though it could have been simple exhaustion from hawking the packing crate and broom all the way from the Falls. 'Ack, Johnny,' he said, 'you make it sound so easy, but that sister of yours... God, she's a case, she gives me such a hard time, and always makes sure I can never get her alone. So if I *do* ask her out to the pictures, I'm gonna have to do it in front of everyone and then, if she turns me down, sure I'm gonna feel like a right eejut. I mean, Jesus, she's *hard*.'

Ronnie was the most handsome of all of Johnny's friends and every girl that Johnny knew fancied him. They fancied him even more because he played the bass in a skiffle group and because, of all the members of the skiffle group, he was the good-looking one, obviously destined to be a rock & roll star. It therefore baffled Johnny that Ronnie, who could have his pick of all the girls, was obsessed with Marlene who, though attractive, always tried not to show it and walked with hunched shoulders to hide her breasts. It just didn't make sense.

'She's not hard,' Johnny said. 'She just acts that way. I'm sure she likes you, Ronnie, but she's never had a boyfriend before and doesn't know how to react when someone like you takes an interest. So just get her alone somewhere - in our kitchen, for instance, when she's makin' tea or somethin' - and then try it on. If she reacts with a "No", say you won't take that for an answer and then keep askin' her every chance you get, day in and day out. I bet she says "Yes" in the end. She'll just despair and give in, like.'

'You reckon?'

'I do.'

While talking, they had turned off the avenue, staggered along the snow-covered Broadway, passing gable ends covered with huge murals of King William crossing the Boyne, then turned again into the street where Ronnie lived. Stopping at his terraced house, they lowered the packing crate to the ground and then straightened up to get their breath back. The snow was still falling, drifting down through the light of the street-lamps to carpet the pavement and road. One of the neighbours, a few doors down, was playing Christmas carols on the radio. Johnny, who professed to hate Christmas, got a lump in his throat. He was thinking of Donna.

'Okay,' he said to Ronnie, 'see you tomorrow night at the party.'

'Right,' Ronnie said, then he hammered on his front door with the knocker, being considered by his parents still too young to have a door key. 'Thanks for the advice,' he added.

'No problem,' Johnny said.

Ronnie's mother opened the front door, letting a pool of light stream out onto the snow-covered pavement. A small woman with delicate, warm features, she smiled fondly at Johnny.

'Would you be coming in for a wee cup of tea, Johnny?'

'Thanks, Mrs. Campbell, but no. Sure I'm expected home for my supper and I'm late already.'

'Aye, I understand that, right enough. Give my love to your Mum.'

'Will do, Mrs. Campbell. Now I'd better be making tracks. See you, Ronnie.'

'Right,' Ronnie said, backing into the house and dragging his packing case and broomstick with him. When his mother closed the door, abruptly shutting out the light, Johnny, hitching his guitar more comfortably on his shoulder, returned to the avenue and walked on, going under the arches, until he reached Donna's house. He stopped, wondering if he should or not, then, given confidence by his guitar, which made him feel like a rock & roll star, he rang her doorbell.

2

Donna's father, Eddie King, answered the door. He had thinning fair hair, Donna's bright green eyes and a boyish, good-humoured fadiece. Though he worked as an electrician in the Short & Harland aircraft factory, he had taken his overalls off and was wearing an open-necked checkered shirt with grey trousers and bedroom slippers. Fond of Johnny, he smiled brightly when he saw him.

'Ack, how are ya, Johnny-lad?' he asked rhetorically, stepping aside to let Johnny enter. 'Come on in.'

'Evenin', Mr. King,' Johnny said, stepping into the small, tidy living room. 'Evenin', Mrs. King,' he added, this time speaking to the attractive blonde-haired lady, Lucy King, who was sitting at the table in the living room, smoking a cigarette. There were plates of unfinished food on the table, with tea still steaming in large mugs. Clearly, they had just finished their evening meal, known locally as 'tea'.

'How are you, Johnny?' Mrs. King said, smiling. 'Been playing with your band again, have you?'

'Aye,' Johnny replied, glancing about the living room. Coloured streamers crisscrossed the low ceiling, pieces of holly and ivy were tucked behind mirrors, reproductions of famous paintings and a framed picture of Queen Elizabeth II, a decorated Christmas tree stood in one corner, its coloured lights turned on, and a coal fire was roaring in the grate of the Devon fireplace. The Kings were one of the only two families in the street to have a television set. 'Sure we were playin' in the Jig, in Coates Street.'

'You weren't!'

'We were.'

'You're takin' your life in your hands, Johnny, when you go to places like that. Sure them Catholics boyos can't be trusted an inch when they have the drink on 'em. An' they're worse when music's playin'. That place is notorious for its fights. It's the talk of the town, like.'

'It's not that bad,' Johnny said, unslinging the guitar from his shoulder and holding it down by his side, out of harm's way. 'I've seen a few fights there, all right, but we've never been bothered.'

'Aye,' Mr. King said, taking a chair near the roaring fire and proceeding to light up his pipe, 'I agree with you, Johnny-lad. That place isn't nearly as bad as it's cracked up to be. Sure didn't I go there myself when I was your age and sewing my wild oats?'

'Before you met me,' his wife retorted.

'Aye, love, before I met you. When I was young, handsome and fancy-free. When all the girls loved me. I went to the Jig and a lot of other dance halls. A regular wee Fred Astaire, I was. Sure I drove the girls crazy.'

'I'll bet,' his wife said with an affectionate, laconic grin. 'The way Johnny drives them crazy when he's playing his guitar. Isn't that right, Johnny?'

Johnny grinned and shook his head from side to side. 'I don't think so, Mrs. King. Besides, I can't even play this guitar; I just strum the chords.' He glanced about him again. 'Is Donna in?'

'Aye. She's upstairs in her bedroom. Just call up to her and check that she's decent.'

Going to the foot of the stairs, Johnny called out Donna's name, shouting because she was playing the Big Bopper's 'Chantilly Lace' at loud volume. When she heard him, she turned the volume down.

'Yes?'

'It's me! Johnny! Can I come up?'

'Yes!'

Receiving a nod of consent from Donna's parents, Johnny made his way up the stairs, being careful not to knock his guitar against the wall or banisters. Donna's bedroom was the first at the top of the landing. Opening the door and entering, Johnny found her wearing a loose jumper over a dress that covered her knees, sitting cross-legged on her bed with a pile of 45rpm records on her lap. The portable record player was resting on a cupboard at the end of the bed, enabling her to just lean sideways when putting on another record. As Johnny closed the door behind him, she changed the Big Bopper for Elvis Presley's 'My Wish Came True', a sentimental ballad released shortly after the singer had commenced his two-year stint with the U.S. Army. There were photos of Elvis and other rock & roll stars pasted up on the walls of the room. Johnny was jealous of Elvis because Donna adored him.

'You've come,' Donna said, flicking the blonde hair away from her green eyes and then patting the edge of the bed with the same hand. 'Here, sit beside me.'

Johnny placed his guitar carefully against the far wall, then sat beside her, self-consciously keeping his feet on the floor.

'How'd it go?' she asked him, referring to the group's performance earlier that evening in the Jig.

'Great,' Johnny said. 'The girls were all screamin'.'

'That's because you shake your legs like Elvis.'

'Aye, don't I know it?' Then he frowned, listening to the record, and said, 'That's one of the worst songs he's ever made. It's real soppy, isn't it?'

Donna closed her eyes and sighed. 'It's real dreamy,' she said. 'When I close my eyes and listen to that song, I can practically see him.'

Johnny felt that familiar stab of jealousy, but he tried not to show it. 'I prefer the other side,' he said. 'I prefer it when he sings rock and roll. I mean, I didn't mind "Love Me Tender", but this one's just sentimental drivel. You can't even compare it to "One Night".'

Donna opened her eyes again to stare steadily at him. '"One Night" is a sexy song,' she said. 'This one is romantic. That's why I prefer it.'

'Not me.'

'You're not romantic, Johnny.'

'No, I suppose not.' When he looked at Donna, at her well developed, seductive body, he felt more romantic than he could say. He felt as if he was melting.

'And now he's over there in Germany,' Donna said, still thinking of Elvis, 'being wasted in the Army, not making any records at all. I think it's terrible. Don't you?'

'Aye, I do. Sure he should be makin' records. And while he's freezin' to death over there, rockin' and rollin' in his tank, all these new guys, none nearly as good as him, are takin' over the Hit Parade. Bobby Rydell, Frankie Avalon, Tommy Sands, Ricky Nelson - all those clean-cut boys with their drippy ballads. Yeah, bring Elvis back, I say.'

'I'm so glad we agree on that,' Donna replied solemnly, removing Elvis from the turntable and putting on another record. 'I don't know if I could stand it, Johnny, if you didn't like Elvis. I mean, that could put a wall between us, couldn't it?'

'Aye, right,' Johnny said.

Actually, as far as he was concerned there *was* a wall between them, though it had little to do with Elvis Presley. As the Teddy Bears started singing another sentimental ballad, Donna obviously being in a sentimental mood, Johnny studied her face, which was, to him, the most beautiful in all the world, inexpressibly attractive, yet somehow a total mystery, absolutely unreadable, and wished he could find a way to get closer to her and let her know how he felt. He still hadn't even kissed her, though he desperately wanted to, dreaming about it night and day. And if she *wanted* him to kiss her, he had no way of knowing it because her steady gaze, though penetrating to his very soul, gave nothing away. Yet he had often made love to her. He had done so in his dreams. In his dreams their lovemaking had been ecstatic, only spoiled when his rude awakening, drenched in his own seed and wracked with guilt, brought him shamefully back to Earth.

> *To know, know, know him*
> *Is to love, love, love him*
> *And I do, and I do, and I do...*

Even listening to the banal, repetitive words being sung by the Teddy Bears, Johnny felt a lump in his throat and was almost overwhelmed by the urge to twist sideways, lean forward and sweep Donna into his embrace, to press his lips on hers and squeeze her tightly. But he couldn't bring himself to do it, not only because her parents trusted him enough to let him stay in her bedroom, which was a rarity hereabouts, but also because he simply didn't have the nerve to do it, being frightened of how she might react. Indeed, every time he sat beside her, as he was doing right now, he found himself wondering how he could *naturally* take hold of her hand, make it seem that it was *normal*, and then gradually draw her to him, into his loving embrace. Finding a way of doing it naturally was his abiding problem and he still hadn't found a way to solve it. He just sat there and stewed.

'That's rubbish as well,' he said, meaning the Teddy Bears' record, needing something to talk about. 'More sentimental drivel,' he added, even though the song had him all choked up. 'Even the name, the Teddy Bears, makes my teeth grind. I mean, that name sounds so *childish.*'

'Elvis recorded "Teddy Bear",' she reminded him with a slight, secret smile, 'and you loved that record.'

'Yeah, well, I mean to call a song that is okay, but to call a *group* that? Thanks, but no thanks.'

Donna's smile widened. 'Well, I like them, Johnny. I mean, I like romantic records. I think you do, too, but because you're a man you just can't admit it. That's the way men are brought up.'

Johnny was taken by surprise at hearing her calling him a 'man' instead of a 'boy'. His cheeks burned slightly with embarrassment and pride, but he turned his head away, as if staring up at some of the rock & roll posters, so she couldn't see him blushing.

'I don't mind some of them,' he said. 'I just hate the drippy ones.'

'What about this one?' Donna put another record on the turntable and Conway Twitty started singing, 'It's Only Make Believe'.

'Ackaye,' Johnny said, 'I like that one. Sure that's a great record.'

'But romantic.'

'Aye, I guess so.' As his cheeks felt normal again, he turned back to face her. 'You have nice eyes,' he told her.

'You think so?'

'Yes.'

'And my nose?'

'That as well.'

'And my lips?'

'Those as well.'

She twisted sideways and leaned towards him until her breasts were almost grazing his chest, then she pouted, forming an O with her lips, let him look at that O for a considerable period of time, then withdrew slightly... but only slightly... to smile mysteriously, perhaps mockingly, at him.

'So why do you like my lips?' she asked, whispering.

Johnny swallowed. 'I...'

'Yes?'

'I...' Johnny shrugged. 'I don't know.'

'You don't?'

'No. I just like them... And your eyes and your nose.'

'So what do you like the most? My eyes or my nose or... my lips?'

Johnny blushed again, so lowered his eyes and glanced down at his hands, clasped in his lap and white-knuckled. Jesus, he thought, I'm all tensed up. Then he shrugged, feeling like a fool, brimming over with all kinds of confusing emotions.

'Your lips, I suppose.'

He raised his eyes to meet her gaze. That gaze was steady and unreadable. She was smiling, enigmatically, like a cat, as she leaned closer to him until, though she wasn't actually touching him, he felt the heat of her body. That heat fired his loins.

'You want to kiss them?' she asked, whispering.

Johnny sucked his breath in.

'Well, do you want to?' she asked, now sounding husky and sensual.

Johnny let his breath out, whispering, 'Yes.'

'Then do it,' she said.

Johnny didn't do it. He let her do it instead. He closed his eyes and the bed squeaked as she moved closer. He felt her breasts grazing his chest and then, with his eyes still closed, heart pounding, he felt her lips pressing gently against his own. They were tender and moist and even warmer than he had imagined, making his thoughts scatter and spin as he melted down through himself. His whole world hung suspended in space; the silence was absolute.

He was just about to put his arms around her, to pull her against him, when she gently withdrew. After what seemed like a long time, though it only took seconds, he opened his eyes and saw her steady gaze, that enigmatic, possibly mocking, smile.

'Did you like it?' she asked.

Speechless, Johnny nodded.

'You want to do it again?'

Johnny swallowed and nodded affirmatively.

'The next time you have to do it to me,' she told him, making his heart race all over again, 'but it can't be in this room.'

'Why not?' He was so breathless, he still had trouble speaking. His voice sounded strange to him.

'Because my Mum and Dad trust us,' she said, 'and we shouldn't betray that trust. The next time, you have to pick the time and place. You understand, Johnny? You have to kiss me - not make me kiss you - because that's the way it should be. Okay?'

'Okay,' Johnny said.

Donna smiled and kissed her own fingers. When she pressed those fingers against his lips, he wanted to swallow them.

'Right,' she said, 'it's a deal.'

Johnny nodded. 'Aye, right.'

Donna sat back, well away from him now, and gave him an even wider smile, this one more open and clearly mischievous. 'Good!' she said chirpily.

The needle was moving repeatedly to and fro, to and fro, at the end of the still spinning record, making annoying scratching sounds, so she took the record off the turntable and replaced it with another. 'Let's have something livelier,' she said, 'so you don't get completely bored. And since it's snowing outside, let's have a wee bit of sunshine.'

This time it was Eddie Cochran singing 'Summertime Blues', a real foot-tapping rock & roll classic - but Johnny was now in the mood for romantic songs. Even as Cochran's guitar was chopping out an irresistible Bo Diddley beat, which should have had Johnny's foot tapping, the maudlin melody and words of 'To Know Him is to Love Him' were repeating themselves relentlessly in his head, with 'him' changed into 'her', convincing him that he was in love with Donna and would love her always.

To know, know, know her
Is to love, love, love her
And I do, and I do, and I do...

'Are you coming to the party tomorrow night?' he asked.

Donna nodded. 'Why not?'

Johnny's Dad was still working in Birkenhead, England, and only coming home every six weeks for a long weekend. Tomorrow night was the beginning of one of those weekends and as it happened to be his birthday, Mary had decided to throw a party for him. Johnny couldn't be certain, but he was pretty convinced that, given the lack of affection between his parents, his Mum was only throwing the party to ensure that lots of friends were present when Albert returned. Invariably, when Albert came home, he and Mary fought tooth-and-nail about everything under the sun, though money was certainly foremost on the agenda, with their separate social lives coming in a close second. Neither Johnny, Billy nor Marlene fully understood what *all* the fights were about, but Johnny had certainly ascertained that the ones about money were based on Mary's insistence that Albert wasn't sending her enough each week and on Albert's equally impassioned insistence that she was being too careless with what he *was* sending her. Johnny had also ascertained that a lot of the fights were about their separate social lives, though here their individual accusations, batted back and forth like tennis balls, were considerably more vague and complicated. Being in love with Donna, the only love of his life, as yet unconsummated, it was difficult for him to imagine an existence where love did not have dominion. Yet it was becoming increasingly clear to him that love did not have dominion in his own home and that his parents were constantly at loggerheads over their separate social lives.

Albert was always accusing Mary of not being a good mother, of being out too much during his absences, leaving the children to fend for themselves, and of having a 'grand time' while he was over there in England, slogging his guts out for the money that she then spent so casually on drink, never mind the 'bastards' she was drinking with, even assuming that that was *all* she was doing with them. Retaliating, screaming histrionically, Mary would remind Albert that he spent more money in England than he sent to her, that her kids were being deprived because of his meanness, that she found it humiliating to be left here alone while her 'so-called husband' worked in England, and that she had no way of knowing what he was doing over there, with or without other women, so how the hell could he possibly accuse *her* of playing around on the side?

While being unable to ascertain the rights or wrongs of this, Johnny certainly knew that his mother went out a lot in the evenings, though never without first preparing a big salad or some other meal that only had to be heated up by him or Billy or Marlene, depending upon who was at home and needed feeding. Certainly it was true that Mary would sometimes ask him or Billy (never Marlene) to either take her to a pub and wait with her until someone escorted her inside or, if for some reason she didn't require that particular service, to wait outside the pub at a prearranged time and then escort her home. Unfortunately, it was also true that just as often she went to a pub alone ((Mooney's in Arthur Square, the Gin Palace in Royal Avenue, the Ulster Tavern in Chichester Street) and invariably, when she did so, returned home with a male friend to whom Johnny, Billy and Marlene would be politely introduced, before being ordered to bed. That introduction would be made either shortly after 11.00pm, when Mary arrived home with her friend, or, if she arrived home even later, when Johnny, Billy and Marlene were already in bed, early the next morning when they came down for breakfast. Though Johnny, Billy and Marlene had always pretended to each other that this was perfectly normal behavior, they were reminded otherwise when their father returned for one of his long weekends. During those periods, angry words were shouted, crockery was thrown, and peace certainly did not reign on Earth. In fact, though the kids were always desperate to see their Dad (who was, after all, the only Dad they had, and a reasonably decent one at that) the long weekends could often be hell on Earth. No sooner did they look forward to their Dad coming home than they wanted him to go away once more. Just thinking about it made Johnny sigh.

'Well,' he said, thinking about tomorrow night but also still reeling from Donna's kiss, 'I suppose I'd better be makin' tracks. Are you comin' over later to see Marlene?'

Smiling ruefully, Donna shook her head from side to side. 'No,' she said, 'not tonight. Sure your mother's havin' one of her séances and I couldn't stand that. My Mum and Dad don't think much of it either, so it's best I don't go.'

Johnny almost blushed again. One of the reasons he wanted to get out of Northern Ireland (if he could take Donna with him) was that both his parents caused him constant embarrassment. His father had long been well known around the city because of his showbusiness activities in the local music halls, and that, as far as Johnny could gather, had embarrassed his mother, who had middle-class pretensions picked up from having been born and raised in the upper Malone Road. (She had, as she had so often stated, married beneath her station.) Johnny had never been embarrassed by his father's showbusiness activities - in fact, he had been thrilled to have a father so well known -

but he had certainly been embarrassed when, at times like Guy Fawkes night or the Twelfth of July, his father had dressed up in some crazy outfit (the Hunchback of Notre Dame, the Charles Laughton version, being his favourite) and ran up and down the avenue, either scaring the life out of passers-by or making them giggle hysterically. Johnny had been even more embarrassed, however, when his mother, distraught at the unexpected death of her beloved elder brother, Neil, had decided to try contacting him from beyond the grave. To that end, she had joined the Spiritualist Church and started conducting weekly séances at home. Johnny sighed again at the thought of it.

'Ackaye, I understand,' he said. 'Sure there's a lot in the street who think it's pretty odd and others who think it's black magic or something. I'm not surprised your Mum and Dad don't approve.'

'My Mum and Dad aren't religious one way or the other, but they think that tampering with the unknown can be dangerous.'

'It's not dangerous,' Johnny said. 'Just a wee bit silly.'

'It scares Marlene,' Donna said.

'Marlene's easily scared. She has a rich imagination. All those stories we picked up as kids are burnt into her brain, and she believes every one of them.'

'What stories?'

Johnny shrugged. 'The kind of stories that Granny Doreen used to tell us. Stories that always seemed to involve the barkin' of distant dogs, the cryin' of dead children tryin' to get back to their parents, fairies at the bottom of the garden, gypsy curses that caused illness and death, ghostly knocks on the walls, pictures falling off their hooks for no good reason, pinches from friendly ghosts trying to tell you that someone close is about to die. Just a lot of old wive's tales, but they all scared the hell out of Marlene and she still believes in them. So naturally, when she watches the séances, she's inclined to imagine things. Marlene *can* be hysterical.'

'You know why she's hysterical, Johnny?'

'Just born that way, I suppose.'

'No, Johnny. No one's born that way. Marlene's that way because she's always felt unwanted. Because you're your Mum's favourite and your Dad doesn't give her any affection. In fact, she told me she thinks that your Dad actually dislikes her, that he probably never wanted her, never wanted a daughter, and that once, when she tried to put her arms around him, he actually pushed her away. That's a dreadful thing for a girl to have to live with - to believe she's unwanted - and that's why Marlene's inclined to be hysterical. I think it's really sad, don't you?'

Johnny didn't know what to say. It had always been his feeling that Donna's parents were more sophisticated than his and that Donna, subsequently, was more mature than he was. Despite his love for her, this had often disconcerted him as, indeed, it was doing right now. What she was saying about Marlene was, of course, almost certainly correct and he was concerned that he hadn't thought of it before. Donna had the disconcerting ability to make him feel immature.

'Yeah,' he said, 'I suppose it is. But there's nothing I can do about it. I mean, I can't make my Dad be more affectionate or make Mum take more notice of her. It may be sad, but there's nothing I can do. It's just one of those things.'

'You could be more understanding and try to give her a bit more attention. You and wee Billy both ignore her more often than not. You're not nasty to her - you just ignore her - and that doesn't help her.'

Johnny nodded, feeling immature and foolish. 'Okay. I'll try to keep that in mind.'

Donna smiled and leaned forward to kiss him impetuously again, full on the lips, then she moved back again before he could grab her.

'You'd better get going,' she said.

'Aye, I reckon,' Johnny responded, reluctantly standing upright and picking his guitar off the floor. 'So I'll see you at the party tomorrow evening?'

'Yes, Johnny, I'll be there.'

The needle was going to and fro, to and fro, at the end of the still spinning record, so she took it off the turntable and put the arm back on its rest. As Johnny opened the bedroom door, she jumped to her feet, stepped up to him, put her hands on his shoulders, and turned him around to face her.

'So who loves me?' she asked.

'I do,' Johnny said, blushing. Then he left the bedroom.

3

Still reeling from being kissed, not once, but three times, by Donna, Johnny said a guilty goodbye to her parents, then stepped out into the cold, dark night. The snow was still falling, the flakes illuminated in the baleful light of the street-lamps as they drifted down to carpet the road and pavements. As he crossed the road to walk along the opposite pavement to his own house, farther along, he thought of the séance about to commence inside and realised that despite a childhood packed with tales of the supernatural, nothing had quite prepared him for his mother's recent turn to spiritualism, brought about by the unexpected death of her elder brother.

Uncle Neil had been something of an exotic mystery to Johnny and the other kids, a jolly man of no fixed abode who turned up at the house only every two or three years, hung around for a few days, sleeping on the couch in the living room, socialised a lot with Albert and Mary, then disappeared again for another few years. Though this had been going on for as long as Johnny could remember, the only thing he had picked up about it from his mother was that Uncle Neil had to keep a 'low profile' because he was a deserter from the Royal Navy. Johnny and wee Billy, in particular, were terrifically excited by the thought of having a deserter in the family (it was just like the movies) and they also admired Uncle Neil because he always brought them presents, played with them, told them exciting stories, and clearly was deeply fond of their mother. Unfortunately, one day late last November, their mother had received a telegram and burst into tears upon reading it. Sent by a relative living in London, the telegram had stated that Uncle Neil had been admitted to hospital for a routine operation, a tonsillectomy, but had died on the operating table after accidentally being given too large a dose of anaesthetic.

Hysterical at receiving this shocking news, more so because Uncle Neil had already been buried in London and she, Mary, had not had a chance to attend the funeral, she had wept profusely for weeks after, refusing to accept that her beloved brother was dead and eventually convincing herself, maybe from something that she had read, that she might be able to make contact with his spirit and at least say goodbye to him that way. In the hope of doing so, she had joined the Spiritualist Church. After attending for almost a year and becoming an ordained spiritualist, she had started having weekly séances at home, using a spirit 'medium' as her link to the other world. With the living room plunged into darkness, she and her spiritualist friends, including the spirit-medium, would link hands around the kitchen table and silently concentrate, attempting to make contact with the dead when his or her voice emerged from the mouth of the spirit-medium or when the spirit answered simple questions by making the table rock slightly, tapping its legs on the floor, one tap for 'Yes', two for 'No'. Johnny had the suspicion that it was all some kind of trickery, but whether it was or wasn't, it was pretty damned scary.

Naturally, the séances had become the talk of the street, then the talk of the whole area, and soon Johnny, Billy and Marlene were having to endure the snide remarks of friends and neighbours. Things came to a head when the minister of the Methodist church that Johnny and the other children had once attended (only stopping when Mary became a Spiritualist and lost interest in their normal church attendances) heard about the séances and came to the house to demand that Mary stop them forthwith. When Mary refused to do so, the minister informed her that the devil was in her house, then he fell to his knees on the floor, in front of the fireplace, and prayed that the evil spirits be exorcised from Mary and her unfortunate children. He then left and never returned. The séances had continued after his visit and there was going to be another one this evening.

When Johnny reached his house, he found the front door unlocked and the door to the living room wide open. About half-a-dozen people were inside, sipping tea and eating sandwiches while standing. The living room had not yet been decorated for Christmas, though his mother had promised to do it the following morning, once this particular séance was over, before Albert came home. The dining table had been moved from the front window to the centre of the room. The adults eating and drinking were only known to Johnny through previous séances, all disciples from the Spiritualist Church, and most of them were too solemn for his liking. Mary had tried and failed to interest her neighbours, including the Catholic Laverys and Devlins, to join in, but so far they'd all responded as if she was inviting them to a Black Magic gathering.

Though about to communicate with the spirit world, Mary, still black-haired and bright-eyed, was smoking a cigarette, letting it dangle from her lips while she arranged the chairs, squinting through her own cloud of smoke. She nodded at Johnny when she saw him, unable to smile because of the cigarette.

Seeing Marlene and wee Billy sitting at the top of the stairs, Johnny started up there immediately, but was called back by his mother, who removed the cigarette from her mouth long enough to say, 'So where do you think you're going, handsome?'

'Up to my room,' Johnny replied, freezing on the bottom stair.

'Got something to eat at the dance hall, did you?'

Johnny shook his head. 'No.'

'So you're going upstairs to starve, are you?'

'I thought I'd better put my guitar away first. Get out of the way, like.'

'Never you mind about getting out of the way. No son of mine is going to come home and starve. We're not starting here for another five or ten minutes, so as soon as you put your guitar away, get back down here and grab a couple of sandwiches.'

'Can I eat them upstairs?'

'If you want. As long as you eat them.'

'Great,' Johnny said.

In fact, he was famished, so he hurried up to Marlene and Billy, both of whom were still sitting on the top stair, waiting to see the séance below. He handed his guitar to the latter.

'Take this into my room,' he said. 'I'm goin' down for some sandwiches.'

'Right,' Billy said, taking the guitar and disappearing into their shared bedroom while Johnny turned back down the stairs, made his way through the standing adults, nodding and smiling artificially at them as he passed on, then went into the kitchen where more plates of sandwiches were laid out. Taking a small plate, he heaped it with cheese and pickle sandwiches, filled a big mug with milk, then made his way back through the crowded living room and up the stairs again to seat himself on the stair just below the top one, in front of wee Billy and Marlene. He wasn't blocking their view, so both of them could look down through the banisters, as he was planning to do.

'How'd it go with the band?' Billy asked him.

'Sure it was grand,' Johnny said.

'Did all the girls scream at the sight of ya?' Marlene asked.

'Aye, and tore my clothes off.'

'They'll go for anything these days,' Marlene informed him, 'now that Elvis is in the army in Germany. They'll even go for someone like you, the poor things are so desp'rate.'

'Lucky me,' Johnny said. He bit into the first of his sandwiches while looking through the banisters at what was going on downstairs.

'So what have you been up to?' he asked of wee Billy.

'Not much,' Billy said. 'Just ran around the centre of town with Harry Patterson, watching him pinch stuff.'

'Pinch stuff?'

'Aye. Not much, like. Only small things that he can pick off the lower shelves of the stands in Smithfield Market - marbles or ciggie packets or packets of stamps or sweets. But he has this great wee system. A hole in the pocket of his short pants. He stands in front of what it is he wants to pinch, puts his hand in his pocket, reaches through the hole with his fingers, picks up the item and then pulls it through the hole into his pocket. Then he walks away whistlin'. Great, isn't it?'

'Borstal,' Marlene said grimly. 'That's where you'll end up. That Harry Patterson's a right wee chancer, he is, and he'll end up in a boy's home for sure – and you with him, I bet.'

'Naw,' Billy said. 'It's only a bit of fun, like. Sure you don't go to a home for pinchin' sweets or wee packets of stamps. Hey, Johnny, you ever been in Robinson and Cleavers?'

'No,' Johnny said, speaking around another mouthful of sandwich.

'Amazing!' Billy exclaimed with reverence. 'That big store is real posh. This really wide marble staircase with white statues on both sides and plush carpets and snot-nosed men and wimmen serving behind the counters. Of course, me and Harry didn't even get as far as the staircase before we were spotted and turfed out.'

'Sure they recognise thieves when they see them,' Marlene said, 'and with you two it stands out a mile.'

'You should get a job in there, Marlene, instead of workin' in that wee shoe shop in Great Victoria Street. I bet they'd pay you twice the money you're getting' right now.'

'They wouldn't hire me 'cause I failed the Qualifying Examination,' Marlene said. 'They're real stuck-up, that lot.'

'So we went into that big Woolworth's on the High Street,' Billy continued, ignoring her, 'and Harry nicked a lot of wee things from there. He had to keep transferrin' the things he pinched from the pocket with the hole in it to the other pocket, but he got it all home in the end. You should see what he's now got in his bedroom. His own Smithfield Market! If his Mum and Dad ever check his room, they'll have heart attacks.'

'Oh, look, they're startin',' Marlene said.

Glancing down through the banister, Johnny saw that his mother had stubbed out her cigarette and was waiting by the light switch while all the others took their places around the table. They all looked, Johnny noticed again, almost comically solemn. It was dead quiet down there.

'Ooooohhhhhh,' wee Billy moaned with pouting lips, imitating an eerie, haunting wind, practically breathing into Marlene's left ear.

Instantly, she twisted around to slap at his face, saying, 'Ack, stop that, ya wee eejut!' He jerked his head out of the way, a big grin on his face.

'QUIET UP THERE!' their mother bawled like an army drill sergeant. 'Either shut your gobs or go to your bedrooms!'

Billy and Marlene settled down, the former still grinning, the latter dead serious. Johnny kept munching at his sandwiches as the last of the spiritualists took his seat and Mary switched off the light, plunging the room into a darkness only relieved by a sliver of moonlight beaming obliquely through the curtains. Johnny heard a chair scraping. When his eyes adjusted to the moonlit darkness, he saw his mother settling onto her chair while linking hands with the people on either side of her. The spirit-medium, an enormous lady with hanging breasts, jowls, fat lips and an abundance of grey-black hair, piled high on her head and held together with a variety of brightly-coloured combs, was sitting at one end of the table, holding the hands of those on either side of her. Mary was one of them.

Everyone around the table closed their eyes.

Silence reigned.

The silence seemed to stretch out forever...

Looking down through the banister, Johnny felt the inexorable rise of tension in Marlene, though wee Billy was gazing down with wide-eyed, fearless curiosity. Johnny knew that Marlene was waiting for the table to rock from side to side, seemingly of its own accord, its legs tapping on the floor, one tap for 'Yes', two for 'No', because they had all seen it do so before and, though they didn't know if it was trickery or not, they were certainly impressed when it happened.

Now, as the silence lingered, Johnny saw the moonlight illuminating his mother's face, saw her closed eyes and pursed lips, head thrown back, face turned towards the ceiling, as she focused all her thoughts on her brother, hoping to will him back from the land of the dead and into the world of the living.

Silence still reigned.

The silence stretched out forever...

The people seated around the table were still holding hands, all with closed eyes, some breathing deeply as if they were sleeping, others twitching and rolling their heads as if trying to shake off a disturbing dream. Eventually, sounding eerily disembodied, the spirit-medium, also putting her head back, face turned toward the ceiling, though with eyes still closed, said, 'We are gathered together here, waiting to make contact, and I can feel you... You are coming through... Do not be afraid. We are here and we are here just for you. Who are you? Speak to us!'

Despite his skepticism, Johnny felt the hair stand up on the back of his neck, a shiver slithering down through him, as the subsequent silence took on a resonance of its own, spreading out to embrace the whole house, upstairs and down. Then that eerie silence was broken by the voice of the spirit-medium.

'I feel something,' she said, though her voice seemed oddly distorted. 'I hear something. I *see* something. Yes! I can see you! I can feel you! Who are you? Please speak to me!'

One of the women at the table started sobbing.

'You cannot speak,' the spirit-medium said, ignoring the sobbing woman, sounding more English than Irish. 'You can only speak with signs, we know, through material objects. So can you speak to us by using the table? Can you answer me, "Yes" or "No"?'

The people holding hands around the table visibly tensed up. The sobbing woman abruptly went silent and leaned forward slightly, as if listening. Mary, with her eyes still closed, licked her lips and took a deep breath. The silence held. The silence stretched out forever... Then the table appeared to lift slightly and drop down again, lightly tapping one leg on the floor, indicating, 'Yes.'

Most of those around the table let out audible sighs, expressing either relief or gratitude.

'Oh, Jesus!' Marlene exclaimed in a melodramatic whisper, grabbing hold of Billy's shoulder and squeezing it. 'That table's really movin'! Oh, Jesus, God help me, it's movin'! The spirits are rockin' it!'

'Be quiet!' Johnny whispered.

Yet he, too, was impressed, slightly scared and disbelieving, caught between his scepticism and his inability to explain what it was that he was seeing down there in that hushed, moonlit darkness. He was transfixed by his mother's face, which looked at once familiar and indefinably different, normally pale but now washed out to a more perfect, death-like whiteness by being upturned in the darkness in that sliver of moonlight, eyes closed, lips unnaturally tight, features tightened by ferocious concentration and the desperate need to believe.

Johnny hardly recognised his mother.

'Yes!' the spirit-medium cried out. 'You have indicated that you can hear us! Can you tell us who you are? Can you speak through me? Or do I have to ask you? Let me ask. Let me help. Have you come here to speak to someone special?'

Silence reigned in the dark room. A lone woman sobbed. Moonlight fell on the clasped hands, the upturned faces and closed eyes, on the combs in the piled hair of the spirit-medium, and, transfixing Johnny, on his mother's white, beautiful, upturned face. He recognised her at that moment, his *mother*, but then he lost her again. She moved her head to the side, less than an inch, and thus moved out of the sliver of moonlight that had made her stand out. The instant she did that, she disappeared and might never have been.

The table moved again, rising up on one side and then dropping down to tap the floor once. The table was saying, 'Yes.'

The distraught woman sobbed even louder, letting everything pour out, while the others around the table moaned, groaned or sighed. Mary came back into view. She opened her eyes, taking a deep breath, then closed them again. She seemed to be in a trance.

'Oh, Jesus,' Marlene whispered, gripping wee Billy's shoulder as if it was a rock in a stormy sea, 'that bloody table moved. Did you see it? It really moved! Oh, Jesus, I'm scared. Sure it must have been moved by a ghost. There must be somethin' down there.'

'Be quiet,' Johnny said again.

'Who are you?' the spirit-medium asked.

The table did not respond.

'Can you tell us who you are?' the spirit-medium asked.

The table tapped once, indicating, 'Yes.'

'Are you related to anyone seated around this table?'

The table tapped once, indicating, 'Yes.'

'Which one of us are you related to?'

The table did not respond.

'Are you related to Charlotte Moore?' the spirit-medium asked, referring to the woman stifling her sobs.

The table tapped twice, indicating, 'No.'

'Are you related to Daniel Pearson?' the spirit-medium asked, referring to the man seated beside the woman who had been sobbing.

The table tapped twice, indicating, 'No.'

'Are you related to Mary Hamilton?' the spirit-medium asked.

After a lengthy silence, the spirit-medium started to repeat her question: 'Are you related to Mary - ?'

She was cut off in mid-sentence when the table tapped once, indicating, 'Yes.'

Johnny's mother choked back a sob. 'Oh, dear God!' she whispered. 'Who is it? Is it...?'

'Can you tell us who you are?' the spirit-medium repeated.

The table did not respond.

'Let me rephrase that question,' the spirit-medium said. 'Are you Mary Hamilton's brother, Neil?'

After another lengthy silence, broken only by Mary's harsh breathing, the table tapped once, indicating, 'Yes.'

Mary burst into tears.

'Oh, Jesus! Oh, dear God!' she said, weeping. 'It's him! It must be Neil! Can I talk to him?'

'Can you hear your sister, Neil?' the spirit-medium asked, still with eyes closed. 'She needs to talk to you. Can she talk to you, Neil?'

There was another lengthy silence, during which nothing could be heard but the heavy breathing of those around the moonlit table. Glancing sideways, Johnny saw that Marlene had jammed her clenched fist into her mouth and was staring down with wide, frightened eyes. Wee Billy, on the other hand, was staring down fearlessly, with a big grin; he turned his head to glance at Johnny, his grin widened even more. He was just about to say something when Johnny put his index finger to his mouth, indicating that his brother should be quiet. Understanding, Billy nodded and turned away to once more look down through the banister.

The silence was broken when the table tapped once, indicating, 'Yes.'

Mary sobbed again, but managed to stifle it when the spirit-medium lowered her head and started breathing deeply, as if she had just fallen asleep. She remained that way until Mary had fully controlled her weeping, then, when another lengthy silence ensued, Mary said, tentatively, like a child, 'Neil, is that really you?'

After a considerable pause, the table tapped once, indicating, 'Yes.'

Johnny heard his mother sucking her breath in, before asking, again speaking like a child, 'Are you all right, Neil?'

The table tapped, 'Yes.'

'Are you happy where you are?'

The table tapped, 'Yes.'

'Are others with you where you are?'

The table tapped, 'Yes.'

'Loved ones? Family?'

The table tapped, 'Yes.'

'Are you reunited with Mum and Dad?'

The table tapped, 'Yes.'

Mary burst into tears for the third time, but eventually regained control again. 'Can I speak to Mum or Dad?'

The table was still for a long time, then it tapped out, 'No.'

'Why?'

The table did not respond.

'Is it difficult for you to talk from the other side?'

The table tapped, 'Yes.'

'Is it tiring?'

The table tapped, 'Yes.'

'Can you see me, Neil? Can you see me right now?'

The table tapped, 'Yes.'

Johnny heard his mother choking back another sob.

'Can you make yourself visible to me, Neil?'

There was another long pause, then the table tapped, 'No.'

'You can't make yourself visible to me right now?'

The table tapped, 'No.'

'Will you ever be able to make yourself visible to me?'

Another lengthy silence... so drawn out that Mary began to speak again. 'I repeat: Will you ever – '

The table tapped, 'Yes.'

'When will that be?'

The table did not respond.

'Will that be soon, Neil?'

The table did not respond.

'Can you still hear me and see me, Neil?'

The table did not respond.

'Are you still there, Neil?'

The table did not respond.

'Are you still there, Neil?'

The table did not respond.

Mary opened her eyes and glanced at the spirit-medium, who was still breathing deeply, head bowed. In the moonlight, Johnny saw his mother open her mouth to speak, but before she could do so, the spirit-medium jerked her head up and opened her eyes. Taking a deep breath and releasing it again, she said, sounding exhausted, 'The spirit has departed. This séance must end for tonight. Let us all pray.'

All those seated around the table bowed their heads to let the spirit-medium murmur a prayer. When the prayer was finished, she raised her head again and said, 'Mary, please turn on the lights.'

The linked hands were unclasped and then Mary, wiping tears from her eyes, pushed her chair back and went to switch on the light. As soon as she had done so, even as the others around the table, most blinking to readjust to the light, were either climbing to their feet or simply moving their chairs to another position, she lit up a cigarette.

'Ah, God,' she said, speaking to no one in particular, but sounding emotionally overwrought, as she inhaled and exhaled the smoke from her cigarette, 'sure wasn't that wonderful? Oh, God, I'm all shaking! It was Neil. I could tell that right away. It was my lovely wee brother. He's alright. He's doing fine on the other side. That was a miracle. *A miracle!*'

'It was a trick,' wee Billy whispered to Johnny, as he and Marlene stood up on the landing. 'That fat oul bag made the table move, one way or the other.'

'What way?' Marlene said, looking rattled.

'How do I know?' Billy whispered. 'But she did it, I'm tellin' ya. If you're dead, you can't rock a table. I mean, your hand would just go straight through it, like.'

'How do you know?' Marlene asked, the fear still in her eyes.

'Because even if there's life after death,' Billy whispered, 'it's not *physical* life, is it? And a non-physical bein', a ghost, couldn't push a physical object. That oul bag is a faker!'

Marlene, who believed in everything, was about to protest when Johnny cut her short with: 'Be quiet or they'll hear you downstairs. Let's go into our bedroom. You two can do all your arguing there.'

'Aye, right,' wee Billy said. 'Let's put on some records. That'll be better than goin' downstairs and listenin' to all them eejuts getting' excited over all that bloody nonsense. Look at Mum. She's a head-case!'

Glancing down through the banister, Johnny saw his mother, distinctly wide-eyed, exhaling smoke through her nostrils while talking animatedly to the solemn spirit-medium and those gathered around her. They were all excited down there. They were pouring themselves drinks, lighting up cigarettes and trying to shout each other down in their excitement.

Johnny wasn't too sure what it was that he'd just witnessed - a genuine paranormal event or clever fakery - but whatever it was, it had certainly made him feel uneasy and a bit disorientated. Some rock & roll music, maybe even the Teddy Bears, would hopefully cure that.

'Come on,' he said, turning into the unlit landing to go to his bedroom, 'let's go.'

Marlene screamed.

Johnny nearly jumped out of his skin. Turning around, he saw Marlene staring at him and through him, her eyes as big as spoons, her hands cupping her face, mouth open as her terrified screaming continued and silenced all those downstairs.

'Jesus!' Billy exclaimed.

Marlene kept screaming.

Without a second's hesitation, Johnny stepped up to her and slapped her once across the face, shocking her into a temporary silence.

'What's the matter?' he asked, as Mary, a cigarette between her lips, rushed up the stairs.

'It was him! It was *him*!' Marlene gibbered, pointing past Johnny to the end of the short, dark landing. 'Sure he was standin' right there!'

'Who?' Johnny asked, glancing back over his shoulder to see only the empty landing.

'Uncle Neil! He was standin' right there! It was the ghost of Uncle Neil, and he was...'

At that moment, Mary reached the top of the stairs, grabbed Marlene by the shoulders, and spun her around until they were face to face.

'What's going on?' Mary asked, using her upper Malone Road accent because the people downstairs were all listening.

'It was Uncle Neil!' Marlene exclaimed. She then burst into tears and jabbed her index finger back over her shoulder, indicating the far end of the dark landing, while refusing to look in that direction. 'He was standin' right there, I tell ya. Sure I saw him clear as daylight! It was his ghost and I saw him standin' there, and I could see right through him to the wall behind him. It was Uncle Neil, I'm tellin' ya! His ghost! *It was him!*'

'She's talkin' shite,' wee Billy said.

Mary belted him on the ear, making his head jerk to the side. 'Don't you dare use that language in this house! One more word and I'll tear your tongue out.' Then she turned back to Marlene, still sobbing, and shook her gently, insistently. 'Are you sure you didn't imagine it?' she asked.

'He was there, I'm tellin' ya! He was there! Oh, Jesus, it was him, it was his ghost, and he was starin' straight at me with his great big, glassy, dead eyes! Oh, God, Mum, I'm scared! I won't be able to sleep a wink tonight! Oh, God help us, *he's here!*'

'Mary!'

It was the big, fat spirit-medium, calling up to Mary from the living room. Most of the spiritualists were filing out of the house, though a couple were sticking close to the spirit-medium. They all looked uncomfortable.

'Yes?' Mary said.

'I think we should leave now,' the spirit-medium said. 'Your daughter's had a bit of a scare, so it's best if we leave you to comfort her. She might have simply imagined it, but it's also possible she actually saw *him*: your departed brother's spirit. Either way, it's clearly shaken her about, so we'll all take our leave now. Same time next week?'

'Aye, right,' Mary said.

Wrapping the still sobbing Marlene in her arms, she patted her on the back, trying to calm her down, though she was clearly as overwrought as her daughter. Eventually, when the living room had emptied out, when silence reigned again, she ran her fingers through Marlene's hair in a rare display of affection and said, 'Come down for a cup of tea, love, and then, when you want to go to bed, we'll go together. There's nothing to fear, love.'

'All right,' Marlene said, sniffing back her tears. 'Aye, let's do that, Mum. I can't go into that bedroom on my own. I'm too scared. I know I won't sleep a wink.'

'Right, love, let's go downstairs. And you two,' Mary added, turning to Johnny and Billy, 'you can play your records if you want, but keep the sound down. Alright?'

'Aye, Mum, okay,' Johnny said.

He and Billy went into their shared bedroom as their mother took Marlene back downstairs. Billy flopped across his bed, clasped his hands behind his head, and looked up at the ceiling with a big grin splitting his cherubic, scarred face.

'Well, we don't need a party after all this,' he said. 'Sure we've already had the fuckin' cabaret.'

'Aye, I reckon,' Johnny said, thinking about how he had slapped Marlene's face without even thinking about it, unemotionally, pragmatically.

There were sides to him that he'd never known he had, but now at last he was starting to see them. The merest glimpse of his shadowy other half made him tremble with dread.

4

The birthday party had been well planned and most of the guests had already arrived when, the following evening, a Friday, Albert walked through the front door with his battered suitcase in his hand. He was wearing a brand new overcoat, covered in snow, over a new suit with shirt and tie, making it clear that he was earning good money, even if he mailed little of it home. Though certainly taken by surprise to find the house, now decorated for Christmas, packed with people, Albert responded with enthusiasm, tickled pink to be the centre of attention and also, like Mary, relieved to know that he and she would be distracted from the potential arguments that invariably erupted when they had these reunions alone. So when he stepped into the living room and saw the mass of friends, relatives and their children packed in like sardines, even flowing back into the narrow kitchen, wreathed in cigarette smoke, all instantly bursting into 'Happy Birthday To You', he simply dropped his suitcase on the floor, grinned with genuine delight, then placed his hands over his ears, pretending that he was blocking out the song.

'Happy birthday, dear Albert,' the song ended. 'Happy birthday to you!'

Hands were clapped and his back was slapped, then someone shoved a glass of whisky into his fist, even as Mary was putting an arm around him to kiss his cheek and say 'Happy birthday!' as if she really meant it. Albert knew better, of course, but he wasn't complaining, since here he was, the centre of attention, about to have an evening of boozing, talking and singing. He liked nothing better.

Seeing Johnny, Billy, Marlene and the latter's hapless admirer, Ronnie Campbell, all seated on the stairs, Albert, even before he took his first sip of whisky, shouted, 'Hey, Johnny! Get this suitcase out of the way! Take it up to the bedroom!'

307

'Okay, Dad,' Johnny said, descending the stairs to pick up the suitcase. 'Happy birthday. Me and Marlene and Billy put together for a present for you and – '

'Sure that's grand,' Albert interjected, hardly hearing what Johnny was saying, but slapping him excitedly on the shoulder. 'Now get this suitcase out of here. Hi, Roy!' he exclaimed, after having a sip of his whisky, pretending to punch his lanky, distracted friend in the belly as Johnny, shrugging his shoulders and rolling his eyes at Billy and Marlene, proceeded to hump the suitcase up the stairs.

'There goes your bedroom,' he said to Marlene, as he passed her on the stairs.

'Aye,' Marlene said, sighing, obviously recovered, at least temporarily, from the shock of seeing the ghost of Uncle Neil. 'Sure the grown-ups have all the luck. Though they're lettin' me sleep up there tonight because of the party. I mean, they're gonna be up half the night, aren't they? So Dad's gonna sleep on the sofa, at least for tonight.' She rolled her eyes. 'Lucky me!'

There were only two small bedrooms upstairs and Johnny, Marlene and Billy had formerly shared one of them. However, when Marlene had had her first period a few years back, her mother had insisted that she move out of the boys' room and sleep downstairs on the sofa. Later, when Albert had gone to work in England, Marlene had shared her mother's bedroom, sleeping in a narrow single bed, but she had to vacate the room every six weeks when her father came back for one of his long weekends. Sleeping downstairs, she was always up first and could put the kettle on for the rest of them.

'So how are things with you, Roy?' Albert asked.

'Right as rain,' Roy replied, handing Albert a gift wrapped in birthday paper. 'Happy birthday, Albert.'

Unwrapping the parcel, Albert found a carton of Benson & Hedges filtered cigarettes, generally considered an exotic luxury hereabouts. 'So where did this come from?' he asked, grinning. 'Fell off the back of a lorry crossing the border, did it?'

'Somethin' like that,' Roy said, also grinning, as Albert placed the carton on the table, now covered with plates of sandwiches and cakes, as well as tumblers and bottles of whiskey, sherry and stout, much of it brought by the guests.

'Here,' Mary said, blowing smoke in Albert's face as she gave him another wrapped parcel. 'Happy birthday.'

Unwrapping this second gift, Albert found a brand-new harmonica, which he turned this way and that, grinning with pleasure. 'What a great wee present,' he said. 'Thanks, Mary.' He pecked her nervously on the cheek, then gave the harmonica a few experimental blows, before launching into 'Rock Island Line', a recent hit for Lonnie Donegan's skiffle group. When the room burst into applause, Albert grinned triumphantly and slipped the harmonica into his coat pocket. 'Later,' he promised.

By the time Johnny came back down the stairs, having left his father's suitcase in the bedroom, people had gathered around Albert and were taking turns giving him presents, which he unwrapped with the enthusiasm of a child. The guests included Mary's Catholic neighbours, the Devlins and the Laverys, as well as her fun-loving sister, Auntie Babs. The latter's husband, Malcolm Craig, wasn't coming because he didn't like parties and disapproved, in particular, of the parties given by Mary and Albert, which were notorious locally for their loud music, heavy drinking and mixed guests, meaning Protestants and Catholics. Albert's mother, Doreen, had also been invited but refused to come when she learnt that Mary's Catholic neighbours would be present - a decision that had secretly delighted Mary, who couldn't stand the old witch. The other guests were composed of relatives and friends, most of whom lived locally.

Albert glanced at the coloured streamers crisscrossing the ceiling and at the Christmas tree standing in a corner, covered in silver tinsel, its tiny lights blinking on and off.

'Nice one,' he said to Mary.

'Aye,' Mary responded indifferently, hardly hearing him, her bright eyes flicking this way and that, not wanting to miss a thing. 'So how are things across the water?'

'Not bad,' Albert said cagily. 'Could be better, of course, but not bad.'

'That's a fancy new coat you're wearing,' Mary said. 'And a new suit an' all.'

'Aye,' Albert responded, taking another gulp of his whiskey and glancing at Roy Williams, who was grinning knowingly at him. 'Have to look good for auditions, haven't I?' he explained without much conviction. 'Sure you have to look like money to make money. It's the way of showbiz.'

'Aye, right,' Mary said, also lacking in conviction. 'I can't remember when I had a new dress or the kids had new shoes.'

'Hey, Matt!' Albert deliberately called out to Matt Fletcher, an old boozing partner from Sandy Row, turning towards him, deliberately, in order to turn away from Mary. 'How's the world treating you?'

'Thunder, lightnin' and rain,' Matt replied. 'In other words, nothin's changed. Can I help myself to more whiskey?'

'Lap it up like cat's milk, Matt.'

Seated on the stairs with Marlene, Billy and the love-smitten Ronnie Campbell, Johnny was looking forward to the arrival of the King family, including Donna. Marlene had their father's present wrapped up and resting on her lap. It was a bottle of Jameson Irish whiskey, which they had purchased illegally on the Black Market from their Dad's friend, Roy Williams. It was their Dad's favourite tipple, even though it came from down South.

'So who's goin' to give it to him?' Marlene asked, since she could never anticipate how her father would respond to any form of affection, including birthday presents, and was always frightened of being humiliated by him.

'You,' Johnny said.

'Not me!' Marlene retorted, glancing nervously down the stairs at all the people gathered around her Dad, slapping him on the back or kissing his cheek and offering best wishes, shouting to make themselves heard above the noise of the record-player, which right now was playing Connie Francis' raucous hit song, 'Stupid Cupid'.

'Why not?' Johnny asked.

'I'm not goin' down there to hand him his present in front of all them people. Sure I'd die of embarrassment.'

'It's only a wee present,' Billy said. 'What's the matter with that?'

'I'd be embarrassed, I tell ya, with all them people lookin' at me. Why don't *you* give it to him?'

'Okay,' Billy said fearlessly, 'let me have it.'

'You should *all* give it to him,' Ronnie Campbell said. 'I mean, you should all go down at the same time, like, and then just, you know, *shove* it at him.'

'Ack, shut yer gob, Ronnie,' Marlene said in nervous annoyance. 'Sure what would you know?'

Ronnie blushed with humiliation. 'Just tryin' to help,' he mumbled.

'We'll take it down later,' Johnny said, 'when we catch him on his own, like.'

'I'm goin' down now,' Billy said. 'I'm gonna get some of that grub before all those pigs gobble it up. So why don't we all go down and help ourselves to some food and then, you know, just give Dad his present while we're there? That way it'll seem real natural, like.'

'Aye,' Marlene said. 'Let's do that. I mean, I'm starvin' myself. Here, Johnny, you take the present and give it to Dad, you bein' the eldest an' all.'

'Okay,' Johnny said.

Emboldened, they followed Johnny down the stairs and pushed their way through the people, adults and children, and a couple of other teenagers, packed into the small living room and kitchen. Already the air was stinking of cigarette smoke and the smells of whiskey and stout.

'Hi, kids,' Roy Williams said, staring down at them over the rim of his glass of stout. 'Long time no see, eh? What's that I see in yer hand, Johnny? Some kind of contraband?'

'You should know,' Johnny retorted.

'You wee bootlegger,' Roy said.

'Aunt Babs!' Marlene called out, so delighted to see her favourite adult that she briefly lost all inhibitions and threw herself into Babs' welcoming embrace. 'Sure I never even saw you arrivin'. You must've come in on yer hands and knees.'

'Ha!' Babs exclaimed, squinting down at Marlene through the smoke spiralling up from the cigarette balanced precariously on her lower lip. 'I came in the way I always do, but you weren't here when I arrived. You were still up in your bedroom. And how are you lot?' she asked of the three teenage boys.

'Doin' alright,' Johnny said.

'Starvin',' Billy added unsentimentally, pushing past everyone to get at the table. He was just about to reach out for a sandwich when his mother slapped the back of his wrist.

311

'Get away from there, you greedy wee pig,' she said. 'Sure what do you think you're doing? We've guests here - or didn't you notice? You wait until the guests have had their fill and even then you *ask* first.'

'Ack, for God's sake, Mary,' Babs said, 'let them have some grub. Sure there's enough to feed an army on that table and most of *us* are having drinks now. So let them tuck in first.'

'Aye, right,' Albert added, automatically agreeing with Babs, as he nearly always did.

'I'm just trying to teach them manners,' Mary said, glaring at Albert. 'Not to behave like them desperate children starving in Africa. Of course, if *you two* think they should just grab what they want before anyone else has had a chance to get near the table, then who am I to complain?'

'Am I in your way, kids?' Nelly Devlin asked, standing with her back to the table, beside her husband, Sammy, both oblivious to the exchange between Mary and her sister. 'Here, step right in.' They stepped aside to leave a clear path to the table. 'Help yourselves, you wee savages.'

Always hungry, Billy rushed in to grab a plate and heap it with sandwiches, while Marlene, so happy in the company of Aunt Babs that she had forgotten she was starving, remained with her. Ronnie Campbell, happy just to look at Marlene, stayed close by her side. Though there were two girls of Ronnie's age in the room, the teenage daughters of neighbours, both looking at him with helpless adoration, he only had eyes for Marlene. Marlene knew that other girls adored Ronnie and she had no wish to join the queue.

Johnny was just about to step up to his Dad and give him the wrapped present when Sammy Devlin said, 'So how are tricks across the water, Albert?'

'Not bad at all,' Albert said, letting the truth slip out because Mary wasn't within earshot. 'A lot better than here, like. I'm still workin' for the furniture factory in Birkenhead, but I'm also playin' a lot of pubs and clubs at night in Liverpool. More variety across the water, isn't there? A man gets more encouragement there.'

'I always said that bein' across the water was the right place to be.'

'So why don't you pack up and go there?' Nelly Devlin said tartly to her husband. 'No one's holding you down, like.'

Sammy grinned. 'Sure you couldn't survive without me if I went. Your poor wee heart would be broken.'

'Oh, would it, indeed?' Nelly turned to Bernadette Lavery. 'Don't these men always think they're the ant's pants? They think all goodness flows from them.'

'It flows at the wrong time, into the wrong place,' Bernadette replied laconically, 'to give us poor women life-long misery. Bein' a midwife, you'd know what I'm talkin' about.'

'Sure I do, right enough,' Nelly said. 'But they have their wee uses now and then.'

'Praise at last,' Patrick said.

'She said *wee* uses,' Bernadette retorted, exhaling streams of cigarette smoke from her nostrils. 'I wouldn't say that was praise.'

Billy returned to Johnny's side, holding a plate of sandwiches in one hand and a bottle of Gratton's lemonade in the other. He glanced at the wrapped bottle still held by Johnny.

'So give it to him,' he said.

'Right.' Johnny held the parcel up, preparing to hand it to his father. 'Hey, Dad, we – '

'Thing is,' Albert interjected excitedly, turning away from Johnny to address Patrick Lavery, 'I might even get on the telly soon.'

'Go on!'

'No, really. You know the Hughie Green show?'

'Ackaye. Sure it's real big news here. I mean, I watch it myself. Some quare good performers on there, despite bein' amateurs. Are you sayin'…?'

'I'm not sayin' it's certain, but I did a first audition and they've called me back for another, which is always a good sign in showbiz. So though I can't say for sure, you just might be seein' me on the telly soon.'

'Away with you!' Patrick exclaimed.

'Sure that's grand,' Sammy Devlin added. 'We'll soon be able to say we know someone famous.'

'Maybe,' Albert said with ostentatious modesty. Glancing sideways, he saw Marlene deeply engaged in conversation with her beloved Aunt Babs. When the latter glanced in Albert's direction and threw him a warm smile, he turned quickly back to his Catholic friends. 'I'm not guaranteeing it,' he said, coughing to clear his throat, though it wasn't blocked at all, 'but I'd say there's a good chance.'

'Let's drink to it,' Sammy said.

Johnny was just about to hand his wrapped present to his Dad when he and the others raised their glasses in a toast.

'To the Hughie Green Show!' Sammy said.

'I'll second that,' Patrick added.

The women raised their drinks as well and everyone in the group touched glasses, none noticing Johnny.

'For God's sake, give it to him,' Billy whispered.

'I will in a minute,' Johnny said, still holding the wrapped bottle and feeling agitated because he couldn't find the right moment to hand it over. 'Dad,' he began tentatively, 'me and Billy and Marlene want to wish you – '

'So how are you, you silly wee bugger,' someone whispered in Johnny's ear.

Startled, Johnny jerked his head around and, to his relief and delight, saw Teddy Lavery. Teddy had joined the Royal Navy when he was twenty years old, which was how Johnny most remembered him; but he was now twenty–seven, out of the Navy, and putting on an awful lot of weight because of his drinking. But as he still had his good-natured face and ebullient nature, Johnny chose to ignore his potbelly.

'Jesus!' Johnny exclaimed, 'you gave me a shock. But I'm doin' great, Teddy. So how are you? I mean, I thought you'd disappeared. I haven't seen you for six weeks or so. Where have you been?'

'In Beryl's house,' Teddy said.

'Oh,' Johnny replied, temporarily lost for words and blushing. 'So how are you?' he repeated, making up for his lost words.

'Great,' Teddy said, brandishing a glass of what looked like whiskey, though it may have been a double brandy, and defiantly holding the hand of the middle-aged woman standing beside him. She had slightly reddish brown hair and a warm, inviting smile. She was stout but attractive. 'Grand, really. Oh,' he added as an afterthought, 'this is Beryl.' He took a deep breath. 'Beryl's a friend of mine.'

Johnny knew Beryl. She was a former friend of his mother's. His mother wasn't speaking to Beryl anymore, and neither was anyone else. Beryl was at least fifteen years older than Teddy. She was the wife of Charlie Adams, also a former friend of Johnny's mother and an occasional boozing companion for his Dad. According to gossip, Charlie had moved out of his house, located just down the avenue, to go and live with another, younger, woman out in Bloomfield. So Johnny's parents, as well as most of the Laverys, not to mention most of the neighbours, were embarrassed by the fact that Teddy, who had seen the world with the Royal Navy and, beyond doubt, picked up some disgraceful foreign morals, had moved in with Beryl and now lived with her, only a few hundred yards from where he, Teddy, had been born and raised. Though he had done this ostensibly as a paying tenant, insisting that his parents had no spare room for him, now that he was too old to share a room with his brother Mark, everyone knew that he was sleeping with Beryl, even though she and Charlie had never divorced. Though this may have been perfectly normal in somewhere like London, it was scandalous in Belfast, a deeply religious, puritanical city. Naturally, it made Johnny admire Teddy all the more - though it also embarrassed him.

'Hi,' Johnny said to Beryl.

'Hi,' Beryl said to Johnny.

'Do you still have that Egyptian wallet I gave you?' Teddy asked with his customary enthusiasm.

'Ackaye,' Johnny said. 'Sure I love it, Teddy. It's the best thing that anyone ever gave me and I'm right proud to have it.'

'An Egyptian wallet,' Teddy explained to Beryl. 'I bought it in Port Said. I wanted Johnny to have it because I knew he was intelligent and could handle money if he knew where to put it. So I bought him that wallet to put his money in.'

'You're so sweet,' Beryl said.

Teddy smiled.

'It wasn't that kind of wallet,' Johnny reminded Teddy, always needing to get his facts right. 'It was a wallet containing things you need for drawing. You know? A drawing pad and coloured pencils and so on. It was hand-made by Arabs.'

'Really?'

'Yeah,' Johnny said.

Beryl smiled at Teddy and repeated, 'You're so sweet.'

'Aye, right,' Teddy said. Confused, he turned back to Johnny. 'So do you use it or not?'

'All the time,' Johnny said.

'You're still drawing?'

'Yeah.'

'You picked that American word up from your rock and roll records.'

'Yeah,' Johnny repeated.

'This kid,' Teddy said, turning back to Beryl, who, despite her advancing years, seemed as young as he was, 'could be a great artist if he was given half the chance. So will he get it?' He shook his head from side to side, grimacing to signify his disgust. 'Naw! They'll shit all over him like they shat all over me - and that'll be the end of it.'

'Not necessarily,' Beryl said, smiling at Johnny.

'Yeah, they will,' Teddy insisted. 'Because Belfast always shits on its best. And why? Because whether or not you're its best, you're either Catholic or Protestant, Fenian or Prod, and in the end, that's what you'll be judged by.'

'With the Prods doing the judging,' Beryl said, still smiling at Johnny.

'No,' Teddy said. 'Because the Prods, though dumb, are no dumber than the Fenians, and both sides, not knowing the outside world, don't know shite from shinola. So this kid here, my wee Protestant friend Johnny, will be whipped up in shite and shinola and come out of it dizzy and confused. I love him, but he's just like me: fucked by the simple fact that he was born here, manure for the future.'

'You're drunk,' Johnny said, without malice, filled with affection for his old friend.

'Aye, I am,' Teddy responded, not offended, 'and why shouldn't I be? Sure these hypocrites, all these Catholics and Protestants alike, are treating Beryl and me like we're not even flesh-and-blood humans. And why? Because I'm a Catholic, because she's a Prod, because we've twenty-odd years between us, and, worst of all, because she's still married. Well, to hell with them! I've been to sea, I've seen the world, I've come back and I'm not as dumb as I used to be. I love this woman, twice my age and a Protestant to boot, and no one's going to stop me living with her. So to hell with them all, Johnny-boy. Let them rot in the weeds of the Lagan River. Now will you take me home, Beryl?'

'Aye, I will,' Beryl said. She put her arm around him, holding him upright, then smiled again at Johnny. 'He's a Fenian and a bad boy,' she said, 'but he's talked an awful lot about you and that means he's your friend. And despite what he just said, he thinks you're bright and could be someone special. Don't disappoint him.'

'I won't,' Johnny said.

Beryl half-carried, half-dragged Teddy out of the house.

'Hey, Albert!' Matt Fletcher bawled from another part of the room, being mere feet away, but having to shout above the heads of the packed guests and, more pertinently, above Perry Como's smooth rendition of 'Magic Moments'.

'What?' Albert called back.

'How's about turning that record-player off and havin' a bit of a singsong?'

'Aye, why not?' Albert responded. 'Billy!' he bawled at his youngest son, presently sitting beside the record-player, shoving the remains of a sandwich into his bulging cheeks. 'Turn that bloody thing off.'

'What?' Billy could hardly speak because of the sandwich.

'I said turn that bloody record-player off!'

'Why?' Billy managed to ask.

'Because we're goin' to have a singsong,' Albert said.

'Aw, shit!' Billy exclaimed without thinking.

Instantly, appearing as if by magic out of the crowd, Mary swung the back of her hand at the side of his head, trying to clip his ear, saying, 'How dare you use that kind of language in this house!' Billy ducked and the swinging hand just missed him. 'You should be drinking a bottle of disinfectant instead of that lemonade.' But Billy was gone already, having shot off the chair, grinning broadly, and plunged back into the tightly packed guests to cheers and applause. Mary smiled and shook her head from side to side, as if to say, 'Well, what can a mere mother do?' Then she removed the needle from the spinning record and turned the machine off by placing the arm back in its cradle. 'There, that's *that*,' she said.

Billy emerged from the crowd to rejoin Johnny. 'They're gonna have a bloody singsong,' he said. 'I feel like throwin' up.' Glancing down, he saw the wrapped bottle still in Johnny's hand. 'You haven't given it to Dad yet. Why ?'

'In a minute,' Johnny said.

At that moment, however, he saw the unlocked front door opening and Donna entering the room with her parents. The three of them were wearing overcoats covered in snow. Johnny's heart skipped a beat. He still vividly recalled those three kisses and felt dizzy at the very recollection. Donna and her parents took their overcoats off and slung them over the banister of the stairwell, where other coats were already draped, then pushed their way, shivering and rubbing their hands, to the living room table, where there was still plenty of food and drink to be had. Leaving his Dad with the Laverys and Devlins, Johnny joined Donna and her parents at the table. They all smiled when they saw him.

'So you've come,' Johnny said.

'Aye,' Mr. King said. 'But not soon enough, judging by this crowd. Where's your Dad?'

Johnny jerked his thumb back over his shoulder. 'Right behind me.'

'Hey, Albert!' Mr. King called out to Albert.

'Who's that?' Albert's voice came back from behind Johnny. 'Eddie! Lucy! Hold on! I'll be over there in a tick!'

Within seconds, Albert was standing beside Johnny, shaking the hands of Donna's parents and nodding politely to their daughter. Albert was flushed with drink and in good humour.

'So what'll you have?' he asked when the customary greetings had been exchanged.

'A wee sherry,' Lucy said.

'A Bushmills for me,' Eddie said.

'Comin' up!' Albert said grandly. He poured both drinks, handed them to his guests, then at last turned to the silent Donna. 'And what about you, gorgeous?'

Johnny could have killed him.

'A lemonade would be great,' Donna said.

'QUIET EVERYONE!' Matt Fletcher bawled. 'We're goin' to have a wee singsong, takin' turns, like, and since I proposed it, I'll kick off the proceedings.'

Albert turned away from Donna's parents to bawl, 'Quieten down, everyone! Be fair! Give the man a chance! Let the man sing!'

'Ah, God!' Johnny whispered, blushing and glancing shame-faced at Donna because, rightly or wrongly, he thought that her parents were above this kind of thing. Certainly he couldn't imagine them having this kind of party in *their* house. It just didn't seem right, somehow. Matt Fletcher began to sing...

Where Lagan stream sings lullaby
There blows a lily fair
The twilight gleam is in her eye
The night is on her hair
And like a love-sick lenanshee
She hath my heart in thrall
No life I own, nor liberty
For Love is lord of all

Considering that he was just an old drunkard, Matt had a fine tenor voice that caressed the lyrics of the song 'My Lagan Love' as delicately as the fiddle for which the melody had first been written nearly a hundred years ago. Singing about his love-sick 'lenanshee', his fairy mistress, who had his heart in thrall, he did indeed, in his maudlin, drunken way, convey the sense of beauty and aching loss conveyed by that unknown composer and the lyricist who had added the words much later. Matt's singing silenced the house.

And sometimes when the beetle's call
Hath lull'ed the eve to sleep
I tip-toe to her sheeling low
And thru' her doreen peep
There on a cricket's singing stone
She saves the bogwood fire
And hums in soft sweet undertones
The song of heart's desire

Thereafter, as one individual followed another with a song, there was an admirable lack of religious prejudice in the choice of material. Bernadette Lavery's moving rendition of 'The Ould Plaid Shawl' was followed by Roy Williams' rousing, laughter-inciting chanting of 'The Old Orange Flute'. Auntie Babs' intensely romantic rendition of 'The Londonderry Air' (which, Johnny noticed, reduced his Dad to tears), was followed by Sammy Devlin's jaunty 'Cockles and Mussels', with everyone joining in on the chorus. Even as Johnny was about to squirm with embarrassment because of his belief that the King family was above this kind of working-class, embarrassing nonsense, Eddie King astonished him by stepping forward to contribute 'The Mountains of Mourne' to the proceedings, singing it with surprising skill and feeling. He was then followed by Nelly Devlin, who presented the gathering with her rather wickedly phrased 'Old Maid in the Garrett':

> *I can cook and I can sew, I can keep the house right tidy*
> *Rise up in the mornin' and get the breakfast ready*
> *But there's nothin' in this wide world*
> *would make me half so cheery*
> *As a wee fat man who would make me his own dearie*

The songs ranged from the sentimental to the funny, the singing ranged from good to atrocious, but every adult took his or her turn and a good time was had by all. Though Johnny normally hated the singsongs, which made him feel embarrassed on behalf of his parents, his latent snobbery was wiped away when Eddie and Lucy King also joined in with obvious pleasure. Had it not been for that, Johnny might have either gone for a walk or retired to his bedroom, in which case he would have missed one of the highlights of the evening. This occurred when it was Mary's turn to sing and she demurred, insisting that she couldn't; then Matt Fletcher, one of the men that Mary sometimes asked to escort her into pubs in Albert's absence (also one of the men who occasionally came back to the house with her) said, 'Okay, Mary, recite *The Stitcher* for us. Sure you always do a swell job on that.'

'Aye,' Babs added. 'You've been a stitcher for most of your life, Mary, and you do that well because you know exactly what you're talking about. So let's hear *The Stitcher*.'

'Sure I can't even remember it,' Mary protested, clearly nervous and frantically puffing clouds of cigarette smoke. 'I can't do it. *I can't!*'

'Yes, you can,' Johnny said.

It surprised him to hear his own voice. He hadn't meant to speak at all. He was shaken to hear how steady his voice sounded (the contradiction was apt) when he told her, practically *ordered* her, to recite the words of that famous old poem. Though normally he was shy, his voice was steadied by outrage, by the knowledge of how hard his mother had worked all her life, and by the gratitude he felt for her, knowing that she had done it only for him and Marlene and Billy. After surviving the linen mills, which had killed as many as they had fed, she had worked in marginally better conditions as a stitcher in various factories, including the Albion in Sandy Row, though she had still been compelled to suffer (and was, of course, still suffering) mercilessly long days of repetitive, mind-draining, exhausting work. She knew *The Stitcher* by heart. So did most of her friends. It was a poem, written in 1918 but still relevant today, about all the women in Belfast who had sweated blood and tears to keep their children fed when their husbands couldn't manage it on their own. Though Mary insisted that she couldn't remember all the words of the poem - or, just as likely, didn't want to - what she *did* remember, or choose to recall, she spoke with passionate conviction. Now, as they had done before, those words deeply moved Johnny. He heard his mother speaking, her voice quavering with emotion, the words that summed up most of the days of the life that had made her what she now was, for good and for ill...

> *Monday morning till Saturday,*
> *I sit an' stitch my life away,*
> *I work an' sleep an' draw my pay,*
> *An' every hour I'm growin' older,*
> *My cheek is paler, my heart is colder,*
> *An' what have ever I done or been,*
> *But just a hand at a sewing-machine?*
> *The needles go leapin' along the hem,*
> *An' my eyes is sore wi' watchin' them;*
> *Och! everytime they leap an' start,*
> *They pierce my heart - they pierce my heart!*

With tears in her eyes, Mary paused and repeated the last line, with emphasis: 'They pierce my heart - *they pierce my heart*!'

The applause nearly lifted the roof off.

'Jesus,' Albert said, looking distraught, his nose put out of joint, 'sure she's brought the house down!'

'Here, Albert,' Eddie King said, holding a flat, square-shaped package out to him. 'A wee birthday present from me and Lucy. We hope it's appropriate.'

Smiling again, being the centre of attention again, Albert placed his glass of whiskey on the table and unwrapped the parcel to find something he'd never had before.

'It's one of them new ten-inch records,' Eddie explained as Albert looked with growing pleasure at the cardboard folder illustrated with a photograph of Danny Kaye. 'It's his latest record,' Eddie explained. 'And since we think you're the greatest thing since Danny Kaye - you know? singing, dancing, doing comedy routines and impressions – '

'And looking just like him,' Lucy added.

' - we thought this was an appropriate gift.'

'It sure is!' Albert exclaimed, turning the ten-inch record this way and that, as if examining the world's biggest diamond. 'This is great, folks. It really is. I can't imagine a better birthday present.'

'Dad...' Johnny began, starting to hold up the wrapped bottle of Jameson Irish whiskey.

'Shut yer gob for a minute, Johnny.' Albert turned to Eddie and Lucy. 'Sure this is a great present. Words can't do it justice. What I'm goin' to do is listen to it over the weekend, learn it off by heart, then work on a new miming act, doing Danny while playin' it behind me. Right now, though, I'd better do somethin' for this crowd – somethin' I already know, like.' Turning away from them, he shouted at Mary, who was sitting in a cloud of cigarette smoke beside the record-player.

'What?' Mary shouted back.

'Have you still got that record by... Whatsisname?'

'Lord Rockin'ham the Eleventh,' wee Billy, unseen, said from somewhere in the crowded, smoke-filled room.

'Aye, that's him,' Albert said.

'"Hoots Mon",' Billy explained to his mother.

'Oh, *that*!' Mary responded dispiritedly.

'Aye, that,' Albert insisted. 'Put it on and I'll do a number for all our friends.'

'Ah, Christ!' Johnny whispered in despair as his mother started flipping over her pile of 45rpm records, trying to find what it was that Albert wanted.

Despite the fact that Donna's parents had enjoyed the singsong - and, indeed, taken part in it - Johnny couldn't bear the thought of what his father was now going to do. 'Hoots Mon', recorded by Lord Rockingham's XI, was a so-called 'novelty' song (a song for idiots, in Johnny's view) that was presently riding high in the hit parade, a rocked-up version of a Scottish folk melody with nonsensical words and the shouted break 'Hoots Mon!' coming after every couple of lines. Albert would roll his trouser bottoms up as far as his knees (as he was starting to do right now), loosen his tie and open his shirt, pull the jacket of his suit halfway down his arms to make it look like a strait-jacket, shove a set of false teeth into his mouth, ruffle his red hair until it looked a real mess, then proceed to tap-dance and contort his body into grotesque postures while miming to the record. Every time he came to the shouted words, 'Hoots Mon!' he would thrust his groin out in a comically lewd gesture.

Johnny couldn't bear it.

'S'cuse me,' he said to Donna's parents, 'but I've got to go upstairs for a moment.'

'Aye, right,' Eddie King said, his bright gaze focused on the centre of the room, near the record-player, where Albert had managed to place himself in good view of everyone, with Auntie Babs standing right in front of him, smiling warmly at him. 'God, I've got to see this one!'

'I'll come with you,' Donna said to Johnny.

'But you'll miss Albert's performance!' Donna's mother said.

'We'll have a better view from upstairs,' Donna lied, 'looking down through the banister.'

'Ah, right,' her mother responded, not really listening, focused, as was her husband, on where Albert, possibly soon to be seen on TV, on the Hughie Green Show, no less, was popping a set of false teeth into his mouth, having already rolled up his trousers, jerked his jacket down his arms and ruffled his hair to make himself look like a maniac. 'You do that, love.'

The opening chords of 'Hoots Mon' blasted through the whole house, shaking the very walls, as Johnny hurried up the stairs with Donna close behind him. He was not surprised, when he entered his bedroom, to find that Billy and Marlene were already in there, both sitting on Johnny's bed while Ronnie Campbell, the idol of most normal girls, sat on the floor, practically at Marlene's feet, which were dangling off the bed, looking up at her with romantic brown eyes that were completely, deliberately, ignored by the object of his undying affection.

'You've still got Dad's present,' Billy said, the instant Johnny walked into the room.

Johnny held the bottle up on high, surprised that he still had it, then he grinned and said, 'Aye, I do, right enough.'

'So what do we do now?' Marlene asked.

'Play some records?' Ronnie asked hopefully.

Marlene glanced at him, then rolled her eyes contemptuously. 'Sure we can't do that, you eejut,' she said, 'while our Dad's down there miming to that stupid record. He'd come up here and strangle us.'

'Sorry,' Ronnie mumbled.

'Hey, Johnny,' wee Billy said, 'are we gonna give that present to Dad or not? I mean, so many of his friends have brought him drink, includin' bottles of whiskey, it's not likely he's gonna remember tomorrow mornin' who brought him what. And since we haven't managed to give it to him yet, why don't we just..?'

When Johnny sat on the edge of Billy's bed, Donna sat beside him.

'Just what?' Johnny asked.

'Well,' Billy said, glancing at each of them in turn, trying to gauge their reactions to avoid getting himself into trouble, 'we can sit up here all night but we can't play our records. We can't even listen to Radio Luxemburg, 'cause they'll be playing records downstairs, so why don't we just..?' He nodded at the wrapped bottle in Johnny's hand. 'Well, Dad's not goin' to miss it, is he? I mean, he's not going to remember tomorrow whether we gave it to him or not, and since we can't do anything else, like, why not just... You know? *Drink it!*'

'You wouldn't dare!' Marlene said.

'*I* would,' Ronnie said, still trying desperately to impress her.

'You dumb eejut,' Marlene said. 'You'd try anything 'cause you're thick as two planks.'

'I *like* whiskey,' Donna said.

'You do?' Johnny asked, surprised.

'Aye,' Donna said. 'My Mum and Dad let me have a wee drink now and then - sometimes sherry, sometimes a wee drop of whiskey - because they think it'll get me used to it gradually and stop me from becoming an alcoholic. You know? Like the people in France and Italy do. Drinking with every meal and thinking it's normal. So I get a drink, a drop of sherry or a whiskey, two or three times a week. I mean, it's normal to me.'

'Right,' Johnny said, instantly starting to unwrap his Dad's present. 'We haven't any glasses up here, so we'll have to drink it straight from the bottle.'

'Just like in the fillums,' Billy said.

They passed the bottle from hand to hand.

5

When their Dad led them out of the house shortly after noon on Sunday, Johnny and Billy were both feeling fine, though they'd been hungover the day before. Marlene was still ill, moaning and groaning when they left, wailing that she would never drink again in her life, but Johnny still didn't know how Donna felt, because he hadn't seen her since having that forbidden experience with her, under the arches right beside where she lived, close to midnight, while the snow was falling about them and her parents were hopefully fast asleep in the house. Johnny couldn't be sure that it had actually happened and now he felt frightened, exultant, guilty, bewildered, triumphant, and not a little ashamed. He felt confused beyond reckoning.

'Now shut your gobs,' Albert was saying as they walked along the snow-covered avenue, having been practically thrown out of the house by Mary, who wanted to tidy it up after Friday's party and a Saturday given over to more carousing. 'You've no reason to complain. We'll just spend a couple of minutes with Granny and then go on to the Custom House steps for an hour or so. That's not too much to ask, is it?'

'Let's give Granny a miss,' Johnny said, 'and just go straight to the Custom House.'

'So what's the matter with your Granny?' Albert asked. 'She's just old, that's all, and a bit short of something in the head. Apart from that she's alright.'

'It's not Granny,' Johnny said, 'it's that dog. Some day it's goin' take a lump out of one of us.'

'Don't talk shite,' Albert said.

They were approaching the arches, passing Donna King's house at the far side of the road, and Johnny glanced in that direction, desperate to see Donna, but also nervous at the thought, given what had taken place between them on Friday night. His gaze was drawn inexorably to the far arch, the one located right next to the railway lines, and he recalled the falling snow, the stench of urine under the arch, the ground shaking beneath his feet each time a train passed, Donna's naked breast cupped in his hand, her tongue in his throat as their lips mashed together, both gasping for air. Just recalling it, he started hardening, felt breathless, a little dizzy. As they passed under the main arch and emerged to the other side, he tried to push the recollection out of his head by thinking of something else. He tried, but he failed. All he could think about was Donna, him and her both drunk, sneaking out of the house while Albert was still performing, holding everyone's attention, and putting on their coats and running down to the dark arches, through the falling snow. They had gone into the last arch, the one beside the railway wall, and there, in that freezing darkness, both drunk, they had tentatively explored each other for the first time. They hadn't gone all the way (they were standing upright, after all) but they had touched each other's bodies, the bare skin beneath the clothes, her blouse pulled off one shoulder, his shirt unbuttoned, each taking turns to tongue the mouth of the other, both hot with passion and yearning, despite the freezing cold. It was something forbidden and even slightly sordid, taking place under the curved roof of the arch, where so many other lovers had illicitly discovered each other in days gone by, and maybe that had made it all the more exciting while it was actually happening. Only the next morning, when Johnny awakened with a hangover, had it seemed a bit unreal, as if it might not have actually happened, and then, when he realised that it had, the guilt gradually crept over him. He had wondered all day, then through that night, as he was wondering right now, if Donna would still be speaking to him when next they met. He silently prayed that she would be, because now, despite his guilt and latent shame, he loved her more than ever.

'I don't mind goin' to Granny's,' Billy said, jerking Johnny out of his reverie as they turned into the Broadway. 'The dog doesn't scare me. I mean, I don't think it's as vicious as it seems. It just puts on an act, like.'

'I haven't noticed you patting it,' Johnny said.

'Aye, well...' Billy said, trailing off, wondering how to answer that one, then eventually coming up with, 'I mean, you just never know, like. Why take chances?'

'It's just a fuckin' dog, for Christ's sake,' Albert said, much quicker to swear and blaspheme in their presence these days because they weren't really children anymore. 'Leave it alone and it'll leave you alone - just like people, really. They won't bother you if you don't bother them. That's a rule of life, kids.'

That philosophy, as far as Johnny was concerned, was his Dad's justification for his avoidance of big Barney Johnstone, who had threatened, a couple of years back, to give him a good hiding the next time he saw him. Clearly not wishing to be bothered by big Barney, Albert had avoided passing his house from that day to this.

They turned off the Broadway, into Granny's street, then walked past some of the houses in the terrace until they came to her front door. The instant Albert hammered on the door with the brass knocker, the big Alsatian inside, still called only 'You', started barking and snarling, then pounded the inside of the door with its paws.

'It's only me, Mum!' Albert shouted above the noise, his lips practically pressed to the door. 'Put that animal on its leash and open the door!'

The usual performance commenced, with Granny bawling at the dog, then taking a strap to it, then putting a leash on it and dragging it, whimpering piteously, back into the living room, with furniture banging and squeaking on the floor as it was pushed aside by the wriggling monster. Eventually, however, the front door opened. Granny stared suspiciously at them for a couple of seconds, then, satisfied that it was really them and not some potential molester, she stepped aside to let them enter. When they did so, they found the huge Alsatian resting as usual on its belly and paws in the small space between one end of the sofa and the wall, breathing heavily and making those piteous whimpering sounds. The instant they entered the living room, however, it stopped whimpering and emitted a low, threatening growl instead. Johnny and Billy both froze where they were standing, with Albert just behind them.

'YOU!' Granny bawled, stepping in front of the boys and raising the leather strap above her head. 'Stop that nonsense or you'll get the biggest tannin' of yer life with this strap of mine. You hear me? BE QUIET!' She cracked the strap like a whip. Instantly, the Alsatian stopped growling and started whimpering again.

'Right,' Granny said, satisfied. 'You can all sit down now.'

Knowing that they had no choice in the matter, Johnny and Billy sat on the sofa, right beside the panting, drooling animal. Albert took the armchair near the fireplace and lit a cigarette. Granny glanced at the clock over the mantelpiece, which indicated eleven in the morning.

'You're always so punctual,' she said to Albert. 'I respect a man that's punctual. Of course, that's how you were brought up. There's no respect for punctuality these days and the world's worse off for it. A cup of tea, boys?'

'No, thanks,' Johnny said, dreading what might be served up.

'No, thanks,' Billy added, dreading the same thing. 'We've just had breakfast, Granny.'

'Sure I knew you were comin', so I put the kettle on and I've put a plate of biscuits on the tray. Just let me go fetch the tray.'

'No, Granny, we don't really – '

'A cuppa tea and a few biscuits won't do you any harm,' Granny said, placing the leather strap over the back of her own chair and heading determinedly for the kitchen. 'I'm sure you never get a biscuit in that house, the way that mother of yours carries on. I'll be back in a tick, lads.'

While Granny was out in the kitchen, collecting the tray, Johnny glanced at the huge Alsatian, saw that it was pacified, then cast his gaze around the small, gloomy living room and noted that it was dustier than ever. Johnny hated coming here. The place was filthy and smelt of decay; even the photo of the Queen, hanging above the fireplace, was drained of all colour, adding to the funereal atmosphere of the place. When Johnny came to visit Granny Doreen, he thought he was in a morgue.

'Here we are,' Granny said proudly, returning with a tray containing a pot of tea, cups and saucers, a bowl of sugar, some spoons, and a plate of what looked like brown biscuits. She placed the tray on the small table in front of the sofa, between it and the two tattered, stained armchairs, poured the tea and milk, passed the cups and saucers around, then held the plate of biscuits out to Albert, always favouring her son first in all things. Albert, though still smoking, took a couple of the biscuits, set them on the side of his saucer, exhaled a cloud of cigarette smoke, then picked up one of the biscuits and stared at it with raised eyebrows and disbelieving eyes. He looked across at the boys.

'Here, lads,' Granny said, holding the plate out to Johnny and Billy. 'Have a couple of biscuits.'

Catching their father's glance, they looked down at the plate and saw that the brown biscuits were dog biscuits. Glancing again at their father, they saw him surreptitiously slip his two dog biscuits into the side pocket of his jacket. Then he nodded at them, indicating that they should take some dog biscuits and somehow dispose of them when Granny wasn't looking.

'Come on,' Granny said, shaking the plate under their noses. 'Sure them biscuits are grand. What are you waitin' for?'

'Aye, they look great, Granny,' Billy said, picking a couple of dog biscuits off the plate and setting them on the side of his saucer. Johnny then did the same.

Granny turned back to Albert and saw that his biscuits had vanished. 'Some more?' she asked, holding the plate out dog biscuits out to him.

Albert shook his head from side to side. 'No, Mum, I've had enough. Sure they were grand but I'm not big on the biscuits. Have to watch my weight, like. I'll just have a wee sip of my tea and maybe have another biscuit in a minute. Just leave the plate on the tray there.'

'Aye, I will right enough.' Placing the plate back on the tray, Granny said to the boys, speaking over her shoulder, therefore not seeing them slip the dog biscuits they were holding into their jacket pockets: 'And you two can have as many as you want. Sure there's plenty more where they came from. Just help yourselves, like.'

'We will,' Johnny said.

'Aye, right,' Billy added.

By the time Granny had taken her chair by the fireplace, facing all three of them, the dog biscuits had vanished from their saucers.

'You two were right quick,' Grandma said with a smile. 'Sure you must have been starvin'. That because you're never fed proper at home with that woman in charge. Have some more. Help yourselves.'

'Aye, I will in a minute,' Johnny lied.

'Me, too,' Billy said. 'I'll just have a few sips of my tea first.'

'Right, childern, that's grand.' Granny turned away from them to get all the gossip from her son. 'So how did the party go, Albert?'

'It was brilliant,' Albert said. 'A real surprise and good fun. Sure we all had a grand time.'

'All except me,' Granny said with a martyred look.

'You were invited,' Albert reminded her.

'Sure that wife of yours only invited them Fenians because she knows my Christian principles won't permit me to go to a do that has their kind as guests. She invited them just to keep me away. That woman doesn't want me in her house and that's all there is to it.'

'That's not true, Mum.'

'Yes, it is. That Mary of yours has never liked me and never will. She knows that I disapprove of her flighty ways and she resents me for that. So I had to sit here on my own, with my radio, while you all had your party.'

'Well, Mum, it wasn't really your kind of – '

'Not that I could have gone anyway,' Granny interjected, 'what with my lumbago playin' up and those other excruciating' pains, maybe the cancer, shootin' through my oul bones.'

'So how are you feelin' today?' Albert asked, as the boys, seeing that Granny was distracted, removed some more dog biscuits from the plate on the tray and slipped them into the pockets of their jackets, to be disposed of later.

'As good as can be,' Granny said with another martyred look, 'though that's not sayin' too much at my age. But if God wants me to suffer, I'm sure He has His reasons and I'll suffer without complainin' about it. His will be done.'

'Amen,' Albert said, exhaling a stream of smoke from his cigarette while throwing the boys a wink. 'So are you eating alright, then?'

'Well, I can't afford luxuries, but I get enough to sustain me. The odd sandwich and a wee salad now and then, with the tripe and onions on Sundays. Sure that's all an oul stomach like mine can hold down these days.'

'How are you passing the time these days? Do you ever see any old friends?'

'I go to church every Sunday, as regular as clockwork, though apart from that and a wee bit of shoppin', I don't get out too much. The body just won't take it. My bones ache night and day. I meet a few friends at church, but sure most are dead and buried and the neighbours, the ones livin' around here, aren't worth the spit of a decent Christian. I can't tell you what they do behind closed doors because those childern are sitting there.'

Trying not to grin, Albert glanced at Johnny and Billy, then returned his gaze to his mother. 'So what's happenin' out back?' he said. 'Out there in the entry?'

Granny opened a small, round tin, picked some snuff up with her fingers, sniffed the snuff up her nostrils, then sighed with deep satisfaction.

'It's a disgrace,' she said. 'There's no shame out there at all. Sure they're couplin' out there like dogs in heat and they're not quiet about it. They're the same kind you find under those arches up where you live. What kind of man would take a woman under those arches in the dead of the night? What kind of woman would be willin' to go there with him? Sinful creatures of the most debased kind, may God strike them dead. I'll say no more about it.'

Despite the fact that Granny was obviously mad, Johnny instantly burned up, feeling guilty and ashamed, recalling him and Donna under that arch in the darkness of Friday night. While they had still been passionately embraced under the arch, Donna's parents had returned from the party and entered their house. The gable end of the house directly faced the arch where Johnny and Donna were hiding. Clearly thinking that their daughter was still upstairs in Johnny's house with him and Billy and Marlene, they had decided to leave the party and make their way home, trusting her to do the same later, on her own. That trust had already been betrayed but neither Johnny nor Donna cared (or, at least, didn't think about it) as they continued, once Donna's parents had entered their house, to passionately kiss and grope each other, oblivious to all but their own feelings. They remained there for another hour or so before Donna, smiling like a Cheshire cat and readjusting her clothing, finally entered her home to go to bed. If her parents had heard her enter, they would have assumed that she had just come directly from the party; they wouldn't have dreamt for one second that their beloved daughter, like Granny Doreen's sinful, debased creatures, had been under the arches with a boy in the dead of the night. Now that boy, Johnny, was writhing with guilt as he listened to his Granny's moral outrage.

'If I had my way,' she was saying, having decided, after all, to say something about it, 'I'd have them entries and those arches patrolled every night by decent Christians and anyone found couplin' in them dragged out and exposed for the sinful creatures they are. Tarrin' and featherin' would be too good for them, but that's the least I'd do to them.' She turned to Johnny and Billy, wagging her index finger at them. 'And you two,' she said, 'take heed of what I say. Keep away from the entries and them arches, particularly when tempted there by some trollop. That kind of woman will only ruin your life and condemn you in God's eyes.' Her beady gaze moved down to the plate of dog biscuits. There were very few left. 'Sure that's a sight for sore eyes,' she said, pleased, then turned triumphantly to Albert. 'See what I mean, son? These boys of yours ate most of the biscuits, so they must have been starvin' as usual. That's because they're neglected at home, though I'm not namin' names. So how are things across the water, son?'

'Grand,' Albert said, stubbing his cigarette out and instantly lighting up another. 'I'm doin' swell, Mum. Makin' a lot more money than I was makin' in the Yard and also getting a lot of work in nightclubs.'

'Pubs and clubs,' Billy corrected him.

'Nightclubs,' Albert repeated, giving Billy an angry glance before turning his most winning smile back on his mother. 'Some are real posh as well.'

'Only what you deserve, son.'

'So all in all, I'm a lot better off than I'd be back here.'

'Sure that's grand news, son. I always knew you'd do well. It's the way you were brought up. My only concern is for the welfare of your family, left alone here while you're across the water. I have concern over that, like.'

'No need to worry, Mum. There's no problems at home. The kids are doin' well at school and Mary's working in the Albion and I'm sending her enough extra money to keep everyone comfortable.'

'It's their moral welfare I'm concerned about, son.' The Alsatian, which had been sleeping, opened its brown eyes, saw the boys and started growling in a threatening manner. 'Hey, you, shut yer gob!' Granny said, reaching for the leather strap that lay across the back of her chair. The Alsatian went quiet again. 'These boys,' she continued, turning back to Albert, 'don't have proper supervision – '

'Mum works six days a week,' Johnny reminded her, refusing to let his mother be blamed for anything. 'That's why she isn't at home much.'

' - and all childern need their father,' Granny continued, blandly ignoring what Johnny had said, 'so I think, if you're not plannin' to come back to Belfast, you should give some thought to movin' them across the water to join you in Birkenhead.'

'Well...' Albert said doubtfully, glancing at the boys, both of whom were staring at him with raised eyebrows.

'You don't have to worry about me, son,' Granny interjected nobly, assuming that he was concerned for her, which was far from being the case. 'The Lord be praised, I'm still in good health and can look after myself. I just feel that no family can profit by bein' split up like this. I'm not one to interfere, but it has to be said that a wife's place is by her husband's side, not runnin' around on her own for all the world to see.'

This, Johnny realised, was as near to subtlety as Granny could possibly manage when it came to talking about her daughter-in-law. He could almost hear the grinding of her back teeth.

'Anyway,' she continued, 'I'll say no more for now. I just think you should give it some thought, given how things are.'

'Aye, I'll do that,' Albert said.

'So when are you goin' back to Birkenhead?'

'Tomorrow night,' Albert said.

'Well, good luck to you, son.'

'Aye, Mum, thanks.' Albert ostentatiously checked his wristwatch and then raised his eyebrows in surprise. 'Hey, kids, we're running late,' he said. 'Get off your backsides and let's go.'

Everyone stood up, including Granny Doreen. Distracted and confused by the movement of more bodies than he was normally used to, the Alsatian opened his rheumy eyes, raised himself slightly and started to growl in a hopefully threatening manner. Without a second's hesitation, Granny grabbed the leather strap off the back of her chair and slammed it down violently across the sofa, making everyone jump. 'Shut up, you brute!' she snapped, leaning down over the dog and glaring at it. 'Bark once and I'll flay the skin off ya to leave ya in misery.' Instantly, the dog ceased its growling and started whimpering piteously again. Granny straightened up and turned back to Albert.

'So where are you goin' today, son?'

'A couple of hours at the Custom House steps,' Albert told her, 'to hear a few of the speakers.'

'That's a good place to take 'em on a Sunday,' Granny said. 'They'll get their fill of decent Christian sentiments down by the steps. Sure some of those men there are saints. The Fenians won't be takin' over Belfast as long as those men are speakin'. But will I see you again before you leave, son?'

'Aye, I'll call in tomorrow.'

'Alright, son, that's grand.' She held her cheek out for Albert to kiss it, which he did, then she held the same cheek out to Johnny and Billy, both of whom kissed her with reluctance. Albert opened the front door to let the boys rush out, both grateful for the fresh air, despite the cold, then he gave his mother a final wave, closed the door, caught up with the boys and proceeded to lead them to the centre of town and, ultimately, the Custom House steps. The snow had stopped falling.

6

Though most Catholics loathed the Custom House on principle, a lot of Protestants loved it and Orange supporters of a certain type viewed it as virtually a sacred place. The Custom House was the forum for Protestant Belfast, the storm centre of Orange aggression. Located in Donegall Quay, down by the river and docks, the building, designed by Charles Lanyon, was architecturally most notable for its sculptured pediment portraying Britannia, with Neptune and Mercury overlooking the waterfront. In front of the building was a vast open space where hundreds could comfortably gather, as they did every Sunday, and steps led from this space, 'the square', up to a flagged esplanade with a balustrade. This was raised a few feet above the level of the pavement, thus making it an ideal platform for the public orators, who would always be in full view of their audience.

Every Sunday afternoon hundreds of Protestants gathered in the square in front of the Custom House steps to castigate the Catholics in general and the Pope in particular, with Popery and all its pernicious works denounced, threatened and torn to shreds by men with booming voices, purple faces, flaring, fanatical eyes and melodramatic gestures. By the time Albert arrived with his two sons, the snow-covered square was already packed and the orators on the raised esplanade, standing just behind the balustrade and often practically leaning over it, as if to get closer to their audience, were expatiating on the creed and politics of Papists, interrupted only by shouts of encouragement and enthusiastic applause.

Though this was a Sunday, when the pubs were closed, a lot of the men were secretly imbibing from hidden hip flasks.

While the Loyalist demagogues bawled and waved their hands frantically, histrionically, on the esplanade, various Lambeg drummers moved amongst the crowds, creating a deafening racket, and the Salvation Army, standing well back, near the road, worked to bring in its own kind of converts. Men with orange sashes and black bowler hats wandered through the crowd, smiling.

'Sure isn't this a grand sight?' Albert said to his two boys as they pushed their way through the milling crowds to get near the esplanade.

Albert wasn't an Orangeman and he certainly wasn't political, but the showman in him enjoyed large crowds and applauding audiences, even if not his own.

'Aye, it's grand,' Billy said, already excited. 'A lot of my pals come here every Sunday, so I might bump into some of them.'

Billy had not left the Sandy Row Orange Lodge as he had planned to do shortly after that Twelfth of July march a few years back. Instead, he had been so exilerated by the march, at being a part of *something*, not ignored as he normally was by his father, that he had gone back to the Lodge after the Twelfth with more enthusiasm than he'd had before it. Now he was, if not fanatical, certainly a committed Lodge member who rarely missed a meeting and viewed his fellow Orangemen as an extended family. Johnny, who still admired his friend Teddy Lavery, had been embarrassed for a long time about this, but gradually he had come to accept it, if not actually approving of it. He was hoping that Billy would grow out of it, but so far there was no sign of that happening.

Though the main speakers were gathered together on the raised esplanade, others, including the patently deranged, were wandering through the crowd, bawling their own brand of demagoguery and carrying placards raised up on poles in order that they might be read by one and all.

NO FENIANS HERE!
DOWN WITH THE POPE!
ACCEPT CHRIST AS YOUR SAVIOUR
POPERY IS HOKERY
PROTESTANT IRELAND - NOT IRISH IRELAND

The last particularly intrigued Johnny, because he had never quite worked out why so many Irishmen in Belfast were so passionate about being considered British rather than Irish; to the degree, indeed, where they viewed the Catholics as 'Irish' who didn't belong in Northern Ireland and certainly not in the Orange State of Ulster.

'Some of those men carrying placards look crazy,' Johnny observed.

'Aye, they are that, right enough,' Albert said, 'but sure they're good for a laugh.'

'Hey, how are you, Leonard?' Billy said, slapping his hand on the shoulder of a small, plump, middle-aged man who was wearing a black bowler and orange sash. 'Good to see you, Leonard.'

The man smiled when he saw who was speaking to him. 'Ack, Billy-boy,' he said, 'sure it's good to see you, too.' He spread his hands in the air, indicating the crowd gathered in the square. 'A good turn-out, eh? Sure doesn't it make you proud to be a Protestant?'

'And an Orangeman,' Billy said.

'Aye, that too,' his friend said.

'Hey, Dad,' Billy said, turning to Albert. 'This is Leonard Graham, one of my friends in the Lodge.'

'How ya doin'?' Albert said, offering a cocky grin, but keeping his hands in his pockets.

'Pleased to meet you,' Leonard said. 'Nice to meet Billy's Dad at last. It's a pleasure to have wee Billy in the Lodge. He gives us all a good laugh, like.'

'And this is my brother, Johnny,' Billy said.

'Hi,' Johnny said.

'Good to meet you, too, Johnny,' Leonard said. 'Sure Billy's told us all about you. So why aren't you in the Junior Lodge?'

Johnny shrugged. 'I dunno.'

'Not a joiner, eh?'

'I guess not.'

'Well, each to his own, I say.' Leonard turned back, smiling, to Billy. 'Just wanderin' about, are you?'

'Aye. We just came down for a bit of a lark.'

'Sure there are worse ways of spendin' a Sunday afternoon. Right now I'm lookin' for a couple of pals. I might see you later on, Billy-boy.'

'Okay,' Billy said.

When Leonard wandered off, Albert led Johnny and Billy deeper into the noisy throng in the snow-covered square until they reached a bunch of onlookers gathered around a man who was dressed like a tramp and holding up a placard stating: SAINT PATRICK WAS A PROTESTANT! This man was spitting as he screamed his beliefs - and he screamed all the time.

'So what *about* Saint Patrick?' he was screaming, spitting over those standing nearest to him. 'Well, let me *tell* you about Saint Patrick! Sure haven't those bloody Fenians, tryin' to steal Ulster from us, stolen Saint Patrick and made him the saint of their Papish republic.'

'Let them have him!' someone, sounding drunk, called out from the depths of the crowd. 'Sure we don't need any Fenian saints here!'

'But Patrick *wasn't* a Fenian!' the tramp screamed, spitting vigorously. 'He was a Protestant just like us! Sure we went across the water in the middle of the fifth century, when Roman Britain was at its weakest, and we looted the land and brought back thousands of slaves, including Saint Patrick.'

'Bollocks to that!' another onlooker bawled, boldly unscrewing the top of his silver hip flask, his face already flushed with alcohol.

'Bollocks yerself!' the tramp screamed back, still spitting with every word. 'Shut yer stupid gob and listen!' Laughter rippled through the crowd. 'In the ancient *Book of Armagh*, where written Irish history began, if you ignoramuses did but know it, Saint Patrick, in his Confession, said he was a simple country man, though a sinner, and that he'd been taken from his home in Protestant England, with thousands of other prisoners, and carried away into captivity in Ireland.'

'Where he had a pint of stout,' someone called out, 'and saw the light instantly.'

More laughter from the crowd, but the tramp was not amused. 'You blasphemous bastard!' he screamed. 'In the Pope's back pocket, are ya? No! No!' he continued, waving his free hand frantically when the crowd broke into laughter again. 'Now listen to this, will ya! After six years as a slave, tending his sheep near the western sea of Ulster, desp'rately alone, like, Patrick saw the light - *Yes, you heathen blasphemer, Patrick saw the light!* And what did he say in his Confession? "*The spirit seethed in me.*" Yes, that's exactly what he said! And so, inspired by God, he walked a couple a hundred miles to the east coast of Ulster and from there, with a ship-load of pirates, he returned to England.'

'Good riddance to the English bastard!' someone in the crowd bawled, slurring. 'We don't need any Englishmen here!'

More laughter and applause, though, again, the tramp was not amused.

'We needed Patrick!' he screamed, spitting worse than ever, raising his clenched fist in the air as if wanting to bring it down on someone's head. 'Because in those days we were pagans, steeped in sin and idolatry, falling to our knees before false gods. And we got him. *He came to us!* Over there, across the water, in Protestant England, he had a vision and heard someone talking to him, a messenger from the Lord, sayin', "We beg you, holy boy, to come and walk among us again." And he was so moved by that, so touched by the spirit, like, he took holy orders and then returned here, to Ulster green and fair, to preach the gospel and convert the pagan populace. So Saint Patrick belongs to us here in Ulster - *not* to those Papish heathens down south. Yes! *Saint Patrick's a Protestant*!'

As this final line was screamed with maximum hysteria, some of those up front actually had to duck to avoid more gobs of spittle from the tramp's lips. Others burst out laughing and applauded, enjoying themselves.

'Let's get up to the real preachers,' Albert said, moving away to lead Johnny and Billy towards the esplanade. 'Christ,' he added, 'it's cold. Sure I could do with a pint.'

They had only managed to advance a few steps when a Lambeg drummer started playing just a few feet ahead of them, making a tremendous, deafening, bloodcurdling din. Stopping to watch, they saw that the man was Bert Wilson, the Lambeg drummer from their own avenue, who lived only a few doors away, was a good neighbour, and always played his drum on special occasions, such as Bonfire Night and the Twelfth of July. Watching him play, Johnny was stirred and slightly frightened, recalling that as a child he had been told by his mother that if he misbehaved, he would be placed inside a Lambeg drum and taken away in it, never to return, while the drummer was pounding it. For years after first hearing that old wive's tale, Johnny had suffered nightmares about being locked up inside one of those drums, bunched up like a ball in total darkness, that relentless drumming resounding in his head for all of eternity, gradually driving him mad. He no longer had those nightmares, but even now, when he heard or saw a Lambeg drum being played, he vividly recalled those nightmares and could not help but feel slightly frightened, even as he could also feel the relentless, primitive rhythms stirring his blood. The Lambeg drum had been created to send men into battle, stripped of their normal, civilised senses and all too ready to revert to primitive savagery. It was a dangerous instrument.

Bert played the hell out of his drum, hands moving so fast that they became a mere blur, sticks striking the skins at a pressure of several tons to the square inch, creating a constant, unbroken pounding that threatened to blot out the whole world. Bert also danced with his drum, actually dancing as he played, turning this way and that, leaning sideways, then backward and forward, spinning on the balls of his feet with the big drum, strapped to his shoulders, seeming to be glued magically to his chest. The men around him, some already drunk, having imbibed secretly from hip flasks hidden under their jackets, were growing excited, shouting too loudly and slapping each other too hard on the backs, obviously getting carried away with excitement.

Johnny thought that some of them might actually start fighting, but then, perhaps sensing the mood he was creating, Bert decided to take a break. When he stopped playing, the men around him, after shouting congratulations or obscene praise, drifted away to listen to some of the other speakers scattered around the square, well away from the esplanade. Slipping the straps off his shoulders, Bert placed the brightly decorated drum on the ground beside him and rested his elbows on top of it while lighting a cigarette. When he saw Albert with Johnny and Billy, he offered a big, toothless grin.

'Well, look at this, will ya!' he exclaimed. 'The Village contingent has arrived. So how are the Hamiltons?'

'Ack, we're doin' fine, Bert,' Albert said, lighting a cigarette to ensure that his friend didn't smoke alone. 'Sure that was a grand bit of drummin'. You can still hack it, can't you?'

'I do my best,' Bert replied, 'but I'm startin' to feel my age. My arms ache like hell these days.'

'Is it hard to beat that thing?' Billy asked.

'Aye, it is, son. A good Lambeg drummer's like a hundred-ton gun - he can only be used a limited number of times. I mean, the strain always makes a man fart far too much - it does his stomach in, like - and his elbows get battered to hell, until he can't play no more. That's what's happenin' to me.'

'Jesus!' Billy exclaimed admiringly.

Exhaling smoke through his nostrils, Bert turned back to Albert. 'You don't play yourself, Albert, but you know all about it, I suppose.'

'Aye,' Albert said, 'I know.' He turned to Johnny and Billy. 'During a busy time, say the Twelfth, when a drummer's workin' real hard, he beats the hides out of his drum so many times, he has to replace them. And just as often the drummers drum so hard and so long, they have a fit and then have to be sedated. One man even drummed so hard, he had a heart attack out there in Finaghy Field. It's a strange business, drummin'.'

'Aye, right,' Bert said, grinning mischievously at the two boys. 'And I'll tell you somethin' else, kids. After a really excitin' day, when a drummer's been playin' nonstop, it's often necess'ry for his wife to take precautions, 'cause he's likely to try drummin' in his sleep.'

'Bollocks!' Billy said, cheeky as always.

'Not bollocks,' Bert insisted, though he winked at Albert. 'Now here's a true story. There's a drummer in Belfast who drummed so violently in his dreams, he actually started drummin' in bed, then out of bed, marching constantly up and down the room. You know? Like a sleepwalker. And he was clenching his fists so hard and waving his arms so violently, he broke up half the things in the room and then accidentally killed his missus before waking up.'

'That's pure blarney,' Billy said.

'No, it's not.' Bert grinned broadly, exposing naked gums. 'And I'll tell you somethin' else. There's a lot of undertakers in this city who won't put a dead drummer in his coffin without first puttin' him in handcuffs. That's a fact of life, Billy-boy.'

'Ack, away with ya!' Billy said in mock disgust. 'Sure you're just pullin' m'leg.'

Bert burst out laughing, convulsed by his own jokes, then, controlling himself, he shook his head from side to side and wiped tears from his rheumy eyes. 'Well, a drummer can only believe what he's told by older drummers and those are the kind of stories I was told. And who knows, kid? Maybe they *are* true. As your Dad just said, drummin's a very strange business. Sure there's none other like it.'

'Those drums make people violent,' Johnny said.

'Aye, they do that, son. More so somewhere like this, where they get themselves whipped up by the preachers and booze, and then, incited by the drums, go on the warpath, marching into the Catholic areas, wavin' their Union Jacks. Sure that's why I'm proud to be a drummer. I'm an Orangeman through and through.'

With his cigarette between his lips, Bert hoisted his big drum off the ground, slipped his arms through the straps, adjusted the straps until the drum was positioned properly against his chest, then proceeded to make his way towards the Custom House steps, repeatedly shouting, 'Move! Step aside!' Because he was a Lambeg drummer, an honoured man, the crowd parted like the Red Sea to let him through. Albert and the two boys stuck close behind him, making it all the way to the esplanade, despite the density of the noisy, excited crowd.

More than one man, hidden from view by those packed tightly around him, therefore out of sight of the odd policeman wandering about on the outskirts, was drinking from his hip flask and passing it on to his friends, many of whom were already drunk.

While Bert took up his position just below the esplanade, Albert and the boys were able to stay near the front of the crowd and get a clear view of the speakers. One was speaking (or, rather, shouting) at that moment. He was a heavy-set man with a thick neck, barrel chest and aggressive features, including lascivious lips, a solid block of a face, flushed cheeks, flaring eyes and an extraordinary, histrionic bellow that would have carried to the back of any balcony and could certainly be heard at the far end of the square. Right now he was shaking his ham fist and bellowing impressively.

'That could be the Reverend Ian Paisley,' Albert said to the boys. 'If it is, he's a real firebrand preacher. He hates the Fenians like nobody's business and has a hell of a lot of followers. It's said he's gonna shake Belfast up if given half the chance. I'm not sure if that's good or bad, but he puts on a great show.'

'He looks like a big bully,' Johnny said. 'Like a schoolteacher who likes the cane too much.'

'Shut your gob and let's hear him,' Albert retorted.

'So I tell you,' the bulky man on the platform was bellowing histrionically while repeatedly shaking his right fist and flicking his hair back from his forehead with his other hand, 'that we have to defend the glories of our Protestant heritage, never letting ourselves forget King William's crossing of the Boyne, the Battle of the Diamond, the Seige of Londonderry - not *Derry*, as the Fenians would have it, but *Londonderry* as we Protestants prefer to call it for the obvious reasons.'

The crowd roared its approval of that last remark, but the preacher, who may or may not have been the Reverend Ian Paisley, was quick to silence them with another melodramatic outburst.

'We Protestants are Christians, saved by the blood of Jesus Christ, shed on the cross at Calvary, but our enemies - the disciples of the Church of Rome and its heretical Pope, unfortunately living right here in our midst, in the very heart of our beloved province - are even now plotting to destroy us and make Ulster, despite the wishes of its Protestant majority, an imprisoned part of their corrupt Fenian Ireland. Yes! Sure don't they believe that if they destroy what *we* believe in, they can then destroy the greatness and glory of the whole Orange State? But they cannot and *will* not!' The crowd roared again. 'Because the Lord will lead us on, from victory to victory, opening us to the glory of God, to the revelations of the saints, to the salvation of lost souls, to the punishment of the sinner, to the defeat of soul-damning Popish heresy and all the moral vileness it brings with it. We won't accept Fenian filth! We'll flush it out and deal with it! Sure we'll make war on the very battlements of hell, sin and apostasy, crying, "Glory be to God!" and "Hallelujah!" Now let me hear it from all of you!'

'HALLELUJAH!' the crowd of men, women and children roared as one, their faces flushed with excitement and reverence, despite the bitter cold.

'Yes!' the preacher bellowed when the crowd had fallen silent again. 'The Protestant faith in Ulster is neither dead nor dying, but marching on to the greater glory of God Almighty. We won't give up our heritage, our beliefs, our religion, to the heresies of Rome, nor to the Popish barbarians standing at our gates. No! Instead, we'll insure that the dark and sinister shadow of that so-called republic, that Fenian state across the border, which encourages the heathen hordes to multiply and overwhelm us, will not deprive us of our political and religious liberties, which are, for us, one and the same, indivisible, eternal. No! And again - *No!* To those heretics and their consorts, to all those who'd threaten us, we proudly cry out, "No Popery!" *Let me hear it!*'

'NO POPERY!' the crowd roared in unison. 'NO POPERY! NO POPERY!'

'No Popery!' the preacher repeated when the crowd had quietened down again. 'For there can be no reconciliation between us and our Popish neighbours, no marriage between Christ and Beelzebub, until the heretics of Roman Catholicism fall to their knees, beg forgiveness for their sins, renounce their pagan ways, and accept the one true Church, the *Protestant* church, as the guiding light and beating heart of Ulster.'

More roars from the crowd.

'Until then we can have no truck with the vipers of Rome, with Popish deviltry and religious subversion; nor with that new Sodom and Gomorrah, the so-called Republic of Ireland.'

More roars from the crowd.

'No! And again - *No!* For so long as we're surrounded by the enemies of the true Christ, the despisers of Ulster and its proud Protestant heritage, we must continue to protest against the iniquities of Rome, to repudiate all Popish lies, and to brand as traitors all those who'd attempt to convert us to the blasphemous fables and dangerous deceits of Popery and damned Republicanism! We must... *And we will!*'

This time the crowd roared even louder, more hysterically, than before, as if about to explode into violence. The preacher cleverly waited until his audience had calmed down, then he took a deep breath, thrust his barrel chest out, let his head fall back, face turned to the cloudy heavens, stared straight at the crowd and bellowed:

'Praise the Lord! *Hallelujah!*'

'HALLELUJAH!' the crowd roared.

Instantly, as if planned, Bert Wilson started pounding his Lambeg drum, faster and faster, louder and louder, until even Johnny was helplessly swept up in the mounting excitement. Aroused to burning point by the inflammatory sermon, set on fire by the drumming and, beyond doubt, further inflamed by drink, the crowd suddenly went wild, surging this way and that, a great wave at high tide, and then it parted again to let Bert Wilson through, as he headed back across the packed square, now beating his drum like a madman, his hands a mere blur.

The crowd closed in on Johnny, pushing between him and his father, and then he found himself crushed against Billy and pushed forward with him. They were being pushed by the crowd, a great mass on the move, drawn inexorably by the pounding of the drums and advancing, as if hypnotised, to an unknown destination. Johnny lost sight of his father. Men were bellowing on all sides. He felt suffocated, half deafened, his head ringing, as if he really *was* inside that Lambeg drum and being carried away. Fear whipped through him and then subsided, was replaced by pure excitement. He caught a glimpse of Billy's flushed, grinning face and then he, too, disappeared, swept away on another tide of seething humanity.

The drum up ahead kept pounding - obviously Bert Wilson's drum - but then it was joined by another, then a third, and then a fourth, until the noise blotted out Johnny's senses and made him part of the crowd. The drummers played as one, a perverted Pied Piper, hypnotising those behind them, drawing the crowd onward, and Johnny went with the flow, a piece of flotsam on the rapids, not knowing and not caring where he was going, simply experiencing every second as it came and went, feeling lit up inside.

The drummers led them through the centre of town, into Royal Avenue, across to Castle Street, then up Divis Street, and then finally, fatally, into the narrow, packed streets of the Pound Loney, until they came to a Catholic church. There the drummers stopped marching, though they didn't stop playing. They played their Loyalist rhythms in the heart of that Catholic ghetto, in front of that Catholic church, as the Catholics, offended, emerged from their homes to confront what was now a mob of ecstatic, aggressive, red-faced Prods with their proudly fluttering Union Jacks.

Abruptly, the drummers stopped playing and a stark, unreal silence took over the street.

The silence lingered until...

'Fuck the Pope!' a man bawled.

'Fenian shites!' another bawled.

'You filthy Protestants!' a woman screamed hysterically. 'Go back where you belong!'

'Fenian bitch!'

'Orange bastard!'

'Who are *you* calling a bastard, you Taig whore?'

'Let's get 'em!' Another man shrieked, sounding close to demented. 'Let's beat the shite out of 'em!'

The battle commenced.

7

Johnny didn't know what was happening. It all happened so fast. He saw the Catholics opening their doors, stepping out into the street, saw fists waving and then heard the Catholics shouting and then his own kind responding. The abuse went back and forth, like balls on a Ping-Pong table, then the two sides suddenly rushed at each other and mayhem ensued. The violence was shocking. Both sexes were involved. As the adults collided, punching and clawing, tearing hair, gouging eyes, the children on the pavements started throwing stones and bottles, often hitting friends or the members of their own family, as they, too, were swept up in the hysteria.

Johnny was caught in the middle of it. Though confused, he felt calm. In fact, he had never felt calmer in his life, more in control of himself, though his perceptions seemed immeasurably heightened and everything that was happening around him had a startling clarity. There was shouting and screaming. A lot of the screaming was caused by pain. He saw a man putting his boot through the hides of a Lambeg drum as a woman, middle-aged, wearing a shabby dress and apron, grabbed another man by his hair to violently slam his face into a brick wall. Women clawed at each other. Men threw punches at one another. There were couples rolling about on the road, interlocked, their fists rising and falling. Windows were smashed. Skin was slashed by flying glass. Time froze and seemed to stretch out forever as the violence spread.

Johnny heard the police sirens when he was running away. He saw an RUC paddy wagon turning into the street as Billy emerged from a convulsion of heaving bodies, his scarred face smeared with blood.

'Jesus,' Billy gasped, 'let's get out of here. All these people have gone mad.'

'Are you alright?'

'Aye,' Billy said.

That's when it ended for Johnny. It ended just as they were escaping. He saw Bert Wilson crawling along the road on hands and knees, blood on his face and hands, the broken frame of his Lambeg drum dragging along behind him, held onto him by its straps, and then he saw Billy jumping up and running back to help Bert, until brought down in what looked like a rugby tackle by three or four men. Those men buried wee Billy in a heap of writhing bodies, then, when they had him on the ground, they started in on him.

Johnny went to the rescue, not pausing to think about it. He felt as cool as a cucumber, as serene as the moon, as remote as the most distant planet, when he ran back the way he had come to grab the first of that heaving bunch and jerk him off Billy.

'What the fuck...?' he heard the man muttering as he fell to the road.

Johnny grabbed another man, pulled him backward, pushed him sideways, and then, as the man tried turning around, Johnny kicked him in the side of the head and heard the sound of bone breaking. The sirens were still wailing. Men bawled and women screamed. The man that Johnny had kicked went rolling over the road, his head bouncing on the tarmac, as Johnny grabbed the third man, punched him hard with his clenched fist, given strength by his cold fury, to let Billy push the fourth man off him and scramble back to his feet.

'Let's go!' Billy shouted.

But Johnny didn't go. He had too much to do. There was nothing in his head but the logic of the moment and it told him to silence that third man and go on to the fourth. He battered the third man into the ground. The blood was warm on his knuckles. He pulled back and started clambering to his feet and then the fourth man came at him.

The police sirens tapered off and were replaced by police whistles. People were running in every direction around Johnny as a darkness, abrupt and disorientating, descended upon him.

There's a fourth man. Where the hell is he? Oh, Jesus, what's that... The pain! Christ, I...

The darkness came and went. Johnny opened his eyes. He saw wee Billy staring down at him, his face partially obscured by someone's shoulder. Johnny realised that he was lying on his back on the road with an RUC officer straddling him, sitting upon him, pressing his head down onto the road with a black billy-club.

'You dumb cunt,' the RUC officer said, despite being a fellow Protestant. 'There's two Taigs lying here and they've both got smashed heads and one of them looks ready for the morgue. Sure normally I wouldn't mind, I might even be grateful, but a lot of these wankers, Prods and Taigs, saw you do it, and that means I can't do a thing to help you. You're fucked, you young eejut, 'cause there's witnesses and now no one can help. It's a Borstal for you. A few years in prison. Now sit up and let me put on these handcuffs and don't aggravate me.'

Johnny sat up and they put the handcuffs on him as Billy burst into tears.

Unable to stand the sight of wee Billy weeping, Johnny closed his eyes.

Time then turned the pages...

Chapter Eight

1

Making his way through the pouring rain across Shaftesbury Square, packed with buses and cars, a cold October wind beating at him, Sean was set on his life's course and had no intention of deviating from it. His father, he knew, had been bitterly disappointed when he, Sean, had been asked to leave Queen's University and refused permission to sit his honours degree in history, thus forcing him to leave with no formal qualifications. This had been his punishment for refusing to 'moderate' his 'disruptive political activities' and for openly petitioning fellow students to support nationalism in some form or other. Despite being reminded repeatedly that he was in his last university year and inviting, with his behaviour, a summary expulsion, thus wasting his previous three years of exemplary work (so good, he had been informed, that his honours degree was practically guaranteed and a Research Fellowship at the Institute of Irish Studies strongly hinted at), he had continued what he was doing until told that he had stretched the patience of the university's governing body to its limits and therefore had to leave immediately, with no chance of sitting for his exams.

'Suicidal, dear boy,' Brendan Coghill had said sardonically when he heard the news over a pint of stout with Sean and his Da. 'What ever made you do it? Surely you could have kept your mouth shut for a few more months, until you graduated. What on earth got into you?'

'The changing world,' Sean replied. 'That's what got into me, Brendan.'

'Complete madness,' Barry said in disgust. 'Four years of education down the drain.'

'*Alas! our young affections run to waste!*' Brendan quoted rather flippantly. '*Or water but the desert.*'

'I watered my own garden,' Sean said, 'by sticking up for my principles - and I'd do it again.'

'I *bet* you would,' Brendan said.

In fact, Sean had not always been so committed and recalled, as he made his way through the pouring, freezing rain, that he had indeed, like a lot of other students, been strongly affected by the changing world beyond the shores of Ireland. Far from being a fecund breeding ground for political radicals, Queen's University was, in 1960, when Sean entered it, one of the most politically docile campuses in Western Europe, with hardly enough radicals to form a CND march or organise an anti-apartheid demonstration. 'About as radical as a convent,' Brendan had said, 'and not much more productive.' Things had started to change, however, in the sense that Sean and others like him were not the rarities that they would have been a few years earlier, when there would have been less students and practically none from the working class. By 1960, the post-Second World War Education Act had brought into the university a greater number of less privileged students, most from the lower-middle class, but some, like Sean, from the Catholic working-class minority. Initially, few of those students had been fired by political passion, but all that gradually changed as events in the world outside the province, brought into most households by television, impinged upon the consciousness of Northern Ireland and inspired its young people in particular.

'We're not as docile as we used to be,' Sean had told Brendan, in response to his sardonic remark, when they were having a lively discussion in a pub a few days ago. 'The last couple of years have seen to that. Fidel Castro and Che Guevara. Sharpeville, South Africa. The sit-ins and freedom rides of the civil rights movement that took place the same year in America. All those events, and others, radicalised us, making us relate what was happening elsewhere to what was happening here. And don't forget, Brendan, that in 1963, the year Terence O'Neill took over as Northern Ireland Prime Minister, Martin Luther King said, "I have a dream". Well, his dream for the blacks of America was our dream for the Catholics of this province. That's what changed the students of Queen's. And that's what changed me.'

Which was true enough, he thought, as he walked through the rain, drenched and shivering with cold, dazzled by the lights of the passing traffic, wishing he could afford to buy a car. That's what changed me forever.

It had, indeed. Though already a member of Sinn Féin and the Wolfe Tone Society, in January of 1964, when the Campaign for Social Justice was set up, he had promptly joined that as well. Formed by a group of largely middle class and professional Catholics, the Campaign for Social Justice, backed by the Nationalists, the National Democrats and the Northern Ireland Labour Party, had set itself the task of collecting and distributing facts and figures about various forms of discrimination in the province. Thus, while continuing to ignore the warnings that he'd already received about his 'political agitation' within the walls of the campus, Sean had soon added to his image as a trouble-maker by distributing to his fellow students leaflets printed by his new civil rights friends. As far as the governing body of Queen's was concerned, that was the last straw and he was thrown out in March of that year.

Which hadn't pleased Barry at all.

Sean knew that his Da, inching into his early forties and still bereft at the loss of Eleanor, had been deeply shocked by his dismissal from the university, not only because he'd set his heart on having his son graduate with honours and, perhaps, going into law, but because he knew only too well that career prospects were more problematical for Catholics than for Protestants, and that his only son, with no formal qualifications, was going to find it difficult to find decent work in Belfast, once it was known that he had been barred from university. This had turned out to be true, though Sean, more politically committed than ever, had solved the problem by working for Sinn Féin, writing their propaganda leaflets under the supervision of Brendan Coghill, who, having finally discarded his political cynicism, was also working openly for them. Sean also contributed by teaching Irish history at Sinn Féin educational classes, by involving himself in the debates and discussions of the Wolfe Tone Society, and, more recently, by working in his spare time for the Campaign for Social Justice, which is where he had met Moira O'Shaughnessey.

Right now, he was on his way to a meeting with her.

Gratefully stepping into the warmth of a busy pub in University Road, he shook the rain off his gabardine coat, then pushed past a lot of noisily babbling Uni' students to get to the bar. The barman, Lennie

Duggan, once red-haired, now balding, looked him up and down, grinning, and said, 'A bit on the wet side out there, is it?'

'Rainin' shoemakers' knives, so it is' Sean replied, also grinning. 'Where are they? The usual place?'

Lennie nodded, indicating a door at the far side of the bar. 'At the top of the stairs.'

'Is there drink available up there?'

'Shit, no. Sure you have to buy your own. All you activists are a bit on the tight side, aren't ya?'

'Anyone else drinkin' up there?'

'Aye, most of 'em took something up, so what'll you have?'

'A pint of Guinness, thanks.'

'Sure that should warm your insides,' Lennie said.

As he was waiting for his drink to be poured, Sean glanced around the pub and recalled how he used to come here with fellow students when at the university. This was a popular student rendezvous, the room upstairs traditionally being used for student meetings and parties. Moira would have known this, since she, too, had attended Queen's, though she and Sean had not crossed paths there. Born in Derry, she had been educated at Magee University College and then Queen's, graduating from the latter in 1962 with an honours degree in psychology. Since then she had been a social worker for the Community Services Department of Belfast City Council, while also immersing herself in a variety of civil rights causes, including the Campaign for Social Justice. It was at one of the latter's meetings that she and Sean had first met and, perhaps drawn to each other by their shared political commitment, fallen in love.

Sean liked being in love. He liked sharing his life *and* his politics with someone he loved. He liked sharing the bed of a woman whose mind he respected. He liked being wrapped in the limbs of the woman who had that mind. He liked the feeling that although he was in love, he was grown-up with it. He liked being alive.

Eventually receiving his pint, he went up the stairs and found Moira seated around one of the tables in the room with another unmarried couple, Des Galloway and Iris Lurgan, both also members of the Campaign for Social Justice. All three of them were drinking stout, though none were smoking. Solid, shapely, black-haired and brown-eyed, Moira was looking casually attractive in a loose, light-

352

grey sweater with a roll-neck collar, a dark-grey skirt and high-heeled, black-leather boots. Casting Sean a warm smile, she indicated the chair beside her.

'I've been keeping it just for you,' she said.

'It must be true love,' Des said sardonically, looking his usual trendily dishevelled self in a duffle coat, baggy corduroy trousers, and rumpled, open-neck striped shirt, his gaunt face showing the beginnings of a beard, his dark hair in need of a barber, his brown eyes slightly bloodshot.

'I should be so lucky,' Iris said. Almost as thin as Des, she looked only slightly less dishevelled in her black raincoat, thick pullover and flower-patterned cotton dress, black hair piled up on her head, above a pretty, though undernourished face in which the green eyes seemed too large. 'All I get is a glass of stout and a pitiful smile.'

'You poor thing,' Moira said, then turned away to kiss Sean on the cheek. Leaning back, she grinned at him. 'Hi, handsome. You're all wet.'

Sean sighed and removed his gabardine, slinging it over the chair beside him. Then he took a handkerchief from his pocket and mopped his wet hair.

'She called him handsome,' Iris said to Des. 'Do you ever tell me I'm beautiful?'

'You don't tell me I'm handsome.' Des grinned, then he turned to Sean. 'I'm told that women only tell their men they're handsome when they're lousy in bed. Any truth in that, Sean?'

'No point in asking me,' Sean said. 'I'd just lie about it. You have to ask Moira.'

Des raised his eyebrows, forming two question marks, staring boldly, cynically at Moira.

'Words can't even begin to describe it,' Moira said. 'Sure doesn't the very thought of his skill in bed make me tremble and moan?'

Des lowered his eyebrows and gazed sombrely at Sean. 'The lady's obviously in love with you,' he said, 'and I feel like throwing up.'

'Just don't do it in my lap,' Iris said. 'I washed and ironed this dress with my own hands and I don't want you ruining it.'

'Is this the level of conversation I have to endure,' Sean said, 'when I'm sitting here soaking-wet and expecting some intellectual stimulation? Who do I have to pay to get out of here and go somewhere else?'

But in truth he was amused, glad to be here in this company, pleased to hear this kind of liberated, good-humoured *craic*, instead of the sexually repressed evasions that had haunted his childhood. The old puritanism was gone, swept away by the changing times - by Elvis and the Beatles and the Rolling Stones and Bob Dylan; by the radicalism of university life and the worldwide student movement; by the rebelliousness of a whole new generation - and Sean was proud to belong to that generation, to be rebellious with it, and to have a woman, Moira, who had been nurtured by it, and friends, such as Des and Iris, who represented the best of it.

'Actually,' Moira said, 'we were just discussing whether or not our relatively new Prime Minister, Captain Terence O'Neill, is going to be better than his predecessor. I say he won't be.'

'Why? He doesn't appear to have an anti-Catholic bias and reportedly even disdains the Orange Lodge.'

'Are you joking?' Iris said. 'Can I just remind you that the O'Neill we're talking about is a direct descendent of Sir Arthur Chichester, the Lord of the Protestant Plantation in Ulster under James I? So he comes from a long line of Irish aristocracy and Conservative MPs. I mean, Jesus, even as we speak, one of his cousins is the chief whip at Stormont, another is the Stormont MP for North Antrim, and two others are MPs at Westminster. Sure isn't O'Neill one of the last of the Big House grandees? So how is a man like that, totally out of touch with the problems of the Catholic community, never mind the Prod *and* Catholic working classes, going to change the status quo? He won't do a bloody thing, believe me.'

'Ah!' Des exclaimed. 'A serious conversation at last! Actually, folks, he's also a technocrat. From what I've gleaned from friends in Stormont – I have friends in all the right places - he's already accepted the decline of Northern Ireland's industries as irreversible and intends concentrating, instead, on attracting new industries from outside. To replace all the lost jobs, as he put it.'

'Noble intentions,' Iris said. 'But if he neglects what's left of our traditional industries and doesn't manage to bring in new ones, that'll be thousands more jobs down the drain.'

'With the Prods given priority when it comes to getting what jobs are left, my beauty.'

'You can bet your arse on that,' Iris said.

'I just said you were beautiful,' Des said.

'No, you didn't. You just called me your beauty - in that sarcastic way you have about you. I'm not melting just yet.'

'I never win,' Des said.

'And even under O'Neill, they're still building Unionist power-bases,' Moira said, always tending to turn serious, even grim, when it came to political discussions. 'I mean, just look at what they're doin' to Derry, my home city, a city with a Catholic majority. First they cut one of the two rail links to the city *and* the county, leaving most of the county, plus Fermanagh and Tyrone, with no railways. Next they cut its vitally important shipping link with Glasgow. Then, instead of developing the city, as recommended by their own town-planner, they commission a new city, Craigavon, pointedly named - and can you believe this insult to the Catholic population? - after Lord Craigavon.'

'Who is, of course...' Des drawled sardonically, dryly leading Moira onward.

'Right. The founding father of the six-county state. The very same bastard who declared Stormont to be a Protestant parliament for a Protestant people. Now, to top all that, instead of extending the university facilities of my old college, Magee, as they should have done, they're talking about ignoring Derry altogether in favour of a new university in Coleraine.'

'Which, apart from anything else,' Iris said, getting the drift of the conversation, 'only has a quarter of Derry's population.'

'They're as slippery as snakes,' Des added, 'and every bit as venomous.'

'And is there a single Catholic on the committee who's considering this matter?' Moira asked rhetorically, glancing at each of them in turn. 'Of course not! Every single committee member is a bloody Unionist!'

'The last thing they want us to see,' Iris said, 'is more educated Catholics coming out of Derry - or anywhere else in the six counties. So they'll build a new university in Coleraine to educate more Prods.'

'Some of whom will end up right here in Queen's,' Des said, having had another taste of his pint and finding it good, 'as political activists of the wrong kind. Let's bear *that* in mind, folks.'

'I'll tell you something.' Moira was waving her index finger, like a blackboard pointer. 'I know the people of my own city and if that university gets built in Coleraine, the people of Derry will be outraged. There'll be riots, believe me.'

'Maybe,' Sean said, 'but that won't be decided until next year.'

'There could be riots before then, though,' Des said, straightening up in his chair and looking more serious, withdrawing a packet of cigarettes from his coat packet, groping about for his lighter.

'Over what?'

Des took his time igniting his cigarette, inhaling and then exhaling a cloud of smoke. 'The antics of the Reverend Ian Paisley. That maniac's starting to get a lot of attention - and he certainly knows how to milk it for all it's worth.'

Sean knew about the Reverend Ian Kyle Paisley. Everyone did. Paisley sprang from a long line of fundamentalist, anti-Catholic political evangelists, though he seemed even worse than his predecessors. Born in Armagh, he was the son of a Baptist minister so ardently Unionist that he had been one of the original members of Edward Carson's notorious Ulster Volunteer Force before going on to form his own church. Paisley had become a preacher while still in his teens and had then, like his father, formed his own church, the Free Presbyterian Church of Ulster, with himself as its highly immoderate Moderator. Right from the beginning, he was virulently anti-Catholic and ruthless with it. He first came to the attention of the media in 1956 when he became involved in the proselytising of a fifteen-year-old Catholic girl who had been kidnapped from her home. He was back in the news three years later when he threw a Bible at the moderate Methodist minister, Dr. Donald Soper, during the latter's visit to Ballymena. He then formed the Ulster Protestant Action Group, whose objective ure that Protestant workers were always given preference over Catholics and that a similar preference should be given when it came to the allocation of housing. In 1959, after he had addressed a 1,500-strong Protestant rally at one of his UPA meetings, the crowd attacked a fish and chip shop owned by Catholics. In 1962, realising the value of publicity, he deliberately got himself arrested in Rome for protesting at the opening of the Second Vatican Council. Since then, he had kept his media profile high by giving inflammatory anti-Catholic sermons in his church, on the Custom House steps and in other areas where his quasi-Biblical thundering against the Catholics could do maximum damage. Paisley was, in short, the Elmer Gantry of the Orange State, a mesmerising orator and ruthless manipulator of the most base emotions of his congregation or, as some would have it, his audience, since he was, indeed, a natural performer who loved the limelight. He was also rapidly becoming one of the most dangerous Protestants in Belfast.

'So what's that mad bastard up to?' Sean asked.

'It's to do with the election,' Moira said. 'I got this from a Protestant who can't stand Paisley, though I can't be too sure if it's true or not.'

Sean shrugged. 'So what is it?'

'That flag hanging out of the window of your office?' Moira said.

Sinn Féin was contesting the West Belfast seat in the present Westminster election and the Irish national flag, the tricolour, was presently fluttering from the upstairs window of an SF election office in Divis Street.

'What about it?'

'It's in breach of the Flags and Emblems Act.'

'So what? For Christ's sake, Moira, even the RUC's given up interfering with the tricolours hung in Catholic areas.'

'Well, they may not ignore this one, because according to my source, Paisley's planning to tell his audience, at the meeting he's holding tomorrow in the Ulster Hall, that if your tricolour isn't removed within two days - that means Tuesday at the latest – he's going to lead a march to Divis Street and remove it himself.'

'Ack, Jesus,' Sean said, 'sure that man's the very devil himself. I mean, one wee national flag hanging out of a single side-street window, completely ignored by everyone else, and he has to go and make an issue out of it. Sure he's no more than a common rabble-rouser!'

'With fanatical followers,' Des reminded him. 'So Moira's right. If that flag isn't removed, there'll be trouble. A whole *heap* of trouble!'

Sean sighed and straightened up in his seat. He swallowed some Guinness, placed the glass back on the table, then looked from Moira to Des and Iris, shaking his head from side, not wanting to accept what he was hearing, wanting only good news tonight.

'It was Liam McMillan,' he said, referring to the Sinn Féin candidate, 'who hung that flag out there. And I don't think he's going to remove it just because he's being threatened by a Protestant bully with a mouth big enough to match his belly.'

'Hear, hear,' Des said, exhaling smoke through his nostrils and wearily rubbing his bloodshot eyes.

'Well,' Moira said, 'it's not your responsibility, but I think you should at least pass on this information and give them the option of doing something about it or not.'

'Aye, I will,' Sean said. He finished off his pint and stood up. 'Are you home this evening?'

Moira smiled and nodded, indicating, 'Yes.'

'Then let's go out for a wee meal,' Sean said.

'Why not? That sounds great.'

It was great for Sean, as well. Living with his father and Theresa in their tiny house in the Pound Loney did not offer many opportunities for privacy. So apart from the occasional grope in the back row of a local cinema or a female student's bed-sit, Sean had had practically no sexual experience when he first met Moira. Luckily, being two years older than him, she believed in female emancipation, including sexual freedom, and was therefore bold enough to seduce him and teach him what he needed to know, which she did in her own small apartment in Chlorine Gardens, off the Stranmillis Road. So though Sean still lived at home with his father and sister, he spent most of his free time with Moira, in her apartment. Now he could scarcely imagine life without her.

'See?' Iris said, nodding at Des. 'Some men take their women out for meals; they don't just bring home fish and chips, wrapped in greasy newspapers.'

'If you offer to take *me* out for a meal, I won't say no, I promise.'

'Sure you're a man in a million.'

Sean grinned at Moira, feeling warmed by her presence, looking forward to bedtime, but he put his gabardine back on and left the pub, intending to go straight to the Sinn Féin office in Divis Street for a good talk with his friends. Outside, the rain had stopped falling, though the wind was still cold. He headed into that cold wind.

2

At one time or another most of Theresa's girlfriends had told her that her father looked young for his age, even though he also seemed sad. Now, as she came down from her bedroom to find him sitting in a tattered armchair by the blazing coal fire, in a living room that seemed to magically, gloomily, decrease in size every year, smoking a cigarette and staring dreamily at the flickering flames, obviously elsewhere, she sensed the sadness in him, as she had done many times since Eleanor's passing. Nevertheless, she still couldn't work out if he looked young or not, because she couldn't remember him any other way and, perhaps more pertinently, couldn't imagine him as anyone other than her father: admittedly still a good-looking man, with thick black hair and a dark, distracted gaze. By the same token, when she looked in a mirror, at her own changing face, now twenty-two,, she could not even imagine what she had been like all those years ago, when her mother died. She only knew that her father had seemed sad, or possibly disappointed, even in those days.

She often thought that his sadness, or disappointment, was due to something that had happened in his younger days when, as she had picked up in asides uttered when he was drunk, he had been involved with the IRA. As far as she knew, he was no longer actively involved with the organisation, though he was still friendly with most of its local members, all older than him, and spent a good deal of his time, between visits to the dole office, in the Sinn Féin headquarters in the Falls Road, performing minor, thankless tasks for them.

His former involvement with the IRA and present involvement with Sinn Féin (which was Sean's particular passion) didn't bother Theresa much, because certainly, these days, neither organisation had much support in Belfast, let alone down south. Nevertheless, she often found herself wondering if his sadness was caused by something relating to either one, or both, of those organisations, rather than by Eleanor's death at a relatively young age. Most times, however, Theresa leaned towards the theory that her father's increasingly heavy drinking was caused by the fact that he could never get a decent job because his former involvement with the IRA was well known; because, like his own father, he had served time in prison for it; and because, though only in his early forties, he was like a piece of flotsam, just drifting with the tide in the hope of landing up somewhere safe.

Now, when she came off the stairs and into the living room, she saw that same sadness in his face, or, perhaps, a mixture of disillusionment, bewilderment and guilt.

I may be relatively inexperienced, Theresa thought, but I'm pretty sure I can see that.

'Sure you gave me a start, Da,' she lied. 'I didn't hear you come in.'

He looked up and smiled. 'I only got back about five minutes ago, darlin'. When I heard the Beatles waftin' down from upstairs, I thought I'd just sit here quietly and leave you to your records.'

Theresa smiled. 'So where were you?'

'At the broo,' he said flatly, meaning the dole.

'Any prospects of a job?'

'Not a hope. So why are you all dressed up at noon?'

'The prospect of a job, Da. Can we have a wee talk?'

'Aye, darlin', of course. Sure I'm just sittin' here, havin' a wee drink and a smoke, tryin' to relax. So sit down and let's talk. We don't do that enough these days.'

Which was true enough, Theresa realised. They didn't talk much because Barry spent as much time out of the house as in it, usually in a pub with his former IRA cronies, probably reliving past glories, while she, who had always done badly at school, and nearly cracked up after the death of her mother, worked night and day at a variety of mostly rotten jobs and, when not so slaving, either went to the pictures and pubs with Gerry Donovan or, when Gerry wasn't available, went dancing with girlfriends. Gerry never took her dancing because he simply couldn't dance and was too big and clumsy to learn. But at least he took her drinking and certainly she drank a lot, trying to deaden all thoughts of her future which seemed, when she thought about it, to be hopelessly lacking in promise. If she didn't do something about it, a bleak life lay ahead of her.

Dressed up to the 'Nineties, though certainly not fashionable by, say, London standards, Theresa took the chair facing her father and lit up a cigarette. He did not reprimand her. He was smoking himself, after all. In this family, only Sean didn't smoke. Even Grandda Eddie smoked like a train.

'So what's this job prospect?' Barry asked. 'I mean, why do you even want to talk to me about it? Sure you must know that any job you can get would be fine with me.'

'Aye, normally,' Theresa said. 'You knowin' that I can't get a decent job because I'm a bad girl.'

'You're not a bad girl,' Barry said gallantly. 'Just a wee bit wild on occasion. A bit of a tomboy, as they say, but that's no sin in my book.'

'Some times you're a real gentleman, Da.'

'I wouldn't recognise a gentleman if he was shoved up my arse with a pitchfork. So what's this job, that it has you so nervous you have to talk about it?'

'It's an opportunity that came through a Protestant friend.'

'A girlfriend?'

'Aye, Da, a girlfriend. Carol Bell. I'm not bein' sucked in by any man here.'

'Good. Glad to hear it.'

'Da, I'm startin' to feel desperate. We both know that ever since leavin' school I've been in and out of too many different jobs, none of them good. I've served in pubs and cafes, worked in different shops - a butcher's, a baker's, even a bloody chippie - and now I'm twenty-one and in a meat-packing factory where the stench is enough to knock you dead. I'm getting' nowhere, Da.'

Barry sighed. 'Aye, I know that alright. It's because you have no real education - and you're Catholic to boot. Not much joy in that hereabouts.'

'So I've got this opportunity, Da, but it came about through my friend, Carol, who happens to be a Prod.'

'No harm in that, Theresa. So what's this opportunity?'

'This friend is a housemaid and kind of general assistant to a Protestant industrialist who lives in a big house out on the Malone Road. She cleans the house, cooks the meals, serves at table when he has guests, does the shopping, and also acts as a general secretary, arranging his business meetings and booking his trips away and so on. She's leavin' to go and work elsewhere and she's recommended me to take over her job.'

'Why you? You don't have that kind of experience. To be blunt about it, darlin', you wouldn't even know how to lay a table in a fancy house. We don't live that way here in the Pound Loney.'

'She's recommended me because I'm her best friend and she knows how desperate I am for an opportunity to better myself. She's recommended me on the grounds that I have a month to work with her and learn the job. I can learn all I need to know, Da. And believe me, I will.'

'You think that bein' a housemaid, in this day and age, when there aren't many around anymore, is bettering yourself?'

'No, I don't. But I think that being a housemaid to a man like that could eventually lead to work in a hotel, particularly across the water, and I'm also dead keen to learn the secretarial side of the job. Add that to what I'd learn about running a big house and I'd certainly be in a better position to pick up decent work somewhere else – like London, for instance. And that's what I'm after, Da.'

'My wee daughter wants to leave home?'

'Your wee daughter has no future here and both of us know it.'

Barry nodded, sipped at his drink, inhaled on his cigarette. 'Aye,' he said, exhaling smoke through his nostrils, 'sure that's true enough. So why do you feel the need to talk about it? Why not just go and do it?'

'Because this man's a Prod, and – '

'I'm not that set against the Prods anymore. I just happen to disapprove of the Orange State.'

'He's a Prod whose Da owned a couple of the old linen mills. When his Da died, he inherited the mills and ran them until the linen trade died away and the mills were closed down. Now, according to Carol, he's semi-retired, but has involved himself with a variety of smaller businesses, just to keep his hand in.'

Barry shrugged. 'I still don't see what this has to do with me. A lot of Catholics have to work for Protestants. They work for the Protestants who'll have them, though there aren't all that many. I don't see what's so different about this job, why you feel you have to clear it with me.'

'I thought you might be upset because this man once owned a couple of linen mills. It was the mills that killed Ma. The flax dust.'

'That and her heavy smoking,' Barry said, though he was smoking himself - as, indeed, was Theresa. 'We can't blame the mills for all of it. Besides, we might have starved without the mills, so it's swings and roundabouts.' He smiled sadly and shook his head from side to side, his face moving in and out of shadow, first white and then dark. 'No, I'm not goin' to hold that against him. I'll put it out of my mind. So you go and try for the job, darlin', and the best of luck to you.'

Standing up, Theresa threw the remains of her cigarette into the burning fire and then leaned forward to kiss her father on the cheek.

'Thanks,' she said. 'I'll be seein' ya.'

'Aye, later,' Barry said.

After checking herself in the mirror in the hall, taking note of the healthy sheen of her shoulder-length auburn hair, the carefully applied make-up that brightened her brown gaze and emphasised her full lips, making her seem more sophisticated than she actually was, Theresa adjusted her jacket and skirt, which revealed a fine, fully mature, woman's figure, then slung her bag over her shoulder and stepped out of the house.

A cold wind was blowing outside, but thankfully the rain had stopped and sunlight was starting to break through the clouds in the early afternoon sky. Theresa did not walk far. She simply cut diagonally across the road to knock on Gerry Donovan's front door. It was opened by Gerry's mother, a cheerful, overweight woman with a flowery apron over her dress and a scarf tied around her head. She gave Theresa a warm smile.

'Ack, Theresa,' she said, 'sure you're lookin' real pretty today. Where are you off to?'

'Job interview, Mrs. Donovan.'

'Well, the best of luck, child. Gerry's up in his room.'

When Mrs. Donovan stepped aside, Theresa stepped in, calling out Gerry's name.

'Yes?' he called back down, having to shout over the Beatles' 'A Hard Day's Night' being played at full volume.

He has a tolerant mother, Theresa thought.

'It's me! Theresa! Can I come up?'

The volume was turned down a little. 'Aye! Come on up!'

As she ascended the stairs and entered the bedroom, Theresa recalled how Gerry had once shared the same room with his dismal, overweight sister Martha, who at that time had been one of Theresa's less interesting friends. But Martha didn't live here anymore. At seventeen years of age she had suddenly lost weight, became shapely and much happier, then found herself a Protestant boyfriend, Martin Stone, thus scandalising both sets of parents. At eighteen, she became pregnant by him and he had to become a Catholic in order to marry her. This had made it difficult, if not impossible, for him to remain in his own home in the Shankill or, as an alternative, to move into Martha's home in the Pound Loney. Subsequently, shortly after they were married, the pregnant Martha and her husband had moved out of Belfast altogether. Now living in Camden Town, north London, they were the struggling parents of four children. According to Gerry, Martha had put all her weight back on and was now as dismal as ever.

It won't happen to me, Theresa thought, as she entered Gerry's bedroom. I want to live a life first.

Wearing a roll-necked pullover and corduroy trousers, Gerry was stretched out on his bed with his hands clasped behind his head, listening to the new Beatles' album. He grinned when he saw her, leaned sideways to turn the volume of the record-player down some more, then patted the edge of the bed and said, 'Sit here and give me a kiss.'

Smiling, Theresa sat on the edge of the bed, but pushed his hand away when he reached out to her. 'No,' she said. 'You'll only spoil my make-up.'

Looking deprived and also a little suspicious, Gerry lay back on the bed and said, 'Sure you look like a million dollars, Theresa. What's the occasion?'

'I'm goin' for an interview,' she told him. 'A chance for a job in a big house out on the Malone Road.'

Gerry gave a low whistle of appreciation. 'Sounds fancy,' he said.

'It's for this Protestant businessman who lives out there.'

'They're the ones with the money,' Gerry said without malice.

'Catholics with money live out there as well,' Theresa reminded him.

'Aye, I suppose so. Sure I wish I was one of them.'

'Still on the broo, are ya?'

'Aye, but they think they might have found me something new - a job with an electrical repair shop up in the Falls. They say I might be able to work there and also go to tech' school in the evenings. That'd be great, wouldn't it? I wouldn't feel that I was wastin' my time if I was goin' to night-school.'

Theresa worried about Gerry. Failing the Qualifying Examination, thus unable to go to grammar school, he had left school at fourteen and found himself unemployed for nearly six months, being rejected by every Protestant that he applied to for work. Eventually, he had found work as an apprentice bricklayer for a Catholic builder located in the Falls. He had worked there for a few years, but his heart wasn't in it and he left when he found another job, this time as an apprentice plumber with a Catholic company in the Ardoyne. He stuck that out for another year, but just couldn't settle to it, so transferred to an electrical repair shop where he learnt his trade while attending the Belfast Technical College three evenings a week. He liked electrical work, but unfortunately that particular shop went out of business, thus putting him back on the dole. He'd been on the dole for four months now. Luckily, he'd had the sense to continue attending night school, still studying electrical engineering, which clearly was why he was being considered for this new job, even at the relatively late age of twenty-two. The job, if he actually got it, would be his reward for his rare display of common sense. Theresa was pleased for him, but she still worried about him, because although he was kind and loving and good-humoured, he wasn't all that bright and was certainly far too restless for his own good. If he lost this job, or got it and failed at it, it would be too late for another and he would have no decent future in Belfast - or anywhere else.

Standing there, gazing down upon him, Theresa realised that she had, without thinking, placed her right hand behind her back and crossed her fingers for luck.

'Do you want to come with me?' she asked him. 'We could go by bus. Save me from workin' up a sweat before meeting that man. Then we could go for a drink afterwards, either to celebrate my getting' the job or to drown my sorrows if I don't.'

'Great,' Gerry said. 'Why not?'

Rolling off the bed, he put on his windcheater jacket and then followed her downstairs, where they said goodbye to his mother before leaving. Once outside, they walked to the Falls Road and caught a bus to the centre of town, sitting upstairs, up front, in order to watch the world go by. Rain clouds had already passed across the mountains and the wet pavements were drying, making the busy streets look more welcoming.

'Sure it's a grand wee city, isn't it?' Gerry said. 'I always 'like drivin' through it.'

'You never fancied leaving?' Theresa asked.

Gerry shook his head. 'No. It never entered my head. Sure I'm content where I am. I mean, everyone I know who's gone across the water has ended up desp'rately unhappy. Just like my sister.'

'Martha has four children,' Theresa reminded him, 'and she's still only twenty-one.'

'Aye, but that's not all that makes her unhappy. It's the English, she says. They're not friendly like the Irish. And she misses the family as well: Ma and Da, the aunts and uncles that used to visit, friends she went to school with. It's the loneliness over there.'

'Old friends and relatives aren't everything,' Theresa said, looking down on bustling pavements that ran past pubs and bookies, clothes shops and furniture stores, a plethora of cafes and cheap restaurants - lively, certainly, but not sophisticated. Not like you saw in the films about London and New York and Paris. Not remotely like that. 'I mean, you can't live in the past all your life.'

'I can,' Gerry said.

That single remark sank into Theresa's head and stayed with her as they disembarked in the centre of town and caught the bus that would take them up the Lisburn Road.

'I'm still a bit early,' Theresa said, trying to shake off Gerry's remark, 'so let's get off at the King's Hall, then walk along Balmoral Avenue.'

'Okay,' Gerry said, agreeable to anything. 'As long as the sun doesn't make you sweat before you have your interview.'

'It's not that hot,' Theresa informed him, 'and it's not a long walk. His house is just past the Weir and the Malone Playing Fields.'

'Right,' Gerry said.

As the bus took them up the Lisburn Road, Theresa gazed down on the seemingly endless rows of bleak terraced houses, broken up only by blocks of newsagents, fish-and-chip shops and the occasional cinema. She could not shake from her head what Gerry had said and what it might, in the end, mean to her. She loved Gerry with all her heart - had possibly loved him since childhood - but she often found herself wishing that he was more imaginative and adventurous than he was. She was convinced that if they married, he would always treat her kindly, but she wasn't sure that kindness alone would be enough. She was still a virgin, which was partly her own doing; but even though she'd always resisted his tentative attempts to go 'all the way', frightened of becoming pregnant, sometimes, perhaps perversely, she had resented his timidity and the fact that he didn't try hard enough. Though renowned amongst her friends for her sharp tongue and cynicism, she lived with the dread that they would discover she was still a virgin. She blamed Gerry for that as well.

'Here we are,' Gerry said.

They were at the King's Hall, a 1930's monstrosity of cream-painted concrete with vast windows rising from its first floor to its big clock. Surrounded by the show grounds of the Royal Ulster Agricultural Society, the building was the venue not only for that society's annual May exhibition, but also for the Ulster Motor Show and the Ideal Home Exhibition. The clock above the main doors showed the time as 1.35pm. Theresa's appointment was set for 2.00pm.

Disembarking from the bus, she and Gerry walked back a short distance and then turned into Balmoral Avenue. Instantly, they found themselves in another, more tranquil world of detached and semi-detached middle-class houses, secluded in gardens bordered by hedgerows or trees, with flower beds and neatly mowed lawns. The perennial clamour of the city could not be heard from here. This was an area of playing fields, sports grounds and golf courses. It was where the people with money, Catholic and Protestant alike, lived out their quiet, anonymous lives. Theresa longed to be part of it.

'Nice out here, isn't it?' she said as she and Gerry walked the length of the tree-lined avenue, passing those attractive middle-class homes secluded in their own gardens, hearing only the occasional car passing by, the tinkling bell of a child's bicycle, the singing of birds.

'You're fuckin' jokin', aren't you?' Gerry responded, glancing about with distaste. 'Sure I'd die a death if I lived out here. Look at it! There's hardly a soul out in the street and not a sign of a shop or pub. It's the end of the world.'

'Pubs and shops aren't everything,' Theresa said.

'Oh, no? Pull the other one!'

No more was said until they turned into the Malone Road and were walking between the undulating greenery of the Malone Playing Fields and the Weir, located at the other side of the broad road. In this relatively pastoral area the homes were much grander, big houses and villas set well back in their own grounds, often hidden from the road, protected by locked gates and high fences. Seeing some of those houses and their expansive grounds, Theresa started feeling nervous for the first time.

'Jesus,' she said, almost whispering, 'I don't really belong out here, do I?'

'Not really,' Gerry said, then added kindly, 'but I'm sure you'll do fine, love.'

'Thanks. I think this is the place.'

They were at a pair of wrought-iron gates that stretched from one high red-brick wall to another. An immaculately polished brass plaque cemented into the wall at the right-hand side of one gate stated: *Stoneykirk Manor.* Peering through the black-painted, wrought-iron bars of that gate, Theresa saw a gravel driveway curving away between a broad green lawn and glorious flowerbeds, before looping to the right, around hedgerows and trees that hid all but the gable end of what seemed like a very big house.

Theresa's heart almost skipped a beat at the mere thought of walking up to that big house.

'How do I get in?' she asked nervously, glancing left and right, at the concrete posts at the end of each wall.

'You probably just open the gates,' Gerry said, grinning. 'I don't see any chains.' Stepping forward, he tried the handle of the right-hand gate. It swung open immediately. Gerry pushed it back some more, then turned to face Theresa. 'The house is all yours,' he said gallantly.

Suddenly overwhelmed with emotion, Theresa ran up to him and threw her arms about him. 'Give me a hug,' she said.

Gerry chuckled and hugged her, though he didn't actually kiss her, not wanting to muss her lipstick before she had her appointment.

'Do you love me?' Theresa asked him.

'Aye, I do. Sure you know that alright.'

'Are you gonna wait here until I come out?'

'As arranged,' Gerry said. 'Now in you go, love.'

Theresa stepped away from him, smiled nervously, took a deep breath, then walked resolutely past the gate, advancing into the unknown terrain of Stoneykirk Manor.

3

When Theresa left the house, Barry sat on for a while, thinking of how much like Eleanor his daughter now looked and of how she was, just as Eleanor had been, a young woman of quick and dangerous impulses. Looking at Theresa, he was always reminded of what Eleanor had been like when he first met her, when she was a member of the Cummann na mBann, the female wing of the IRA, and he was an IRA gunman. Eleanor had been an attractive woman, nothing special, but certainly attractive, and they had been drawn together as much by sexual passion as by politics. The passion had faded away as the politics soured, Eleanor becoming bitter, he merely disillusioned; but now, when he thought of those days, he felt the dreadful weight of all that had been lost and of the high price he had paid for so little. Yet despite all of that, he was still committed to the cause.

He was also haunted by the recollection of all the men that he had killed for the cause. They came back to him in dreams, in nightmares, that left him sweating and shaking.

'Don't think about it,' he said aloud.

Someone knocked on the closed door of the living room. This being the Pound Loney, where people trusted their neighbours, the front door was always left unlocked.

'It's only me!' Barry's father, Eddie, called out.

'Come on in!' Barry called back.

Eddie entered the room, stooped over with the burden of his years and the wounded left shoulder that gave him more pain every month. He was still surprisingly slim for his age, though, and had an abundant head of silvery-grey hair over his weathered face. His smile was lively as well.

'How are you, son?'

'Not bad at all, Da. Sit yourself down.' Eddie sank gratefully into the armchair at the other side of the blazing fire. 'Can I offer you anything? A bottle of stout? Whiskey? Cuppa tea?'

Eddie shook his head. 'No. Sure I just turned the corner for a walk. Comin' here and goin' back home's the only exercise I can manage these days. Lucky you.'

'Aye, lucky me. But you know I'm always glad to see you. What's the state of play your side?'

'Ack, I'm fine, when all's said and done. Not about to win the Olympics, but not bad otherwise. And you?'

'I'm survivin'.'

'Still on the dole?'

'I reckon.'

'It's the curse of this family. The price you pay for bein' a Catholic and, worse, a Republican. So what else is new?'

'Not much,' Barry confessed.

'How's Sean? Still beaverin' away there for Sinn Féin while pursuin' all his other young dog's passions?'

'Aye. Though one of his passions might be a serious woman. I mean, I think he's involved there.'

'Wouldn't do him any harm if he was. Has he talked about it?'

'Are you kiddin'? Sure he's a decent wee Catholic lad who never talks about sex. But I'm convinced he's got someone out there. I mean, he never comes home at night. At least not until midnight. And he seems a lot more confident than he's been in the past. That suggests somethin' other than politics.'

'Well, good for him, he deserves it. Nothin' wrong in sewing your wild oats while you've still got the spunk.'

'I'm not complaining,' Barry said.

'And Theresa?'

'She's fine as well. I think she might even be startin' to settle down. She came to me today, just before you arrived, to tell me she was fed up with getting' nowhere and was tryin' for a job up in one of them big houses in the Malone Road. Kind of maid and secretary all in one. She's particularly interested in the secretarial side of it. Thinks it might help her get out of here, maybe even to London. Aye,' he added when he saw his father opening his mouth to speak, 'she wants to get out of Belfast eventually and go across the water. I can't say I blame her.'

'Me, neither' Eddie said. 'So what about you, son? How are *you* faring these days. Any woman in sight?'

Barry grinned ruefully. 'Nope,' he said like Gary Cooper, one of his screen idols. 'I get the odd look and occasional fling, but somehow I never settle on anyone. I just don't have the enthusiasm these days. Don't know why. It just dried up, I guess.'

'You're only forty-two,' Eddie said. 'That's too young to be dyin' on your feet.'

'I'm not exactly dyin'. I mean, I've had some relationships. I'm havin' one right now, in fact. But I just can't bring her back here - mainly because I'm worried about what Theresa would think. But also because... Well, you know, there's precious little privacy in these wee houses. Theresa's bedroom is right next to mine. So... I always go to see Meg – that's her name - in her place up in Turf Lodge.'

'How long have you been involved with her?'

'Six months or so.'

'That's a quare good time, son.'

'Aye, it is. I mean, we're pretty close, like.'

In fact, Barry wasn't too sure about how deeply he felt for Meg, though he certainly enjoyed her company a lot, not to mention her bed. She was roughly his age (a few years older, he suspected, though he hadn't dared ask), with a fine figure and a ready, rough wit that always managed to charm him. They'd met through mutual friends, around a table in Sean McGeown's bar, and though both had sensed immediately that their friends were trying to set them up, to put them together because they were on their own, neither of them had felt offended by it, which had to be a good sign. Indeed, it *was* a good sign. Once their mutual friends, artfully guiding the conversation, had let each of them know that the other was free, they'd both relaxed and ended up drunkenly telling each other how they had come to be living on their own. After Barry told Meg about Eleanor, Meg told him that she lived in Turf Lodge, that she ran her own hairdressing business in the Falls, that she had four grown-up children, all of whom were now married with children of their own, and that her husband had died of a brain tumour three years ago. She and Barry had not become involved for a few weeks after that, but they had started seeing each other with increasing frequency, until going to bed together became inevitable. When they did so, it seemed natural to them and the affair simply took off.

Now, six months later, Meg still hadn't been to this house, but when he had told her about Theresa and where they both lived, Meg had said that she could guess just how small the house was, being in the Pound Loney, and understood his problem. She was content, she had said, to let Barry keep their relationship a secret from his family, at least for a few more months or until they had both decided if it would last. Barry had thought that this was admirably sensible of her. Subsequently, they had agreed that if their relationship continued, they would move into her house in Turf Lodge, which was a good deal bigger than Barry's. Though Barry liked the idea, he was still thinking about it.

'Do you want to talk about this?' Eddie asked him.

'Not yet,' Barry said.

Eddie stared steadily at him, then said, 'What's troubling you, son?'

'Troubling me?'

'I'm sixty-three years old and half deaf. You haven't reached that stage yet.'

Barry grinned painfully. 'Okay, Da, I heard you. What's troubling me?' He shrugged. 'I don't know. I just can't decide on anything anymore. I don't know *what* I believe in.'

'You mean this woman?'

'Yes, her... and other things.'

'Such as?'

Barry shrugged again, but said nothing.

'You're worried about what you've done in the past? What you did for the IRA?'

Barry nodded. 'Yeah, maybe that's it.'

'So what do you worry about?'

'About what a kid like Theresa would think if she knew that her father had shot men. Even worse: shot them at close range, on their own doorsteps, with their kids looking on.'

'Does Sean know about that?'

'Yes, but he's a man. He also happens to be committed to the cause.'

'So how much does Theresa know?'

'Not much. Not nearly as much as Sean - and I've told him not to tell her. She only knows that I was active in the organisation and that I served time for it; but she thinks I was involved in a non-violent way, as a kind of driver and courier, just like her mother. One day, when she asked me outright if I'd ever shot anyone, I blatantly lied and said, "No." She seemed relieved to hear that.'

'What age was she then?'

'Fifteen or sixteen.'

Eddie shrugged with his good shoulder. The other shoulder, the one wounded during the street battles of 1935, was so bad that he could hardly move it these days.

Some wounds last forever, Barry thought.

'She was a lot younger then,' Eddie said. 'She didn't understand the issues. Maybe now, though she wouldn't actually *approve*, she'd understand how, as a young man, you could do that for a cause you believed in, even if you have certain regrets now, as I certainly have. Best not to tell her, of course, if you don't have a reason. Silence is golden.'

'You still have regrets?'

'You mean, even at my age?'

'Aye, even at your age. I'm not suggestin' you're old, you understand. I'm just sayin' you're not sixteen any more.'

'I won't be seein' my sixteenth birthday again, that's for sure. But, yes, I still have regrets. I didn't do anything *too* bad. No wimmen or childern hurt. And if I *did* shoot someone - and I can't be sure of that - it would have been done from a distance, in the heat of one of those awful riots. But I still have regrets.'

'Why?'

'Because I believe you can never win this kind of conflict with violence, that violence only encourages the Brits to oppress us even more, giving more powers to the Orange State. The only way to win, I reckon, is to take the long road.'

'Which is?'

'Passive resistance - like Ghandi. Gradually shame them in the eyes of the world and force them to the negotiating table. Just keep resisting them in every way possible, short of violence, until world opinion forces them to get out, like it did in India and Africa.' He was silent for a moment, as if considering what he had said, then he nodded, as if confirming the point to himself. 'Ackaye, that's the only way. Now I'm pretty damned sure of it. But then, as we both agree, I'm no longer sixteen - and maybe we grow soft in our old age. You're on the way there already.'

'Aye, right,' Barry said. 'I'm turnin' soft - even as Sean is fillin' up with salt and vinegar.'

'So it goes.' Eddie sighed, pushed his chair back and stood up. 'Well, I have to be makin' tracks. Thank God I still live just around the corner. That's about as far as I can walk these days. My legs are startin' to ache as much as my shoulder. Growin' old isn't easy.'

'You're doin' swell,' Barry said.

'I'll drop in tomorrow,' Eddie promised.

'Do that. See ya, Da.'

When Eddie left the room, closing the inner door behind him, Barry stood up to pour himself another bottle of stout. He changed his mind, however, thinking of Meg and feeling lonely, recalling Theresa and feeling haunted (all those dead men in his past), and decided, instead of drinking more, to pay a visit to the Sinn Féin election office in Divis Street. Hopefully, he would find some small task to perform there, or, failing that, persuade someone to join him in the nearest pub for a jar and a good bit of *craic*.

Since he was leaving the house empty, he closed and locked the front door, then walked to the end of the street, initially shivering from the cold wind but gradually warming up. He turned left to make his way down the Falls. As usual, despite the weather, the pavements were bustling and he passed a few old friends during the brief walk to Divis Street. As he approached the building being used as a Sinn Féin election office, the tricolour fluttering proudly from its upstairs window, he wondered why it was that he still stubbornly came here despite the fact that he was generally treated by all, except Brendan Coghill, as some kind of has-been and only tolerated because he performed menial, unpaid tasks for them. This offended him all the more because neither the IRA nor Sinn Féin had much credibility these days in the local community, let alone down south. The failure of the Border Campaign had spiked all their guns.

So fuck them, Barry thought.

Entering the building, he was relieved to see that Brendan was present, seated behind a desk piled high with the electioneering pamphlets that had been composed either by him, by Sean, or by both of them working together. After years of resistance, Brendan had finally been persuaded by Sean to lend his literary talents and solid reputation as a local poet to the Republican cause. He may have done it, also, because of his growing disgust at the continuing British and Unionist intransigence regarding the most basic rights of the Catholic community and because, as he had hinted to Barry, age was catching up with him (he was now sixty-two) and he didn't want to die knowing that his literary talents, while certainly admired in academic quarters, had not helped his own kind one bit. So Barry had more than one reason for being delighted to see the renowned man of letters in this otherwise dismal room with its hard wooden chairs, desks piled with pamphlets and correspondence, and walls plastered with Sinn Féin propaganda posters. The two men at the desks, Liam O'Hanlon and Joe Mallon, were chain-smoking, shuffling papers and answering the telephones. Only Brendan looked up when Barry entered.

'Ack, you've come,' he said to Barry.

'Aye,' Barry replied, pulling a chair up in front of Brendan's desk and lighting a cigarette. 'Thought you might have something for me to do. Either that or you might like a pub break.'

'If you want to shuffle papers, you can certainly do so. But if you'd rather go out for a pint, I'm amenable. We're so busy, I haven't even had lunch yet.'

'How's it goin'?'

'I don't think we'll win, but we might at least gain a propaganda victory. If William Boyd of the NILP takes enough Prod votes off that Unionist, James Kilfedder, and Diamond gets most of the Catholic votes, they'll lose their seat.'

'So they can't afford to alienate their Loyalist supporters right now.'

'What a bright boy you are.'

Entering the room at that moment, Sean overheard what they were saying.

'Then we could be in trouble,' he said, smiling at Barry, squeezed his shoulder affectionately, then pulling up a chair to sit beside him.

375

'What does that mean?' Brendan asked.

'I've just been informed that the Reverend Ian Paisley's holding a meeting at the Ulster Hall tomorrow.'

'So what's new?'

'He's threatening to tell his congregation that we're displaying the tricolour – '

'Which we are,' Brendan interjected.

' - and that if we don't remove it within two days,' Sean continued, 'he's going to march here with his followers and remove it himself.'

'God Almighty!' Brendan exclaimed.

O'Hanlon and Mallon looked up from their work, both clearly shocked by what they had just heard.

Eventually, after a lingering, uneasy silence, Barry said, 'Surely they can't let him get away with that.'

'They can and they probably will,' Sean replied. 'As you've just confirmed, they can't afford to alienate their supporters in the middle of an election, which they'll do if they try to stop Paisley.'

Barry was always taken aback when he heard his son speaking like this, with an air of quiet authority, seemingly matured beyond his years. He respected him for it, admired him, was certainly proud of him, but he was also made uncomfortable by him; made to feel that his own time was over and that his and Sean's roles were being gradually, subtly reversed, with the son becoming the father and vice versa. This possibility only heightened Barry's conviction that he was increasingly useless.

'I think they'll have to try stopping him,' Brendan insisted, 'despite the possibility of losing Loyalist support. O'Neill sells himself as a liberal, but that image is likely to be demolished if he lets Paisley march here with his followers to take our tricolour down by force.'

'If it's a choice between the Catholics and the Loyalists,' Sean said, 'O'Neill will lend his support to the latter and take a chance on his image. Besides, who believes that O'Neill's really a liberal, other than the grand man himself? His liberal image would be tarnished in the eyes of the Catholic minority; but it would actually be given a shine in the eyes of those that matter the most to him: the Protestant majority. O'Neill, despite what he says to the contrary, is still heading an Orange State.'

Barry knew what Sean meant. Despite the publicly expressed liberal sentiments of Captain O'Neill, the Catholics were still living as an oppressed minority in their own country, as second-class citizens, with constant gerrymandering creating artificial Unionist majorities and the Special Powers Act giving the Unionist government almost limitless power. That power had been used to ban any organisations, meetings or publications that did not meet with Stormont's approval, to seize Catholic property at will, to restrict the movements of Catholics or throw them out of their homes, to suspend trial by jury and to imprison suspects without trial. Those powers were not, by and large, used against the Prods; they were used *by* the Prods, with the support of the B-Specials, against the Catholic community. Nothing had changed much.

'What's your feeling about Paisley?' Brendan asked. 'Do you think he'll actually carry out his threat? Or is the Big Man just blowing his horn again?'

'If previous experience is anything to go by,' O'Hanlon said from behind his cluttered desk, 'he'll do what he says he's goin' to do. Sure there's nothin' that particular Prod likes more than a good, highly publicised confrontation - and that's exactly what he'll get if he comes here to pull down our flag.'

Brendan sighed. 'And his meeting takes place tomorrow?'

'Yes,' Sean confirmed.

'Then there's nothing we can do but wait and see if he actually makes good his threat.'

'And if he does?'

'Then we spread word of his intentions throughout the Falls and rustle up some support.'

'And after that?' Barry asked.

'We pray,' Brendan said.

4

Theresa felt more nervous with each step she took into the grounds of Stoneykirk Manor, not only because it was so obviously a grand estate, but also because she was half expecting some huge slavering guard-dog to come bounding around the bend in the gravelled driveway and pounce upon her. Even when she had rounded the bend, which she did with great reluctance, and saw no sign of movement in front of the house, she remained nervous.

Stopping for a moment, straining to hear an approaching animal, she heard only the water gushing out of the ornate fountain that dominated the grounds directly in front of the house. The driveway circled around the fountain, passing the front door, and continued on back to the main gates. The fountain, which was working, was made of white marble and giant water lilies were floating in the pool around it.

The sheer size of the manor house overwhelmed her.

It was an unusually large, cream-painted Georgian mansion with two floors, high windows, soaring chimneys all the way along the apex of its roof, indicating a lot of bedrooms with their own fireplaces, and wide steps leading up to a colonnaded entrance, with double doors made of varnished oak. It was the biggest house that Theresa had ever seen outside of the movies.

Glancing left and right, she noted that the circular driveway was lined with trees, presently bare, and that there were well tended lawns and gardens behind the trees. Glancing along the western gable end, to which she was standing parallel, she saw vegetable gardens and part of what looked like a fenced-in tennis court. It certainly seemed like the house of a wealthy man.

Taking a deep breath, then letting it out in a sigh, she walked up the steps to the double doors. She was just about to use one of the polished brass knockers, as she would have done in the Pound Loney (though the knockers would not have been so fancy), when she saw a bell embedded in the plinth to the right of the door frame. Taking another deep breath, she rang the bell, holding it down for two or three seconds, then jerking her hand away as if it had been scorched. She waited for what seemed to be an awfully long time but was, in fact, less than a minute. She was just about to ring again when she heard footsteps approaching the other side of the doors. One of the doors was opened by her Protestant friend, Carol Bell, tall and slim in a black blouse, matching skirt and starched white apron, with her ink-black hair pinned up on her head. She was holding a feather duster in her hand and held it upright, almost brushing her own cheek, when she saw Theresa.

'Theresa!' she exclaimed with a big smile. 'You've come! Good girl. He's expectin' you.'

Stepping aside, she waved Theresa in, then curtsied jokingly as Theresa inched past her, entering a spacious rectangular hallway. The floor was covered with blue-grey tiles, paintings in gilded frames hung from the walls, plants stood in large pots in every corner, and there were wide, carpeted stairways at both ends. The far wall, directly facing Theresa, was broken up with doors, most of them presently open, giving her glimpses of more rooms, more paintings, and shelves packed with books. A balcony ran around three sides of the upper floor, offering glimpses of the doors of other rooms behind its darkly varnished wooden balustrades. Putting her head back to stare up at the high ceiling, she saw two crystal chandeliers. She only knew they were chandeliers because she had seen them in films and magazines; this was the first time she had seen them in real life.

'Oh, God Almighty!' she exclaimed softly, lowering her gaze and turning back to Carol, as the latter closed the front door behind her.

'Pretty impressive, eh?' Carol said, grinning.

'Ackaye,' Theresa said. 'Sure I'm shakin' in m'boots just lookin' at it.'

'First lesson,' Carol said. 'Try not to use words like that. "Ackaye" and "sure" and so on. They'd sound a bit common to some of them that come here. Don't worry about your accent, but try to use only proper words, like "yes" and "no." No "ackaye", no "Jasus!" and certainly no "fuck!" when you can use another word instead. "God!" instead of "Jesus!" "Sugar!" instead of "shite!" Don't make the mistake of trying to speak posh, but *do* try to keep the vernacular to a minimum. You get my meaning, Theresa?'

'Aye... I mean, yes. I get your meanin'.'

'Mean*ing*,' Carol emphasised.

'Yes... mean*ing*. Jesus - I mean, God! You already have me a bundle of nerves, Carol, and I've only just walked in through the door. I'm practically wettin' my knickers here.'

'Don't be nervous,' Carol said, still grinning. 'And certainly not of him. He's not a snob and he's dead easy to work for, though he has a few little eccentricities. I mean, you can't be a rich bachelor at forty if you're not at least a *wee* bit strange. Anyway, let's get the worst part, the first meeting, over and done with. We've still got a minute or two, so I'll show you a bit of the house as we go. Come with me, love.'

Crossing the hallway, they entered one of the rooms off it: a spacious living room, dominated by an ornate, hand-carved wooden fireplace, with a glittering chandelier overhead, in the centre of the ceiling. The room was filled with antique furniture, including soft chairs, sofas, tables and sideboards covered with expensive-looking bric-a-brac, including various Chinese puzzles, vividly painted boxes-within-boxes, Victorian toys, and wooden birds. Though the room was immaculately clean, it had a musty smell, as if used but rarely.

'The living room,' Carol explained as they walked through, weaving around chairs, sofas and tables. Stopping at one of the tables, she picked up a wooden bird that had a pile of ivory counters beside it. After picking up a couple of the counters, she pressed the side of the bird to make its jaws pop open. She then dropped the ivory counters, one after another, into the bird's open jaws. The jaws closed and opened again, swallowing the counters with a metallic clicking sound. When she pressed the other side of the bird, the ivory counters dropped out of the birds arse. Carol chuckled and placed the bird and ivory counters back on the table.

'A Victorian toy,' she explained, walking on with Theresa trailing behind her. 'They were fashionable amongst the aristocracy when his father was a child.' Waving a hand airily, she indicated the Chinese puzzles and vividly-coloured boxes-within-boxes on the sideboard they were passing at that moment. 'They collected those as well,' she said, 'on their travels - and apparently they travelled a lot. This house is like a museum: big and packed with treasures, though as far as human beings are concerned, it's mostly empty. It seems sad somehow, doesn't it?'

By now they had left the living room and were moving along a short corridor, past a wide variety of paintings in gilt frames, hanging from the cream-coloured walls. Most of the paintings were portraits of people wearing 19th century or Victorian clothing.

'The members of his family,' Carol explained. 'That's his grandma.' She pointed to a portrait of a rather severe beauty wearing a crinoline dress, with what looked like a dead animal on her head. 'The last of the real aristocrats. By the time he was born, they'd stopped commissioning the paintings and were into photos, just like the common folk. So there are no paintings of his parents. But apart from them, most of the family line is shown in those paintings and they give me the shivers. Their eyes follow you up and down the corridors, day in and day out.'

Theresa studied the paintings as she passed them and noticed that the eyes did, indeed, seem to follow her as the moved along the corridor. They seemed eerily, disturbingly, alive.

'In here,' Carol said, leading Theresa into a room where every wall was covered by darkly varnished bookshelves. Most of the books had old-fashioned bindings, with intricate gilt lettering. The carpets were faded and worn. Again, there was a musky smell that came, Theresa judged, from the worn leather of the old armchairs, and, perhaps, the book-bindings. The room seemed unnaturally quiet, almost as if it was haunted.

'His father's old study,' Carol explained. 'He keeps it the way it was when his father was alive, though he never uses it himself. Instead, he uses the study adjoining it. Through that doorway there.'

Theresa saw a closed door at the far side of the study and instantly felt nervous again. Grinning, Carol turned around to face her.

'I repeat, don't be nervous. Try to moderate your language, but otherwise just be your natural self. If he asks you something you don't know, just tell him the truth - that you don't know the answer - because he knows that I'm going to be training you and that's all that concerns him. Like a lot of people in his position, he finds it difficult to get domestic help these days, so he'd rather take on someone recommended by someone he knows, even if they're not experienced, than take a chance on someone totally unknown. So this meeting isn't to do with your experience; it's really only to let him see you and check that you haven't two noses or three eyes, or whatever. When you come out, I'll introduce you to the other staff – there's only three - and show you the rest of the house. Okay?'

'Ackaye,' Theresa said… then instantly corrected herself: 'Yes.'

Grinning, nodding approval, Carol stepped up to the closed door and rapped lightly upon it with her knuckles.

'Yes?' a slightly world-weary man's voice responded.

'Miss Coogan to see you, sir,' Carol announced.

'Oh, good. Show her in, please.'

After opening the door, Carol stepped aside to wave Theresa into the room. Theresa entered, suddenly feeling dead calm.

'This is Theresa Coogan, Mr. Stewart,' Carol said.

Seated behind his desk, Mr. Stewart was not what Theresa had imagined him to be. Though forty years old, he looked about ten years younger, with a boyish face, smooth skin, healthily flushed cheeks, fair, slightly reddish hair, and sky-blue eyes that seemed a little out of focus. Instead of a suit with shirt and tie, which is what Theresa had been expecting, he was wearing a powder-blue, open-necked shirt under a light-grey V-necked pullover. When Carol introduced him, he pushed his chair back, stood up and, smiling pleasantly, offered his hand.

'Hello, Theresa,' he said in a friendly, informal manner, with only the slightest trace of an Ulster accent. 'Pleased to meet you.'

As Theresa stepped forward to lean across the desk and shake his hand, she heard the door closing behind her, indicating that Carol had left the office. Theresa shook Mr. Stewart's hand, which felt warm and soft, certainly not a worker's hand, then, when he indicated the wooden chair just behind her, she took a step backward.

'Please,' Mr. Stewart said. 'Take a seat.'

Theresa sat on the chair. Mr. Stewart resumed his position behind the big desk. On the wall behind him were black-and-white photos of two people: a withdrawn, moustachioed man and a chillingly handsome woman. His parents, Theresa assumed. The photos were clearly the oldest items in the study, since everything else, including furniture and filing cabinets, was modern. The desk was stacked high with folders, documents and correspondence.

'Well, now,' Mr. Stewart said, clasping his hands under his chin, 'Carol tells me you're keen to work here, though you have no experience.'

'That's right, sir, I have no experience, but I'm certainly keen to work here and learn. I know I can do it.'

Smiling, Mr. Stewart looked even more boyish. 'Yes, I'm sure you can, Theresa, given what Carol's told me about you. You've worked at a lot of other jobs, I take it.'

'Aye... Yes, sir. Though few of them were good. I failed the Qualifying Examination and left school at fourteen. That doesn't stand you in good stead hereabouts.'

'No, I suppose not.'

'But though they weren't good jobs, I did all of them well and never got fired from any of them. I've good references right here.'

She started opening her bag, but Mr. Stewart waved his hand languidly. 'There's no need,' he said. 'I'm not interested in seeing them. The worst workers in the world can get a good reference if their employer wants rid of them badly enough. So I don't read references. I'd rather take the recommendation of someone I know - in this instance, Carol. She said you were bright and hungry to learn. That's good enough for me.'

Theresa closed her handbag again. 'Right, sir. If you say so.'

Mr. Stewart gazed steadily at her, though his sky-blue gaze, she noticed, still seemed slightly unfocused, as if he was really gazing inward, trying to find something lost. He seemed kindly, but distant.

'Do you smoke?' he asked.

'Yes, sir, but I can do without them. And I won't smoke here while doing my duties. You can take that as read, sir.'

Smiling again, he picked a packet of Benson & Hedges cigarettes and a lighter off the desk in front of him. 'I only asked because I want a smoke myself.' He opened the packet and held it out towards her. 'Yes?'

'No, thanks,' Theresa said. 'Not right now.'

'Are you sure?'

'Aye... Yes, I'm sure.'

'You already have the job, Theresa. You won't lose it by having a smoke. Have one. It might help you relax.'

'I'm relaxed, sir. Honestly, I'm fine. I just don't want to smoke right now.'

Mr. Stewart nodded, smiling. 'As you wish.' Leaning back in his chair, he lit his cigarette and then gazed dreamily at the ceiling while dreamily blowing smoke rings.

'Did Carol tell you much about the history of this place?' he asked eventually.

'Not much. She said your family originally came from Scotland.'

'Correct. From a place called Stoneykirk, near Luce Bay, in the south-west of Scotland. Belfast is located almost directly opposite. The south-west of Scotland is where many of the first Protestant plantationers came from. My ancestors were among the first of those.' He lowered his gaze to look directly at her. 'Do you mind that?'

'What?'

'You being a Catholic and so on.'

Theresa found herself blinking repeatedly. 'No,' she said, and the rapid blinking ceased.

Mr. Stewart nodded. 'Good. Anyway, this house was named after Stoneykirk to remind my ancestors of their old home. It's stood here since about 1750. In other words, it's *very* old, not in the best of conditions, and I'm fighting a losing battle to maintain it. Though hopefully it will still be here long after I'm gone.'

'Why a *losing* battle?' Theresa asked.

'I can tell you're listening,' Mr`. Stewart said, smiling again. 'It's a losing battle because of the costs. The building needs constant maintenance, a lot of the work is highly specialised - tinted windows, antique fittings and so forth - so it really is remarkably expensive. And what with our mills being closed down and so forth...' Trailing off, he shrugged forlornly. 'Well, that's why I have so few staff. Only a gardener, a cook, a general maintenance man... and now, of course, you. So you'll be one of four full-time staff in all.'

'Sure that's grand,' Theresa said.

'Your main duties will be secretarial,' Mr. Stewart continued, 'but because I can't afford any more domestic staff, you'll be expected to dust the rooms every day, change my bed linen once a week - I make my own bed - and serve at table, but only when I have guests; otherwise, I just eat in the kitchen. Twice a week, a cleaning woman, Gladys Webb, comes in to spend a full day, washing or polishing floors, vacuum-cleaning, and so on. Does that sound alright to you?'

'Yes, sir,' Theresa said.

'It's straightforward dusting, but there *are* a lot of rooms, so Carol does it every morning, finishing by lunchtime, then she starts working for me, serving lunch if I have guests - Mrs. Ward only cooks; she doesn't serve at table - and doing the secretarial work every afternoon. Does that still sound alright?'

'It sounds grand,' Theresa said.

Mr. Stewart nodded. 'Carol tells me you can start Monday week.'

'Aye... Yes, that's right. I have to give a week's notice where I am, so Monday week would be perfect.'

Mr. Stewart pushed his chair back, stood up and extended his hand for the second time. 'Welcome aboard, Theresa.'

Theresa stood up and shook his hand.

'Thank you, sir.'

'My pleasure.'

Coming around the desk, he walked her across the room and then opened the door for her. 'See you Monday week.'

'I'll be here,' Theresa promised. She stepped out of the room and heard the door clicking shut behind her. Carol had been sitting on a chair in the other, older study, waiting for her. Now she stood up expectantly.

'So, how did it go, love?'

'Grand,' Theresa said. 'I start Monday week.'

Carol smiled and gave her a hug. 'Terrific,' she said. 'Come on! Let me give you another quick tour before I go back to my work. I'm so pleased for you, love.'

She did, indeed, give Theresa another quick tour, showing her the rooms on the ground floor that she hadn't already seen, including the drawing room and a library completely separate from the old study. The kitchen, Theresa noted, while being old-fashioned, was as large as the whole downstairs of her house in the Pound Loney. The six upstairs bedrooms all had adjoining bathrooms and were, Theresa judged, about as large as the whole upstairs of her house. The basement, which was the same size as the expansive ground floor, contained the central heating and hot-water boilers, a couple of facility rooms, a canned-food store, a huge freezer packed with food, and a walk-in wine cellar, with hundreds of bottles laid out in high racks, many covered in dust.

Having shown her the house, Carol then introduced her to the cook, Mrs. Ward, a plump, good-natured, bustling woman who scarcely blinked when learning that Theresa was a Catholic from the Pound Loney.

'Sure you'll have a nice time workin' here, love,' she assured Theresa. 'Mr. Stewart's as good an employer as you'd find on either side of the border. There aren't many like him anymore.'

More excited every minute, Theresa let Carol lead her out of the building and into the garage that stood facing the eastern gable end of the house. There were two cars in the red-brick garage: an immaculately polished, silvery-grey Mercedes Benz saloon and a bright-red, open-topped sports car. Six bicycles, two motorcycles and half-a-dozen sets of snow skis were propped up against the walls.

'Mr. Stewart goes skiing in Switzerland every year,' Carol explained as she led Theresa out of the garage and into the rear gardens. Like everything else to do with the house, the gardens were extensive, including vegetable patches, glass houses, wooden sheds, and a fenced-in tennis court with a Swiss-chalet styled building beside it.

'That's the bar used by him and his friends,' Carol explained, 'when they're playing tennis. Just like Wimbledon, isn't it?'

'Very nice,' Theresa responded, growing even more excited, scarcely able to believe that she would soon be working here, learning how the wealthy lived. 'It must be real grand when his friends come.'

'Not *that* grand. He doesn't seem to have too many friends. A bit of a loner, really. I think this place was used more when his parents were alive. His life style is considerably slower these days, which at least makes *my* life a lot easier. Since I only have to serve at table when he has guests, I don't have to do it that often - and neither will you.' She sighed melodramatically, raising her hands in the air, indicating the big house and all around it. 'Well, Theresa, that's it. You've seen all there is to see. I'd better get back to my work now. Come on! I'll walk you around to the front of the house and then send you packing.'

'Aye,' Theresa said automatically, before correcting herself. 'Yes. All right.'

They walked along the path that ran between the garage and the gable end of the house to lead them back to the front driveway. There Carol gave Theresa another hug.

'See you Monday week,' she said, then she waved farewell and entered the house by the front doors.

Theresa stood there for a moment, studying the big house, trying to take it all in. Then, with rising excitement, she walked back along the driveway and left the grounds by the main gates, where she found Gerry waiting patiently for her. Walking up to her, he kissed her on the cheek, and said, 'How did it go?'

'I start Monday week,' Theresa replied, trying not to let him see just how excited she was.

'That's great,' Gerry replied, falling in beside her as she started walking along the Malone Road, back the way they had come. 'So what was he like?'

'Who?'

'Yer new boss.'

'Mr. Stewart.'

'Aye, him.'

'Not bad,' Theresa said, shrugging as if indifferent. 'He seemed nice enough. No airs or graces, like. I think we'll get along just fine.'

'Good,' Gerry said. 'Now if I can just get this job bein' offered to me, we'll *both* be doin' fine.'

'Fingers crossed,' Theresa said, though she was actually thinking of Mr. Stewart's languid, graceful movements, his quiet voice, his soothing accent, the way he had called her by her first name, offered her a cigarette, and even held the door open for her. A real gentleman.

When she glanced sideways at Gerry, though she still felt that she loved him, he suddenly seemed slightly different to her... somehow diminished... Yet she couldn't quite grasp why this was so.

'Let's celebrate with a drink or two,' Gerry said.

'Yes, let's do that.' The word 'Ackaye' never even entered her head. 'Yes,' she repeated, speaking quietly, precisely. 'Let's have a real celebration. Let's go and get drunk.'

'Now yer talkin', Gerry said.

5

Looking down from the window, past the fluttering tricolour, Sean saw that a lot of men, women and children had gathered in response to the news that the Reverend Ian Paisley was threatening to march with his followers to Divis Street and personally pull the flag down. Paisley had made that threat yesterday, a Sunday, giving Sinn Féin only two days to voluntarily remove the flag, but Sean believed that he was likely to come earlier and his belief had been made known to the local population. Now, on Monday, an already large crowd of Catholic demonstrators was growing rapidly down below, covering the pavements and the road. Some were active Sinn Féin supporters, but others were merely locals who would have taken no interest in the matter had Paisley not made his threat public.

'A good turn-out,' Brendan said as he, too, glanced down through the window.

'Aye,' Sean said. 'And the Falls Road is packed as well, with hundreds, maybe more than a thousand, turned out to lend their support.'

'To do battle with Paisley's mob,' Brendan corrected him, 'if they come marching into the Falls. This could lead to violence.'

'That's exactly what Paisley wants,' Sean said. 'The Big Man's after blood.'

Certainly it had seemed that way to Sean when he had gone to watch Paisley rant and rave on the stage of the Union Hall, working his congregation up into an unholy, certainly unChristian, fury with his rabble-rousing mixture of biblical and sexual imagery, smearing it like excrement over Catholics in general and the Pope in particular. Sean had been shocked at Paisley's ability to suggest unspeakable sins committed by priests and nuns, even by the Pope himself, without actually stating what those sins were; by his melodramatically bawled references to 'vile Vatican plots' and 'Popish deviltry' and 'Fenian fornicators' and 'Roman whores'; by his ability, in particular, to incite sectarian hatred and arouse violent emotions. Sean would not quickly forget how the men and women of Paisley's audience had entered the Union Hall like perfectly respectable, modest, Christian souls, only to emerge, an hour or so later, as an almost frenzied, potentially violent mob. Now, as he turned away from the window, sighing, he thought of those same people marching into the Falls with Paisley at their head. The very thought was depressing.

'Have you any idea of what's happening?' he asked of Brendan, having just arrived in the office five minutes ago.

'Not yet,' Brendan replied, 'but O'Hanlon's out there in the streets, sniffing the wind. He's going to let us know if Paisley's mob starts marching or if the Big Man has a change of heart.'

'If he said he was going to march here - and he did - the only thing that'll stop him is the news that we've removed the tricolour.'

'We can't do that, Sean. We'd only lose what little credibility we still have here in the Falls. I mean, look at those people down below, then think of the hundreds, maybe thousands, that you saw gathering earlier in the Falls Road. Most of those people, who'd forgotten all about us, or despised us as being useless, only turned out to demonstrate a single point: that they won't be bullied by a Protestant rabble-rouser like Ian Paisley. In that sense, at least, Paisley's doing us a favour: he's actually getting us back a lot of the support we lost after the failure of the Border Campaign. But if we give in to him now, if we remove that tricolour, those same people will feel betrayed and turn away from us again - so the flag has to stay.'

'I agree,' Sean said. 'I just wish I knew what was happening. The tension's killing me, Brendan.'

'You're not alone, Sunny-Jim.'

They stayed on in the office, doing little of real worth, merely smoking, drinking tea and talking to those who came and went, for another forty-five minutes, by which time the crowd outside had grown considerably. Luckily, just as the tension was becoming unbearable, Liam O'Hanlon arrived, flushed, out of breath, and clearly excited.

'So what's happening?' Brendan asked.

'The Minister for Home Affairs has struck a deal with Paisley, promising to have the flag removed by the RUC, if necessary by force, if he promises to stay away from the Falls. They're on their way here right now - the RUC, I mean - and Paisley's cancelled his march. He's staging a meeting outside the City Hall instead.'

'It's the lesser of two evils,' Brendan said, 'but we still can't take the flag down ourselves. Joe,' he added, turning to Mallon, 'go downstairs and lock the front door. If they want in, they'll have to break in. We won't open the door for them.'

Nodding affirmatively, Mallon rushed down the stairs.

Suddenly, police sirens started wailing in the distance, somewhere along the Falls, but becoming louder as the RUC squad cars approached Divis Street.

'That's them,' O'Hanlon said.

As the door was slammed shut downstairs, they all went to the window to look out. With the sirens growing louder, approaching rapidly, the people down on the road broke into applause and then started shouting words of encouragement. The wailing sirens drew nearer, tyres screeched on the road, then the RUC vehicles, a mixture of squad cars and armoured vans, were suddenly racing along the street, as if intent on ploughing into the demonstrators.

'Such enthusiasm,' Brendan said sardonically. 'Let's go downstairs and greet them.'

'I thought we weren't opening the front door,' Sean said.

'We're *not* opening the front door. We're simply going to talk to them *through* the door, reminding them that this is private property and insisting that they stay outside.'

Sean grinned, though he felt a little queasy. 'I don't think they'll take much notice of that.'

'It's just my version of street theatre,' Brendan retorted as he turned to face O'Hanlon and Mallon. 'You two stay here. If they break in and come up the stairs, stand in front of the window - in front of the tricolour - and don't move until they push you aside or drag you away. The people down there will see them do it and won't be too pleased. That's one up for us, at least.'

'Right,' O'Hanlon said.

The sirens were still wailing when the RUC vehicles screeched to a shuddering halt in the road below. As the doors were flung open and RUC policemen poured out, some wearing helmets, armed with batons and pistols, the onlookers booed and shook their fists. More helmeted policemen dispersed from the vans behind the squad cars, then fanned out to form a circle designed to hold back the crowd, which was growing excited and looked threatening. As the policemen took up positions, facing the shifting, heaving crowd, a uniformed RUC officer, surrounded by two men in riot-control gear, both wielding sledgehammers, approached the locked door of the building.

'Come on, Sean.' Brendan was heading for the stairs. 'It's time to go down there.'

Sean followed him down the stairs to the ground-floor office, entering just as the RUC officer at the other side of the door was trying the handle. Discovering that the door was locked, he shook it a few times in frustration and then called out, 'Police! Open up!'

Brendan approached the door. Leaning towards it, practically brushing it with his lips, he called out, 'This is private property, officer. You don't have the right to enter the premises without our permission.'

'You're displaying a tricolour in contravention of the Flags and Emblems Act,' the officer responded, speaking politely but firmly through the closed door. 'If you don't remove that flag within five minutes, we'll be forced to enter the building and do it ourselves.'

'We don't recognise your right to forbid us flying the Irish national flag. And I repeat that you don't have the right to enter these premises without our permission.'

'You fuckin' eejut!' the officer snapped, no longer pretending to be polite. 'You know we can do what we like if you don't take that flag down. Now remove it before we smash this door in.'

'That flag is staying where it is, officer.'

'I'm warning you, we'll smash this door down!'

'I insist upon my right as a free citizen to fly any kind of flag I want. If you wish to enter the building, you'll have to do so without my consent.'

'Fuck the five minutes, you Fenian bastard, we're comin' in right now.'

Sean glanced at Brendan and saw, to his surprise, that his friend was grinning. He was, however, careful enough to step away from the door. Sean did the same.

'Get set,' Brendan said, as if playing some kind of game.

The first sledgehammer slammed into the door, making a resounding racket, causing the door to shake violently and the hinges to come partially out of the wall, with dust billowing out from the breaking cement. The second sledgehammer completed the job, nearly splitting the door in two, forcing the hinges out completely, then the door fell inwards and crashed to the floor, raising more clouds of dust. Sean heard the crowd outside booing and bawling angrily, as four baton-wielding RUC men came charging in through the doorway, emerging from swirling clouds of dust. The officer marched in behind them.

'I insist...' Brendan began, attempting to step in front of the officer. But one of the other policemen charged into him, butting him hard with his shoulder, bowling him backwards into the wall. Before Sean could make a move, he was grabbed roughly by the shoulders and also slammed into the wall. Pain shot across his back, forcing his eyes closed. He heard the clatter of the policemen's boots on the stairs as they rushed up to the top floor. When the pain passed away, Sean opened his eyes again, wiped tears from his cheeks, blinked repeatedly and saw Brendan doing the same. The RUC officer was standing stiffly on the dust-covered fallen door, flanked by the men with the sledgehammers. The other men were bawling upstairs. O'Hanlon shouted in protest, there was the sound of breaking glass, something thudded on the floor, then the police came clattering back down the stairs, one of them holding the tricolour in his clenched fist.

'Let's go,' the officer said. Turning aside, he offered Brendan a slight nod, a bleak smile, while saying, rather formally, 'Good day to you, sir.' He then spun on the ball of his left foot, turning away, and marched stiffly out of the building, followed by his six men.

Outside, the onlookers booed and bawled.

When Sean ran up the stairs to check that no one had been hurt, he found O'Hanlon picking himself off the floor, pressing a hand to his belly. The window had been smashed, as Sean had suspected, and the floor was covered with shards of broken glass.

'You all right?' Sean asked.

O'Hanlon nodded. 'Ackaye. One of 'em hit me in the belly with his baton, then threw me down on the floor. I thought he was gonna kick the shite out of me, as the others were hauling Joe here away from the flag, but luckily he managed to control himself. Sure I'm more shocked than hurt.'

'And you?' Sean asked of Mallon.

'I'm grand. Apart from draggin' me away from the window, they didn't lay a hand on me.'

Going to the broken window, Sean looked down and saw that the crowd, still booing and bawling, was surging like a great wave against the police cordon as the RUC squad car made a tight U-turn and moved off along the street, heading back the way it had come. As the other squad cars did the same, the policemen forming a protective wall broke up and ran for their vans with the angry crowd, finally set free, pursuing them.

Brendan stepped out of the office, into the street, holding his hands on high, bawling, 'Let them go! Calm down! It's all over! Please go back to your homes!' But the crowd took no heed, ignited by a common anger, sweeping irresistibly around the police vans, reaching out to grab or strike the policemen as they were scrambling back into their vehicles. The policemen retaliated even as they were moving off, hammering with their batons at those out front. Some of the people fell, men and women alike, blood pouring from their heads, but others knelt to help them up as the last of the police vans moved off and the crowd pursued it along the street, heading for the Falls.

The sound of an explosion came from that direction.

'What the hell was *that*?' O'Hanlon asked.

'I don't know,' Sean replied. Glancing down on the street again, he saw Brendan following the crowd. 'I think I'd better get down there. You two stay here and man the telephones. Call an ambulance for those wounded people left down there on the street. Let the press know what happened.'

'Will do,' Mallon said.

Sean hurried down the stairs and left the building. As he turned in the direction of the Falls, following Brendan and the noisy crowd in front of him, he saw a few men and women either lying or sitting upright on the road, their heads covered in blood, being helped by concerned friends or relatives. Detouring in that direction, he told the people surrounding the wounded to remain there until an ambulance came, then he hurried on after Brendan and the angry, clamorous crowd. He heard the sound of another explosion somewhere in the Falls.

'Jesus!' he whispered automatically, addressing only himself.

Then he started running.

Up ahead, the crowd of demonstrators poured out of the street and into the Falls. Brendan followed them, disappearing around the corner, into the main road, and Sean then ran even faster. As he reached the end of the street, black smoke billowed up to the sky and blew across the rooftops, like spilt ink spreading across blotting paper. Sean smelt the smoke even before he plunged into it, turning into the Falls Road. Brendan was just ahead of him, catching up with the tail end of the angry crowd, now spread across the road from one pavement to the other, though it had ground to a halt, unable to go any farther, forced back by the fierce heat of two double-decker buses, set on fire and now blazing furiously.

Even as Sean stopped running, freezing where he stood, looking on in disbelief, some men with scarves tied around their faces, hiding their features, were herding the frightened passengers away from a third bus, while other men, also hiding their faces with scarves or towels, threw petrol bombs. When the bottles smashed through the windows of the bus, sending shards of broken glass flying out in all directions, the petrol, ignited by burning tapers, exploded into flames that swept through the vehicle, setting the seats on fire and making the other windows explode, with more flames licking out of them. A pall of smoke now covered the Falls Road, turning day into night.

6

Three days later, the Falls was still covered in a pall of smoke and the general situation was worse than ever. Even as he was buttoning up his shirt in his small house in the Pound Loney, preparing to return to the Sinn Féin office in Divis Street, Barry, who could scarcely credit what had happened, was concerned for the safety of his children.

'Stay indoors,' he told Theresa, 'until all this blows over. The temperature on both sides has been goin' up every day and the whole of the Falls could explode. So you stay indoors, you hear me?'

'I'll be alright, Da,' Theresa replied, speaking more precisely than usual, while ironing clothes on the ironing board set up in the living room, having taken over the household duties since the death of her mother. 'I'll only be going to the shops and back, getting the groceries. I've no intention of getting into trouble, now that I've got this new job starting soon. Besides, nothing much is happening out there. It's all died down, I'm telling you.'

'It hasn't died down. This is just the lull before the storm. The second riot last night was a clear indication of that. And since the boyos down there in Divis Street have replaced the smashed door and plan to hang a second tricolour in defiance of the ban, you can be sure they'll get the trouble they're askin' for and that the trouble will spread. There's people out there ready to explode and I don't want you near them when they do.'

Temperatures had, indeed, been rising in the area ever since that first tricolour had been forcibly removed by the RUC. The blackened shells of the buses set on fire by the rioters two days ago were still there in the Falls Road to remind the locals of what had happened. Since then, gangs of youths and older men had been gathering at street corners, some genuinely concerned that Paisleyite mobs might suddenly invade the area, others, particularly the teenagers, simply looking for the slightest excuse to cut loose. Barry had been hoping that it would all die down, but last night, the night after the bus burnings, a Sinn Féin meeting had broken up in rioting and baton charges by the RUC. Barry had not been present, but he had heard all about it from friends who had been there. Reportedly, the baton charge had been especially brutal, leaving a lot of the rioters with broken limbs and bloody heads, while increasing the anger of even those who had formerly been unsympathetic to the Republican cause. That anger was building and would certainly explode into violence if the RUC returned to forcibly remove that second tricolour from the same Sinn Féin building. The tricolour had become a red flag to a bull.

'So why are Sean and his Sinn Féin friends,' Theresa asked as she folded an ironed shirt and laid it carefully on top of the clothes already done, 'deliberately putting out another tricolour, if they know it's asking for trouble?'

'Paisley's left them no choice,' Barry told her as he put on his jacket, preparing to leave the house. 'The RUC only removed the first tricolour under pressure from the Big Man. If Sinn Féin lets them get away with it, they'll be seen to be giving in to the Big Man as well. They can't afford to let that happen – they'd only lose what little credibility they have left with this community - so they have to display the tricolour again. I'm not sayin' it's right, but that's the general feeling around the Falls. Now I have to make tracks.'

'You shouldn't go down there,' Theresa said, laying another shirt across the ironing board. 'You could get into trouble.'

'I'll take my chances,' Barry said, flipping a cigarette into his mouth and lighting it. 'I have to find out what's happening.'

'The RUC know you, Da. They know you served time before. If you get caught in any shenanigans, you could end up with a really heavy sentence.'

'I won't get caught,' Barry said.

'If this thing ends up in another riot, you could get caught by the police or badly hurt. That goes for Sean, too. You should both keep away from it.'

'I can't keep away from it. I just can't. Sure I'd never forgive myself if I ignored it.'

'You're askin' for trouble,' Theresa insisted, her anxiety making her slip back into her normal mode of speech. 'You an' your eejut Sinn Féin friends, includin' my brother.'

'I'll tell him you said that,' Barry joked.

'Aye, you do that,' Theresa said.

Grinning, Barry blew her a kiss and left the house. Walking along the street, he saw that a lot of unemployed youths were hanging about in gangs, some smoking cigarettes and drinking stout from bottles, all looking restless. Not happy with that sight, he merely nodded as he passed them, not saying a word, and continued along to the end of the street to turn into the Falls Road. Instantly, he saw the burnt-out buses, which had yet to be towed away, their windows smashed, the broken glass scattered around them, glinting like scattered jewellery in the afternoon's grey light. Though the Falls Road had always been a busy thoroughfare, there were even more people out and about than was customary, too many of them simply loitering at windblown street corners, talking each other into a fighting mood. Word that Sinn Féin was going to display another tricolour had swept like wildfire through the Falls; now the locals were waiting for something to happen. Thus, the closer Barry came to Divis Street, the more dense the crowds were, until, when he turned into the street, he found it so packed that he practically had to shove his way through to the office where, he noticed immediately, the new tricolour had still not been displayed. The front door was locked.

Barry banged on the door with the knocker.

'Hey, Barry!' someone called from a large group of people standing farther along the pavement. 'Are they puttin' the flag out or not?'

'I don't know,' Barry replied.

'Well, tell them to put it out or we'll kick the fuckin' door in and display it ourselves.'

The others laughed at that.

'Aye,' the first man said. 'No big fat Prod like Paisley's gonna tell us what to do here in the Falls. So get that tricolour out and let him and his fuckin' Orange pals see it.'

Barry grinned, though he wasn't amused, then he knocked on the door again. This time Liam O'Hanlon called out, 'Who is it?'

'Barry Coogan.'

'Hold on a minute, Barry.' The door was unbolted from inside and then jerked open. O'Hanlon stuck his head around the edge of the door; seeing Barry, he nodded to indicate that he should enter. 'Quick!' Entering the downstairs office, Barry found Joe Mallon leaning against a pine cupboard that he clearly intended pushing across the door, once he had locked it. O'Hanlon closed the door and bolted it, then nodded again, this time indicating the stairs. 'They're all up there, Barry, arguing about whether or not they should fly another tricolour.'

'Right,' Barry said. 'You're going to block the door with that cupboard?'

'That's right,' Mallon replied, grinning. 'It won't actually keep the RUC out, but at least it'll make it harder for the bastards to get in when they come back again.'

'That means you've already decided to display the tricolour.'

'You've got a head on your shoulders, sure enough,' O'Hanlon said, 'and a pair of good eyes to go with it. Damned right, we're gonna display the flag. Okay, Joe, start pushin'.'

As the two men commenced pushing the cupboard across the front door, Barry climbed the stairs to the upstairs room. He entered just as Brendan and Sean, the debate obviously over, were putting the tricolour out through the window. The crowd below burst into cheering and applause. Once the flag was fluttering freely in the wind, above the heads of the watching crowd, the cheering and clapping grew even louder. Grinning, Brendan and Sean waved to the crowd below, then turned around to face the other men packed into a room dense with cigarette smoke. Most of them were members of Sinn Féin, though some, such as Barry, had formerly been with the IRA.

'Hi, Da,' Sean said when he saw Barry. 'You got here just in time.'

'For what?' Barry said. 'Another riot?'

'It's a calculated risk,' Brendan said, 'but one we have to take.'

'What does that mean?' Barry asked.

'None of us want a riot - '

'Don't you?' Barry interjected impatiently.

'No, none of us want a riot,' Brendan repeated patiently, 'and we're working on the assumption that the RUC won't want to risk one by taking the flag down a second time.'

'I'm not so sure about that,' Barry said. 'I think they'll *have* to do it again. Just as we'll lose face if we don't put the flag back out, so the RUC will lose face if they let us get away with it. Sure you know that right enough. It's a riot you want and are inciting. Deliberately, I think.'

'For what purpose?' Sean asked disingenuously.

'Because Paisley's inadvertently done us a favour by reminding the Catholic community that this is a Protestant state, run for and by Prods, including the RUC. We'd practically lost all our support here, but now we're getting' it back and we can't afford to lose it again by showing weakness. If the RUC return to forcibly remove that flag, those people down there are going to riot. They'll be rioting over the tricolour, the Irish national flag, Republicanism, and that's exactly what we need to regain the support we've lost these past years in our own community. Now is that true or not, lads?'

'Yes, it's true,' Brendan said.

'So why do you disapprove?' Sean asked.

'Because people could get hurt,' Barry said.

'That's pretty hypocritical, coming from *you* of all people,' Sean said.

Shocked to hear his son speaking to him that way, brutally reminded of his own violent past, Barry opened his mouth to reply, but no words came out.

Police sirens wailed in the distance.

It was clear from the sound of those sirens that there was more than one vehicle.

'Jesus!' O'Hanlon said, as he entered the room again. 'Sure it sounds like a whole army down there!'

'They've obviously been told there are a lot of people outside this building,' Sean said, 'and they know they'll have to force their way through. They'll be coming in pretty large numbers.'

'Good,' Brendan said, sounding pleased. 'I've already been in touch with the press - '

'Which explains why the RUC knew that you were intending to put the flag out,' Barry interjected.

' - and the reporters and photographers are probably on their way here already. The more police they see, the better for us.' Brendan shrugged. 'Now we wait.'

Not for long. Within minutes, the noise of the sirens had become a demented wailing that was rapidly approaching the building. Instinctively, forgetting his hurt feelings, Barry went to the window, squeezing in between Sean and Brendan, to look down. RUC squad cars and paddy wagons were braking to a halt in a long line, running the length of the street, to disgorge a lot of men in riot-control gear - steel helmets, padded GPV vests and big boots - wielding reinforced shields and truncheons. Two of them were carrying pickaxes.

Instantly, the crowd, already in an aggressive mood, was galvanised into action, surging forward to prevent the police from reaching the Sinn Féin building. This time, however, the police had come in greater numbers and, obviously prepared for the worst, they proceeded to fight their way through the crowd, viciously beating those nearest to them with their truncheons. Men bawled in protest, women screamed. The police with the shields and truncheons spread out to force the crowd back, forming a broad protective ring while the men with the pickaxes attacked the door of the building. Some young men in the crowd started hurling stones and bottles, which either bounced off or smashed against the police shields. Other men in the crowd were soon doing the same, throwing stones and bottles, trying to strike the men who were now hammering at the door with their pickaxes. Stones continued to bounce off the shields and bottles also smashed against them, sending shards of glass flying out in all directions, showering down on some of the bawling, fist-waving onlookers, making them scatter.

Still leaning out of the window, squeezed between Brendan and Sean, Barry glanced to the side and saw that the police convoy ran all the way back to the Falls Road. The police were now dispersing the crowd by spreading out, running down individuals and attacking them with their truncheons, brutally hammering them to the ground. Other policemen, working in teams of three, were pinning men to the walls of the terraced houses, beating at them with truncheons, then half-running, half-dragging them across the road, to throw them, dazed and bleeding and groaning, into paddy wagons.

Lowering his gaze, Barry saw the men directly below him, protected from flying stones and bottles by a ring of raised shields, still hammering furiously at the front door with their pickaxes, causing lumps of shredded wood to fly out of it. Within minutes, the door was hacked to pieces, then pounded off its hinges, though it still remained upright because of the cupboard placed directly behind it. Cursing, the men with the pickaxes leaned against the loosened door and pushed at it until the cupboard was forced back, shrieking and rattling. Then the cupboard fell over, the door crashed on top of it, with clouds of dust billowing upward, and the men with the pickaxes rushed into the building, followed by policemen wielding shields and truncheons. Barry heard their boots pounding up the stairs.

'Form a chain!' Brendan bawled.

Instantly, Barry, Brendan, Sean and the other men joined hands to form a line that stretched across the whole of the room, directly in front of the window and its fluttering tricolour. But the RUC men who rushed into the room were in no mood for talk and they quickly smashed through the chain, swinging their truncheons and hurling aside anyone they could reach. Thrown bodily into a wall, Barry practically bounced off it, but twisted around, trying to find his bearings, feeling battered and bruised, in time to see Sean being pushed by a policeman towards the open door, then brutally propelled down the stairs by a boot to his backside. Brendan, his head bloody, went down next.

Barry felt a sharp pain lancing through his left shoulder, followed by pins and needles darting down that twitching arm, then he was grabbed by both shoulders and hurled violently towards the doorway. Glancing back, he caught a glimpse of an RUC officer hauling in the tricolour, to a concerto of boos and bawled abuse from the street below, then he, too, was kicked out onto the landing, struck with another truncheon, this time in the belly, making him jack-knife, and found himself stumbling down the stairs, holding his hands over his head to protect it from more swinging truncheons. Hurled forcibly out into the street, he stumbled and fell and rolled over a couple of times, being kicked repeatedly. Finally, coming to rest on his belly, he managed to push himself upright.

Chaos reigned on all sides. Helmeted riot-control police were racing in both directions along the street, striking out wildly with their truncheons, attacking men and women alike, while others dragged or pushed protesting men into the paddy wagons. Barry saw Brendan, holding his bloody head, being heaved up into a paddy-wagon, even as

Sean twisted free from the two policemen trying to pin him to a wall, then ran away in the direction of the Falls Road.

Barry followed his son, running as fast as he could and weaving frantically each time he saw a policeman coming towards him. On all sides, men were bawling and women were screaming, some staggering about with bloody heads or lying on the ground while being kicked by the police, others being pounded by truncheons. Barry kept running until he reached the end of the street. Turning into the Falls Road, he saw that another two buses had been set on fire and were blazing furiously, the yellow flames flickering frantically in the wind, the oily black smoke swirling along the pavements and billowing up to the sky. The police were here as well, holding their shields on high, swinging their truncheons as they charged at the men and youths who were hurling missiles at them. Bottles sailed through the air to smash on the road or against walls, with shards of glass flying out in all directions, lacerating faces and hands, causing more blood to flow. Stones ricocheted off the shields or flew past the policemen to smash the shop windows behind them. At various street corners gangs of young men were pushing cars across the road and then rolling them over, bumper to bumper, to form barricades and keep the police out. Already, some of the men behind those barricades had made petrol bombs out of bottles and were igniting them and hurling them at the police. The bottles exploded on the road and against walls, creating more searing yellow flames and billowing black smoke.

Barry had lost sight of Sean, but as he made his way up the Falls Road, hugging the walls where possible and breaking out in a run each time a policeman came charging at him, he saw Sean's friend, Tommy Molloy, now a young man of twenty-two, running out from behind an overturned car to hurl a petrol bomb at an RUC armoured car. Sailing over the armoured car, the bottle smashed through the window of a shop on the far pavement, where it exploded, setting the shop on fire.

'That bloody young eejut!' Barry said aloud, realising that rioters like Tommy were doing as much damage to their neighbours as they were to the police. He was just about to cross the road and shake some sense into Tommy when the young man was attacked by three policemen, who took turns at beating him with their truncheons, virtually battering him to his knees, then grabbed him and dragged him across the road to throw him, bloody and bruised, into a paddy wagon.

'Lord have mercy!' Barry whispered to himself, before turning away and continuing to make his way up the road.

Suddenly, he saw Sean again, standing up on the back of a flat-topped truck, shouting through a megaphone, urging the people to get off the streets and return to their homes. Sean did not speak for long. His voice was drowned out by the wailing of sirens as more police vehicles advanced along the road. Glancing back over his shoulder, Barry was horrified to see that the approaching vehicles were RUC armoured cars carrying water cannons. The first of them rumbled past him, weaving left and right to avoid the fires blazing in the middle of the road and the new petrol bombs being hurled at it. Its water cannon started firing while it was still on the move, sending a high-powered jet of water shooting across the road to hammer the men throwing the petrol bombs. So powerful was the stream of water that it made a calamitous drumming sound against the overturned cars, then bowled over those hiding behind them, punching them with the strength of a giant fist that could break a man's ribs.

A second armoured car rumbled past Barry, overtaking the first vehicle, then fired its own water cannon. That particular jet of water was not aimed at the barricades across the street, but at the flat-topped truck upon which Sean was still desperately calling for the rioters to return to their homes. The jet of water was so powerful that it made the whole truck shudder, then it hammered at Sean and sent him flying backward, limbs akimbo, off the truck and out of sight.

Shocked, fearful, Barry ran obliquely, crouching low, across the road, trying to get to the truck that Sean had been standing upon. He was about halfway there when he saw Theresa's boyfriend, Gerry Donovan, being dragged off the pavement and forced, with repeated blows from a truncheon wielded by a policeman, up into another paddy wagon. Beyond that ugly vehicle, Seamus Magee and Kevin McClusky were standing on an overturned car to hurl petrol bombs at the RUC armoured cars. Their bombs exploded against one of them, covering it in flames and forcing the men firing the water-cannons to jump off and run away from the searing flames. Another jet of water then swept vertically from Magee to McClusky, punching them off the overturned car, one after the other, and sending them spinning back down to the road. Barry kept running, weaving left and right, crouched low. He was just about to reach the truck when he heard sirens up ahead and saw more riot-control police pouring out of a dozen RUC vans, cutting off the rioters who were trying to flee from the police advancing up the road from Divis Street.

Though realising that he was boxed in with the rioters, Barry started making his way around the drenched truck, determined to check if Sean was all right, but something smashed into him, hammering at him with dreadful force, lifting him off his feet to slam him into the side of the truck and then throw him violently to the ground.

Oh, God, he thought, as searing pain was followed by numbness and inrushing darkness. *What..?*

Then he blacked out.

7

Four days later, Sean, physically unharmed, not in prison like many of his friends, but still in a state of shock, was reliving, with Moira, Brendan and Frank Kavanagh, in the patched-up election office of Sinn Féin, the worst rioting that Belfast had seen in thirty years. It was all over now, but the repercussions would last a long time and the cost had been high.

Sean was in a state of shock because Barry was in hospital suffering from mild concussion and broken ribs; because Theresa's boyfriend, Gerry Donovan, was merely one of the many who had been arrested and were now in jail, awaiting trial; and because approximately fifty people were in hospital with wounds received on Friday, the third day of the rioting, when an estimated 350 RUC men, carrying reinforced shields and truncheons, backed up by armoured cars with water cannons, had 'pacified' the Falls by ruthlessly driving the demonstrators off the streets. Now the Falls was quiet again, but certainly not at peace, and armed RUC men were visible everywhere.

'So what happened to your Da?' Brendan asked while tenderly adjusting the bandage around his head. His temple had been split slightly by a blow from a police truncheon, the wound requiring two stitches, but at least he was still a free man.

'He saw me being bowled off that truck by the jet of water from a water-cannon and thought I might have been hurt. So he left the doorway where he was taking shelter and ran across the road to rescue me.'

'A good man and lovin' father,' Frank Kavanagh, the hypocrite, interjected.

'Aye,' Sean said. 'Anyway, I was actually lying on the ground, winded by that jet of water, gasping for breath, when I saw Da coming around the side of the truck. Another jet of water hit him, practically lifting him off his feet and slamming him into the side of the truck. He bounced off the truck and then fell head-first to the ground. That's how he got his concussion and broken ribs.'

'So why didn't you help him?' Kavanagh asked suspiciously, his rheumy, 70-year old eyes blinking repeatedly, but still hard for all that.

'I tried crawling to him,' Sean explained patiently, though he still had no respect for Kavanagh, 'but I still couldn't breathe properly. Then another jet of water hit me and punched me along the road, winding me even more and making me pass out for a few seconds. Just as I came to, I saw two coppers pick my Da up and slide him into the back of an ambulance. By the time the ambulance moved off, I'd gotten my breath back and jumped up and made a run for it. The ambulance took Da straight to the hospital, where they patched him up and put him in a bed.'

'So how is he?' Brendan asked.

'He has a splitting headache, as you'd expect, and his ribs hurt like hell, but apart from that, at least according to the doctors, he should be okay. But he was certainly a bit dazed when I saw him. I mean, he recognised me all right, but he was out of it. He just wanted to rest, he said, so I didn't stay long.'

'Those RUC bastards!' Moira exclaimed with passionate conviction. 'Sure they're just a bunch of Protestant thugs.'

'So what about you?' Kavanagh asked of Brendan. 'Why are *you* still free to walk the streets?'

Brendan smiled, lightly tapping the bandage wrapped around his head, stained with blood over the area of the temple. 'The slightest wound to the temple makes you bleed like a pig,' he said. 'So when I was thrown into that paddy wagon, I was bleeding like a pig and the two officers in there with me, guarding me and the other prisoners, became a little concerned. One of them recognised me. He'd seen my picture in the papers. "Aren't you that famous poet?" he asked. "Yes,"

I replied humbly. "What the fuck were you doing in the streets," he said, "with all those rioting Fenians?" So I confessed, humbly, that I, also, was a Fenian who happened to live in the area and was just out shopping when the rioting started. I was caught in it before I realised what was happening, I informed him, and, being an old man - sixty-two years old, I emphasised - I couldn't push my way out of the crowd of rioters. Then, of course, as I also explained, looking contrite, I was mistaken for a rioter and banged on the head with a truncheon. "Jesus!" the RUC officer said. "That's all I fucking need! To have a fucking Fenian bleedin' to death in my paddy wagon would be bad enough; but to have it happen to someone well known - and, even worse, someone as old as you - would give your Fenian friends all the ammunition they need to vilify the force. So you're getting out of here, Mister Famous Fuckin' Poet, before you bleed to death all over me and become another fucking Fenian martyr." So he dropped me off at the Royal Victoria Hospital, instead of taking me on to a holding cell. Fame has its advantages.'

Though still shocked by what had happened to his father, Sean had to grin. 'That kind of fame is better than riches,' he said.

'Too true, dear boy.'

But Frank Kavanagh was not amused. 'You fuckin' binlids shouldn't have appealed for peace,' he said, referring not only to Sinn Féin, but to Eddie McAteer, the nationalist leader, and his brother Hugh, both of whom had, with Sinn Féin, made unsuccessful appeals for peace before the police arrived in their hundreds to pacify the area. 'You should have let the rioting continue until it was completely out of control. That would have brought those Protestant cunts to the negotiating table.'

'I take exception to your use of the word "cunts",' Moira said, displaying her feminist leanings. 'The word "bastards" is fine.'

Kavanagh was just about to offer a retort, almost certainly vicious, when Brendan brought them back to the subject at hand.

'If we hadn't appealed for peace, God knows where all of this would have ended. Also, it was only *because* of our appeals for peace that the RUC compromised and allowed us to carry the tricolour during that Republican parade yesterday. It was that compromise on the part of the RUC that finally stopped the rioting.'

Kavanagh nodded in reluctant agreement. 'Aye, that's true, right enough, but you still lost in the end.'

In using the word 'you' he meant Sinn Féin, not the IRA, which had virtually been redundant since the failure of the Border Campaign of the 1950s.

'How did we lose?' Moira asked.

'What he means,' Brendan said, 'is that the riots deepened the anti-Catholicism of the Prods and increased the votes for the Unionist candidate. Prior to the riots, there'd been grounds to believe that the West Belfast seat, always notoriously volatile, might have gone to an opposition candidate, but the Unionist candidate came in at 21,337 votes - some 7000 ahead of his nearest rival. So the Unionists hold Belfast again.'

'Even worse,' Sean said. 'That display of Paisley's power - and he certainly proved he had it - forced Terence O'Neill to publicly back away from his liberal stance and show his true Orange colours.'

'What does *that* mean?' Moira asked.

'Instead of condemning Paisley for starting the riots, O'Neill placed the blame squarely on the Catholic candidates, reminded the Prods that the Catholic candidates had backgrounds in the IRA. Then, even more damaging, he said that certain of the Catholic candidates - I quote – "*appear to be using a British election to provoke disorder in Northern Ireland.*" Unquote. That remark was the nail in our coffin.'

'So now we know,' Brendan said. 'Either O'Neill gives in to Paisley and his cronies or he'll have to resign. My bet is, he'll resign.'

'Then we'll have even worse troubles,' Brendan said.

'Yes,' Sean said. 'Civil war.'

Chapter Nine

1

'I'm goin' dancin',' wee Billy informed his Mum and Dad as he dabbed cologne on his scarred cheeks, where he stood in front of the mirror above the sink in the kitchen, stripped to the waist, but with his shirt and tie draped carefully over a hangar dangling from a hook on the wall behind him. Though he was twenty-four years old, everyone still called him 'wee' Billy because he was short and round, with a battered, cheerful, schoolboy's face that seemed to never age. He was also a bit of a dandy like his Dad and took care of his appearance, particularly when going out for the evening. 'Up in the Floral Hall. I still like to go up there 'cause it's a bit like travellin' and makes me feel I'm in another country.'

'Never mind that,' his Dad said from the armchair by the fireplace, wreathed in a cloud of smoke that did not come from the coal fire, which was out, but from the cigarette protruding from his lips even as he spoke. Albert was home for one of his long weekends and waiting impatiently to use the mirror when wee Billy was finished with it. After all these years, Albert was still working in Birkenhead and only coming home every six weeks. He and Mary both liked it that way, having their separate lives. 'I don't want to have to sit here for half the bloody evenin' while you're makin' yourself up like a nancy boy. The lads'll be waitin' for me in Sandy Row and getting' in their first jars already, so get a move-on, thanks.'

'Sure isn't it typical,' Mary said as she cleaned up the table in preparation for her spiritualist friends, 'that the two men of the house should go out every Saturday and leave the poor woman behind?'

'If you changed the evenin' for your spiritualist meetings,' Albert said, 'you could come too. You've been invited, but always refused, so you can't complain now.'

In fact, Albert was delighted that Mary had always refused as he preferred to be as free as a bachelor when out with the boyos.

'I have to have it on Saturday,' Mary said as she carried cups and saucers into the kitchen, brushing past Billy to place them beside the sink, 'because that's when most of my friends are off work and can make it more easily.'

'You and your batty friends,' Albert said, studying the smoke coming out of his cigarette as if it was ectoplasm. 'All fallin' for the bloody tricks of that oul bag of a so-called spirit-medium. Sure ya must be all eejuts!'

'The dead have spoken to us,' Mary insisted as she returned from the kitchen. 'We've received many a message through the tapping of this very table and one of those that spoke was my dearly departed brother.'

'Aye, I'll bet,' Albert said.

'Never mind your sarcasm,' Mary responded as she started picking up the used knives and forks. 'If we're wrong no harm comes of it. And it's better than going out every night and getting drunk like you do.'

'Sure I only get merry,' Albert insisted, 'and there's no harm in that. At least I'm talkin' to my fellow human beings, not the dead, ho, ho. I've still got my marbles, like.'

'All your *drunken* friends,' Mary corrected him, letting the knives and forks clatter noisily to emphasise her point. 'You're only home for four days every six weeks and you go out every single evening during that time. You could try staying home at least one evening just to see what it's like.'

'I *know* what it's like,' Albert retorted. 'Sure I remember it well. Listenin' to some malarkey on the radio and gradually fallin' asleep in front of the fire. Thanks, but no, thanks. Hey, you!' he added, addressing wee Billy, still in the kitchen. 'Are you nearly ready yet?'

'Aye, Dad, I'm finished.'

'Well, thank God for that.'

As Billy emerged from the kitchen, now wearing his pressed white shirt and tightening the knot in his tie, he found himself wondering how his Mum had the nerve to complain about his Dad going out to the pub at nights during his long weekends. While it was true that his Mum stayed in most nights, including Saturday, when Albert was home, Billy knew that she could have held the séances any night of the week, since her friends would be home from work by then. In truth, she only held the séances on Saturday evenings when Albert was home and did so because she would rather spend the evening with her friends than be obliged to go out with him. Billy also knew that while his Mum *did* tend to stay at home during Albert's long weekends here, she certainly went out to the pubs most nights of the week when he was working in England. Indeed it seemed to Billy that his Mum had started drinking a lot more when Johnny got into trouble and that she now drank as much, or almost as much, as his father did. Billy believed that what had happened to Johnny had seriously disturbed his mother, though she tried not to show it. He believed that what had happened to Johnny had damaged them all, including even his Dad, in some way or another. Certainly it had damaged him, though he, too, tried not to show it and laughed a lot to prevent himself from crying.

Life wasn't the same without Johnny.

'The kitchen's all yours,' Billy said as they brushed past each other in the living room.

'Aye, and about bloody time too,' Albert said without rancour. 'I just hope them girls think you're worth it.'

'They do,' Billy said.

Once in the kitchen, Albert started putting on his shirt and tie. Times were changing and he'd already had a bath in the bathroom built as an extension to the kitchen by the local council. Nevertheless, old habits died hard and he and Billy still liked to get dressed in front of the mirror in the kitchen, as they had done when they didn't have a bath. You could talk or listen to the radio in the living room while you did your business in front of the kitchen mirror. That's why they both liked it. Of course a few of their neighbours now had television sets as well as radios, but Albert had refused to let Mary buy one, saying that they still couldn't afford it. Given the price of cigarettes and booze, this was true enough.

Mary, who liked to listen to the news, which Albert detested, had just turned on the radio and a commentator was talking about US troop movements in Vietnam. You couldn't get away from Vietnam these days. Albert wished they would shut up about it, but they rarely did.

'It's disgusting,' Mary said. 'They should get them American troops out of there and let the Vietnamese people settle their own differences.'

'That's what the Fenians say about the Brits,' Billy reminded her.

'What?'

'That the Brits should get out of Northern Ireland and let us solve our own problems.'

'Sure if they did that,' Mary said, 'those Fenians would run all over us and we'd lose all our rights.' Though Mary was still on friendly terms with her Catholic neighbours, the Laverys and the Devlins, she was less liberal than she had been some years back. The Falls Road riots of 1964, only two years ago, had given her a fright and made her view the Catholics (neighbours excluded) in a different light. Now, when she discussed the Catholics in general (as distinct from her neighbours), she was inclined to bring up their propensity for trouble-making and violence. Certainly, despite Johnny's own protestations to the contrary, she had blamed the Catholics for what had happened to him in 1958, commencing that dreadful day in the Falls. The riots of 1964 had, however, made her even more fearful of Catholics and now, apart from her immediate neighbours, she wanted no truck with them. And even though she was still friendly with the Laverys and the Donovans, she didn't visit them nearly as much as she used to and tried to avoid them entirely during Protestant celebrations, such as the Twelfth of July.

'So who are you going to the dance with?' she asked.

'Dan Johnstone,' Billy said, removing his coat from the hangar behind the front door.

'What?' Albert said from the kitchen. 'You're not still runnin' around with him, are ya?'

'Aye, I am.'

'That Dan Johnstone's a head-case like his Dad.'

'He's all right now,' Billy said. 'Not as wild as he used to be. Sure I persuaded him to join the Orange Lodge and it's done him a power of good.'

'He's trouble, mark my words. *All* those Johnstones are trouble. His Dad, the big brute, has terrorised half this street and his son'll end up doin' the same.'

'He didn't terrorise half of this street,' Mary insisted. 'He only terrorised you. He threatened to knock your teeth out if you ever passed his house again, so for the next couple of months you walked to work in the opposite direction. Sure you'd still be doing that if you weren't workin' across the water - '

'No, I wouldn't!'

' - and I note that even during your long weekends back here, you still walk all the way around the block rather than pass his house. So he certainly terrorised you - and still does.'

'Not too many around here,' Albert said in desperation, 'can boast of still havin' their own teeth - and in good nick, as well. So I don't intend risking mine over a trivial matter that took place about fifteen years ago.'

'What matter?' Billy said. 'We've all known for years about his threat, but you never said why he threatened you.'

'It was all Dan's fault. That big eejut you call a friend. Sure the both of you were trouble-makers for as long as I can remember, but he was even worse than you. And every time someone got angry over somethin' he'd done - threw a brick through someone's window; beat up someone's kid; pinched things from shops - you name it, he did it - so every time he did somethin' like that and someone clipped his ear for it, he'd run home and tell his Dad about it. Then that mad bastard would tear out of his house and knock on the neighbour's door and give the man of the house – he'd never touch a woman, like - a bloody good hidin'. So don't tell me he didn't terrorise the street, 'cause he did and you know it.'

'Years back,' Mary said.

'So what about you?' Billy asked, now standing with his jacket on, preparing to leave, but waiting to hear the rest of the story, holding his grin in check.

'That eejut friend of yours again,' Albert said. 'Sure him and you pinched wee Jackie Wilson's scooter and then clambered over the railway wall behind those houses across the street and laid the scooter on the track in the hope that the passenger train, which was due, would be derailed by it. Luckily, Jackie came runnin' to tell me what you were up to and I tore like hell down to the railway track and found you two eejuts just sittin' there on the wall with big grins on your faces, waitin' for the spectacle to begin. So I clambered over the wall and removed the scooter from the tracks just before the express train came roaring through. Then I gave you a good clip around the ear and turned around to do the same to Dan. He responded to me as he did to everyone - said that if I laid a hand on him, he'd tell his Dad and then his Dad would give me a good hidin'. So that angered me all the more and I said his fuckin' Dad couldn't beat his way out of a paper bag - and then I gave him a couple of good belts on the head and sent the wee bastard home howlin'. Next thing I know that mad dog, his Dad, is slavering at the mouth at our front door, demandin' that I step outside and take my medicine.'

'Which your Dad couldn't do,' Mary explained, 'because he was on his way out of the house through the back yard door and he didn't return until midnight, under cover of darkness.'

'Very funny!' Albert said.

'But true!' Mary retorted.

'Well, what would *you* have done?' Albert asked, as he emerged from the kitchen, also tightening the knot in his flashy polka-dot tie. 'Would *you* have gone out to fight him?'

Billy grinned. 'No.'

'I mean, Jesus Christ, that man had fists like hams and the devil's own temper. His foamed like a mad dog! So I took myself down to the pub – '

'By the back door,' Mary reminded him.

' - and stayed there until they closed up, then came back here and tucked myself into bed. Would *you* have gone past that mad bastard's house?'

'No,' Billy lied, though he knew that he would have, even if it meant getting a good hiding.

'I was in showbiz, right? I mean, I was playin' the music halls even then. So I couldn't afford to have my looks altered just because of that eejut. I did the sensible thing, right?'

'Right,' Billy said.

Mary rolled her eyes, distractedly patted down her hair, still as black as ink at forty-five years old, then she lit a cigarette, had a drag and blew smoke to the room. 'You look like a million dollars,' she told

Billy, lying through her teeth, because they both knew that he would never look that way as long as he lived. He was short and rotund and cheerful, but no more than that. The girls, however, liked him because he could make them laugh and that bought him a few little favours up the back alleys. It was hard to find somewhere to bed down around here because most of the girls lived with their parents and the houses were too small to offer privacy. Though Billy had fooled around with a lot of girls, necking and groping desperately, he was still a virgin at twenty-two. So were most of his friends, though they would never admit to it.

'Fancy me, do you?' Billy asked his mother with a cheeky grin.

'You're the ant's pants,' she said. 'Are you going to call in and see Marlene on your way there?'

'Aye, I might as well. She might let Ronnie come out for a spin if I promise not to let him run off with another woman. Ronnie likes to dance, doesn't he?'

'Aye, I know he does and Marlene doesn't, though it amazes me that she lets him do that - go to dances with you single men. That wouldn't have been done in my day, I can tell you that much.'

'She trusts him,' Billie said, 'and she's happy enough to stay home and look after the kids. I mean, remember when they were just runnin' around together, before they got married? She let him go to dances on his own even then. I mean, she knows he's not the kind to fool around. He just likes to dance.'

'Let's hope so,' Mary said.

Ronnie and Marlene had married in 1961 and now they had two children, Steven and Jill. Ronnie had fancied Marlene from the first time he saw her, when he visited the house to rehearse in the skiffle group with Johnny, but it had taken him well over a year to work up the courage to ask her out. Given her studied indifference to him, he had been surprised when she said, 'Why not?' and even more surprised when, a few months later, he had proposed and she had accepted him. Once married, they had moved into their own house, located five minutes from here, just off the avenue. Now, with her and Johnny both gone and Albert working overseas, Billy shared the house with only his Mum and it still felt strange to him. He really missed Johnny.

'Well, I'm off,' he said, glancing down to check that his jacket was immaculate. 'I'll see youse both later.'

'Aye, right,' his Dad said.

'Don't get into any mischief,' his Mum said.

'I won't,' Billy promised.

Leaving the house, he stepped into lamplit darkness, turned left at the garden gate, and headed for the arches, just as Teddy Lavery was coming up the street to enter his own house, three doors down. Seeing him, Teddy smiled broadly and stopped by his gate. Though now in his middle thirties, Teddy still had his shock of red hair, the look of a mischievous schoolboy, and a big, easy grin.

'So how are you, Billy-boy?' he asked.

'Ack, not bad,' Billy replied, stopping, feeling faintly embarrassed. He and Teddy weren't as relaxed with each other as they used to be. Part of this was due to the fact that Billy was in the Orange Lodge, something that even someone as easy-going as Teddy could not ignore, particularly since Billy was a Paisleyite and the Big Man was becoming increasingly well known for his passionate hatred of Catholics. Another part of it was due to the Falls riots of a couple of years back, which had brought to the surface the fundamental differences between Catholics and Protestants. Finally, throughout the early months of this year there had been a number of petrol-bomb attacks on Catholic shops, homes and schools in Belfast, with two or three Catholics killed. So a little distance had sprung up between Billy and Teddy; certainly enough to make them feel uncomfortable in each other's presence. Of course, Teddy had always been Johnny's special friend, not Billy's, but Billy still felt a little odd at how distant he and Teddy had become to each other these past few years. 'So how are things with you, Teddy?'

'Okay, like. You know me, Billy-boy. Easy come, easy go. I'm workin' in a bakery these days and it's a dead easy number.'

Teddy was certainly easy come, easy go. He had left the Royal Navy about ten years ago and drifted through a succession of different jobs, none of them skilled. Then he had caused a scandal by taking up with Beryl Adams, one of his mother's closest friends, twice Teddy's age, married and, even worse, a Protestant. Defying the scandal, Teddy had moved in with Beryl *and* her husband, Lawrence, who lived farther along the avenue, at the other side of the arches, until eventually, after a few months of this *menage a trois*, Lawrence had moved out. Now Teddy lived permanently with Beryl and only dropped in to see his parents about once a week, though never with Beryl, because Bernadette was no longer speaking to her. Even now, though Teddy and Beryl had been living together for five years or so, people still whispered about them.

'You heard from Johnny lately?' Teddy asked.

'Aye, he writes the odd letter. He's sailin' all over the place - just like you did when you were in the Navy.'

Teddy nodded. 'Sure he always loved it when I told him about my travels - he said he wanted to do the same - so I wasn't surprised to hear that he'd gone to sea after his wee bit of bother here. I'm just surprised he hasn't come back, even for a visit, in all these years. Can't stand the thought, I suppose, after what was done to him.'

It still seemed to Billy that Johnny's 'wee bit of bother' had taken place just a few days ago, though it had actually been about eight years ago. They had taken Johnny away and incarcerated him in a Borstal: a boy's home. While in there, he had changed out of all recognition, and eventually, when he got out, he simply slipped away from them, from his family, from Belfast, without saying where he was going. Finally, after a few weeks, the first of his occasional letters had arrived, informing them that he had joined the merchant navy and detailing his travels around the world. He had not come home in all that time and his letters were few. In truth, he was no more than a memory now.

'Anyway,' Billy said, not wanting to talk about his brother and still feeling uncomfortable with Teddy, 'I've got to be makin' tracks.'

'Sure you're dressed up to the nines,' Teddy observed. 'Where are you headin'?'

'Dancin'. Up in the Floral Hall.'

'Jesus,' Teddy said, 'I haven't been there in years! Sure those days are well behind me now. Well, you have a good time, kid.'

'Thanks,' Billy said.

As Teddy walked up the garden path to ring the doorbell of his former home, Billy continued along the windblown, lamplit street to meet his dangerous friend, Dan Johnstone.

2

'Right, well I'll be off as well, then,' Albert said as soon as wee Billy had left. 'Can't keep my fans waiting, like.'

Mary rolled her eyes. 'Fans, are they?' she retorted. 'That bunch of boozers down in Sandy Row. The only thing that makes you interesting to them is your eagerness to set them up with drinks. The instant you stop being so generous, they'll melt back into the walls. You were always a soft touch that way, Albert. A real fool with your money. Buying compliments to satisfy your ego. Do they tell you how grand you were on TV? Is that why you do it?'

'Now, now,' Albert responded, checking himself in the mirror, adjusting the knot on his flashy tie, doing anything except look directly at Mary, 'stop pickin' on me. Just give me some peace. We only have to see each other every six weeks - four days every six weeks - and we can surely be civilised with each other at least for that short time. No need to cast dispersions on my friends or on my wee bit of fame. There's some who'd be proud of me.'

'Proud of you? What for? For making an eejut of yourself in front of the whole of England and Ireland? Sure it makes me blush with shame just to think of it.'

'Always quick with the compliments, Mary. I'll give you that much.'

Albert flipped a cigarette into his mouth, lit it, blew smoke rings and watched them disappearing. Mary knew that he wanted to disappear like the smoke rings, but she wasn't about to let him escape that easily. Though her every instinct told her to be quiet, she just had to fly at him, making him pay for his neglect, for his lifetime's betrayal.

'Why did you marry me?' she asked him.

'What?'

'Why did you marry me?'

'Because I got you pregnant, as I remember. Did I do the wrong thing?'

'It wasn't me you wanted, was it?'

'Sure you knew that all along. You knew that the first night we were together - and you knew exactly what you were doin'.'

'I seduced you?'

'You could say that.'

'I wanted you.'

'No, you didn't. You just didn't want her to have me. You didn't want me until you knew that she did, then you just *had* to have me. That's the difference, isn't it?'

'I've tried not to hate you.'

'You always thought you were above me. You, from the upper Malone Road; me from the Newtownards Road. That's why you resent my bit of fame. It's not that you're embarrassed or ashamed of me at all. It's that it's put your toffee-nose out of joint, makin' you realise that the upper Malone Road isn't the beginnin' and end of the world. But your sister got what you wanted, a middle-class life with a boring civil servant, while you were dragged down to my level - or, at least, so you seem to think. That's all there is to it and it's so banal it's pitiful, not worth the loss of a good night's sleep or a single angry word. Now I'm goin' out to get drunk with my working-class mates and maybe sing a song and act the clown. I'll make a fool of myself and do it gladly. As for you, you're more than welcome to your spiritualist friends and your mad search for a wee bit of crack with your long dead brother. I won't come back till they're gone.'

Albert walked to the front door.

'I've spoken to him,' Mary said behind his back, 'and he's spoken to me. It's not my imagination. When the table rocks, it tells me things that only he could have known, so I know it isn't a trick. It's my dead brother, Neil. He still loves me and he's reaching out to me. He talks to me from the Other Side and gives me what you never did.'

'What's that?'

'Love.'

Albert sighed. 'Well, let's hope so. Now I have to be makin' tracks.'

'Enjoy yourself.'

'I'll sure try.'

When Albert left the house, closing the door behind him, Mary sighed with relief. Staring at the closed door, at Albert's imagined back, she was torn between her contempt for him and the unspeakable pain of her loss: his enduring love for someone else.

'After all these years,' she said aloud, speaking to the empty room. 'And there it is, still eating at him. Sure who'd have believed it?'

Glancing at the clock on the mantelpiece, she saw that it was still early: the first of her guests would not turn up for another half hour or so. Feeling the desperate need for human contact, even the love of the departed, her dead brother, her missing son, she sighed and poured herself a sherry, then lit a cigarette and took a chair in front of the fireplace to think things through.

Smoking and drinking, she thought back on what she and Albert had said to each other, wondering how much truth there was to it. Enough to hurt. Enough to cut her and make her bleed. She had always known he didn't love her, that he loved someone else, and she had seduced him for that very reason, becoming pregnant by him. That first child, also called Johnny, had died shortly after birth, a cot death, inexplicable, forever tormenting, perhaps as her punishment for what she had done, the high cost of her ruthless duplicity. She loathed Albert for that as well: all the bad luck that he'd brought her, including the death of her first child, the first Johnny, and then, even worse, the loss of her second son, Johnny, all those years ago. She blamed Albert for that as well.

What had happened to Johnny would never have occurred if Albert hadn't taken him to the Custom House steps and let him get swept away in that unruly mob. Albert, of course, had kept well out of it, cleverly heading off in the opposite direction, even as his two sons, both impressionable adolescents, were being infected by the violent excitement of the crowd and carried on a wave of sectarian madness all the way to the Falls Road. There, during the ensuing riot between Protestants and Catholics, Johnny had been picked up by the police, charged with bodily assault, and sentenced to three years in a Borstal. That it had happened to him, of all people (Johnny, the quiet one; not wee Billy, the wild one), had struck everyone who knew him as unbelievable. Even now, all these years later, Mary could scarcely credit it.

Inhaling deeply on her cigarette, exhaling slowly, distractedly watching the smoke spiralling away like ectoplasm, she thought of the forthcoming séance, of all the séances that she'd held here, and realised that her need to make contact with her dead brother was all mixed up with her feelings of loss over Johnny. She was convinced, however, that she *was* in touch with Neil, her only, beloved brother, and that when he spoke to her, either by rocking the table or, more dramatically, by speaking eerily through the mouth of the spirit-medium in the trance state, he was trying to soothe the pain she had suffered over losing Johnny, first to the Borstal, then to his new life at sea. Strangely enough, though Johnny had doubtless been influenced by Teddy Lavery's tales of his travels with the Royal Navy, he was also doing what Neil had done when still a young man. Neil, too, had been in the Royal Navy, even though he had ended up as a deserter, spending the rest of his life on the run. Mary thought it strange that though Neil and wee Billy had been so much alike (both adventurous and prone to trouble) it was Johnny, the quiet one, the private one, who had followed in Neil's footsteps. Life was unpredictable.

'Just like Johnny,' Mary now said aloud. 'As unpredictable as life itself.'

The Borstal had changed him, done something to him, though she had never quite worked out the exact nature of that change, nor managed to get him to talk about it. Looking back on those early days, through the mist of the passing years, almost a decade, she recalled how shocked she had been when the sentence was pronounced in juvenile court, how she had screamed out in disbelief, sobbed piteously, protesting, and had to be virtually helped from the building. She recalled, too, the deathly whiteness of Johnny's face when he heard the sentence pronounced, the helpless flickering of his eyes as he fought to hide his emotions, his disbelief and fear; and how, as he was led away by an RUC officer, he had simply glanced in her direction and then waved his index finger from side to side, clearly telling her not to be concerned. She *was* concerned of course. She was deeply, mortally wounded. He was being imprisoned for three years, the most important years of his life, and would not emerge until he was twenty, too late to get an apprenticeship or pick up a trade.

Mary recalled the pain of it, the initially lacerating and eventually numbing shock. Even more vividly, she recalled her first visit to the Borstal and the shock she had felt when she saw the change in him. There were no marks on him, no signs of brutality, yet he was definitely not the same, seemed imprisoned within himself, with a guarded look about the eyes that not even the love she tried to show him could clear away. He was closed off, encased in protective ice, revealing nothing, denying that he had been in any way mistreated, but hiding something for all that. Gradually, as their awkward conversation continued, Mary realised that he had spent the whole time avoiding her gaze. He wasn't looking at her but though her, beyond her, at some space far away. She knew then, with a ruinous grief, that she had lost him for good. He was not the boy she had known. He had matured overnight.

The Johnny she knew never returned to her. The Johnny she had visited regularly for nearly three years was always courteous, softly spoken, seemingly appreciative of the visits, but remained somehow distant, closed up, revealing little of what his life in the Borstal was like, what friends or enemies he had made, what his feelings about the past and future were. He smiled at her, sometimes patting the back of her hand where it rested on the table between them, but his gaze was constantly, furtively shifting, never meeting her eyes. He was like that with Albert, Marlene and Billy when they, too, went to see him.

'He's not the same,' Marlene said one day, after they had all been to visit. 'He is, but he isn't. I don't know what it is, but he's different. They've done something to him.'

'Sure you're just imagining that,' Billy said.

'No, she's not,' Albert said. 'Something's happened to him. He's not the same boy he used to be. He's not the Johnny we knew.'

Gradually, as one year slipped into the next, Mary sensed the hardening in him, a maturity beyond his years, even a coldness that was not quite concealed by the superficial warmth of his smile.

Then he disappeared.

He had been released three months early for good behaviour, but hadn't told them that his release was imminent. Mary didn't know about it until she went to the Borstal to visit him and was told by a puzzled receptionist that he'd been released a few days before. When Mary returned home, not knowing what to expect, he wasn't there and had still not made contact, not even through the mail. He had simply vanished.

The days ran into weeks and the whole time was a nightmare because no one knew where Johnny was, and Mary, with her vivid imagination, began thinking that he might have killed himself. Eventually, out of the blue, a letter arrived from Liverpool, England, letting them know where he was and what he was doing. If anything, that letter was more shocking than his few weeks of silence.

Mary inhaled on the butt of her cigarette, exhaled the smoke with a sigh, then stood up, threw the butt into the cold grate and pulled a small tin off the mantelpiece. Taking the chair again, she rested the tin on her lap, opened it and withdrew a small pile of envelopes held together by a rubber band. After removing the rubber band, she tugged the first letter out of its envelope, unfolded it and held it in both hands, staring down at it. She virtually knew it by heart, but she wanted to read it anyway, to see Johnny's handwriting, his immaculate spelling and surprisingly good grammar. Her eyes misted over with tears as she read...

20th November, 1961.

Dear Mum and Dad and Billy and Marlene,

I hardly know where to begin. I suppose I should start by apologising for not telling you that I was getting out of the home a few months early and for taking so long in letting you know where I am, but I just couldn't do anything about any of it until today, though I don't really know why. I only know that I couldn't do it, that I had to slip away quietly and be on my own for a while, to think things through, to work out my future, and I knew that I couldn't do that if I stayed around to see you, went home, regained all I'd lost three years ago, so I thought it best to just move on immediately, turning my back completely on the past in order to map out my future. That may not be very clear to you, but it's the only way I can explain what I did and what I'm doing right now.

I'm not ready yet to go back where I came from, to face the friends I used to know, to answer questions about what went on in that Borstal, or to apologise for having been there in the first place. I'm not ready yet to be treated as a criminal for an impetuous action taken three years ago, or to be forgiven for sins I never committed. I'm not ready yet to take any rotten job I can find because my three years in a Borstal will ensure that I won't be offered much.

There are other reasons, as well, for my not wanting to return to my old life in Belfast.

Dennis Burton

I'm not who I used to be. I'm not the boy you used to know. I can't say too much about this, because it's not clear in my head, but I certainly know that I've changed and feel removed from what once seemed natural to me. By this I mean that I wouldn't be comfortable at home any longer, wouldn't fit in, would feel caged even more than I felt caged in the Borstal, would hurt you all by seeming a stranger to you, which is not what you need. This has nothing to do with you, only me, but it's real, I can feel it in my bones, and it has to be faced.

In other words, I don't feel that I belong there any more. Maybe I've learnt things that would be better not known, seen things that I'd rather forget, done things that can't be undone and will mark me forever. My three years in that Borstal were a lifetime that made me unrecognisable to myself. I'm not sure that I like what I've become, but at least I've come to accept it.

I've also thought about what happened that day in the Falls Road and I now realise that I have a violent nature that was merely suppressed up to that moment. I've shown that violence before - once in Finaghy Field when I almost brained Dan Johnstone; then in Mackie's factory when I attacked another apprentice - and after what happened in the Falls, what I did personally, I finally accepted that it's part of my nature. I'm not sure I can control it. I'm not sure that I want to. I only know that it ruled me during my years in the Borstal in ways that I would rather not describe. So I didn't want to take that back home with me, bring it into the house, into your lives, and that, also, is why I left the Borstal quietly, without seeing anyone.

I'm here in Liverpool now, leaving Belfast behind me. When I was discharged from the Borstal, they gave me some money, enough to last me for a month, and told me to sign on the dole. I didn't. Instead, I used the money to buy a ticket on the first night ferry to Liverpool and signed on the dole here the following day. They gave me enough of an advance allowance to pay for cheap accommodation and I rented a room in a family house in Toxteth, then got myself a job in the Queen's Dock, not far from where I live.

I'm staying with Mr. and Mrs. Enright, both in their late thirties and with two teenage children. The eldest son, they told me, is nineteen and left home to find work in London, so it's his room I'm renting. They're English. I didn't want to move into another Irish community. Mr. Enright works for an insurance company located near the Liver

Building and Mrs. Enright works as a cleaning lady on the Liverpool-Birkenhead ferries. They're both decent, kindly people and their teenage kids, Peter and Anne, are just as nice. They never ask me any personal questions and I feel comfortable here. I have my own room, but I share the toilet and bathroom and have the run of the kitchen. It's a pretty nice set-up.

As for work, right now I'm working in the docks as a labourer, helping to load dry cargo onto the container ships, but my ultimate aim is to use the friends I'm gradually making here, friends who don't ask questions and can pull a string or two, to get myself a seaman's ticket and go to sea. I want to spend the foreseeable future aboard ship, travelling the world like Teddy did, like Uncle Neil did, far removed from normal society, cocooned in my own world. I want to forget Belfast, the Borstal, the endless conflicts between the Prods and the Catholics, the small-mindedness that leads to the kind of riots that landed me in that boy's home for three years. I want to forget that I was ever a child and become my own man. I want to do that at sea and I hope to be gone soon.

I'll write when I can, but it may not be that often. I don't like to see my own thoughts on paper, so I can't always write. Don't worry if you don't hear from me. I can look after myself. I'm sorry if I've caused you any pain, but some things can't be helped.

Look after yourselves. Keep wee Billy out of trouble. Give Marlene a hug for me.

Love,
Johnny.

Mary wiped tears from her eyes with the back of her hand, then refolded the letter neatly, meticulously, and slipped it back into its tattered envelope. Checking the clock on the mantelpiece, she saw that she had another fifteen minutes before the first of her guests were due to arrive. Though realising that the reading of Johnny's letter had caused her pain, reminding her of everything she had tried to suppress, particularly his references to 'things that would be better not known' and 'things that I'd rather forget' (making her wonder, yet again, just what had gone on in that boy's home to change him so much), she could not resist opening another one.

Again, she opened it with extreme care, as if handling an ancient parchment, then held the pages out between both hands to intently study them. She read the words of the child that she had carried in her womb, nurtured in his early years, protected from a distance, loved hopelessly, completely, much more than she had loved the others, because he was the resurrected one, her first son, the dead Johnny magically reborn. But she failed to recognise him in these words, which were the words of a stranger.

She read the words of that stranger.

3

Billy always met Dan Johnstone under the arch that ran over the avenue, rather than calling on him at home, because Dan was sensitive about being humiliated by his mad Dad in front of his friends and self-conscious about his oppressed mother's visible fear of her husband and understandable reticence with visitors. In fact, in all his years of knowing Dan, Billy had only been in the house twice and both times the experience had been singularly uncomfortable because Dan's huge Dad, Barney, had simply glared at him and demanded to know where he and Dan were going (clearly not believing what his son had told him) while his Mum had sat mute by the fireplace, knitting and keeping her gaze on the floor until both boys had left. So now Billy and Dan always met under the arch.

Dan's house was near the end of the terrace, almost directly facing the home of Johnny's old sweetheart, Donna King. As Billy walked past Dan's house, he glanced across the road to Donna's place, recalled how Johnny had managed to leave without even bidding her goodbye. He wondered what Johnny would think if he knew that Donna had married and then moved to a new place in Dundonald. Donna and Johnny had been mad for each other and the former had wept for days when the latter was sent to a boy's home after being caught up in those riots; but she never saw him again because when he came out of the Borstal, where clearly bad things had happened to him, he virtually disappeared off the face of the earth and was not heard from again until his first letter arrived from Liverpool, He hadn't mentioned Donna in that letter at all or in subsequent letters, and she, deeply wounded, had married the first man who proposed to her. Now, like Marlene, she had a couple of kids. Time stood still for no one.

Dan was, indeed, waiting there for him, about halfway along the wall of the arch, keeping out of the wind and smoking a cigarette. He was a big lad now, almost as tall as his Dad, though not nearly as broad, and like Billy he was wearing his best suit, with shirt and tie and well polished black shoes. His hair was as black as his shoes and slicked down over wild eyes and a crooked, slightly deranged grin. He'd received an awful lot of beatings from Barney and it had done something to him.

'So you've come,' he said by way of greeting, flicking his spent cigarette to the ground and grinding the heel of his shoe onto it.

'Aye,' Billy responded. 'Let's drop in and see Ronnie on our way. Marlene might let him come with us. She sometimes likes to get rid of him.'

'Okay by me, Billy-boy. The three musketeers, like.'

'Right,' Billy said.

They walked side by side along the avenue. As they were approaching the Broadway, Dan nudged Billy and nodded at a terraced house across the road.

'That's where Teddy Lavery lives with that married woman,' he said with a wink and a crooked grin. 'Sure you've got to hand it to him: he's got a brass neck, right enough. It must've been all those years he spent at sea with a different girl in every port and all of 'em, bein' foreign, havin' different morals than us. You think Johnny's doin' the same kind of thing?'

'Maybe. Who knows?'

'Any sign of him ever comin' back?'

'Not so far,' Billy said.

'How long's he been gone now?'

'About eight years, includin' the Borstal.'

Dan pursed his lips to mime a whistle of disbelief. 'Jesus!' he said. 'You can't imagine it, can you? I mean who'd have thought he'd just take off like that and never return. You think he was ashamed of bein' in the home?'

'No,' Billy said. 'I think it was somethin' else, but I don't know what it was. No one does. It's a real mystery, like.'

'Aye, it is, right enough. A real mystery.'

They turned into the Broadway, which ran as straight as an arrow between the gable ends of street after street, many of them decorated with huge Loyalist paintings: King William crossing the Boyne, and so on. This was a strongly Loyalist area. Dan nudged Billy again as they passed the first street. 'Isn't that where your granny lives?' he asked.

'Aye,' Billy said, 'it is. A bit too close for comfort for Marlene's liking.'

'Well, I can understand that. That granny of yours is fuckin' mad. Always cursin' people out in the street. Mad and as tough as nails, I hear. Does she give Marlene problems?'

'A few,' Billy said. 'Bein' so close, she drops in a lot to see Marlene's kids and, of course, to lecture Marlene on how to rear them. That drives Marlene crazy.'

'And Ronnie, too, I'd reckon.'

'No, not Ronnie. You know Ronnie: as easy-goin' as they come. Doesn't give a damn about anything, except drinkin', backin' the horses and collectin' Little Richard records. Nothin' else gets through to him. Granny Doreen can yak on all she likes, drivin' Marlene crazy, but for Ronnie it's in one ear and out the other. He just smiles and agrees with anything she says. He doesn't give a fuck, like.'

They passed a row of small shops, including a busy fish and chip shop and, right beside it, an old-fashioned sweet shop, its illuminated window beaming into the evening's darkness, containing a colourful, if inelegant, display of glass jars and bowls containing Liquorice Allsorts, Dolly Mixtures, Brandy Balls, Gum Boils, chocolate caramels, sticks of pink or striped rock, and a wide variety of chocolate bars.

'Wait a minute,' Billy said. 'I just wanna pop in here and pick up a couple of bags of sweets for Marlene's kids. That should sweeten Marlene up,' he added, in case Dan thought he was a softie for the kids, which he certainly was, 'when we ask her if Ronnie can come out with us.'

'Good thinkin',' Dan said.

While Dan waited impatiently outside, too embarrassed, at his age, to even enter such a shop, Billy darted in, waited patiently in the queue of women and children, and eventually purchased two 'quarters' of Dolly Mixtures, which came in cones of newspaper and were soft enough not to damage the kids' teeth. Holding a cone in each hand, he left the shop and then continued on along the Broadway with Dan, eventually turning into a side street and stopping at one of the terraced houses. When Billy hammered the brass knocker on the door, Ronnie came to open it. Though wearing only a pair of wrinkled pants and an open-necked shirt under a pullover, he was still the most handsome of the old gang. He grinned when he saw them.

'How ya doin'?' Billy asked rhetorically, grinning back. 'We're just on our way to the Floral Hall, so thought we'd drop in an' say hello.'

'Ack, that's great,' Ronnie responded, stepping aside to let them enter. 'Sure we're always glad to see ya. Come on in, the pair of ya.'

Entering the small two-up, two-down house, they found Marlene sitting in front of the television, watching the local news in the expectation that something better was following. She had her two children beside her on the sofa, both babbling happily. Steven, at four, was already handsome, with his father's thick, brown hair and melting brown eyes; Jill, a year younger, looked almost identical. Both children were clearly well looked after and smiled readily, easily.

'How ya doin', Marlene?' Billy asked.

Marlene glanced up from the sofa and threw him a quick smile. 'Ack, I'm grand,' she said, then automatically looked back at the TV.

'And how's my wee darlin's?' Billy said, tickling each child in turn under the armpits, making both of them wriggle and giggle. 'Here, I've brought something for you,' he added, giving each a bag of Dolly Mixtures.

'Not sweets again,' Marlene said, though she was obviously pleased. 'Sure you'll spoil them both rotten.'

'Kids like this are made to be spoilt. Aren't you, kids?'

'Aye,' Steven said.

Jill nodded and beamed.

Billy tickled them again and they both giggled, spilling some of their sweets. When they had calmed down, he helped them pick up the sweets they'd lost and put them back into the relevant paper cone. This done, he gave each of them a kiss on the cheek. They smiled at him and then started stuffing their faces, mouths working, cheeks bulging. Billy always got on with kids. In fact, he got on with everyone.

'There's the Reverend,' Marlene said reverentially

Glancing at the television set, Billy saw that Marlene's hero, the Reverend Ian Paisley, was hotly denying to a BBC journalist that he was in any way, shape or form involved with the Ulster Volunteer Force, which had claimed responsibility for the recent killing of a number of Catholics. Not caving in to Paisley's outraged, histrionic denials, the journalist insisted upon reminding him that the UVF, set up earlier in the year, was known to have been organised throughout the province by Noel Doherty, a member of the B-Specials who had also set up the presses for Paisley's fanatically anti-Catholic, anti-communist newspaper, the *Protestant Telegraph*, launched at roughly the same time. Doherty, the journalist reminded Paisley, was also the secretary of Paisley's Ulster Constitution Defence Committee. Yet despite being faced with these facts, the Big Man continued to melodramatically deny any involvement with the UVF.

'Despite the fact that the IRA campaign collapsed in 1962,' the BBC journalist was now saying straight to camera, briefly cutting Paisley out of the picture, 'and Republicans concentrated, instead, on non-violent forms of protest, that UVF promise was kept, in the early months of 1966, with a series of petrol-bomb attacks on Catholic shops, homes and even schools, as well as the deliberate murder of Catholics. The first victim, John Scullion, was shot and wounded in Clonard Street, off the Falls Road, and died a couple of weeks later. Next, a group of off-duty Catholic barmen from the International Hotel were ambushed as they left a pub, where they were having a drink. One of them, Peter Ward, later died of his wounds. Subsequently, three men were arrested and charged with the murder of Ward. One of those men, Gusty Spence, was a brother of the Unionist election agent for West Belfast and former activist for the Reverend Paisley's Ulster Protestant Action.' The TV journalist turned his head to look accusingly at Paisley, who was still off-screen. 'So what do you say to that, Reverend Paisley?'

With the camera back on him again, the good Reverend, eyes bulging, voice thundering, again hotly denied any personal involvement with the UVF.

'But is it not true,' the journalist asked in response, 'that Spence was an active member of your Ulster Protestant Action Group? That you publicly thanked the UVF for taking part in a march on the seventeenth of April? That you did, furthermore, refer to the UVF again on the sixteenth of June? And finally, as we have already said, that Noel Doherty, a leading member of the UVF, is also the secretary of your Ulster Constitution Defence Committee?'

Ignoring Paisley's angry retorts to his accuser, Marlene leaned forward to turn the volume on the TV down, then said, clearly outraged, 'Now isn't that typical? A few Fenians get shot by one of them unofficial Protestant groups and they immediately try to pin it on Reverend Paisley. They couldn't stoop any lower if they tried.'

'Well,' Ronnie said tentatively, always mindful of the fact that his wife had, over the past few years, developed an explosive temper, 'Paisley *was* friends with – '

'Oh, Jesus, just listen to him!' Marlene exploded. 'Now he's doin' what those English bastards always do on TV: condemning a famous man - a preacher; *a man of God* - just because he happens to meet a lot of people on a daily basis and can't be knowin' what all of them are up to. And remember this, smarty-pants,' she added, glaring red-faced at her husband, 'the Reverend Paisley dismissed Doherty from the UPV and the UCDC, so he's no connection with him at all these days. Just chew on *that* for a minute!'

'Pure luck,' Dan Johnstone said, grinning in that crazy way he had. 'According to my Dad - who doesn't take sides; hatin' everyone, like - the only reason Paisley dismissed Doherty from his organisations was because those killings of Fenians were getting the Loyalists a bad name and harmin' the industrial drive.'

Though Dan was in the Orange Lodge, he had no real interest in politics per se and wouldn't normally know a thing about 'the industrial drive' or anything else; so clearly he *was* parroting exactly what his father had told him.

'Also, it's well known,' Dan continued while Billy rolled his eyes at the grinning Ronnie, 'that Doherty and his mates visited Loughhall to obtain arms and explosives from the local UPV organisation for use against the IRA. In fact, Paisley drove Doherty there and picked him up later, though he wasn't personally present at the talks. So when Paisley learnt that the RUC knew about Doherty's visit to Loughhall, he dropped his old friend like a hot spud. Doherty and his mates were then picked up in an RUC round-up. But Paisley, having already dumped him, was able to hold up his big hands and show that they were clean.'

'Aye, he's right clever that way,' Ronnie foolishly said.

Marlene rounded on him. 'How can you say such a thing? How do you know it's true? Read it in some Fenian newspaper, I suppose! Or one of them English papers that are usin' propaganda to encourage the Brits to wash their hands of the Orange State. So what do *you* know about politics, you big eejit? About the only thing that's ever stuck in your brain are those Little Richard songs. Them songs with really brilliant lyrics like "AwopBopalLooBopAwopBamBoom". Jesus, but you make my blood boil!'

'Alright, alright!' Billy said, grinning and spreading his hands in the air as if pleading for clemency. 'Let's call a halt to this. We just dropped in 'cause we're goin' up to the Floral Hall and we thought you might let Ronnie come with us.'

'Oh? And why should I?' Marlene was still outraged.

'Because he likes to dance and you don't.'

'You mean he likes to feel the fannies of all them girls he cuddles up to on the dance-floor.'

'Ack, come on now,' Billy said, sensing that Marlene was softening already, being soft on Ronnie except when he drank and gambled too much. 'Sure you know he's not the kind to chase the girls. It's just the dancin' he likes.'

'And the odd drop of whiskey,' Dan added.

'The odd drop or two,' Marlene emphasised, though already breaking out in a smile. 'Just make sure you don't bring him back drunk.'

'They don't sell liquor in the Floral Hall,' Billy reminded her. 'Only soft drinks.'

'That won't be stopping him,' Marlene said, nodding in Ronnie's direction. 'If he wants it, he'll find it.'

'You mean I can go?' Ronnie asked.

'Aye, you can go. Sure what woman, apart from an eejut like me, would want to run away with the likes of you?'

Ronnie threw his mates a big grin. 'I'll be down in a minute,' he said, then hurried up the stairs to put on some decent clothes.

Marlene rolled her eyes and turned back to the TV set, automatically sliding her arms around the two children. The news was coming to an end with a summary of recent events that supposedly had a bearing, either directly or indirectly, on the politics of Belfast: a

Labour government sympathetic to the Civil Rights Movement in the province being re-elected in Britain; former Irish Labour party member, Gerry Fitt, being elected MP for West Belfast; and the U.S. civil rights march from Selma to Montgomery in Alabama, to which the growing 'freedom movement' in Belfast was being compared. All of those events, the narrator was saying over news footage of the Alabama march, were indications that social injustices in Northern Ireland - injustices against the Catholic community - were being more widely recognised.

'What a cheek!' Marlene exclaimed as she watched the Alabama footage being replaced by footage covering the Reverend Ian Paisley's activities during the first six months of the year. 'Injustices against the Catholics, indeed! And what about the injustices against us? Sure the Catholics just have to make a complaint to get another concession. Every time they give something more to the Fenians, they take it from us. Sure it's a damned disgrace!'

The footage was now showing a montage of the Reverend Ian Paisley's more recent activities: Paisley forcing the government to mobilise B-Specials for a month and ban trains from the south from coming into Northern Ireland to commemorate the 50th anniversary of the 1916 Rising; Paisley, at a Loyalist rally, denouncing the government for not banning the Catholic parades altogether; Paisley leading an aggressive parade of his Protestant supporters through Cromac Square, thus causing another riot when Catholics tried to block the road; then that violence culminating at the Presbyterian General Assembly where the marchers tried to attack the Governor of Northern Ireland.

'This time Paisley went too far,' the newsreader said off screen. 'Prosecuted on eighteenth July, he went to jail for three months when he wouldn't agree to be bound over for two years.'

'I can't stand any more of this,' Marlene said, jumping up to switch to another channel, thus blotting out the image of the burly, smiling, self-dramatising Paisley being manhandled into an RUC paddy wagon, en route to prison. He was replaced by a popular quiz show, starring the lanky, rubber-limbed, lantern-jawed Bruce Forsyth. 'To throw a man like that into jail!' Marlene continued, ignoring the quiz show. 'And they talk about injustices against the *Catholics*! Sure it's us that are suffering the injustices. We've no rights left at all.'

'That was brilliant of him,' wee Billy said admiringly of Paisley. 'I mean, he knew just what he was doin' when he refused to accept bein' bound over. He took three months in jail instead, to make himself look like a martyr and gain even more support from us Protestants. You remember what happened when he went in?'

'Aye,' Dan said, 'I do. Sure didn't we both take part in it?'

A few days after Paisley was incarcerated, Billy and Dan had joined a demonstration outside the prison and soon found themselves in the thick of a serious riot, with Loyalists fighting the RUC. The following day, the RUC tried to stop about 4000 Paisleyites, including Billy and Dan, from marching in protest from the centre of Belfast, but the marchers broke through and then rampaged through the city centre, breaking shop windows, stoning a hotel owned by Catholics, and going on to Sandy Row, a Loyalist heartland, where they tried to burn down a bookie's shop employing Catholics. That night there was more savage rioting outside the Crumlin Road jail where Paisley was being held, with repeated baton-charges by the RUC. That riot, the last, only ended when heavy rain washed it out.

Since then, Billy had been confused by his feelings over his own part in the riots. On the one hand, he was proud to have taken his part in demonstrating on behalf of the Big Man, whom he viewed as a true Protestant hero; on the other hand, he could not recall that particular couple of days without suffering a hot flush of shame. He had not attended those demonstrations in order to cause violence, but he couldn't forget how, once they started, he and Dan had been so swiftly swept away by them, caught up in the excitement, and had briefly lost their own personalities when they melted into the mob. That mob, a single, amorphous, unpredictable beast, had caused dreadful destruction, and now, mere weeks after the event, Billy was compelled to recall his own part in it, his almost mindless joy as he smashed shop windows, fought baton-wielding policemen, threw stones at the International Hotel and, most shamefully, joined his fellow Protestants in marching along Sandy Row, their own territory, to attempt to burn down a bookie's shop, which, though owned by a Protestant, had openly employed Catholics for years. Billy would live for a long time with the memory of those unfortunate Catholics running away from a jeering, taunting mob that included men who had once been customers. There was something shameful about that, something new to deal with, and Billy wished that he could talk about it to Johnny, who was no longer here to help him out.

'Okay, I'm ready,' Ronnie said as he came down the stairs and entered the living room, wearing his 'Sunday-best' suit with shirt and tie, looking like a matinée idol. 'Can I have a couple of quid, love?'

'What for?' Marlene asked tartly.

'Entrance fee and a few drinks,' Ronnie said.

'They don't sell booze in the Floral Hall,' Marlene reminded him, quoting Billy.

'Just a wee bottle of whiskey,' Ronnie said, grinning. 'Small enough to slip into my hip pocket. That's all I need, love.'

'You're incorrigible,' Marlene retorted, though she stood up to remove a small, brightly-painted tin from the mantelpiece. Opening it, she pulled out a fiver and handed it to him. 'Spend it wisely,' she said.

Ronnie grinned and slipped the note into his wallet. 'I will, don't worry.' He turned to Billy and Dan. 'Okay?'

'Ackaye,' Dan said. 'Let's make tracks.'

'See ya later,' Billy said to his sister.

'Aye, right,' Marlene replied, then she turned back to the television, where Bruce Forsyth was hamming it up with a pair of contestants and one of his long-legged, bespangled, female assistants.

The three young men left the house.

4

8th January, 1964

Dear Mum and Dad and Billy and Marlene,

Sorry for not writing in such a long time (a couple of years, is it?), but as I think I said before, I normally don't like to see my own thoughts put down on paper, so it takes a lot to get me to pick up a pen. But I felt that I might be able to do it this evening, so I'll give it a whirl, like.

Isn't that what we used to say in Belfast? Ending sentences with the word 'like'? It didn't make sense to me then and it doesn't now, but at least it sounds right.

Dennis Burton

Where do I begin? It's been so long I can't even remember what I wrote the last time, so don't blame me if I start repeating myself.

Let's start with the ship.

I'm sailing on the San Diablo, a mixed cargo vessel built in 1962 at the Deutsche Werft in Hamburg, Germany, and the last in line of six similar vessels before the advent of modern containers. To give you an estimation of her size I have to use European (metric) measurements. She's 159.4 metres long, 21.47 metres wide, and her volume is 9998.36 GRT (Gross Register Tons), 5728.65 NRT (Net Register Tons) as a full scantling ship, and with 7626.1 GRT/4116.25 NRT as a shelter-decker. Fully laden she displaces 17,470 tons at 8.46 m draft. Her empty weight is 6,700 tons at 3.78 m draft. She's propelled by a two-stroke engine with nine cylinders and 11,600 horsepower. (If this doesn't interest you, Mum and Marlene, it might interest Dad or wee Billy.) Her maximum speed is 20.3 knots per minute at 118 revolutions per minute. The four auxiliary engines and generators supply the ship with electricity.

Probably doesn't mean to much to you, does it?   But it's all I know these days. This is my world, like.

Let me tell you more about it, because this is where I live and right now I love it. The San Diablo is a conventional cargo ship with five hatches and six tanks for liquid food transport. Some of the hatches are fitted with cooling plants capable of operation down to minus twenty-five degrees centigrade. She carries her cargo in bags, barrels, boxes, bales and unpacked, separated into lots and stowed by stevedores, of which I am one. In this lowly capacity (and lowly it is!) I've helped stow a lot of stuff, including medicines, camera-film and recording-tape, chemicals in bags or drums (some of it toxic, so I had to wear a filter mask), paintings, batteries, electronic equipment of all kinds, cars and tractors, filing cabinets and cupboards, machines and machine parts. Also, tea, coffee, tobacco, alcohol, frozen meat, chilled beef, cooled oranges and apples, all totalling thousands of tons.

Okay, I'm a pack mule!

What's the ship like? Not pretty, I can tell you. Everywhere I look I see a mess of wires, ropes and chains running from winches up the mast to the derricks. There are two cranes on the fo'c'sle and stern, each capable of lifting up to three tons. Most of the derricks can lift three to five tons, four of the derricks can go up to fifteen tons, and the

434

heavy lift boom at the foremast can lift up to fifty tons. All those are maintained by the crew and operated by stevedores, of which, as previously mentioned, I am one.

Nevertheless, it's not a 'tramp' steamer and is, in certain ways, pretty luxurious, with a dining room, lounge, bar, portside pharmacy and hospital (two patients maximum at any given time), as well as cabins for up to twelve passengers. Plus a galley, pantry and single mess for both officers and crew. As a crewman I have to share my cabin with one other man, but luckily the one I share with is almost human. In fact, he's a gentleman.

In general, I like the people I work with. These include other stevedores as well as boatswains, signallers, telegraphists, carpenters and stewards. Also, a doctor, cook, baker, butcher, laundry man and, of course, the deckhands, greasers, wipers and ABs (able-bodied seamen). Not to mention the petty officers, including nautical officers, engineers, apprentices and engineers' assistants and, last but not least, mess-boys, without whom life would be no fun at all.

I get along with most of them and I think I know why. Here, aboard ship, outside all territorial waters, you're judged only by your work - not by your religion, your politics, or your juvenile record. Here you're judged only on what you <u>are</u> at any given moment. You have no past or future here.

Social life? Most of my free time is spent on the palaverdeck - the socialising deck. The crewmen meet here after their watch is over, working in two 4-hour shifts every 24 hours. As there's not much else to do, this kind of socialising is fairly constant, certainly booze-orientated, and only broken up once a month when we have boat drills and fire alarms. There's also a promenade deck and swimming pool, but we (the crewmen) can only use them between seven and eight in the evening, when the passengers are stuffing their guts at dinner.

It's always interesting to see how the upper classes live while you're down there sweating on the lower decks. I sometimes think of the Protestants and the Catholics of Belfast, and assume that even out here, at sea, not too much has changed. But perhaps I'm imagining this.

I feel so far removed from Belfast now, so remote to it. In the intervening years this ship has taken me to an awful lot of places. Lisbon, Madeira, Casablanca, Gibraltar, Tunisia, through the Suez

Canal, stopping at Port Said and Suez and Aden, then on to Colombo (Ceylon), then Freemantle, Adelaide, Melbourne and Sydney, Australia. Back via Tasmania and New Zealand, across the South Pacific to Tahiti, from there to Acapulco, Mexico, and San Jose (Costa Rica), then through the Panama Canal, stopping at Panama City, then Trinidad and Tobago, Madeira and Lisbon again, then finally back to Southampton. I've sailed the Arctic Ocean, been to Greenland and back, though I haven't yet been to Antarctica because this ship's not equipped for that. I was compensated, however, with a journey around the coast of Africa to Marrakech, Freetown, Cape Town, the dreaded Cape of Good Hope (calm when we sailed around it), then Madagascar and the Seychelles and the Maldives, across the Indian Ocean to Jakarta and Sumatra, then Manila and Hong Kong.

So many seas! So many ports! I've seen the sun rise and sink over the Great Bitter Lakes, over the Red Sea, over the Mediterranean, the South Pacific, the Indian Ocean, over the Sinai Desert and the hills of Morocco, over the rain forests of Brazil, over the great harbour of Sydney - so many dawns and dusks of the kind I could scarcely even imagine in Belfast, so colourful were they, so absolutely spectacular. And all the people I've met or seen! The Arabs selling their wares from 'bum' boats when we anchored in Port Said and Aden, swarming like ants along the banks of the Suez, working in the fierce heat of the desert, or packed into the souks and bazaars of Marrakech and all the other bustling towns along the African coast. When I venture into those ports I hardly know myself, so lost do I become in what goes on around me - the exotic sights and smells, the extraordinary bedlam and activity - and my anonymity in those swarms of dusky faces offers me protection.

From what? I'm not too sure. Maybe from what I ran away from. From all the humiliations of the juvenile court, from the pain I saw in your faces when sentence was passed upon me, from the things that I experienced in the Borstal and would prefer to forget - though I can't quite forget them, not entirely, and probably never will. What I experienced was mine alone. It wasn't uncommon and may not be that important, but it changed me and sent me away from home and that has to be reckoned with.

Travelling with this ship, each port becomes a new adventure to me. When I enter those foreign towns with my friends from the ship, I *always leave my old self behind and become, at least for the evening, someone else entirely. We drink a lot when on dry land. We take our chances with foreign food. We talk to strangers, men and women alike, and have diverse experiences. What I've learnt from this is that Northern Ireland isn't the whole world, that what we believed there has no credence elsewhere, that a lot of the problems of Northern Ireland are due to provincialism, to purely local superstitions and prejudices, that there <u>are</u> religions other than the Catholic and the Protestant, and that most people in the world are a lot worse off than those in the province and yet do not necessarily try to kill each other because of what they might lack. What I've learnt from my travelling is that I no longer belong to Belfast or anywhere else. I belong to where I happen to put my feet down. And no matter how strange a country might be, I rarely feel strange in it.*

Now, I believe I'd feel strange in Belfast, which is why I haven't gone back there.

Will I ever? I suppose so. At least, maybe for a visit. I want to see you all again, but I'm nervous about it, not knowing if we still have things in common or if I'll be a stranger in your midst. I'm 23 now. I was 17 when I was arrested and sent away. I'm not remotely like the boy you all remember and I'm certainly not as nice. Life can be tough at sea. You have to learn to defend yourself. I learnt to do that in the Borstal and I've learnt even more ways of doing it since I've been on this ship. There are hard men here. Some are borderline crazy. I have good friends, but I also have enemies and they, too, have changed me. So I'm nervous about going home. I'm not sure you'll recognise me. I have a new life now and it's nothing to do with where I came from. I have new friends and they're not the kind of men that you're likely to understand. In other words, I'm different. I'm not the Johnny that used to be.

I'll probably do it some day - I mean, go home for a visit. I'd like to, but the thought of it also frightens me, so I keep putting the day off. Nevertheless I keep thinking about it.

The sun is sinking here. We're in the Great Bitter Lakes. The sun is like a great ball of fire - all yellow and crimson - seeming to melt along the horizon as it slowly sinks. It looks like molten metal being poured from the vats of Mackie's foundry, but the sea is on fire as well, the sky is crimson, the stars are brilliant, and none of that, of course, *is like Belfast, which now seems like a dark, distant dream. So maybe I <u>will</u> return some day - just to confirm to myself that it's real and that I'm not just imagining it.*

Again, I'm sorry for not writing in such a long time, but I keep putting off the writing of letters, exactly as I keep putting off that promised visit to Belfast - a form of cowardice, I guess.

Look after yourselves. Keep Billy out of trouble. I bet he's not 'wee' Billy anymore. Love to all.

Johnny

Mary wiped more tears from her eyes with the back of her right hand, then she refolded the second letter as neatly, as meticulously, as she had done with the first one and slid it back into its wrinkled envelope. Checking the clock on the mantelpiece, she saw that it was time for her guests to arrive, so she placed the letters back into the tin box and then returned it to its traditional place on the mantelpiece.

Not wishing her guests to see that she had been at the sherry, she removed the bottle and glass to the kitchen, but lit another cigarette and kept it between her lips, expertly blowing the smoke out of one corner of her mouth, as she placed cups, saucers and plates of biscuits on top of the sideboard. She had just finished doing this when someone knocked on the front door, signalling the beginning of the evening.

Opening the door, Mary found the imposing, unattractive spirit-medium standing on the doorstep with two of her spiritualist friends. The friends were women as well. Both, like the spirit-medium, were wearing heavy overcoats and had scarves tied around their heads.

'Ack, you've come, Mrs. Bleakley!' Mary said.

'Aye, as always,' the spirit-medium replied grimly.

Smiling, despite her pain and longing and confusion, hardly able to grasp exactly what Johnny had written, surprised by the eloquence of it, by the talent it had displayed, its surprisingly sure grasp of language, its natural eloquence and clarity, a talent never recognised and now blighted and surely lost, its potential brutally crushed by inexplicable events, Mary stepped aside to let her guests enter and help her find a brief peace.

She was looking forward to making contact with Neil. It did her good to talk to him. The dead were not threatening, as so many people thought. They could, indeed, comfort a troubled soul. It was the living who caused the pain.

5

After purchasing two half-bottles of whiskey from an off-licence on the Donegall Road, Billy, Ronnie and Dan took a bus to Castle Junction in the centre of town. As the double-decker bus was nearly empty, they were able to share the two front seats upstairs, Billy and Ronnie in one, Dan hogging the other, legs wide apart to ensure that no one sat beside him. When the bus set off again, they all lit up cigarettes and puffed away gratefully. Billy didn't normally drink, but when Ronnie, after checking to ensure that the conductor was downstairs, surreptitiously passed his bottle of whiskey to him, Billy, already nervous about going dancing, had a couple of sips. Instantly, he felt light-headed but more confident.

Though rain was threatening, it had not yet started falling and from their high vantage point they could look down on the girls, some alone, others in groups, who were making their way in both directions along the pavements, past the grim terraced streets and the children's park and library. The girls were dressed up to the nines and carrying handbags, because this was a Friday, pay day, and they were going out for an evening of fun. In the wan light of the street lamps they looked more attractive than most of them would have been up close.

'I wouldn't mind havin' a go at that one,' Dan said, squinting down through cigarette smoke at a girl, about his age, who was making her way across Sandy Row, clearly heading for Shaftesbury Avenue. Though she was hardly elegant, being dressed in a loose green skirt, waist-length fawn jacket and flat shoes, with a black beret on her head, she was slim and had a decent set of pins and a good set of knockers.

'You wouldn't know what to do with her if you had her,' Ronnie said, smiling in his sweet manner, his soft brown eyes blinking repeatedly. 'You'd probably both die in silence.'

'Oh, yeah?' Dan retorted. 'You think because you're married you're the only one to know what it's all about? Well, let me tell you...'

Glancing down, Billy saw that Sandy Row was as busy as always, the lights from its many shops, pubs and bookies falling over pavements packed with busy housewives, boozing men, playing children. There was something timeless about Sandy Row, Billy thought. It never seemed to change. It had been frozen somewhere back in the 1930s or '40s, when the great mills had dominated the city and small, eccentric shops had served the tightly knit communities of exploited workers. Sandy Row was such a community, tightly knit, strongly Protestant, always lively and generous to a fault, except when it came to the Catholics. It was a good place to go for a drink and a bit of a sing-song in a back room of one of its many pubs.

He was reminded of this when, still glancing down, he caught a glimpse of his Dad, dressed up like a right wee dandy, a fag smouldering between his smiling lips as he turned off the Donegall Road and into the Row, clearly heading for the first of many watering holes in what would be a lengthy pub crawl.

'Hey, look, there's yer Dad!' Dan exclaimed, pointing down with his index finger, obviously keen to change the subject and avoid awkward questions regarding his strictly limited sexual experience.

Billy sighed. 'Aye, I see him.'

'Out for a night on the town, is he?'

'Ackaye,' Billy said. 'That's all he does when he comes home. He'll drink with all his mates and boast about what he's doin' across the water. Probably give 'em a turn or two in the back rooms - a bit of singin' and dancin'.'

Ronnie chuckled, exhaling cigarette smoke, blinking those distracted soft brown eyes that had melted many a female heart. 'Aye, your Dad always loved doin' that,' he said. 'That's why we all liked him when we were kids.'

'Credit to him,' Dan said, as Albert disappeared into the hustle and bustle of the pavements and Sandy Row fell behind the advancing bus. 'I mean, he's pretty good at it. Did youse see him on that Hughie Green Show a couple of months back? Sure he was really great, wasn't he? A real all-round entertainer. Danced as neat as Fred Astaire, sang as good as Frank Sinatra - I *loved* his "Strangers in the Night" - and his impersonations were absolutely fuckin' brilliant, especially his Red Skelton and Norman Wisdom. Sure, he was really terrific, wasn't he? Belfast's very own Sammy Davis Junior, but white instead of black, two eyes instead of one, and a few more inches on the vertical. He should have *won* that talent contest, but it doesn't make a bit of difference that he didn't. He still did us proud, like.'

'Aye, right,' Ronnie said, always agreeable to anything and certainly fond of Billy's father, who shared his enthusiasm for drink and gambling. 'I mean, who else do we know who's actually been on TV, beamed out of Birmingham in England? Sure wasn't everyone we know really excited for weeks after that? He brought a bit of fame to us, so all credit to him.'

'True enough,' Dan said.

Billy wished his Mum had felt the same way, but predictably Albert's appearance on that popular TV talent contest had only increased her embarrassment and made her tongue sharper than ever. Billy was secretly proud of the fact that his Dad was something of a local celebrity and he'd been thrilled to actually see him on TV, so he'd never quite understood why his Mum found it so distasteful. He could only assume that it was because his Mum, coming from the upper Malone Road, with a father who had lost both his legs at the Somme and had a disability pension to go with his medals, felt that she was socially above her husband and was being dragged down to his working-class level by his showbusiness activities. This was, of course, mere speculation, since in truth you could never fully understand your own parents' relationship. Another of life's little mysteries, like.

'You can tell it's pay day, can't you?' Dan said, nodding to indicate the many people in the broad expanse of Shaftesbury Square, some swarming along the pavements, silhouetted against the brightly lit shop windows, moving in and out of the weaker light of the street lamps, others racing dangerously across the roads that ran off the vast square, weaving through the dense, clamorous traffic. 'They're all out to spend it.'

'Like us,' Ronnie said.

'Aye, like us. God knows, it's hard enough to earn, so we might as well enjoy it while we can.'

'What does that mean?' Billy asked.

'While we're still young enough,' Dan explained. 'Before we grow too old to be able to enjoy it.'

'I'll never grow that old,' Billy said with conviction. 'I'd rather die young than grow that old.'

'I'm that old already,' Ronnie said with his amiable grin, his soft brown gaze focused elsewhere, as it usually was. 'You two just can't see it.'

'It's being married that's done that to you,' Dan said. 'Havin' the kids, like. The responsibilities. What you'd like is to be back in the skiffle group, poundin' away at your bass while the girls scream and wet their knickers. Those were probably the best days of your life.'

'Aye, they were,' Ronnie admitted with that faraway look. 'And they're not comin' back.'

'Jesus!' Billy exclaimed in exasperation. 'Sure you're talkin' like you're forty years old - and you're only twenty-four. What the fuck's wrong with you?'

'Nothing,' Ronnie said. 'Not a thing. Just that those days with the skiffle group, when Johnny was here, were really good times. Good times all round, like.'

'Aye, right,' Billy said. 'And you once shat in your nappies without knowing it, being innocent, like. You can't live in the past, for fuck's sake, so stop lookin' back on the Fifties like some oul Teddy Boy.'

'I *liked* the Teddy Boys,' Ronnie said. 'They revered Little Richard. They thought Little Richard was even better than Elvis, though he was black and not nearly as famous. They had good taste, the Teddy Boys.'

'Ack, you're fuckin' jokin', aren't you?' Dan said, exhaling clouds of smoke as she spoke. 'I mean, *no one* was as good as Elvis in those days. Not Little Richard, not Gene Vincent, not Fats Domino or Jerry Lee Lewis, not that wimp, Buddy Holly. Elvis wiped them all out, like.'

'Aye, right,' Billy said.

The bus took them along Great Victoria Street, past the railway station, the Grand Opera House, the Odeon and the old Ritz cinema, since renamed 'the ABC', where long queues had already formed, then turned right at the Royal Academy Institute, more commonly known as the 'Inst', to go along Wellington Place and into Donegall Square. It passed the City Hall, resplendent in lamplit darkness, its great copper dome flood-lit, and then went down Donegall Place to Castle Junction, the end of the line. Once there, Billy and his friends transferred to another bus that would take them out of town, heading north, along the

Antrim Road to Hazelwood, just north of Greencastle. Again, they found seats upstairs, though not up front this time, with Billy seated behind Ronnie and Dan, on the right-hand side of the vehicle. They didn't find their favoured front seats empty because this bus was crowded with mostly young men and women, all heading, like them, for the Floral Hall, so decked out in their best clothes. The girls giggled constantly, the young men grinned at them, and both groups were highly self-conscious.

As the bus moved off, the rain started falling.

'Aw, shit!' Dan exclaimed in exasperation. '*Now* it starts to rain! If it doesn't stop by the time we get to Hazelwood, we'll get drenched going up to the Floral Hall in that open bus they have there.'

'Yeah,' Billy said. 'And your pompadour will collapse and become a mess and *then* what will you do?'

'Hey, knock it off, Billy!' Dan retorted, nervously touching his greased pompadour to check that it was in perfect alignment with his forehead. 'This is no fuckin' joke.'

'Ack, it's just a passin' shower,' Ronnie said, smiling amiably, not bothered, as usual. 'Sure it'll be over by the time we get there.'

'It better be,' Dan said grimly, lighting another cigarette.

Nearly everyone upstairs was smoking because smoking downstairs was forbidden. The smoke looked like fog, and the bus, both upstairs and down, was a riot of excited conversation.

'Some nice birds on this bus,' Dan observed in a low voice while casting his sly gaze left and right.

'Aye, there are,' Ronnie said in his mild, distracted way, as if he hadn't really noticed. Some girls had noticed him, though, and were giggling and nudging each other, while nodding repeatedly in his direction.

'Hey, Ronnie,' Dan said, his gaze shifting left and right. 'Some of those birds are givin' you the eye and bein' brassy about it.'

'Sure I'm just an oul married man,' Ronnie said. 'They should be givin' you and Billy the eye, not me.'

'Aye, but it's always you,' Billy said. 'I don't how you do it, so I don't. A married man with two kids and you *still* manage to pull all the birds. Sure there's no justice at all.'

Ronnie just shrugged and smiled, watching the rain falling outside as if looking beyond it, at something a lot farther away, in some other universe.

'But if you'd just smile back at them,' Dan said hopefully to Ronnie, 'offerin' some encouragement, that'd give us the opening to talk to them. How's about it, Ronnie?'

'I just want a few drinks,' Ronnie said, 'and a bit of a dance. I don't want any nonsense. I'm a married man with two children.'

'But think of *us*, Ronnie!' Dan was really frustrated. 'The birds never give us the eye – it's always *you* they fancy. So let's use that to at least get close to them when we're in the dance hall. Come on! Be a pal!'

Ronnie shrugged again. 'I'm just an oul married man with – '

'Don't even say it!' Dan took hold of Ronnie's shoulder to give it a vigorous shake and hopefully gain his full attention. 'Just promise us, Ronnie!'

But he didn't get Ronnie's full attention. No one ever did. Ronnie just gazed distractedly out of the bus, at the teeming, gleaming rain, and murmured, with a weary shrug, 'Well, we'll see.'

'Great!' Dan said, satisfied.

As the bus climbed out of the city, taking the Antrim Road, passing through Cliftonville and Fort William, Billy looked to his right, beyond the rows of terraced houses, and saw the broad, glittering sweep of Belfast Lough, running out from the towering cranes and gantries of the shipyard to the cloudy, rainswept darkness over the North Channel. It looked grim out there.

'Oh, shit!' Dan exclaimed. 'We'll soon be there and it's still pissing rain. We're gonna get drenched!'

Hazelwood was so called because of the many hazelwood trees in the area. Billy saw plenty of them as he glanced beyond Bellevue and Valley Park to the distant rooftops of Rathcool and Whitehouse, with the sea dark and rainswept farther on, receding eerily into invisibility. They would be drenched alright.

The bus stopped near the entrance to the Zoological Gardens which, like the Floral Hall, was located on the slopes of Cave Hill, offering panoramic views over the city and Belfast Lough. In summer it could be beautiful, all green hills and trees, but right now it looked dismal in the pouring rain. Disembarking from the bus, Billy and the others hurried through that rain, the young men cursing, the girls giggling, to board a special low-geared, semi-open bus (it had a roof but no sides), with unusually small wheels, for the journey up to the Floral Hall, perched high on the steep slopes of Cave Hill. Most of the women, not having brought umbrellas, had to cover their heads with their coats; some of the men, including Dan, did the same. There was a frantic scramble to get onto the bus, but even on board there was little protection, since although there was a roof, the lack of sides enabled the wind to blow the rain right through the cabin, further drenching the passengers. The females shrieked or cried out despairingly; the males cursed or just laughed. When eventually the bus started off, packed tight, the passengers had to hold on to either the railings or other passengers, because the vehicle leaned over dramatically, dangerously, shuddering and shrieking, while manoeuvring the sharp uphill bends to the dance-hall, located under the brow of Ben Madigan. When it reached the top, some of the passengers cheered, before piling out and hurrying into the colourful Art-Deco building.

Before approaching the ticket booth, Ronnie and Dan removed the half-bottles of whiskey from their jacket pockets and shoved them down the back of their trousers, hidden under their coats, where hopefully they would not be discovered if the doorman, always watchful for illicit drinkers, decided to search them.

'Jesus!' Dan exclaimed furiously as they stood in the queue for tickets and he tried in vain to dry his soaked hair and ruined pompadour with his handkerchief, 'I'm a right awful mess!'

'Aye,' Billy said, grinning as he did the same, 'and you sure enough look it.'

'Thanks a million.' Dan glanced resentfully at Ronnie. 'And look at this cunt, will ya?' he said. 'He's still as dry as a bone!'

Ronnie didn't hear the remark, though he was certainly bone dry. He just stood there, elegant and handsome, smiling at the brunette standing in front of him, though not really seeing her. He was thinking of his next drink.

'It was that wee girl in front of him,' Billy explained, still combing his hair and grinning. 'When she saw him gettin' off the bus, about to step into the rain, she said, "Here, let me share my umbrella; there's no need to get soaked." Then she took his arm and sort of cuddled up to him and held the umbrella over both their heads until we were inside. That's why he's as dry as a bone.'

'I don't believe it!' Dan was shaking his head in disgust. 'I mean, that girl's only about eighteen years old and he's twenty-four. There's no justice, I'm telling ya.'

'None at all,' Billy said.

After purchasing their tickets, they entered the dance-hall, Billy and Dan both nervous, though trying to hide it, Ronnie distracted and smiling benignly. The uniformed doorman didn't bother them as they passed, looking straight ahead, to step into the blue, tangerine and gold splendours of the popular 'Belfast Ballroom of Romance'.

'Let's go straight to the bar,' Ronnie said, raising his normally soft voice to make himself heard above the sudden explosion of music and animated conversation. 'Let's get something to mix the whiskey with.'

'Aye, right,' wee Billy said, feeling drunk already, more confident, and wanting more of that false confidence. 'Let's have a few more drinks before we start.'

'No argument,' Dan said.

6

Before going to see his mates in Sandy Row, Albert dropped into the Laverys, who lived just two doors along from his own house. Albert had always had a soft spot for the Laverys, despite the fact that they were Fenians, because they always managed to make him feel good when Mary gave him a hard time, as she had done just a few minutes ago. They also always offered him a drink and he never said 'No' to it.

'Albert!' Patrick Lavery greeted him with a big grin when he answered the knocking on his front door. 'Back again, are you?'

Albert nodded. 'Just got in last night. Mary's havin' her spiritualist meeting this evenin', so I thought I'd slip out for a pint or two and couldn't pass without sayin' hello, like.'

'Dead on, Albert. Sure it's grand to see you again. Come in. You picked a good night. We've got Nelly and Sammy Devlin in for a drink and I'm sure they'll both be pleased to see you.'

'Right,' Albert said, stepping into the house when Patrick turned aside to let him pass. The instant he entered the living room, he saw Bernadette's flaming red hair and bright green eyes (still a beauty in middle age, he thought), where she was seated in a soft chair at one side of the fireplace, facing the Devlins, side-by-side on the sofa at the other side of the hearth. They all smiled when they saw him and the two women jumped up to give him a hug.

'Sure you're lookin' grand, Albert!' Bernadette said. 'England must be good for you.'

'I could've done worse,' Albert replied, as Patrick closed the front door behind him, then returned to the living room. It was the same as Albert's living room, except for the Virgin Mary over the mantelpiece where, in a Protestant household, it would have been a photo or painting of Queen Elizabeth.

'All dressed up to the nines, Albert,' Nelly said with her brown eyes flashing wickedly. 'Out for a night on the town, are you?'

Grinning, Albert jabbed his thumb backwards over his shoulder, indicating, as it were, his own house, just two doors away. 'The monthly night of madness up there,' he said, 'so I thought I'd take myself away from it. I'm not into talks with the dead myself. I'd rather talk to the living. And you're lookin' as alive as always, Nelly. Sammy must still be treatin' you right.'

'Aye, I am, right enough,' Sammy said, waving his bottle of stout at Albert by way of greeting. 'Spoilin' her rotten as usual.'

'What would grab your fancy, Albert?' Patrick asked, stepping in front of him. Though the same age as Bernadette, he was thinning on top and putting on weight, so he looked a good bit older than his wife, though at ease with himself.

'Sure I'll have whatever's goin',' Albert said, noting that the women were drinking whiskey and the men bottled stout with whiskey chasers. Cigarettes were smouldering between fingers or in ashtrays, so the room was, as usual, dense with smoke.

'What about a stout with a wee Bushmills as a chaser?' Patrick suggested.

'Grand,' Albert said.

'Take that chair beside Bernadette,' Patrick said, 'while I rustle it up.'

Taking the chair indicated, flipping a cigarette into his lips, Albert sat down and crossed his agile legs. 'So how have ya all been?' he asked, lighting his cigarette. 'Anything exciting happenin', like?'

They all shook their heads, indicating, 'No.'

'What would happen to *us*?' Nelly said. 'It's *you* that things happen to, Albert. Sure didn't we see you on that show on television...'

'The Hughie Green Show,' Sammy prompted her.

'Aye, right. And it was so exciting to see you. Sure we could hardly believe it, could we? A bona fide television star – and one from our street!'

'Right,' Bernadette said. 'Weren't me and Nelly here squealin' just like a pair of teenagers? We were over the moon.'

Sammy nodded and smiled benignly, his bottle of stout resting on his pot belly. 'They're not fibbin', Albert. It was just like they say. I mean, most of the street was watchin' you - and those that didn't have TVs visited those that did, so no one missed out. It was a great event, I can tell you. You'd have thought it was the Twelfth of July - or the Coronation. When it was over, we all got as drunk as monkeys, we were so thrilled to see it.'

'Well, I'm glad youse all enjoyed it,' Albert said, trying not to sound smug. 'It was nerve-wrecking to do, I can tell you, so I hope I did all right.'

'All *right*?' Patrick said, holding out a glass of whiskey and a bottle of stout. 'Sure it was more than all right! You were absolutely brilliant! The best in the whole show. No question, you should have won first prize, but that's the English for you. They always look after their own and that's why you lost out.'

'He came second,' Nelly said.

'Aye, right, but he should've come first. If he had, he'd have had a recording contract, but instead it went to a bloody English woman.'

'I've no complaints,' Albert said, though at the time he'd been broken-hearted, seeing all his hopes dashed to smithereens, his future narrowing overnight. Indeed, he still felt crushed when he thought about it. 'They treated me right royally over there and Hughie was great. As for not comin' in first, well, I wasn't all that upset and I certainly didn't think that bein' Irish had anything to do with it. They played it fair and square, if you ask me, and the applause-board is what picked the winner. So that girl, the one who won, deserved it. Besides, she was a pretty wee thing and that counts for a lot on TV. Let's face it, I'm no spring chicken anymore. My mug isn't a selling point.'

'Sure, you're still a handsome man,' Bernadette said. 'Don't do yourself down, Albert.'

'Aye, right,' Nelly said. 'I've seen worse than you in my day.'

Nelly's compliments had always been oblique, if not downright double-edged.

'I'm not doin' myself down,' Albert said. 'I'm just facin' facts. If it comes to a choice between a pretty face and me, the TV audience will always go for the pretty face.' He inhaled and exhaled smoke, gulped some stout, sipped more whiskey. 'It's just the name of the game, like. But I was proud to have made it that far, even though it's probably as far as I'll ever get.'

'Ack, away with ya!' Sammy said. 'Sure you've still a long way to go yet and I'm sure you'll go the whole route eventually.'

'A truer word was never spoken,' Patrick said, nodding vigorously for emphasis. 'Just keep at it and I'm sure you'll go the distance. Well, here's to you, Albert.'

When Patrick raised his glass in a toast, the others did the same, then they drank and puffed on their cigarettes. You could hardly see the Virgin Mary for the smoke, which for Albert was comforting.

'So Mary's havin' another of her séances,' Bernadette said, brushing strands of red hair from her green eyes and smiling mischievously. 'Talkin' to the dead again.'

'Aye,' Albert said. 'I always thought it would be just a passing thing, but she hasn't given up on it. Now she goes to the spiritualist church and believes all they tell her.'

Nelly shivered. 'Personally, I think it's spooky. I wouldn't allow it in *my* house. I'm not saying there's anything to it, but you just never know. It's best *not* to know, I say.'

'Sure I'd never believed it of her,' Bernadette said. 'She never seemed the type for that. Always seemed too level-headed, like.'

Albert gulped some stout, sipped some whiskey, had a drag on his cigarette and then exhaled a couple of smoke rings. 'You're all talkin' as if you hardly know her, yet you used to be the best of friends. What's happened to you?'

Bernadette and Nelly glanced at one another, then the former shrugged. 'Nothin',' she said. 'And maybe that's the problem. I mean, nothing's happened one way or the other, because in truth we hardly see her these days. She used to drop in a lot - practically every day, I'd say - then she started comin' less and less. Now we rarely see her at all.'

'She's still the same when you meet her,' Nelly added. 'Still friendly an' all. And she always promises to drop in real soon, though she never does. So it's not that anything's happened - nothing has. It's just that she never drops in and that's made the difference.'

'You think it's the spiritualism?' Albert asked. 'Because she knows you all secretly disapprove?'

'I used to think it was that,' Nelly said, 'but now I'm not so sure. I think it was because your Johnny was arrested during that riot in the Falls, when those Orangemen he happened to be with caused a confrontation with the Catholics. I think Mary blamed the Catholics for what happened to Johnny and has never looked at us the way she did before, when she used to stick up for us. Now she looks at the Catholics differently, with suspicion, and we're her Catholic neighbours. So although she's still friendly, she's also distant and rarely comes calling.'

'Aye, right,' Bernadette said. 'She's not the friend she used to be, because she doesn't trust Catholics - and unfortunately we all happen to be Catholics. That's the truth of the matter.'

The lingering silence that followed made Albert feel embarrassed. He'd never had this kind of conversation in this house before and he didn't quite know what it meant, except that it made everything seem different. In all the years he'd been coming here there'd never been talk of Catholics and Protestants, only talk about fun things, and these people, his lifelong friends, had even attended parties in his house on the Twelfth and during other Protestant celebrations. Now they were raising subjects long buried and, in Albert's apolitical view, best left that way. The malevolent spirits of Ireland's troubled history were being brought back to life, just as Mary was trying to resurrect the beloved brother who had died. Albert, never keen to face reality, didn't want to face this.

'Well...' he began tentatively, 'Mary's become obsessed with this spiritualist business and has let it take over her completely. If she'd only...'

He was cut off in mid-sentence by the clatter of shoes on the stairs and a male voice calling out, 'Mr. Hamilton!'

Glancing sideways, Albert saw Teddy Lavery and his brother Mark, both now in their mid-thirties, both still with their mother's red hair, standing at the foot of the stairs, having come down from Mark's bedroom. The latter looked as serious as always, but the former was grinning.

'How ya doin', Teddy?' Albert asked.

'Ack, I'm great.'

'And you, Mark?'

'Not bad,' Mark said coldly.

As friendly as ever, Teddy advanced across the room to stand in front of Albert. 'So how are you, Mr. Hamilton?'

'Grand,' Albert said.

'You're *famous*!' Teddy said, grinning. 'You're the talk of the whole street. Ever since you appeared on TV, you've been the ant's pants. We're all as proud as Punch here.'

'Ack, sure it was nothing,' Albert said, though he couldn't help feeling pleased with himself. 'Just one of those things, like.'

'Just one of those things, my arse,' Teddy said.

'Teddy!' Bernadette snapped. 'Watch your language!'

'Sorry, Ma,' Teddy said, still grinning, turning back to Albert. 'You put this avenue on the map, even more than the football grounds did. Are you just back for the weekend?'

'Four days,' Albert said. 'We get it every six weeks. You're lookin' pretty good, Teddy.'

'Ack, I'm fine,' Teddy said. 'No complaints, like. So what about Johnny?'

'What about him?'

'You ever hear from him?'

'He sends the odd letter,' Albert said, 'though he doesn't say much. He's just travelling like you used to do, one port after the other. I think he got it from you.'

'Yeah, maybe he did.'

451

Albert felt uncomfortable again. The very mention of Johnny only reminded him of that dreadful day when he had taken Johnny and Billy to the Custom House steps, when the former was seventeen years old, the latter sixteen. Albert had always known there could be trouble down there, but he'd chosen to ignore the possibility in his enthusiasm to simply get out of the house, away from Mary, and hopefully have a few jars with some pals. Then the Big Man had started bellowing, the Lambeg drummer had started playing, and suddenly a mob was marching to the Falls, to deliberately seek out, or cause, a confrontation. That's when Johnny had been arrested, reportedly with good cause. According to the RUC (this had been confirmed by wee Billy) Johnny, normally reserved, had almost gone berserk, seriously beating up a couple of Catholics, leaving them black and blue and, in at least one case, with broken bones. Of course, he shouldn't have done it, but he'd clearly been aroused by the general atmosphere and lost control of himself. Albert blamed himself for it. He'd secretly blamed himself for years. He could never admit it to anyone, but his feelings of guilt rarely left him. In that moment of carelessness, when he had turned the other way, leaving his boys with that rampaging mob, he had caused the chain of events that had ruined Johnny's life. Now, it seems, he had also indirectly caused Mary to turn away from her former best friends, the Laverys and Devlins, viewing them as Fenians, not just neighbours, which she'd never done before. He was guilty. There could be no doubt about it. And he wanted no part of it.

Shaking himself out of his reverie, he ostentatiously checked his wristwatch. 'Ack, Jesus!' he exclaimed melodramatically. 'Sure look at the time! I'm supposed to be meeting the lads five minutes from now and here I still have my backside on this chair. I'd best be makin' tracks.' After quickly polishing off his whiskey and stout, he pushed his chair back and stood up. Suddenly, for the first time in all the years he had been coming here, he felt that he didn't belong and wanted to leave. 'Thanks a million for that,' he said. 'Sure it got me off to a fine start. Now I'll invade Sandy Row and have a few more and make a fool of myself. I mean, life's for the living, right?'

'Aye, right,' Patrick said with a broad grin.

'Great to see you all,' Albert said, nodding and smiling at each of them in turn. 'Let's have a real party next time. Come up to my place.'

'Just like the good old days,' Bernadette said sardonically.

'Aye, right,' Albert replied, suddenly feeling slightly hysterical or, at the very least, unnatural. 'Okay, then, I'll be seein' youse.'

'Aye, right,' Nelly and Sammy said in chorus. 'Until the next time, Albert.'

'Six weeks from now,' Albert said.

Patrick showed him to the door, opened it for him, gave his shoulder an affectionate squeeze and then let him go. Albert stepped outside, into the lamplit darkness, the evening's damp chill, and heaved a sigh of relief, surprising himself, as he made his way along the pavement to the arches. He had to pass the Johnstone house to get there, but this time he didn't care - it was dark, after all, and in the evening that mad bastard, big Barney, did nothing except watch TV. Passing the dreaded house, he looked up automatically at the window, but no one was there. Relieved, he glanced across the road to Donna King's house and wondered what Johnny would think if he knew what had become of her. Albert had always thought that Johnny would end up marrying Donna, but it wasn't to be. Life was filled with surprises, like.

Halfway along the avenue, he decided to turn into the Broadway and check if his mother was alright. She was. At least the dog was. In relative terms, it was now almost as old as she was, but like her, it was clearly going to live forever. Albert could tell that by the barking, the snarling, the paws pounding the front door when he used the knocker. Doreen let him in eventually, once he had told her who he was, shouting through the letter box, and when he stepped into the dust-covered living room, he saw the enormous, rheumy-eyed Alsatian. Having done its bit by barking like all hell, hopefully keeping strangers at bay, it was already back in its damp corner at the side of the tattered, stained sofa, whimpering with its tongue hanging out, dribbling from its black lips. In truth, it lived in fear of Doreen; no one else concerned it.

'Not staying long, Mum,' Albert said, deliberately not taking a seat and just as deliberately lighting up another cigarette, in the hope that the smoke would diminish the smell of decay. 'I'm on my way out for an evenin' with m'mates and just dropped in to see if you were okay.'

'Ackaye, son, I'm fine,' Doreen said, resuming her seat by the fireplace and staring at him with increasingly mad eyes. 'I mean, apart from the arthritis and the piles and hardened arteries, not to mention my racing heart, I'm doin' grand, like. No change since I saw you six weeks ago. Fine thing when a mother only sees her son every six weeks, but times change, I'll admit.'

'Come on, Mum,' Albert retorted, puffing nervously on his cigarette, 'sure you know I work across the water and only get home every six weeks. A man doesn't always have a choice when it comes to earning his money.'

'Well, at least you've come to see me.'

'That's right, Mum, here I am.'

'And you don't even have time to take a seat, your social life is so hectic.'

'I'm runnin' late, Mum.'

'And why's that, may I ask?'

'I had to drop in and see the Laverys when I was passing their house. Only being polite, like.'

'You stopped off to see some Fenians on your way here and now you haven't any time for your own mother? Well, times certainly *have* changed!'

'Ack, away with ya,' Albert said, exhaling another cloud of smoke. 'Sure you know I couldn't walk past their front door, their front window, with them seeing me an' all, without at least droppin' in to say hello.'

'With a stout and wee whisky thrown in.'

'Well, yeah, that as well.'

'And drank it under the unblinkin' gaze of a framed Virgin Mary.'

'What?'

'Have you no shame at all? You'd tolerate that Popish idolatry for the sake of a free drink?'

'Aw, come on, for Christ's sake - '

'Don't blaspheme in this house!'

'I only stopped in to say hello and they gave me a drink. What's the matter with that?'

'Your wife practises black magic - '

'Spiritualism!' Albert corrected her.

' - and you fraternise with Fenians in their own house, filled with blasphemous ornaments and pictures. Sure you've no shame at all.'

Albert had another drag on his cigarette, exhaling the smoke with a long, drawn-out sigh.

'I'm here until Tuesday,' he said. 'Can I get you anything before I leave?'

'Like what?'

Albert shrugged. 'Food. Tobacco. Snuff. Maybe something to drink.'

'I never let alcohol pass my lips,' she said, lying blatantly.

'I meant tea or soft drinks.'

'I'm in no need of charity. I've always looked after myself and I always will. Don't mention the welfare state to me, because I don't approve of it.'

Albert checked his wristwatch. He did that a lot these days. Raising his head, he said, 'Jesus, it's - '

'Don't blaspheme in this house!'

'It's late, so I'd better be goin'. I'll drop in tomorrow afternoon, Mum, and maybe...'

'Not if you don't want to, son. Don't do it just for *me*.'

'I'd like to stay longer,' Albert said, 'but my mates are expecting me. So I'll drop in tomorrow afternoon and we can talk a bit more. Okay?'

'If you say so.'

Albert took a step forward, kissed her cheek and smelt the decay. A shudder of revulsion passed through him.

'Right,' he said, quickly straightening up again. 'So I'll see you tomorrow.'

'If you want.'

'I want,' Albert lied.

'You'd best be makin' tracks now,' Doreen said.

'Aye, right,' Albert said. 'See you tomorrow.'

'Goodnight, son.'

'Goodnight.'

Heaving a sigh of relief, he left the house and walked to the end of the terrace, turning back into the Broadway. There, even in darkness, the enormous, garish Loyalist paintings on the gable ends of the houses dominated all. As he left the Broadway to enter the avenue, he wondered, for the first time, what his old friends, the Laverys and

455

Devlins, thought each time they either passed, or walked through, this blatantly advertised Loyalist area.

They must have felt humiliated, he thought. Maybe even scared. They must have felt like black men in South Africa or in Alabama, America. They must have felt pretty rotten.

He had never considered this before and it made him feel even worse.

To hell with it, he thought, just get drunk. Drink the whole mess away.

Ten minutes later, he was in Sandy Row, starting to make good his vow.

It was good to get drunk with Protestant friends.

Good to get drunk with anyone.

7

'A pretty good crowd here tonight,' Billy said as he stood with Ronnie and Dan at the packed, teetotal bar of the Floral Hall, sipping his second glass of orange juice laced with the smuggled-in whiskey and looking out over the circular dance floor, where couples were dancing to a live band of the Glenn Miller kind, though not nearly as good, under a multi-sided mirrored globe that revolved from the centre of the blue, tangerine and gold-coloured ceiling, giving a constant, romantic flickering effect. Rows of flags also hung from the round ceiling, but what they represented was hard to discern, so tattered and covered in dust were they.

'Aye,' Ronnie responded, smiling benignly at no one in particular, though a few girls were smiling at him, 'pretty good. But not nearly as good as it used to be.'

'Oh, yeah?' Dan enquired in his simple-minded manner.

'See, a few years back,' Ronnie explained with infinite patience, 'up to about the end of the Fifties, Belfast was a city of ballroom dancers - that was the big thing then - and every dance hall in the city was packed on a regular basis. The Plaza in Chichester Street was the biggest of them all, but the top suburban spot was this place.'

'Still popular,' Dan noted sagely, surveying the crowd.

'Aye,' Ronnie agreed, 'still popular, but not nearly as much as it was back then.'

'Really?'

'Aye. See, though the Plaza and this place could have held about three-thousand dancers between them, they were packed to the gills just about every night. They were really popular, like.'

'So what happened?' Dan asked.

'Rock and roll,' Ronnie said with quiet pride, smiling beatifically.

'Oh, yeah?'

'Aye,' Ronnie said. 'Things changed overnight in 1956 when Bill Haley's "Rock Around the Clock" went into the hit parade. I mean, everyone kept dancin' all right, but it was rock and roll dancin'. Then it was Elvis and Gene Vincent and Little Richard and Buddy Holly and all the other great rock and rollers. After that, the dance halls were never the same, because the young kids wanted their own thing, and it wasn't what you get here or in the Plaza or the other ballrooms.'

'Lots of young kids here,' Dan observed, 'includin' me and wee Billy.'

They grinned at each other, both being single and viewing Ronnie as an old married man, even though he was the one who still pulled the birds.

'Aye,' Ronnie continued, still smiling beatifically, clearly recalling better days, when he and Johnny had played in a skiffle group, once even on the stage of the Plaza during a special rock and roll evening, 'but that's only because Belfast doesn't have too many alternatives. Believe me, this place isn't nearly as full as it used to be and I'd say that in a couple of years it'll probably close down entirely. Along with the Plaza and the Kingsway and all the other ballrooms. Ballroom dancing, if not exactly dead, is on its way out.'

'Well, it won't bother me if it goes,' Dan said with misplaced confidence, 'because I can't dance anyway. I'm only here for a good excuse to rub my dick against the belly of some bird who's agreeable. You can't really do that when dancin' to rock and roll, 'cause you don't touch in that kind of dancin' - you just hold hands and spin about like, sometimes facin' your partner, sometimes side by side with her, but never rubbin' your bellies together. That's why a lot of us still come here, I reckon, if you ask me, I mean.'

'Aye, that's right,' Billy said.

The three of them had taken turns to visit the men's toilet to dry themselves on the towels and comb their wet, windblown hair. Now looking reasonably respectable again, they were keen to get out on the dance floor, though more nervous about it than any of them were willing to admit. Ronnie, of course, probably wasn't nervous at all, because he was a married man with kids, which meant he was experienced, and the girls, who didn't know he was married, kept *asking* him to take them for a dance. When they did do, he just fluttered his long, fine eyelashes, let his brown eyes mist over, smiled distractedly and nodded, indicating, 'Okay,' and then let them lead him away. It happened every time they came here and it drove Dan, in particular, wild with frustration.

'So let's knock back these drinks,' Dan said, clearly itching with frustration, 'and go find a few bellies to rub against.'

'Aye, right,' Billy said, feeling drunkenly bold. 'They're standin' around the dance floor in bunches, practically pantin' for us. I can see them from here.'

'Just drink up,' Dan said.

Finishing their drinks, they wiped their lips dry with the backs of their hands, then moved from the bar to the nearest edge of the circular dance floor. True enough, the girls were standing in bunches around one half of the floor, the boys doing the same around the other half, the two sexes staring across the floor at each other like armies about to commence battle. The light from the revolving mirrored globe above flickered over those already dancing, giving them an exotically surrealistic appearance, temporarily erasing what blemishes they might have, while those standing around the edge, in grinning or giggling bunches, were obscured in a romantic semi-darkness. On stage, the middle-aged members of the band, wearing what had once been fancy uniforms with bow ties, though now they were threadbare, were playing 'Old Devil Moon'.

'There they are, pantin' for us,' Billy said, grinning as he glanced across the crowded dance floor at the girls standing in bunches at the other side, wearing sheath dresses or flared skirts and high-heeled shoes, gossiping, giggling, and either boldly making eyes at the men or acting disdainful. 'At least half have their noses stuck up in the air and the other half aren't worth lookin' at. Okay, who goes first?'

The real challenge was to pick out a girl and then cross the floor and ask her if she'd like to dance. It was a challenge, because as a male advanced on a bunch of girls, usually with one in mind, invariably some of the girls would start giggling and nudging each other, others would roll their eyes, yet others would get ready to make a smart remark, usually a vicious Ulster put-down, and a few would freeze and then turn their noses up in the air. The aspiring Romeo would therefore advance across the floor wondering if he was going to be successful or humiliated, not only in front of a lot of girls but also, even worse, in full view of his mates. It was a challenge indeed, so 'going first' was not something that any of the young men, including Billy and Dan, were keen to do.

'I don't see anyone I fancy,' Dan said, trying not to look nervous.

'The last time we came you fancied that redhead,' Ronnie said, smiling benignly, his gaze fixed on the middle distance.

'Did I?' Dan said in a rising panic, his glance moving blindly left and right. 'I don't think so. What girl?'

'That one there,' Ronnie said calmly, nodding in the direction of a pretty redhead wearing a flared skirt, belted at the waist, emphasising her firm breasts. She seemed to be staring directly at Dan with uncommon boldness. 'You really fancied her, but you just couldn't approach her. She knew that and she clearly remembers you. So go on. Just walk up to her, looking real cool, and ask for a dance.'

Dan shook his head. 'Naw. I don't think so. I mean, it wasn't *her* I fancied. It was a redhead, all right, but someone else.' He made a great show of glancing all around the dance floor and then looking gravely disappointed. 'Naw, she's not here tonight. The one I really fancied isn't here, like.'

'It was her,' Billy said, supporting Ronnie and amusing himself by watching Dan squirm. 'That one smiling at you right now. Sure there's no doubt about it. You couldn't take your eyes off her and she knew it and was givin' you encouragement, and that made you scared shitless. You kept tryin' to approach her, actually crossing the floor to ask her, but you always turned away at the last minute and asked someone else to dance instead. Me and Ronnie were laughin' ourselves sick half the evenin', so we remember it well. Go on, Dan, ask her to dance. I mean, she's standin' there panting.'

'Ack, away with ya!' Dan snorted. 'Why the hell should I? You don't ask a girl who's lookin' directly at you and givin' you the come-on. You go first, Billy, and ask that wee bird you danced with last time. The brunette in that other bunch over there - those four down to the left. You've already danced with her and she liked you, so you should have no bother, like.'

Glancing in the other direction, Billy did indeed see a group of four girls, all wearing flared dresses belted tightly at the waist, including the brunette he had danced with last week. Her name was Valerie, though her friends called her 'Val'. He was certain she'd told him that. She'd also told him, he was convinced, that she lived in a street off Sandy Row. They'd had a couple of dances and he fancied her like hell, getting an erection when his dick touched her belly during the waltzes. He'd been so embarrassed by his erection, wondering if she'd felt it, that he'd avoided her for the rest of the evening, despite the fact that she'd often thrown him glances and what seemed, to him, to be inviting smiles. Now there she was again, standing with her three girlfriends, all staring at him as they nudged each other and giggled and passed remarks back and forth. Convinced that they were talking about him, Billy blushed and turned away.

'Ack, I dunno,' he said quickly, dreading having to cross that floor. 'I mean, she might not remember who I am and give me a hard time when I get there. That one's a factory girl, I can tell, and they often have tongues like razor blades.'

'Hey, Ronnie,' Dan said. 'You like dancin' a lot more than we do, so why not go over and ask someone? I mean, they never turn you down, like. So why not go over and ask that one with the red hair and then, you know, if she says yes and she will, they always do to you, like, you can maybe dance her over in this direction and kind of stop and have a wee chat with us, sort of introduce us, like, and then, you know, she might invite her friends over and we can all have a drink and dance later, if you get what I mean, like, and I'm sure you do.'

'Okay,' Ronnie said, as cool as a cucumber or, more likely, indifferent, then, smiling beatifically, not caring who he danced with as long as he had a dance, he sauntered across the floor, heading straight for the redhead, and didn't stop until he reached her, despite the fact that her girlfriends saw him coming and started nudging each other and giggling in that way most girls had.

'Oh, fuck,' Dan muttered. 'They're gonna give even *Ronnie* a hard time.'

But the redhead hadn't giggled. She hadn't moved a muscle. Ronnie said something to her, obviously asking her to dance, and she smiled and melted into his embrace and then they were hoofing it. Dan couldn't believe it.

'Shit!' he said, 'did you see that?'

'She was dead easy,' Billy said. 'You could've been doin' that instead of Ronnie. You just need to be bold, like.'

'Which *you* are,' Dan snorted.

'I'm not bothered,' Billy said.

'You're not bothered, but you're shittin' your pants. So what about that brunette?'

'*What?*' Billy said, suddenly feeling hot and bothered.

'I think you heard what I said. She's standin' over there and lookin' straight at you, rememberin' the last time, so you've no excuse not to ask her, Billy-boy.'

'What's the big deal?' Billy said with an unconvincing show of nonchalance. 'Sure there's better lookers than her. I'm still eyeing up the available talent, tryin' to decide.'

'Pull the other one,' Dan said.

Glancing around the hall, Billy saw a few men and women wandering about watchfully, dressed in what appeared to be regulation bus driver/conductor type uniforms. In fact, the Floral Hall dances were organised by the Belfast Corporation and those men and women were staff members, whose function was to discreetly monitor the activities of the customers and either prevent trouble, particularly fights between the men, which broke out on a regular basis, or offer first-aid or other assistance if required. In those uniforms, they always made Billy think of prison wardens and that, in turn, made him think of Johnny. He wished that Johnny would come home.

'Look at that fuckin' Ronnie,' Dan said, torn between admiration and resentment. 'He sure knows how to hoof it.'

'Aye, he's a quare good dancer,' Billy said, raising his voice to be heard above the noise of the swing band. 'It's the only talent he's got, like.'

When the floor was crowded, as it was now, inexperienced dancers found it difficult to manoeuvre their way out from the centre of the floor and were constantly hemmed in by the more experienced dancers, such as Ronnie, who were able to remain on the outside of the circle, where they had space to try more elaborate dancing steps as, indeed, Ronnie was now doing with the redhead, clearly impressing her.

'Ack, Jesus!' Dan exclaimed in exasperation. 'Would you look at that bastard? Sure he has that redhead in a trance. I haven't a fuckin' prayer now.'

'At least he's workin' his way around the circle and comin' towards us. Look! Here he comes!'

As the band came to the climax of 'Cheek to Cheek', Ronnie and the redhead spun gracefully towards them and then came to a stop right beside them. When the dancers and onlookers alike applauded the band, Ronnie released the redhead and walked her off the dance floor, stopping in front of Billy and Dan. Ronnie blinked his fine eyelashes as he gave the redhead his amiable, distracted, charming smile.

'Thanks,' he said. 'That was grand.'

'Aye, it was,' the redhead said, only glancing momentarily at the frustrated Dan. Up close, she had smooth pale skin, a pert nose, full lips and brilliant green eyes. Alas, she appeared to only have eyes for Ronnie, a married man with two children. 'Sure you're a real good dancer.'

'Thanks,' Ronnie said, taking compliments for granted and already glancing hopefully towards the bar, yearning for his next drink of lemonade topped up with his smuggled-in whiskey . The band struck up again, playing the opening strains of 'Alone Together'.

'Do you want to go again?' the redhead asked Ronnie, whose gaze was still focused on the bar. He turned back and smiled at her. 'Sorry,' he said, indicating Billy and Dan with an airy wave of his hand. 'These are my friends, Billy and Dan. This is Sarah, guys.'

'How ya doin'?' Billy and Dan said simultaneously, having to nearly shout to make themselves heard above the band.

'Okay,' Sarah said.

'You want to go again?' Ronnie asked her.

'Ackaye. I love dancin'.'

'Why not take her for a spin?' Ronnie said to Dan, startling him, putting him on the spot. 'Sure you haven't had a dance yet.' He looked at the equally startled Sarah and said, 'Dan's a really good dancer. I'm off for another glass of lemonade. Want to join me, Billy?'

'Aye, terrific,' Billy said.

'Well...' Dan started, beetroot-red and practically stuttering.

'Well...' Sarah started, also blushing.

'See youse later,' Billy said, grinning, as he fell in beside Ronnie and walked to the bar with him, leaving a nonplussed Dan behind with his luscious redhead. When they reached the bar, where men without partners were lined up like skittles, knocking back soft drinks laced with smuggled-in alcohol, Billy glanced back over his shoulder and saw that Dan and Sarah, embraced uneasily, were already making their awkward way around the dance floor. Grinning, Billy turned back to the bar.

'Good one,' he said.

'Two lemonades,' Ronnie said to the barman, then he glanced at Billy. 'What do ya mean?'

'The way you put Dan together with that bird. That was a good bit of manoeuvring, like.'

'Sure I didn't do a thing,' Ronnie said. 'I just fancied another drink, is all. Otherwise I'd still be out there, hoofin' it. I love dancin' but I love my drink more. So why aren't *you* dancing?'

'Can't dance, but can drink.'

Ronnie grinned at the remark. 'Aye, that might be true enough, but what about that brunette Dan mentioned?'

Billy shrugged. 'Sure he was just talkin' shite,' he lied brazenly. 'I just happened to dance with her a couple of times the last time we were here. She was okay, but nothin' special. I might ask her for a dance later on, when I've had a couple more drinks.'

'Dutch courage,' Ronnie said.

'Ackaye, I'll admit that. I hate askin' birds for a dance. Sure they're so unpredictable.'

'Don't I know it,' Ronnie said, clearly referring to Marlene. 'So how's Dan gettin' on?'

Briefly turning their backs to the bar, they gazed at the dance floor beyond the people milling about in the semi-darkness. The floor was still packed and the more experienced dancers were, as usual, making their way with fancy movements around the outside of the circle while the inexperienced, including Dan (clinging grimly to Sarah and discernable only intermittently in the flickering lights from the illuminated glass globe spinning hypnotically overhead), were trapped in the middle, not able to move so freely.

'He's workin' hard at it,' Ronnie observed.

Billy chuckled. 'Aye. Probably trampin' on her toes every couple of seconds and breakin' her spine with his sweaty paws, but he should do okay.'

Turning back to the bar, they found their glasses of lemonade waiting for them. They picked the glasses up, then turned their backs to the bar. Ronnie glanced carefully about him, looking out for the watchful staff members of the dance hall. Seeing that none were in the vicinity, he surreptitiously removed his bottle from the side pocket of his jacket, to where he had transferred it upon entering the building, and poured a good dose of whiskey into each glass; he then slipped the bottle back into his pocket. Billy didn't smoke, but Ronnie, who had all the vices, lit a cigarette, exhaled a cloud of smoke, then, having properly prepared his throat, had a mouthful of the whiskey-laced lemonade. Billy, though not smoking, also had a drink, becoming drunker on the instant, then wiped his lips with the palm of his free hand. Glancing sideways, he was startled to see that the brunette, Val, had come up to the bar and was standing at the other side of Ronnie, practically rubbing shoulders with him as she feebly raised her left hand to try gaining the busy barman's attention. Ronnie glanced to the side and gave her his irresistible smile. To Billy's amazement, Val instantly smiled back.

'What are you after, love?' Ronnie asked in his soft-spoken way.

'A lemonade,' Val replied, then she shrugged. 'But the barman hasn't even seen me.'

'Cigarette?'

'Aye, thanks.'

'I'll get that drink for you,' Ronnie said, giving her a cigarette and then gallantly lighting it for her.

Billy was dumbstruck.

While Val was inhaling and exhaling, Ronnie, raising his right hand but not his voice, caught the barman's attention by forming a ring with his thumb and index finger and merely *mouthing* the words, 'A lemonade, thanks.' The barman nodded that he understood. Ronnie turned back, smiling, to Val, saying, 'He got the order okay.'

'Thanks,' Val repeated, this time admiringly, not even glancing in Billy's direction, possibly not even remembering him.

'I'm Ronnie...'

'Valerie, but my friends call me Val.'

'... and this,' Ronnie continued, nodding in Billy's direction, 'is my brother-in-law, Billy.'

Val looked at him for the first time, not smiling, then she nodded and said, 'Ackaye... Billy... We met last week. I don't suppose you remember me.'

'Aye, I do right enough,' Billy said, more quickly than he had intended, feeling the heat rising to his cheeks, mesmerised by her hazel eyes and auburn hair, by the full breasts and tightly belted waist above the flared skirt. 'We danced a couple of times, didn't we?'

'Aye, we did.' Val turned back to Ronnie. 'So you're married, then, are you?' She sounded disappointed.

'Aye,' Ronnie said, practically fanning her with his fine, long eyelashes and staring at her with his glistening brown eyes. 'With two kids thrown in.'

'You don't *look* married,' Val said, glancing sideways at Billy, then just as quickly returning her gaze to Ronnie.

Ronnie sighed forlornly. 'Well, so it goes. Now, Billy, here,' he added, smiling amiably again and nodding in Billy's direction, making him blush, 'is still single and dances like a dream, so why don't you take him out there for a wee spin around the dance floor?'

'I haven't finished my drink yet!' Billy blurted out.

'And my lemonade's just arrived,' Val said, picking up her glass.

'So let's all get drunk instead,' Ronnie said. After glancing carefully about him again, he withdrew the bottle from his pocket and poured some whiskey into Val's glass.

'What's that?' Val asked, looking suspicious.

'Whiskey,' Ronnie said.

'Oh, that's wicked,' Val retorted with a smile.

Ronnie recapped the bottle, put it back into his pocket and then held his glass up in the air. 'Cheers.'

Val tapped Ronnie's glass with the rim of her own and then held her glass out to Billy.

'Cheers,' she said.

'Cheers,' Billy said.

The three of them were still drinking when Dan returned from the dance floor, beaming triumphantly, with Sarah clinging possessively to his arm.

'Sure that was great!' Dan said, sounding breathless. 'I worked up a real sweat out there and now my throat's parched. I could do with a drink.'

'You have a bottle in your pocket,' Ronnie said, 'and we could all do with topping up.'

Dan grinned. 'Aye, right. I'll be back in a minute.' He went to the bar, returned with two glasses of lemonade, surreptitiously laced them with whiskey and gave one to the brassy redhead, Sarah. He then topped up the glasses of the others, furtively slipped the bottle back into his jacket pocket and then held his glass up in a mock salute. 'Cheers!' he said.

They all drank a lot after that, alternating the drinking with dancing, becoming drunk from a combination of alcohol and sheer exhilaration, rendered magically unreal in the flickering lights from the revolving glass globe, sucked into the music, dissolving into the romantically-coloured ambience, briefly set free from reality, enchanted with little things. They left just before midnight, returning to the city in the same bus, the men laughing, the girls giggling, glad to see that the rain had stopped, then going off, staggering drunkenly in different directions, under an unclouded sky, an umbrella of stars, to return to their own beds and, at least in Billy's case, to be changed for all time.

Though he would never quite remember how he had managed it, Billy, in a drunken stupor, with no previous experience, hardly knowing what he was doing and doomed to scarcely remember it, impregnated Val in her own bed, in that small terraced house just off Sandy Row, in the early hours of that morning, oblivious to the fact that her parents were sleeping unaware in the adjoining bedroom. Despite his vague recollections of how they had come to be there and what they did in that bed, Billy would always recall the full moon beaming in through the window, illuminating the rumpled sheets, Val's shapely, enfolding legs, the smooth plain of her belly, the milky-white curve of her bosom, making everything seem dreamlike, romantic... almost unreal... Even though it turned out, in dawn's pearly-grey, revealing light, to be very real indeed.

One stolen moment can change a whole life and Billy's life changed overnight.

8

It was just before midnight when the séance ended and the last of Mary's spiritualist friends left the house. Once they had gone, having had their tea with buns and biscuits, Mary poured a whisky, lit a cigarette, then removed the tin box from the mantelpiece and sank back into a chair, resting the tin box in her lap. She did not immediately open it.

The séance that evening had been particularly successful, with a wide variety of spirits making contact, using the primitive Morse code of the rocking table, to each of those linking hands. Mary had been talking to her departed brother, Neil, for a long time now and each time had been exalted by the experience. However, this evening, for the first time, she had made contact with her first child, the Johnny who had died shortly after birth, a cot death, inexplicable, and had only done so through the intervention of Neil, who had told her, though the spirit-medium, speaking in the trance state, that Johnny, the first Johnny, having died while still a baby, could not actually speak to her, but could only let her hear him as she remembered him. Mary had agreed to this and then, to her astonishment, the crying of a child had emerged from the lips of the semi-conscious spirit-medium and Mary had known, on the instant, beyond any shadow of doubt, that she was hearing the crying of her first-born son, as he had been just before he tragically died. Hearing him, she had broken down and wept.

Beyond that, of course, there could be little contact, as the first child, the original Johnny, had died before learning to speak. Nevertheless, simply learning that her first child was all right, that he existed on the Other Side, that he was being looked after by Neil and her other departed relatives - her mother and father, various aunts and uncles - Mary had felt a transcendent uplifting. That's when she had broken down, sobbing out of sheer relief, all the years of grief finally swept away. Now, with the last of her guests gone, she felt the peace of acceptance.

Her first child, Johnny, was alive and well on the Other Side and her other Johnny, the one she had named after the dead child, was still writing letters and promising, albeit time after time, to come home one day. That day might soon be dawning.

When Mary read Johnny's letters, she realised that he had indeed changed, was more mature, less innocent, perhaps even hardened, but she was convinced that despite what had happened to him, where he had been, what he had seen and done, he was essentially still the same Johnny, her formerly dead, resurrected first child, and that he would be as right as rain once he stepped through the door.

She was convinced that sooner or later he would do just that.

She was, however, still deeply moved by the recollection of that ghostly child's crying, that eerie babble emerging from the trembling lips of the spirit-medium, and this drove her to read the last letter that Johnny had sent to her, as if, by reading it, she would somehow be in contact with the other Johnny, the first son, her lost one. Thus convinced, she opened the tin, withdrew the pile of letters, removed the rubber band, and separated the last envelope from the rest - the one that had just come that morning. After tugging the letter out, using her thumb and index finger, she unfolded it and then took a deep breath and started to read through tearful eyes...

9th August, 1966.

    Dear Mum and Dad and Marlene and Billy,

    As usual, I have to start by apologising for my tardiness in writing (was my last letter last year or the year before that?), but they've been keeping me busy and, as I think I said before, I'm intimidated by writing and reluctant to put words down on paper.

    Since last writing to you I've been all over the place - particularly the Far East and the South Pacific - and I now feel that I've seen all there is to see - at sea, ha, ha, and ashore. It's become so commonplace that every port is now beginning to look the same to me and the different languages, none of which I can speak, all sound like the same babble. I no longer find it exciting when, after days at sea, we see land on the horizon and know that we're going to get ashore. In fact, in recent months, when we've docked, I've found myself staying aboard ship more and more, preferring the privacy and silence of my cabin (when my cabin mate is ashore) to the hustle and bustle of the ports we stop at. I've also become more private even when we're at sea, sticking pretty much to myself and not saying much to anyone. Some of the crew, I know, think I'm a bit strange, but that doesn't bother me and, indeed, it's probably useful in making them keep their distance. I want this because although I have, in the past, made good friends aboard ship, I've also made enemies and seamen, when angered, can be dangerous, even when not downright psychotic, which some of them are.

Because I like to keep busy, I volunteer for a lot of jobs and now do a wide variety of things. While I still work as a stevedore when the ship is docked and loading, I now also work in the engine room as the engineer's assistant. It's hard, hot work. When the ship is travelling at maximum speed (approximately 20 knots at 118 revolutions a minute, gobbling 40 tons of fuel a day) the temperature in the piston room soars as high as 40 degrees centigrade. It's dark and noisy down there. I pant and sweat a lot. The commands from the bridge are sent down to the engine room by telegraph and used by the engineer to control the engine. As the engineer's assistant, I help to start and stop the ship, slow it down, go into reverse or speed up, by using compressed air. The four auxiliary engines and generators on the starboard side supply the ship with electricity (the main switch-board is on the port side) and during loading and refrigeration operations often three, and sometimes all four, auxiliary engines have to be kept running. Though I assist the engineer, I'm helped in turn by the storekeeper, the greasers and the wipers. We all work like dogs.

The engineer and I have to regularly inspect the engine room, checking the temperature of all the bearings in the shaft tunnel, applying more grease and ascertaining that the stuffing box seal isn't drawing water. (I know that you, Mum, and you, Marlene, won't be interested in this, but you, Dad, and you, Billy, might be.) When the inspection is completed to our satisfaction, all of the crew from the piston room and the centre station are allowed to go up to the palaverdeck to take in some fresh air, get away from the heat and din of the engine, and have a cool beer and smoko. That's one of the few times I socialise with the other men, but don't ask me why. I really don't want to.

Why have I become so private? I'm not at all sure, but I suspect that it's a combination of fear of my own violence (the violence I first expressed at Finaghy Field on that Twelfth so long ago, then expressed again in Mackie's foundry when 14, and finally expressed in full a year later, during that awful riot in the Falls Road) and growing discontent with this life of constant travelling.

The fear of my own violence springs from my knowledge that there are similarly violent men aboard this ship and that they and I can easily provoke each other. There's a kind of unspoken hierarchy to this insular shipboard society in which some men automatically assume authority over others and the others either bend or get broken. I won't bend and I refuse to let myself get broken, and my quiet stubbornness in this particular direction has often led to trouble. Over the years, however, as my time with the ship grows longer, I have automatically been accorded more respect, more privacy, and I find that by keeping a certain distance, maintaining a polite aloofness, I gain even more respect (or, perhaps, make others nervous) and am not bothered by the violence of the bullies. Silence sometimes speaks volumes.

That's one reason, I believe, for my increasing isolation and need for privacy. The other is, as I have stated, my growing discontent with this life of constant travelling. I am now 25 years old, but I feel a lot older, more experienced than my years, and as the novelty of new ports, new faces, gradually fades, as 'a girl in every port' becomes no more than a sour joke, I find myself thinking increasingly of home, of Belfast, and yearning to return to my own kind.

I once wrote to you, I know, saying why I couldn't go home, why I'd feel a stranger there, would be uncomfortable there, but that was only me at a particular time and that time has long gone. I've changed over the years (as I changed in the Borstal, though not for the better) and now I find that I'm beginning to feel 'Irish' in a way that I never did before. I realise that we in Belfast are 'British', at least according to our passports, and that we tend to feel more 'British' than Irish in certain ways. Nevertheless, we are Irish, very different from the English, and I now feel that I have to go back home to regain my roots.

Does this make me too old for my age?

Sometimes I think so. Certainly, I find myself, like an old man, reliving my past with increasing frequency, recalling my childhood, my school days, my adolescence (How is Donna, by the way? Has she forgiven me for not getting in touch? I'll understand if she hasn't.) and yearning to somehow, at least partially, get them back, perhaps simply by walking the streets I used to walk and talking to the people I used to know, including all of you. I'm withdrawing into myself, becoming obsessed with my former life, growing discontent with travelling, with the rootlessness of it all, its lack of family feeling, and so I want to regain what I lost when I went into that Borstal. I want my family back, my old friends, the streets I know, and so despite the fact that I've said it so many times in the past, promised so many times, I think this time I can say with complete confidence that when the ship docks next month at Southampton, I'll be...

Mary was just about to read the final line of the letter when someone opened the front door and entered the house. Sniffing back her tears, resting the letter in her lap, she looked up to see Albert entering the living room. Though he had been out all evening and was pink-faced with drink, he still looked like a bit of a dandy, his hair still neatly combed, his suit still immaculate, tie knotted precisely between the pristine collars of his shirt, the rings still flashing on his fine fingers. He was drunk, of course.

'You're still up,' he said. 'I thought you'd be in bed.'

'No,' Mary said. 'I'm not in bed. Sorry to disappoint you.'

'That's enough of that, Mary.'

As if sensing the change in her, furrowing his brow as he looked at her, his blood-shot eyes squinting, he stepped closer to her, but stopped again when he was standing right above her. She noted that he was swaying a little, taken over by the drink, but typically, he soon managed to steady himself.

Staring up at him, his greying head haloed by the rays of the ceiling light, his shadow stretched out to her feet, she had to admit to herself that he was still a handsome man, despite the lines in his face, despite the bags under his eyes, despite the ruination caused by his years of constant drinking, but he remained, despite all of that, the father of her children - Marlene's father, Billy's father, more importantly, Johnny's father - and even though she despised him on many counts, she owed him for that. Though he had never really wanted her (she knew who he had really wanted) he had lain with her in their tormenting bed and fathered their children. Reluctantly accepting this undeniable fact, this dividing line between them, she thought of what she had just read in the letter from Johnny and was torn, like someone stretched on the rack, between sorrow and joy.

'What's up?' Albert said. 'Have you been crying? You look like you've been crying.' Then he noticed the letter in her lap. 'What's that? Another letter from Johnny?'

Mary couldn't help herself: she started crying again. The tears rolled silently, uncontrollably, down her cheeks and dripped onto the letter.

'What's the matter?' Albert asked, concerned. 'Why are you crying?'

Mary sniffed back her tears, glanced again at the letter, then raised her head and offered Albert a healing smile.

'Johnny's finally coming home,' she said.

Chapter Ten

1

The march began peacefully enough. Leaving their house in the Pound Loney just after eight in the morning, Sean and Moira walked to the centre of town, in the bitter cold, through a darkness illuminated only fitfully by street lights, or by the lights of the odd passing car, the shops, normally opening at this hour, being closed for New Year's day. They both had small rucksacks strapped to their shoulders, containing food, drink, fresh underclothes, sleeping bag and toiletries. Sean felt like a Boy Scout.

Arriving at the City Hall, they were pleasantly surprised to find what appeared to be a group of about fifty people, mostly students from Queen's University, both Catholics and Protestants, but including slightly older members of the Civil Rights Movement and the recently formed Peoples Democracy, gathered together in front of the imposing building, gradually forming a marching column that blocked the road. Helpfully, the roads were virtually free of traffic at this early hour, this particular day. The copper dome of the City Hall, seemingly scraping the fast-drifting clouds of a leaden sky, had turned a leprous green with age and looked, in the morning's wintry gloom, like a giant, rotting cabbage.

A bunch of Paisleyites, mostly males, wearing gabardines or heavy overcoats with scarves, peaked caps or hats on their heads, were standing around the fringes of the crowd, already waving Union Jacks and bawling abusive remarks for the benefit of the gathered TV cameramen, news photographers, sound-recordists and journalists. Uniformed RUC policemen were also spaced at regular intervals around the edge of the marchers, though they appeared to be doing nothing to subdue the aggressive Loyalist demonstrators.

Though formally headed by the PD activist, Michael Farrell, this proposed march to Derry had been organised by the Northern Ireland Civil Rights Association, which had been set up in 1967 by the Campaign for Social Justice, the Republicans and other opposition groups as a multi-party lobbying group on civil rights issues. It was therefore no surprise to Sean and Moira that they should find Des and Iris in the middle of the excited, idealistic crowd. Iris looked as undernourished as always, though her short-cropped hair, anorak, loose pants and boots gave her the appearance of a Queens Uni' radical; whereas Des, previously clean-shaven, now had the untidy beard and long hair of a Haight Ashbury hippie. He also had eye pupils unnaturally enlarged by his regular intakes of marijuana.

'Ack, Jasus,' he exclaimed, emulating a cod Ulsterman, or, perhaps, the histrionic Reverend Paisley, blowing into his clenched fists to warm them as the marchers formed into a lengthy column, 'it's like bloody Siberia here today. Sure this is going to be a march to numb your balls.'

'If you have any,' Iris said.

'Thank you for those kind words, my darling little woman, who clearly has more balls than me and is willing to prove it.'

Iris grinned and rolled her big eyes, then turned to Moira. 'So who's looking after Michael and Deirdre?' she asked, referring to Sean and Moira's children, three and two years old. But before a reply could be given, the noisy Paisleyites surged forward in a single, protoplasmic mass, deliberately heading for the front of the column.

'So what are *they* up to?' Des asked.

'Go and find out,' Sean told him.

'I think I will,' Des said and promptly hurried after the Loyalists.

'My Da and Meg,' Sean said to Iris, replying at last to her question, picking up their conversation as Des left. 'They've taken the kids to their house and they'll stay there until we get back.'

Sean and Moira had married almost five years ago, with the latter moving into Sean's family home in the Pound Loney, shortly after Barry married the widowed Meg Connolly and moved out of his own home to join her in her bigger Turf Lodge house. Now three years short of fifty, with no IRA work to do, since the organisation was practically redundant, and with Theresa no longer living at home, a lost cause, Barry adored his grandchildren, as did Meg, and both were always keen to look after them.

'It's nice to have loving grandparents living near you,' Iris said, 'if they're helpful instead of interfering. You should both count your blessings.'

'We do,' Moira said. 'No sign of any kids with you and Des?'

'Sure you're joking me, aren't you?'

'You're still living together, though.'

'In sin,' Iris emphasised, shrugging and grinning. 'We're still not married and we've no plans for children.'

'Wouldn't you like to be married?' Moira asked.

'Not at all,' Iris said. 'Sure it's only a bourgeois invention, designed to keep women in bondage. I'm a female liberationist, aren't I? Also, I'm too committed to my civil rights activities to have time for kids of my own.'

'What does Des think about it?'

'Well, you know Des. He's into rock music and dope, the counterculture and civil rights, so he's happy enough with our situation. Maybe some day, when we're older and more settled, but not right now, thanks. So how are Barry and Meg these days? Settled down just like any other old married couple?'

'Correct,' Moira said. 'Sure they're as happy as Larry. And with four kids of her own, all grown up now, Meg knows what *not* to do with her in-laws . She loves our two wee'uns.'

'Lucky you.' Grinning, Iris turned her wide-eyed gaze to the front of the column, where most of the men with Union Jacks had formed a solid mass, a human barrier, directly in front of the civil rights marchers at the head of the column. 'So what's goin' on up there, I wonder?'

She had barely spoken when Des returned from the front of the column, blowing into his cupped hands to warm them, clearly frustrated. 'Lord have mercy,' he said. 'Wouldn't you think they'd leave us alone for once?'

'What's happening?' Sean asked, dead keen to see the march commence, but feeling slightly nervous as well. Having heard too many rumours about what the Prods were planning, he was worried about what they might do this morning.

'Paisley's right-hand man, Ronald Bunting, that former British Army major, now Loyalist fanatic, is up there with a bunch of his fellow wankers, informing Farrell that the march is going to be harassed and hindered all the way by Paisleyite binlids.'

'Sure there's nothing new there,' Moira said. 'How did Farrell respond?'

'He said we won't give in to threats, that this is a peaceful, legal march, and that it's going to commence at 9.00am sharp, a couple of minutes from now, no matter what Bunting or his flag-wavers do.'

'So what *are* they going to do?' Iris asked.

'They're going to march directly in front of us, waving their Union Jacks in full view of the media.'

'The RUC has to stop them,' Iris said, her cheeks flushing with outrage. 'This march is perfectly legal, formally arranged, so they've no right to walk in front of us like that, waving their filthy British flags.'

'One of our organisers has already tried that theory with the RUC and was told that this is a free country.'

'Meaning?'

'That the Prods can do what they want.'

'They wouldn't say that, the bastards, if this was an Orange Lodge march and we insisted on marching in front of it, waving the tricolour, the true flag of this country.'

'No, they wouldn't,' Des agreed. 'But this is an Orange State and we all know whose side the RUC is on. All those morons are Protestants.'

'So are a lot of those marching with us,' Sean reminded him, always keen to pour oil on troubled waters, 'so let's not automatically use the word "bastards" when discussing Protestants.'

'Sorry,' Des said, grinning. 'All that Protestant bawling's done my head in.'

'That and Mary Jane,' Iris said laconically. 'Just try to keep that hippie's head straight.'

'Christ!' Moira exploded in exasperation. 'This was supposed to be a *peaceful* demonstration!'

'It will be,' Sean reassured her. 'I don't think Bunting and his lot will walk in front of us too long. This is going to be a four-day hike and I can't imagine they'd want to share it with us. They're just trying to gain themselves more publicity before we leave Belfast.'

'They do it every time, don't they?' Iris said. 'They won't bend an inch.'

True enough, Sean thought, aware that Paisley and Bunting had become the thorns in the side of the whole Civil Rights Movement. Though the prime aim of the movement was to put an end to gerrymandering and introduce the principle of 'one man, one vote' by peaceful means, time after time, as Sean recollected all too clearly, when the movement had announced a planned demonstration or march, Paisley and his followers had done all in their power to stop them or, at least, harass them, often by creating violent confrontations, for which the civil rights marchers were then blamed. The Paisleyites had done this despite knowing that the Republican clubs had been banned under the Special Powers Act, Sinn Féin had been classified as illegal in the north, and the IRA had been rendered virtually redundant as a fighting force, lacking weapons, men and even the support of the Catholic community. And they had done it, as far as Sean could see, out of nothing more rational than a sectarian paranoia so absolute that it bordered on racism. Small wonder that the Civil Rights Movement in the Six Counties had based itself on the original movement in the United States. The Catholic Irish were beginning to view themselves as the blacks of the Orange State, with the Paisleyites as their very own Klu Klux Klan. To Sean, with his interest in all matters historical, the parallels were painfully obvious.

'Brilliant,' Des said, 'we've started moving.' He checked his wristwatch to confirm that it was 9.00am exactly. 'And dead on time, despite those flag-waving Orange baboons.'

As the column moved off, some of the marchers held hands and started singing, 'We Shall Overcome', which they had picked up from the American Civil Rights Movement and now used as their own theme song. Because this particular march was being modeled on the Selma-Montgomery march in Alabama in 1966, which had exposed the vicious racism of America's Deep South and forced the U.S. government into major reforms, the song was both appropriate and encouraging.

Looking over the heads of the singing crowd, Sean could see the Union Jacks of Bunting and his henchmen fluttering in the wind as they boldly marched out front, hoping to hide the civil rights marchers from the television cameras and news photographers.

'Arseholes!' Iris exclaimed, always quick to offer foul-mouthed invective to relieve her frustrations.

'They won't last,' Sean assured her, grinning despite himself, amused even while secretly concerned. 'I'm pretty sure they're just doing this for the benefit of the local media - propaganda for their fellow Orangemen. They'll pack it in once we get out of town.'

'Let's hope so,' Moira said.

Proving Sean right, Bunting and his fellow Paisleyites only marched ahead of the column as far as Carlisle Circus, the traditional gathering place for the Orange Lodges on the Twelfth and the beginning of the road that led to Antrim. Once there, in full view of the gathered media, the Paisleyites divided into two groups, one at each side of the road, but they continued waving their Union Jacks and shouting abuse at the civil rights marchers passing between them, heading out of town. The RUC policemen following the march did nothing to stop the abuse, which was purely vocal at this point, and eventually, as the marchers continued along the Antrim Road, the Paisleyites dropped out of sight and the shouting faded away.

'Thank God for that,' Moira said, holding Sean's hand and smiling at him as she walked by his side, with Iris and Des on her right, also holding hands. 'Maybe it *will* be a peaceful march, after all.'

'Peace on Earth, good will to all men,' Sean intoned sardonically, though he was truly relieved to be out of the city, now marching in relative safety through quiet suburbs, between wet, green fields, over which, forming bizarre, spectral shapes, a few clouds of morning mist still hovered. The sky remained dismal.

'I'm breathless already,' Moira said, 'so this exercise can only do me good.'

'You'll get plenty of exercise before we're finished. We've a long way to go yet.'

'Not all at once, thank God. So what's the plan for today?'

'We hope to make our way to Antrim, getting there in the late afternoon and stopping for tea, then we'll bed down in a local county hall for the night and march on to Derry from there.'

'Great. I could do with a good tea and a kip. A bit of both should revive me.'

As they continued the march, first in silence, then singing the songs adapted by the American Civil Rights Movement for their own marches, Sean glanced frequently at Moira, at her luxuriant jet-black hair and brown eyes, her solid yet shapely figure, full lips open as she sang along with the others, and found himself swelling with secret pride that together they had stuck with the movement. Through all of its vicissitudes, its successes and failures, they had both remained determined to do their modest best in helping resolve the problems of the Six Counties by peaceful means. He was pleased that they had.

The times they certainly are a-changing, he thought, as he joined the others in singing the Bob Dylan song, while holding and frequently squeezing Moira's hand. Even former IRA men, the hard men, are taking part in this march. That, at least, is *some* kind of progress.

'This march,' he said, glancing out over the sea of heads that formed an arrow pointing towards Antrim, cutting a swathe through the Ulster mist, 'is reminding me of what the last couple of years gave us.'

'Oh, yeah?' Moira said, sounding slightly American, subconsciously influenced, as most of them were, by the intonations of Folk music and Protest songs. 'And what was that, my love?'

'The possibility of justice.'

'God, pass me the smelling salts!'

But Sean merely smiled at her remark. He knew she wasn't a cynic. Throughout the whole of the past year, she had been as moved as he was by the events taking place overseas: the Tet offensive in Vietnam, the student demonstrations in Paris, the 'Prague spring' in Czechoslovakia. Like the majority of the students of Queen's, he had been radicalised by them.

'Don't give me that smelling-salts nonsense,' he said. 'Remember last year's civil rights march, in August, from Coalisland to Dungannon?'

'Who could forget it?'

'Four thousand people took part in that march and "We Shall Overcome", deliberately sung as a civil rights anthem, was heard in Northern Ireland for the first time. After that, there was no going back for us. And that includes you.'

Moira smiled. 'Okay, I admit it. Now climb down off your high horse.'

'That march passed off peacefully, didn't it?'

'Yes, it did, but what did that prove? The next march was a nightmare.'

She was referring to the march that took place the previous year: the year that had ended yesterday. It was the second civil rights march to Derry, planned to go from the Waterside Station area, across Craigavon Bridge, through the ancient city walls, then on into the Diamond - a predominantly Protestant route, leading to what was virtually the Loyalists' Weeping Wall. It had ended brutally, however, when the marchers, men, women and children, were indiscriminately baton-charged by the police and hosed with the first water cannon to be deployed in the city. The police then lost control, viciously attacking everyone in sight, including prominent politicians, businessmen and other innocent bystanders. That evening, the Bogside had its first riots, with the stoning of police cars, the smashing of shop windows, and petrol bombings. More ominously, barricades were put up in the streets of Derry for the very first time.

'Aye, a nightmare,' Sean agreed, 'but it gained us a lot. That riot was shown on English and Ulster television, outraged those who saw it, increased liberal opinion in the North, and greatly enlarged the membership of our movement. So here we are, marching on Derry again – again demanding our civil rights.'

'There speaks the born politician,' Moira said with soft, affectionate sarcasm. 'That could be your downfall.'

'I'm not a politician,' Sean insisted.

'You're on your way, love.'

But Sean didn't mind what she said. She kept his feet on solid ground. She was as committed as him, maybe more so, but she knew how to hold herself in check. She was his anchor, his port in a storm, his safe harbour when doubts crept in to paralyse him. In truth, she was stronger than he was, though she tried not to show it. He had often thought that if push came to shove, she'd be the one who pushed hardest. That belief gave him the moral support he needed when he temporarily lost faith in himself, as he did too often for comfort these days.

'Do you think what we're doing's right?' she asked, her voice raised against the howling, freezing wind. They were now about halfway between Belfast and Antrim, and it seemed, at least to Sean, that they'd been marching for an eternity. No one in the column was singing at the moment, perhaps being too tired to do so, but most of them still seemed of good cheer, laughing and joking as they rubbed frozen hands together, stamped their feet to get the blood circulating, blew steam from numbed lips.

'What do you mean?' Sean asked, glancing in both directions at frost-covered fields and grassy hills, over which the shadows of black clouds were inexorably, ominously creeping.

'Deliberately marching through Loyalist towns. I'd call that provocative.'

'It *is* provocative. Sure it's *meant* to be provocative. What was new about that first big march into Derry, the one in August last year, wasn't just that it was one of the first civil rights marches, but that it was Catholics marching instead of Orangemen. Prior to that, it was only the Orangemen who could march by right, while we had to get official permission. So that first march into Derry was certainly provocative, but deliberately so, letting the Orangemen know that we're demanding the right to march as freely as they do. This march, in going through Loyalist towns, is making the same point.'

'The million-dollar question being: Will those Loyalists actually *let* us march through their towns?'

'I don't believe ordinary people will bother us. If we meet with resistance, it's going to be organised, probably by the Ulster Protestant Volunteers. We'll just have to deal with it when it comes.'

'Do you believe the RUC will help us?' Moira indicated the many unformed policemen in plain view. Some were marching along with the civil rights demonstrators, but others were positioned around the column in paddy wagons, prepared to haul the marchers away at the first sign of trouble.

'If they're in the sight of the media, they might. Otherwise, I wouldn't depend on it.'

'That's comforting,' Moira said.

In fact, they had already passed a variety of Protestants on the country roads outside Belfast and received no more than curious glances and even, on the odd occasion, a friendly grin or encouraging wave. Sean was hoping that this kind of reception would persist, but his hopes were dashed when, as they approached Antrim, about four in the afternoon, in light dimming to darkness, a handful of Paisleyites gathered on the bridge outside the town, some of them brandishing wooden clubs.

'Well, well,' Des said. 'Looks like we might have a wee problem here.'

'More Orange binlids,' Iris said as the RUC vehicles up front ground to a screeching halt, blocking the road and stopping the marchers. Other RUC men spilled out of the paddy wagons and took up positions along both sides of the road, while those in charge went up to talk to the menacing Paisleyites. Those policemen, as Sean could see clearly, were smiling and offering the Protestants cigarettes.

'Why don't they just crawl into bed together,' Des drawled, 'and stick their tongues up each other's arses?'

'Maybe they're just being diplomatic,' Moira said hopefully.

'Yeah, right, they're just being diplomatic... and I'm Santa Claus.'

Even as the RUC officers were supposedly pacifying the gathered Paisleyites, a Lambeg drummer started pounding his instrument, calling more Loyalists to the bridge. As the marchers waited impatiently, smoking or having sandwiches and drinks from thermos flasks, many sitting on blankets on the frozen road, exhaustion clearly etched on their faces, the drummer pounded his instrument more relentlessly, hypnotically, creating a blood-stirring din, making the very air vibrate, until the bridge was blocked by a huge crowd of agitated, red-faced, bawling Protestants. Most were dressed in plain clothes, drab suits and overcoats, with peaked caps or hats on their heads, but a lot of them were holding make-shift clubs in their fists, raised on high to let the marchers see them.

Sean noticed that the RUC made no attempt to order the Protestants off the bridge.

No violence broke out, but the marchers could not continue until, with the fall of darkness, the RUC persuaded them to get into the paddy wagons for their own safety and then drove them across the bridge, through the chanting, club-waving Loyalists, to the county hall that they had originally intended marching to from the centre of Antrim. There they bedded down for the night, most stretched out in sleeping bags. Sean lay in a sleeping bag beside Moira, with Des and Iris sleeping nearby, but he still reached out to hold her hand and squeeze it reassuringly.

Sleeping, he dreamt that he was a child, back in the Pound Loney, when a Scottish Protestant band, led by a Lambeg drummer, entered the street as if they owned it, creating a dreadful, frightening din. Sean, the child, was standing on the pavement, watching the band with a mixture of fear and excitement, when a man, a veritable giant, his features obliterated by the sunlight behind him, rendering him terrifyingly faceless, reached down and picked him up off the pavement, saying, 'Here's what we do to you wee Fenians.' The dream then dissolved into a deep well of terror, cosmic darkness, spinning stars, and Sean returned to his senses, though still in the dream, to find himself *inside* the Lambeg drum, curled up between the two hides that vibrated demoniacally, to a shocking, relentless rhythm, as the drummer pounded on them with his drumsticks, while carrying Sean away, still tucked up inside the drum, to a fate worse than death, because it was unknown...

Sean, the real Sean, the mature man, awoke pouring sweat, relieved to find Moira sleeping beside him, also in a sleeping bag, in the moonlit darkness of the county hall located just outside Antrim. Though relieved to see his loving wife still lying there, still holding his hand, he faced the new day with trepidation.

His fear of Loyalists, heightened by his dream, was given concrete form when the civil rights march, continuing after breakfast, reached the town of Randalstown, near Lough Neagh. There, another group of Loyalists, armed with sticks and cudgels, were blocking the bridge leading into town. This time, the police stopped the march and then diverted it around the Catholic town of Toome. Shortly after, at the far side of the town, they blocked it again.

Standing well behind the police blockade, almost hidden by the police line that covered the whole road, from one side to the other, Sean caught a glimpse of local MP, Major James Chichester-Clark, and another man wearing a pinstripe suit, who looked distinctly like a Stormont politician. Now he knew where the blocking orders were coming from.

'So what's happening?' Moira asked when Sean returned from his brief visit to the front of the blocked column.

'The RUC's just informed us that a hostile crowd of vigilantes is blocking the main road, so they're diverting us up some back roads.'

'Sounds sensible enough,' Des said, though his eyes, despite the glaze of marijuana, expressed cynical disbelief.

'I wouldn't trust them as far as I can spit,' Iris retorted, before inhaling deeply on the joint she was sharing with Des. 'And I can't spit at all.'

Ten minutes later, when the marchers were taking the diversion recommended by the RUC, which did indeed channel them along a couple of country lanes, then into a back lane, narrow and winding, flanked with tall, dripping hedgerows, they were attacked by a mob of Loyalists, who were waiting for them at an isolated crossroads.

Sean was shocked at the hatred he saw in their faces, as they bawled abuse, threw large stones, and struck out at the marchers with cudgels. No response was forthcoming. The marchers simply ducked and weaved, trying to avoid being hurt, until they made it through the gauntlet of flushed, heavily breathing, violent men. Only when the last of them had made their way through, humiliated and bruised, did the RUC move in, halfheartedly pushing the vigilantes back into the hedgerows.

'Very clever,' Sean said to the leading RUC officer, as he marched past the squad car parked by the side of the road, under the bare, frost-covered branches of the overhanging trees. 'You must have known exactly where those Prods were waiting for us. You deliberately led us right into them.'

The officer smiled thinly, shaking his head in denial. 'Not true, sir. Sure they know this area better than we do. More likely, when they saw us diverting the march, they took a short cut and reached that crossroads before us. I'm real sorry about that.'

'Yeah, I bet you are,' Sean said, feeling rage boiling up for the first time.

'That was mean,' Moira chastised him, as they trudged on in the middle of the column with Des and Iris, both stoned, but just as weary and dispirited, sticking close to them. 'He might have been telling the truth, after all.'

'I doubt it,' Sean retorted, now too angry to be reasonable. 'They deliberately led us straight into those bastards *and* their ambush.'

'Didn't you recently tell us,' Des said, grinning, 'to stop using the word "bastards" when referring to Loyalists?'

'Not *those* Loyalists,' Sean said.

Darkness was falling when they reached the nationalist hamlet of Gulladuff. There they were warned that another crowd of vigilantes was waiting for them on the road to Maghera, their destination for the following day. Truly weary by now, not in the mood for another fight, they decided to bed down in Gulladuff for the night. This wise decision bought them a peaceful sleep, but the following morning, just before setting out again, they were informed that the Loyalists who had been waiting for them the previous evening, incensed when they didn't turn up, had vented their frustration by rampaging through Maghera, attacking Catholic shops and homes. As a result, Major Chichester-Clark had met a deputation of Loyalists at his home and promised to try have the march banned. Luckily, he hadn't succeeded in doing so. Nevertheless, when the marchers continued on to Maghera, the RUC blocked their way into the village and diverted them over the Sperrin Mountains, along empty country roads, past isolated farmhouses, where they were whipped by fierce winds and often drenched in rain, until they reached the outskirts of Dungiven. There they were stopped by another RUC blockade.

'What is it this time?' Moira asked in exasperation when Sean returned from the front of the stalled column.

'Those RUC officers are trying to tell us that there are hostile crowds in the next two villages along the main road, but this time we don't believe them. So we're going through their damned blockade, despite what they say to the contrary.'

Looking ahead, Sean saw that the RUC men had lined up across the road and along both sides of it, forming a wedge designed to keep the marchers back. There was a lot of noise up there, with men shouting threats, women screaming abuse, and a lot of civil rights marchers waving clenched fists. To calm themselves down as they began their advance, some of the civil rights marchers linked hands and again started singing, 'We Shall Overcome'. When the rest of the marchers did likewise, with the massed singing sounding like a choir in a cathedral, the police reluctantly parted to let them all through. The marchers burst into spontaneous cheering as they passed the barricade.

Moving on, they soon reached the first village, Feeny, where, despite what the police had said, there was no hostile crowd waiting for them. Relieved, but growing angrier at the repeated police deceptions, they continued on to the second village, Claudy, which they reached in the afternoon. Again, they found that the promised crowd of Loyalist vigilantes did not exist. Now tired, frustrated and angry at the police, who were supposed to be protecting them instead of deceiving them, they settled into Claudy for the night.

Before bedding down again, Sean was informed by Des, who had been talking to the DP's Michael Farrell, leading the march, that while there had been no hostile crowds waiting for them at Feeny or here in Claudy, as promised by the RUC officers, there had certainly been a mob of armed Loyalists waiting for them on the diversion route recommended by the same officers.

'Those RUC bastards are trying to set us up,' Des said. 'If we'd taken that route they recommended, there would've been a riot. Sure isn't it now as clear as day that we can't trust a damned word they utter?'

'Clear as day,' Sean agreed. 'But did Farrell have anything else to say?'

'Yep. He said that earlier this afternoon, the Reverend Ian Paisley and his buddy, Major Bunting - who boldly promised us this harassment and is certainly trying to deliver - had a meeting with William Long, the Home Affairs Minister, again asking for the march to be banned. Long didn't agree, but later in the afternoon, Paisley and Bunting addressed a rally at the Guildhall in Derry, deliberately whipping up the crowd, putting them in the mood to harass us tomorrow, when we start our march into the city.'

'I think the trouble tomorrow could be serious.'

'You're real brilliant,' Des said.

However, Sean was encouraged when, the following morning, at the start of the fourth day, the ranks of the civil rights marchers were swollen by several hundred additional men and women who, incensed by Paisley's rabble-rousing of the previous afternoon, had come out from Derry to lend their support. The march therefore continued with a great deal of renewed enthusiasm. Yet they had only marched a few miles out of the village when they were halted again by the police.

Instantly, Sean ran to the front of the column, where he heard an RUC officer warning Michael Farrell that there might be 'a spot of bother' up ahead.

'Are you saying we can't continue the march?'

'No. I'm simply warning you that there might be some trouble.'

'How much?'

The officer shrugged. 'A wee bit of stone-throwing.'

'That's all?'

'I think so. There are some Loyalists ahead, in a field beside the road. They might throw a few stones, but I think you'll be okay if you stick close in to the hedge on the right-hand side. It's up to you, of course, if you want to risk it.'

'We'll risk it. Can we move on now?'

'Of course,' the RUC officer replied, stepping aside and indicating that his men should do the same, which they did, glancing at one another and smirking.

Sean saw those knowing grins, those smirks, and instantly became suspicious, exchanging a glance with Farrell, who merely shrugged and raised his hands in the air as if silently praying.

The marchers advanced again. Just as a concerned Sean had rejoined Moira, who looked tired and tense, they started along the narrow lane that ran downhill to Burntollet Bridge, located a few miles outside Derry. Suddenly, a large crowd of Loyalist vigilantes, all wearing identifying armbands, poured out of a side lane that had been hidden by the hedgerows, bawling abuse, hurling stones and bottles, then attacking the shocked marchers with planks of wood, iron bars, bicycle chains and wooden clubs studded with nails. The marchers scattered, men shouting, women sobbing or screaming, some running back up the lane to be trapped by the vigilantes circling around behind them, others heading downhill, towards the bridge, pursued by more vigilantes.

'Fuckin' Fenian cunts! Taig bastards! Take *that*, ya Papish bitch! *Hold this bastard down for me!*'

As the marchers scattered on all sides, Sean grabbed Moira by the hand and ran her towards the bridge, behind Des and Iris. The noise was dreadful, a cacophony of bawled abuse, cries of pain and screams of panic, made worse by the sickening thud of clubs against bodies, of nails piercing skin to strike bone. As he ran downhill, weaving this way and that, ducking the swinging cudgels, while holding Moira close to him and trying to protect her, he saw civil rights marchers, men and women, staggering about like blind people, sobbing and holding bloody heads, or being hammered to the ground, sometimes by three or four Loyalists, all swinging cudgels.

Almost directly in front of Sean, Des was struck by a club, his head jerking sideways, his body convulsing, while Iris, enraged, hurled herself at Des' assailant, trying to claw his eyes out. Pushing her back, the Loyalist bawled, 'You fuckin' Fenian bitch! I'll...' He grabbed her by the throat, forced her onto her knees, and was raising his club over his head, preparing to strike, when Sean, hardly aware of what he was doing, ran pell-mell into him, bowling him sideways and knocking him to the ground.

'Keep going!' Sean bawled to Iris, as he released Moira's hand and roughly pushed her ahead of him. 'I'll look after Des!'

Wide-eyed and raging, though clearly also shocked, Iris nodded and grabbed Moira's hand, to drag her downhill. As Des, obviously dazed, clambered back to his feet, he was attacked by another vigilante. Sean saw the man's flushed face, his features distorted by hatred, a blurred mask in a nightmare, as he threw himself at Des, bowling him over, still cursing as they both went down, then he reached out to grab Des by the shoulder and tug him upright.

'The bridge!' he shouted. 'Start running!'

They ran along the lane together, crouched low and weaving, ducking the swinging clubs, pushing the vigilantes aside. Moira and Iris were farther down, approaching the bridge, but when their path was suddenly blocked by more bawling vigilantes, they turned away and headed for the river. Despite the fact that the water was close to freezing, the vigilantes were pursuing the marchers all the way to the muddy bank, forcing them into the river, then hurling stones and bottles at them, even as they were wading across to the other side.

'Keep going!' Sean bawled.

He was aware of Des by his side as he fought his way down to the riverbank, ducking the swinging cudgels, pushing vigilantes away from him, helping other marchers who had fallen or been beaten to the ground. Moira and Iris were already wading into the river, having no choice, being pursued by two vigilantes, the latter wearing peaked caps, normal suits and big black boots, their nail-impregnated clubs raised on high, preparing to strike.

'Protestant bastards!' Sean bawled at them.

Still feeling that he was dreaming, losing all self-control, he hurled himself at one of the vigilantes. He caught a glimpse of Des and another vigilante plunging into the river, then he felt the shocking cold of the water as he and his opponent sank together, locked silently in a primal, violent embrace, before breaking apart, choking and coughing, kicking wildly, falling backward in opposite directions. Surfacing, gasping for air, his heart pounding, chest aching, he saw the vigilante rising out of the river, water pouring off him as he hammered his own broad chest with clenched fists. Moira and Iris were straight ahead, both waist-deep in the water, shivering as stones and bottles rained upon them, splashing into the river.

'Keep going!' Sean bawled again.

As they turned towards the far bank, a bottle struck Iris, smashing against her forehead, making her scream and fall back into the river. Moira grabbed her before she sank, hauled her up, dripping blood, as Des, breaking the surface, coughed repeatedly, spat water, and then saw what had happened. Sean and Des reached their women at the same time, wading in deeper, as the Loyalist vigilantes bawled obscenities from the bank while throwing more stones and bottles, only turning away to attack other civil rights marchers, who, unable to cross the bridge, were trying to reach the river.

More screams of pain and fear, more bawled oaths and threats. Sean grabbed hold of Moira, whose gaze was wide and blind, while Des embraced the blood-soaked, sobbing Iris. Together, they waded across the river, following other lucky marchers, and at last collapsed on the far bank, gasping for air like hooked fish.

Eventually recovering, sitting upright, Sean glanced at Moira and saw that she was unharmed. Lying on her back in the grass, breathing heavily, she offered a weak smile, her gaze in focus again.

'How's Iris?' she asked.

Glancing in the other direction, Sean saw that Iris' forehead was badly slashed and that Des was trying to stem the flow of blood by tying a towel around her head. Iris was shaking and sobbing profoundly. By now, most of the civil rights marchers had managed to cross either the bridge or the river, though some unfortunates remained trapped on the other side and were still being attacked by the vigilantes. There was no sign of the RUC. Glancing over his shoulder, Sean saw other marchers gathering at the top of the hill on this side of the river, safe from their attackers.

'Those vicious bastards,' Des said as he tied a knot in the blood-soaked towel that was now wrapped around Iris' head. 'They ought to be hung for what they've done here.'

'Oh, Jesus!' Iris sobbed, resting her head on Des' shoulder and tentatively touching the damp towel where it covered her bloody wound. 'Sure I'm going to be scarred for life, Des. Oh, Jesus, how could they *do* this? We're just *marching*, for God's sake!'

'Animals, all of them!' Moira said. '*That's* how they could do it.'

Des embraced Iris. 'There, there, it's alright. I don't think you'll even need stitches. Sure there's nothing to fear, love.'

'Let's get up the hill,' Sean said. 'Farrell's telling everyone to meet up there, so we'd best go now.'

'Aye, right,' Moira agreed. 'Let's all get the hell out of here.'

With Iris still sobbing, clinging desperately to Des, they made their way up the grassy, windblown hill to join the other marchers. Iris was not alone. A lot of the women up there were hysterical and sobbing. Some, men and women alike, had been badly beaten and were, like Iris, bruised and bloody. Others, clearly in a state of shock, were being comforted by friends or relatives. The place looked like a war zone.

'Jesus Christ!' Des exclaimed softly. 'Look down there, will you.'

Glancing back down the hill, Sean saw that the last of the civil rights marchers, some badly beaten, were making their way across the bridge, being bothered no more by the vigilantes, who were, at the far side of the river, otherwise engaged. Over there, around the bridge and trailing up the steep lane, the vigilantes, identifiable by their armbands, still holding their cudgels, were relaxing by smoking, drinking bottles of stout, and talking sociably to groups of the very same RUC men who should have been protecting the marchers.

'Well, now we know,' Sean said without thinking. 'We can't win by peaceful means.'

'No way,' Moira said.

Sean stewed in his new rage.

2

'Well, they fell for it,' wee Billy said. 'The Civil Rights Movement is being wiped out and now the IRA, though not really active since 1962, is being blamed for the bombs we set off. Sure it worked a treat, like.'

Billy, now all of twenty-seven, married with one kid and another on the way, was celebrating the Twelfth with some fellow members of the Ulster Protestant Volunteers, including Dan Johnstone and Rob McKenzie. Billy hadn't touched alcohol since that fateful evening at the Floral Hall and was presently drinking only orange juice; the other two were downing pints of stout.

'Aye, right,' Dan said. 'The whole of this city comes close to dyin' of thirst and we cause it and the IRA gets the blame. Fuckin' beautiful, right?'

He was referring to the series of bomb explosions that had taken place earlier in the year. The first bomb had exploded in an electricity station at Castlereagh, causing an estimated £2 million worth of damage. The next two had destroyed the water pipes of the Silent Valley reservoir, leaving the whole of Belfast drastically short of water.

'I think the UPV's beautiful,' Rob said. 'I think we're all brilliant.'

Billy didn't know *what* to think. After a lot of soul-searching, he had joined the UPV only because it had been organised by Noel Doherty, the man who set up the Reverend Ian Paisley's *The Protestant Telegraph*, was the secretary for the Reverend's Ulster Constitution Defence Committee, and was also a member of the Ulster Volunteer Force. While it was widely accepted that the UVF was the group responsible for all those homicidal attacks against Catholics three years ago, in 1966, and while Billy, personally, had not approved of them, he had found it next to impossible to avoid joining the UPV, child to the UVF, for a couple of reasons. First, there was no hard evidence to link Paisley to the homicidal activities of the UPV, so Billy couldn't use the Big Man's involvement as an excuse for staying clear of it. Secondly, most of Billy's mates had already joined the organisation and peer pressure, particularly in his age group, was hard to ignore. On top of which, he had previously, openly, perhaps *too loudly*, admired the Reverend Ian Paisley, extolling his virtues to all and sundry, so he could not, when it would have been helpful to do so, change his opinion. It had therefore become virtually impossible for him *not* to join the UPV when called upon to do so by his friends.

It was at times like this that he wished Johnny was here to give him advice. But Johnny, despite his promise of three years ago, had still not come home.

'Yeah, fuckin' great,' Rob McKenzie said, running his fingers distractedly through his flame-coloured hair and glancing around the packed, smoke-filled pub with his wild blue eyes. Rob had been the drummer in the skiffle group that Johnny and Ronnie Campbell had played with when they were younger, so talking to him always reminded Billy of Johnny. 'And you've got to give Paisley's men credit. *The Protestant Telegraph* was as quick as a fucking rat up a drain in blaming the bombings of that electric substation on the IRA.'

'Aye,' Billy said, trying to sound more enthusiastic than he was, 'and they were even smarter in suggestin' that the sheer professionalism of the operation - *our* professionalism - was an indication of how well equipped the IRA is. Now even the Prods think those bombings are a clear indication of what lies ahead for the province - mass destruction by a revitalised IRA. I mean, we couldn't have done any better, could we?'

'A brilliant fuckin' joke to blame the IRA for *anything*,' Dan said. 'I mean, since the collapse of the Border Campaign, that organisation's practically fallen apart and the few men remaining have turned to politics instead of bombings and shootings. As far as I can gather, the only thing they do these days is act as stewards during those eejut civil rights marches. I mean, things are so bad that even the Cummann na Mbann - '

'The *what*?' Rob asked.

'The women's wing of the IRA,' Dan explained.

'Oh, right.'

'As I was sayin', even the Cummann na MBann has been disbanded for lack of something to do, other than makin' tea for their wanker husbands. And apart from that, the IRA, these days, has practically no support in the local community, yet they're gettin' the blame for those bombings we did. Now everyone, including the pinstripes in Westminster, is convinced the IRA's about to go on the warpath all over again.'

'And that's why,' Billy concluded, 'Terence O'Neill's reform package was placed on the choppin' block and the poor fucker, the aristocratic darlin', bein' out of touch completely, was finally forced to resign. That's what the Big Man wanted all along. I think Paisley's brilliant.'

'Aye, he is,' Dan agreed. 'And now he's sayin' that if he can bring down one prime minister, he can bring down another. So who's really runnin' the country? Not Chichester-Clark, that's for sure. It's the Big Man that's runnin' it.'

'Thank God,' Rob said. 'As long as we've got the Big Man on our side, the fucking Fenians won't get far.'

Glancing around the packed bar, Billy saw that it was filled mostly with members of the Sandy Row Orange Lodge, now relaxing after marching in the annual Twelfth of July parade, from Carlisle Circus to the Field at Edenderry and back again. As Billy, Dan and Rob were also in the Orange Lodge, they, too, had marched in the parade and were still wearing their orange sashes over their jackets. Some of the men at the bar had started a sing-song and right now they were singing, appropriately enough, 'The Sash My Father Wore'.

'Bit dirty, though,' Billy said distractedly, expressing his secret doubts without thinking.

'What's dirty?' Rob asked.

'Well... you know... gettin' the IRA blamed for things they didn't do. I mean, I'm not sure that's strictly necessary.'

'*Of course* it's necessary!' Rob exclaimed, his blue eyes widening, displaying the hot temper of his Scottish ancestors. 'You think just because the IRA's havin' a snooze, the fuckin' Fenians have gone to sleep as well?'

'Well, I...'

'What do you think those so-called civil rights marches are? They're the Fenians's new way of wresting control out of our hands and into their own.'

'Aye, right,' Dan said, before having another slug of his stout and sighing contentedly.

'Damned right, I'm right!' Rob said. 'I mean, look at what those bastards have been up to this past six months, startin' with that so-called civil rights march from Belfast to Londonderry last January. Sure that was pure provocation! I mean, the Diamond is the centre of Protestant Londonderry, symbolising the plantation, and no anti-Unionist parade had ever marched through the walled city to the Diamond - at least not since that Anti-Partition League tried to do it way back in the 'Fifties.'

'Which they failed to do,' Dan said, 'because the RUC, God bless 'em, batoned the Fenian fuckers off the streets.'

'Right,' Rob said. 'But that march in January was a triumph for the Fenians, a real propaganda victory, and just look at the gains they've made since then: John Hume and other so-called moderates elected to Stormont, the People's Democracy gaining over 23,000 votes, and that Republican bitch, Bernadette Devlin, elected as an MP and flouncin' off to Parliament in her miniskirt. And what's the first thing she does there? Gives a speech callin' for the abolishment of Stormont and direct rule from Westminster! So don't tell me we shouldn't use dirty tricks, 'cause that's just what the Fenians are doin'.'

'Aye,' Dan said, trying to gain political wisdom, though finding it hard to grasp. 'Those so-called civil rights marches are doing us more damage than the IRA ever did, so let's go the way of the Big Man.'

'Damned right,' Rob said emphatically. 'Encourage everyone to believe that the Civil Rights Movement is merely a front for an IRA build-up. Otherwise, all this liberal thinkin's going to rob us of everything and put those Fenian bastards in power. And we don't want that, do we?'

'No, we don't,' Dan said, his eyes glazed with incomprehension. 'But let's talk about something more entertaining. I mean, this is the Twelfth, for fuck's sake, and we're supposed to be here celebratin', so let's do just that.' He held his glass up on high. 'To King William of Orange!'

They touched their glasses together before having a ritualistic swallow. When Billy had placed his glass of orange juice back on the table, he glanced around the bar again and saw that his Dad had arrived and was drinking at the counter. Though not in the Orange Lodge and so not wearing an orange sash, Albert would use this day as an excuse to have a good pub crawl and see a lot of his old mates. Clearly, he was flushed with drink already.

'There's m'Dad,' Billy said.

Dan glanced back over his shoulder, saw Albert and grinned. 'Sure he never misses a chance for a bit of fun. He'll be doin' the rounds, like.'

'Aye, he will, sure enough,' Billy said.

'Drinkin' with all them Orangemen,' Rob said resentfully, 'and he's not even in the Orange Lodge.'

'He's not in anything,' Billy clarified. 'He's just not a joiner.'

'The day's comin',' Rob said, 'when a man might not be able to keep his hands clean.'

'It's not comin' for m'Dad,' Billy said. 'He doesn't give a damn, like.'

'So how come you're not celebrating the Twelfth with your missus?' Dan asked, wanting to change the subject to something more amusing.

Billy shrugged. 'No problem,' he said. 'Val watched the parade from the Lisburn Road until she saw me passin'. Then, knowin' I'd be away most of the day - first out in the Field with the Lodge, then marchin' back again - she decided to spend the day with her Mum and Dad. Our second baby's due any day now, so her mind's easier with them than it would be if she spent all day with just Frances for company.'

'So how's married life so far?' Rob asked, being single, like Dan, and curious about friends who tied the knot.

'Sure it's grand,' Billy lied, since it wasn't grand at all, having brought him little joy, only the pain of disillusionment, the belief that Val didn't love him at all, possibly never had, and had deliberately lured him into her bed that drunken night, after the Floral Hall dance, only because she knew a sexual innocent when she saw one and she wanted a husband. 'It has its moments, like. Having kids makes you feel older, more responsible, and that's a pretty good feeling.'

'Aye, that must be somethin',' Rob said, lighting a cigarette and exhaling a cloud of smoke. 'I just don't fancy it, that's all.'

Nor did Billy. Even now, he could scarcely recall what had happened that night, only that he'd been drunk, that they'd sneaked up to her bedroom, tiptoeing past her parents' door, and had then somehow come together in her bed, in fractured, moonlit darkness, their clothes scattered on the floor, and that everything had then slipped away from him as he surrendered to sleep. When he'd awakened the next morning, still in darkness, before dawn, badly hungover, feeling sick, he'd crept out as quietly as he'd sneaked in, not looking back. Then, a few months later, Val had come to see him, waylaying him outside his house when he was coming home from work one evening. He hadn't seen her since that morning after the Floral Hall dance and he'd imagined that what had happened was well behind him.

'I'm pregnant,' she informed him. 'Two months pregnant, so I'm told. It could only have happened that night, so you're the dad, Billy. You'd best do the right thing.'

So he did the right thing. He married her two weeks later. They had a girl, Frances, and Billy really loved her, but he didn't have the same kind of feelings for his wife and the pain was like a daily crucifixion. They had a relationship of sorts, perhaps united by the child, and although they only had sex occasionally, being awkward with each other, self-conscious in bed, eventually Val became pregnant again. That child was due any day now and Billy looked forward to it. He had always liked kids. But he hadn't had an alcoholic drink since that one night of sin.

'So what about you, Dan?' Billy asked, feeling uncomfortable and wanting to change the subject. 'When are you and Sarah gonna tie the knot?'

Sarah was the redhead that Marlene's husband, Ronnie, had introduced to Dan that same night in the Floral Hall. She and Dan still saw each other on a regular basis, but so far there had been no talk of marriage.

Dan shrugged. 'Fucked if I know, Billy. Probably never. I mean, we still see each other and... you know... *do* it now and then... but we're not really serious about each other and we both have other friends, like, if you know what I mean, like, and I'm sure you do.'

'Ackaye,' Billy said, grinning. 'Sure I know what you mean.'

'So, you know, it just hasn't happened, like, and I don't think it will and I'm not, I mean, come to think of it, that interested in kids or in bein' what you call responsible, like, so I suppose I'll just drift along, like, and die with a fuckin' strong right wrist, havin' used it a lot, like.'

'As good a way to live as any,' Rob said. 'That's how *I* like to do it. The women, they can drag you down real quick, and I like my freedom.'

At that moment, Albert polished off his drink, waved airily at the men he'd been talking to at the bar, then sauntered across the smoky room to Billy's table. The drink having gradually corroded his good looks, he was starting to resemble his true age of fifty, but he was still a wee dandy in his polyester suit, flash tie and immaculately polished black shoes. Also, he still had a full head of hair, though the red was turning grey at last. Flushed with drink, he offered the table a chirpy grin and waved both hands eloquently as he spoke, letting his fancy rings flash brilliantly in the overhead lighting.

'So here you are, Billy-boy,' he said. 'Sure I saw you in the parade from up there on the Lisburn Road, but I couldn't find you later in the Field - there were just too many people there. I saw you again when you came back, but I decided to come down to the Row and have a few jars. Got a wee bit worried when I heard about that Unity Walk business, so I'm relieved to see you sittin' here, all safe and sound, like.'

'What Unity Walk business?' Billy asked. 'What happened there, Dad?'

Unity Walk was a complex of Catholic flats located at the very edge of the Shankill Road. Representing a large Catholic presence at the very entrance to the city's major Protestant ghetto, it had always aggravated the Orangemen and was widely viewed by both sides of the divide as a potential trouble spot.

'Well, apparently,' Albert said, puffing smoke as he spoke, waving his hands to show off his glittering rings, 'even before breakfast this morning, Orange bands with Lambeg drummers were coming down the Shankill to parade in front of the Unity Walk flats. Naturally, the Fenians protested, but the bands weren't moved on, and according to my source - '

'What source?' Billy asked.

'A *Belfast Telegraph* reporter,' Albert said. 'An old drinkin' buddy of mine.'

'Okay. What next?'

'According to my friend, who was there at the scene, an RUC officer told the residents' representatives that the Twelfth was the Orangemen's day and if the residents didn't like it, they could take themselves off and live down south.' Albert rolled his eyes. 'Puttin' the cat in with the pigeons, as it were.'

'That officer said the right thing,' Rob offered. 'Let 'em know where they stand, like.'

Albert, who had no sectarian inclinations, simply stared at Rob for a moment, as if examining some kind of zoological specimen, maybe one up in Bellevue, then he shrugged and continued. 'Anyway, earlier this evening, as the bands were returning from the Field, trouble flared up again. This time, the Unity Walk's residents had gathered on the forecourt of the flats and they hurled stones and the like at the passing Orange Lodge bands and their followers. The Orangemen responded with some of the same, so naturally a riot ensued.'

'Any casualties?' Billy asked.

'Aye, a few, but only one serious: a kid, a wee boy, hit on the head by a flying bottle and apparently hurt pretty badly - he's in intensive care now. So, Billy, I thought you might've been one of the Orangemen down there and I was certainly a bit worried, like.'

'No, we weren't there,' Billy said. 'We didn't march back in that direction. Did the RUC put a stop to the rioting?'

'Not for a long time. Apparently, they occupied the balconies and forecourt of the flats, but didn't attempt to stop the Orange bands from passin' and didn't interfere with the fighting - at least not until the last of the bands had passed. Naturally, when the Orangemen finally left, the Catholics stopped throwing stones and the RUC then cleared out of the area.'

'Sounds pretty trivial to me,' Rob said. 'Nothin' worth worryin' about.'

'That's not what my reporter friend said.'

'Oh?' Billy looked at his Dad with raised eyebrows.

Albert flicked ash from his cigarette, studied the fancy rings glittering on his fingers, then pursed his lips and said, 'He thinks it's just a beginning. He said the Unity Walk is dynamite, just waitin' for the fuse to be lit. He said the Fenians there have viewed the RUC's lack of action as evidence that the police always favour the Orangemen. More crucial, he said, is that the incident's convinced the

Orangemen that their parade was deliberately attacked from the flats and that the insult couldn't be taken lyin' down.'

'What does that mean?'

'He thinks the Orangemen are plannin' to deliberately march past the Unity Walk flats again - maybe in a week or so - and if they do, the riots are likely to be even worse. That place could go up in flames.'

'So it should,' Rob said.

Albert stared steadily, disbelievingly, at Rob for some time, then he sighed, turned away, gave Billy's shoulder a rare, affectionate squeeze and walked out of the pub.

3

14th August 1969

Dear Sean,

Ave atque vale! Hail and Farewell! I write to you from the flaming bowels of Derry - or, as the Prods would have it, Londonderry. As I write, I can assure you, I do not have to remind myself that I am now 67 years old. The shakiness of my hand, which you can judge from this letter, is eloquent testimony to my increasing frailty. Growing old is a curse, leaving a man no shred of dignity, and I am writing this from a hospital bed, to which I was rushed unexpectedly in the early hours of the morning, the day before yesterday. The old ticker, of course. Not ticking properly, so I'm told. Malfunctioning at the very worst of times, which, at my age, is every damned second of every damned day. To add to the varicose veins, the crippling arthritis, lungs congested by years of heavy smoking, and a liver done in by drink. Truly, there are no best times at my age, as my fellow poets and human wrecks have always known.

> *An aged man is but a paltry thing,*
> *A tattered coat upon a stick, unless*
> *Soul clap its hands and sing, and louder sing*
> *For every tatter in its mortal dress.*

Yeats, of course! My hero and tormentor. Who also wrote:

> *What shall I do with this absurdity -*
> *O heart, O troubled heart - this caricature,*
> *Decrepit age has been tied to me*
> *As to a dog's tail?*

But no more of the poetic whimsy of my worthless competitors. I write to you, dear Sean, because I came here for a purpose, to find out what was happening in Derry, this ancient city of Fenians surrounded by Prods, to find out and write about it, spread the word to the troubled masses, but alas, the old ticker gave out and will not, so I am reliably informed, tick in the manner required for very much longer. Thus, Ave atque vale! Hail and Farewell! This letter, which contains my fond greetings, could well be my last.

I write to you, my young friend, to give you fair warning that war is undoubtedly coming to this fair land.

(London)Derry is, as it were, in flames and its recent history (in which you played a small role) eloquently demonstrates why this is so. While this has always been a troubled city, its last year (from August '68 to this August of '69) has surely shown us exactly where we are heading, which is into the abyss. So let us look at the grim facts.

In August 1968, the Dungannon-based branch of the Campaign for Social Justice, backed by NICRA, decided to hold a protest march from Coalisland to Dungannon. Approximately 2500 people turned up, this being twice the population of Dungannon. Instantly, Ian Paisley announced that he would hold a counter-demonstration in the centre of Dungannon, and the RUC, being an agreeable organisation, particularly with regard to its dealings with the Orangemen, promptly barred the civil rights march from the centre of town. Naturally, some of the younger marchers tried to break through the police cordon, but they were beaten back by RUC batons.

A second civil rights march, this one in Derry, was planned for 5th October. The route was to be from the Waterside Station on the east side of the Foyle, across Craigavon Bridge and on to the Diamond, centre of the plantation walled city and the symbol of

Protestant supremacy, located strategically high above the Catholic masses down there in the Bogside.

Instantly, the Apprentice Boys (that Protestant and Loyalist organisation so similar to the Orange Order) announced that they would be having their 'annual' parade on the same day as the civil rights march, taking the exact same route as the civil rights marchers.

Realising that the civil rights movement and the Apprentice Boys could not possibly march the same route at the same time without a clash, William Craig banned all parades, except in the ghetto, on 5th October. However, the Derry civil rights groups and the Belfast Young Socialists decided to go ahead with their parade, despite the ban, and approximately 2000 marchers duly assembled around the Waterside Station on the 5th October, only to find that William Craig had drafted in a massive force of police, including the hated RUC Reserve force, armed with the usual weapons, plus two water cannons.

Setting off, the marchers only managed to travel about 200 yards when they were met by a solid wall of RUC policemen, a couple of whom batoned MP Gerry Fitt, at the head of the march. Incensed by this, the Young Socialists tried to break through the cordon and were baton-charged by the RUC. Caught between two lines of police in a narrow street, the marchers had to run a gauntlet and were hammered savagely, then hosed with the water cannons. Subsequently, fighting broke out throughout the city and culminated in the Bogside, where barricades were put up and petrol-bombs used for the first time in Derry. An estimated 77 civilians were injured and a greater number arrested.

So much for civil rights!

On the other hand, to the good, that particular march had been covered by television, so viewers both in Ireland and in England saw RUC brutality being waged against a peaceful demonstration. A wave of revulsion swept through the country and even stirred liberal opinion in the North, leading to demonstrations in Belfast and the formation of the highly influential People's Democracy.

Another civil rights march over the original route in Derry was planned for 16th November. Learning of this, William Craig banned all marches inside the walled city for a month. Defying the ban, 15,000 people marched on the 16th, but were stopped again by a massive police force. Luckily, the organisers, including the moderate Citizens

Action Committee led by John Hume and Ivan Cooper, managed to prevent a confrontation. Nevertheless, for the next few days, Derry factory workers marched in, out and around the walled city, deliberately breaking Craig's ban several times a day and making it clear that the city was in revolt.

Desperate, Terence O'Neill announced his package of reforms, which turned out to be too little too late, though it was still enough to outrage the Loyalists, even while leaving the Catholics disappointed. As a result, the whole civil rights campaign came to be based on the principle of 'One man, one vote' and control over the gerrymandering councils. O'Neill, however, could not concede this - it would have split the Unionist Party - and so another civil rights march, this one in Armagh, was planned for 30th November.

In the early hours of that morning, Ian Paisley and his followers occupied the centre of Armagh, armed with cudgels and clubs. Capitulating to this threat of violence, the RUC made no attempt to remove Paisley's men, but stopped the perfectly legal civil rights march when it reached the edge of the Catholic ghetto.

So why am I telling you this, which you probably already know?

Because what happened in Belfast and Armagh, as described above, had strong bearing on what was happening here in Derry.

You, of course, know about the next civil rights march on Derry because you and Moira personally took part in it. The marchers were harassed and assaulted brutally by vigilantes who were clearly given support by the RUC. Now it transpires that over a hundred of the vigilantes who took part in that dreadful assault at the Burntollet Bridge (which you and Moira endured heroically) were actually off-duty B-Specials, that the stones thrown were collected throughout the night before, and that the vigilantes had been gathering there since early morning. In short, it was not only planned, but also planned with full RUC knowledge.

That evening, as you also know, after the battered, bloodied survivors of the civil rights march had entered Derry to a hero's welcome, the RUC, enraged, went on a rampage through the city, breaking windows and doors, bellowing abuse and beating up everyone in sight. As a result, the barricades went up in the Catholic ghettoes and Free Derry was born.

So what's happened since the birth of Free Derry?

Instead of condemning the violence of the vigilantes and RUC, Terence O'Neill only mildly rebuked the former, was silent about the latter, but was vehement in his condemnation of the civil rights marchers. All the support he had gained amongst the Catholic community was lost there and then.

On 23rd January, Brian Faulkner resigned from the government in protest against a government commission to investigate the recent disturbances and their causes. On 3rd February, twelve Unionist backbenchers called for O'Neill's resignation. That evening, O'Neill announced an election for 24th of the month.

The subsequent election left O'Neill's party more divided than ever when, on the opposition side, John Hume, one of the new civil rights leaders, ousted the Nationalist candidate, Eddie McAteer, by a majority of 3653 votes; a second Nationalist was ousted by another civil rights leader, Ivan Cooper, a Protestant; and a third Nationalist was ousted in Armagh. The People's Democracy, challenging both Unionists and Nationalists, won an unprecedented 23,645 votes and only narrowly failed to oust another Nationalist in South Down.

On 17th April there was a by-election for the Mid-Ulster seat at Westminster and Bernadette Devlin, a 21-year old student member of PD, won the nomination as a united anti-Unionist candidate, then won the election with the biggest anti-Unionist majority since the seat was created in 1950.

Two days later, there was a minor riot in the centre of Derry. The RUC beat the rioters back to the edge of the Bogside. A group of RUC men then broke into a house in William Street and beat the owner, Sam Devenny, so badly (in front of his family) that he died three months later from his internal injuries. That same evening, however, while the unconscious Devenny was being carted off to intensive care in hospital, the rioting spread and the hated RUC Reserve force, in full riot-control gear, was called in to occupy the Bogside. The next morning, Bogsiders woke to find their streets occupied by armed police and to learn about the Devenny beating. The atmosphere became charged. Most of the Catholic women and children evacuated the area, but the menfolk gathered on Creggan Heights, arming themselves for a fight.

There can be no doubt about it, my heroic young friend, that for a couple of hours there, with God's metronome ticking, Derry was on the brink of war.

Luckily, a frightened Minister of Home Affairs ordered the RUC to withdraw and peace was restored. However, by that stage, NICRA and People's Democracy had already mounted a series of protests, most of which ended in riots; while in Belfast, as you know, the IRA, formerly redundant, retaliated by petrol-bombing a number of post offices - their first action since the civil rights campaign began - and, as you also know, there was rioting in the Falls Road for a number of days.

We have only the Unionists to thank for this.

On 22nd April, O'Neill took the only step that could possibly deflate the situation: he finally accepted the principle of 'One man, one vote'. O'Neill resigned five days later and the parliamentary Unionist Party then elected O'Neill's cousin, James Chichester-Clark, as their new leader.

NICRA immediately called a halt to the demonstrations, but the RUC couldn't let sleeping dogs lie. Their intervention in a row in a pub on Crumlin Road, Belfast, ignited the smouldering resentment of the Catholic working class and led to several weekends of violent rioting in the Ardoyne ghetto. This in turn led to the formation of the extreme Unionist Shankill Defence Association (SDA), led by the notorious Loyalist, John McKeague. In June, while a proposed Connolly commemoration parade was banned from the centre of Belfast, John McKeague and his supporters were allowed to occupy the centre of the city.

So much for equality under the new regime!

As it was in Belfast, so it was here in Derry. On the 12th July this year, an Orange Parade through the city was stoned, leading to three days of fighting between the RUC and Bogsiders, with three civilians shot and wounded by the former. In Dungiven, another Orange Parade led to two days of rioting and attacks on the local Orange Hall. A 66-year-old Catholic man was killed in an RUC baton-charge and a platoon of B-Specials fired over the heads of a Catholic crowd coming out of a dance. As a consequence, the Orange Hall was burned down and several police tenders wrecked.

That same day, as you know, an Orange Parade deliberately marched past the Unity Walk flats in Belfast, causing a minor riot. As you will also know, a couple of weeks later, on 2nd August, to be precise, there was a second march of Orangemen past the Unity Walk flats, this time leading to major rioting. One man, a Catholic, died after being beaten up by police in an RUC barracks. Because of this, the rioting worsened and lasted three days with Loyalists, led by John McKeague's SDA, attacking both the Unity Walk flats and the Ardoyne. That rioting was only stopped when the B-Specials were mobilised and used instead of the RUC.

Meanwhile, however, as a chilling indication of what was to come, some Catholic families were forced out of their homes in the mainly Protestant area located opposite Ardoyne. The SDA then attempted to force out Catholics living in the Ardoyne itself.

So where were the British in all this?

In fact, British troops had already been moved quietly into a naval base in Derry as a precautionary measure. Shortly after, British Prime Minister, Harold Wilson, appointed Roy Hattersley as a Minister of State for Defense with instructions to prepare for intervention in Northern Ireland, if necessary. At the beginning of August, another detachment of British troops were moved into the RUC headquarters, for possible use in Belfast.

Here, in Derry, there was no doubt at all that the flash point would be the 12th August, the day of the Apprentice Boys' parade, when thousands of Orangemen from all over the province would parade through the city and around the walls overlooking the Bogside, to commemorate the Siege, celebrate the plantation, and remind the Catholics that they were living under sufferance in a Protestant state.

That march went ahead, it was stoned by the outraged Bogsiders, the RUC launched a baton-charge, and battle commenced.

The newly formed Bogside Defence Association, led by veteran Republican, Sam Keenan, built barricades all around the Bogside and defended them with petrol-bombs. Using armoured cars, CS gas and 700 men, the RUC attempted, and failed, to break through. The moderate Citizens' Action Committee, still led by Hume and Cooper, was swept aside and leadership returned to the hands of the hardline Republican activists. Despite the fact that the CS gas was everywhere like a poisonous smog, saturating the narrow streets and the small, terraced houses, damaging eyes and racking lungs, causing torment to the old and those with respiratory problems, the Bogsiders bravely fought on. The tricolour and the Starry-Plough were flown from a block of flats, and Bernadette Devlin, Westminster MP, was amongst those stoically manning the barricades.

The siege continued all that day and throughout the night, with the Catholics, ironically, now playing the defensive role of the original Protestant Apprentice Boys, who shut the gates of Derry against the forces of King James II during the Great Siege of 1688.

A crude field hospital was established in the Candy Corner sweet shop and ended up treating over a thousand casualties, with the more seriously injured being ferried across the border to Letterkenny Hospital. Rebel songs were broadcast from a radio reportedly stolen from the Athlone army barracks in the Republic. When the Bogsiders used that same radio to appeal for help, NICRA and the PD arranged mass demonstrations for a dozen different locations, hoping to stretch RUC resources to breaking point. All of those rallies ended in more rioting, notably in Dungannon and Belfast.

In the former, armed B-Specials were called in and fired into a crowd of Catholics, wounding two men and a girl; in the latter, several buildings were burnt out in the Falls Road, two RUC barracks were attacked by angry crowds, and a grenade was thrown at an RUC vehicle. The RUC then fired into a crowd, wounding two men.

Instead of pulling the RUC back from the Bogside, Chichester-Clark announced the mobilisation of the hated B-Specials, thus simultaneously frightening and enraging the Catholic population. In Dublin, three cabinet ministers called for the Irish Army to invade the North and seize Derry and other mainly Catholics areas. Taoiseach Jack Lynch refused to do this, but announced that the Irish Army would establish field hospitals along the border for people injured in the North. He also called for a UN peacekeeping force to be sent to the six counties.

Clearly, the North was on the brink of war.

British troops, fully armed, moved into the centre of Derry at 5.00pm today. The Catholic rioters, who believed that they were going to be massacred by the B-Specials, fell silent as they watched the troops taking up their positions. After consultations between the Bogside Defence Association and the British Army commander, the *latter agreed to place his troops between the Bogside and the RUC and B-Specials. He also agreed not to enter the Bogside.*

The siege here in Derry is over, but for you, up there in Belfast, the war is just beginning.

Last night, shortly after learning that the British Army had ttaken control, I slept very badly, then awakened in the middle of the night, suffering another heart attack. I am not, of course, suggesting that it was caused by what has happened here, though I <u>will</u> insist that it seems rather symbolic.

I am dying, dear Sean, though it may yet take some time, and before I depart this earth, this bloodied soil, this tarnished country, I would like to thank you for persuading me, all those years ago, to use my modest talents for the benefit of my oppressed fellow Catholics. I am proud to have done so, to have worked for Sinn Féin, whether legal or illegal, and to have made my small contribution to my country's fight for freedom. I have no doubt that you will continue to do the same in troubled Belfast.

The six counties have already changed beyond recognition and undoubtedly there are grim days ahead. This may, indeed, be the time for realism. To quote Yeats again:

> *Romantic Ireland's dead and gone*
> *It's with O'Leary in the grave.*

Ave atque vale, my dear young friend. Hail and farewell!
Yours with deep affection and respect.
The (almost) late...
Brendan Coghill

4

Theresa and Neil Stewart heard the gunshots coming from the television set, still turned on, in the adjoining room, though at first, not understanding what they were hearing, they took no notice. They were having an early evening meal in the conservatory of Neil's second family home in Cultra, part of the North Down constituency, the most affluent in Northern Ireland, the so-called 'gold coast' located between genteel Holywood, with its bewildering array of churches, and the more flagrantly materialistic Crawfordsburn. The house, though not as grand as the one in the Malone Road, was still an impressive, red-brick Victorian edifice, perched high on the green lawns and thickly wooded slopes above Belfast Lough, offering splendid views of Newtownabbey, at the far side of the darkly glittering water. Belfast lay a few miles to the south-west, Carrickfergus to the north. The Liverpool, Heysham and Isle of Man ferries departed from and arrived at the ferry terminals daily, passing almost directly in front of the house, though a good distance away, often looking like ghost ships in the fading light of early evening or during misty days. To Theresa, even though she was now used to the view, it still seemed impossibly romantic

'You must try to understand,' Neil said, continuing his conversation, sounding so quiet, so gentle, so *withdrawn*, as he always did when he talked about his past. 'My parents were born in a Belfast that even *I* can scarcely imagine. They were both brought up by *their* wealthy parents in the golden age of the linen trade: the period following the American Civil War and the blockade of American cotton. In those days my parents drove in a horse-drawn four-wheeler to attend balls in Edenderry House, the red-brick Georgian mansion located in a grove of beech trees near the banks of the Lagan, just above Shaw's Bridge. It was owned by the people who owned the linen mill nearby. As I recall, my father always wore black coats and white gloves with a white silk scarf. My mother wore fur coats, had fur rugs in her carriage during her winter drives, and viewed those walking by the roadside as serfs. She was perfectly at home in the Malone and the lower Lagan valley, though felt that Belfast, with its factories, mills and smoke, was an ugly and - I quote - *vulgar* town.'

Theresa smiled, feeling good, loving the way he always qualified things, hoping to convince her that he wasn't some kind of privileged plantation snob who despised the working classes, as, clearly, his parents had.

'Well,' she said, sipping her champagne, 'Belfast *is* a vulgar town, though that isn't necessarily a bad thing.'

Mr. Stewart (*Neil*, she still had to remind herself, even when in his bed) smiled, his sky-blue eyes a little out of focus (as usual) under his slightly-reddish hair, his pale skin, though flushed with alcohol (as usual), still smooth enough to make him seem at least ten years younger than his forty-five years. Theresa, now twenty-seven but feeling older, certainly more sophisticated than when she had first come to work for him, was utterly charmed by his smile, even though it had removed her from a comprehensible past and placed her in a luxurious present with an uncertain future. She loved him and that's all that mattered. To hell with the guilt, the lingering shame. She'd get over that sooner or later; then life, which wasn't bad at the moment, would be even better.

'Tell me more about your mother,' she said, between sips of her champagne, wondering what brand it was. She still had a lot to learn.

'Well,' Neil said, sighing, as if recalling a bad dream, 'despising Belfast so much, she only went into it for occasional shopping expeditions - to Linday's or Robinson and Cleaver's. When she socialised, which she did a great deal, she only did it in her own home or in the homes of people from the same class.'

'So you didn't get out much,' Theresa said. 'I mean, you wouldn't have had too many chances to meet a nice wee girl like me, let alone a Catholic.'

'Dear God, no!' Neil said, smiling shyly, his eyes widening, drifting sideways to look over the darkening lough and the interweaving necklaces of lights winking on beyond it, on the rolling, darkening hills of Newtownabbey. 'Absolutely not! Naturally.'

'So what do you remember?' Theresa asked, speaking better English than she had spoken when she first came here all those years ago, when she had thought that she was in love with that big idiot, Gerry Donovan, only recently released from the Crumlin Road jail and, according to Sean, now desperate to see her. The very thought was embarrassing.

'Not much,' Neil said. 'I think I blocked a lot out. But I still recall the constant tinkle of tea-cups, an endless stream of lady visitors in wide-brimmed hats, birthday parties at the end of the garden, with treasure hunts and so on, and, certainly, of course, my pet dog, Foxy, an Airedale terrier, probably given to me by my always busy parents, to keep me from being lonely in their absence. It was a sheltered, cloistered, protected life and I still suffer from it.'

Theresa loved him, but she couldn't believe her ears. There were times when he baffled her.

'You still... *suffer* from it?'

'Oh, yes,' he said, nodding affirmatively, the light from his champagne glass reflected in his eyes, to make them even more romantically blue than they normally were. 'I had to go off to boarding schools for three months at a time, and wasn't even allowed to come home for weekends or during half terms. Even when I *was* at home, I wasn't allowed to go out on my own. I was privileged - oh, yes, I certainly was - but I had no real life of my own. My family home was my prison.'

Prison, Theresa thought, recalling the Pound Loney, the unemployment, the poverty, the daily grind that encouraged suffering women to hide pain with rough humour. Lots of humour in the Pound Loney. Lots of humour all over the Falls. You could kill yourself listening to them laughing about their lack of a real life. Of course, she, Theresa, had always wanted to get out, escape, run away, flee to England, the Big Smoke, London, the real world, where the Paddies weren't particularly welcome, though they could always at least get paid work and live *some* kind of decent life. That had been her intention, her plan, her secret dream, but instead she'd come here (or, more precisely, to Stoneykirk Manor, Neil's big house located up the Malone Road, by the Lagan River, in alluvial fields of green, under smoke-free azure skies) to work for the man now sitting in front of her, across that long table, with the tablecloth and the candles and the fancy flute-glasses and, best of all, the champagne. That had been the end of it, the destruction of her ambition, because as soon as she had started to work for him, gotten to know him, to find out, as Carol Bell had informed her, that he was a decent man, kind, not sectarian at all, perhaps even guilty about inheriting his position, the industrial wealth of his Scottish antecedents. So she had fallen in love with him, despite having once loved Gerry Donovan, also sweet, kind, but picked up in a sectarian riot and sent off to rot in prison for the best years of his young life, his whole future destroyed. And didn't that say it all, her heart breaking in silence, thinking of her and Gerry, of the growing up together, of the love and the shared hopes and the awful ruination because of fucking religion and politics? So no way, she thought, not for me. I'm going to cling to this sweet, good-natured, slightly naïve man, this Prod, despite the fact that I'm a Fenian and my family disapprove of what I'm doing. Despite that. Despite them. Because I love him and because he loves me; and because, although we come from different sides of the track, we recognised each other on the instant and have never looked back.

I will never look back.

'So what *do* you remember about your childhood?' she asked him. 'I mean, what did you do when you couldn't play out in the street with the other kids? Did you ever even go to the fillums – I'm sorry, I mean the films, the movies. Did you ever do that?'

Though smiling, he shrugged his shoulders forlornly. 'In the whole of my adolescence, until I went to university, I never went to a corner shop to buy sweets for myself and I saw no more than three or four films in the whole of my childhood. I could cycle around the grounds of Stoneykirk Manor - and, of course, around this house - but I couldn't go outside on my own. It was a protected, secure, absolutely lonely life, though I wasn't to know that at the time. Having no friends of my own age, I had nothing with which to compare it. So I thought it was normal.'

'Well, maybe it was,' Theresa said, feeling slightly drunk and uninhibited. 'I mean, how can you lose what you never had? You just accept what you get.'

'Did you?'

Theresa smiled. 'No.'

'So why should I?'

'Because what you had... what you *have...* is more than I could possibly imagine having. And it makes life worth living.'

Mr. Stewart - Neil - raised his eyebrows and smiled, looking like a mischievous schoolboy. 'Please accept my apologies for having inherited my privileged position. I will now slit my wrists in atonement.'

'Please don't.'

'Why not?'

'Because I love you and need you.'

'Love me? Yes. Need me? No.'

'Why "no"?'

'Because no matter how much you love me, you're a woman who'll never let herself depend on any man, rich or poor. You're a woman who'll always go her own way, irrespective of the consequences.'

'So why do you love me?'

'Because you won't let yourself be dependent on anyone and that means you're not sharing my bed just because of the money. I love you and I hope you love me, which for me, in my position, isn't always that easy to believe. For most people it isn't easy to separate me from my wealth, and that fact, which cannot be ignored, has always contaminated my personal life, including my love life. With you, the problem doesn't exist. We're a natural couple.'

'I'm a Fenian and you're a Prod.'

'So what?'

'You really don't believe it makes a difference?'

'No, Theresa, I don't.'

'You're very unusual,' Theresa said.

Shrugging, Neil sipped some more champagne, then said, 'Well, we were known as a pretty unusual family. Solid. Stubborn. Calvinist to the core. Not given to petty emotions, or the expressing of personal opinions that had no direct bearing on business. I mean, business was everything. That's why, when the plantation brought us to Ireland, we knew how to exploit it. It came naturally to us.'

'*Us*? Just who am I sleeping with?'

Neil smiled. 'Unusual? Of *course* I'm *unusual*! For a start, I'm the only son out of five generations. There were no daughters at all. My earliest ancestors came here from Scotland in 1605. According to family tradition, King William rested in Stoneykirk Manor on his way to Belfast - but don't tell your Catholic friends *that*!'

'I won't.'

Neil smiled again and shrugged. 'Anyway, whether or not that story's true, various antiques in the house are said to have belonged to King William: a shaving mug, the jug he drank from, and so on. Certainly Stoneykirk Manor is in an area where that class of person, at that particular time, would have come to visit or stay for short periods. In fact, the house actually stands on the site of an ancient fort - '

'I felt the hauntings!' Theresa joked.

' - and other forts and churches are known to have been scattered all around here. So I must accept that I have illustrious ancestors.'

'You don't have to sound ashamed of your background,' Theresa said, 'just because I'm working class and, even worse, Catholic.'

Neil reached across the table to take her hand and shake it gently, affectionately.

'I'm not ashamed,' he said, 'but I don't want you to think I'm boasting. You asked me about my background and I'm telling you. That's all there is to it.'

'So tell me more,' Theresa said.

'I can't think of anything else.'

'Please! Give me a scandal!'

'What kind of scandal?'

'Like why, at forty-five, you're still a bachelor, even though you're attracted to women. At least, you find *me* attractive!'

Neil was clearly amused. 'I don't really know. All I can say with confidence is that my forefathers all waited until middle age before marrying, and then, invariably, they married a woman as strong and as well placed as they were.'

'Were they like you?'

'A bit. Certainly red-haired and Scottish. Silent. Speculative. Shrewd men who cared for little other than their duties.'

'Which were?'

'To take care of the mills and make fine cloth. I'm sure they'd have been disappointed in me. Though I am, at least in one sense, following in the family tradition, by still not being married at my age and by having no children.'

'Can I ask why?'

'You can ask, but I can't give you a satisfactory, truthful answer. It just hasn't happened, that's all. Maybe because I simply haven't met the right person. Maybe because I *don't want* to meet the right person. Maybe because I feel awkward being a wealthy plantationer in Belfast, where the resentment, in my view, will never end. Maybe because my parents rarely showed their emotions and I'm probably the same as they were: essentially decent but generally lacking in emotion. Who knows?' He shrugged again in defeat. 'Not me, that's certain.'

Theresa thought of Stoneykirk Manor, that large Georgian house nestling in its own grounds in the upper Malone Road, surrounded by trees, high hedges and a stone wall, with well-tended lawns and flower beds out front, a tennis court and vegetable gardens at the rear, the very epitome of Protestant supremacy in Ulster. Did that place explain why, after working for Neil for two years, she had gone to bed with him? Was it love or just the knowledge that her first love, Gerry Donovan, had been picked up by the RUC during yet another mindless sectarian riot and ended up in the Crumlin Road jail like a common criminal, thus losing the last chance he'd had of learning a trade and getting a decent, long-term job? Had she simply given up on Gerry then? Given up on her whole working class, Catholic background and decided to go instead for something, or someone, grander? Like this perfectly nice, gentle, slightly irresponsible, plantation Prod who'd inherited the wealth of the very same mills that had killed her mother back in the bad old days? She had asked herself those questions many times, but hadn't yet come up with any answers. Maybe because, in the end, deep down, she did not want to know.

What she *did* know - and what she wanted to forget - was that when she had told her Da she was leaving home to live with Neil Stewart in his manor house in the upper Malone Road, out there with the non-sectarian nobs, all tied together by money, not divided by poverty and religion, Barry hadn't exactly insulted her (he hadn't called her a whore or anything similar) but had certainly made it clear that he was deeply disappointed in her and would rather not meet the new man in her life. And from that day to this, he had not been out to Stoneykirk Manor; nor had he invited her and Neil back to his pitifully small house in the Pound Loney. Not that he could seriously have done the latter, since even *she* couldn't bear the thought of Neil sitting in front of the tiled fireplace in that tiny two-up, two-down house in that narrow, terraced street, with the kids playing outside, the overweight housewives, the gangs of unemployed men loitering at the corners. Jesus, no! No way! Because in truth she'd always had ideas way above her station and was now, she believed, as snobbish as the nobs she'd once despised.

Fuck Gerry. Fuck her whole past. You couldn't live with losers like Gerry without losing yourself. At least with Neil, with this wealthy, planted Protestant, she felt civilised. So fuck her Da and his working class, Catholic resentment. Fuck the whole fucking world. Life was too short for guilt.

'Do you like it here?' Neil asked.

'You know I do. I love it.'

'I love it, too,' Neil said. 'I always did. Even when I was a child. I never realised that most people don't have second homes, so I had no guilt about it at all. Now... Well, though I feel a *little* guilty, I must confess I still love it. Maybe because it's a lot *smaller* than the house in Belfast; maybe just because it's out here in Cultra. Either way, I feel grand here.'

Theresa knew what he meant. From the lounge of this house, modest in size but cocooned in its own gardens, you could look out over Belfast Lough, fourteen miles long, its rippling surface littered with passenger ferries, steamers and sailboats, the sky cloudy or sunny above it, but always seeming to offer distant horizons. Also, the place *felt* different. As Neil had told her, King John had spent the night in nearby Holywood, in 1210, being ferried over the lough from Carrickfergus. The Franciscan Monastery, once located in the Holy Wood, had been burned down in 1572 by the O'Neill of Clannaboy to prevent it from becoming a refuge for Thomas Smith's expedition. The big ships, as distinct from the ferries, sailed past here even now, not too far from the front window, on their way in and out of Belfast docks. When Theresa saw them, she always had the urge to travel, which is what she had been planning to do before becoming involved with Neil. Her aims had been modest. She had only wanted to go to the Big Smoke, London; but those ships, she knew, went an awful lot farther, to places she couldn't even imagine. Crimson dawns. Purple sunsets. Golden beaches and palm trees. But Neil could not, or would not, take her there, because he didn't like traveling farther than Europe.

Settle for what you can get, she had thought, to soothe her disappointment.

'Shall we have the brandy outside?' Neil asked.

'Aye... Yes,' she corrected herself. 'Why not?'

When Neil had poured two large brandies and handed one to her, they left the dining table and went out onto the patio overlooking the glittering, now moonlit, waters of the lough. At the wall of the patio, caressed by an unusually warm August breeze, Neil slid his arm around her waist and held her close to him. He had stolen her virginity and she hadn't resented him for it, had actually been grateful, because in truth she had wanted to lose it and had frequently been frustrated by Gerry's lack of aggression in that particular area. Now a mature woman, living in sin (as her father and the priests would have it; though not Sean, thank God), she felt comfortable as his secretary and mistress, less frustrated, more secure, at ease with herself. She still hadn't been across the water, not even to London, let alone tropical beaches, but what she had was enough for the moment, despite what she had sacrificed: the loyalty of her father, close neighbours, a few old friends. Not much to lose, really. And at least she still met Sean once or twice a month, in a bar or restaurant in the centre of town. That was enough, given Sean's calm acceptance of her situation, to make her feel that she wasn't doing anything wrong. Sean was brilliant that way.

'Looks nice out there,' Neil said.

'Aye,' Theresa said, 'really nice.'

If she looked to the south-west, the view wasn't too appealing, showing only the three channels of the docks, all lined with cranes and gantries, though minute from this distance. A foul black smoke, even darker than the incoming night, billowed up from the tall chimneys of the oil refinery and, farther on, the chemical works, the few remaining mills and the other factories scattered around the vast sweep of water, covering it in a leaden pall, streaked eerily with irregular lines of crimson light. Much closer, more romantically, a passenger ferry was advancing from the direction of the Liverpool Ferry Terminal, its many lights winking on as night's darkness descended. Other lights, on the move, like stars in an inverted sky, were the lights of ships and other boats that she'd seen clearly just an hour ago. They looked more romantic at night, under stars, in the moonlight. They could lead her thoughts elsewhere.

'God,' she said, 'it looks really gorgeous. It's not like that in daylight.'

'It's romantic,' Neil responded. 'More so when you know about it. Did you know, for instance, that it was from Bangor Bay - '

'Is that out there?'

'Yes, on the southern shore.'

'Sorry. Go on.'

'It was from Bangor Bay that St. Colombanus and his twelve companions set out as missionaries to Gaul, Germany, and Switzerland.'

'When?'

'In the year of 575.'

'Lord, that was a long time ago.'

She had problems when Neil became pedantic, which was one of his failings. In love with history, he droned on like a schoolteacher, making her eyelids droop. But now he smiled and squeezed her hand.

'Before you and I were born,' he said. 'And in 882, the Viking long-ships sailed into that lough to enable the Vikings to murder and plunder and burn their way across Ulster.'

'Real historical, Neil, but too far back for my liking. Give me something a bit more up-to-date to hold my attention.'

'Well,' Neil said, as patient as always, 'in 1944, which is as modern as I can get, the American fleet assembled here in preparation for the Normandy landings. So one way or the other, give and take, we're looking out on an important body of water.'

'It's not important if you can't drink it,' Theresa said.

'Oh, you're such a crude realist, Theresa.'

'The sky's red,' she informed him, ignoring his gentle chiding. 'Sure I never thought I'd see a red sky over Belfast at night.'

'Red? Where?'

'Over there.' She pointed with the index finger of her free hand, to indicate a flickering red-and-crimson light that had formed an immense fan to the south-west, over part of West Belfast.

Neil gazed in that direction, his brow furrowing, then he blinked a couple of times and looked again, more intently, as if bewildered by what he was seeing.

'That's not natural light,' he said. 'It's flickering and it's stained with dark patches. I think what we're seeing is fire, or a series of fires, with smoke billowing up from the flames.'

At that moment, the sound of gunfire came again from the television set in the room adjoining the conservatory, making Theresa twitch involuntarily. 'God!' she said. 'That must be a violent movie on the TV. Can I turn it off?'

'My fault,' Neil said. 'I forgot to do it. I'll go and do it right now.'

Resting his glass of brandy on the wall of the patio, he made his way back through the conservatory, to the room adjoining it. Theresa stared across the lough, in a south-westerly direction, wondering what kind of fires could be causing those expanding fans of crimson light in the distance. She heard the gunshots again: Neil still hadn't turned the TV off. She glanced back over her shoulder, across the conservatory, to see him in the other room, staring down intently at the flickering screen. Eventually, when it was clear that he was engrossed in what he was seeing, she placed her glass of brandy on the patio wall, beside his, glanced once more at the crimson sky above West Belfast, and then crossed the conservatory to join him.

Looking down at the TV screen, she saw burning buildings, shadowy figures firing rifles, people fleeing from homes pouring smoke, some pushing prams piled high with personal possessions. It was all taking place in what looked to Theresa like hell.

'It's not a movie,' Neil said, sounding distraught. 'What we're seeing is happening in Belfast. It's happening right now. The Protestants and Catholics are at war.'

'God help us,' Theresa said.

5

The telephone call came at seven in the morning when Sean was still lying in bed beside Moira, not fully awake, though certainly not asleep, repeatedly going over in his mind the contents of Brendan Coghill's letter. The letter had shocked and saddened him for a couple of different reasons. First was the shock of learning that Brendan had suffered a heart attack to add to the many other health problems that he'd had over the past five years or so. Certainly, knowing that Brendan would never exaggerate his problems, it seemed to Sean from the tone of his old friend's missive that his health was now in serious decline and could not be reversed. Sean was even more convinced of this when he thought of how suddenly Frank Kavanagh had become ill and how rapidly his condition had deteriorated, until, a mere ten days after first complaining of breathing problems (though he had aged and withered away dramatically in that time; down from his formerly massive physique to mere skin and bone), he had collapsed and, mere hours later, died in the intensive care ward of the Royal Victoria Hospital. Though Sean had always secretly despised Kavanagh, he had still been shocked by his death and viewed it as the end of an era.

It's that time of life for their generation, Sean thought. The generation of hardened Republicans. They're all passing away now.

Saddened by that aspect of Brendan's letter, Sean had also been given a restless night by his old friend's vivid reminder of what had happened at the Burntollet Bridge. Though he and Moira had escaped unscathed, Iris had taken a bad blow to her forehead, which had been impregnated with pieces of glass, and was taken away, with a distraught Des, in an RUC ambulance. Iris still bore the scar to this day, was traumatised by it, thinking it made her look ugly; and Des, in particular, hated the Loyalists even more because of what they had done to Iris in particular and to the Civil Rights Movement in general. Formerly a moderate, Des was, like a lot of his friends, now doubtful that the problems of the Six Counties could be solved by peaceful means.

'Maybe the IRA were right,' he said one day to Sean. 'Those Loyalists are fascists and there may be only two ways to deal with them: the bomb and the bullet.'

While not necessarily agreeing with that point of view, Sean still clearly recalled how, after the attack at the Burntollet Bridge and River Faughan, the civil rights marchers, bloody though they were and badly diminished in numbers, had defiantly gone on to Derry, only to be attacked twice more before reaching the city. The final attack, at the Irish Street estate, had included a fusillade of stones and, for the first time, petrol-bombs. Shortly after, the RUC had deliberately stopped the marchers and refused to let them continue, even as they were being pelted with rocks thrown by Loyalists perched on a hilltop quarry. Nevertheless, the marchers, minus Farrell, who had been knocked unconscious and taken to hospital, finally arrived to a hero's welcome in Guildhall Square.

Alas, their exultation had been short-lived. That night, the RUC Reserve force, most of its members drunk and clearly furious that the marchers had broken through, rampaged through the Catholic Bogside, breaking windows and doors, demanding that the 'Fenian bastards' come out of their homes, and either beating or stoning anyone foolish enough to do so, or merely unlucky enough to be passing by. The people were outraged, the barricades were raised, and at the entrance to St. Columb's Well, someone painted the statement: 'You are now entering Free Derry.'

Thus, Free Derry was born.

Sean was recollecting all of this when the telephone rang. The phone had been installed for him by the Campaign for Social Justice in Northern Ireland. Still half asleep, he picked the receiver up and held it to his ear.

'Yes?'

'Are you Sean Coogan?' a harsh, unfriendly, male voice said.

'Yes, I am.'

'The bastard who belongs to Sinn Féin?'

Instantly, Sean snapped awake. 'Sinn Féin is an illegal organisation.'

'So's the IRA,' the unfriendly male said, 'but those cunts are still out there, bombing and shooting Loyalists to their heart's content.'

'Who is this, please?'

'You're one of them communistic civil rights traitors, aren't you?'

'I'm a member of the Campaign for Social Justice, if that's what you mean.'

'You're a communist agitator and Fenian subversive.'

'I'm putting this phone down right now.'

'Don't. Heed this warning instead. If you don't want your house to be burnt over the heads of you and your family, leave it today, because we're going to burn all you Fenians out before the Brits come in to protect you. Now spread the news to all your friends in the Falls. If they're not gone by the time we get to them, they'll regret ever having been born.'

The line abruptly went dead.

Shocked, Sean held the receiver in his right hand, staring stupidly at it, until snapped out of his reverie by Moira, who rolled onto her back, yawned, then sleepily asked him who had called at this ungodly hour of the morning.

'An anonymous caller,' Sean said, placing the receiver back on its cradle on the bedside cabinet. 'And not a pleasant one either. Some Prod warning us to get out of the house before he and his friends burn it down.'

'*What?*'

'You heard me. That's exactly what he said.'

With her brown eyes widening, awakening, Moira pushed herself upright. 'Jesus, Sean, do you think it's serious? Or just the joke of some sectarian deep-breather?'

Sean shook his head from side to side in perplexity. 'I'm not sure, but I'm inclined to take it seriously. The heat's been rising in the Protestant communities for days, given what's been going on in Derry and, more crucially, given the rumour that the Irish Army's about to invade the North.'

'Who'd believe that bloody nonsense?' Moira said, now fully awake and swinging her long legs off the bed. 'Sure didn't Lynch only say he's going to get the Irish Army to establish field hospitals along the border, for people who get injured in the North? He said nothing else.'

'But the Loyalists, encouraged by Ian Paisley and his friends, believe that Lynch's statement is just an excuse for moving his army to the border in preparation for an invasion of the North, at least to rescue Derry.'

'The British Army's now in Derry.'

'To protect the Catholics from the Loyalists. At least that's what the Loyalists of Belfast believe. So that anonymous caller's reference to burning us out before the Brits arrive should be taken seriously.'

'Oh, God!' Moira exclaimed, her eyes widening.

'I think we should take the kids to my Da and Meg. If the Prods come, they'll come from the Shankill, which means they'll come here, to the Falls - not to Turf Lodge. So I think we should get the kids out of here.'

'I'll make breakfast,' Moira said, 'then take the kids to your Da's while you do whatever you have to do.'

'That's my girl,' Sean said.

When Moira had left the bedroom, he kept turning the anonymous phone call over in his mind and decided that it was definitely a serious threat. The tension had been building in Belfast ever since early in the month - the second of August, to be exact - when the Junior Orangemen had deliberately marched down the Shankill to parade for the second time past the Unity Walk flats. Once more the residents had turned out to protest. When, after a few stones had been thrown, the

BBC's local news included the information that the marchers had been attacked at Unity Walk, it was inevitable that there would be a confrontation when the parade returned that evening. The situation was only exacerbated when, early in the afternoon, a Protestant crowd, led by John McKeague of the SDA, had advanced on the flats, loudly demanding the arrest of the leading Republican, Jim Sullivan, who had been seen in the courtyard and was therefore, in the eyes of the Loyalists, obviously planning some Republican mischief. By late afternoon, a vast crowd from the Shankill Road had gathered behind Unity Walk. The waving of a tricolour at the window of one flat provoked the expected attack, with a variety of missiles, including stones and bottles, being thrown in both directions, as men bawled obscenities and women screamed. Eventually, all the windows down one side of the apartment block were smashed, and the police, short of men, had to devote their energies to preventing an invasion of the flats by the returning Orange parade. Then they baton-charged the stone-throwing Protestant crowd and drove them back to the Shankill. Unfortunately, in the hope of preventing another Protestant mob from invading through an unprotected side entrance to the complex, a police unit drove there just as the expected Protestant mob arrived. To the besieged Catholics, it looked as if the police were actually leading the Protestant onslaught, so the Catholics, infuriated, attacked the police. When a second police unit, guarding another entrance to the complex, went to assist their colleagues, more Protestants invaded through that unguarded area, thus confirming Catholic fears that the police were slyly aiding the Protestants. Finally, to make matters worse, the police, being attacked on all sides by the Catholics, became convinced that they had been ambushed by the very people they were trying to defend. This suspicion turned the police against the Catholics. From that day on, the tension had been building in Belfast, with both sides convinced that the other was preparing to attack them. Sooner or later, the situation was bound to explode… and this could be the day.

When he had finished dressing, before going down to breakfast, Sean put through a call to Des, now working these days in the offices of the Campaign for Social Justice.

'Des Galloway at your service.'

'Des, this is Sean.'

'*You're* up bright and early!'

'Do you still have eyes and ears in the Shankill?'

'Naturally. Why?'

'Is there any sign of agitation there?'

'Damned right there is. We're monitoring the situation and we're seriously concerned. There were more people than normal out on the Shankill yesterday evening and half of them remained on the road throughout the night. They seemed unusually agitated, standing around in large groups, arguing and shouting, and some were being egged on by their women. Most of them are still there as we speak - and they're still agitated.'

'I think this could be serious trouble,' Sean said. 'I've just received an anonymous call from a Prod, warning me that if the people in the Falls don't leave their homes, they're going to be burnt out. I don't think he was kidding me.'

'Jasus!' Des exclaimed. 'So what...?'

'I'm sending Moira and the kids to stay with my Da and Meg, then I'm going to have a sniff around.'

'Don't go near the Shankill,' Des warned him. 'Any stranger there's going to be challenged.'

'Your people are okay?'

'They're familiar faces, so they *should* be okay, but given the mood of that crowd...'

'Okay,' Sean said, when Des' voice had tapered off uneasily. 'Keep monitoring the Shankill and I'll call you back about lunchtime.'

'Aye, right,' Des responded.

Sean went down to have breakfast with Moira and the kids, Michael and Deirdre, three and two years old respectively. Though he could not ignore the anxiety in Moira's eyes, he joked with the kids as if everything was normal, then informed them that they were going to spend the day with Grandda and Granny, meaning Barry and Meg. Since Barry and Meg always spoilt them rotten, both children were thrilled.

'Once I leave them there,' Moira told Sean, 'I'm coming straight back. If those mad Loyalists *do* invade the Falls, I'm not going to budge from this place. I'll protect my own property.'

'I don't think that's wise,' Sean said gently.

'I'm not interested in whether it's wise or not. I won't be pushed out this way. Besides, if anyone gets hurt, I can help with first aid.'

Sean smiled. 'Aye, right, you do that.'

Once Moira had gone off with the kids, he, too, left the house. But ignoring Des' advice, he crossed the Falls Road and then went along Northumberland Street, heading for the Shankill Road, less than a mile away. He had only walked for ten minutes, about equidistant between the Falls and the Shankill, when he saw that the far end of the road, if not exactly blocked, was virtually solid with a gathering of men. Those men, he knew, had to be Protestants.

Sean stopped walking. Since the side streets here merged into Protestant territory, to advance any farther would place him in a situation where he could find Protestants coming up behind him. At the same time, he was frustrated because he was still too far away to see what those men at the far end of the street, where it ran into the Shankill, were doing. He had seen enough, however, to know that they were there in great numbers and had gathered together for a purpose.

Immediately, he turned around and hurried back to the Falls, then made his way to an office located near Divis Street and now used as an informal meeting place for members of Sinn Féin, though the organisation was officially banned. Inside, in a masculine squalor of old filing cabinets, badly scratched tables, piles of pamphlets and other papers, overflowing ashtrays and unfinished cups of tea or coffee, he found Liam O'Hanlon and Tom Mallon, as busy as always on their telephones, both speaking with cigarettes in their mouths.

'Hi, Sean,' Mallon said, squinting through smoke, the smouldering cigarette jumping up and down between his thin lips. 'What's brought you here? I thought the Campaign for Social Justice was takin' up all your time, it bein' that *we're* an illegal organisation an' have closed shop, ho, ho.'

'What's your reading of the situation hereabouts?'

'Grim,' Mallon said without hesitation. 'The general belief is that the Prods are about to explode an' that we won't be given too much assistance if they attack - because Stormont doesn't want to offend the Unionists. The general belief is that the Prods are preparing to attack - specifically - the Falls, and that this time the rioting won't be minor.'

'What about Turf Lodge?' Sean asked, still concerned for his kids, now with Barry and Meg in that very place.

'I can't guarantee that it'll stay out of trouble,' O'Hanlon said grimly, putting his phone back on its cradle. 'If the Prods attack, they'll move out north and south from the Shankill, meaning the Falls and the Crumlin Road area, including the Ardoyne. To get to Turf Lodge, they'd have to go all the way through the Falls and then across Ballymurphy. I don't think they'll do that. It's the Falls and the Ardoyne they'll be after. But who knows, in a situation like this, what they'll end up doing? So Turf Lodge *could* be in danger.'

'You make it sound like a real war,' Sean said.

'If they move, it *will* be a real war. You mark my words, boyo.'

'I will,' Sean said. 'Thanks.'

Leaving the office, he made his way back to his home in the Pound Loney, noticing en route that the streets were more crowded than usual, particularly for this time of the day. They were more crowded, specifically, with gossiping women and shabbily dressed, unemployed youths, most of the older men being at work. The youths were everywhere, mostly gathered together in large groups that hogged the street corners. Though few of them were likely to comprehend what was happening, they were young and had the instincts of animals, so sensed that *something* was coming down. They were talking too loudly, pretending to box or wrestle, and laughing too hard to be sincere. The atmosphere was hysterical.

Once back in his empty house, Sean rang his father. Meg answered the phone, assured him that Moira had brought the kids, then she passed the phone to Barry.

'Hi, son,' Barry said. 'How are ya?'

'Fine. I'm just a bit worried, Da. I suppose Moira's told you what happened here.'

'Of course. But as she said, the kids are here, safe and sound. They're both watchin' TV.'

'Has Moira left already?'

'Aye, she has. She was goin' straight home.'

'Da, I've just been to see Liam O'Hanlon and Tom Mallon. Though they both think Turf Lodge will be safe in the event of an attack, they couldn't really guarantee it. So I think you and Meg should take the kids out of this area altogether. What about that sister of Meg's? The one out in Newtownards?'

'You want us to take the kids there for the day?'

'I want you to take the kids there and *stay* there until I phone to say it's safe to return.'

'Are you sure that's strictly necessary, son?'

'Yes, Da, I'm sure.'

'Just a moment, son.' There was a lengthy silence at the other end of the line as Barry conferred with Meg, then he came back on to say, 'Right, son, that's grand. No problem. We'll take the kids out there this afternoon.'

'Great. What's the number of Meg's sister?' As Barry gave him the number, Sean jotted it down in his address book. 'Thanks, Da. I'll give you a call when I'm convinced it's safe to come back.'

'Stay out of trouble,' Barry said.

'I'll do my best,' Sean replied. He pressed his fingers on the cradle, cutting his father off, then instantly put a call through to Des. 'Hi, Des. It's lunchtime.'

'I never leave my desk.'

'Dedication is a wondrous thing. So what gives in the Shankill?'

'Bad news,' Des said bluntly. 'Loyalists are pouring into the streets connecting the Shankill to the Falls and arming themselves with stones and bottles, possibly petrol-bombs, plus a variety of cudgels, some of them reportedly spiked with nails. Even worse, they've been joined by hundreds of mobilised B-Specials, armed with rifles, pistols and sub-machine guns. There's a lot of drink being taken as they work themselves up into a frenzy. I think we should barricade the streets.'

'I think you're right,' Sean said. 'Send a lot of men out there with megaphones and start spreading the word.'

'Shite!' Des exploded.

'What?'

'We've just received a message. Rioting's already started at the Hastings Street barracks and mobs of Loyalists are pouring down the side streets towards the Falls, attacking Catholic homes, smashing windows and... *What?* Aw, Jesus! They're smashing the windows, hammering doors in with sledgehammers, and throwing petrol-bombs into the houses... Sorry, Sean, but I've got to hang up now. We've just heard gunshots from the area under discussion. I think we've got a real war on our hands. I'm going to ring the RUC.'

'Aye, you do that, Des.'

Sean put the phone down just as Moira entered the house.

'What's happening?' she asked. Sean told her. 'Oh, God help us! What about Turf Lodge?'

'They're not likely to go that far, but I'm taking no chances. The kids will be taken to Meg's sister, out in Newtownards. They'll stay with her until I call them back.'

Moira sighed. 'Thank God. So what are *you* planning to do?'

'I've already talked to Des. He's organising for people to go around the Falls - at least those areas not yet under attack - and encourage the building of barricades to keep the Prods out. Apart from that, the only way we can fight back is by using any weapons we can lay our hands on.'

'Bricks and stones and bottles,' Moira said.

Sean shrugged. 'That's it, I suppose.'

'Is there shooting? Are those B-Specials using their weapons?'

'Des heard gunshots where the Prods were attacking, so *some* of them must be armed with real weapons.'

'The B-Specials.'

'Probably.

'So what about the IRA? I know they haven't done a damned thing in years, but they must have *some* weapons.'

'I'm just about to go and find out,' Sean said. 'But what if the Prods reach this street? What about *you*?'

'I'll worry about that when it happens. Meanwhile, I'll go out there and help organise some kind of resistance, including barricades.'

'Most of the mature men are still at work - which may be why the Prods picked this particular time to start, having only women and kids to deal with.'

'Then I'll organise the housewives and teenagers. Those kids are already straining at the leash, so I'm sure they'll be more than willin' to throw bricks and bottles, or build some kind of barricade. You'd better be off now.'

'Aye, I reckon.' Leaning forward to kiss Moira on the cheek, Sean realised that he still loved her and certainly respected her; that their mutual interests in politics, though frequently causing rows, had not necessarily been a mistake. 'You look after yourself.'

'Aye, you too.'

Leaving the house, Sean walked along the street to the Falls Road, noticing en route that most of the housewives were out on the pavements, talking to each other, most looking anxious, and that the youths were still in gangs at the corners, gazing in the direction of the Shankill, their attention drawn by the smoke rising from the burning houses of the Catholic areas and, more chillingly, by the sound of distant gunfire. Seeing that they were working themselves up into a lather, already egging each other on, challenging each other to do something about the situation, Sean knew that reciprocal violence was now unavoidable and that it was bound to escalate out of control. Frightened by that thought, he hurried down the Falls, to where he knew he would find the late Frank Kavanagh's old IRA pals, Seamus Magee and Kevin McClusky. Though Sean had never particularly liked the two men, he knew that he now needed them and more of their kind; so, having turned off the Falls again, he entered McGahan's bar in the Albert Road without hesitation. Magee and McClusky practically lived in this bar or, rather, relived their dreams of past glory in it, so they were there as expected, sitting at their usual table, but now surrounded by a bunch of men their own age, most dressed in shabby suits, peaked caps and scuffed shoes, all hazed in a pall of cigarette smoke, all talking excitedly.

'Sure the Prods are swarming down through the side streets like bees!' one of the younger men, John Leary, exclaimed melodramatically. 'They're comin' down here to slaughter us!'

When Sean stopped at the table, everyone stared at him, recognising him, this being a small, intimate community. 'So what are you doin' about it?' he said, trying to sound like his old self, in the days before he went to Queen's University; trying, in fact, to sound like one of them. 'Apart from sittin around this table, drinkin' and yappin'?'

'What the fuck does *that* mean?' another young man, Eamon McFeely, asked.

'It means that the women an' children of the Falls are already out there, collectin' weapons and gatherin' material for barricades, while you lot just yap on and on. So why not get out there an' help them?'

'So what are *you* doin' in here?' an unknown, hard-faced, middle-aged man, almost certainly a former member of the IRA, asked with barely concealed contempt.

'I'm here to see these two,' Sean said, nodding to indicate the red-haired Seamus Magee and the lean, dark Kevin McClusky, the former now in his late forties, the latter fifty years old, time stopping for no man. 'And I'd rather talk to them privately while you go out there and try to help the women and kids. That mob could be here any time now, but you could help slow them down.'

'You're Barry Coogan's son, right?'

'Aye,' Sean said.

'That's good enough for me,' the unknown man said, smiling. 'Me and Barry, we did a lot together - a lot of time, like. Aye, and all for the cause.' He turned to the rest of the men gathered around the table. 'All right, lads, let's go and do what the man says. We haven't got all day.'

'Damned right,' young McFeely said.

Spitting a cacophony of insulting remarks about those Loyalist bastards from the Shankill, all of the men, except Magee and McClusky, hurried out of the pub. When the last man had departed, Sean pulled up a chair and sat facing Frank Kavanagh's two old friends.

'Very clever the way you handled them,' McClusky said, looking as lean and mean as ever, though his formerly ink-black hair was streaked with grey and his face, which had never been creased with humour, was now creased with age. 'So what the fuck are you here for?'

'I'm here for the Falls,' Sean replied.

'I thought you'd given up on the IRA,' the red-haired, still boyish, though visibly edgy Seamus Magee said, 'in favour of all them nancy-boy radicals from Queen's.'

'Those so-called nancy-boys from Queen's are the ones who created worldwide sympathy for our cause when the IRA had virtually given up. So you've no right to sneer at them now.'

'Grand,' Magee retorted. 'I stand reprimanded. So what the fuck are you doin' here, talkin' to us IRA no-hopers?'

'You know what's happening out there.'

'Damned right we do. What's happenin' out there is that the Civil Rights Movement has fallen on its arse and now you've got a war on your hands.'

'That's close enough,' Sean said, though he was gritting his teeth, 'so now's the time for you no-hopers to contribute.'

'Oh, yeah? How?'

'By putting weapons into the hands of our people and, if necessary, showing them how to use them.'

'What weapons?' McClusky asked blandly.

'You must have weapons. We all know you still have weapons. You may not have many and what you have may be primitive, but anything would be useful right now, so stop playing games with me.'

'You want weapons?'

'Yes.'

'So here's what *we* want.' McClusky glanced at Magee, received a nod of silent agreement and then turned back to Sean. 'If we bring in arms, we get to organise the defence of the area and you people only deal with the politics.'

Sean sighed. 'Agreed.'

'If we put up the barricades, they only come down when we say so - and we won't say so until certain demands are met.'

'What demands?'

Again, McClusky glanced at Magee and received another nod of approval. Smiling thinly, he turned back to Sean. 'One,' he said, raising his thumb, 'Stormont has to be suspended. Two,' he added, raising his index finger as well, 'the RUC has to be disarmed and the B-Specials disbanded. Three,' he continued, adding his forefinger to the other two digits, 'the Special Powers Act has to be revoked.' He stared steadily at Sean for a moment, then spread all of his fingers outwards like a fan. 'So what do you say?'

Sean didn't like it, but he didn't have a choice. 'You have an agreement.'

McClusky and Magee glanced at each other, both smiling slightly, then Magee leaned across the table to stare coldly at Sean and say, 'You realise that this puts you and your civil rights mates in the passenger seat?'

Sean mutely nodded his agreement.

'And you're willin' to wear it?'

'What's my option?'

Magee smiled more broadly, perhaps even admiringly. 'Sure that's a good answer,' he said. 'Almost as good as a signature.'

'How soon can you help?' Sean asked, feeling personally humiliated but hopeful. 'We don't have that much time.'

McClusky nodded to indicate that he understood. 'We can start right away - in fact, the minute we leave this pub - but we've an awful lot of people to contact and some of them can't get here too quickly, comin', as they will be, from places as far out as South Armagh.'

'I understand,' Sean said.

'But I'll guarantee you this much - '

'Anything,' Sean interjected.

'The Falls might suffer tonight, the Prods might have their fling, but by tomorrow you'll have weapons - not many and not good, but weapons all the same - and the barricades, *proper* barricades, will have been raised to seal off the area. Then, when the Brits march in, we can feed 'em tea and cakes, at least for the first few days. Make peace, not war, right?'

Sean nodded and smiled bleakly. 'Right. I think I'd better leave now.'

'Aye, you do that,' Magee said.

Sean pushed his chair back and left the pub. Briefly dazzled by the light, though it wasn't all that bright, he then saw smoke billowing up over the area between the Falls and the Shankill. He heard gunshots from that area, imagined the sound of breaking glass, screams and shouts, and then, feeling defeated, he hurried back to his home in the Pound Loney, silently praying that the Loyalists hadn't managed to get that far, despising himself for his rising fears.

The Civil Rights Movement had been destroyed. The IRA would soon be in control again. The clock had been turned back by fifty years.

6

The first wave of Loyalists had already moved out and were smashing their way through the side streets when wee Billy arrived at the Shankill with Dan and Rob. He was stunned by what he saw. The whole road was like a war zone, with men in ordinary suits and peaked caps parading back and forth, too restless to stand still, while wielding a variety of clubs, including cudgels with large nails protruding from them. Others were kneeling behind coal sacks filled with stones, handing the stones out by the fistful. Yet others, mostly teenagers, were filling bottles with petrol and stuffing the mouths of the bottles with dry rags to make crude petrol-bombs. Men were queuing up to obtain those as well. More surprisingly, mingling with the crowd was a great number of grim-faced B-Specials armed with rifles, pistols and sub-machine guns.

'It's a fuckin' war all right,' Billy said.

'About time,' Rob retorted.

Billy, too, despite his initial reservations, now felt that the time had come. At first he had been frightened by how serious it was all becoming (the siege of Derry; the riots throughout the province), but gradually, as he had attended hastily convened Orange Lodge meetings and 'strategy discussions' with the Ulster Protestant Volunteers, of which he was one, he had been caught up in the mounting hysteria and became convinced, like his friends, that the Fenians were preparing themselves for a major attack on the Protestant communities, particularly the Shankill, and that the IRA were arming themselves for a return to the fray.

This was ironic in that only a few months back the UPV had deliberately bombed electrical and water installations in order to have the IRA blamed for it and consolidate Unionist power in the province; but Billy and his UPV friends had forgotten that already and were, like their fellow Loyalists, convinced that the IRA, redundant this past seven years, was obtaining arms from the South with a view to starting a new, all-out war. Any residual doubts they may have had about this dirty trick had been swept away when Taoiseach Jack Lynch announced that he was planning to establish Irish Army field hospitals along the border for people injured in the North. Those so-called 'field hospitals', at least as far as Billy and his friends were concerned, were merely an excuse to get the Irish Army to the border in readiness for an invasion of the North. If that happened - and many Loyalists were convinced that it would - the Catholics in the Falls, led by a re-armed IRA, would most likely come surging through the side streets to engage in an ethnic cleansing of the Shankill. Thus, Billy and most of his friends now felt justified in doing the same thing in reverse - and, more importantly, in advance. Their own brand of ethnic cleansing had therefore commenced.

From where he was standing, between Dan and Rob, near the corner of Northumberland Street, where stones, clubs and petrol-bombs were being handed out, Billy could hear the distant bawling of men and the screaming of women. He also heard occasional gunshots.

'Those fuckin' IRA assassins,' Rob said grimly. 'They've got weapons an' they're firing at our lads.'

'The B-Specials have weapons as well,' Billy reminded him, 'so they could be the ones doin' the firin'.'

'What the hell does it matter?' Dan said, his grin slightly crazy, his gaze bright and wayward. 'Let's fill our pockets with stones, get some petrol-bombs and clubs, then go an' help clear out them Fenian fuckers. I don't want to miss this one.'

'Me neither,' Rob said.

Glancing straight ahead, they saw the backs of a mass of men much farther along, near the Falls Road, and smoke billowing up from the side streets.

'That smoke's comin' from Fenian houses,' Dan said. 'That means our lads are getting' the Fenians out and then settin' fire to their homes. They've got the Taigs on the run. Come on, boys, let's go.'

Together they crossed the road to get in the queues for stones, petrol-bombs and clubs. As there were three of them, each of them took a separate queue and Billy ended up in the one for clubs. The boy handing out the clubs, about seventeen years old, his face covered in acne, his hair an uncombed mess, initially offered him a club spiked with nails.

'No, thanks,' Billy said without thinking. 'Sure I don't think I could bring myself to hit anyone with somethin' like that. Just give me three ordinary clubs.'

'Just remember that it's Fenians you're attackin' and you'll do it all right.'

'I don't mind crackin' the odd skull,' Billy lied, since he wasn't sure if he could do even that much, 'but I couldn't bear to stick those nails in anyone, Fenian or otherwise, so just three plain clubs, thanks.'

The boy shrugged. 'Your choice,' he said, handing him three black-painted wooden truncheons.

'Where did you get these?' Billy asked.

'Ask no questions an' I'll tell you no lies, mister.'

'Were they supplied by the RUC or B-specials?'

'Ask no questions and… '

'All right, forget it.'

'Best of luck.'

'Thanks,' Billy said. Leaving the queue, he found Dan and Rob already waiting for him, the former holding a small sack containing six petrol-bombs, the latter with a cut-down coal sack filled with heavy stones.

'For breakin' windows with,' he exclaimed excitedly, as they knelt facing each other on the ground.

'Or Fenian faces,' Dan said, grinning.

Billy gave each of them a truncheon, filled his trouser pockets with as many heavy stones as they would take, then took two of the petrol-bombs and shoved one into each of the side pockets of his jacket.

'Do any of youse have a lighter?' he asked as an after-thought, realising that he personally, being a non-smoker, did not have a lighter or box of matches.

'Aye, I do,' Rob said.

'So let's make sure we stick together,' Billy said.

'Aye, right,' Dan said. 'Now let's go and join that crowd over yonder.'

The crowd to which he was referring was virtually blocking the entrance to Northumberland Street. Surprisingly, it included a good number of women. Many of them were holding up fluttering Union Jacks; others were holding out aprons which, still tied around their waists, were sagging with stones. It was clear that they were just about to march into Northumberland Street, but just as the first of them started moving off, there was the distant roaring of a submachine gun, followed by more bawling and screaming. The marchers at the end of the street faltered, but then stopped altogether when they saw the first wave of Loyalists, a good way down the street, emerging from a pall of smoke and either running back towards the Shankill or disappearing into one of the side streets.

'What the fuck…?' Rob glanced about him in confusion, not completing his question.

'They must have been fired at by that machine gun,' Billy said. 'Where the hell did *that* come from?'

'Those IRA bastards,' Dan said.

Confirmation that the Loyalists had been fired upon by a submachine gun came when the first of them arrived back at the Shankill, out of breath, panic-stricken and, in more than one case, splashed with blood.

'Ah, Jasus!' one of them gasped to no one in particular, trying to get his breath back, wiping blood from a gash in his forehead. 'Those Fenian fuckers have found a submachine gun and they're not shy of usin' it. We were doin' well until they opened fire with that, then we had to retreat.'

'What happened up there?' Billy asked. 'How far did you get?'

'A good distance, I tell ya. We went almost as far as the Falls, playing the Lambeg drums to let 'em know we were comin', wavin' our Union Jacks, shoutin' insults, and scarin' most of 'em out of their homes. We smashed their windows with stones, hammered their front doors down with clubs, then threw petrol-bombs in through the windows or open doors to set the houses on fire. Any Fenians in our way got a damned good hidin', though most of them had fled with their hordes of childern before we got there. We had 'em on the run, like, no question, until some IRA shite, right there on the Falls, at the end of the street, opened fire with that submachine gun.'

'How do you know it's the IRA?' Billy asked.

'Who else would it be? We all know that those bastards are gettin' arms from the South, so they'd obviously be the ones to have the weapons.'

'They could be old weapons,' Billy insisted. 'Not new ones from the south. They could be old weapons from the Border Campaign days. And if that's the case they won't have many of them.'

'Even a few's too much for us,' the man retorted. 'That's why we had to retreat.'

'If they don't have many weapons,' Billy said, 'they'll have to move that submachine gun from place to place, to prevent the Prods from attacking down other streets.'

'So?'

'So,' Billy responded, now trying to assert himself and put his doubts to rest, 'I say the man firing the submachine gun has probably moved elsewhere already. That means we can march back down Northumberland Street, into the Falls.'

'I'm with you,' Rob said.

'Me, too,' Dan added.

'Let's go!' a barrel-chested, florid-faced man near the head of the crowd bawled, his voice pitched high with excitement, then he ran into the street, waving his club above his head, and was followed instantly by the rest of the crowd, including the women. The latter were there to cheer their men on, defiantly wave their Union Jacks, and throw stones at the windows of Fenian houses or at the Fenians themselves.

Even the faces of the women, Billy realised, were distorted by hatred.

A Lambeg drummer, coming up behind the bellowing, screaming crowd, started pounding his instrument, adding dramatically to the general bedlam.

As he marched in the thick of the noisy, excited crowd, almost deafened by the Lambeg drummer, though helplessly excited by the savage, relentless rhythms, Billy inexplicably thought of his mother and knew that she would be angry to see him here. Though her attitude towards Catholics had changed since the Falls Road riots that Johnny had been caught up in, leading to his imprisonment and subsequent flight from Belfast, Mary still didn't approve of the Orange Lodge or militant organisations like the UPV. While more suspicious of Catholics than she had been before the riots, and while certainly not socialising as frequently with her Catholic neighbours as she had done before, she still strongly disapproved of overt attacks on the Catholics and had warned Billy not to come to the Shankill this particular day. Billy, however, had not been able to resist, being a member of both the Sandy Row Orange Lodge and the UPV; now, as he marched with a lot of men known to him, he felt removed from himself, set free from his normal inhibitions, swept away on a wave of excitement that made his skin tingle. He felt slightly unreal.

'Fuckin' fenians!' Rob bawled as he advanced beside Billy, waving his club wildly above his head. 'Start runnin', you bastards!'

'All Fenians out!' Dan was chanting repeatedly, in chorus with others in the advancing mob. 'All Fenians out!'

Similar remarks where being shouted by the various members of the crowd, including the flag-waving women, as the people out front, approaching the Falls Road end of the main street, started breaking up to swarm into the narrow, mainly Catholic, side streets.

Smelling smoke, Billy glanced to his right and saw houses burning in one of the Catholic streets. Smashed glass fell to the pavements, men bawled, women screamed, then a distraught mother emerged from the swirling smoke with three frightened children clutching desperately at her dress as she frantically pushed a pram piled high with her possessions. She was sobbing and the children were all crying. An unseen man bawled,'Get goin', you Fenian whoor, and take the spawn of your fornication with ya!' Instantly, the woman stopped pushing the pram, just stood there as if frozen, then closed her eyes, placed her hands over her ears and wailed like someone demented.

Billy kept walking, his thoughts starting to spin and scatter, his vision slightly obscured by the smoke swirling out of burning houses to drift across the debris-strewn road. A rifle snapped close beside him, making him jump. Glancing to his right, he saw a B-Special firing his weapon into a crowd of Catholic youths hurling stones. One of the youths flung his arms back, convulsed and fell away. The B-Special, smiling grimly, shifted his aim and fired another shot.

Just before the Falls Road was a terraced row of untouched Catholic houses. Instantly, the men and women behind Billy hurled stones at the houses, noisily smashing the front windows while screaming abuse. Burning up in a kind of fever, aware that his heart was racing, Billy glanced over his shoulder and saw that the women not waving Union Jacks were hurling stones with the men and that their faces were contorted with hysterical hatred. Facing the front again, he saw that some of his fellow Loyalists had ignited the tapers of their petrol-bombs and were either hurling them through windows or into doorways. The bottles burst inside the houses, exploding into balls of fire, and the smoke, black and oily, giving off a rich aroma, billowed out to spread over the road.

A young woman ran screaming out of her blazing house, holding a baby in her arms, with her husband beside her, but Loyalists swarmed like flies over the man, clubbing him repeatedly to the ground while his wife, now hysterical with fear, fled with her child.

Billy couldn't join in. He had a weakness for women and children. But ignoring the burning houses, he continued along the street, still heading for the Falls Road, just as a large group of Catholics, grown men and teenagers, used their combined strength to topple a truck over onto its side. It crashed down with a noisy, metallic clattering, smashing the concrete, causing clouds of dust to boil up, forming a barricade across the end of the road, blocking the exit to the Falls. Catholic youths hurled stones and empty bottles from behind that barricade.

'Let's get 'em!' Rob shrieked.

They ran forward automatically, as if magically joined together, and kept advancing as stones sailed past their heads and bottles exploded.

A bottle smashed against the head of the man running in front of Billy. He screamed and staggered blindly, turning this way and that, as blood splashed down his face. Billy ran past him, weaving around him, and then felt a short, sharp pain in his ribs where a large stone had struck him. Rob and Dan were straight ahead, both kneeling on the ground, the latter setting a match to the petrol-bomb of the former as missiles rained down on all sides. As Billy knelt beside Dan, Rob jumped up and hurled his smouldering petrol-bomb at the overturned truck blocking the road. The bottle smashed against the truck, exploding into a sheet of flame, as other petrol-bombs sailed over the same vehicle to explode amongst the youths hiding behind it. The flames looked like torn white sheets, became fingers of phosphorescence, then dissolved into swirling black smoke that darkened the daylight. Dan lit Billy's petrol-bomb. Billy jumped up and hurled it. It fell in a languid arc behind the overturned truck, then exploded with a muffled bellowing, followed closely by others, and more jagged sheets of flame briefly brightened the gloom before the smoke darkened all again.

'Wow!' Billy exclaimed, helplessly awed by what he was witnessing.

At that moment, a couple of B-Specials fired sustained bursts from their submachine guns, aiming at the gaps on either side of the truck, clearing those areas to let hordes of Loyalists rush through, swinging wildly with their clubs, while one group formed a protective cordon around a man holding up a Union Jack. When they disappeared through the gaps, turning down the Falls Road, heading for Divis Street, Billy went after them, followed by Dan and Rob, advancing carefully through the narrow gap formed by the end of the truck and the gable end of the last terraced house. Glancing left and right, he saw only some young men, obviously Catholics, retreating up the Falls

Road as best they could while half-supporting, half-dragging wounded comrades, all looking like ghosts in the smoke that covered the road. Ignoring them, Billy turned right, heading down towards Divis Street, following that fluttering Union Jack, now raised on high.

Overwhelmed by the sheer numbers of Loyalists and the ferocity of their attack, the Catholics were backing into Divis Street while constantly hurling stones, empty bottles and anything else they could lay their hands on. Meanwhile, the Loyalists, supported by the B-Specials, advanced inexorably to where the old Sinn Féin election headquarters had been located.

A single shot rang out. The man marching beside Billy grunted, gasped, glanced down, bewildered, at his own chest, which was bloody, then sank to his knees and keeled over.

'This man's been shot!' Billy bawled at no one in particular.

'By a Fenian sniper!' Rob added grimly.

Instantly, the submachine guns and pistols of the B-Specials roared, all aiming at the corner of a street running off Divis Street, tearing the gable end of the first house to shreds, with pieces of pulverised cement flying out in all directions in billowing clouds of choking dust. Cheering in chorus, the Loyalists up ahead ran on into Divis Street, forcing the Catholics still there to scatter into the side streets; then they swarmed along the pavements on both sides of the road, smashing the windows of houses, shops and offices as they passed, hurling petrol-bombs inside. The houses went up in flames as the B-Specials chased the last of the Catholics into the side streets and the Union Jack, carried all the way from the Shankill, was planted proudly in Divis Street. The Loyalists cheered again.

'We made it!' Dan shouted exultantly, grinning at the breathless Billy and Rob. 'We've cleared the Fenians out!'

'What now?' wee Billy asked.

7

The battle raged throughout the day and well into the night, though in darkness the fighting was more desultory, more widely scattered, with a bombing here, a shooting there, and with burnt-out Catholics using the relative respite to either return to their homes for more belongings or to leave the area for good, often escorted by an armed IRA man who would give them covering fire in the event that they were attacked by a sniper.

Seamus Magee and Kevin McClusky had made good on their promise to find weapons, though certainly they were few in quantity and not that good in quality. Nevertheless, apart from rifles and pistols, they had managed to find one old Heckler & Koch MP5 submachine gun which had, the previous day, been shifted from one location to another, wherever it was felt to be most needed. When dawn broke on the second day of fighting, the gunfire was sporadic, mainly coming from snipers, both Catholic and Protestant, on the rooftops. The sky above the Falls was still black with the smoke from the many burning houses. As Sean quickly discovered, some of the Catholic streets had been burnt out completely, hundreds of the residents had been rendered homeless, some people on both sides had lost their lives, and many had been wounded.

Sean's street in the Pound Loney was one of those not attacked, but Moira had been outside during most of that first long day, giving first aid and comfort to the wounded. Meanwhile, Sean had liaised between the various civil rights groups and the IRA to ensure that they didn't conflict with one another. Insisting upon their right to organise the defence of the area, Magee and McClusky had personally distributed the weapons to those that they felt could handle them, had gathered the Catholic youths into gangs that could operate around the clock in shifts, and had supervised the raising of more barricades across both ends of the endangered Catholic streets.

Shortly after seven on Friday morning, when Sean and Moira were planning to snatch some sleep, the telephone rang. Answering it, Sean learned from Des, calling from the offices of the Campaign for Social Justice, that a survey undertaken by civil rights volunteers had ascertained that 650 Catholic families had been burnt out in one night; that Protestants living near besieged Catholic areas had also been forced to flee, though their numbers were considerably less; that the Protestants had generally fled to the east of the city, while many of the Catholics had crossed the border into the Republic, some availing themselves of the facilities in the Irish Army camps set up to cope with the flood of refugees. When Sean also learned that hundreds of other homeless, traumatised and wounded people were being looked after in the two most important local churches, he and Moira decided to visit both churches and offer their assistance.

As they made their way to the Redemptorist church in the Clonard district, they saw Catholic people in streets not touched by the rioting being dragged from their homes and taken away in RUC paddy wagons. In streets that had been attacked, Catholics, men and women, young and old, were massed behind barricades of overturned, burnt-out cars, trucks and even buses. Elsewhere, whole streets had been burnt out and were mostly deserted, except for looters or families who were removing what few possessions had not been destroyed when their houses went up in flames. Most of the streets were littered with broken glass, stones, wooden planks, iron bars, chair legs, bin lids and other items that had been used as missiles or clubs. Smoke was still billowing up from burning buildings, guns were firing from all directions, and the RUC was patrolling most of the Falls in Shorland armoured cars equipped with Browning heavy machine-guns. Some of those weapons were firing at that very moment from what appeared to be the Divis Street area.

The Redemptorist church was located at the top of an incline that sloped up from the Falls Road and overlooked the militant Protestant Sandy Row district. Stopping there briefly, with Moira by his side, Sean could look over the monastery wall to Sandy Row; glancing back over his shoulder he saw Protestant Belfast sweeping out in both directions to the sea. From here, also, he could look down Clonard Road and see, only a couple of hundred yards away, Cupar Street, a Catholic thoroughfare running into a Protestant area. To the immediate right, mere yards behind one end of the church, was the network of streets known as 'little India', including Kashmir Road, Bombay Street, Cawnpore Street and Lucknow Street. Despite the exotic names, this was another staunchly Catholic area, renowned for its close ties to the Republican movement and the number of IRA heroes who had been born and bred in it.

'We're practically living on top of one another,' Moira said as they both studied the interconnecting Catholic and Protestant areas spread out around the church. 'How will we ever be able to forget this and become decent neighbours again?'

'God knows,' Sean said, feeling helpless. 'Let's go inside.'

Once indoors, they could scarcely believe their eyes. Every spare room in the monastery, including the kitchen, was filled with hysterical women, weeping children and battered or bloody men, with local volunteers distributing food and drink, applying first aid, and in general trying to offer comfort. As they stood there, looking on in disbelief and growing rage, a Redemptorist priest, Father Riordin Parnell, came up to talk to them.

'Sean and Moira!' he exclaimed, surprised to see them, neither being a member of his congregation. 'What brings you here?'

Sean nodded, indicating the crowded monastery kitchen. 'This,' he said. 'We heard you had your hands full, so we came up here to see for ourselves. You certainly have a lot of needy people here.'

Father Parnell glanced about him and sighed. 'Yes, a lot. Unfortunately, we're running out of food and medicine. Can you help?'

'Yes. If you tell me what you need, I'll get in touch with the NICRA and I'm sure they'll be able to find what you need.'

'Wonderful.' After groping about under his black smock, Father Parnell withdrew a sheet of paper and, smiling, gave it to Sean. 'I was keeping this list for the first soft touch to walk through that door. I'm pleased it was you.'

Sean returned the smile as he slipped the paper into his jacket pocket. 'Have you been bothered by anyone?'

'Not yet. But this morning I received an anonymous phone call, formally warning the Community of Clonard, through me, that they'd better clear out or be burned out. As you can see, so far that hasn't happened.' He waved his right hand, indicating the hysterical women, weeping children and battered, bloody men. 'I mean, where would we go?'

'This place is as good as any, I suppose.'

'Yes, I think so.' Father Parnell looked about him again, then said distractedly, almost whispering, 'Hard to believe, isn't it, that Catholics and Protestants alike huddled together in the monastery cellars of this very church to avoid the German air-raids during the Second World War? It seems such a long time ago now.'

'And a long way away. I don't think it's likely to happen in the near future.'

'No, I suppose not.'

'Well, I'd better start making tracks, Father.'

'I'll stay,' Moira said on an impulse, her stricken gaze taking in the sad scenes on all sides. 'Sure I can make myself useful.'

'Aye, right,' Sean said. 'I'm sure Father Parnell would appreciate it.'

'I would indeed,' the priest said.

'See you later, Sean.' Moira smiled weakly. 'You take care of yourself.'

Sean nodded, also smiling, then he turned away and left the monastery. Once outside, he glanced again over the wall at Sandy Row, wondering what was going on in that militant Protestant area, just as militant as the Shankill, then he made his way back to the flames and boiling smoke of the Falls, all the way to the Pound Loney and, close to it, St. Peter's pro-cathedral, with the spires of its twin towers soaring high to pierce the smoke-smeared sky. As he entered the building, advancing into striations of rainbow-coloured light falling obliquely through stained-glass windows, illuminating motes of dust at play, he recalled the last time he had been here, many years ago, when, shortly after his mother's funeral, he had gone into the Confession box only to tell the priest that he was renouncing the church and devoting himself to politics instead. That priest, Father Paul Connolly, was standing there right now, looking out over his cathedral which was filled, like the previous church, with the victims of the Loyalist onslaught. When Sean approached him, he raised his eyebrows in surprise.

'Sean Coogan! I never thought I'd see *you* in here again. Have you seen the error of your ways at last? Or is it…?' Smiling wearily, he cast his glance around the victims of what now seemed distinctly like a pogrom… '*This?*'

'Aye,' Sean said, following the priest's gaze. 'It's this. I've come on behalf of the Campaign for Social Justice and, of course, the NICRA, to see if we can offer any assistance.'

'Thanks for the thought, Sean, but you're too late. Your friend, Des Galloway, has already been here and I gave him my costly shopping list. But how thoughtful of both of you, nonetheless, to even consider us. So how are you, my boy?'

'I'm as good as can be, Father, given what we're all going through right now.'

'The wife and children are alright?'

'Ackaye, they're fine as well. Moira's helping out at the Redemptorist church in Clonard and the children are staying with my mother-in-law's sister out in Antrim, so they're safe enough for the moment. How have things been here?'

'As good as can be expected. At least, we haven't been attacked. But things are awful generally, aren't they? I mean, I went out there yesterday and I've been out again this morning, giving absolution and anointing dying men. I never thought our troubles would come to this and I'm truly saddened by it.'

'Religious differences are always the worst, Father. That's one of the reasons I left the church.'

'I respect your decision, Sean, though I never agreed with it. Without the moral laws imposed by religious faith, the world would be in a worse state than it is. Religion may have its defects, its dishonest practitioners, but not everything that's going on in those streets can be blamed on religion, whether Catholic or Protestant. The problems of the Six Counties are too complex by far to be reduced to mere religious differences. And, if I may say so, I think you're too intelligent not to understand that.'

Sean smiled. 'That's a compliment with a cutting edge, Father, but then you always knew how to use a razor to cut out our nonsense. And, yes, I agree that my remark may have been a bit impetuous. Sure I wouldn't have joined the Civil Rights Movement if I hadn't believed that the problems of this country aren't based solely on religion.'

'Thank you, Sean, for those kind words.'

'But I don't have time to discuss this now, Father. Since Des has already taken your list of requirements from you, I think it's best that I start makin' tracks. Sure I've an awful lot on my plate right now and I can't catch my breath.'

Smiling sadly, Father Connolly nodded his understanding, then he placed his right hand on Sean's shoulder to give it an affectionate, paternal squeeze. 'You come back some day,' he said, 'when all of this nonsense is over and sanity has returned to the community. We can have a good blather about politics and religion without putting on our boxing gloves.'

'I'll give it a thought, Father. Meanwhile, you know you can always call me if you need any help.'

'Ack, I've always known that, Sean. Sure you've built up quite a reputation for your invaluable community work. Come back soon, Sean. God bless.'

Unable to return that blessing, Sean simply smiled, nodded and left the building. Once outside, he made his way to Des' office in the headquarters of the Campaign for Social Justice, now part of the NICRA. To get there, he had to pass rows of burnt-out houses, many still blazing furiously, and the barricades of burnt-out vehicles, some of them still smoldering, with crowds of noisy, excited youths behind them. Gunshots could still be heard all over the area, punctuated every so often by the roaring of the Browning heavy machine-guns of the RUC's roaming Shorland armoured cars. Frequently, he saw men running desperately across the littered, smoky roads, from one street corner to the next, one gutted house to another, some armed with rifles or pistols. Though scarcely able to credit this, he kept expecting to be struck down by a bullet. Eventually, however, he reached Des' office and was glad to step into it, unbloodied and with no broken bones, still in one piece.

'Ack, there's Des!' he exclaimed jauntily, trying not to show his deep sense of relief at being indoors again. 'Still hard at work at his desk - and stuffing his mouth with a sandwich.'

'The working man's lunch,' Des retorted, running the fingers of his free hand through his long black hippie's hair and distractedly scratching his thick beard.

'So what's happening?' Sean asked.

'Nothing good.'

Between bites of his sandwich and sips from a cup of coffee, Des informed Sean that the general situation had not improved and that the violence was still continuing, both in the Falls Road area and in the Ardoyne. Indeed, Des had just received a phone call telling him that a Shorland armoured car had fired into the Divis Flats, killing a nine-year old boy and a young British soldier home on leave. The violence, however, had not been limited strictly to the Falls. According to a typed report that had just landed on Des' desk, the RUC had charged into the Catholic Ardoyne estate, followed by an angry Loyalist mob, and in the ensuing confusion had fired into the streets with submachine guns, shooting two Catholic men, though that hadn't prevented the Loyalists from burning out half of Hooker Street. Finally, Des told him, the Loyalists had managed to plant a large Union Jack in Divis Street and were continuing to hold the area with the help of well-armed B-Specials.

'Sure we can't let that continue,' Sean said. 'No way in the world. No matter what it costs, we've got to have that flag removed from there. If we don't, we'll lose the psychological war and then we'll lose *everything*.'

'I repeat,' Des said, 'that the Loyalists are being helped by the B-Specials - and those bastards are looking for any excuse to fire their weapons at Catholics.'

'I don't give a damn,' Sean said. 'I'm going to make sure that Union Jack is removed, despite the presence of the B-Specials. If necessary, I'll use that IRA machine-gun, enlisting the help of Magee and McClusky. They'll enjoy a bit of excitement - and as long as they're personally involved, I'll get the machine-gun.'

'Sure you're a man in a million,' Des said with a slight, mocking smile. 'May God bless and protect you.'

'I'm sure he will,' Sean retorted.

Leaving the office, he went straight to the Falls Road pub, now boarded up for protection, but being used by Magee and McClusky as their temporary IRA HQ. Sean found them sitting in a blue haze of cigarette smoke, surrounded by some of their men, studying a map of the Falls and the areas around it, with the intrusions of the various Loyalist gangs shown in yellow marker pen. The map looked like a game of snakes and ladders.

'They're swarming in from all directions,' Magee was saying, 'and spreading out all over the place.' He glanced up at Sean. 'So what do *you* want, Coogan?'

'The Loyalists have been flying a Union Jack in Divis Street and have been holding the area since yesterday. That's going to wreak havoc with Catholic morale, so we have to remove that flag and chase those Loyalists out of there.'

'Those Prods are being protected by B-Specials,' McClusky said, 'and those fuckers are heavily armed.'

'We can get them out of there,' Sean insisted. 'We go in there with your single submachine gun and as many armed men as you can spare, backed up by as many kids as we can find to throw stones and petrol-bombs. We simply spray them with the submachine gun, turn the place into a furnace by using the petrol-bombs, then rush in with all those kids throwing everything they can carry. My bet is that if we do that, even the B-Specials will have to retreat.'

'What makes you think the B-Specials will retreat when they can simply retaliate in kind, but with more and even better weapons?'

'The B-Specials can shoot the odd Catholic if they have an excuse - he was a sniper, or throwing a petrol-bomb, or whatever - but they can't be seen massacring a whole bunch of ordinary Catholics, including teenagers. Diplomatically, that's simply not on. So rather than get involved in a potential propaganda disaster, they'll beat a retreat with those lunatics from the Shankill.'

'Which would certainly be one hell of a propaganda victory for us,' Magee noted dryly.

'Right, let's try it,' McClusky said, after giving it some thought, 'but not until darkness has fallen. That'll give us the element of surprise.' He glanced at each of the men around him. 'You men have all been put in charge of separate areas, so I want you to pick up as many armed men and teenagers as you reasonably can without leaving your area totally undefended. Bring them at precisely 7.30pm to the corner of Northumberland Street and the Falls, just above Divis Street. Okay, boys, get goin'.'

As the men filed out of the building, McClusky turned to Sean. 'So what about you, Coogan? Are you comin' with us or not?'

'Yes, I'm coming with you.'

'Can you fire a pistol?'

'Yes, my Da taught me how. But I don't want to fire one. My role in all this is still political, so I don't need a weapon.'

McClusky and Magee glanced at each other, both grinning cynically, then the former nodded, indicating his agreement. 'Aye, right. So meet us at Northumberland Street and let's see what happens.'

'I'll be there,' Sean said. 'But what about that submachine gun?'

Magee grinned, reached down under the table, pulled up the Heckler & Koch MP5 submachine gun, and held it above his head while smirking triumphantly.

'You want it, you've got it,' he said.

'I'll see you at seven-thirty,' Sean said, then he left the pub.

By now so exhausted that he could hardly think straight, he returned to the Pound Loney, passing the all too familiar, deeply distressing sight of overturned vehicles, burnt-out houses, streets littered with broken glass and other debris, gangs of scruffy, unruly youths, and RUC Shorland armoured cars with their ugly Browning heavy machine-guns. Once home, he phoned the Redemptorist church in Clonard to check that Moira was still safe and was informed by another volunteer worker that she was having an enforced three-hour sleep before returning to her second shift of the day. Pleased that she was being used and made part of the team, Sean went to bed, lying on top of it, fully dressed, having set his alarm clock for four hours later. When the alarm woke him up, at seven that evening, he rolled off the bed, splashed water on his face, made himself a cup of tea, then phoned the church again to ask for his wife. The female who answered the phone was clearly distraught, but said she would fetch Moira, who came on the phone shortly after. She, too, was upset.

'The British Army's here, Sean.'

'*What?*'

'You heard me.'

'I'm not sure…'

'It's been hell since you left here,' she said.

'What happened?'

'Jesus!' Moira exclaimed softly, before sighing and becoming silent, obviously crossing herself, silently begging God's forgiveness for her blasphemy. 'Okay,' she continued eventually, thoughtfully, as if rehearsing a written speech. 'Let me try getting this straight.'

'Just tell me, sweetheart.'

Moira took a deep breath and released it as she spoke. 'At about three this afternoon a large mob of Loyalists, armed with stones, sticks and petrol-bombs, emerged from the Cupar Street area, only a couple of hundred yards from the church. They stoned, smashed and burned their way towards us. Since most of the men in this area were still at work, we had few to defend us, so the kids - I mean the teenagers - hurled everything they could find at the advancing mob. Father Parnell then called the local police station, asking for protection, and although they responded encouragingly, no policemen actually turned up to help.'

'Those bastards!' Sean exclaimed softly. 'Sorry. Continue.'

'As the Loyalists advanced, attacking every Catholic they came across and setting fire to the houses, women, many sobbing and screaming, poured into the church.'

'And you already had enough refugees from the other burnt-out areas.'

'Don't I know it,' Moira said. 'Anyway, as those hysterical women poured into the church with their frightened kids, we heard the sound of gunshots outside. Looking through the monastery window, we saw a body lying on the pavement of Waterville Street. Father Parnell immediately ran outside to give the poor soul absolution and anoint him. Then an ambulance arrived to take him away, but he died, as we were later informed by the hospital, before he got there.'

'Those bastards!' Sean repeated, now whispering.

Moira sighed again, sounding even more forlorn. 'So Father Parnell went off to the local police station to appeal for help. But although there were a lot of police officers lounging about, he was informed that they were under orders to remain in the barracks, despite what was happening to our community.'

'A conspiracy!' Sean whispered, hardly recognising his own voice, let alone being able to grasp exactly what he was implying. 'And then?'

'Receiving no help from the police, Father Parnell returned to the church, just as the mature men of the community, having heard what was happening, came hurrying back from their work to lend their support to the women and kids. By this time, of course, a lot of the streets were in flames and the fear of a real massacre had gripped everyone.'

'It's a damned disgrace,' Sean said bitterly.

'Aye, it is. More so because the Loyalists kept advancing, burning everything in their path, causing women and children to flee, with no interference at all from the local police, who were under orders, as Father Parnell had been told, to stay in their barracks. *Whose* orders? I wonder.'

'But the church was alright?' Sean asked anxiously. 'You're okay as well?'

'Ackaye. Sure I'm as right as rain, love. I mean, the church wasn't touched because the British Army, about thirty minutes ago, arrived to beat back the Loyalists and form a protective cordon around the area. So we're safe - at least for the moment. What about you?'

'I'm fine,' Sean said, deciding not to mention the problem of Divis Street. 'I'm just sitting here on the phone, trying to keep in touch with everyone. Are you sleeping there, in the monastery, tonight?'

'Yes, Sean. We're working here in shifts.'

'So when's your next break?'

'In a couple of hours.'

'Enjoy it,' Sean said.

Moira blew him a kiss over the phone. 'Take care.'

'You, too,' Sean said.

He left the house, locking the door behind him, then walked along the street, which, though unharmed so far, was packed with curious or frightened neighbours. Turning into the Falls Road, he made his way, stepping on broken glass, stones and other debris, past burning vehicles, burnt-out buildings, barricades and even larger crowds of agitated locals, until he came to Northumberland Street. He was not disappointed with what he found there. Despite his distaste for Magee and McClusky, he had to admit that they'd delivered as promised. A great number of men and teenage boys, some armed with pistols and antiquated rifles, the rest holding fistfuls of stones, clubs and petrol-bombs, had gathered together at the junction, waiting for someone to give the order to advance upon Divis Street. Other men, armed and with walkie-talkies, were standing a good distance away in both directions, keeping their eyes peeled for RUC patrols. McClusky was standing on the back of a flat-top truck, holding a megaphone, and Magee, beside him, held the Heckler & Koch submachine gun, not only preparing to use it, but also employing it as a dramatic gesture. They all looked slightly unreal, almost spectral, in the deepening twilight, rendered darker by the pall of dense smoke that still covered the area.

As McClusky raised the megaphone to his mouth, Sean instinctively jumped onto the truck and took up a position beside Magee, where he would at least be seen and remembered. This could be invaluable if the mission, already being widely viewed as an IRA assault, failed and rebounded upon the organisation, sending it back to its recent state of disgrace.

Even from where he stood, in the deepening twilight, Sean could see, across the road, the hand-painted statement that had been appearing on gable ends all over the Falls:

IRA = **I R**an Away

Given that statement, it was reasonable to assume that if this attack failed and that Union Jack remained flying over Divis Street, the recently resurrected IRA would be doomed yet again and the Catholic community would be looking elsewhere for salvation. In which case, the Civil Rights Movement could hopefully be reborn.

Though Sean was now so outraged by what the Loyalists had done - and, even worse, by the collusion of the RUC and B-Specials, the supposed forces of Law and Order - he was still clinging desperately to his original ideal of a Northern Ireland, if not united with the South, at least run along democratic principles, with civil rights to the fore. The thought that this might not come to be was simply too much to bear.

'Your task,' McClusky said, speaking to his gathered men, his voice booming out over the megaphone like the voice of God, 'is to attack those Loyalists in Divis Street, capture their Union Jack, publicly burn the filthy thing, then chase them back to where they belong and, if necessary, do to them what they've just done to us. Chase them out of their own homes, burn their houses to the ground, and encourage them to leave Belfast for good, leave Northern Ireland for good, letting this country become what it was meant to be...' At this point he took a deep breath, before bawling melodramatically: '*A Catholic country for Catholics!*'

The crowd cheered and applauded. When the truck then moved off, carrying Sean, McClusky and Magee towards Divis Street, deliberately moving slowly to let others come up behind it, the whole crowd of men followed it, marching silently, with grim determination.

Within minutes, there it was... The Union Jack raised over Divis Street and surrounded by many Loyalists, some of whom were B-Specials, all bathed in moonlight as well as the flickering light of the flames that had reddened the sky above the Catholic houses burning in the nearby streets. That sight filled the Catholics with rage and that in turn gave them courage.

Before the Loyalists had realised what was happening, the truck containing Sean, Magee and McClusky suddenly raced ahead, its engine whining, then screeched to a shuddering halt about fifty feet from the Protestants surrounding the raised Union Jack. Magee's submachine gun roared, sending a hail of bullets into the bunch of shocked Loyalists. They scattered in all directions, weaving frantically, trying to dodge the bullets, but one of them convulsed, shuddering like an epileptic, then staggered backwards and collapsed, falling into the pole of the Union Jack and knocking it over. As a couple of B-Specials fired, using submachine guns and pistols, the Catholics advanced, a few firing pistols, but most throwing stones and petrol-bombs. The latter exploded all over the road, creating sheets of silvery-white fire that illuminated the night and then filled the air with black smoke. Instantly, most of the Loyalists retreated into the side streets that led back to the Shankill, some firing their weapons as they went. They were given covering fire, also, by the retreating B-Specials, but those shots, as Sean had anticipated, were deliberately aimed high, the purpose being to keep the Catholics at bay, rather than have the kind of massacre that would only gain the police a bad reputation in the British press.

One of the Loyalists, bolder than the others, tried to rescue the Union Jack, now lying on the ground, but just before he reached it a petrol-bomb exploded, causing the flag to burst into flames. As the Catholics cheered and applauded, the remaining Loyalists fled, following the others into Percy Street.

Sean jumped off the truck, followed by Magee and McClusky, and was surprised to see his father, Barry, running along the street to catch up with the advancing Catholics. Sean was even more surprised when he saw that Barry was holding a pistol in his right hand.

'What the hell are you doing here?' Sean asked, when his father stopped in front of him, looking grim. 'Why aren't you still with the kids?'

'Sure when I heard what was happenin' in the Falls,' Barry replied, 'I just couldn't bring myself to stay away - I had to do my bit, like. Especially when I learnt that Meg's hairdressing salon on the

Falls Road was burnt out by the Loyalists. The kids are still in Armagh with Meg and her sister, so they'll be well looked after.'

'Where'd you get that pistol?'

'It's my old handgun. The one I used for IRA business in the good old days. I never thought I'd have to use it again, but this is clearly the right time.'

'You stay out of this,' Sean said. 'No point in taking unnecessary chances. Let these men take care of it.'

'To hell with that,' Barry said, then he skirted around Sean and ran to catch up with the rest of the advancing Catholics. Concerned, Sean ran after him.

By now the Loyalists and B-Specials had retreated into the flame and smoke of Percy Street, which led back to the Shankill, and the Catholics, a few still firing weapons, the rest reduced to throwing stones (the petrol-bombs were clearly used up), started pursuing them. Sean briefly lost sight of Barry as he followed the Catholics into Percy Street, now an inferno of burning houses and swirling smoke. He could hear, from up front, the staccato barking of Magee's submachine gun and the desultory answering fire of the B-Specials. As he advanced farther into the street, almost choking in the smoke, he noticed that the ground was littered with broken glass, stones, chair legs and even smashed radios and television sets, obviously dropped accidentally as the fleeing Catholics, or looters, had tried to make their escape. Seeing this, he was filled with an almost uncontrollable rage that made him want to bend down and pick up some stones and start throwing them at the retreating Loyalists. Resisting this urge, he continued along the smoke-filled street, passing more burning houses, their doorways strewn with rubble and smashed furniture. The Loyalists were retreating by moving backwards along the road, throwing stones and other missiles as they went, though some were ducking into the open doorways of houses that had been deserted but not set on fire, from where they fired off the occasional shot at the advancing Catholics.

About halfway along the street, when it was clear that the Loyalists were retreating all the way to the Shankill, some of the Catholics gave up the chase and either stopped to have a rest or turned around to make their way back to Divis Street.

Barry was one of them.

Emerging from the smoke of the houses burning on both sides, holding his pistol down by his side, not looking remotely like his forty-seven years, he offered a surprisingly boyish smile when he saw Sean.

As he raised his left hand in greeting, a single shot rang out, fired from farther along the street.

Instantly, the smile was wiped from his face, his eyes widened in shock, and he took a single step forward, then stopped and bowed his head as if praying. He quivered like a bowstring, legs shaking and buckling, then dropped to his knees and fell sideways to roll onto his back. His fingers opened, releasing the pistol, then he choked and was still.

'*Da!*' Sean screamed.

Hardly aware of what he was doing, he knelt beside his father, grabbed his shoulders, tried raising him, but then saw the blood around his lips, his blind gaze, and understood, with a shock, that he was dead.

Sean sobbed. Hugging Barry, his father, his Da, he whispered, 'Jesus! Oh, no!' Then he filled up with an all-consuming grief that quickly turned to rage. Lowering his father back to the ground, he picked up the pistol, jumped to his feet and then grimly advanced along the street, passing Catholics coming back the other way. Eventually he started running, blinded by rage and hatred, and fired a shot at the first Loyalist he saw. The bullet ricocheted off the wall just behind the man's head, spewing dust over him, and he ducked and threw his cudgel at Sean before running away.

Here the Loyalists were in a panic, being set upon by the Catholics, who were stoning them or beating them with clubs and iron bars, forcing some of them to run for cover into the houses that had not yet been wrecked.

Sean saw one of them do just that. Being attacked by three Catholics, all wielding wooden clubs, the Loyalist tried protecting his head with his crossed arms, but he was hammered to the ground and left there, bleeding, as the Catholics moved farther along the street.

Sean aimed his pistol at the Loyalist, preparing to fire at him, but the man managed to raise himself onto his hands and knees, then made his way, still on hands and knees, across the pavement and in through the open door of a house that had not been set on fire.

Lowering his pistol to his side, Sean ran up to the house just as the Loyalist, though still on hands and knees, tried kicking the door closed behind him. When Sean kicked the door open, the Loyalist tried standing upright, but Sean planted his boot between the man's shoulder-blades and sent him sprawling face-down on the floor of the small, wrecked living room with its framed Pope and Virgin Mary, both hung reverentially above the fireplace. The Loyalist rolled onto his back and stared up as Sean stood over him, one foot planted on each side of him, and aimed Barry's pistol at him, holding it steadily with both hands.

'You Protestant bastard,' Sean said without thinking, barely recognising his own voice. 'You murdering Orange shite. You won't be killing any more Fenians. It all ends for you right now.'

As he aimed more carefully with the pistol, his hand becoming steadier, sirens started wailing in the distance.

The Loyalist on the floor closed his eyes, waiting for Sean to fire, but when Sean failed to squeeze the trigger, he opened his eyes again.

'Sure I never killed anyone,' the Loyalist said, staring up with wide, slightly shocked eyes in a round, good-natured, slightly battered, now bloodied, oddly ageless face. 'I may be a Prod, but you can't accuse me of that, like. I may have got a bit carried away, but I didn't harm anyone, let alone *kill* anyone. So shoot me and you might regret it tomorrow when tempers have cooled. Why have me on your conscience?'

Sean remained where he was, standing over the Loyalist, aiming the pistol at him, looking into his face, that appealing, boyish face, albeit badly bruised and bloodied, and gradually realised that he couldn't squeeze the trigger, despite what had happened. Yet he was still boiling over with grief and rage. There were tears in his eyes.

'What's your name?' he asked.

'Billy Hamilton,' the Loyalist said. 'My friends call me wee Billy. I'm from up near the Bog Meadows. Sure I've had Catholic neighbours all m'life and we've never had cross words. I shouldn't have been here - sure I know that - but we all make mistakes, like.'

'Remember me, Billy Hamilton. Take a good look at my face. If we ever meet again, if I ever see your face again, I won't be as generous as I am now. Now get off that fucking floor, that Catholic floor, and get the hell out of here. If you leave by the back yard and go down the entry, you should make it out in one piece.'

'Right,' wee Billy said. 'Dead on.'

He clambered to his feet, nodded at Sean, left the living room, and then hurried through the narrow kitchen to the back door. He opened the door, stepped into the back yard and closed the door quietly behind him. Sean waited until he was sure that Billy Hamilton had left the back yard before he lowered the pistol to his side. After glancing at the framed Virgin Mary and Pope, he turned away and left the house.

The sirens were still wailing in the distance.

Sean walked back along Percy Street, passing the burning houses, trampling on broken glass. He shoved the pistol down into his belt when he reached his dead father. Looking down upon him, he started weeping again, but eventually, when his tears had ceased to fall, he picked Barry up in his arms and carried him back to Divis Street.

Turning in the direction of the Falls Road, still carrying Barry, still hearing the wailing of the sirens in the distance, he saw a regiment of British Army troopers, all heavily armed, marching towards him, past the smoldering, barricaded streets and their temporarily silenced inhabitants. He stood there for some time, holding his father in his arms, watching the British Army take command of the Falls, understanding, beyond any shadow of doubt, that the real war was only beginning.

8

Johnny saw the British soldiers even before he stepped off the Liverpool-Belfast ferry. It was only seven in the morning, dark and foggy and quiet, but shortly after the boat had docked, before the first passengers had disembarked, the silence was broken by the wailing of police sirens and an RUC paddy wagon trundled onto the quay, braked to a halt, and just sat there, the policemen not getting out, though doubtless keeping their eyes peeled, as British Army half-tracks with machine-gun crews in the rear, also arrived to spread out along the whole length of the bleak harbour. The machine-gun crews aimed their weapons at the ship as the passengers disembarked.

No trouble ensued, though the police were unusually rigorous with their security checks.

Eventually let through the recently raised police barricades, Johnny, carrying only a medium-sized travelling bag, since he had gathered few possessions over his years at sea, decided to walk all the way home in order to check what was happening to the city of his birth. He had left this place about ten years and he was now twenty-eight years old, though he felt a lot older. He certainly felt a lot older when he saw the changes wrought in the past few days to his hometown. It looked and felt like a war zone.

Leaving the dock area, which was being protected by British Army troops and half-tracks with machine-guns, he made his way through the centre of town, still relatively unchanged, though he had to adjust to how small it now seemed, compared to his recollections of a childhood spent in a sprawling, geographically complex city. Apart from the clouds of smoke hovering over the Falls, he saw little evidence of war between the dock area and the City Hall, the latter's vast copper dome gleaming eerily in the foggy early-morning light. But as soon as he entered Great Victoria Street, he saw the troop trucks and half-tracks, growling and clanging ominously as they entered and left the Protestant Sandy Row area. The troops, all heavily armed and helmeted, looked extremely tense.

As it was still too early to go home, Johnny stopped off at a workers' cafe in Shaftesbury Square to have a fry-up for breakfast. Glancing about the cafe as he was having his meal, washed down with hot tea, he saw how weary and anxious most of the other customers looked and he briefly yearned to be back at sea, warmed by tropical humidity, bathed in exotic light. Smoking a cigarette, deliberately trying to pass more time, wanting everyone out of bed by the time he reached home, he thought of his Mum and Dad, of wee Billy and Marlene, wondering if they had changed very much and if, indeed, he would still be able to relate to them. *He* had changed, he knew, being older and wiser, and although his family had to be older and wiser as well, their experiences, always limited to Belfast, would have been very different from what he had seen and done in the far-flung shores of the Empire and other, even more romantic, climes. He had left here as one kind of person and returned as another, so his family might find him unrecognisable: a stranger in their midst.

He wasn't uneasy about this, merely curious, because in truth few things made him nervous these days; his pragmatism protected him.

After finishing his cigarette, he paid his bill and left the cafe, then made his way up the Donegall Road, dominated by the Black Mountain, the Cave Hill and the rock face known locally as Napoleon's Nose. Those mountains and hills were beautiful, pastoral, suggesting peace and quiet, but when he glanced north, over the slate rooftops of the Protestant streets to his right, he could still see black smoke billowing up from the fires in the Falls. Thus reminded of the war that was being engaged in this city, he wondered why he had chosen, after so many years of indecision, to return at this particular time. He couldn't come up with a reason. He only knew that when he had read about the fighting, he had felt compelled to come back. He didn't have to travel far. He had simply taken the night ferry. For the past three years he had been living in Liverpool, working once more in the docks, frequently planning a return to his hometown, his former house, his family, and just as frequently putting it off. He still didn't know why.

Just before reaching the Windsor Picture House, where he had spent so much of his childhood, he turned into the familiar avenue which, in his childhood, had seemed to go on forever, though it now seemed of merely reasonable length. As he passed the Broadway, where Granny Doreen had lived and might, indeed, still live, he glanced along it and saw no evidence of rioting. The gable ends of the houses were still covered with Loyalist paintings, the Broadway still cut a straight line all the way to the Bog Meadows, the Whiterock Road, the Black Mountain, and the terraced streets running off on either side looked as bleak as he had always remembered them. It was clear, however, that the sectarian riots had not come this far, that no Catholics had come here to attack the Protestants, and that the place, at least so far, remained unchanged.

Well, not quite…

As Johnny passed the house where his dear friend, Teddy Lavery, a Catholic, had lived with Beryl Adams, an older, married woman and Protestant, he saw that the front windows had been smashed and the front door hammered almost off its hinges. Curious, he opened the door, sensed the emptiness within, but called out to Teddy and Beryl, just in case he was wrong. Receiving no response, he walked into the small living room and saw that it had been wrecked and, given the lack of material possessions, either cleaned out by the occupants or looted after they had fled. To be doubly sure, he called upstairs, again received no response, so went up and found the bedrooms empty, though the beds had been smashed to pieces and anti-Catholic graffiti had been painted over the walls, including those in the bathroom. Realising that Beryl and, possibly, Teddy had been forced out by vigilantes, Johnny went back down the stairs and gratefully left the house.

The familiar bridge and arches were straight ahead, with the shorter section of the avenue lying beyond them, leading to the football grounds, where Johnny, as a child, had spent many a happy Saturday afternoon. That part of the avenue looked unchanged, except for one thing... it was now filled with people.

Still not feeling nervous, but certainly becoming cautious, Johnny continued walking until he reached the arches, covered with Loyalist and anti-Catholic graffiti. Passing under the main arch, he walked on until he reached a house in the middle of the terrace that ran parallel to the railway tracks. It was Donna King's house. Seeing it again, he felt the sudden rise of an unappeasable, adolescent hunger. Surprised by this wanton, unexpected resurrection of former feelings, both exalted and anguished, he gazed about him and saw that most of the neighbours were either standing at their front doors or in separate groups on the road and pavements. They were unusually, grimly quiet, watching something that was taking place near Johnny's former home.

Stopping briefly at Donna's house, he cast his gaze over the crowd, checking if Donna was there, wondering if he would recognise her, but he saw no woman roughly the age that Donna would be now or who even looked remotely like her. Assuming that she wasn't in the crowd, feeling an odd mixture of disappointment and relief, he glanced directly across the road, at Dan Johnstone's house, and saw Dan, almost ten years older yet still recognisable, standing at his front gate with his huge father, Barney, and his pitiful mother and two wild brothers, looking in the same direction as all the others. Not wanting to be seen by them, certainly not today, Johnny made his way farther up the pavement, pushing through the eerily silent crowd, until he was standing opposite to where the Lavery and Devlin families lived, only a few doors down from his own house. Again glancing across the road, he saw that the windows of the two Catholic houses had been smashed and that a Ford saloon car with a trailer attached to it was parked in front of them. The trailer was piled high with furniture.

The gathered neighbours were staring at those two houses.

As Johnny looked on in disbelief, Sammy and Nelly Devlin emerged from their house and trampled over the broken glass on their short garden path until they reached the parked car and trailer. Though all of the neighbours were staring at them, they didn't say a word. Sammy Devlin had his arm around his weeping wife's waist. There was no sign of Teddy or Mark.

Even as Sammy was helping his wife into the rear of the Ford saloon, Patrick and Bernadette Lavery were emerging from the house next door to also walk on a carpet of broken glass the short distance to the parked car and trailer. Bernadette was not weeping. She had her hand on Patrick's shoulder, gripping it tightly, as if trying to give *him* courage, and she walked down the short garden path with her head held proudly on high and her long red hair shivering in the breeze like a royal banner. Patrick glanced at her and smiled. She smiled back and squeezed his shoulder. In a dead silence that seemed to have enveloped the whole world, Bernadette joined Nelly in the rear of the car, while Patrick sat beside Sammy in the front, the latter in the driving seat.

It wasn't much furniture to have come from two homes, Johnny thought, but it was probably all they'd been able to take in the time allowed to them. That time would have been limited.

The Ford's engine coughed into life. As the vehicle moved off slowly, pulling the trailer behind it, and as the crowd moved in upon it, still silent but oddly threatening, Johnny walked a few more yards up the street until he was facing his own house. He gazed across the road. There was no sign of his father, but he saw Mary, his mother, sitting on the front doorstep, holding a handkerchief to her face and weeping profoundly. Wee Billy was standing beside her, watching his former friends depart, still baby-faced despite being ten years older, though badly bruised from what was clearly a recent beating. He looked deeply troubled.

Gazing in the other direction, Johnny saw the Ford saloon and trailer moving away from the kerb, heading for the arches. Johnny kept expecting the neighbours to throw stones or scream abuse, but the car and trailer went under the arches and then continued along the avenue with nothing louder than a whisper to be heard.

It must be shame, Johnny thought.

He returned his gaze to his own house. His mother was still weeping. Wee Billy was distractedly exploring his bruised face with his fingertips while staring intently, as if bewildered, or simply stunned, possibly ashamed, at the arches through which the car and trailer had gone without trouble, taking the Devlins and the Laverys away to an unknown destination.

Johnny crossed the road, pushing his way through the crowd, not speaking to a soul, not even to those he recognised. He opened the garden gate and walked up the short path to his weeping mother and badly bruised younger brother.

'I'm home,' Johnny said.

TO BE CONTINUED...

Lagan River, Black Mountain
Volume 2
Divide and Rule

Dennis Burton

Lagan River, Black Mountain is an immense work of fiction, a 2-volume novel dramatising the whole history of 'the Troubles' in Northern Ireland through individuals drawn from both sides of the divide.

Beginning where the first volume ended, in 1969, when war broke out in the province and the British Army arrived, Volume 2, *Divide and Rule*, takes the story on from there to the precarious peace initiative of 1996.

With a gallery of finely drawn characters, young and old, good and bad, *Divide and Rule* covers another period of nearly thirty years, as 'sectarian' Belfast becomes 'criminalised' Belfast, political ideals crumble into corruption, and the leading individuals, as they age, move inexorably towards their tragic or redemptive destinies.

This second volume, *Divide and Rule*, is an extraordinary combination of historical epic and political thriller.

The two volumes of *Lagan River, Black Mountain* will, between them, constitute the most ambitious and riveting work of fiction to come out of a deeply troubled, divided city.

This is the 'Belfast' novel to end them all.